THE OXFORD HISTORY
OF ENGLAND

Edited by SIR GEORGE CLARK

THE OXFORD HISTORY OF ENGLAND

Edited by SIR GEORGE CLARK

THE REIGN OF ELIZABETH
1558-1603

BY

J. B. BLACK

Emeritus Professor of History
University of Aberdeen

SECOND EDITION

OXFORD
AT THE CLARENDON PRESS

Oxford University Press, Amen House, London E.C.4

GLASGOW NEW YORK TORONTO MELBOURNE WELLINGTON
BOMBAY CALCUTTA MADRAS KARACHI LAHORE DACCA
CAPE TOWN SALISBURY NAIROBI IBADAN ACCRA
KUALA LUMPUR HONG KONG

FIRST EDITION 1936
REPRINTED 1937
SECOND EDITION 1959
REPRINTED 1963, 1965

19571

PRINTED IN GREAT BRITAIN
AT THE UNIVERSITY PRESS, OXFORD
BY VIVIAN RIDLER
PRINTER TO THE UNIVERSITY

PREFACE TO THE SECOND EDITION

THE reader will find numerous alterations in the text of this edition—due to expansions of the matter, corrections of error, modifications of the emphasis, together with other adjustments suggested by the desire to enhance the interest as well as the helpfulness of the book. In particular, I would draw attention to the new passages dealing with the queen of Scots, which I venture to hope will do something to place that unfortunate lady in a more attractive light than seemed possible when the first edition was published. For one thing, the notorious Casket Letters—the Pandora's box from which a host of troubles emerged—have been set aside as thoroughly untrustworthy evidence, which no court of law today, provided it were free from political interference, would seriously consider, much less give credit to. I make this change without apology; for I feel that the time has come boldly to eliminate the 'Buchanan myth' and the 'legend of the good lord James', which between them have bedevilled our text books and distorted the truth beyond recognition.

Apart from this major alteration the reader will note that I have devoted more space and attention to Essex than is customary: not because hitherto unexplored material has come to light during the last two decades, but because there is a manifest tendency today to present this notable Elizabethan as a kind of 'playboy of the western world', who misbehaved himself and met the fate he deserved; whereas, seen against the turbid political welter of the age, he was probably more sinned against than sinning—the victim of unscrupulous rivals, who waylaid him at every turn, and of a jealous queen, whose surrender to a sadistic impulse subsequently brought her hours of remorse. I have also altered the balance of the book by enlarging the space given to the later years of the reign with matter which, though not new, is often forgotten, concerning the 'succession question', the machinations of Robert Persons, and the episode of the Spanish infanta.

Finally, the reader will discover some interesting changes in the text, in connexion with matters barely alluded to in the first edition because of lack of space: this is particularly true of James VI and Scotland, and in a lesser degree of the references to literature.

It remains for me to say that Sir John Neale will doubtless recognize references and quotations drawn from his invaluable volumes on *Elizabeth and her Parliaments*; albeit the use made of them may not always correspond with his own ideas, or tally with his own opinions. Nevertheless, like all 'Elizabethans', I owe him a great debt of gratitude, which I acknowledge gladly.

To Sir George Clark—editor, counsellor, and friend—I record once more my grateful thanks.

J. B. B.

King's College, Aberdeen
November 1958

PREFACE TO THE FIRST EDITION

THE purpose of this book is to consider, so far as the space allows, all aspects of the reign of Queen Elizabeth I, giving more emphasis than usual to social and cultural as distinct from political affairs. Obviously the arrangement of the matter cannot be decided simply on the chronological principle; for no historian, however skilled in the art of narrative, could hope to carry forward the whole burden of fact from year to year without involving himself and his readers in confusion. Moreover, a strict adherence to chronology would make it impossible to treat any one subject consecutively and intelligibly. On the other hand, the substitution of a topical for a chronological treatment, although it might simplify the issues at stake, would have the effect of sacrificing unity, and would leave the book in the form of a series of essays, more or less disjointed, which is equally to be deprecated. As a working compromise between these two opposite methods, we have adopted the plan of arranging the chapters in rough chronological sequence, and at the same time keeping each chapter focused on the particular topic with which it deals.

While this is, broadly, the plan of the volume, it had to be modified in one respect, in order to accommodate the discussion of certain matters which have a central importance for the period, but cannot be treated adequately in the general body of the narrative. In books of this kind, non-political questions are frequently relegated to the end, or at least the latter part, as if they were in the nature of addenda. The reader will find that we have incorporated them in the central portion of the volume, side by side with discussions of the catholic and puritan problems, and of the constitution. In short, the scheme as a whole works out thus. First come four chapters dealing with the Religious Settlement, England and France, Mary Stuart and the Succession, and the critical years 1568–75, which follow each other in approximately chronological order. Then this method is frankly abandoned in favour of specialized studies of the catholic and puritan challenges to the establishment, of the working of the constitution, and of the economic, social, literary, artistic, scientific, and cultural features of the age. In chapter ix, which deals with England's relations with the Netherlands, the method employed in the first four chapters is resumed and continued through chapter x (the Execution of Mary Stuart, and the Armada) and chapter xi (the Later Years of the Reign). The final chapter deals with the Irish problem, not because Ireland is important only at the close of the reign, but because this is the only point in the narrative where it can be discussed comprehensively.

In regard to the matter contained in the book, it need hardly be said that a completely objective account of events in Elizabeth's reign, however desirable it may be in theory, cannot in actual fact be written. From time to time one treads on embers of controversies that still flicker with a baleful light as soon as they are disturbed. And there are questions on which historians will probably be divided to the end of time, for the simple reason that their points of view differ so greatly that the gulf between them is unbridgeable. Of such a nature is the question of Mary Stuart's responsibility for the fate that eventually overtook her. No catholic historian will accept the view that Elizabeth, or her minister Walsingham, was not animated by a deadly hatred of the Stuart queen, whose claim to the English throne was the *fons et origo* of most of the troubles of the reign. Similarly it may be doubted whether a well-informed Scottish historian, working intelligently over the state papers now available for the reign of James VI, could come to any other conclusion than that English policy, after Morton's fall, was directed towards keeping Scotland in a continual welter unless and until those who controlled affairs in Edinburgh were 'at England's devotion'. And who would venture to suggest that a Spaniard, a Frenchman, or even a Netherlander could be expected to take any but a hostile view of the inner working of the same policy in regard to his own country? In the present volume we have been compelled to observe events predominantly through English eyes, or, to be more correct, through the eyes of the English government— to look upon the kings of France and Spain, the popes, Mary Stuart, and James VI as 'problems' to be solved rather than as beings entitled to a separate and sympathetic consideration. But the writer is aware, and the reader ought also to be aware, that there is another point of view which must be taken into account before we begin to speak of objective history in the proper sense of the words. An attempt has been made to keep this in mind while writing the book, but the paramount necessity of placing the reader at the standpoint of the queen and her ministers has prevented a rigorous following out of the principle. In accordance with the general rules governing the series of which this volume forms a part, notes and references have been very sparingly used, only in fact when for one reason or another some elucidation of the text seemed to be necessary, or a ruling had to be given on a disputed point, or it was deemed advisable to lighten the narrative of its heavy burden of fact. Spelling has been modernized for the convenience of the reader, without, it is hoped, any violence being done to the sense. The sources are indicated in the bibliography, which aims at giving a fairly representative selection of authorities, but is not to be regarded as exhaustive on any topic. The researcher will naturally turn to Conyers Read's *Bibliography of British History: the Tudor Period* for further guidance in his work.

To sum up one's indebtedness to other writers is never easy, and to particularize it would perhaps be invidious. Nevertheless I should be singularly ungrateful and neglectful were I not to put on record how much I owe to the labours of Queen Elizabeth's most recent biographer, Professor J. E. Neale, whose researches in English political and constitutional history of the later six-teenth century have placed all students of the period under a lasting obligation. The extent of my debt to his various writings is by no means covered by the references in the text.

It remains for me to thank heartily those who have helped me in the later stages of my task. I am profoundly grateful to the editor, Professor G. N. Clark, for his unfailing courtesy and for the many suggestions he made on points both of matter and of style. His critical acumen and wide knowledge saved me from more errors of omission as well as of commission than I care to remember. To Mr. J. M. Henderson, lecturer in British History in the University of Aberdeen, I am also greatly indebted for the care and discrimination with which he read the proofs, for much fruitful interchange of opinion, and for the numerous occasions when his eye detected ambiguities which I myself failed to discover owing to too great familiarity with the written word. Both have in different ways contributed materially to the read-ableness and, I dare hope also, to the usefulness of the book.

J. B. B.

King's College, Aberdeen
January 1936

CONTENTS

IV. YEARS OF CRISIS: 1568–75

V. CATHOLIC AND PURITAN

VI. THE CONSTITUTION

VII. THE EXPANSION OF ENGLAND AND THE
ECONOMIC AND SOCIAL REVOLUTION

VIII. LITERATURE, ART, AND THOUGHT

IX. ELIZABETH AND THE NETHERLANDS

XI. THE LATER YEARS OF THE REIGN

CONTENTS

LIST OF MAPS
(at end)

GENEALOGICAL TABLES
(at end)

NOTE ON THE CHANGE IN THE CALENDAR, 1582

In order to rectify the error of ten days which had crept into the Julian calendar, Pope Gregory XIII, by the bull *Inter gravissimas*, ordained that 4 October 1582 should be followed by 15 October, the intervening days being dropped. The alteration was adopted at the exact time in Italy, Spain, and Portugal. Brabant, Flanders, and most catholic countries followed suit shortly afterwards. Protestant countries, however, with the exception of Holland, Zeeland, and Denmark, held to the 'old style'. The change was not made in England until 1752. We have decided, therefore, to keep the old style of dating when referring to events throughout the period 1582–1603. The only exceptions to this general rule will be found on pp. 400, 401, 402, where both styles are given.

I

THE QUEEN AND THE RELIGIOUS SETTLEMENT

FEW rulers have impressed themselves so forcibly on the memory and imagination of the English race as Queen Elizabeth I. It may be admitted, of course, that much of the lustre surrounding her name is adventitious; that her reputation as a queen, like that of Louis XIV, lies bathed in the reflected glory of the people she governed. Even so, however, 'Elizabethan England' was, in a very real sense, Elizabeth's England. She it was who nursed it into being, and by her wisdom made possible its amazing development. Her characteristic virtues and defects, her sympathies and antipathies, her very whims and caprices are writ large across its political firmament. She inspired its patriotism, its pageantry, its heroisms, stimulated its poetry, and shaped its destiny. And when she died she left behind her a kingdom that had won a commanding position among the great powers of Europe.

On 17 November 1558, when she succeeded her half-sister, Mary, on the throne, there was no glimmering of the splendid future in store for her. England was 'ragged and torn with misgovernment'; the treasury was empty; the principal fortresses of Portsmouth and Berwick were falling into ruin; the country was bare of munitions; and a huge debt of more than £266,000 had to be liquidated, part of which was owing to foreign creditors, and charged with a 'biting' interest. The French king, Henry II, bestrode the realm like a Colossus, with one foot in Calais and the other in Edinburgh; and the alliance with Spain had played itself out with the loss of England's last continental possession. The prospect was rendered gloomier by the uncertainty of the young queen's title, and the probability that the Stuart claim, barred by Henry VIII, would be revived by the French dauphiness, Mary Stuart. So insecure did the state of affairs appear that few expected the new régime to last, and many calculated on its speedy downfall. To one competent observer, at least, it looked as if the two great continental monarchies, taking advantage of the defenceless state of the country, would turn it into a second Piedmont.

As for the queen, what contemporaries saw was a tall, 'comely rather than handsome' woman of twenty-five summers, with fair hair, 'fine' eyes, and a delicate 'olive' complexion. While, in some respects, she took after her mother, Anne Boleyn, her temperament and bearing were those of her imperious father, in whom, we are told, she 'gloried'. Close beneath her winsome, debonair exterior lay the *terribilità* of the Tudor 'lion'. Her character, however, was largely an unknown quantity, and her capacity for government altogether untried. Few probably realized, and time alone would show, that this slip of a woman, ignorant as yet of the technique of statesmanship, had already graduated in the hard school of experience, and was, in all essential respects, mistress of her destiny.

Wisdom, indeed, had come early to Elizabeth. Fate had deprived her of a mother[1] at the tender age of two years and eight months; but, as a sort of compensation for the loss, had developed in her a remarkable precocity of intellect. She became an observant, introspective child, apt to learn both from books and from life. Growing up, as she did, in a world of swift political changes and sudden reverses of fortune, when the fragility of happiness, the insecurity of power, and the uncertainty of all human affairs were the recurrent themes of philosopher and poet, it would have been strange if this intelligent offspring of Henry VIII had not pondered deeply on these things. But it was experience rather than books that disillusioned her of any tendency she might have had to romanticism, and converted her plastic and unformed mind into the calculating machine it afterwards became. She ripened quickly, almost too quickly to preserve that balance between emotion and restraint which is the true glory of womanhood. At the age of fifteen, an unsavoury but harmless love-affair with Admiral Seymour, which cost the admiral his life and involved the princess herself in public disgrace, had given her a first bitter taste of the power of scandal, and shown her the importance of keeping a tight hold over her natural impulses. It was, in fact, the fiery crucible in which all that remained of irresponsible childhood was remorselessly burnt to dross and ashes: out of it came a woman with a purpose, schooled to self-repression, prudence, and mistrust. Following upon this crude awakening came the five momentous years of her sister's reign, when, as heir presumptive to the throne, she

[1] Anne Boleyn was executed on 19 May 1536.

became willy nilly the centre of every plot against the existing régime, and had to pick her steps with care between the calculated malice of her enemies and the pitfalls dug by her friends. For Elizabeth it was probably the most trying time in her life: her stamina was tested to the uttermost. For weeks she lay a prisoner in the Tower for alleged complicity in the Wyatt rebellion, a prey to gnawing anxiety lest this gloomy keep, which had been for so many the antechamber to death, might be for her also the end of all things. But she escaped disaster by her own innate shrewdness and by the lack of convincing evidence against her. Seldom, very seldom, did she allude to those anxious days in after years. But in 1566, when she was hard pressed by parliament to declare a successor, she lifted the veil for a few seconds and then dropped it again. She was addressing a delegation from the commons on this burning question, and since all of them had taken part in the debate and knew what lay behind her seemingly obscure phraseology, they must have listened with rapt attention. She was sure, she said, 'there was not one of them that ever was "a second person" as I have been, and have tasted of the practices against my sister—who, I would God were alive again. I had great occasions to hearken to their motions . . . and I stood in danger of my life, my sister was so incensed against me: I did differ from her in religion, and I was sought for divers ways.' That was all: it was a bitter memory, better forgotten, but useful as a moral to adorn a tale!

Danger had sharpened her wits: she had learnt to screen her thoughts from others, to prevaricate, to dissimulate, to deceive, and to overcome difficulties less by vanquishing than by circumventing them. Circumstances had bred in her a hard, self-regarding type of mind, not particularly sensitive to fine issues, nor open in its acceptance of life, but strong in the grain and pliant as steel. She was wise with this world's wisdom—resourceful, self-reliant, cautious, and morally courageous in moments of stress. But she had lived too long in an atmosphere of plot and intrigue to cultivate the virtue of magnanimity—it was a luxury she could ill afford; and suspicion was a second nature to her. It cannot be said, therefore, that, as she stood on the threshold of her reign, she was a particularly heroic figure, or that her personal character, abstruse and recondite as it was, would be likely to provide material for the lyric or the tragic muse. In short, she was like one who had been 'saved, yet so as by fire': the marks of the scorching she had received, during the most impressionable period of her life, remained with her—a psychological inheritance which the passage of time would never alter. Of religious feeling, in the ordinary sense of the word, she probably had little. Her cold, entirely humanist outlook, nourished by classical study, kept her apart from the deeper spiritual currents of her time. Moreover she had seen too much of the ravages of fanaticism, both protestant and catholic, to set any store by the dogmatic formularies of either side. The only religious faith she can be said to have held with any degree of conviction was a belief in an over-ruling Providence—the refuge of all distressed human beings.

The speculations of theologians were to her no better than 'ropes of sand or sea-slime leading to the moon', and the doctrines for which they slaughtered each other merely a 'dream of fools or enthusiasts'. As she grew older, however, and experience brought self-assurance and a consciousness of triumph, visible in the mounting prosperity of the nation and the amazing loyalty of her subjects, there came a dawning conviction that she was, in some special way, favoured of God. This note of spiritual satisfaction—if it can be so called—may be traced in her speeches to parliament. In 1576, for example, she closed her remarks with these thrilling words: 'And as for those rare and special benefits which many years have followed and accompanied me with happy reign, I attribute them to God alone, the Prince of rule . . .'; and, again: 'These seventeen years God hath both prospered and protected you with good success under my direction. And I nothing doubt that the same maintaining hand will guide you still, and bring you to the ripeness of perfection.'

In regard to her culture it is possible to speak with more confidence. In an age that could boast of such feminine prodigies as Jane Grey, Mildred Cecil, and the accomplished daughters of Sir Thomas More, Elizabeth was notable for her learning. 'Among them all', wrote Roger Ascham, 'the brightest star is my illustrious Lady Elizabeth.' She could speak French and Italian as well as English: Latin readily and well, and Greek moderately. She had read the Greek Testament, the writings of Cyprian, and Melanchthon's *Loci Communes*; together with the orations of Isocrates and the tragedies of Sophocles. Quite a liberal education for a princess—even if Ascham's eulogy is overdrawn! Her knowledge of Latin must have been surprisingly good; for, at the age of sixty-four, she replied to a somewhat bombastic speech of the Polish ambassador with a torrent of Latin that must have taken his breath away, and certainly astonished the listening court. After the gale had blown past, she burst into laughter, saying: 'God's death, my Lords! I have been enforced this day to scour up my old Latin!'

But learning apart, the most precious possession of Elizabeth as a princess was the knowledge that the stability of her throne would depend upon the success with which she interpreted the national aspirations and gave them articulation—the very point, be it noted, on which her sister had blundered so badly. Whatever mistakes she might make at the commencement of her reign, there would at least be no repetition of 'Spanish' rule and 'Rome' rule, which had been linked together in the public mind as the causes of England's troubles at home and abroad. The future policy of the country would be based upon its vital needs. Thus did Elizabeth strike the key-note to a new age when she resolved to identify herself with her people, and become, in fact as well as in name, the 'most English woman in England'.[1]

The accession was a memorable occasion in the civic annals of London; and London in those days was like Paris in the days of the French revolution—the heart and brain of a kingdom. Something of what people felt may be gathered from the glowing exordium with which Holinshed begins his chronicle of the reign:

After all the stormy, tempestuous, and blustering windy weather of Queen Mary was overblown, the darksome clouds of discomfort dispersed, the palpable fogs and mist of the most intolerable misery consumed, and the dashing showers of persecution overpast: it pleased God to send England a calm and quiet season, a clear and lovely sunshine, a quitsest[2] from former broils of a turbulent estate, and a world of blessings by good Queen Elizabeth.

From the first day of her arrival in the capital, 23 November, to her coronation day, 15 January, the young queen revelled in the enthusiastic loyalty of her subjects, feasting their eyes

[1] The best account of Elizabeth's youth is L. Wiesener's *La Jeunesse d'Élisabeth d'Angleterre*, 1878, trans. C. M. Yonge, 2 vols., 1879; but cf. J. E. Neale, *Elizabeth*, 1934, chaps. i, ii.   [2] i.e. release, a corruption of *quietus est*.

with equipages through the city and on the Thames. The popular rejoicing reached a climax on the eve of the coronation, when the glittering royal procession wound its way from the Tower to Westminster, stopping from time to time, so that the queen might admire the splendid pageants set up by the Londoners in honour of the occasion, and make suitable responses to their greetings. There could be no mistaking the meaning of the pageantry: tableau after tableau was charged with significant references to past miseries and future hopes. There was the pageant of the Roses in Gracechurch street; the pageant of the 'Respublica Ruinosa' and the 'Respublica Bene Instituta' in Cheapside; and the pageant of Deborah in Ludgate and Fleet street. The allusion to Deborah, 'judge and restorer of Israel', was merely one of the many allusions that day to religion, for London was overwhelmingly protestant. At Temple Bar, where a chorus of children sang a farewell to the queen as she left the city, stress was laid on the establishment of truth and the suppression of error; and it was observed that when religion was mentioned Elizabeth lifted up her hands and eyes to heaven, expressing the wish that all around should respond—Amen! More striking, perhaps, than the popular rejoicing was the affability of the queen: she entered into the spirit of the celebrations with a frankness that disconcerted at least one foreign spectator, who thought that she exceeded the bounds of gravity and decorum. But there was method in this wooing of the people. Elizabeth's first care was to show that she had their interests at heart, and thereby to recover for the Crown the favour her sister had so recklessly squandered.

Meanwhile signs of an impending revolution in national policy were beginning to be visible in the political world; and one of the first to notice them was the count de Feria, Philip II's ambassador, who had been dispatched from Brussels shortly before Mary's death to present the king's felicitations to Elizabeth. With a confidence strangely out of keeping with the circumstances of the time, this proud Spaniard had journeyed down to Hatfield to inform her that her succession was assured, and that she owed her good fortune to the kind services of his master. To his chagrin he was firmly but politely told that in this matter her gratitude was due solely to her people. The privy council treated him even more perfunctorily. 'They received me', he commented, 'as a man who came accredited with the bulls of a dead pope'; and again: 'They are all as ungrateful to your Majesty as if they had never received anything from your hands.' Worse still, Spain's representative soon found that he was denied the courtesy of a room in the palace, after the queen took up residence at Whitehall; nor could he get any reliable information as to what was going on behind the scenes, for every one shunned him 'as if I were the devil'. He concluded angrily that the realm was in confusion, and that the best way to deal with it was 'sword in hand'. This cavalier treatment of de Feria was more or less inevitable: it was a gesture to the world that English policy was henceforth to be modelled on English interests and not as the Spaniard should dictate.

In regard to religion also changes were imminent, but here the signs were more difficult to discern. This was due to the fact that the political question of the queen's personal and dynastic security took precedence over all other matters. Doubtless if the throne could have been secured by means of a concordat with Rome, involving concessions on both sides, this would have been the method employed. The queen herself, despite outward friendliness to protestantism, had no vested interest in the movement, nor was she in favour—rather the reverse—of the prevailing Calvinism of the time. But the character of the reigning pope, Paul IV,[1] and the fear of French machinations at Rome in support of Mary Stuart, rendered such a plan impossible, even if it were seriously considered. On the other hand, so radical a step as a decisive breach with the papacy was too dangerous to be contemplated in the present military and financial weakness of the kingdom. Extreme caution was the only feasible line to follow. Matters must not be brought to a crisis until the new government was properly in the saddle, and until a religious policy had been formulated that would secure the allegiance of as many of the queen's subjects as possible.

The preliminary moves were by no means reassuring to catholics, but moderate enough not to arouse their resentment. Elizabeth chose as her principal secretary Sir William Cecil—

[1] 'Fully conscious of his own dignity, he regarded princes not as his sons but as his subjects. . . . He told the ambassadors that the place of kings was at the feet of the pope, from whom they should receive their laws as his pupils. . . . The utterances of his volcanic nature were as sudden as the eruptions of Vesuvius.' (L. Pastor, *History of the Popes*, vol. xiv, chap. iii, pp. 69–70.)

an eminently safe if not heroic figure, who had already served under Somerset and Northumberland in a similar capacity, and had so cleverly dissimulated his protestant leanings during Mary's reign as to be employed by her in an important embassy to the Netherlands. Cecil belonged to the 'politique' group of Englishmen, to whom might be applied the description—*non ex quercu sed ex salice orti*. His greatness as an administrator still lay in the future, when he became, if not the brain, at least the regulative balance in the Elizabethan government for more than thirty years: so that in selecting him to be her chief co-operator at the beginning of the reign the queen showed great discrimination. Even the Spanish ambassador could find nothing worse to say of him than that, so far as he could discover, Cecil was a man of intelligence and virtue; indeed he thought it worth while to recommend him for a Spanish pension, although there was no likelihood of such a bribe being accepted. Cecil was sworn in by the queen with the following words: 'This judgment I have of you that you will not be corrupted with any manner of gift, and that you will be faithful to the state, and that without respect of my private will you will give me that counsel that you think best.' To the best of our knowledge the secretary preserved the letter as well as the spirit of his pledge until his death in 1598. In the choice of her council Elizabeth was no less discriminating. Discarding the majority of her predecessor's advisers, all staunch catholics, she retained only those who were likely to prove pliable; and to these she added seven of her own choice, all of whom were protestants, and some related to herself by marriage. The new board could hardly be described as a revolutionary junta, and de Feria exaggerated when he remarked that the kingdom was 'entirely in the hands of heretics'; but he was right to this extent that the really significant part of the council was protestant.

In regard to policy, again, the note of caution was especially prominent, not unmingled with a touch of dissimulation. Thus, for example, the first important proclamation of the reign forbade, under severe penalties, 'all manner our subjects of every degree' to attempt of their own authority any alteration of the established order of religion. Ostensibly the purpose was to quieten the catholics, but observant critics, reading between the lines, came to the conclusion that, as the proclamation bound only subjects, it reserved to the Crown the right to make any innovation it pleased, and was really an announcement to that effect.[1] Similarly the Marian ambassador at Rome, Sir Edward Carne, was not only allowed for the time being to remain at his post, but instructed to inform the pope that an important mission would shortly be sent to him from England, although such a mission was inherently improbable from the very first. It was also observed that the royal title which the queen affected omitted all reference to the supreme headship, Elizabeth being content to style herself simply 'Queen of England, France, and Ireland, etc.' But the use of the 'etc.' left her the loop-hole to restore the obnoxious phrase if she saw fit to do so. It was no ordinary brain that devised so clever a subterfuge.[2]

All these measures might be described as anticipatory of coming change; but they were of a negative rather than a positive nature; and the queen steadfastly refused to communicate to any one what use she intended to make of them. Yet, in spite of her caution, Elizabeth was not quite consistent in her behaviour, and many indications were given long before parliament met of how the land lay at court. The first divine to preach at Paul's Cross—a regular court appointment—was a known protestant, William Bill; and when Bishop Christopherson of Chichester dared to refute him, on the following Sunday, he was reprimanded and confined to his house. In December, when the requiems for Mary and Charles V were celebrated, in strict accordance with the old ritual, Bishop White, who preached the sermon at the former, ventured to refer to coming changes in religion. For this he was punished in the same way as Christopherson. On Christmas day, however, came a marked change in the queen's demeanour. She instructed the officiating bishop at the royal chapel, Oglethorpe of Carlisle, to omit the elevation of the host from the service of the Mass; and when he refused to mutilate the rubric she left the chapel as soon as the reading of the Gospel was concluded. Meanwhile the return of the 'wolves from Germany'—the

[1] 'It is true that in the proclamation by the queen "that no one was to dare (of his own authority) . . . to alter the present state of religion", the phrase "of his own authority" is construed to imply that the queen, at her own time, will herself give the authority.' (Michiel Surian to the Doge and Senate, 10 Dec. 1558: *Venetian Calendar*, 1557-8.)

[2] The 'etc.' had indeed been used by Mary until Wyatt's rebellion; but with the opposite intention, i.e. as a means of dropping the supreme headship.

Marian exiles for conscience' sake—became the signal for an outburst of theological polemics, little to the queen's liking; and scurrilous attacks were made by pamphleteers against the hierarchy. To still the uproar, a proclamation was issued on 28 December, forbidding all preaching, but permitting the use of the Gospel, the Epistle, and the Ten Commandments—which were to be recited in English. By this time the catholics were becoming thoroughly alarmed: so that it was difficult to find a cleric willing to officiate at the coronation ceremony on 15 January. Eventually Oglethorpe consented, and the queen took the oath in the accepted manner, being proclaimed 'Defender of the True, Ancient, Catholic Faith'. But at the subsequent service in the Abbey she repeated her tactics of Christmas, left before the elevation of the host, and refused to receive the communion which was given in one kind, according to the old rite. The final scene of this interim period occurred a few days later, on the occasion of the state opening of parliament, when the queen was met on her way to the house by the abbot of Westminster and his monks bearing lighted tapers. 'Away with these torches,' she cried, 'for we see very well.'

It was now beyond dispute that great alterations in religion were about to be submitted to the verdict of the nation's representatives.[1] For weeks committees had been busy drafting bills and preparing business, and when parliament met, on 25 January, the government was ready for the fray. The lord keeper, Sir Nicholas Bacon, in his opening speech, explained that 'her Majesty's desire was to secure and unite the people of the realm in one uniform order to the glory of God and to general tranquillity'; and for this purpose she required them to avoid 'contumelious and opprobrious words, as heretic, schismatic, and papist, as causes of displeasure and malice, enemies to concord and unity, the very marks they were now to shoot at'. On 4 February Carne was recalled from Rome, his presence there being no longer necessary; and on the 9th a bill for annexing the supremacy of the church to the Crown was laid before the commons. The great controversy had begun.

Much criticism has been expended on the composition of this first parliament of the reign, on the assumption that the validity of the Elizabethan settlement must depend primarily

---

[1] 'The catholics are very fearful of the measures to be taken in this parliament.' (De Feria to the king, 31 Jan. 1559: *Span. Cal.*, 1558–67.)

on the integrity of the legislative body that gave effect to it. Doubtless the narrowness of the franchise, the susceptibility of the electoral system to interference, and the enormous strength of the Crown have given rise to the belief that all Tudor parliaments suffered from 'packing'; and, of course, 'packing' could easily be accomplished by the simple device of circulating lists of 'approved' candidates to the sheriffs. Mary's third parliament was apparently doctored in this way—albeit not very profitably, for the queen's policy was already doomed. But there is no clear evidence that the new government of Elizabeth found it necessary or advisable to indulge in pressure tactics. There was, in fact, no need to coerce or prod the constituencies: the young queen had been borne to her throne on a wave-crest of popularity—and this in itself was sufficient to sway the elections. When all is said and done, however, the question of 'packing' is really of small importance; for, if the conduct of Tudor parliaments be examined, it will be found that, despite government interference, they had a mind and will of their own, which they sometimes asserted with disturbing emphasis. Mary could not move her parliaments to redistribute the ecclesiastical lands that had passed into the hands of the laity in Henry VIII's reign; nor could Somerset touch the agrarian question in his day without creating trouble for himself. Packing a parliament, therefore, did not mean making it a slavish servant of the Crown.

In point of fact discussion was prolific in the parliament of 1559, in spite of the strength of the government's supporters. Harding, the catholic apologist, writing a few years after the event, asserts that 'many learned in parliament' spoke against the proposed changes; and there is plenty of evidence from other sources to corroborate him. For example, the bill to secure uniformity in the church service created wide divergencies of opinion, and in the last resort was only passed by the narrow margin of three votes. It has been pointed out, also, that there were no less than three supremacy bills introduced before the act took its final shape and won the approval of both houses. Not only so: the last draft of the measure shows, according to Maitland,[1] traces of extensive erasures and interlineations, which can only be explained on the assumption that the clerk of the house of commons was kept busy with his pen as the discussion proceeded.

[1] F. W. Maitland, *Collected Papers*, iii. 185–204.

Naturally the strongest opposition was encountered in the house of lords, where the forces of the old order were entrenched. But even here the full conservative weight of the catholics was not brought into play, because there were no less than ten sees unrepresented through death or illness and the carelessness of 'the accursed cardinal',[1] and the dissolution of the monasteries had, of course, deprived the abbots of their seats; while several catholic peers were either absent or voted, by an incredible slackness, through protestant proxies. But such as it was, the opposition in the upper house, particularly the episcopate, presented an unbroken phalanx to the measures sent up from the commons, and succeeded to some degree in modifying the resultant legislation in the conservative interest. Altogether three months elapsed before the two key statutes of the Reformation became law—a fact that seems to show, apart from all other indications, that discussion was not suppressed nor the action of the government unduly precipitate.

A more difficult question now emerges, to which, unfortunately, it is impossible to give a precise answer. Granting that parliament was not inordinately 'packed' and that debate was not 'gagged', how far may it be said that the voice of the nation's representatives expressed the conscious will of the nation? Simpson in his *Life of Campion* caustically describes the anglican settlement as 'originally an abasement of religion before *a supposititious public opinion*[2] for the convenience of statesmen'. Some colour for this view is lent by the statements of the Spanish ambassador, de Feria, and of Dr. Sanders, the catholic apologist and refugee, both of whom were eyewitnesses and had some opportunity of acquiring information as to the state of public opinion. Both assert categorically that the catholics were greatly in excess of the protestants. De Feria places the non-catholic part of the population at one-third;[3] Sanders at one per cent.[4]

---

[1] i.e. Reginald Pole, who died on 19 Nov. 1558.
[2] The italics are ours.   [3] *Span. Cal.*, 1558–67, p. 39.
[4] 'The English common people consist of farmers, shepherds, and artisans. The two former are catholics. Of the others none are schismatic except those who have sedentary occupations, as weavers and shoemakers and some idle people about the Court. The remote parts of the kingdom are still very averse from heresy, as Wales, Devon, Westmorland, Cumberland, and Northumberland. As the cities in England are few and small, and as there is no heresy in the country, nor even in the remoter cities, the firm opinion of those capable of judging is that hardly one per cent. of the English people is infected.' (*Cath. Rec. Soc.* I: Report to Cardinal Morone.)

It will be noted, however, that there is a very great discrepancy between the estimates; and the reason for this is plain: there was, as yet, no means of ascertaining the relative strength of parties, nor can it be said that parties, as such, existed. In January 1559 there was no definite issue before the country regarding the religious question, for the government had, as we have seen, carefully refrained from divulging its programme. Twenty years were still to elapse before public opinion, under the pressure of government action, jesuit and seminarist propaganda, and puritan agitation, began to take shape and cleave England into two passionately opposed camps. At the beginning of the reign the credal conflict was entirely subsidiary. While, therefore, it is true to say that the vast bulk of the nation were untouched by any desire to revolt from the old faith, it is equally true to affirm that they were not moved by any marked desire to defend it. The whole dispute about England's relations with Rome was beyond the lay mind. We must also remember that this was the fourth religious settlement within the space of less than a generation; and during these momentous years England had allowed herself to be bandied about from the caesaropapalism of Henry VIII to the protestantism of Edward VI and back again to the catholicism of Mary with singular indifference: showing that collective thinking on the issues involved was unformed, or that ecclesiastical questions did not deeply interest the country. Possibly also the memory of recent fanaticism, both catholic and protestant, had caused a general languishing of religious enthusiasm similar to that which prevailed during the Restoration period. All three explanations are probably true.

The only organized body capable of expressing a considered opinion on the religious policy of the government was the clergy; but their co-operation was not invited, and they were given no opportunity of influencing the course of events except, as we have seen, through parliamentary channels. Convocation, the official organ of the church, was deliberately ignored. Nor were the returned protestants better treated in this respect than their opponents. On the contrary, they were rather worse off; because being without cohesion or organization, and prohibited from preaching by law, they could make no use of the stores of learning they had acquired abroad, and had to look on passively while the catholics freely voiced their views in convocation and defended the old order in the house of lords. Thus, on 28 February, convocation under Bonner's presidency passed a series of articles reaffirming its belief in transubstantiation, the sacrifice of the Mass, the papal supremacy, and condemning the usurped right of the laity to decide matters affecting the faith, sacraments, and church discipline. Obviously the balance seemed to be tilted unfairly against the reformers. It was to remedy this grievance as well as to afford the reformers a chance of fleshing their weapons on their opponents that the government planned a conference between both parties shortly before Easter. On 31 March a debate was staged at Westminster Hall by royal command, at which the rival theologians might discuss in public certain of the questions already pronounced upon by convocation. There was no intention, be it noted, of giving the debate anything more than an academic character: it cannot, for example, be compared with the celebrated colloquy of Poissy which the French government arranged two years later; nor was it in any sense a free interchange of opinion. No sooner were the proceedings opened than the disputants began to wrangle over the method of presenting their arguments, the catholics alleging, with some justification, that they had not been correctly informed beforehand of the arrangements.[1] Sir Nicholas Bacon, who acted as president, ruled that, in refusing to abide by the conditions laid down, they had shown contempt of the Crown, and forthwith dissolved the assembly. A few days later two of the ringleaders, bishops White of Winchester and Watson of Lincoln, were sent to the Tower, and heavy fines were inflicted on the others. Probably the only notable result of the conference, apart from a certain propaganda value, was to deprive the catholic cause of its most redoubtable champions and to weaken the episcopal defence in the house of lords.

The work of parliament, which received the queen's approval on 8 May, may now be conveniently summarized. By the Act of Supremacy the whole of Mary's reactionary legislation was swept away, the anti-papal statutes of Henry VIII revived in all essential points, and the supreme power over the national church vested for ever in the Crown. At the same time the Act of Uniformity restored the second Edwardian prayer book, slightly modified, as the directory of public worship. Both of

---

[1] e.g. that the debate was to be in English and not Latin, and spoken not read.

these acts carried their penal codes. Refusal to take the oath of supremacy was punishable with loss of office, and any attempt to maintain by 'writing, printing, teaching, preaching, express words, deed or act' the authority of a foreign prince, prelate, or potentate, within her majesty's dominions, exposed the offender, on the third committal, to death for high treason. The oath was compulsory for all the clergy, judges, justices, mayors, royal officials, and persons taking orders or receiving degrees at the universities. The provisions of the Act of Uniformity, on the other hand, applied to the entire community, clerical and lay alike: clerical offenders against the prayer book being liable, on the third committal of the offence, to imprisonment for life, and the laity to a fine of 12d. for every absence from church.

When Elizabeth sanctioned the Act of Supremacy she took care to point out that her position was substantially the same as her father's under the earlier supremacy statutes. She claimed, as he did, that the power vested in the Crown was merely a jurisdictional authority over the clergy (*potestas jurisdictionis*), or, as the Thirty-nine Articles afterwards expressed it, the right 'to rule all estates and degrees . . . whether they be ecclesiastical or temporal, and restrain with the civil sword the stubborn and evil doers'. This would seem to imply only a temporal authority over ecclesiastical persons akin to that exercised over the laity. Such a statement, however, is a gloss upon the statute rather than an exposition of its content. Although the supremacy did not transfer to the Crown the spiritual authority in the church (*potestas ordinis*), that is the right to minister the rites of religion, which can only spring from consecration, it did transfer, as the subsequent publication of the royal Injunctions clearly shows, the right to make ordinances touching spiritual matters. Some of the queen's counsellors went so far as to maintain that she had power under the law equal to that of the pope or the archbishop of Canterbury, extending even to the articles of the faith. There is, then, a marked discrepancy between the gloss put by the queen on the statute and the powers it actually conferred or was believed to confer. Why was this so? There seems to be only one reason, namely, a desire on the part of the government to quieten public opinion on the catholic side, which strongly resented anything in the nature of a regal supremacy by a lay person over the church. A jurisdictional authority, merely temporal in character, would not carry the same obnoxious implications. For the same reason also the title accorded to Henry VIII of 'the only supreme head in earth of the church of England', which was followed without variation by Edward VI, was altered in the Elizabethan statute to 'the only supreme governor of this realm, as well in all spiritual and ecclesiastical things or causes as temporal'. This qualitative difference in the wording, be it noted, sacrificed nothing of the substance of power, but it was intended to soften the impact of the measure on the catholic conscience, and to make the transference of ecclesiastical power to the Crown as little obtrusive as possible.[1]

The same spirit of compromise is noticeable in the prayer book. The petition to be delivered from the tyranny of the 'bishop of Rome and all his detestable enormities' was struck out of the litany; the rubric declaring that by kneeling at the sacrament no adoration was intended to any corporal presence of Christ was expunged; and in the delivery of the sacrament to communicants the Zwinglian wording of the second Edwardian compilation was tempered by the addition of the catholic wording of the first. These were undoubtedly concessions to those who were attached to the old order; and it may be questioned whether, in view of the queen's moderation, the average Englishman was conscious at first of any marked change in the ministration of religion beyond, perhaps, the use of English in the service in place of Latin, and the Communion in two kinds.

Actually, of course, the settlement satisfied no one. The catholic leaders refused to have anything to do with it—for obvious reasons; and the émigrés who had returned to their native land, with banners flying and drums beating, to see the New Jerusalem of their dreams built in England's 'green and pleasant land', either condemned it as papistical, or sorrowed over its incompleteness. As for the queen herself, there is little room for doubt that, if she had had her way, she would have preferred—as she told the Spanish ambassador, de Feria, at the beginning—'to restore religion as her father had left it', taking the first prayer book of Edward VI as a *ne plus ultra*. But the heavy pressure from the enthusiasts who had imbibed the teaching

---

[1] For the philosophical basis of the supremacy see Richard Hooker, *Ecclesiastical Polity*, bk. viii; and for its legal implications, Sir William Holdsworth, *History of English Law*, i. 589–91; cf. also W. P. M. Kennedy, *Elizabethan Episcopal Administration*, vol. i, chap. viii, and F. Makower, *Constitutional History of the Church of England*, pp. 251–9.

of continental divines in Zurich, Strassburg, Geneva, and elsewhere, and who would have liked to jettison the Edwardian prayer books altogether in favour of a new revolutionary system based upon 'the best reformed churches', compelled her to sink her prejudices and allow more scope to the zealots than she had intended. After all, she had to depend almost entirely on these very men for the officering of her new state church, since catholic co-operation was definitely out of the question. But when all is said and done, it was the establishment of peace with France at Cateau-Cambrésis early in March 1559, that eventually induced Elizabeth to yield. This is evident from a statement by Edmund Grindal, who was shortly to become bishop of London under the new régime: 'We were indeed urgent from the first that a general reformation should take place. But the parliament long delayed the matter and made no change whatever until a peace had been concluded between the sovereigns, Philip, the French king, and ourselves.' Shortly afterwards, John Jewel who was to become bishop of Salisbury in 1560, summed up the predicament of his fellow *émigrés* in these words: 'The scenic apparatus of divine worship', he wrote to Peter Martyr, 'is now under agitation, and those very things which you and I have so long laughed at, are now seriously and soberly entertained by certain persons (for we are not consulted) as if the christian religion could not exist without something tawdry.' By 'scenic apparatus' Jewel meant the 'ornaments and vestments', which the queen so much loved and determined to retain at all costs in her revised version of public worship.

Thus the compromise of 1559, like all compromises, became in the minds of many a *terminus a quo* rather than a *terminus ad quem*: time would test its validity, and might even disrupt it, or attempt its disruption. For the present, however, it served its immediate purpose and allowed the *via media* a chance of success.

One other important enactment remains to be noted, that confirming the queen's title. Technically Elizabeth's position was somewhat dubious. By the succession statute (35 Henry VIII) she was the lawful inheritor of the crown after Mary; but an earlier statute (28 Henry VIII) had declared her 'preclosed, excluded, and barred to the claim', and this statute was still unrepealed. Her half-sister Mary had been placed in exactly the same position, but had taken steps to have herself legitimated by act of parliament. It was therefore a moot point whether Elizabeth should follow her example, or simply let sleeping dogs lie, and ground her claim entirely on the statute of 1544. Bacon, who was her legal adviser in the matter, decided on the latter course; and an act was passed establishing the royal title on Henry VIII's later statute and the queen's descent from the blood royal of England. Thus the question of Elizabeth's 'legitimacy' was ignored and continued to trouble her for many years to come.

From a strictly legal point of view the Bill establishing the royal title was perhaps a matter of urgency. From the standpoint of the commons, however, the future security of the dynasty was even more important. Consequently as early as 4 February 1559, before the government had introduced its Act of Supremacy, the house of commons proceeded—with apparent unanimity—to draft a petition to the queen requesting her to marry and provide the country with an heir; and two days later Mr. Speaker (Sir Thomas Gargrave), accompanied by the privy council members of the house and thirty others, was granted an audience at the palace. Camden devotes two pages of his *History* to an account of what transpired at the interview, giving what purports to be a genuine abbreviation of the speeches on either side.

Gargrave, who presented the petition, was fully aware of the delicacy of his task, the gravity of the occasion, and the need for caution against giving offence; but his speech was nevertheless both vigorous and forthright. He steered clear of the dangerous pitfall of naming a candidate—which, in any case, would have been the acme of folly and an insult to boot, even if the general feeling in parliament favoured an Englishman. His whole utterance was honest, humble, and objective: and, so far as was humanly possible in a matter so intimate, devoid of provocation. Emphasis was laid on the fact that, while princes are mortal, commonwealths are immortal: that a husband 'availeth more for the effecting of matters than the joint industry of many men': that 'the kings of England have never been more careful of anything than that the royal family might not fail of issue'; and that if a princess 'in whose marriage is comprehended the safety and peace of the Commonwealth' were to remain 'unmarried and, as it were, a vestal virgin' it would be 'contrary to the public respects'.

That Elizabeth was somewhat taken aback by the frankness and temerity of the commons in daring to discuss her marriage at all, is fairly obvious from the first words of her reply: 'In a matter most unpleasing', she said, 'most pleasing to me is the apparent good-will of you and my people.' If she had chosen the single life, it was not because she had not been offered marriage by 'most potent princes'; and she could not be considered childless, since she had married her kingdom, and 'every one of you, and as many as are Englishmen are children and kinsmen to me'. She commended the deputation that they had not 'appointed' her a husband, 'for that were most unworthy the Majesty of an absolute princess. and unbeseeming your wisdom who are subjects born'. She promised that if she entered upon another course of life, she would do nothing prejudicial to the Commonwealth, but would take such a husband as would have as great a care for it as herself. Finally, she remarked that if she continued in the kind of life she had begun, she had no doubt that 'God would so direct mine and your counsels that ye shall not need to doubt of a successor, who may be more beneficial to the Commonwealth than he who may be born of me, considering that the issue of the best princes many times degenerateth'. And so she concluded with the well-known passage: 'To me it shall be a full satisfaction both for the memorial of my name, and for the glory also, if when I shall let my last breath, it be engraven upon my marble tomb, "Here lieth Elizabeth, who reigned a virgin and died a virgin".'

With this evasive answer, flavoured with a dash of irony, parliament had to be content for the time being.

After the passing of the Acts of Supremacy and Uniformity, the government lost no time in putting them into execution. The bishops as protagonists of the old order were the first to be brought to the test; and with a single exception—Kitchen of Llandaff—they refused to have anything to do with the supremacy oath or the prayer book. Dogged determination to stand by their guns at all hazards was perhaps to be expected of serious-minded men who had fallen once already and been pardoned: any other course of action would have argued an inconceivable weakness of character. Consequently during the summer they were deprived of office; but since it was not the policy of the government to make martyrs of them and thereby weaken its own position, they were not subjected to the full rigour of the law. Some were detained in a condition of semi-imprisonment in the custody of the new state bishops who took their place; others were given their liberty conditionally upon reporting themselves to the council from time to time; eight were sent to the Tower; and one at least, Bonner, for whom the queen manifested an unqualified dislike, was sent to the Marshalsea, where he subsequently died. Heath, archbishop of York and chancellor of the kingdom in the previous reign, was allowed to retire to his estates in Surrey, and seems to have remained on excellent terms with Elizabeth until his death. Likewise also fared the aged Tunstall of Durham, whose adherence to the settlement the government was particularly anxious to secure. 'The recovery of such a man', said Cecil, 'would have furthered the common affairs of the realm very much.' But Tunstall was not to be won over: having come through the whole stormy period since the first attack on the church by Henry VIII, he was proof against cajolery, and remained a stalwart defender of the ancient church to the end.[1]

The courage and unanimity of the episcopate was not, however, supported by a similar attention to conscience and principle on the part of the lower ranks of the clergy. On the contrary their surrender to the government in the day of adversity was so complete that even catholic writers describe it as a *débâcle*. The government commissions that began their perambulation of the country in August returned to London in October with the comfortable feeling that 'the ranks of the papists have fallen almost of their own accord'. It is impossible, of course, to prove this statistically, for the simple reasons that we do not know the number of priests then in England, there is no accurate record as to the number of subscriptions to the oath. All estimates, therefore, are the result of ingenious and elaborate guessing; and they are so discrepant that little profit can come from considering them.[2] The one indubitable fact is that the Marian

---

[1] For the subsequent history of the deposed bishops see Bridgett Knox, *The True History of the Catholic Hierarchy deposed by Elizabeth* (1889), and G. E. Phillips, *The Extinction of the Ancient Hierarchy* (1906).

[2] The following figures show the extraordinary discrepancy in the estimates. Camden (*Annales*) places the number of livings at 9,400 and the non-jurors at 175. H. N. Birt (*The Elizabethan Religious Settlement*) reduces the former figure to 8,000 and increases the latter to 700. J. H. Pollen (*The English Catholics in the Reign of Queen Elizabeth*) follows Birt fairly closely, but scales down the non-jurors to 600. Both writers, however, reckon between 1,000 and 2,000 unexplained 'disappearances', which may have been due to non-acceptance of the religious changes. A. O. Meyer

pastorate in overwhelming numbers passed over into the service of the establishment without a murmur. The small minority who resisted and were deprived of their livings, or resigned their charges for conscience' sake, were either reabsorbed into the general body of the laity, or became the 'lurking' priests of later days; or they left the country for a more agreeable domicile in the Netherlands and other friendly parts.[1] It must be added, however, that the success of the government, great as it was, did not mean the total extinction of the old church. True, it disappeared as a visible organized body; but the loyalty of the priests who took the oath demanded by the government was often qualified by time-serving, and a watchful readiness to revive the past whenever fortune's wheel should take another turn. The situation in 1559 was far from irremediable. The queen might marry a catholic prince, or she might die prematurely like her sister; and who was to say that in either of these contingencies the new religious settlement would survive? Impermanence had been the lot of the previous religious revolutions: impermanence might also be the fate of this one. Hence many who accepted Elizabeth's innovations and paid lip-service to the new liturgy were buoyed up with the hope that a day would come when the old religion would again be restored to favour.

The surrender of the pastorate, however, was substantial enough to ensure an overwhelming acceptance by the laity of the religious changes imposed upon them. The success of the government, of course, was by no means uniform or complete, but varied greatly in different parts of the country. It soon became apparent, for example, that whereas the south, southeast, and midlands found little difficulty in adjusting themselves to the new conditions, the north and north-west harboured a good deal of 'recusancy'. It was here that the so-called 'massing priests' were to find a congenial outlet for their activities. Plying their profession precariously on the hills, or, more securely, in the houses of the nobility and gentry, they contrived to supply the needs of a spiritually backward population, whose attachment to the catholic faith was nevertheless the deepest thing in

(*England and the Catholic Church under Queen Elizabeth*) is content with the remark that out of about 8,000 clergy only 200 or 300 were deprived during the first six years of the reign. The question cannot be settled by the data available at present.

[1] According to Pollen (op. cit.) there were 68 refugee English priests in Flanders in 1566.

their lives. When the new bishops came into office and took stock of their dioceses, the reports they sent to the council of the difficulties and problems confronting them were dismal in the extreme. Pilkington of Durham, whose sphere of influence included the pestilent border region, the haunt of 'arrant knaves and stark thieves', complained that he was 'fighting wild beasts with Paul at Ephesus', and that the cleansing of his diocese was more than the labour of a Hercules. At Carlisle matters were no better; for persistent rumours of change were being blown about the countryside by priests and 'evilly disposed persons'; while the cathedral church was in a state of decay, and all the prebendaries save one were 'ignorant papists or monks'. The noblemen of Westmorland, on the other hand, repressed protestantism among their peasantry by threatening eviction. Lancashire was a veritable hot-bed of 'rampant popery'. Even in Yorkshire the reformed faith could not be regarded as secure. It should not be concluded, however, that the north was rebellious. The fact that eleven years of the reign passed without civil strife beyond Trent is a sufficiently valid testimony to the non-existence of anything more than passive disaffection.

Between the comparatively small minority who resisted the law and became recusants, and the great majority who continued from a sense of use and wont to attend the parish churches, there was a considerable number of the laity who found it necessary to compromise with their consciences in deciding their attitude to the new religious régime. Naaman bowed in the house of Rimmon while his heart was in the temple of the true God: so too, it was argued, might a true catholic be present, from a bodily point of view, at the heretical services of the anglican church, and yet remain a faithful adherent of the Roman creed. This silent compromise of conscience was in conflict with a strict interpretation of the canon law, which left no such loop-hole of escape for the tortured conscience of the individual. The pope, the committee of the council of Trent which considered the matter, and prominent English catholics like Dr. Sanders and William Allen, were unanimous in their verdict that attendance at heretical services was a heinous sin. Yet in spite of it a sort of dual loyalty was conceived to be possible by many catholics in England, and became the source of much anxiety to all who had the recovery of the country for catholicism deeply at heart. On the strength of it some went to the anglican service, but left before the end; others attended morning and evening prayer, but scrupled at the communion; and others again received the 'Lord's Supper' in accordance with the new ritual, but afterwards enjoyed the 'Lord's Body' in secret to satisfy their consciences. In other words, the distinction was drawn between inner belief and outward conformity. In the confusion of the time all manner of irregularities prevailed. Sometimes the same clergyman was both anglican minister and catholic priest in one, balancing his functions between the formal and the real needs of his flock. But the government showed no inclination at first to inquire into these doubtful proceedings: it was satisfied if the letter of the law was obeyed: the private opinion of the subject was a matter that lay outside its province. This was in keeping with the queen's remark that she did not wish to 'make a window into men's souls' nor to force their consciences. Time and the slow moral attrition of repeated church attendance might be relied upon to convert unwilling obedience into a real conformity.[1]

It has been said also, with some justification, that the substitution of English for Latin in the service was as acceptable to catholics as to protestants, and that this may have helped forward the settlement. The demand for the bible in the vernacular was certainly common to both catholics and protestants; and we know that it was with difficulty that those catholics who had possessed themselves of English bibles in Edward's reign could be got to give them up under Mary. Nor must one forget that one of the principal achievements of the catholic seminary at Rheims was the translation of the New Testament into English. The use of the vernacular in the anglican service may, therefore, have acted as an attractive force on the side of the reformation.

It is clear, however, that when the second parliament of the

<hr>

[1] Not to 'force consciences' remained the pervading and animating principle of the royal policy throughout the reign, albeit it partially broke down after 1581, when the intensification of the penal laws against catholics made it a capital offence to 'become' a catholic, and 'hearing Mass' an offence punishable with a fine of 100 marks and a year's imprisonment. Even so, however, it was still contended that no alteration in the government attitude had taken place. As Francis Bacon put it nearly a decade later: 'Her Majesty, not liking to make windows into men's hearts and secret thoughts . . . tempered her law so as it restraineth only manifest disobedience, in impugning and impeaching advisedly and maliciously her Majesty's supreme power, and maintaining and extolling a foreign jurisdiction.'

reign met, in 1563, the government was by no means satisfied with the progress of the settlement. Many influential people who were in a position to hinder the establishment of the church had been able to escape the oath of supremacy, either because they were not included in the classes specifically required to take it, or because the officials entrusted with its administration were lax in the discharge of their duty. The bishops, too, were much handicapped in the enforcement of the secular penalties of excommunication, their principal weapon against the froward, by the lack of support from the sheriffs on whom they depended. The only way to remedy these defects was to amend the law. Consequently when parliament assembled in 1563 two supplementary acts were passed. The first, an act for the assurance of the queen's power, increased the penalties for upholding the authority of the pope, and swept several new classes into the circle of those to whom the oath of supremacy was applicable: e.g. members of the house of commons, schoolmasters, lawyers and barristers, sheriffs, and 'all persons whatsoever who have or shall be admitted to any ministry or office belonging to the common law or any other law within the realm'.[1] At the same time the administration of the oath was placed in the hands of the archbishops and the bishops: the lord chancellor was authorized to issue similar powers to any one he considered fit to be entrusted with it; and the court of king's bench was made the general supervisory authority. In the second, an act for the better execution of the writ *de excommunicato capiendo*, the censure of the church was strengthened by penalizing officials who stood in the way of its enforcement.

Even so, however, the irregularities could not be eradicated. It is observable that in most cases the episcopal reports on the condition of the northern dioceses take the form of complaints against the hostile or doubtful attitude of the justices of the peace. In 1564, when, for the first time, an official inquiry was made into the matter, it was found that practically half of the

---

[1] The penalty for a first offence was a *premunire* (i.e. loss of lands and goods, and imprisonment at the queen's pleasure) and, for a second offence, death for treason. The measure was severely criticized in both houses for its harshness; but it passed with considerable majorities. Cecil's comment is interesting: 'Such be the humours of the Commons' House, as they think nothing sharp enough against the Papists.' Archbishop Parker, who was similarly minded, instructed the bishops not to administer the oath a second time (i.e. to ecclesiastics) without obtaining his sanction in writing. (See Neale, *Elizabeth I and her Parliaments, 1559–1581*, p. 121.)

justices in the country were either unfavourable or openly adverse to the policy of the government; and in the north the proportion of the 'evilly disposed' to the loyal was much greater. Clearly the private opinions and affinities of the magistracy were a serious obstacle to the successful establishment of the church. Nor was it possible for the government, in view of its own moderate religious policy and the nature of Tudor local administration, to purge the roll of the justiceship too drastically. As late as 1578 complaints were rife that owing to the slackness of the justices in divers counties 'not only is God dishonoured and the laws infringed, but very evil example given to the common sort of people'.

Let us now take a wider view. The religious revolution introduced by the legislation of 1559, however carefully prepared and cautiously carried out, was not a thing that could be confined in its effects to England alone: it was bound to create widespread concern throughout the length and breadth of catholic Europe. In particular, the pope as guardian of the spiritual integrity of christendom could not remain passive while a kingdom that had been reunited so recently to the Holy See again proclaimed its independence. Theoretically his course of action was clear enough. The law of the church in the sixteenth century, as in the thirteenth, prescribed that temporal rulers who were guilty of maintaining heresy in their dominions should be proceeded against by ecclesiastical censure and deprivation.[1] If, therefore, the English question had been susceptible of treatment purely on grounds of justice and religion, the punishment of the queen ought to have followed as soon as plain evidence of the fact convicted her of malevolent intentions towards Rome. It is noteworthy that Paul IV was ready to move in this direction as early as the spring of 1559. But in point of fact the pope was not free to act on spiritual grounds alone. Besides launching the ecclesiastical thunderbolt, he had to consider how it might be made effective. Expediency, practicability, and the convenience of the secular power on whom would fall the burden of carrying out the will of the church had to be consulted; to pronounce sentence and find no suitable means of executing it would reduce disciplinary action to a mere absurdity. Moreover, there was the mortifying fact to be taken

[1] Pollen, p. 49.

into account that in the sixteenth century princes no longer
stood in the same dread of papal bulls as formerly. Henry
VIII's excommunication had shown that the foundations of
secular sovereignty were too secure to be shaken by a discharge
of the papal artillery. It may be doubted, too, whether the
papacy was not now afraid of its own weapon, and inclined to
hesitate before using it, however great the provocation. But the
principal danger, so far as the pope was concerned, lay not so
much in the promulgation of the bull of excommunication as in
its execution.

In virtue of his position as 'King Catholic' and mightiest
catholic monarch in the world, Philip II of Spain was the pre-
destined champion of the old order. Of his anxiety to save
catholicism in England from destruction there is plenty of evidence in the documents. But worldly cares and the conviction
that a conflict with England would redound to his own disadvantage in the struggle for power in Europe made him unwilling to sponsor violent measures against the English queen.
Consequently his constant advice to the pope was to delay
extreme action and trust to the diplomatic means which he
himself could employ through his ambassador in London. Thus
while the English catholics living in exile on the Continent, the
imprisoned bishops in England, and many in high position in
the catholic church were in favour of immediate corrective
measures regardless of consequences, Spanish influence at Rome
never ceased to counsel patience and restraint. This conflict of
opinion may serve to explain the wavering and uncertain attitude of the papacy towards Elizabeth during the early years of
the reign, and that curious mixture of menace and suavity, of
energy followed by supineness, that prevented both Paul IV and
Pius IV from taking the only decisive step capable of retrieving
to some extent the downfall of the old religion in England.

A contributory cause of the indecision of the popes might
perhaps be discovered in the prevalent misconception at Rome
and elsewhere as to the real state of affairs in Elizabeth's dominions. The general tenor of reports reaching the Holy See from
interested catholics was that things were not so bad as they
appeared to be: that the English people were overwhelmingly
loyal to the ancient faith: that the religious revolution was the
work of a handful of greedy nobles, apostate priests, and adventurers who, having possessed themselves of power and poisoned

the queen's mind, had imposed their will on the country; but that Elizabeth herself was not hostile to the church, and might even be induced to restore it, if only she were freed from the evil advice of her counsellors. Spain as well as Rome was the victim of this hallucination; and such was the queen's ability to dissimulate her true sentiments that she succeeded in keeping up the convenient illusion for a considerable time. Discreet 'asides' in conversation with the Spanish ambassador, the use of candles in her private chapel, affectation of innocence on points of doctrine, &c., were all pressed into the service of her artful make-believe.

Nevertheless, in spite of all countervailing influences, no less than three major efforts, and several subsidiary, were made by Pius IV during the years between 1559 and 1565 to pave the way for a catholic revival in the country. In the spring of 1560 he dispatched Parpaglia, abbot of San Salvatore, with a letter to the queen adjuring her to return to the bosom of the church. If this envoy did not reach England but found himself stopped by the Spanish authorities at Brussels, the blame for the failure rests not with the pope but with the king of Spain, who represented that the time was unpropitious. Parpaglia was therefore recalled to Rome at the end of the year.[1] The following spring, after the bull announcing the early summons of a general council (the council of Trent) had been published at Rome, another papal nuncio, the abbot Martinengo, was sent to England, with instructions to invite the queen to send representatives. But again the effort failed. In common with the German protestants, England refused to have anything to do with the council, and the envoy was denied access to the realm (May 1561). The reasons for this drastic decision—which, incidentally, was largely the work of Cecil and Bacon—were that the queen had not been consulted as to the summoning of the council, that the council would not be 'free, pious, and christian', and that the pope was seeking at the very moment of the invitation to stir up trouble for the government in England and Ireland. It was not, therefore, through Spanish influence that Martinengo was turned away from our shores: on the contrary, the Spanish ambassador, de Quadra, did what he could to win acceptance

---

[1] Parpaglia was a bad choice: he was regarded in Spanish circles as a partisan of France; only eighteen months before, he had been expelled from Flanders for espionage; and, as a friend of Pole, he was certain to be disliked by Elizabeth.

for him; but after the rebuff was administered, Spain played an important part in warding off the retaliatory blow of the pope, which in normal circumstances would have been a bull of excommunication. Nor was this all. After the council met at Trent, and the question of the queen's excommunication was submitted to it in a memorandum from the English catholic refugees at Louvain (June 1563), it was through the influence exerted by the Habsburg rulers, the emperor Ferdinand and Philip II, that nothing was done to give effect to the petition. They pointed out that such a step was dangerous to the peace of Europe and therefore to the hope of re-establishing credal unity. After these outstanding failures Pius contented himself with indirect attempts to restore relations with England by means of individuals like the cardinal of Ferrara, Thomas Sackville, and the Italian Gurone Bertano.[1] But the queen resisted all advances.

It will be apparent, then, that if catholicism in England succumbed to the government the explanation must be sought for not only in a lack of morale among the Marian pastorate, but also in the impotence of their friends abroad to render effective aid when it was most needed. But Philip II must bear by far the heaviest share of the responsibility for what happened. Although he claimed to be the patron and protector of the English catholics, his attitude was that of an obstructor rather than of a helper. He would neither allow others to lend assistance nor himself intervene materially to remedy the situation. The only attempt at friendly intervention came not from him but from his kinsman Ferdinand, who, at the pope's request, indited a letter to Elizabeth, in 1563, urging her to modify her laws in favour of the catholics, to the extent at least of granting them freedom of worship in specified places. Needless to say, this appeal also met with a firm, albeit courteous, refusal.

We have seen how the religious settlement was reached, and have discussed its nature and success: it remains to be seen how the church was reconstituted.

By November 1559 the last of the Marian bishops had been removed from office and the filling of the vacancies began.[2] On

---

[1] On the subject of these missions see C. G. Bayne, *Anglo-Papal Relations, 1558–66*, and Pastor, vol. xvi, chap. vii.

[2] The installations were not complete until 1562: London, Ely, Bangor, Worcester (21 Dec. 1559); Salisbury, Lincoln, St. David's, St. Asaph's, Rochester, Bath and Wells, Lichfield and Coventry, Exeter, Norwich (1560); York, Winchester, Peterborough, Carlisle, Durham, Chester (1561); Gloucester (1562).

17 December Matthew Parker was consecrated and installed as primate at Canterbury. Elizabeth and Cecil had long marked out Parker for the onerous and responsible task of piloting the half-manned ship into port, but it was with considerable reluctance that he would consent to undertake the office. He was over fifty years old, he said; he suffered periodically from the quartan ague; his voice was somewhat decayed; he was lame of a fall from horseback. Above all, being a man of backward and retiring disposition, he pleaded that he could never hope to influence the world by his personality, though he might hope to do so by his pen. He therefore asked to be allowed to remain in obscurity. But Elizabeth and Cecil were imperative, and Parker, betraying all the shrinking diffidence of the scholar, was dragged into the theatre of public life. Perhaps the government knew their man better than he knew himself; the archbishop was indeed a remarkable man.[1] Although cut out by nature for the university and the school rather than public affairs, he did not lack courage nor practicality of mind. By all accounts, too, he was a model of wisdom and piety and generosity. 'How prudent, how grave, how learned he was,' wrote one person, 'that one would think that Cato or Quintus Fabius lived again in him.' These were the qualities the government wanted. A church founded on a compromise, whose path was to be a *via media*, required a pilot whose mind and character were resolute, albeit opposed to all fanaticism and recklessness. Parker had an excellent tradition behind him. He had been one of the little society, 'little Germany' as it was called, which gathered round Bilney at Cambridge in the earlier days of the Renaissance; he was a thorough-going believer in schools and universities and learning; and he had personally known the great protagonists of the English Reformation, Cranmer, Bucer, Latimer, and Ridley. Above all he had no taint of presbytery, which marked most of the prominent protestants in 1559, who had spent years on the Continent.

The archbishop's task was one of colossal difficulty. The situation as revealed by the ecclesiastical commissioners and the new bishops was chaotic in the extreme. Many parishes had no

---

[1] He had already had considerable administrative experience as master of Corpus Christi College, Cambridge (1544), and vice-chancellor of Cambridge (1545, re-elected 1549). He had also been chaplain to Anne Boleyn (1535) and to Henry VIII (1537), and dean of Lincoln (1552).

clergyman; and out of the few who administered the sacraments there was scarcely one who was both able and willing to preach the word of God. 'Incredible ignorance and superstition' prevailed among the people. Doubtless the desolation which had settled down on the church is partly to be explained by the deprivations or voluntary withdrawals which had removed the better and more conscientious clergy; but there were many causes. The universities, which, in the last resort, maintained the level of intelligence among both clergy and people, had suffered practically continuous decay since Henry VIII's time. The confused revolutions of the preceding generation had depraved the tone of religious life everywhere. Moreover, the church had failed to keep pace with the growth of the population and the shifting of the centres of population. Cities, market towns, and boroughs where the greatest concourse of people was, writes a contemporary, were destitute of learned men, and many were lapsing into pure heathenism. To some extent, also, the problem was the creation of the protestant conscience. Under a catholic hierarchy the so-called 'superstition' of the people, the 'rank ignorance' of the clergy, the lack of 'reverence' for church buildings and the other 'evils' which bulked so large in the reports of the new episcopate, might have caused little stir. It was a condition into which the catholic church fell from time to time, to be rescued by a reactionary wave of reform whenever the public conscience was deeply touched. But with the establishment of protestantism these things took on a new colour; for the protestantizing of the church meant not merely a change in the personnel of the pastorate, but also a change in the religious attitude of the community. The new service with its greater inwardness of appeal, which took the place of the ritual of the Mass and the more outward and symbolic observances of catholicism, demanded, if not an increased intelligence on the part of both clergy and laity, at least a new point of view. And this was the root of the matter to men like Parker. The queen might be satisfied with outward conformity and leave the conscience alone, but to her bishops the problem presented itself in exactly the opposite form. If protestantism was to have a foothold in the country it was necessary to alter the religious outlook of the nation. This, briefly, was the work the new governors of the church had taken in hand. But owing to the indifference of the queen, its accomplishment was slow.

The establishment of the church was completed, so far as Elizabeth was concerned, by the issue of the royal Injunctions of 1559. For any subsequent effort to give it a real corporate and self-conscious existence, the archbishop had to depend upon his own ingenuity and assume the responsibility: it was sufficient for the political purposes of the government that the papal control should be broken and the superstitious practices of the middle ages abrogated. The consequence was that for some years there was neither a distinctive doctrine nor an effective discipline in the anglican church. At first the only legal standard in matters of belief was the subscription to the oath of supremacy by the clergy and church attendance by the laity. The Act of Supremacy, it is true, prescribed the Scriptures, and the decrees of the first four general councils, as the test for heresy; but this was the common heritage of all christians, and cannot be compared with the Confession of Augsburg and the other elaborate formularies that gave individuality to the protestant churches abroad. The *Book of Homilies* published by Parker in 1562, for the use of the pulpit, carefully refrained from mentioning points of doctrine and confined itself to moral precepts concerning the heinousness of rebellion, the reverence due to church buildings, excess of apparel, and other matters of a socio-political character. It was not until the Thirty-nine Articles were adopted by convocation in 1563, and published by royal ordinance, that the church acquired a definite body of doctrine. Even so, however, the Articles had really no binding force in law until they were sanctioned by parliament in 1571, in the so-called Subscription Act (13 Eliz., cap. 12). Thereafter priest's or deacon's orders, or transference of benefices with cure of souls, were granted only after subscription. The reason for the long delay was the rigid refusal of the queen to allow parliament to introduce a bill affecting religion: as she explained to Archbishop Parker in 1566, only the royal prerogative could deal with such matters. And furthermore, the Articles as they were originally drafted by convocation contained non-doctrinal clauses that were repugnant to the puritan or radical element among the clergy. Thus it was not until the third parliament met in 1571, when these clauses were removed by strong puritan pressure, that the Articles were given full statutory authority.[1]

On the disciplinary side, too, the reconstruction of the church

[1] See Makower, p. 171.

was accompanied by great difficulties. Parker found that his freedom to exercise authority was weakened by the lack of support from the queen, and by open or secret obstruction from certain of her councillors. It was only after extensive disorders had broken out, too glaring to be passed over, that he ventured to issue his *Book of Advertisements* (1566); and he was careful to temper his regulations with the remark that they were merely for the preservation of order and decency in the church service. Thanks to his efforts, however, there gradually emerged a national church with a distinctive service, a distinctive creed, and a distinctive clergy.

Meanwhile, in 1562, Bishop John Jewel of Salisbury published his *Apology* in order to explain and justify the principles of the settlement. This celebrated work, although it lacked the balance and repose of Hooker's greater apology a generation later, remained the basis of the anglican reply to catholic controversialists throughout the period. Jewel took his stand on the theory already embedded in the Acts of Supremacy and Uniformity, and contended that the archetype of the anglican church was the christian church as it existed prior to the establishment of the universal power of the Roman bishop, and of the elaborate ritualistic accretions of the middle ages. 'We have planted no new religion,' he wrote, 'but only have renewed the old that was undoubtedly founded and used by the apostles of Christ and other holy fathers in the primitive church, and of this long late time, by means of the multitude of your traditions and vanities, hath been drowned.' The importance of the argument lay in the fact that it boldly appealed to the church of the first six centuries as the standard of christian belief and practice. On this firm historical foundation the Anglican defence rested until the 'judicious' Hooker still further strengthened it by introducing the appeal to pure reason. Meanwhile the *Apology* found its way, either in its original Latin garb or in translations, into every European country, and gained wide-spread recognition as one of the most notable books of its time.[1]

The coming into force of the anti-papal legislation, and the diocesan visitations of the ecclesiastical commissioners, were

---

[1] The publication of the *Apology* led to a furious controversy (1564–7), no fewer than forty volumes of catholic polemic being written in reply by those who had settled in the Netherlands. The revolt in the Low Countries extinguished the controversy.

accompanied, particularly in London and adjacent parts, by an ebullition of public feeling against the church; and a considerable amount of looting, burning, and destruction took place. In the autumn of 1559 'papist gear' of all kinds—roods, crucifixes, images of Mary and John, copes, altar-cloths—were pillaged from the churches, piled up in the streets, and given to the flames in what has been called a protestant Bartholomew. Possibly some degree of violence was unavoidable on the occasion, but the appetite for destruction once whetted did not confine itself to 'things savouring of superstition', whose abolition the queen sanctioned by her Injunctions. It passed into an insensate *furor* of vandalism, in which valuable monuments and family memorials were defaced. To meet this contingency a proclamation was issued (September 1560) prohibiting the destruction of monuments of antiquity set up in the churches for memory and not for superstition. But much irreparable mischief had been done by mob violence before it could be arrested. Patrons of cures appear to have been no less rapacious. Responsible churchmen like Bishop Jewel speak of them as 'latrones', robbers, rather than patrons, and complaints were frequent that valuable church property disappeared, to say nothing of the plunder of bells and lead roofing. Even the attitude of the court savoured of vandalism, though in a more subtle way. Elizabeth took over the most eligible of the 'lands, manors, tenements, and castles' belonging to the bishoprics in exchange for the much less valuable 'tithes and parsonages impropriate' which had been annexed by the Crown at the dissolution of the abbeys.

Many protestations were addressed to the queen to prove that the step was both iniquitous and dangerous. Would it not lead directly to the decay of learning? Were not bishoprics rewards for studious men? Did not the bishops voluntarily maintain scholars at the universities out of their revenues, and how could they do so if they were cramped? Besides, a married clergy needed a larger income for purposes of hospitality and the education of their families than the old celibate prelates. But however good the arguments, the installation of the primate and the consecration of the bishops elect was delayed until the lands had been surveyed and the exchange carried out.

The effect of all this was incalculable. Destruction and desecration of sacred things brought about a general growth of irreverence in both the destroyers and those who watched the disappearance of the symbols they held dear; and it is questionable if the public mind recovered from the shock to which it was subjected. 'It cannot cause surprise', says a well-known writer, 'that to many people, and those the best, even the abuses of the old system were more dear than the reforms of the new.'[1]

[1] W. H. Frere, *The English Church in the Reigns of Elizabeth and James I.*

II

ENGLAND AND FRANCE

MEANWHILE Elizabeth had made her first experiments in foreign policy with a boldness that hardly corresponded with her slender resources.

For some weeks previous to her accession commissioners representing France, Spain, Savoy, and England had been engaged, at Cercamp, a Flemish village near the French border, in winding up the last of the great wars between the house of Valois and the house of Habsburg. War-weariness, financial exhaustion, and indecisive results rendered it comparatively easy for the two chief belligerents, France and Spain, to settle their differences on the basis of a mutual withdrawal from conquered territory, and a return to the *status quo ante bellum*. But the fate of Calais, which England had lost to France in the course of the struggle,[1] still hung in the balance, delaying indefinitely the conclusion of a general peace. It was a matter that admitted of only one rational solution, namely, the formal cession of the town to its captors; for the time had come when England must cut herself adrift from territorial commitments on the Continent, and launch out on her true destiny as an island kingdom. The wounded pride of a defeated nation, however, would not brook such a solution. The loss of Calais, over whose walls the English flag had floated for two hundred years, whose gates once bore the haughty inscription:

> Then shall the Frenchman Calais win
> When iron and lead like cork shall swim:

had created as much excitement in London as, let us say, the loss of a place like Gibraltar might be expected to produce at the present day. So much glamorous sentiment had attached itself to this 'brightest jewel in the English crown', as the saying then went, that its recovery by diplomatic means would have done much to mitigate the gloom that surrounded the death-bed of Mary Tudor. But France was adamant: under no circumstances would she include Calais in the general programme of restitutions; rather than surrender it, said the French king, Henry II,

---

[1] 7 Jan. 1558.

he would hazard his crown. So Mary went to her grave with Calais written on her heart; and Elizabeth found herself confronted with a bad debt, which prudence suggested should be abandoned at the earliest possible moment, but the recovery of which might well prove to be a splendid augury for the success of the new reign, an earnest of better things to come. Naturally she resolved to make the recovery of Calais the prime object of her diplomacy, and a proof that the vindication of the national honour was her deepest concern. She could hardly have acted otherwise.

But the quest was hopeless from the start. The French were in effective occupation; they had won the place in fair fight in a legitimate war; its acquisition completed the territorial unity of the kingdom, and ended once for all the medieval anomaly of an English settlement in the midst of a community homogeneously French. Nothing, therefore, would induce them to reconsider their decision, although they were willing enough to fall in with any verbal subterfuge whereby England's humiliation might be softened. The duke of Guise, whose prowess had resulted in the original capture of the town, only voiced the opinion of his fellow countrymen when he stated that he would rather sacrifice a hundred thousand lives than evacuate it. Against this stubborn attitude all juridical and canonical arguments beat in vain. Nor could King Philip II of Spain, in whose interest England had entered the war, prevail upon France to abate one jot of her demand. His desire to see the English again in possession of Calais was undeniable.[1] He was in honour bound to do what he could for his unfortunate ally and fully cognizant of his obligation; it was also important that a place of such strategic value for his dominions, commanding, as it did, the sea route between Spain and the Netherlands, should be in friendly hands. Besides, there was the over-riding consideration that Spanish *Weltpolitik* and the maintenance of the existing balance of power in Europe required the continuance of Anglo-Spanish co-operation. But Philip was not a free agent. His treasury was empty and his need for peace very great.[2] He was worried with the many distractions incidental to a ruler whose

---

[1] 'As the English entered into this war for our cause the treaties which bound them to do so also bind us not to treat without them, and we are determined to fulfil this obligation and to conclude no peace without their consent.' (The king to de Feria, 28 Dec. 1558, *Span. Cal.* i.)

[2] A. de Ruble, *Le Traité de Cateau-Cambrésis*, pp. 8, 9.

empire reached from the North Sea to the Mediterranean, from the confines of Germany to Peru. The Turkish fleet had made an onslaught on Minorca; the Moors had inflicted a serious reverse on the Spanish forces in Morocco; the plague of heresy was making headway in the Netherlands and even in Spain itself—in short the position, as the Spaniard saw it, was so desperate that ruin stared him in the face if the peace negotiations miscarried and war broke out again in northern Europe. All things considered, then, King Philip could not give England unconditional and unlimited support in her demand for Calais; nor, indeed, was he prepared to continue his support unless he had ample assurance that the change of government in London would not mean a change in the direction of English foreign policy. If, however, he could feel sure that England under the new régime would remain, as before, the client state of Spain: if, better still, Elizabeth would marry him and keep her hands off the catholic religion, he would do his utmost to give her satisfaction in regard to Calais; otherwise he would be compelled to let matters take their course. These conditions were perhaps reasonable enough from the Spanish point of view; but any hope the king may have had of their acceptance was rudely dashed by the incalculable audacity of Elizabeth. Politely but firmly she turned aside his offer of marriage and pursued her preparations for the religious revolution in England uninterruptedly. Thus Philip's interest in Calais gradually faded. In March 1559, after the conference had resumed its meetings at Cateau-Cambrésis, he announced the transference of his matrimonial offer from Elizabeth of England to Elizabeth of Valois, eldest daughter of Henry II—a plain intimation that the conclusion of a Franco-Spanish peace was not far off.

There was now nothing left for Elizabeth to do but to get the best terms she could from France; and so, on 2 April, she compromised on the following conditions. Calais was to remain in the possession of the French for eight years, at the expiry of which it was to revert to England, under penalty for default of half a million crowns. The French undertook to send hostages as a token of their honourable intentions, and the question of ultimate sovereignty was deferred to the end of the probationary period. It was also stipulated—an important reservation, as we shall see—that the fulfilment of the bargain should be dependent upon mutual abstention from acts of aggression in the meantime, and that Scotland, as France's ally, should be included in the protective guarantee. Under this transparently face-saving device was Calais virtually ceded to France—not in intention but in effect; for no one doubted that the French government would find a pretext, under the clause of reservation, for retaining the place when the allotted period ran out. On the other hand, events were soon to show that Elizabeth, for her part, did not hold herself bound by the treaty, but would attempt to recover Calais by force or stratagem as soon as a fair opportunity offered. The morality of governments in relation to international obligations was proverbially low in the sixteenth century, and treaties were regarded as binding only in so far and for so long as they subserved the interests of the states that made them. Of such a nature was the Anglo-French section of the treaty of Cateau-Cambrésis. Mutual distrust, rancour, and unfulfilled hopes dogged it like a shadow.

Elizabeth had good reason to be suspicious of the French. From the first, their attitude to her accession had been one of ill-concealed hostility. Already the dauphiness had quartered the English insignia on her shield along with those of France and Scotland; and more than once during the discussions at Cateau-Cambrésis the malevolence of the French delegates had broken through the thin crust of diplomatic suavity. Rumours were also current that Henry II was using his influence at Rome to draw the papal thunders against the daughter of Anne Boleyn, and that preparations were in train for an invasion of England. The tension was probably increased by the publication of the bull, *Cum ex apostolatus*, on 16 February; for although Paul IV did not mention any ruler by name, he declared that all sovereigns who supported heresy in their dominions fell from their right by the mere fact of their heresy. Circumstances therefore seemed to point to the likelihood of a French crusade on behalf of Mary Stuart, and de Feria thought it necessary to warn his master on the subject on 11 April. But Henry II was too circumspect a prince to risk a fresh European conflagration on the morrow of a definitive peace settlement. So long as he lived the Stuart claim to the English Crown would be no more than a tacit threat.

In July, however, fate took an unexpected hand in the game. The king died suddenly of a lance-thrust at a tournament held

in honour of his daughter Elizabeth's marriage to Philip II; and
the crown passed to the dauphin, Francis, and his consort, Mary
Stuart. The house of Guise was now dominant in France. The
queen's uncles, the duke of Guise and the cardinal of Lorraine,
formed along with the chancellor a secret cabinet for the direction of national policy.[1] All offices in the patronage of the Crown
were at their disposal, and were filled with their partisans. In
Scotland another member of the same family, Mary of Guise,
ruled in trust for her daughter. Is it surprising that Elizabeth
should view with grave concern the amassing of power by so
formidable a group, whose enmity to herself was the common
talk of Europe, and who put family aggrandizement before all
other considerations? What was to hinder them, now that they
had the resources of both France and Scotland at their feet,
from seeking to establish a Guise ascendancy over England as
well? The lure was great: their niece's claim would furnish a
colourable pretext for the enterprise; and Scotland would make
an admirable *point d'appui*.

A French intervention in Scotland was indeed overdue, if the
protectorate established by Henry II was to be maintained; for
the country was in a state of appalling disorder, and administration had become difficult. The Scots, whose love for their
'auld' ally had never been a positive sentiment nourished by
community of culture, but an artificially created affection rest-
ing on the negative basis of enmity to England, had given way
to a francophobia. The Frenchman was too much in evidence
everywhere—in the high seat of government, in society, in the
army; and everything seemed to point to his making himself
master of the country, to the destruction of its independence.
In many respects the position tallied with that which obtained
in England shortly before Elizabeth's accession. Just as the
London populace cold-shouldered the Spaniard in the streets,
so the Scots rabbled the bodyguard of M. d'Oysel in the streets
of Edinburgh. The government of the regent was watched with
suspicion and distrust, and her efforts to enforce the laws was
met with the cry of outraged liberties. 'And now that it is a question of my determination to see justice take a straight-forward

[1] 'Before the "Council of Affairs" assembles, the Cardinal of Lorraine, the duke
of Guise, with the chancellor meet first, either in the king's chamber or in that of
the queen mother, where they discuss privately all matters of the greatest importance, without communicating their deliberations to others.' (*Venetian Cal.*, 1558–
80, Tiepolo to the Doge and Senate, 16 July 1559.)

course, and they find me a little severe,' wrote Mary of Guise to her brother the cardinal of Lorraine, 'they will not endure it, and say that these laws are the laws of the French.'[1] Racial antagonism, however, was of small moment compared with the vast social and political upheaval caused by the growth of protestantism. After a decade of propaganda, persecutions, and martyrdoms, the followers of the new doctrines had secured the support of an influential section of the nobility, and banded themselves together in a covenant for the defence of the gospel, under the title of the 'Congregation'. In 1559 the movement was greatly strengthened by the fiery apparition of John Knox, who brought with him to Scotland a militant Calvinism excelling in severity anything that had hitherto appeared in Europe. It was Calvinism with a 'war-head' attached, similar in character to that which prevailed among the Huguenots in France. Immediately the whole structure of religious and political life in Scotland, which had enjoyed the prescription of centuries, was shaken to its foundations, and a fury of destruction, popular in origin, laid waste historic churches and abbeys at Perth, Scone, Stirling, Linlithgow, Edinburgh, and, spreading rapidly through Fife, reduced St. Andrews to a ruined and depopulated city. In Perth the mob attacked and gutted the monasteries of the grey friars (Franciscans), the black friars (Dominicans), the white friars (Carmelites), and completely destroyed the Charterhouse of the Carthusians. 'Down with the nests', cried Knox, 'and the rooks will fly away.' The ancient abbey church of Scone, where Scottish kings had been crowned for hundreds of years, perished among the ruins. It was as if a cyclone had struck the country: 'All kirkmen's goods and gear', says the *Diurnal of Occurrents*, 'were spulzeit and reft fra' them in every place where the samyn could be apprehendit.'

The devastation continued through the early summer months without abatement; and on 29 June, Sir William Kirkaldy of Grange deemed it advisable to explain to Sir Henry Percy what was actually happening north of the border. 'We mean nothing', he said, 'but reformation of religion': 'the manner of their proceeding in reformation is this: they pull down all manner of friaries and some abbeys, which willingly receive not the reformation. As to parish churches, they cleanse them of images and all other monuments of idolatry, and command that no Masses be

[1] See J. H. Pollen, *Papal Negotiations with Mary Queen of Scots*, 1901.

said in them, in place whereof the book (i.e. prayer-book) set forth by godly king Edward VI is read in the same churches.' Knox corroborated: 'Persuade yourself and assure others', he wrote to Percy, 'that we mean neither sedition nor rebellion against any just and lawful authority, but only the advancement of Christ's religion and the liberty of this poor realm.'

At first the queen regent, moved by a natural desire to save the French alliance, the sheet anchor of her policy, tried to steer a middle course between the 'reformers' and the catholic church: she temporized, prevaricated, did everything in her power to moderate the *tempo* of the anti-clerical party; but the inflammatory preaching of Knox, and the vandalism of the 'rascal multitude' which it provoked, soon led her to the conviction that 'it is not religion, nor anything thereunto pertaining, that they seek, but only the subversion of our authority, and the usurpation of the crown'. Accordingly she published a proclamation which had the effect of arraigning the whole 'reform' party as sedition-mongers and enemies of the state. She had no option in the matter, if the French protectorate was to be maintained; but the step she took was fraught with the gravest consequences.

If the catholic church in Scotland had been worthier of support: if the secular arm had been longer and stronger: if the papacy had been alerted in time and less dilatory in action: if the French king had been guided by his conscience and not by material interests—if any or all of this formidable catalogue of 'ifs' had been realized, matters might have taken a different course. But in reality the rotten fabric of the church, long since known to be tottering and in need of the most drastic treatment 'in head and members', merited most of the censures showered upon it by Knox and his followers; the forces at the disposal of the regent were inadequate to cope with the turmoil; and Henry II of France was not interested, he said, in 'the consciences of Scotsmen'—he would be prepared, however, to hazard his crown and all he had, rather than that the young queen of Scots should lose her right. But if it were a matter only of religion that moved them, *as he had been informed*, 'we must commit Scotsmen's souls unto God, for we have enough ado to rule the consciences of our own countrymen'. Consequently the reformers boldly defied the regent's authority, and sought to paralyse any coercive measures she might take against them by recourse to arms. Safety, as Knox said, consisted in numbers. Nay, he went farther, and in the name of a most revolutionary political philosophy, deduced from the Scriptures as a precept of Almighty God, proclaimed that a wicked ruler setting herself up against the 'godly' might with divine sanction be deposed. Being also an idolator—as all worshippers at Mass appeared to him to be—she might lawfully be put to death; for did not the Scriptures plainly command that idolators should die the death?[1] Thus a holy war was begun against France and the catholic church, and protestantism became identified with patriotism. The die was cast when the Congregation, after vainly attempting to arrest the military precautions of the government by a peremptory demand to stop the fortification of Leith, formally declared the regent deposed at the market cross of Edinburgh (October 1559).

In the ordinary course of events, and granted free access to the port of Leith, a powerful military state like France should have had little difficulty in suppressing the rebellion. Ill-armed peasantry and burghers, without experience in war, were no match for infantry trained in the tradition of Bayard and Gaston de Foix. Herein, precisely, lay Elizabeth's peril. She could not help the Scots openly because she was pledged to a policy of non-intervention by the treaty of Cateau-Cambrésis; and yet, if the French conquered them, the next step might be the invasion of England. Clearly something would have to be done to checkmate France before this danger materialized. Subsidies and munitions might, for example, be smuggled into Scotland from Berwick: the earl of Arran might be brought back from France, in order to give the rebellion a show of legality and a titular head: an army might be mobilized in the northern English counties, as a precautionary measure, and to lend moral support. All these things Elizabeth did on the advice, and with the warm approval of Cecil, who had been secretly engaged for months in stimulating the ardour of the rebels.[2] But the situation in Scotland grew steadily worse as the autumn wore on, and the subsidies were as good as wasted. Not only were the Scots defeated in the field, but defeat greatly damped the fiery ardour which, in the first flush, had brought men to the standard in

---

[1] Knox's 'murderous syllogism'. He relied on the Old Testament denunciations of the Amalekites, and Elijah's slaughter of the prophets of Baal.

[2] See Conyers Read, *Mr. Secretary Cecil and Queen Elizabeth*, chap. vii, for a full account.

such numbers that it 'rained steel bonnets'. Sorrowfully Knox had to admit that the arm of the flesh was a failure. 'The whole multitude standen in such doubt', he wrote to Cecil, 'they cannot tell to which party they shall incline.' 'For God's sake', wailed Cecil to Sir Ralph Sadler at Berwick, 'comfort them to stand fast.'

The military weakness of the Scots was bad enough, but not so serious as their lack of a navy. The North Sea in winter might be a fickle friend to the French, as they found to their cost in December, when two expeditions bound for Leith with men, guns, and stores, were blown back and wrecked, only a few stragglers reaching the haven in safety. Nevertheless, it was confidently stated in France that by Candlemas there would be an army of ten thousand on Scottish soil; and in any case these disasters did not greatly hinder the plans of the garrison at Leith. On Christmas eve, a detachment crossed the Forth to Burntisland, and set out on a rapid march to St. Andrews accompanied by their ships. The Congregation, whose numbers had been much thinned, owing to the season of the year, could do nothing to arrest their progress. Obviously the time had come for Elizabeth, if she wished to save the Scottish cause from destruction, to throw off the mask of neutrality with which she had been vainly trying to delude the regent.

For weeks she had been watching the darkening prospect with an anxious eye, fully aware of the extensive military preparations in France and the bellicose utterances of the Guises, but reluctant to commit herself to war because of doubtful reports from the Netherlands as to Spain's attitude, and her own unpreparedness. However, she had mobilized 4,000 men beyond Trent for service on the border under the duke of Norfolk and Lord Grey de Wilton, and—more important still—had instructed Admiral Winter to take a fleet to the Forth and 'impeach' the French in whatever way he could, provided he acted on his own responsibility. Then at length, on 24 December, the privy council resolved upon open intervention in Scotland, and instructions were sent to Norfolk on the following day. He was to proceed in aid of the Scots with the utmost care and deliberation, and not to unleash the army under Grey's command until he was reasonably certain that the regent would not agree to the removal of the French troops by negotiation, and that the combined forces of England and Scotland were sufficient for the enterprise. Five days later, these orders were countermanded, the duke being informed that he must limit his action to sending secret succours—captains, powder, shot, and guns—into Scotland, and rely mainly on Winter and the fleet.

Meanwhile the admiral, who left Queenborough on 27 December, was slowly making his way northward through heavy weather to strike the first blow against the French. It took him three weeks to reach Berwick; but on 23 January he was safely in the Forth. Fortified by words of encouragement from Norfolk, and more detailed instructions, he sailed boldly for the narrow passage between Queensferry and Burntisland, which formed the line of communication between Leith and the French army in Fife. The effect was immediate. Hardly had his guns begun to speak at Inchkeith than the campaign on the north side of the Forth came to an abrupt termination. Seeing the English in command of the sea, and fearful of being marooned in Fife, the French abandoned their ordnance, set their stores in a blaze, and retreated swiftly by the circuitous route of Dunfermline and Stirling to their base on the southern side of the firth.

By this time Norfolk and Grey were getting into position on the border; but the formalities of a treaty arrangement with the Scots delayed action for a month. Eventually, on 27 February, an offensive and defensive alliance was made between Norfolk and the Scottish lords, whereby Elizabeth took over the protection of Scotland, its civil and religious liberties, so long as the marriage of the queen of Scots and the French king endured, and one month longer; the Scots undertaking, for their part, to aid England with 2,000 foot and 1,000 horse in the event of an invasion by France. The object of the alliance was not to abrogate the sovereign rights of Queen Mary—these were safeguarded by the treaty—but to prevent the overthrow of Scottish independence by the French.

Elizabeth, however, did not yet see her way clear to give the treaty its military expression. She had to keep a wary eye on the Netherlands, where the Spanish troops employed in the late war were still under arms, and the viceroy, Margaret of Parma, was urging the king to use them for the preservation of European peace.[1] At the same time Granvelle, president of the Spanish *consulta* at Brussels, took the English ambassador, Sir Thomas Challoner, to task for his mistress's rashness in provoking

---

[1] The Spanish forces were not recalled to Spain until the autumn of 1560.

a war for which she was utterly unprepared. 'Is it not strange', he asked, 'that ye believe the world knoweth not nor seeth your weakness? ... Is there one fortress or hold in all England, that is able for one day to endure the breath of a cannon?' 'The cock may scrape so long in the dunghill', said another Spaniard in high position, 'till at last he discovereth the knife to cut his own throat.' Challoner was much perturbed by what he heard, but more so by the hostile chatter in Spanish military circles, where intervention was regarded as certain. He therefore wrote to Cecil: 'Whiles two cocks fight, beware the still cock, looking on and taking breath, when he seeth them tired, do not set upon both.' Very different, however, was the tale which Sir Thomas Gresham had to tell. Gresham was Elizabeth's financial agent in the Low Countries, and had his finger on the pulse of the merchant community, as well as access by his extensive system of espionage to the innermost secrets of the *consulta*. He therefore knew just how much or how little importance to attach to rumours of Spanish bellicosity. He had discovered among other things that the royal finances were so chaotic, and the royal credit so low, that it was morally certain King Philip could not raise a finger against England; that all the gold of the Indies would not suffice to extinguish his mountainous debts; and that the Flemings who lived by commerce with England would not tolerate a war between the two countries.

Gresham's exploits at this time were literally amazing. Keeping an open house and a bounteous table, he dined the great financiers of Antwerp, the Fuggers and the Schetzes:[1] 'dried up' the Bourse by the loans he contracted, and 'robbed the city of Antwerp of all its fine gold and silver': bribed the customs officers of the port, especially the chief searcher, and was able by their connivance to snap his fingers at proclamations prohibiting the export of arms and munitions. Thus, under the very eyes of the government, consignments of precious metals and ship-loads of ordnance, arquebuses, morions, corselets, pikes, dags, and gunpowder left the quays at Antwerp for the Tower of London. By the aid of his accomplices he even plundered the royal arsenal at Malines. 'I will confess here', he wrote to Cecil, 'that by trickery I have drawn 2,000 corselets from the royal arsenal at Malines and they are now in England. You will understand that their disappearance has created no small stir among the officers.

[1] Gaspard Schetz was *trésorier-général des finances* at Brussels.

Meanwhile, very heartening news was coming in from Sir Nicholas Throckmorton, the English ambassador in Paris, who began to allude, as early as 4 February, to 'factions in religion springing up everywhere' in France, and urged the queen to 'beat the iron while it is hot'. 'Many wise men', he wrote, 'agree that now is the time and good occasion offered to abate the French pride.' About the same time Christopher Mundt transmitted startling news to Cecil from Strassburg about a conspiracy hatched in France against the Guises, of which, he remarked, 'some of the first rank in France are cognizant'. Then came the actual outbreak of the Tumult of Amboise, on 16 and 17 March, the attempted capture or assassination of the duke and cardinal of Guise, and the temporary paralysis of the government. Four days later Throckmorton was jubilant. 'The queen may now see', he wrote, 'what advantage she has over the French, who are so troubled that they know not where to levy any force. . . . It will be to her advantage to have gained somewhat of the French before the king of Spain interposes himself in these matters.'

The chance was not to be missed. On 28 March word was sent to Lord Grey to set the English army of 6,500 in motion from Berwick, and to join the Scots at Prestonpans. Thus, when a messenger[1] arrived from King Philip on 5 April, with urgent representations that an armistice should be declared and war avoided, he was confronted with a *fait accompli*: Grey had effected a junction with the Scottish army, and was on his way to the siege of Leith. The war of the insignia had begun.

It is not necessary to follow the course of the campaign. It was by no means glorious, except, perhaps, to the defeated French. The besiegers were numerous enough to contain the enemy in their entrenchments, but insufficient to carry the place by assault. Nor did they agree at first as to the objects of the war. The Scots demanded the deposition of Mary of Guise, the evacuation of Scotland by the French, and the transference of the administration to a committee of themselves. Elizabeth was interested only in the ulterior motives of the French, and the defence of England; and if she could have security by treaty she was prepared even to aid the regent in reducing her rebellious subjects to order. It was not until Mary of Guise, buoyed up by

---

[1] De Glajon, a Fleming by birth and friendly to England, who secretly advised Cecil to continue hostilities.

false reports of coming succours from France, refused to recognize the Anglo-Scottish alliance, or to consider a settlement, that the aims of the allies became focused on the same object—the expulsion of the French bag and baggage. Even so, however, events moved with leaden foot, and the siege was grossly mismanaged. The grand assault on 8 May ended disastrously for the attackers, from inadequate preparation and lack of proper siege-tackle, and was not repeated. In the end it was not military defeat but sheer starvation and want of support from France that caused the gallant garrison to capitulate. Throckmorton had been a true prophet.

The peace negotiations, which were begun at Edinburgh while the siege was still in progress, were much delayed by Elizabeth's insistence on the restoration of Calais to England and an indemnity of 500,000 crowns for her losses; but eventually, on 6 July 1560, after threatening to break off the conference and reinforce Grey for another assault on Leith, Cecil compelled the French to surrender on all essential points. The dowager had meanwhile died in the castle. The Treaty of Edinburgh, as it was called, solemnly reaffirmed the provisions of the previous treaty, pledged both France and England to a policy of non-interference in Scotland, handed over the government to a Scottish council of twelve (of whom five were to be chosen by the lords of parliament and seven by Queen Mary), and provided for the evacuation of the kingdom by the French and the destruction of their fortifications at Leith, Dunbar, and Eyemouth. No mention was made of religion or of the Anglo-Scottish alliance, both subjects being regarded as too burning to be touched. In regard to the question of the insignia, however, it was agreed that Francis and Mary should abstain 'for all time coming' from using the style and arms of England and Ireland.

These were substantial results to have achieved after so indecisive a war and a great personal triumph for Cecil. They would have to be ratified later by the king and queen of France; but for the moment Elizabeth might rest assured that she was safe from a French attack through Scotland. Moreover, the reformation was now securely established north of the Tweed, and a bond of common interest forged between the two kingdoms, of incalculable use to herself and the Scottish reformers in the future. Yet in spite of it all the queen was far from contented with the settlement. She bitterly upbraided Cecil for his failure to secure the town of Calais and the indemnity, and on his return to London treated him with studied disfavour, even to the extent of leaving him out of pocket for his expenses.[1] Worse still, he learned, to his surprise, that she had no intention of following up her victory and consolidating the favourable position she held with the Scottish lords. In vain he argued that the 'union of hearts' brought about by the war should be strengthened by a policy of lavish money grants to men like Lord James Stuart, the earl of Glencairn, the Lords Maxwell and Hume, and the lairds of Lethington and Grange.[2] In vain, also, Throckmorton pointed out, in dispatch after dispatch from Paris, that £20,000 yearly was not too much to pay for 'the assured amity of Scotland'. Neither his advice, nor his reports that France was still bellicose and unlikely to ratify the treaty, made any impression on the stubborn refusal of the queen to spend another penny on Scotland: it had cost her enough already (£133,886. 4s.), and the short-distance loans contracted by Gresham would have to be repaid at an early date. Likewise she received the proffered hand of friendship from Edinburgh with a cold indifference; and when the 'lords of the parliament of Scotland' sent an embassy urging her 'to join herself in marriage with the earl of Arran' as the most effective way of establishing the security of both kingdoms, and of making herself 'the strongest prince in christendom upon the seas', she placidly remarked that while she prized the amity of Scotland she thought the two countries could work together for common political ends quite as effectively without marriage as with it. Nay, she went farther and seized the occasion to tell the embassy that the conduct of the Scottish parliament in carrying out a thorough reformation of the church and religion, since the close of the war, was jeopardizing the ratification of the treaty by the French government.

This was a dangerous line to follow; but fortune favoured Elizabeth. In December (1560) Francis II died—'of a rotten ear', said the unsympathetic Knox: the Guises fell from power: the widowed Mary Stuart was thrust into the background of French politics; and the queen mother, Catherine de Médicis, assumed the regency during the minority of the new king, Charles IX.

[1] It is worth while noting, however, that five months later she appointed him Master of the Court of Wards—a lucrative office, and six months after that, she made him a substantial grant of lands: see Read, p. 192.

[2] 'With one thousand pounds I durst undertake to save £20,000 in five years, and with £2,000 to save £40,000. And yet it is no good counsel.'

To Throckmorton these unexpected events seemed like a crowning mercy from Heaven. 'The queen', he wrote, 'has now cause to thank God for so well providing for her security by taking away the late king.' Up to a point he was right. The new French government was not disposed to reopen the war with England, nor to fight the battle of the Guises and their niece; and within a few months Elizabeth was able to boast that 'save for manners' sake she needed no ambassador at the court of France'. But if Throckmorton had been able to pierce a little farther into the mysterious ways of providence he would not have been so optimistic—as we shall see presently.

Meanwhile let us look at what was happening behind the scenery of the political pageant. If Cecil was perturbed at the nonchalant way in which Elizabeth gambled away the amity of Scotland, he was still more perturbed, on his return from Edinburgh, to find her sunk in amorous dalliance with one who bore the most tainted name among the aristocracy of England. After solemnly assuring her first parliament that she intended to live and die a virgin, and, in the spirit of this assurance, rejecting several suitors much higher in rank—including the archduke of Austria and Eric prince of Sweden—she had seemingly fallen a victim to the charms of Lord Robert Dudley, son of the arch-traitor Northumberland who perished on the scaffold in Mary's reign.[1] It may be assumed as practically certain that Elizabeth entertained the hope of marrying Dudley as soon as the way was clear: that is, as soon as he was freed from Amy Robsart, who had been his wife for eleven years. He had already been

---

[1] The precise nature of the liaison with Lord Robert cannot be determined by the recorded facts of history. Men of the world, taking their stand on the statements of the Spanish ambassador, will probably always believe that the queen was Dudley's mistress, in the full sense of the word. But the evidence in favour of such a view comes, it will be observed, from a hostile source, and cannot, therefore, be accepted *simpliciter*; while, on the other hand, we have Elizabeth's own assurance, given to her council at a solemn moment (Nov. 1562), when she was seriously ill of the small-pox and believed herself to be dying, that 'nothing unseemly' had ever passed between them. For a vigorous defence of the queen and Dudley, consult F. Chamberlin, *The Private Character of Queen Elizabeth* (1921), pp. 176 and 212–16. Chamberlin points out that the case against them rests on a mis-translation of two words in the letter from the Spanish ambassador (de Quadra) to the duchess of Parma, 11 Sept. 1560. The words are *privança* and *desórdenes*, which are rendered in English as 'intimacy' and 'misconduct' respectively: thus giving an immoral meaning to each. According to Chamberlin, however, *privança* means favour, protection, familiar intercourse *between a prince*, or great personage, *and a person of inferior rank*; and *desórdenes* signifies disorder, confusion, irregularity. Neither word, therefore, should be construed as 'illicit relations'.

promoted to the Order of the Garter and was Master of the Horse. Moreover, it was believed by many that considerations of propriety, morality, or the public interest would not deter Lord Robert from using fraud or violence to attain his end, if either promised a chance of success; and rumours were afloat as early as November 1559 that he intended to poison his wife. It was noted also that he became an assiduous cultivator of the Spanish ambassador, de Quadra: a sign, presumably, that if public opinion countered him he would carry through his project with the help of Spain. Thus the potential danger to the state was twofold. If Dudley killed his wife, or procured her death, or even if she died in circumstances that gave rise to a suspicion of violence, the queen could not escape a share of the obloquy; and if she married him thereafter, under Spanish auspices, it could only be at the price of far-reaching concessions, tantamount to a complete reversal of all she had hitherto achieved, and the renewal of Spanish influence in England.[1]

Such, then, was the posture of affairs when Cecil returned from his peace labours in Scotland. He found Lord Robert in the seat of power, the queen listless and apathetic in matters of business, and de Quadra a prime favourite at court. In fact, the stage was set for the amazing drama about to burst on the world.

On 6 September 1560 the secretary, pocketing his pride, approached the Spaniard with a doleful tale of coming ruin to the state, and besought him to remonstrate with the queen on her misgovernment. He had decided, he said, to retire to the country 'even if they sent him to the Tower for it'. At the same time he communicated the startling information that a plot for the murder of Amy Robsart by poison was actually in train, and that she was already reported to be ill, although, he said, he knew that at the moment she was quite well. The very next day, on her return from hunting, Elizabeth herself told de Quadra, in confidence, that Lord Robert's wife was dead or nearly so—a strangely significant remark if Cecil was right about the state of her health. Twenty-four hours later Lady Dudley was found dead, with her neck broken, at the bottom of a stair in Cumnor Place, her husband's Berkshire residence. The news of the occurrence was not published at Windsor until the 11th, when it was represented to be the result of an accident: she had broken her neck, said Elizabeth to the Spanish ambassador: she must have fallen down

[1] See footnote to p. 52 below.

a stair. If this was the official version of the tragedy, it was also the view of the coroner's jury, who returned a verdict of death by misadventure, and acquitted Lord Robert of all responsibility in the matter. But public opinion, cognizant of the long intrigue preceding the event, refused to accept the accident theory. Before this unconventional tribunal Dudley stood condemned, and the queen was regarded as consentient to the crime.

It stands to reason that we can never know the truth about the Cumnor tragedy. It may have been a case of suicide—Amy Robsart had plenty to grieve and distract her; but, in the opinion of the most competent historian[1] who has investigated the facts, so far as they are available, the presumption is strong that she was deliberately murdered; and, if this be so, the candid critic might reasonably conclude that Elizabeth was just as much a party to it as Mary Stuart was to the Darnley murder. The only material difference between the two cases is that Mary married Bothwell after the murder, and Elizabeth did not marry Dudley; but this was due to a difference of temperament, not of intention. The 'queen' had mastered the 'woman'.

Everywhere in Europe the worst construction was put upon the deed. Either it was believed that Dudley had killed his wife in order to marry the queen, or that he was already secretly married to her. Throckmorton was so affronted with the abominable reports circulating in Paris that 'every hair on my head stareth and my ears glow to hear'. 'The queen your mistress', said the Spanish ambassador to him, 'doth show that she hath honour but for a few in her realm, for no man will advise her to leave her folly.' In Germany, where the protestant princes had begun to build their hopes on England, consternation was the prevailing note.

Now although Elizabeth might—and did—affect an attitude of bland indifference, she could not be altogether impervious to

---

[1] E. Bekker, *Elisabeth und Leicester* (*Giessener Studien*, v, 1890). Bekker's conclusion is that Amy Robsart was probably murdered by poison, and then her neck was broken and the body placed at the foot of the stairs, so as to give the appearance of death by a fall. Froude's comment on the episode is as follows: 'The conclusion seems inevitable, that although Dudley was innocent of a direct participation in the crime, the unhappy lady was sacrificed to his ambition. She was murdered by persons who hoped to profit by his elevation to the throne.' But the reader might consult with advantage Professor Ian Aird's article in *Eng. Hist. Rev.*, Jan. 1956, entitled 'The Death of Amy Robsart—Accident, Suicide, or Murder—or Disease; in which he propounds 'spontaneous fracture' of the spine, due to disease, as the cause of death.

the shafts of criticism that struck her from all quarters. She was angry at first, and for a time matters hung in the balance, but she soon realized that she had committed a *faux pas*. The marriage with Lord Robert was definitely given up, and Cecil was called in to help in the extrication of the queen and her lover from the consequences of their conduct.[1] Once Cecil was back at the helm, the ship of state, which had been momentarily deflected from its true course by gusts of passion, was guided into safe and charted waters; de Quadra was ousted from his favoured position at court; and the queen never again allowed her private impulses to endanger the safety of the state. Marriage-negotiations in the future were entrusted to statesmen.

Meanwhile, as a protective measure against possible aggression from abroad, Elizabeth had begun her quest for allies on the Continent. During the recent war, English agents had been busy in the chief heretical centres of Europe, pleading for union and co-operation with England; and Throckmorton had shown by his dealings with the huguenots, at the time of the Amboise conspiracy, how effective the plan could be, it it were pursued with secrecy and resolution. 'As the king of Spain advances his greatness', he wrote, 'by countenancing papists in his own and other countries, so it will be to the queen's advantage to sustain the protestants in her own realm and abroad.' As if to emphasize the need for some such *rapprochement*, continuous reports were reaching England from various sources of projected leagues among the catholic powers for the destruction of the reformed faith. Generally speaking, there was no solid foundation of fact behind these reports—merely vague surmises, fears, and suspicions engendered by the perfervid imagination of a world oppressed by a nightmare of uncertainty and widespread espionage. Nevertheless it was as easy to believe in the existence of hostile combinations among catholics as it was difficult to disprove them; and protestants everywhere lived under the demoralizing conviction that a day was surely approaching when a bloody deluge would break over them and submerge their religion for ever. Germany was a factory of rumours. Situated in the heart of Europe, and being the principal recruiting-ground for mercenaries, it became, in effect, a gigantic whispering gallery,

---

[1] See Read, pp. 207–8 for a careful study of Cecil's effort to defeat the Lord Robert–de Quadra plan to re-catholicize England.

where the military secrets of the catholic powers were overheard, speculated upon, and distorted out of recognition. Throckmorton heard some of the whispering in Paris, and, having a *flair* for anything in the nature of a plot against the reformation, passed on the information dutifully to London.

However unreal these alleged catholic leagues may have been, there was no unreality about Elizabeth's efforts to knit up the protestant communities of Europe in a common policy of defence. The relationships she entered into with them cannot be dignified by the name of alliances, since they were not established with sovereign independent authorities, and as a rule carried no binding obligations; but they had much the same effect as alliances, for they linked up the protestant communities with a secret network of intelligences and promises of mutual support, which stimulated and strengthened the hands of each. Ostensibly the basis of co-operation was the defence of the Gospel—it was so understood by the Lutherans and huguenots; but, to Elizabeth, the religious aspect was quite subsidiary. What she wanted of her friends abroad was that they should enable her to shift the strategic frontier of England into Germany, France, and the Netherlands.

It was difficult for the queen to reconcile such a policy with her avowed hatred of rebellion and solicitous regard for the rights of sovereignty. Probably she never troubled to rationalize her position in the matter. But the representatives of foreign states, whose interests were damaged, remonstrated bitterly. 'This woman', wrote de Quadra, the Spanish ambassador in London, 'desires to make use of religion in order to excite rebellion in the whole world'; and again, 'If she had the power today she would sow heresy broadcast in all your Majesty's dominions, and set them in a blaze without compunction.' Events were soon to show that the Spaniard was substantially right in his prognostications, and that although the object was self-protection rather than aggression, the friendly relations Elizabeth had set up with foreign protestants might easily be used as an instrument of offence as well as defence. It was France, not Spain, however, that was to feel the first blow.

In the spring of 1562 the French nation was moving rapidly towards one of the gravest crises in its history. Religious fanaticism, temporarily suppressed after the Tumult of Amboise, was now rampant again, playing havoc with social order, disorganizing administration, and even threatening to obliterate from men's minds all sense of political obligation. The authority of the Crown had sunk to its lowest ebb for a century. After a vain attempt to avert bloodshed by the *Édit de Janvier* (1561), granting a wide measure of toleration to the huguenots, Catherine de Médicis saw the rival religious groups fall to blows in various parts of the kingdom. Plunder and sacrilege by the huguenots led to murderous retaliation by the catholics. In the south, free companies (*pieds nus*) were formed, and hired out their services to whichever side offered the more attractive rewards. Pitched battles became the order of the day: the highways became unsafe: trade languished: husbandry was neglected; and the very foundations of civil society seemed to be shaken like a vessel in a storm.[1]

Meanwhile the duke of Guise, observing from his retirement in Lorraine the rising tide of religious passion, decided that the hour had struck for him to play his familiar role of catholic champion. Setting out at the head of his retainers, late in February 1562, he directed his steps towards Paris, permitting his men by the way to flesh their weapons on a huguenot congregation in the village of Vassy. Early in March he entered the capital to the plaudits of the masses, the incarnation of militant catholicism. In quick succession followed the flight of the huguenot members of the council, the reconstruction of the government under a triumvirate consisting of Guise, the constable Montmorency, and the marshal St. André—all staunch catholics, and the coercion of the king and queen mother into acceptance of the *coup d'état*.

On 31 March Throckmorton, who had watched the course of events closely, informed Elizabeth that the huguenot leaders, the Prince de Condé and the admiral Coligny, were in arms, and that civil war was imminent. Early in April, in defiance of the royal command to lay down their arms, they seized Orleans and issued an apologia for their action, calling upon all good subjects to resist the aggression of the house of Guise and rescue the tottering throne of France. At the same time appeals for

---

[1] For a description of the condition of France see Félix Rocquain, *La France et Rome pendant les Guerres de Religion*; also the memoirs of Gaspard de Saulx-Tavannes, Michael de Castelnau, Blaise de Montluc, &c., in the *Collection des mémoires*, ed. by J. F. Michaud and J. J. F. Poujoulat. Tavannes boldly asserted: 'Il faut que les raisons d'état et les raisons humaines cèdent à la religion, d'autant que l'âme est plus que le corps.'

help were sent to England and Germany, and an effort was made to rally the whole of protestant Europe in defence of the Reformation.

How did Elizabeth respond to the appeal? In the first place she was fully aware of the issues at stake in France, and, generally speaking, she knew what would follow if the Guise faction succeeded in annihilating its opponents, or at all events she could make a pretty shrewd guess. Not only would the reformed cause in Europe receive a blow the effects of which might prove to be fatal, but the triumphant Guises, in collusion with Spain, whose interest in the suppression of heresy was notorious, would inaugurate a great crusade for the faith, and on the crest of this movement rise to the political domination of the Continent. Then would come England's turn. Mary Stuart would perhaps marry Don Carlos, the heir to the Spanish throne, the English catholics would rise in support, Spain would launch an armada, and Elizabeth would lose her crown. In other words, the flank attack through Scotland, which had proved a miserable failure in 1560, would be retrieved in 1562 by a gigantic frontal attack on England, supported this time by both France and Spain. If these surmises were anywhere near the truth, clearly the huguenots must not be allowed to quail for lack of support. Their cause was in large measure England's cause: their defeat would be tantamount to the removal of the strongest bastion in Elizabeth's system of defence. But in what form should the assistance be given? Would moral support be enough? Would it suffice for the queen to act through the ordinary diplomatic channels and offer her services as mediator between the court and Condé? The idea pleased her because it entailed no expenditure of blood and treasure, did not commit her to the objectionable policy of aiding rebellion, and, if successful, would greatly enhance her prestige. Moreover, a pacification of France by means of a compromise would have the special advantage of preserving the huguenot faction intact and more than ever dependent on her good graces: whereas war, if it did not actually result in the annihilation of the huguenots at the hands of Guise and his supporters, would certainly weaken them. Accordingly, at the end of April 1562, Sir Henry Sidney was dispatched from London to join Throckmorton in urging the French government to accept an offer of mediation from Elizabeth. But Catherine de Médicis was suspicious—suspicious of some ulterior motive at

work behind the scenes, and especially suspicious of Throckmorton, who was a bosom friend of the huguenot leaders. She
had not forgotten the conspiracy of Amboise; and her dislike of
the ambassador was fully sustained by the Parisians, who vented
their hatred of the accursed Englishman by shooting arquebuses
into his house and molesting his servants in the streets. The queen
mother had no compunction, therefore, in giving Elizabeth's
offer a blunt and uncompromising refusal. She would deal with
Condé herself and in her own way.

Meanwhile the fertile brain of the English ambassador had
been busy turning over a scheme whereby the turmoil in France
might be used to the great advantage of England. As early as
17 April he divulged his plan in a letter to Elizabeth. 'It may
happen', he wrote, 'that in these garboils some occasion may
be offered as that again you may be brought into possession of
Calais, or some port of consequence on this side.' It was a subtle
suggestion by one who thoroughly understood the *Realpolitik* of
his mistress, and, like the seed that fell on good soil, it took root
and germinated at once. To Cecil, with whom he could afford
to be more explicit, he wrote in more detail, explaining possible
ways and means of bringing about the desired consummation.
'Our friends the protestants', he commented, 'must be so handled
and dandled, that in case the duke of Guise, the constable, the
marshal St. André, and that sect, bring the king of Spain into
France and give him possession of some places and forts, then
the protestants for their defence, or for their desire of revenge,
or affection for the queen, may be moved to give us possession
of Calais, Dieppe, or Newhaven,[1] perhaps all three.' Here indeed
was a way in which assistance to the huguenots, necessary now
in any case, could be combined with an excellent stroke of business. But would the huguenot leaders be willing to make their
appeal for help—the necessary preliminary—in the terms required by the queen for the realization of the Throckmorton
scheme? Would they accept succour from England at the price
of a betrayal of their country? Their need for money was patent
and urgent, and England alone could supply it in the necessary
amount; but so far there was no indication that troops were
wanted, still less was there any likelihood that a port would
be conceded. So the queen drew tight her purse-strings, and
resolved to 'creep into the matter' with caution. In June Armigil

---

[1] i.e. Le Havre.

Wade, who had been sent to sound the pro-huguenot governor of Dieppe as to the reception of English assistance, reported that the time was not yet ripe for such a move and that it would be better to wait until the pinch of adversity had begun to operate. As a matter of fact negotiations between the court and Condé were still going on, and on 25 June it was rumoured that a settlement had been reached—a rumour soon dissipated when it was learnt that the huguenot demands included not only the removal of Guise and his party from the council but the republication of the Edict of January.

In the meantime a campaign was on foot in France for the settlement of the quarrel by force. The duke of Guise and the constable were on the way to Orleans and the Loire, while the dukes of Aumâle and Bouillon were moving into Normandy to cut off communications between England and the huguenot centres in the north. Early in August Cecil responded by a naval demonstration off the Norman ports. But still Condé and Coligny would not speak the words of concession that would bring England to their rescue; and at the beginning of September Elizabeth, falling back on her old policy of mediation, sent Sir Thomas Smith to tender her services to Catherine de Médicis. By this time, however, the huguenot cause, despite certain financial aids from the German protestants, was in desperate straits, and its leaders were in a mood to grasp at any conditions. The royal army against them was daily increasing: the Rhinegrave was on the march to Paris with substantial German catholic levies: Spanish forces were concentrating in the neighbourhood of the Pyrenees; and papal troops were at Avignon. The only way out of the peril was to yield to Elizabeth and throw themselves on her mercy. About the middle of September, accordingly, the vidame de Chartres and La Haye were sent over to London with a blank sheet already signed by their principals and instructions to procure the most reasonable terms they could. The queen was now able to dictate the conditions of her intervention and to drive, incidentally, one of the hardest bargains of her life. On 20 September 1562 the secret treaty of Richmond was signed. Its terms were few. Le Havre was to be garrisoned by 3,000 English troops and held as a pledge until Calais was surrendered; a further 3,000 men were to be placed at Condé's disposal for the defence of Dieppe and Rouen in case of necessity; and a sum of 140,000 crowns was to be paid as a loan into the huguenot war chest—repayable by the huguenots when the English were in possession of Calais.

From the French point of view it would be difficult to imagine a more humiliating contract. The huguenot clergy, who represented a kind of protestant cosmopolitanism, might gloss it over with the flattering formula that it was for the glory of God and the good of religion; but in reality the cession to England of the mouth of the Seine was simply a throw-back to the bad old days when France, a prey to the strife between Burgundians and Armagnacs, fell under the domination of the Lancastrians. Even the huguenot leaders must have had their qualms when they learned the terms of the treaty, for they asserted later that their plenipotentiaries had misunderstood their instructions; but it was not until the time came for the fulfilment of the bargain, some months later, that they fully grasped the baseness of the concessions they had made. For the moment the heat of passion and the urgency of the cause thrust reflection into the background. Elizabeth, of course, was perfectly aware of the machiavellian character of her diplomatic victory. In a proclamation issued immediately the treaty was signed, she expatiated on the justice of her intervention in France. It was in defence of Condé 'who requires nothing but the maintenance of the honour of God, and repose of the realm, and the liberty of the king', and the occupation of the coastal places by English troops was merely to preserve them from falling into the hands of those 'who have advanced themselves in force beyond the authority of the king'. Furthermore, she laid stress on the religious aspect of the struggle she was about to enter upon: the cause (i.e. of Guise) had become 'a manifest enterprise not by teaching but by the sword to force men's consciences', and the quarrel would spread to all other countries, being really part and parcel of a great catholic league for the suppression of the protestant faith. To Philip of Spain, however, she could not present the issue in this fashion with any hope of winning his sympathy. As the Most Catholic King he could not be expected to give his blessing to a war for the defence of heresy. So on 20 September Elizabeth explained her intentions to him quite frankly. She was at war, she said, not against the king of France but against the house of Guise: with the king she intended to live in peace; but she must safeguard her right to Calais, 'which she manifestly sees they do not mean to deliver', and as soon as this object was accomplished she would withdraw her forces. Moreover, since Philip had been at least in part responsible for the loss of the seaport, and presumably regarded it as a debt to be wiped out, she ventured to solicit his help in its recovery.

This was hardly Philip's intention. He had hoped, subject to French approval, to intervene in the struggle against heresy and rebellion, on the side of the Crown; and his offer of help had been provisionally accepted by the queen mother. Spanish troops were therefore moved up to the French frontier in July, and orders were sent to the duchess of Parma to prepare a Netherlands contingent. Here the assistance of Spain to Charles IX came to a dead stop; for not a man could be sent from the Low Countries, and Philip soon found himself in much the same position as the king he was so anxious to help. The Netherlands were, in fact, seething with an incipient revolt against Spanish rule and the religious policy which it practised. As Thomas Windebank put it in a letter to Cecil: 'If the Low Countries of Flanders had a head, the likelihood is of such troubles as was at the enterprise of Amboise, and so forth greater to come.' Moreover, the sympathies of the Flemings—thanks to the activities of Gresham and others, who followed Throckmorton's tactics in France—were as strongly on the side of England in regard to the huguenot crisis as they had been when the Franco-Scottish crisis occurred three years before. 'All men, saving the papists', remarked Windebank, 'do wish the Queen's Majesty to make her profit, thinking it should be the profit of all christendom.' Gresham corroborated, and on 1 August he informed Cecil that 'now is the time (they say here) to recover those pieces we have lost of late in France, or better pieces'.

Elizabeth was thus in the happy position of being able to dispatch her expeditionary force to Normandy without any possibility of interruption from the side of Spain. Nay, the position of affairs in the Netherlands became so alarming in the autumn that Philip was compelled to execute a rapid *volte-face*. In December the duke of Alva, speaking in his master's name, informed Challoner in Madrid that he was in favour of the English right to Calais, and that the king would willingly mediate with the French for its restoration. To Granvelle, in Brussels, he wrote at the same time that the only way to stop the English from helping the huguenots and creating trouble in the Netherlands was to let them have Calais.

Meanwhile the war in France was going badly for the huguenots. In spite of the gallant help of Captain Leighton and an English company, the royalists had captured Rouen on 26 October, thus breaking the chief link between the huguenot forces and the Norman ports; and in December they completely defeated Condé and Coligny at the battle of Dreux, taking the former prisoner and driving the latter with the remnant of the army back on the Loire. By this time the occupation of Le Havre by the English under Sir Adrian Poynings and the earl of Warwick had excited the liveliest concern in catholic circles. Rather than see the country dismembered, the queen mother now approached Condé with the most enticing inducements to disown his perfidious ally, who had taken the opportunity of domestic troubles to seize one of the most important seaports of the kingdom. Circumstances favoured her appeal—Navarre, the senior member of the house of Bourbon, was dead, killed at the siege of Rouen; the constable was a prisoner of the huguenots; and the duke of Guise was soon to be removed by the stroke of a fanatical huguenot.[1] Why should not Condé clasp the proffered hand of friendship extended by the court, and join with the government in expelling the impudent foreigner? Already wavering in his attachment to the English alliance, which had profited him nothing, and seeing the way open for a general conciliation, Condé succumbed, and in March 1563 signed the peace of Amboise, thereby gaining toleration for the huguenot religion, and political recognition for himself and his coadjutor Coligny.

Elizabeth, whose information was perfect—thanks to the plentiful communications of Smith and Throckmorton—was greatly perturbed at this trend of events; and Condé was not allowed to make his surrender to the court without many caustic reminders of his treaty obligations. Tormented by his conscience over Le Havre, and urged on by the feeling that duty as well as interest left him only one line of policy to follow, the unfortunate prince prevaricated, excused himself, urged the queen to moderate her terms, made eloquent but futile suggestions about a possible marriage between her and the French king; but in the end it was clear he would do nothing to implement his promise with regard to Calais. While the unedifying wrangle was in progress, a great movement of national feeling began to surge

[1] Feb. 1563.

through France. Grievances that had seemed irremediable, divisions that apparently cut deeper than life itself, were salved as by the stroke of an enchanter's wand. The intervention of the foreigner had re-established the moral unity of the nation. 'D'ici à Bayonne', exclaimed Montmorency, 'tout crie: Vive France!'[1]

The defence of Le Havre which followed is one of the many minor episodes of heroism and tragedy that crowd the reign of Elizabeth. All through the winter and spring (1562-3) Warwick and his little garrison of 5,000 men had toiled unceasingly at the fortifications, sleeping in their harness, badly provided with arms and munitions, lacking food, drink, and clothing, but in excellent spirits and able to hold the attacking forces of the Rhinegrave at a distance. 'This is as noble a garrison', wrote its gallant commander, 'as ever served a prince. They fight like Hectors, labour like slaves, are worse fed than peasants, and are poorer than common beggars.' But the hand of fate was soon to descend upon them with a crushing blow. On 7 June Warwick noted in a communication to the council that a strange disease had come amongst them 'whereof nine died this morning and many before very suddenly'. By the third week of the month this new and unforeseen enemy, more terrible than 'all the cannon of France', was carrying off two hundred a week. At the end of June the mortality more than doubled itself, and Warwick was reduced to desperation; half his men were out of action, either dead or dying. Recruits were hurried across from England to make good the wastage; but they were raw, untrained louts, unacquainted with the use of firearms, hastily dispatched without leaders; and if they escaped the raging furnace of the plague, they merely added to the troubles of the harassed commander. Meanwhile, with the royal army of 20,000 under the constable closing in on all sides, with huguenots as well as catholics rallying for the assault, with his ovens smashed by the enemy guns and his bakers mostly dead, Warwick found himself unable to feed his rapidly diminishing troops. On 15 July his effective strength was only 1,200; and five days later the position was so bad that Sir Thomas Smith, who had contrived to negotiate with the queen mother, sent an urgent message to Cecil advising the immediate conclusion of peace if England's right to Calais was to be preserved. But before diplomacy had got properly to work,

[1] A good account of the whole episode is given in the duc d'Aumâle's *Histoire des Princes de Condé*, tome i.

the plague and the investing army had sealed that fate of Le Havre. On 24 July Warwick lost command of the harbour and saw his communications with England cut. At the same time contrary winds set in, preventing the approach of Admiral Clinton with new succours. On the 26th he decided to make the best terms he could with the constable, and intimated his willingness to parley. Two days later he hauled down his flag, and the remnant of the plague-stricken and war-weary garrison, with its honour intact, dragged itself and its baggage to the ships to begin the evacuation. France was again freed from the foreigner.

It was a terrible blow to Elizabeth's pride; and the humiliation was deepened by the severity of the terms imposed by the victorious French. Arguing that she had forfeited all claim to Calais by her entry into Le Havre and by making war on the kingdom, they steadily refused to accept any compromise; and against this resolute attitude Smith and Throckmorton (who had now joined him) bent their diplomatic skill in vain. Elizabeth might threaten to stop the import of French wines into England, or to 'impeach their great west and north fishing', or to deprive them of Newcastle coal, or to bombard their coasts with her navy: it was all to no good. Eventually, after hanging fire for nine months, an agreement was arrived at in April 1564, when the queen, relaxing her demands, allowed her ambassadors to accept 120,000 crowns in lieu of the hostages she had held since 1559,[1] and satisfied herself with the empty proviso that the rights of both princes in regard to Calais should be reserved. In this way the treaty of Troyes (11 April) to all intents and purposes annulled the obligations of the French under the treaty of Cateau-Cambrésis, and gave them effectual possession of Calais.

---

[1] As a matter of fact many of them had escaped.

III

MARY STUART AND THE SUCCESSION

IF Francis II had lived, it is more than doubtful whether Mary Stuart would ever have set foot on so uncongenial a soil as Scotland. Neither the land not its inhabitants had any attraction to offer comparable to that of the rich inheritance she had enjoyed as queen consort of France. Turbulent and still heaving with the ground swell of revolution, Scotland must have seemed to its exiled sovereign little better than a semi-barbarous outpost on the frontier of civilization: a *triste pays*, stubborn and self-willed, whose people had rebelled against her mother's well-intentioned rule, and perhaps hastened her untimely end. But her career in France was finished. All she had to look forward to there was the flat, stale, and unprofitable existence of a dowager, and the still more disagreeable prospect of playing second fiddle to the jealous daughters of Catherine de Médicis, who monopolized the court. In Scotland she would at least be a queen; and who was to say that the journey to Edinburgh, circuitous as it might appear, would not be the shortest way to the goal on which her affections were set, the establishment of her right to the English succession? From conversations she had held with those of her subjects who visited her in France, she learned that she might reckon on the support of a large and influential section of the nation. The return to her patrimonial kingdom was not, therefore, a blind leap in the dark, but an adventure, the end of which might be crowned with glorious success.

Mary was in many respects the antithesis of her cousin the queen of England. Brought up at the court of France, at that time the most brilliant and gayest in christendom, she had enjoyed a comparatively sheltered existence, unharassed by the grim experiences that had shaped and disciplined the character of Anne Boleyn's daughter. True, the French court in the days of Henry II and Catherine de Médicis was not the *vrai paradis du monde* depicted by the poet Brantôme, but it was certainly not the 'school of depravity', described by the historian Mignet, where the *petite reine d'Écosse* 'could not fail to see what was evil and afterwards to imitate it'. On the contrary, what evidence there is seems to point in the opposite direction. France has always had the reputation of looking well after her royal ladies, and Mary was, potentially at least, one of them. She was educated along with the dauphin and his sisters by the best schoolmasters in the kingdom, Claude Millot and Antoine Fouquelin; and her *gouvernantes* were chosen with care. The dowager duchess of Guise, her grandmother, had a trusteeship over her general up-bringing; and her uncle, the cardinal of Lorraine, albeit he was no saint, was too much concerned about his niece's dazzling future to permit irregularities in the household.

If the education Mary received was thorough, it was in no way remarkable, nor was the princess afflicted with 'bookishness'. If it had suited the introspective Elizabeth to become a scholar, and to find in books compensation for the straitened circumstances of her childhood, there was nothing of this in Mary's make-up. She never fell a victim to the New Learning, now sweeping across Europe like a whirlwind, nor was she driven to it by the need for sympathy in a somewhat bleak and comfortless universe. She grew up as a woman of the world, preferring the romances of chivalry and the satires of Rabelais to the grave, edifying works of Greek and Latin writers. The library she left behind at Holyrood in 1567 was not impressive. In regard to languages, she could understand Latin, but could not write it; and if she had a smattering of Italian and possibly (in later life) some acquaintance with Spanish, she was completely ignorant of English, which she only began to pick up when she was a prisoner in Tutbury castle. Her knowledge of the Scots tongue, again, was almost negligible except on the colloquial level: she could not write it, but she could conduct conversations in it with John Knox and Sir Nicholas Throckmorton. Of course French was the language in which she was nurtured: it was the only tongue she really mastered, or cared for, or corresponded in. She could indite a sonnet after the manner of Ronsard, like all the court poetasters of the day; and her letters are fluent compositions written in a beautiful hand. In disposition she was expansive, eager, and cheerful, much given to the gentle arts of music, dancing, masking, and *joyeuseté*[1]—in a word, she was objective and sanguine in her outlook on life. Her favourite recreations were needlework, embroidery, and tapestry, in all of which she excelled.

[1] i.e. merriment.

Physically, Mary was not gifted with a strong constitution. Her father died at the early age of 31, her mother at 44, and her two brothers did not survive infancy. Moreover she seems to have suffered from a chronic complaint of the spleen, which assailed her in moments of fatigue or excitement. Yet she could perform feats of endurance on horseback, that might have taxed the strength of a man; and her gallops from Holyrood to Dunbar, from Jedburgh to Hermitage, from Langside to the Solway have become almost legendary. Evidently she was no delicate or cloistered heroine of romance, but a bold, self-reliant, indomitable woman with a masculine feeling for comradeship and high adventure. Stimulated by the Guisan blood within her to a consciousness of her great destiny, she loved to hear of brave deeds, of hardships endured, of perils overcome—not with the passive wonder of a Desdemona, but with the eager longing that she herself were a man, to bear the buckler on her arm, the sword upon her thigh, and to share the life of the soldier on the tented field.

Unlike Elizabeth she had a warm, passionate temperament, in which the primitive emotions of love and hate, hope and fear, found an unusually free expression. She was violent in her attachments and equally violent in her hates; but in neither was there much constancy or permanence. Nevertheless her loyalty and kindness to those who served her, and stood by her faithfully in emergency, were unstinting. More sensitive than Elizabeth to the changes of fortune, and probably finer in the grain, she was easily moved to take a rosy view of events, and just as easily plunged into black despair. Success brought jubilation: failure was accompanied by weeping. But her natural buoyancy of character was remarkable, and her recuperative power immense—until both were broken and crushed by her long imprisonment in England. Emotionally she was capable of greater heights than her rival; but she lacked precisely those prudential qualities that make for success in the world of practical affairs. And although she could attract men by her charm, her vivacity, and her urbanity, she was woefully ignorant of how to govern them, or even to single out those whom she could trust. In the Scotland of her day she was little better circumstanced than a sheep among wolves.[1]

[1] Froude's portrayal of the queen's character (*History of England*, vol. vi, pp. 509-10) is a brilliant piece of work from a literary point of view: it is highly

F

The moment at which she severed her connexion with France was not unpropitious. A crisis had arisen in Anglo-Scottish affairs, which brought about a revulsion of feeling among the Scots against Elizabeth. It had developed out of the English queen's second and final refusal to marry the earl of Arran. This marriage proposal had been the rallying cry of the protestant party in Scotland ever since their war against the regent, and so strongly committed were they to the idea that when Elizabeth finally brushed it aside they jumped to the conclusion that she intended to snub the whole nation. Was not a Hamilton good enough for a Tudor, especially a Tudor whose descent was not above demur? *Amour-propre* was a force to be reckoned with at all times north of the Tweed, but never more so than when the two countries were beginning to draw towards a common understanding and to cast off their medieval antagonisms. In any case, the effect of the ill-starred marriage negotiations was to galvanize into life the latent jealousy of the Scots for all things English, and to carry the politicians of Edinburgh back once more to their old stereotyped formula of national independence. Driven back on this primary instinct, so to speak, they began to reconsider their bearings. They had fought for the overthrow of French rule and the establishment of spiritual liberty, and hitherto they had feared their queen as the ally of the reactionary forces they wished to destroy. Now, by a happy turn of fortune's wheel, they saw her a widow, and no longer queen of France. She was young and a political cipher so far as the direction of French policy was concerned. If she would only be reasonable, there seemed to be no apparent reason why she and her subjects should not pull together in the common task of national effort. At all events they were prepared to give her the benefit of the doubt and receive her as became good citizens.

Still, it must not be supposed that antipathy to Elizabeth meant any warmth of feeling for their own queen. On the contrary, the prevalent attitude among the people seems to have been one of reserve. It could hardly be otherwise considering the trying circumstances through which the nation had so lately passed, and the fact that the queen's character and intentions at this time were largely unknown quantities. In the prevailing

picturesque, subtle, and suggestive. But it is clearly a *tour de force*, a fantasia, a false and misleading creation, which cannot be taken as having any real historical worth. We still await a genuine reliable 'portrait' of the historical Mary.

ignorance, all sorts of rumours and exaggerations took shape in men's minds. Keen protestants like Knox feared lest her arrival might herald another revolution, involving the loss of all they had fought for. They knew, for example, that Mary was a staunch catholic, like her uncle the cardinal, and to their excited imaginations it seemed not improbable that she would take advantage of the still precarious condition of the new religion to crush it once for all, and on its ruin to restore the Mass, the hierarchy, and the burnings. If she did not venture to make this clean sweep of the Reformation and all its works, she might quite well endeavour to arrest its development; for no catholic sovereign could rightly countenance the growth of heresy in her dominions. There was also another disquieting fact to be taken into account, namely the French upbringing and sympathies of the queen. Presumably she was ignorant of the temper, tastes, outlook, and mentality of the Scots; and if she came as an apostle of French culture there would be a barrier from the very start between her and the nation. Scotland had had enough of the French for the time being: it desired above all things a thorough-going national existence. Would Mary fall in with the common will, or would she take a line of her own and thwart it?

For these reasons, therefore, Scotland was in no very confident mood on the eve of the queen's return. Randolph, the English ambassador, spoke of a 'mad world' as likely to supervene when she arrived. Maitland of Lethington,[1] probably the acutest politician in Scotland, hinted that 'wonderful tragedies' might ensue. And the 'godly' brethren of the kirk, who had most to lose by an upsetting of the existing order, steeled themselves to resist, if need be, 'to the uttermost'.

Accordingly, when Mary landed at Leith in August 1561,[2] she

[1] William Maitland of Lethington, the son of a poet and essayist, the laird of Lethington in Lauderdale, was by far the most cultured, fascinating, and attractive personality in Scotland. He was known in England as the 'Scotch Cecil', and Elizabeth herself styled him the 'flower of all the wits of Scotland'. In Scotland, however, he enjoyed the sobriquet of 'Michael Wylie' (i.e. Machiavelli). He was allied by marriage to the earl of Atholl, and in times of acute danger he took refuge in the Atholl country, beyond the Tay and the Pass of Killiecrankie. He was behind the scenes, and 'held the threads of all the plots'. He won, and lost, the queen's confidence, became one of her enemies, and eventually died a Roman death in Edinburgh castle.

[2] There is still some dubiety about the traditional belief that Elizabeth sent out warships to 'stay', or intercept, the passage of the Scottish queen from Calais to Leith. For a full discussion of the matter consult Hay Fleming's *Mary Queen of Scots*, chap. iv, pp. 250–1. 'Possibly', says Fleming, 'all these fears and rumours' (i.e.

received a poor reception from the good people of Edinburgh. Hardly was she settled in Holyrood when she was treated to a protestant *auto da fé*, in which the effigies of the old Testament idolaters, Korah, Dathan, and Abiram, were committed to the flames. The meaning of this fiery tableau was too obvious to be missed.

Little did the pessimists know their sovereign! True, she was a catholic; and before leaving France she had the hardihood to tell the English ambassador, Throckmorton, who questioned her on the subject of religion, that she had no intention of altering her faith. 'Constancy becometh all folks well, but none better than princes', she said; '. . . I am none of those that will change my religion every year.' Nevertheless, she had not come as a missionary or crusader to Scotland. She said quite sincerely that she harboured no designs against the religious freedom of her subjects. She was probably too fond of hunting and amusement to give much consideration to the graver questions of the hour. Her motto was liberty of worship for all, herself included: constraint of conscience was to be a thing of the past. In politics, still more clearly, the same note of friendly conciliation was sounded. Evidently, then, Scotland was not to be compressed, as so many had expected, into a French or 'papist' mould; the queen had made it plain that her policy would be, simply and solely, secular and national. By this wise moderation, which came as a great relief to all reasonable men, she soon gathered round her a strong following—every one, in fact, who desired to see the country freed from the tutelage of France, and dreamed, it may be, of one day seeing a Scottish dynasty seated on the English throne. Court life, which had virtually disappeared on the death of James V and the subsequent influx of French adventurers, was now resurrected at Holyrood, and the young nobles flocked eagerly to the capital to take their lawful place at the queen's side. In order still further to strengthen her position, as well as to bring all the resources of the country under her

relating to the 'interception') 'owed their origin to Elizabeth's rash speech to d'Oysel', Mary's special messenger to Elizabeth requesting a passport. Apparently d'Oysel reported to Mary on his return that the English queen had said she would make provision to keep her from passing home. While there is no clear indication that warships were employed for this purpose, 'it is certain', says Fleming, 'that arrangements were made to stay her if she entered any north-of-England port'. This affirmation is based on the Historical MSS. Commission, *Twelfth Report*, App. iv, pp. 73–77. The easterly 'haar' was only encountered by the French galleys when they approached the Scottish coast.

control, Mary formed her council of twelve lords, representing all the national interests, religious and territorial: including, on the one hand, the catholic earls Atholl and Huntly, and on the other the well-known pillar of the Reformation, the Lord James Stuart,[1] and the laird of Lethington. So successful was she in winning the hearts of all that Knox complained bitterly of the waning enthusiasm of those who had formerly been so 'hot for the Gospel'. 'The holy water of the court', he remarks in his *History*, took the 'fire-edge' off their zeal. He alone of the leading men in Scotland refused to take the proffered hand of fellowship, and kept sounding alarms from time to time; but it was difficult even for him to preserve his 'fire-edge' when the whole people was fast drawing to the queen. Lethington strikes the true note when he writes, 'The queen behaves herself as reasonably as we can require; if any thing be amiss, the fault is rather in ourselves.' In short, a wonderful feeling of loyalty seems to have sprung up practically at once between the nation and its queen.

Thus did Mary successfully navigate the troubled waters of Scottish politics, disarm the critics, and attach to herself, by unmistakable tokens of good sense, a naturally warm-hearted people. Not only so: the whole country, so much disturbed of late by civil war and dissension, settled down, after her arrival, *in pacem incredibilem*.

Meanwhile she had turned to the question of her title to the English succession, the dominant interest of her life, and the source of all her subsequent troubles. In what mood and under what auspices did she approach this grave matter? Clearly in no spirit of bravado. The 'trial by battle', two years before, had sobered and chastened her mind: she was no longer under the control of her imperious uncles, whose sabre-rattling she had left behind her in France. What Mary now wanted was simply the

---

[1] Lord James Stuart, the queen's bastard brother and former prior of St. Andrews, was one of the important *dramatis personae* of the period. He was destined to play a dominant role in the unhappy fate of his sister. The Scottish historian, T. F. Tytler, depicts him as a man whose 'peculiar art' was to 'appear to do nothing whilst, in truth, he did all'; and he adds the caustic remark—'there is perhaps no kind of man more dangerous in public life than he who conceals matured purposes under a negligent and careless exterior'. His most remarkable quality was caution: he was always ready with an *alibi* when circumstances demanded one; and, like many of the leading nobles in Scotland, he was a pensioner of Elizabeth, and therefore a potential traitor to his own country. History sees him as Lethington saw him, 'looking through his fingers', an inscrutable, enigmatic man, courageous, ambitious, bold, and unscrupulous. 'God' and 'Honour' were always on his lips, but deceit and cruelty ruled in his heart.

right to be designated 'second in the kingdom', or heir presumptive to the English crown; and her quarrel with the Treaty of Edinburgh was that, if she signed it as it stood, she would be deprived of this humbler satisfaction. Clause 6 of the treaty, to which she took exception, ran as follows: '. . . that the Most Christian King and Queen Mary and both of them shall at all times coming abstain from using the said arms and title of the kingdoms of England and Ireland. . . .' Undoubtedly these words could only be construed to mean one thing—total exclusion; and Elizabeth never ventured to suggest that they were susceptible of any other meaning. The point was not arguable: it was undeniable. The question was, would Elizabeth be willing to have the obnoxious clause revised? Lord James Stuart put it in this way: 'What if your title did remain untouched as well for yourself as the issue of your body? Inconvenient were it to provide that the queen my sovereign her own place were reserved in the succession to the crown of England, which your Majesty will pardon me if I take to be next by the law of all nations, as she that is next in lawful descent of the right line of king Henry VII, and in the meantime this isle to be united in a perpetual friendship?'

Accordingly, fortified by the moral support of Scotland, Mary dispatched Lethington, two weeks after her arrival in Edinburgh, to find out how the land lay at the English court and to discover whether Elizabeth would consider a revision of the treaty. Lethington handled his mission with a frankness that betokened complete conviction as to its reasonableness. He argued that the belief in his sovereign's right was widespread and incontestable, whereas Elizabeth herself was generally held to be a usurper. Consequently, if she insisted on ratification of the treaty as it was, such a settlement could not last; for if Mary were successfully forced into signing away her claim, she would seize the first opportunity to cancel her signature. On the other hand, if she were acknowledged 'second', there would be no further trouble. Elizabeth was equally frank in her reply. She admitted that she knew of no better title than Mary's, and solemnly stated that she intended no harm to her. Her objection was not to the justice of the claim, but to the consequences that might flow from a public declaration of it. To give Mary the position of heir presumptive would rouse controversy, not only in regard to the propriety of the step, but also on the subject of her own title—a contingency she contemplated with the liveliest apprehension. Moreover, she doubted whether, in the event of her acceding to the request, she could retain the loyalty of her own subjects; for 'more people worship the rising than the setting sun'. As 'second' in the kingdom, the queen of Scots would inevitably become, as she herself had become during her predecessor's reign, the centre of rebellion and plot against her rule. With a curious touch of pathos, she remarked: 'It is hard to bind princes when hope is offered of a kingdom. . . . Do you think I could love my own winding-sheet?' Here, then, was the core of the whole matter, so far as Elizabeth was concerned; in Lethington's words, she was resolved 'to be queen while she lived, and after her death, let that one succeed who had most right'. As for the equivocal clause in the treaty, round which the discussion moved, it was to stand, and each of them could take her own meaning out of it—*unusquisque in sensu suo abundet*.[1]

Although his mission was only a qualified success, Lethington was not discouraged, nor was his mistress; and when Sir Peter Mewtas appeared shortly afterwards in Edinburgh with a fresh demand from Elizabeth for ratification of the unrevised treaty, Mary took advantage of the occasion to reaffirm her desire for amity between the two kingdoms and her love for her 'good sister'; but Mewtas could get nothing positive from her in regard to the treaty, only a reiteration of her objections and a request for revision. In October the duke of Guise took a hand in the game, and stated the case for his niece with such cogency that he won over Throckmorton to his side, and caused him to write a letter to Cecil urging acceptance of the Scottish proposal. Lethington, too, concentrated his guns on the English secretary of state, pointing out to him that 'if this be overthrown . . . it may be judged that God wills that one nation shall ever be a plague to the other'. In January, after waiting many weeks for some answer to her message by Mewtas, Mary took up her pen and wrote a personal letter to Elizabeth protesting her love and pleading for an interview, 'when the unfeigned nature of her good meaning would appear more clearly than in her writing'.

[1] Lethington, however, elicited from Elizabeth the verbal offer 'that if the queen, her sister, would require that commissioners were appointed to review the treaty, she would be content thereof, and by them come to a qualification'. (See *Scot. Hist. Soc.* xliii, App. 1.)

Then, in May, Elizabeth yielded to the persuasion of Lethington and agreed to meet the queen of Scots in amicable conference. Mary had won her first success. Alone with Elizabeth all their difficulties which the politicians boggled over would vanish as by the stroke of an enchanter's wand. In a mood of girlish exultation, she wrote a letter to her uncle the duke of Guise: 'You can think', she said, 'how astonished others will be when they see us, the queen of England and me [agreeing] so well.'

Alas for her anticipations! No sooner had Elizabeth agreed to the conference proposal than Throckmorton's dispatches poured in from Paris with alarming reports of the imminence of civil war, the March *coup d'état* of Guise, and the perilous position of the huguenots. On 17 April he urged the queen seriously to consider the danger of leaving London when the situation abroad was so menacing. Three weeks later came the news of Sidney's failure to mediate a settlement between the government and the huguenots, and on 7 June Elizabeth decided to postpone the conference 'pending the troubles'. But Lethington, who had returned to London, succeeded in persuading her to change her mind; and she concluded, against the will of her council, that 'go she would' to the conference, unless she had further news from France 'that might cause her to stay'. On 18 June instructions were sent to the earls of Northumberland and Cumberland, the earl of Rutland, president of the council in the north, the archbishop of York, and many other dignitaries to prepare for the reception of the queen of Scots. Meanwhile Throckmorton, acting on Elizabeth's advice, put pressure on Guise to make an accord with Condé, by representing to him that unless there was a settlement in France the conference in England was doomed; and on 29 June he informed the queen that the troubles were successfully composed. On receipt of this report Elizabeth at once made arrangements for the court to move north to the rendezvous with Mary, which was now fixed to take place at Nottingham on 3 September; and Lethington left for Edinburgh with the articles for the conference in his pocket, in high spirits at the success of his mission. Then, like a bolt from the blue, came a dispatch from Throckmorton intimating that he had spoken prematurely, and that the negotiations between the court and Condé had been broken off. On the strength of this disconcerting news Elizabeth was reluctantly compelled to postpone the conference. Thus, while Mary was jubilantly preparing for her journey south, fortified by the assurances of Lethington that all was well, Sir Henry Sidney was dispatched to Edinburgh, on 15 July, with the melancholy information that the whole business was off until the 'early summer of the following year'. With the failure of the plan for an amicable conference we enter into a new phase of the queen of Scots' chequered career. At first Mary was deeply affected by the destruction of her high hopes, and kept to her bed all that day. But the acuteness of depression soon wore off, and her naturally buoyant temper reasserted itself. She was shrewd enough to see that if nothing had been gained by the efforts to win Elizabeth's favour, nothing, at all events, had been lost; she could begin again, if need be, from the beginning. On the other hand, she was convinced that some pressure must be brought to bear on the English queen, if any further progress was to be made. The question was what form the pressure should take. War was farther from her thoughts than ever, though there was an excellent opportunity for intervention in the Anglo-French struggle of 1562–3. But she did not desire to irritate the English nor to render a peaceful and diplomatic solution impossible: so she preserved her neutrality. There was a much more feasible way, namely to marry 'powerfully' and strengthen her feeble resources. If she could procure some rich and influential catholic prince as a husband, it might be possible, she thought, to overawe Elizabeth and wring the desired concession by a kind of tacit threat. At any rate there would be weight behind her representations, and she could carry on her attempt to persuade the English queen in the confidence that if the worst came to the worst, she had something to fall back on.

Mary's marriage was indeed a serious matter to Elizabeth, for the queen of Scots was no mean attraction to suitors by reason, it was said, of what she had title unto and 'is *in potentia propinqua* to obtain'. To her ardent admirers she was the best match in Europe. Elizabeth's main concern, of course, was to see that whoever was selected to husband her rival should not be a scion of the royal houses of Austria, Spain, or France: such a person might easily become a real source of danger. Consequently if Mary moved in any of these directions, the only thing to be done was to head her off by threats of enmity or by diplomatic measures of a subtler sort, while at the same time urging her in a friendly way to accept a husband of less august status, preferably an English nobleman. On this point there was bound to be trouble, for, as Lethington averred, his queen would 'never yield to any marriage how fit or profitable soever it be to her, unless she sees that her reputation [i.e. royal position] shall not diminish by the match'. Nevertheless Elizabeth pursued her plan with considerable success for the next two years, albeit in the end the husband chosen by Mary did not correspond to her wishes.

Of all the eligible princes the only one in whom Mary was really interested, and who could be of any use to her, was Don Carlos, ¹heir of King Philip and first catholic prince in Europe. The archduke Charles of Austria, whose claim was favoured by the cardinal of Lorraine, was eventually ruled out by his poverty; and Charles IX of France, whose name was also mentioned, was also dropped. All things considered, the heir of the Spanish empire appeared to be the man marked out by destiny to husband the Scottish queen and re-establish her fortunes. But it was no easy matter to carry through so grandiose a project with the secrecy it demanded; and the politicians of Edinburgh found they had undertaken the impossible. Elizabeth, of course, opposed the match tooth and nail. To Mary she intimated bluntly that if she proceeded with it, she could not avoid being her enemy, and therefore charged her to consider well her steps, for if, on the other hand, she married agreeably to her (i.e. Elizabeth), she would not fail to be her good friend. Concurrently but independently Catherine de Médicis, greatly fearing an alliance between Spain and Scotland and profoundly suspicious of the Guises, strove to attract the prince to a marriage with her own daughter Margaret. Mary's chance of success was probably lessened by the death of the duke of Guise in February 1563—an event that plunged her into deep melancholy. But the event that finally shattered her hopes was the grave illness of Don Carlos in the autumn of the same year. Thereafter King Philip seems to have lost all interest in the matter. By the month of August 1564 it was as good as dead.

It is impossible to say what would have happened if Mary had been successful; but in all probability it was fortunate for her that she failed. She had not consulted her people in the matter, and she knew that she had no general support in the furtive

---

¹ Don Carlos is usually described as a cruel, sullen, gluttonous epileptic; but Brantôme depicts him as 'a brave and gallant prince'. See R. H. Mahon's *Mary Queen of Scots* for the negotiations.

policy she was pursuing. Moreover, the prince of Spain was both a foreigner and a catholic. If the protestants, in alarm for religion, poured out their vials of wrath on the secret negotiations, the rest of the community was almost certain to take offence at his being a Spaniard. And if Don Carlos had set foot in Edinburgh with a Spanish guard, the old cry that had rallied the nation against the French in 1560 would have been repeated against the Spaniards in 1563; and either Mary would have reenacted the tragedy through which her mother had passed three years before, or she would have been precipitated prematurely into the humiliating position in which she found herself in 1567. It was well that the Spanish match of 1562–3 vanished into thin air like its more famous successor some sixty years later.

Meanwhile, in August 1563, Elizabeth made an unexpected move in the fascinating game of heading off her rival from undesirable suitors: she sent Randolph to Edinburgh to say— 'as of himself'—that no candidate would content her better than 'some person of noble birth within our realm, having also conditions and qualifications meet for the same, yea perchance such as she could hardly think we should agree unto'. The allusion, of course, was to the notorious Lord Robert Dudley,[1] Master of the Horse, and 'loved and favoured by Elizabeth as a brother'. For the moment, however, no name was mentioned; but the lure was clearly expressed, viz. 'our wish to favour by all means we can to try and determine her [i.e. Mary's] right and title, whether she be, or ought to be, by the law of God and man, our next cousin in blood . . . to succeed us in this crown of England, if we shall depart this life without children'.

When the message was expounded by Randolph in Edinburgh, the Scottish queen received it with a bland indifference. Who among the English nobility, she inquired, would be

---

[1] It has been asserted by historians—for different reasons—that the offer of Dudley was seriously intended by Elizabeth as the best solution of Mary's marriage problem. Beesly, for instance, argues that if the queen of Scots accepted Dudley, the English queen 'would have no suspicion or fear of any usurpation before her death, being assured that he was so loving and trusty that he would never permit anything to be attempted during her time'. Neale, on the other hand, penetrating more deeply into the circumstances of the case, is of opinion that Elizabeth was virtually driven into offering her favourite by the 'mental torment' of the succession debates of 1563. Of course, it is impossible to know what motive actuated her; but there were many intelligent men in Scotland who believed that the proposal of Dudley, even if elevated to the highest rank, was merely another example of English 'time-serving' or 'time-driving'.

regarded by her 'good sister', as suitable, and who unsuitable? It was a fair question; but since the ambassador was not at liberty to divulge any name, he had to return to London empty-handed for fresh instructions. Many weeks elapsed before he returned to the Scottish capital; but when he eventually did come it was merely to say that his mistress could not change her former judgement, nor could she name anyone or say who was fit; but she thought that 'none fitter could be found than some nobleman of her realm, who would have special desire to unite the two countries in perpetual concord'.

The New Year and Twelfth Night (1564) came and went, accompanied by feasting, dancing, and masking at Holyrood; but Randolph waited in vain for an answer to his sovereign's repeated offer. All that Mary would say was: 'let me know what your mistress's mind is, that I may the better devise with myself, and confer with others, and so give you a more resolute answer'. The ambassador was puzzled at the delay; and on 21 January he wrote:—'I judge her heart is in Spain.' A little later, however, he shelved Don Carlos, remarking:—'Divers reasons make me think that in the end she will be content with some party nearer home.' A month passed; and then Randolph unbosomed himself to Cecil with conviction:—'This queen's noble stomach can never embase itself so low as to marry in place inferior to herself. ... The thing of greatest moment is that, if our queen marry with the greatest, this queen by marrying a subject both loses the honour, commodity, and profit that might ensue by matching in high room ... whereby she will be better able to come by her right, if the same were refused.'

All this time Randolph was pestered by the inquisitive Scots asking him to reveal his private instructions, to divulge the name of the candidate his mistress favoured; and they refused to be satisfied with the retort that 'the choice' must lie with their own queen. In all probability Mary increased the prevailing uncertainty by her inexhaustible love of chatter. 'Sometimes', writes the ambassador, 'she likes well to hear of marriage—many times the widow's life is the best': 'sometimes she may marry where she will, sometimes she is sought of nobody. I pity her state and case, the loss of her time, the hurt of her country—commending the felicity of marriage, the joy and pleasure of such children as God may send her; and I suggest that she at least will take compassion on the four Maries, her worthy daughters and mignons, that for her sake have vowed themselves never to marry if she be not the first.' After three months of questioning and discussion with the queen and her advisers Murray[1] and Lethington, the ambassador had nothing of significance to communicate to London except this: 'They would acknowledge nothing in particular, and said that as my proposition was "only general", their sovereign for lack of full knowledge of my sovereign's mind, could but give as uncertain an answer as I came with a doubtful message.'

Since matters had now reached a deadlock, Elizabeth decided on 5 March 1564 that the time had come to lift the embargo on the naming of the nobleman she favoured as the husband of the Scottish queen; and Randolph was informed that he could now speak without 'generalities' or 'obscure terms', with 'simple plainness and sincere meaning'. Mary was immediately informed; but, whatever she thought at the moment, she professed that she was taken by surprise—'upon the sudden', she said. Meanwhile, she would have a palaver with the ambassador. Said Mary:—'Now Mr. Randolph, doth your mistress in good earnest wish me to marry my lord Robert?' When Randolph answered that it was so, he was at once confronted with the question: 'Is that conform to her promise to use me as her sister or daughter, to marry her subject?' He replied that no worthier man could be found, and went on to rehearse the good such a marriage would bring to her realm, and how her own people desired it. When Mary retorted: 'Are you so assured of my subjects' minds that you dare assure that?', Randolph hedged. 'It would be to Scotland's interest', he said, 'to live in obedience with so friendly a neighbour as England.' Mary was not impressed: 'The Queen your mistress', she remarked, 'being assured of me, might let me marry where it may best like me; and always I remain friend to her as I do now.' She continued:— 'What if the queen my sister should marry herself and have children, what have I then gotten? Who will judge this wisely done of me, or who will allow it? . . . These are things uncertain, and it is not safety for me to give any such adventure. Though I have little cause to mistrust your mistress, or to think otherwise than well of her: yet in matters of such difficulty good and long advisement must be taken, as for my part in this I intend to do.' The upshot was that on the following morning Lethington,

---

[1] Lord James Stuart was created earl of Murray in Feb. 1562.

who had been up all night discussing the matter with Mary, stated to Randolph that his mistress required further information as to what Elizabeth would do, what the conditions would be, and what the assurance? She had no disliking for Lord Robert *per se*—had he not been recommended by her 'good sister'?—but she would like a conference of English and Scottish representatives at Berwick to thrash out the details of the problem.

Lethington was now tired and irritable at the slow progress of events, and somewhat bewildered as to the direction they were taking. On 30 March Randolph wrote:—'Many terrors I have to deal with in so weighty a cause: I see Lethington, so wise a man, almost tremble to talk in the matter. He compares himself to Blind Bayard, whose heart served him well, but his sight failed to guide him the way.' A fortnight later the ambassador quoted a friend as saying:—'Wheresoever she hover, and how many times soever she double to fetch the wind, I believe she will at length let fall her anchor between Dover and Berwick, though not perchance in that port, haven, or road that you may wish she would.' Meanwhile the proposed conference at Berwick, mooted by Mary, was gradually allowed to fall into semi-oblivion. Lethington lapsed into despair, fearing that 'God, provoked to anger by the ingratitude of both nations, will not suffer us to attain so great worldly felicity as the success of that negotiation must bring with it, if once it is brought to a happy end.'

Complications were now beginning to develop in another quarter. The day was approaching when the earl of Lennox, whom Mary had invited to return to Scotland at Elizabeth's request in order to be re-instated in his lands and property, would appear in Edinburgh and present his claim for restitution. And a rumour was circulating that soon the countess and her son, the young Lord Darnley, would follow in his train. There was considerable speculation as to the meaning of this sudden development; and Kirkaldy of Grange, staunch protestant and violent anti-papist, glimpsed the 'writing on the wall'. On 19 September 1564 he informed Randolph that in his opinion Lord Robert's chances were now nil: 'he has not descended from a great auld hows', said Kirkaldy, 'and his blood is spotted. . . . I fear we shall not accept him, but if ye will earnestly press it, ye may cause us to take Lord Darnley.'

Kirkaldy was clearly well informed. The Lord Robert marriage proposal was definitely losing its momentum; and on 7 October, Elizabeth, having decided to humour Mary's request for a conference of representatives, briefed the earl of Bedford and Randolph to meet Murray and Lethington at Berwick. But she made no change in the formula; and the Scots complained that the dealings of the English were 'marvellous strange', a 'mere drift of time'. They appealed, therefore, to Cecil for assurance that his sovereign 'means to deal frankly in this matter', and suggested that 'she might send to the Border men of good credit, privy to her own conceptions, and nighest about her, with full authority not only to devise but also to resolve and conclude'. Randolph gave his support, emphasizing the deadly earnestness of the Scots, and saying that 'no man in England wishes more than they do that the Queen's Majesty's desire . . . take sooner effect'. The English secretary of state was obviously impressed; for immediately he penned an apology of sixteen pages in defence of Elizabeth's position—one of the longest epistles he ever wrote, and one of the craftiest.

Pretending that he was mystified by the Scottish demand for 'plainer speech', he insisted that his sovereign's goodwill was beyond question: that she was anxious to advise what would be most beneficial for the maintenance, or augmentation, of the queen of Scots' right, and for the preservation of her country and people. He alluded to the Scottish demand that Elizabeth should, by parliament, establish the succession in her right, placing her 'next to herself and her children'. On this point, which was the very kernel of the problem, Cecil pleasantly admitted that he 'could desire with all his heart that, if his queen had children', Mary 'should be established in the very second place'. Then followed a eulogy of Lord Robert, and of the advantages likely to accompany the marriage. And, said the secretary, 'you will have with him the establishment of your sovereign's title'; but it will have to be 'in order and time, not against order and not before due time'.

The really crucial part of the letter, however, had still to come. If, wrote Cecil, Lord Robert were accepted, his sovereign 'will cause willingly investigation to be made of your sovereign's right, and so far as shall stand with justice and her own surety, by honourable means to be provided, she will abase such titles as shall be proved unjust and prejudicial to her sister's interest, and to leave to her sister her whole right, whatsoever it be'. He pointed out, however, that anything Elizabeth had in mind to do would have to be 'ruled and directed by her laws, and by consent of her three estates . . . and therefore she can promise no more in deed but that which she may jointly with their assent do'. Finally, he said, 'her Majesty was bent to proceed wholly herein in terms and conditions meet for friendship, but *not by way of contracting*; and he advised the Scots *not to let their negotiation be converted to a matter of bargain or purchase* . . . to compass at my sovereign's hands a kingdom and crown, for it may be sooner lost than gotten; and not being craved for, may be as soon offered as reason can require'.

Complete disillusionment was the order of the day in Edinburgh when Cecil's epistle was received and studied. Disappointment, anger, and dismay must have swept over Murray and Lethington by turn; and their reply was reproachful and bitter. Instead of 'plain speech', they wrote, they had been beguiled with 'obscure words and dark sentences' and 'in a manner so many words as there be, so many ambiguities do result thereof'. They insisted that if their sovereign accepted the terms submitted, she would become 'a thrall in her own time'; whereas Elizabeth by yielding to the Scottish demand, would gain complete surety both for herself and for those who descend from her. If things so fell out, she (Elizabeth) would only leave to the right heir 'that which she cannot carry to the grave with her'. With a touch of irony, they confessed themselves to be novices in handling princes' affairs, but they believed that the order of managing them should be to negotiate by way of contracts, bonds, promises, and such like. If the English queen was determined 'not to establish the succession to her crown, then (to speak roundly) Cecil may conclude, also absolutely, that they would never have credit to induce their sovereign to marry an Englishman, lacking the chiefest argument, that may work persuasion'. The tail of the letter carried a sting: 'the declaration of a title to the second place', said the Scots, 'is neither kingdom nor crown . . . it is just a toy, and if we misconstrued your advice, might we not suspect that it is not merely for friendship you make this match, but you also hunt for a kingdom, and go about under that pretence to make an Englishman king of Scotland?'

Fortunately this supercharged letter, born of irritation, was not communicated to Cecil—thanks to the mediatorial services of

Randolph; but the time was coming nearer when the impulsive and emotional Mary would cast her patience to the winds and fight free from the frustrations that had beset her. Meanwhile, on 5 February the hard-worked English ambassador, who had journeyed to St. Andrews, where the Scottish court was now assembled, in order to find out whether Mary was still averse to the English offers, reported that the queen had said to him: 'This I say, and trust me I mean it, if your mistress will, as she hath said, use me as her natural born sister or daughter, I will take myself either as the one or the other as she pleases. . . . But if she shall repute me always but as her neighbour queen of Scots, however willing so ever I be to live in amity and to maintain peace, yet must she not look for that at my hands, that otherwise I would, or she desireth.' Then suddenly, about the middle of March, Elizabeth seems to have made up her mind to end the long-drawn-out debate; for on the 15th she promised that if her good sister 'would marry Leicester,[1] she would promote him to all the honour she could, and would also favour her title as far as she could, although she would not proceed to the examination, or declaration of the same, until she herself had married or notified her intention of never marrying, one or other of which she meant shortly to do'.

This was cold comfort to the queen of Scots: on hearing the news, she 'wept her fill': it was obvious that the 'great game' was coming to an end. By this time Lord Darnley, whose licence to return to Scotland had been granted, apparently with Cecil's approval and suggestion, had been attending the Scottish court for at least a month, and was already established in Mary's good graces. He had also made a favourable impression on many people. 'A great number', wrote Randolph, 'wish him well'; albeit, said the same writer, 'others doubt him and deeplier consider what is fit for the state of their country than (as they call him) a fair jolly young man'. But others, again, suspected his religion, and some believed that if he married the queen, 'it would be the utter overthrow and subversion of them and their houses'. Murray was, of course, among the pessimists. 'What mind will he bear me', said he, 'that knoweth how much I do mislike therewith? If he be a papist, either we must obey or fall into new combers, and I ever to be thought the ring-leader.' Lethington, however, sought comfort in the company of the

[1] Lord Robert Dudley, created earl of Leicester (1564).

'lusty' Mary Livingstone, one of the queen's Maries—'a most singular remedy', remarked the sarcastic Randolph, 'for all diseases of all persons'.

It was now Easter, and the celebrations were on an unprecedented scale. Randolph, who was present, was struck not only by the magnificence of the display, but also by the boisterous optimism of the queen.

Greater triumph [he remarked] there never was in any time of most popery, than was this Easter, at the resurrection and at the High Mass. Organs were wont to be the common music: she wanted now neither trumpet, drum, nor fife, bag-pipe, nor tabor. On Monday she and divers of her women apparelled themselves like bourgeois wives, went upon their feet up and down the town, of every man they met they took some pledge of money to the banquet; and in the same lodging where I was accustomed to lodge, there was the dinner prepared and great cheer made, at which she was herself, to the great wonder and gazing of man, woman, and child.

This outburst of *joyeuseté* was, in large measure, a symbol of the enthusiasm with which Mary now embarked upon what was to be the greatest adventure of her life—and alas! the source of its tragic end.

Meanwhile Darnley was at Stirling castle with the queen, and 'great expectations' were entertained of 'what will come of this great favour'. There was 'more than a bruit', wrote Randolph on 15 April, to the effect that the queen was so fond of the young nobleman, that she 'can be content to forsake all other offers'. Other rumours were also circulating of a very different nature, e.g. that Darnley had been sent to Scotland to 'match the queen meanly and poorly; rather than to live long in amity'. In fact public opinion was in a state of confusion. The duke of Châtellherault was convinced that the house of Hamilton was doomed, and the 'godly' were crying out that they were 'undone'. On Palm Sunday (23 April) mob violence had broken out: a priest was taken at Mass in Edinburgh, hustled off to the Market Place, tied up and exposed to a merciless bombardment with eggs, and only saved from being battered to death with batons by the appearance of the provost, who had the unfortunate wretch removed to the Tolbooth. 'Such discontent, large talk, and open speech', says Randolph, 'I never heard in any nation, and for myself I see not but it must burst out in great mischief.' To make matters worse, the queen fell foul of Murray, Châtellherault, Argyll, and others of the nobility, who began to form a 'band' for self-protection. The decisive moment came when, on Sunday 6 May, Mary attempted to line up the leading nobles on her side by getting them to sign a document, 'granting and consenting unto' her marriage to Darnley. Murray at once refused: his chief objection was that 'he would be loth to consent to a marriage with anyone, of whom there was so little hope that he would be a favourer of Christ's true religion'. But many believed that he was 'led by England', and said that they knew 'from whence he had his lesson'. In any case, the earl left the court in anger, pursued by the queen's taunting words: 'He would set the crown on his own head'!

A few days before this crisis arrived, Lethington had been sent to London to inform Elizabeth of Mary's intention to take Darnley as her husband; and the English privy council was at once informed. Its decision was unanimous, viz. that the marriage 'would be unmeet, unprofitable, and perilous to the amity between the queens and both realms'; but a supplementary resolution recommended that 'a free election' should be offered to the queen of Scots 'of any other of the nobility, either in this whole realm or isle, or in any other place, being suitable for her estate, and agreeable to both the realms'. This was the posture of affairs when Sir Nicholas Throckmorton received his instructions to proceed to Scotland and endeavour to 'stay' the marriage (24 April–6 May). He carried the privy council resolution in his pocket, so that Mary might have ocular demonstration, if she wanted it, that the whole council was behind the resolution —'not one of the nobility known to be of the contrary'. He was to say that 'only with Leicester we mean to inquire into, judge, or publish her title. And this is the bottom of our mind hereon at present.' In regard to the Darnley marriage, his message was: 'We do simply mislike it, as a matter dangerous to the common amity.'

When Lethington was well on his way to London to deliver his mistress's message regarding her intention to marry Darnley, Mary herself became involved in a whirlwind of activity, which staggered and angered her secretary as soon as it was revealed to him. First, she dispatched John Beaton to intercept Lethington and hand to him a fresh commission, viz. to transmit a letter of defiance to Elizabeth. It was a virtual ultimatum, according to Throckmorton, stating in effect that the Scottish queen would no longer be beguiled with 'fair speech', nor fed with 'Yea and Nay', but with the advice of her estates would use her own choice in marriage. 'You would have thought', remarked the English ambassador, who had a glimpse of the document, 'there had neither wanted eloquence, despite, anger, love, nor passion.' Beaton met the Scottish secretary, who was making his way back to Edinburgh, somewhere between Newark and Grantham; and to his surprise, no doubt, the secretary had no sooner read the epistle he was to deliver to Elizabeth than he stuffed it into his pocket and calmly resumed his journey to Edinburgh. Throckmorton, also on the way north, accompanied him. At Berwick, where the two men arrived on 12 May, they found news awaiting them of the goings-on in the Scottish capital, and Lethington was handed another letter from Mary, peremptorily ordering him to 'stay' the English ambassador from entering Scotland for two or three days. 'I never saw him' (i.e. Lethington), says Throckmorton, 'in so great perplexity nor passion' ; nevertheless, both envoys jogged on via Dunbar to Edinburgh, defying the frantic orders of the queen; and subsequently they headed for Stirling, where Mary and the court were resident.

The explanation of all this astonishing sequence of events is plain enough. Mary was in desperation to gain time for the elevation of Darnley to the highest rank in the Scottish peerage, before Elizabeth's envoy could intervene with further opposition. Already he had been promoted lord of Ardmanach, earl of Ross, and duke of Rothesay—three honours 'never before given to any but the king's own sons'. The last step had still to be taken, viz. the award of the dukedom of Albany; but by this time Throckmorton was hammering on the gate of the castle at Stirling. When the Englishman at length received an audience, he presented his orders for Darnley and his father to return forthwith to England, 'having failed in their duty by their arrogant and presumptuous attempts to enterprise such a matter, without making Elizabeth privy, being her subjects'.

By the end of June the situation in Scotland was, from the English standpoint, fast deteriorating. A considerable number of the nobles had ranked themselves with the queen and Darnley: the council had sanctioned the marriage: Throckmorton's mission had ended in a failure; and Elizabeth had instructed

Randolph to establish contact with the party at variance with Mary—Murray, Châtellherault, Argyll, and Glencairn—and to assure them that so long as they intended only to 'uphold the true religion', and to 'support their queen with good advice', preserving amity between the two countries, they would have her sympathy and assistance. At the same time Mary was, with feverish haste, endeavouring to win the approval of her relatives and friends abroad; and the bishop of Dunblane was deputed as a special envoy to Rome to seek a papal dispensation for the removal of the 'impediment of blood' between her and Darnley.[1] Before all these preparations were completed, certainly before the dispensation had even been considered by the pope, Mary took the irrevocable step of publishing the marriage banns on Sunday 22 July, in St. Giles, Holyroodhouse, and the Chapel Royal. On the same day, Darnley was raised to the dukedom of Albany: on the 28th he was proclaimed king; and in the early morning of the 29th the marriage ceremony was performed with full pomp and magnificence. This was, however, in flagrant contradiction to the promise made to Throckmorton before he left, that the final steps would not be taken for another three months.

Elizabeth therefore seized the occasion to send yet another messenger, John Thomworth, to remonstrate with Mary for breaking her promise, for antagonizing her own nobility, and for threatening the extirpation and subversion of the religion established by law; and at the same time to urge reconciliation with Murray and his party. Above all, he was to do his best for the preservation and continuance of peace and amity with England, so that the Scottish queen would not be provoked to revive the 'auld alliance'.

But Thomworth was unable to make any impression. Mary flatly refused to compound with her rebels: she swore she would 'pursue them to the uttermost', being 'marvellous stout'. Thus two days after the Englishman's arrival at court, Murray was 'put to the horn'.[2] The Lennoxes were allowed to remain in Scotland; and Mary, defying Elizabeth's demand for their return, put the coping-stone on her 'insolence' by saying that matters inside Scotland must not be interfered with. Thomworth must have returned to London 'with a flea in his ear'; and, to add to his discomfiture, he was arrested for crossing

---

[1] For Darnley's relationship with Mary and his position *vis-à-vis* the English succession see genealogical table II.   [2] i.e. outlawed.

the frontier without a passport. Meanwhile, events took their fateful course in Scotland.

The rebellion, if it may be so called, lasted about two months and a week: that is, from Murray's 'horning' on 6 August until 19 October, when Mary and Darnley 'rode the whirlwind', occupied Edinburgh with their troops, and the confederate nobles fled across the border to Carlisle, under English protection. Elizabeth was now in a quandary: she had rashly assured Murray and his associates of assistance, but had done nothing to implement her promise, except to allow driblets of monetary help to be smuggled surreptitiously across the border. This policy of cautious restraint was not entirely due to a disinclination to support rebels: it was imposed upon the English queen by the vigilance of the French ambassador, de Foix, who made no secret of his knowledge that France would move in favour of Mary if England supported Murray. An English frigate, however, patrolled the Forth estuary to see that munitions or arms from the Continent were not being landed; while English money continued to percolate through Berwick to Murray's exchequer. On 14 October, when the rebels had successfully eluded pursuit by slipping across the frontier under cover of Scrope's protecting troops from Carlisle, Murray wrote a singularly revealing letter to Leicester. Owing to Elizabeth's 'cold feeling', he said, 'a great part of my friends are ruined, and I and the rest of the nobility here put to this extremity . . . to which we are brought by following her Majesty and her Council's advice'.

Mary had indeed secured a triumph; but it was not complete, for the sanctuary at Newcastle, where the rebels collected with Elizabeth's connivance, became a valuable base for plots and plans against the Marian government in Edinburgh. It was all very disconcerting to the Scottish queen; but more trouble had already overtaken her from a quite unexpected quarter. On 22 September, when victory seemed to be within her grasp, a certain Captain Cockburn arrived with the news that France had become a broken reed, and that it would be advisable to seek reconciliation with the insurrectionists. A few days later, an official envoy from Paris—the sieur de Mauvissière, corroborated the bad news. Help from France was doomed. Mary listened to what the Frenchman had to say, and 'with a tear in her eye' protested that her hope was in France, praying Mauvissière not to divulge to anyone the subject of his mission, since reconciliation with her rebellious subjects was impossible without loss of honour. A painful discussion went on for two consecutive days, Mary pleading with anguish for a respite, Mauvissière driving home his arguments with illustrations from the horrors and disasters of the civil wars in France and the French disaster at Leith in 1560. In the end, the Frenchman agreed to place the letters from Paris in the queen's hands, to do with them as she wished, but he put a final question: 'Would she rather hazard her estate and life by giving battle?' And when she answered that she would, 'rather than languish and not be a queen', he saw that the game was up. In a letter to the king, he admitted his failure, commenting wryly: 'Il semble que Dieu ne veuille pas encore les laisser en repos!'

In the meanwhile, Murray, who had been warned by Elizabeth to remain in Newcastle, made the foolish mistake of hastening to London to plead his cause. He was quickly disillusioned. Instead of receiving comfort and consolation from a friend and ally, he was trounced unmercifully by a seemingly irate queen, in the presence of the privy council and the lynx-eyed de Foix. Was it a carefully rehearsed melodrama? Above all, was the Frenchman deceived?

When the news of Murray's 'discomfiture' reached the Scottish court it was received with great jubilation; while Elizabeth's conduct was generally interpreted as a confession of fear. In November the movable goods of all who had taken part in the rebellion, already declared forfeit to the Crown, were dispersed by public auction, being 'greedily taken up and sold for ready money at half their value'. Three months later Randolph was summarily dismissed from Edinburgh, on the ground that he had helped the rebels with money. In an age when ambassadors were often left to shift for themselves this did not necessarily mean a declaration of war; but it certainly indicated that Anglo-Scottish relations were rapidly drifting into the danger zone. For three years Randolph had worked whole-heartedly in the interests of peace and goodwill between the two realms— a highly respected and diligent frequenter of Holyrood, whose advice was much courted by the queen, and by his own admission, one of her most devoted admirers. But now the fateful marriage had ruined everything: replacing the amity he had striven for by a seemingly implacable enmity, and bringing the sovereigns, whose co-operation and conciliation had been the inspiration of his life, to the very brink of war. Anger mingled with disappointment. With a bitter and jaundiced mind he turned to rend the idol he had formerly worshipped: 'And in the whole world, if there be a more malicious heart towards the queen my sovereign than she is that here now reigneth, let me be hanged at my home-coming or counted a villain for ever.'

But the activities of the queen of Scots at this time had a much wider range than the facts just recounted would appear to show. Until the Darnley marriage she had acted on a very narrow basis, relying principally on her own resources and the skill of the able politicians in Edinburgh. She had consistently avoided any semblance of 'papistical' intentions; and nothing was farther from her thoughts than to stir up a religious war in Scotland. Indeed so strong was her desire to maintain the goodwill of her subjects, protestant as well as catholic, that she resisted even the direct appeals of the Holy See itself, and thus gave all her catholic friends at home and abroad the impression that she had not the good of the church at heart. Sending no representative to the council of Trent, she had hustled Nicholas of Gouda, the nuncio, out of the country in 1562, pleading that the times were unpropitious for a religious revival.[1] Not unnaturally, therefore, the construction put upon her actions was that she was cold in the cause of religion and a time-server. Likewise, too, in the political field, she had disappointed her friends by her neutrality and apathy. Now, however, all this was dramatically changed. Throwing aside the mask of forbearance, Mary made a strenuous appeal to both the supreme pontiff and the king of Spain. In the autumn of 1565, when the civil war was rampant in Scotland, the bishop of Dunblane was in Rome beseeching the pope for ten or twelve thousand men and a sum of money to enable her to overcome her enemies; and a certain Yaxley was accredited to the Spanish government of the Low Countries with the message 'that the queen of Scots, having reason to doubt the credit of her uncles in the court of France, was advised to address all her causes to the king of Spain, and would commit herself, her husband, and her country to his protection'. Philip was to understand that she would follow his advice without swerving so much as a hairsbreadth.

Great was the joy in Rome and Brussels at this news. Now at

[1] J. H. Pollen, 'Papal Negotiations with Mary Queen of Scots, 1561–7' (*Scot. Hist. Soc.* xxxvii, 1901).

last, it seemed, there was ocular demonstration of the fact that
Mary was sincere in her protestations of loyalty to the faith;
many thought that the counter-reformation in Britain was begun.
The amazing energy of 'this woman with a man's heart' stirred
the enthusiasm of the aged pope to an unwonted degree. Despite
the embarrassed state of his finances and the many other cares
distracting the head of the church, he responded to the appeal
for succour with alacrity. The aggressive Turk might conquer
Malta, the anarchy in the papal states might continue, but the
heroic queen must not be left alone in her war against heresy.
If need be, he would even stint his table and sell his plate rather
than see her beaten for lack of money. Had he been younger he
would willingly have spent life itself in her service. Pius V was
a born crusader, and, like a true knight, credited Mary with
the same high intentions as he himself possessed. He offered her
all she asked, 200,000 crowns, payable in monthly instalments of
40,000; and urged the Spanish king to send the necessary military aid.

Much was expected from this combination of forces; and for
a brief space, as we have just observed, the queen enjoyed the
satisfaction of riding the whirlwind. But the foreign element,
which had lent so imposing and dangerous a character to the
scheme, on which Mary principally calculated for its ultimate
success, hardly came into action at all. The English catholics,
whose active help the Darnley marriage was specially designed
to enlist, remained unresponsive, preferring their 'silent compromise of conscience' to the dubious hazard of war; the promised Spanish troops never landed—were, in fact, never sent—
because Philip, afraid of precipitating a war with England for
which he was as yet unprepared, 'shamelessly deserted the young
princes', leaving them 'naked to the assaults of heresy'; while,
of the papal subsidy, only 40,000 crowns reached Edinburgh,
the remainder being delayed at the pope's express order, until
the queen's intentions became clearer. Thus prop after prop
crumbled and fell away. But the mortal blow was delivered in
Scotland by a confederacy of the malcontents.

Murray and his associates were living in penury at Newcastle,
hoping against hope that Elizabeth, whose interests they had
served, would do something to see them restored. But their
wailing letters brought no comfort. And, to make matters worse,
news reached them in November that their 'movable' property,

now forfeit to the Crown by their treason, had passed under the auctioneer's hammer at throw-away prices. Rumours were also circulating that they would soon have to leave England and seek asylum abroad. Then, in December, the summons went forth from Edinburgh ordering them to appear before parliament on 12 March to hear the forfeiture of their lands and estates. By Christmas Murray was in the depths of despair.

It was at this juncture that Sir James Melville and Sir Nicholas Throckmorton tried their hands at mediation. Full of foreboding at the stubbornness of the queen, and knowing full well that the friends of the banished nobles would work unceasingly for their return, Melville advised clemency towards Murray. 'Clemency', he said, 'would be more profitable than rigour, for extremity frequently brings on desperate enterprises.' But the queen replied 'with choler': 'I defy them: what can they do?: what dare they do?' Whereupon Melville tried intimidation: he had heard 'dark speeches' that we should have news 'ere parliament was ended'. To which Mary retorted that she herself had heard such rumours, but set no store by them: 'our countrymen', she said, 'are talkative'. Throckmorton fared no better. In a letter full of political shrewdness he spoke of the advantages of moderation: let the queen be merciful, he asserted, and the English protestants who were under the impression that her quarrel with Murray was entirely on the score of religion, would rally to her side in the matter of the succession. He spoke with authority and conviction. But Mary would have none of it. She preferred the advice of her French friends, particularly the cardinal of Lorraine, and the archbishop of Glasgow, who counselled her to stand fast. On 19 February 1566 she summoned Randolph to the council chamber, accused him of perfidy, and ordered him to leave the kingdom within three days. The dismissal was undoubtedly warranted; but nearly a week of wrangling ensued, in which the 'outraged' Englishman stoutly denied his culpability, and refused to accept a passport signed by the king; eventually he packed his baggage and allowed himself to be conducted to Berwick.

In the meantime what Melville had feared and the queen had derided, began to take shape with a grim and awesome speed. One of the most brutal plots of this cruel and conscienceless age was hatched in Edinburgh and executed with appalling barbarity. This was the murder of David Rizzio. Little is known about the man except that he was an Italian, probably of bourgeois origin, who came to Scotland in 1561 in the train of Moretta, the Savoyard ambassador. He was a skilled musician and a man of attractive wit—which may have been the reason why Mary appointed him one of her secretaries, in place of Raulet who had left her a year before. Perhaps he brought with him just that light-heartedness and *joie de vivre* of the Mediterranean people that the queen found missing in Scotland. He was also a catholic, and so far as we know quite incorruptible by anyone. The removal of this comparatively harmless and insignificant Italian, albeit he was trumped up as a papal emissary and an inspirer of the queen's strong action against Murray and his friends, was merely incidental to the main issue. Fundamentally the plot was directed against the queen herself—and her unborn child, whose birth was expected within two months; and the hope of the plotters was that the shock of the murder (which was to take place in the royal presence) would not only throw the government out of gear, but enable them to set up Darnley as a puppet king, while they would bring back Murray and the exiles to their old dignities and offices. If the queen and her child perished in the *coup d'état*, so much the better for the conspirators: with the feeble Darnley as head of the state, they could do as they pleased; and if he, too, became *difficile*, there were plenty ways of disposing of him! Such was the queen's own interpretation of the plot in the light of events, and it must be admitted that no other meets the case so completely or satisfactorily.

The leverage by which the plot was to be carried out, and without which it would have proved a dismal failure, was supplied by the king, with whose consent and known support the various elements were drawn together.

A few months of married life had completely disillusioned Mary as to the true character of the man she had so blithely taken into partnership—the pleasant, music-loving, sporting lover of yester year had now shown himself in his real colours: an addict to drink and boon companions, promiscuous in his relations with women, violent in temper, unstable, volatile, and quite incapable of business. Like most weak men, he was inclined to stand upon his 'rights', and to claim his share in administration. Nay, he demanded more than this: he wanted—probably at his father's instigation—the 'crown matrimonial', which would secure for him the privileges of royalty during the rest of his natural life. No wonder the queen turned away from the sot in disgust: instead of giving her the moral support, counsel, and advice she gravely needed in the contest with her unruly and domineering nobility, he presented the latter with the means of destroying her. And when it was beyond dispute that the Italian had the queen's confidence, as her private secretary, and sat with her in her boudoir, Darnley's suspicious and weak mind, probably goaded by others cleverer than he, led him from suspicion to jealousy, and from jealousy to the conviction that 'David' was carrying on a clandestine love affair with his wife. This drove the unhappy man to distraction. The peace of mind of the unfortunate Rizzio was also shattered; for the astrologer Damiot, whom he consulted, warned him 'to beware of the bastard', meaning George Douglas the natural son of the earl of Angus, and one of the worst desperadoes of the entire group of plotters. The Kirk, too, added its voice to the confused babble, and the cry arose that the Italian was an emissary of the pope, an enemy of the established religion. Even Melville, for all his wisdom and shrewdness, accepted this trumpery, despite the assurance given by the queen that 'David' 'meddled no further than in her French writings and affairs'.

The first indication that something in the nature of a murder conspiracy was afoot was conveyed by Lethington in a letter to Cecil on 9 February 1566. After a year of courtship, described by Randolph as his 'stark, staring madness', Lethington had just married Mary Fleming, and was now staging a 'come back' in politics. In cryptic words he informed the English secretary that he saw no certain way to restore matters in Scotland to their former state 'unless we chop at the very root—you know where it lieth'. The reference is probably to Rizzio. About the same time Darnley took George Douglas into his confidence about the great concern agitating his mind, and through him appealed for help to his kinsman by marriage, Lord Ruthven. He in turn called in Morton, the most unscrupulous noble in Scotland. Darnley's father, the earl of Lennox, was also 'art and part' in it, and so, too, was Lord Lindsay, who like Ruthven had married a Douglas. Quite a family compact, in fact, or a clan feud—the Douglases *versus* the Stewarts! Others like Ker of Faudonside came in later. Details of what was brewing must have come to Randolph's ears on or about 13 February—

perhaps it was deemed advisable to inform him because of possible English repercussions—for on that date he sent the following startling tidings to Leicester: 'I know that there are practices in hand between the father and son to come to the crown against her [i.e. Mary's] will. I know that if that take place which is intended, David with the king's consent shall have his throat cut within these ten days.' More significant, however, is his further communication that 'many worse and grievouser things', which he could not commit to paper, were likely to happen to the queen. We shall never know what were the things he was afraid to communicate in his dispatch; but one of them at least may have been the denigration of Mary as a strumpet. Why, otherwise, did Cecil tell de Foix, the French ambassador in London, that Rizzio was slain in the arms of the queen—*reginam nefario stupro polluens*?

Speed was, of course, essential to success, for the meeting of parliament on 12 March was barely a month ahead. So, on the first day of the month two 'bands' were drawn up and signed: between Darnley and the conspirators in Scotland—Argyll, Morton, Ruthven, Boyd, Lethington, George Douglas; and between Darnley and the banished lords—Murray, Rothes, Grange, Pitarrow, and the rest. The former envisaged not only the slaughter of the Italian, but also of others close to the queen, possibly Huntly, Bothwell, and Atholl; for, as the wording of the 'band' ran, 'it may chance that there be sundry great personages present, who may make them to gainstand our enterprise, where through some of them may be slain'. The king was therefore to grant the would-be murderers his protection to the uttermost . . . 'because it may chance to be done in the presence of the queen's majesty or within the palace of Holyroodhouse'. The second 'band' was supplementary: it concerned the exiles and Darnley alone. They were to fortify and maintain him in his just title to the crown of Scotland 'failing the succession of their sovereign lady', to be friends of his friends and enemies of his enemies, to give him the 'crown matrimonial', and to maintain the established religion; while he, for his part, was to pardon Murray and his followers, to stay all proceedings for their forfeiture in parliament, and to restore them to their lands and dignities. All this was arranged before Randolph left Edinburgh for Berwick on 2 March, for he and Bedford informed Cecil on 6 March of the substance of the plot, together with a list of the 'chief doers' as well in England as in Scotland.

In a covering letter addressed to Elizabeth they divulged that the 'attemptate' was to be carried out 'before Tuesday next' (i.e. 12 March) and referred to the letter they had sent to Cecil for full information. There is, therefore, no reason to doubt that government circles in London were pretty well informed beforehand of the approaching tragedy, although, as a matter of fact, the miscreants carried out their foul design only three days after the Randolph–Bedford dispatch was sent off from Berwick to the English court. Probably they accelerated their preparations in order to prevent any possible interference from London. Saturday night (9 March) was the chosen date, not Tuesday (12 March).

The details of the sordid murder, together with the kaleidoscopic revolution to which it gave birth, belong to Scottish history, and are too well known to be recounted here. But several salient facts emerge from the confusion, with a direct bearing on Anglo-Scottish relations, and may therefore be emphasized. In the first place, although Murray's part (if any) in the crime is obscure, his well-timed appearance in Edinburgh immediately after its perpetration, and the masterful way in which he handled the situation, suggest that the deed in itself was secondary, and the *coup d'état* that followed the really important thing. In the second place, the effect of the upheaval was to destroy Mary's plan to establish personal government in Scotland, and to place both her and the state once more under the control of Murray and his associates. It would be too much to say that the revolution was engineered in England's interest—the facts do not warrant such a conclusion; but it cannot be denied that the outcome was eminently in England's favour.

So far we have considered the succession question mainly as affecting the two queens. But it had a wider import; and before we resume the thread of our history, a glance at the matter from a different angle is advisable.

Ever since 1559, when Elizabeth replied to her first parliament's recommendation to marry, with honeyed words about her care for the public weal and the advantages of virginity in a queen, who, as she said, had already given herself in marriage to her kingdom, the problem of dynastic security and the safety of the religious settlement, which depended upon it, had grown to be the dominant theme in English politics. Parliament at first did not know what to make of the queen's evident antipathy to marriage. An unmarried queen was an intriguing novelty; but to men of the world it was unnatural, and, in view of the prevailing uncertainty as to the future, distinctly disconcerting. After all, as the commons had hinted in their petition, princes are mortal and commonwealths immortal, and the kings of England had always shown great solicitude about their issue. Therefore the queen must marry and provide an heir, her private preferences notwithstanding. The force of the argument was incontestable; and it received an accession of strength when, in October 1562, Elizabeth fell ill of the smallpox, and for several days seemed to hover between life and death. It was an anxious moment for the council and, indeed, the country at large; for it needed no flight of imagination to foresee the chaos that would supervene if she died prematurely. Protestants, confronted with the likelihood of an unconditional catholic succession, in the person of Mary Stuart, began at once to canvass the claims of Lady Catherine Grey,[1] the representative of the Suffolk line which, failing heirs by Henry VIII's children, had the 'remainder' in the succession by act of parliament. Others favoured the earl of Hertford or the earl of Huntingdon;[1] and doubtless the catholics and all partisans of the principle of strict hereditary succession secretly hoped to revive the Stuart claim, which Henry had barred. Consequently, when the second parliament met in January 1563, there was a general desire on the part of both houses to have the order of succession established by law. Petitions were presented to the queen by the lords and the commons. Let the queen marry, said the former, and designate a successor: 'thereby she shall strike a terror into her adversaries and replenish her subjects with immortal joy.' If she followed the example of Pyrrhus, and left her kingdom to the person with the sharpest sword, it would mean calamities innumerable, civil war, the destruction of religion, foreign invasion, and bondage. The commons argued on much the same lines, but laid more stress on the necessity for delimiting the succession than on marriage.

Elizabeth was perturbed; but again she had recourse to evasion and procrastination. Her own safety and theirs, she said in reply to the commons, was her paramount consideration, but

[1] See genealogical tables II and III.

she could not 'wade into' so 'deep a matter' without deliberation. Let them not talk about her death: she knew now as well as before that she was mortal. She would give them an answer 'upon further advice'. In conclusion she assured them that 'though after my death you may have many stepdames, yet you shall never have a more natural mother than I mean to be unto you all'. To the lords she pointed out that it would cost England much more blood if she declared her successor: let them consider well what they were urging her to do. As for marriage, it was not impossible: they must not mistake the marks left on her face by smallpox for the wrinkles of age; and if she did marry, even although she were old, God would provide her with children as He did Saint Elizabeth:—once more the familiar assurances about the public weal and hints that she might marry, but no pledges or commitments of a positive kind, and, above all, no indication that the question of the succession would be settled in the immediate future. Admittedly the queen played her cards well. She finessed boldly, employed all the cunning she knew, or ingenuity could suggest, and so mingled firmness and reproof with an evident desire to conciliate that she circumvented her difficulty with comparative ease. After parliament was prorogued, in April, she imprisoned John Hales, a chancery lawyer, for writing a pamphlet against the Stuart claim, and defending that of Lady Catherine; and Bacon, his patron, was exiled from court. So matters stood until the ominous events in Scotland following the Darnley marriage—the expulsion of the protestant lords, Mary's machinations with the pope and the king of Spain, and the birth of Prince James—exposed in startling light the peril in which England was placed by an unmarried queen and an unsettled succession.

Needless to say, when the third parliament assembled, in November 1566, a lively session was inevitable. Acrimonious discussions began almost at once on the all-important question of the hour. 'So far brake forth the sharp and hot spirits of the Commons', writes Camden, 'that they taxed the Queen as if she neglected her country and posterity, defamed Cecil with slanders and scandalous books, as a corrupt counsellor in this matter, and cursed the Queen's physician as a dissuader of her marriage for I wot not what womanish impotency.' The debate lasted several weeks, rising to a crescendo towards its close. The secretary and the lord chamberlain, acting on Elizabeth's instructions, tried to pour oil on the troubled waters by announcing that she was now 'moved to marry, and that she mindeth, for the weal of her Commons, to prosecute the same'. But instead of rousing enthusiasm, as the solvent they were looking for, the intimation was apparently swept aside without even an acknowledgement. In the upper house, greatly to the queen's annoyance, many of the peers, including Norfolk, Leicester, and Pembroke, took sides with the commons; and both Leicester and Pembroke were excluded from the presence-chamber, having to sue for pardon on their knees. But in the lower house excitement drove men to an astonishing licence of speech. It was contended by two lawyers, Bell and Monson, supported by Paul Wentworth and others, that monarchs are bound in the interests of their peoples to make known their successors. If Elizabeth refused to do so, she was no mother to her country but a step-mother, nay a parricide; for she would rather that England 'which now breathed with her breath, should expire with her than survive her'. Not princes, they said, but cowards and timorous women have ever stood in fear of their successors. The wrath of God and the alienation of her subjects' hearts would be her portion if she refrained from so obvious a duty.

This was plain speaking with a vengeance, the like of which would have caused her illustrious father—if he had heard it—to turn in his grave. But the daughter rose to the occasion with a vigour and concentrated passion that must have surprised the staid Cecil, whose effort to find some sort of compromise amid the turmoil was side-tracked as totally inadequate. On 5 November, thirty members of each house were summoned to the palace, where the queen, without inviting them to state their case, bluntly announced that she would now do the talking. It was a long speech she made, partly truculent and vituperative, partly conciliatory, somewhat illogical, but definitely the outpouring of an angry woman. 'I muse', she said, 'how men of wit can so hardly use that gift they hold': they reminded her of 'bridleless colts whose mouths had never been snaffled by the rider'. Did they know who she was? Was she not born in the realm? Were her parents born in any foreign country? Was there any reason why she should alienate herself from being careful over this country? Was not her kingdom here? They had not taken notice of her assurance that she would marry; but she would say it again; and she hoped to have children, otherwise she would never marry. As for limitation of the succession, she had 'stayed it' for their benefit; 'for if they should have liberty to treat of it, there would be so many competitors . . . that it would be an occasion of a greater charge than any subsidy'. But, if her will had not bowed to reason, it (i.e. the succession) 'would be that thing she would gladliest desire to see them deal in'. For herself, she cared not for death because all men are mortal. But one thing she would not do: she would never be by violence constrained 'to do anything'. 'I thank God', she continued, 'I am endued with such qualities that if I were turned out of the realm in my petticoat, I were able to live in any place in Christendom.' She finished characteristically: 'As soon as there may be a convenient time, and it may be done with least peril unto you—though never without great danger unto me— I will deal therein for your safety, and offer it unto you as your prince and head, without request; for it is monstrous that the feet should direct the head.'

With these pointed words, and a promise, Elizabeth dismissed the deputation, instructing its members to pass on her remarks to both houses. Of course, she had considerable justification for what she had said. While the succession remained open, she was safe: both catholics and protestants were her bondsmen, the former from hope, the latter from fear. And in her safety lay the stability of the state. History, moreover, had shown that there were dangers to successors as well as to those in possession, if a public pronouncement were made in the matter of the succession. She herself had been in peril at the time of the Wyatt rebellion; and the fates of Roger Mortimer, earl of March, and John de la Pole, earl of Lincoln, signalled still graver warnings from the more distant past. Is it surprising that Elizabeth felt justified in her resistance to parliament's demands? Their way was the way to chaos: hers was the way to peace. On the last day of the session she took a high hand with the assembled lords and commons: hectored them for their disingenuousness in making a 'vizard of liberty and succession' in order to triumph over her; but finished her harangue by assuring them, in characteristic manner, that 'a more loving [prince] towards you ye shall never have'. 'Thus by a woman's wisdom', says Camden, 'she suppressed these commotions, which Time so qualified, shining ever clearer and clearer, that very few, but such as were seditious or timorous, were troubled with care about a successor.'[1]

We return once more to Scotland, where events were moving with accelerated pace from tragedy to tragedy. The lacerated body of Rizzio had not been long underground when the Fates began to weave their toils about the wayward and luckless Darnley. Instead of winning the 'crown matrimonial' as a reward for his share in the murder at Holyrood, he found himself loathed and despised by the queen, whom he had deceived, wronged, and insulted beyond forgiveness on the night of the crime; and regarded with a mortal hatred by Morton, Ruthven, and the other accomplices whom he had abandoned and betrayed on the following morning, who were now nursing their wrath and longing for the day when they would be able to punish the royal poltroon. As for the rest of the greater nobles—Murray, Argyll, Huntly, and Bothwell—they cold-shouldered him with contempt, as one who had no further significance in the political arena. Thus Darnley, shut out by the queen from public affairs as incompetent and untrustworthy, began to feel himself the butt of everybody's aversion. He became a 'man with a grievance': his resentment drove him deeper into a dangerous and sulky solitude—brooding, suspicious, disgruntled, rebellious, for ever prying into the queen's doings, and creating the worst impression by his own. He corresponded with the pope and the catholic party in Scotland, condemning Mary's dilatoriness in promoting the counter-reformation and proclaiming himself the true champion of catholicism: he talked of leaving the country for Flanders, in order to plead his case in foreign courts and to acquaint the world with his ill-treatment: a ship had been chartered for him and lay at Glasgow in readiness. In short the fretful Darnley was making himself a nuisance and a public danger; and his movements had to be watched in case he drifted into fresh conspiracies. Eventually, in September 1566, the queen and the council decided to bring him to book. He was asked by them to account for his behaviour; but he refused to give any rational answer and left the room with the sullen words: 'Adieu, madam, you shall not see my face for a long time.'

Of course Mary had other things on her mind than the vagaries of her besotted husband. The summer and autumn of

---

[1] For further details as to the constitutional crisis see chap. vi.

1566 brought her alternately days of rejoicing and of gloomy despair. In June Prince James was born in Edinburgh castle; and even the 'barren' Elizabeth, who had previously wished her 'a short pain and as happy an hour as she herself could wish for', joined in the thanksgiving. 'I too', she said, 'am big with desire for the good news.' Undoubtedly the birth of an heir was a triumph; for it seemed to bring the settlement of the English succession appreciably nearer. Hence the joy and excitement in Edinburgh. But exaltation turned to blank despair when, early in October, Mary fell ill at Jedburgh with an obscure ailment that nearly killed her. For hours she lay as if dead—'all her members cauld, her eene [eyes] closit, mouth fast, feit and arms stiff and cauld'. Her servants prepared for her funeral, and prayers were offered up, while the great bell of St. Giles tolled for her recovery. She made her will, and drafted arrangements for the government of the country in the event of her death, protesting her loyalty to the catholic church and the French alliance. When at last the haematemesis passed off and convalescence was on the way, Mary wrote (18 November) to the English privy council concerning her claim to the succession—a subject that had greatly agitated her mind during the illness. In this letter she expressed the hope that the council would 'have respect to justice with indifferency whensoever it shall please your sovereign to put the matter in deliberation'. Melville had already paved the way by his mission to Elizabeth after the *accouchement*; and he had the assurance from her lips that she 'was resolved to satisfy the queen [Mary] in that matter, which she esteemed to belong most justly to her good sister, and that she wished from her heart that it should be that way decided'. Melville took this with his customary scepticism; but Mary was overjoyed: she believed that the achievement of her life's ambition was now within sight—the more so, since Elizabeth had admitted to the ambassador that the birth of the prince would be a 'spur to the lawyers' to get on with the job, and that the matter would be proceeded with 'before her nobles now assembled left for their houses' on the dissolution of parliament. Melville concluded his dispatch with the words: 'Seeing the great mark which her Majesty shoots at . . . being so near to be obtained . . . let her Majesty be more careful and circumspect that her desires . . . be not overthrown for lack of secrecy, good management, and princely behaviour.'

Unfortunately there was a fly in the ointment—the persistent discontent of the king, which showed no sign of abatement as the autumn wore on. Du Croc, the French ambassador in Edinburgh, was of the opinion that Darnley suffered from hurt pride—'il veut être tout et commander partout'. In October Lethington, writing to Mary's ambassador in Paris, Archbishop Beaton, commented: 'It is a heart-break for her to think that he is her husband, and to be free of him she sees no outgate.' 'I could wish to be dead', she is reported to have said to du Croc; and at Christmas the latter wrote in a gloomy strain: 'I cannot pretend to foretell how it may all turn, but this I will say that matters cannot subsist long as they are, without being accompanied by sundry bad consequences.'

Meanwhile the fateful conference of Craigmillar had considered the question of the 'outgate': Murray, Huntly, Argyll, and Lethington were present with the queen. Divorce was mentioned as a possible solution, but was dropped when Mary objected that it might prove prejudicial to her son—she would rather endure all torments and abide the perils that might chance her in Elizabeth's lifetime: indeed it might be better if she retired to France until Darnley changed his mind. Lethington assured her that they, being of the council, would find the *moyen* to be quit of him without prejudice to the prince, and 'albeit my lord of Murray here present be little less scrupulous for a protestant than your Grace is for a papist, I am assured he will look through his fingers thereto and will behold our doings, saying nothing'. To Mary's objection that she would prefer that the matter were left as it was, lest believing to do her a service they might hurt and displease her, Lethington's reply was: 'Madam, let us guide the matter among us, and your Grace shall see nothing but good and approved by parliament': on which the queen retorted that nothing must be done to stain her honour and conscience. There the discussion ended; but it would seem as if the murder 'band' was drawn up by the lords before they dispersed.

It is, of course, arguable that Mary must have known, or guessed, what was in Lethington's mind when he made his somewhat sinister suggestion; but there is no ground whatever for believing that she sanctioned the 'band', or was 'art and part' in what followed. The only reasonable conclusion is that, knowing something was intended against Darnley, she did not warn him nor try to protect him from his enemies. Instead, she let things take their course.

Shortly after the conference, the prince was baptized (17 December) with full catholic ritual—the last grand papal pageant in Scotland—accompanied by banqueting, masking, and firework display. To Mary it was to be—or it might be—the harbinger of a catholic revival throughout the country. At the same time, the presence of the earl of Bedford as Elizabeth's representative appeared to her to be an unmistakable token of her 'good sister's love and good-will'. Darnley was not present at the function; but hearing that Morton had been pardoned, he decided to leave Stirling for Glasgow and the Lennox country in the west (24 December). Here he fell ill of the smallpox or, as one writer suggests, an attack of virulent syphilis. On his return to Edinburgh in the queen's company, apparently reconciled but not yet free from infection, he was taken on a litter to the old provost's house at Kirk-o'-Field to be 'cleansed' before re-entering Holyrood, where the infant James was domiciled. Here, in the early morning of 10 February, he was strangled and the house itself blown up with gunpowder.

The murder of the king is a veritable 'Serbonian Bog'—a trap to the unwary, a challenge to the adventurous, and a nightmare to historians. It is true, of course, that we now know with some degree of certitude how the foul deed was accomplished— R. H. Mahon has explained the technique, destroying in the process Buchanan's fantastic tale;[1] but a thick fog still hangs over the movements of those who, for one reason or another, seem to have been involved, either as accessories or as participants. The so-called 'evidence' which the Scottish lords produced at the Westminster conference (November–December 1568) when they accused their queen of being Bothwell's lover, accomplice, and instigator—the celebrated Casket Letters (discovered conveniently four months after the murder), the Lennox Indictment (also *ex post facto*), the Confessions of Paris, &c.—all this mass of 'documentary' material, which puzzled and shocked the English commissioners, has been sifted, explored, and adjudicated upon by some of the best brains in the intellectual world for more than two centuries. But it is more than doubtful whether anyone with even a modicum of knowledge about legal

[1] R. H. Mahon, *The Tragedy of Kirk o' Field* (1930).

procedure, and a balanced mind, would care to assert that the evidence would pass muster in a modern law court.

There are moments, indeed, when the candid critic perusing the documents would be inclined to dismiss the whole affair of the Scottish queen's indictment as little better than a *crime policier* or, in common parlance— a 'frame-up'. The plain fact is, that the earl of Murray and his associates, having complete control over all the agencies of government, could rig parliament and the law as they pleased, despite their solemn asseverations of legality: they could, and did, suppress evidence that threatened to interfere with their aims and plans, and were prepared to manufacture it if they found it necessary to do so, with the same disregard for moral scruples, and the same security from detection as the authorities in a modern totalitarian state. They were able to do this, moreover, not merely because they were masters of the situation in Scotland, but also because they were in close alliance with Mary's implacable enemies at the court of Elizabeth, whose unalterable aim was to prevent a Stuart succession. The true motive that linked this formidable combination together was not the bringing of Bothwell to justice as Darnley's murderer—that was merely the dust they threw in the eyes of the world—but the political annihilation of the queen of Scots.

It is probable that the fairest verdict on the whole matter is still that of Andrew Lang nearly half a century ago, before he submitted to what he termed 'the superior logic' of T. F. Henderson. Observe what he says in the last edition of his brilliant book, the *Mystery of Mary Stuart*, published in 1912, one year after the famous debate finished. 'This book does not profess to establish the innocence of Queen Mary, but rather to show that the methods of her accusers—some of them, if she was guilty, her accomplices—were so clumsy and so manifestly perfidious, that they all but defeat the object of the prosecution. When measures so dishonourable and so unjust were employed, and when, even thus, no definite verdict was pronounced, it is natural, even if illogical, to doubt the guilt of the accused. . . .' A 'not-proven' verdict in Scots legal procedure! Thus, to Lang and those who ponder the problem with the same thoroughness, the real issue is to find an explanation of the 'Mystery', viz. how it could come about that a woman, whose *naturel* was the antithesis of cruel, who was opposed to violence and bloodshed, who steadfastly refused to display her loyalty to the counter-reformation by making a holocaust of her protestant counsellors, as the papal legate, Laureo, insisted she should do: a woman, moreover, whose character was probably nobler than that of the majority of the men who surrounded her—how could such an one descend so suddenly, and so low, in the moral scale as to become an accomplice in an abominable crime, and so devoid of common sense, self-interest, and self-respect, that she gambled away not only her good name and her Scottish crown, but also her hope of the English succession, which had been her unalterable aim ever since she set foot on Scottish soil? Nay, the 'mystery' deepens when we remember that only a short time before the murder she sent Robert Melville to London to open negotiations for a conference on this very matter, in accord with Elizabeth's 'direct' and express desire. It may be worth while noting that the 'not-proven' verdict of Lang corresponds with Elizabeth's statement in January 1569, viz. that nothing had been 'sufficiently shown' against the queen of Scots.

To resume the narrative: the main fact on which everything turned is not legal but moral, and is connected with Mary's behaviour after the crisis, not with her doings at the time of the murder or before it. Hardly was the deed known when mysterious voices were heard in the streets at night crying out that Bothwell had murdered the king; and placards began to appear in public places—on the door of St. Giles cathedral, on the abbey gates at Holyrood, on the Tolbooth, in the market place, and elsewhere, professing to disclose the names of the criminals who had taken part in the murder. Portraits of Bothwell, drawn to the life, were scattered through the streets, bearing the superscription: 'Here is the murderer of the King.' The most famous of the pictorial bills that were posted up was the so-called 'Mermaid and Hare': it appeared towards the end of February and depicted Mary as the mermaid, armed with a whip, protecting the hare, Bothwell, from the pursuing hounds. To the candid inquirer, the whole of this affair of the placards seems to bear the imprint of a carefully organized, methodical campaign of vilification, directed to the utter destruction of the queen of Scots's reputation, as well as Bothwell's. In the boldest of all the placards, which was posted up in the market place, the earl is described as 'he who murdered the husband of her whom he intends to marry, whose promise he had long before the murder'. What super-subtle brain was capable of this extraordinary glimpse into the future revelations of the Casket Letters? It would be an interesting speculation: but had better be left among the unsolved problems of the time.

The purpose of the denigrators was undoubtedly well served. Elizabeth went into action quickly with a letter to Mary, professing a genuine sincerity and imploring her to bring the criminals to justice, and do her duty as a noble princess and loyal wife. De Silva, the Spanish ambassador in London, wrote to his master in Madrid on 1 March, saying:—'Every day it becomes clearer that the queen must take steps to prove that she had no hand in the death of her husband.' There was plenty 'good advice' to tell the queen of Scots what she should do; but whether she was a free agent during the weeks following the murder—a large assumption—or whether she had already decided to throw in her lot with Bothwell for better or worse—which is probable—she took no notice of Elizabeth's letter or any other. Thus she roused a presumption that, even if she was not actually the instigator of the crime, she was accessory to it and sympathized with it. And when Bothwell was 'cleansed' by the assize, promoted to the dukedom of Orkney, and eventually married to the queen on 15 May with protestant rites, having been divorced from Huntly's sister only twelve days before for the purpose of this marriage, Mary's depravity in the opinion of many was firmly established.[1]

[1] The marriage to Bothwell is another enigma in the life of Mary Stuart. She may have been lured into it by the so-called Ainslie Tavern 'band', by which the majority of the nobles pledged themselves 'as they will answer to God' to defend Bothwell to the uttermost, and to advance his marriage with the queen. On the other hand, her 'ravishment' by the earl, when he carried her off to his stronghold of Dunbar, may have made the marriage inevitable. But probably the simple truth is that, after the Darnley murder, which must have reduced Mary to a state of mental collapse and stupefaction, she did not know where to turn for help; and help was the one thing she most needed in the appalling confusion. Her memory may have flashed back to the night of Rizzio's murder, when she also was threatened by the dags of the blood-drunk perpetrators of the crime, and shut up all night alone in a room, fearing the worst. In her plight on that memorable occasion, it was Bothwell (and Huntly) who, 'taking no regard to hazard their lives', arranged a plan for her escape. She may also have remembered—she could hardly forget it— that Bothwell was the man who gave unswerving support to her mother when, as regent, she was engaged in a bitter struggle with the 'lords of the congregation'. It is not altogether surprising, therefore, that James Hepburn should become Mary's 'man of destiny'.

In the catholic world it was widely held that her downfall extinguished the last hope of better days for the old faith in Britain. 'The catholic religion,' said one, 'which in Scotland had no greater foundation than the good intention always evinced by the queen to support it, now is, according to general opinion, deprived of all hope of ever again raising its head, because she, without fear of God, or respect for the world, has allowed herself to be induced by sensuality or else by the persuasion of others to take one who cannot be her husband, and gives thereby a suspicion that she will go over by degrees to the new fashion.' The papal nuncio, writing from Paris to the pontiff, contented himself with the remark that 'one cannot as a rule expect much from those who are subject to their pleasures'. James Beaton confessed that 'it would have been better in this world that she had "lossit" life and all'; and the bishops of Ross and Dunblane pleaded witchcraft and destiny respectively, as the source of the catastrophe. Pius V, after weighing the pros and cons, expressed himself in some doubt which of the two queens in Britain was the worse. It was mortifying that the plans of the Holy See for the spiritual regeneration of Britain should be so badly thrown out of gear by the caprice of a passionate woman!

The queen's position was, indeed, that of one who has just made the great renunciation of her life. Disowned by her own party and anathematized by her subjects, she figured in the popular imagination as some monstrous Clytemnestra, who, to satisfy an illicit passion, had imbrued her hands in her husband's blood. Yet such was the infatuation of the woman, in this moment of dire extremity, that the words of condemnation and execration sounding in her ears only served to goad her into more desperate courses. With Bothwell she would defy the world. Less than a month after her marriage the lords of the council summoned the lieges to their banner, proclaiming their intention of executing justice upon the 'murderer of the king and the ravisher of the queen'; and at Carberry hill, on 15 June, the brief drama came to an end with Mary's surrender. Bothwell, under cover of his wife's self-sacrifice, made his way safely to Dunbar, the Orkneys, and Denmark where he was imprisoned and subsequently died in 1578. Days of anguish followed for the captive, while the fanatical mob of Edinburgh clamoured for her blood, and her captors sat in solemn conclave, as a committee of public safety, to decide her fate. As a precautionary measure they sent her a prisoner to Loch Leven castle.

At this point Elizabeth found it necessary to intervene with more than hortatory epistles. Mary's incarceration and the deliberations of the Scottish leaders cast a totally new light over the relations of the two queens: far-reaching political issues, involving the rights of crowned heads in general, were at stake. Thus although Elizabeth disapproved strongly of the Scottish queen's marriage to 'him whom public fame had charged with the murder of Darnley', and although she was also firmly resolved to see the murderer punished, she was no whit less determined to help Mary to recover her liberty from subserviency 'to them that by nature and law are subjected to her'. This was the burden of Throckmorton's new mission to Edinburgh early in July 1567. He was to seek by all means in his power (1) to establish concord between the queen and her lords; (2) to secure her liberation by persuasion and treaty, or by force; (3) to urge the punishment of the king's murderer; and (4) to preserve the prince from danger. It was a heavy assignment—so heavy that the ambassador confessed, in a private letter to Leicester, that it was 'the most dangerous legation in his life'. Well might he say so; for the Scots were not only extremely touchy on the subject of their independence, and deeply suspicious of Elizabeth's intentions: they were also fanned to a flaming and furious hatred of their queen by Knox and others of the clergy, who backed their clamour for condign punishment by 'many arguments, some forth of the Scripture, some forth of histories,[1] some grounded (they say) upon the laws of this realm, and some upon conditions and oath made by their prince at her coronation'.

In the circumstances, it is not surprising that Throckmorton found his request for an interview with the imprisoned queen resolutely denied: the rebel lords, who were now masters of the situation, made it quite clear that they intended to exploit their success to the uttermost, whatever might be the protests and injunctions from London. The best the ambassador could do was to pass a note to Mary by Robert Melville, urging her to renounce Bothwell and suffer a divorce to be carried out—this seemed to him to be the only way to recover her freedom. But the 'poor prisoner' remained unmoved in her determination to

[1] Presumably Hector Boece's fabulous *Scotorum Historiae*, 1527.

cling to the earl: she would, she said, leave her kingdom and dignity to live as a simple damoselle with him, and would never consent that he should fare worse than herself. Meanwhile Knox and his fellow clerics threatened 'the plague of God to this whole country and nation' if the queen were spared the punishment due to her; and the mob cried out that the queen was 'no more privileged to commit murder or adultery than any other private person'. In Throckmorton's eyes Mary's position seemed well-nigh desperate: 'When they [i.e. the lords] have gone so far, they will think themselves unsafe while she lives, and take her life'; and a little later: 'It is to be feared that this tragedy will end in the queen's person after the coronation [i.e. of the prince] as it did begin in the person of David the Italian and the queen's husband.'

The fury of the Scots, however, was matched by the anger of Elizabeth. On 27 July, she instructed her ambassador to read the rebellious lords a lesson in political science. 'What warrant have they in Scripture', she asked, 'to depose their prince? Or what law find they written in any Christian monarchy, that subjects may arrest the person of their princes, detain them captive and proceed to judge them? No such law is to be found in the whole Civil Law.' But Elizabeth went farther than this. If they should, in their blind fury, deprive their queen of her crown, she would 'take plain part against them to revenge their sovereign, for an example to all posterity'. This was the daughter of Henry VIII at her very best; but although her message was an implied threat of war in certain contingencies, it proved to be *un coup manqué*. And so, in the last week of July, under threat of a public trial, exposure, defamation of character, and possibly death, Mary signed her abdication; and three days later, Prince James was crowned at Stirling to the plaudits of the misguided multitude. When the whole grim drama was over, Throckmorton unbosomed himself to Leicester: he said that he had at least saved the life of the queen of Scots, but any attempt to secure her liberty could only end in her death. He was also thankful that he had succeeded in convincing her of his own sovereign's desire to help her—'which I am sure the poor lady doth believe'.

Meanwhile, the well-intended English intervention had only succeeded in achieving the opposite effect from what was hoped for. It brought both countries to the verge of war. 'Therefore take heed', said Lethington to Throckmorton, 'that the queen your sovereign do not lose altogether the goodwill of this company irrecuperably. For although there be some amongst us which would retain our prince, people, and amity to England's devotion, yet I can assure you if the queen's majesty deal not otherwise than she doth, you will lose all.' More pointedly still: 'For now we begin to hold all things suspected that cometh from you: and if you be overbusy with us, you will drive us faster to France than we desire to run.' And again: 'My lord ambassador . . . I assure you that if you should use this speech unto them [i.e. the nobles] which you do unto me, all the world could not save the queen's life three days to an end.' Still Elizabeth persisted with her adjurations and threats, to the despair of her ambassador and the dismay of Cecil and Leicester, who had never seen her so incensed as she now was against the Scots. She not only refused to acknowledge the *faits accomplis*, but tried to frustrate the establishment of the regency under Murray, and entered into negotiations with Lord Herries and the Hamiltons for the release of the captive by force. Eventually, when these efforts also proved fruitless, she withdrew Throckmorton without recognizing the legality of the new government in Edinburgh, and approached France with a proposal for joint action against Scotland by means of a blockade. But by this time Murray had the situation well in hand: all the strongholds of the country, except Dumbarton, were in his possession, and the revolution was virtually complete.

Fortune's wheel, however, had not yet come to rest. Before seven months were past it took another turn. On 2 May 1568 Mary escaped from her island prison, joined her partisans, the Hamiltons, and again the torch of civil war was brandished in Scotland. Elizabeth hastened to offer her congratulations, help, and mediation. But before the messenger had started on his way the campaign came to a sudden and unexpected end by the defeat of the Marian troops at Langside and the flight of the queen to the border. In a tempest of baffled rage and wounded pride, and with a blind passion for revenge, she crossed the moors of Galloway and the Solway, placing herself, as she fondly hoped, in the friendly protection of Elizabeth. 'I have endured injuries, calumnies, imprisonment, famine, cold, heat,' she wrote to her uncle the cardinal, 'flight not knowing whither, ninety-two miles across the country without stopping or alighting, and then I have had to sleep upon the ground, and drink sour milk, and eat oatmeal without bread, and have been three nights like the owls, without a female in this country.' Her thoughts were far from complex: her one hope, when she touched English soil, was to procure Elizabeth's aid for the destruction of her enemies. 'What she most thirsteth after', wrote Sir Francis Knollys, who met her soon after her arrival, 'is victory . . . and in respect of victory, wealth and all things seemeth to her contemptuous and vile.'

Elizabeth was now in a quandary. When she offered help to Mary she had not contemplated the possibility of being called upon to restore her to the throne by force of arms. A war with Scotland for such an object was, indeed, unthinkable. On the other hand, to surrender her to Murray would be an act of gross inhumanity and folly. Nor would it be politic to accord her freedom of movement in England, because of her position *vis-à-vis* the English catholics and the succession. Nor, again, would it help matters to allow her to go abroad and seek the aid of France, for French influence in Scotland was a contingency more to be feared than any other. From whatever point the problem was approached, the difficulties seemed to be insuperable, and yet some solution was imperative. In the circumstances, Elizabeth decided that for the present her own interests might best be served by detaining Mary under observation in England.

Lord Scrope and Sir Francis Knollys, who were sent north to take over the supervision of the fugitive at Carlisle, were instructed to explain that it would be impossible for her to be admitted to her majesty's presence 'by reason of the great slander of murder, whereof she was not yet purged'. Hard upon this came a letter from Elizabeth, in which the English queen elaborated the point further. 'If you find it strange not to see me,' she said, 'you must make a "metamorphose" of our persons, and then you will see it would be "malaise" for me to receive you before your justification. . . . But once honourably acquitted of this crime, I swear to you before God, that among all worldly pleasures *that* will hold the first rank.' Mary was not impressed by this 'cold dealing'; and on 13 June she answered, with a sense of offended dignity:

Remove, madam, from your mind that I am come hither for the preservation of my life . . . but to clear my honour and obtain assistance to chastise my false accusers; not to answer them as their

equal, but to accuse them before you. . . . Being innocent as, God
be thanked, I know I am, do you not wrong me by keeping me here,
when I am just escaped out of one prison, as if I were in another,
encouraging by that means my perfidious foes to continue their
determined falsehoods, and dispiriting my friends by delaying the
aid others have promised if I would employ it. . . . Here I neither can
nor will answer their false accusations, although I will with pleasure
justify myself to you voluntarily as friend to friend, but not in the
form of a process with my subjects.

Meanwhile the English privy council, actuated no doubt by
Cecil, who was in communication with Murray, resolved unanimously and decisively that 'her Majesty can neither in honour
nor with surety aid her [Mary], nor permit her to come into
her presence, nor restore her, nor suffer her to depart without
a trial'. And about the same time (22 June), a packet of letters
addressed to Murray by his servant, John Wood, who was
in London working up the case for the Scottish lords, fell accidentally into Mary's hands, giving her for the first time a lurid
glimpse into the plotting and planning of her enemies, and also
of the grim fate that awaited her. The suspicion grew upon her
that she was to remain in England securely guarded, but never
to return to Scotland; and any hope of playing the part of
accuser or plaintiff in the prosecution of her rebellious subjects,
slowly but surely faded from her mind. A 'trial of her innocence'
was impending before an English tribunal—albeit the word 'tribunal' was not actually mentioned. It was to be a 'conference'.
But Mary was not deceived by the shifting of the terminology.
In an outburst of anger, she protested that she would have
no other judge but God, that she knew her degree of estate
well enough, and that none could compel her to accuse herself; 'but', she went on, 'I see how things frame evil for me. I
have many enemies about the queen my good sister, and such
as do all they can to keep me from her at the solicitation of my
rebellious subjects.' In this she was not far wrong, albeit her
optimism regarding Elizabeth was hardly justified.

At the same time as the English privy council and Cecil were,
in conjunction with Murray, preparing to retain the queen of
Scots in England—and incidentally to ruin her reputation—
between June and July 1568, Elizabeth, *tenant sa voix haute*, informed the French ambassador, la Forest, that 'she would take
the cause of her sister the queen in hand, and was resolved to

place her again in her country in her former degree and authority royal, either by a good appointment and reconciliation, which she would try to arrange between her and her subjects, or by force'. Later (11 July) la Forest informed the French government that the English queen had assured him 'par serment et parolles bien expresses et pleine d'affection, qu'elle n'avait autre intention que de remettre la dite dame d'Écosse en son royaume, avec l'entière obéissance de ses sujets . . . et il ne s'y traiterait rien que fût à son prejudice, ou qui tant soit peu touchât son honneur'. No wonder the Frenchman concluded that Mary would be better off in England than in Edinburgh!

Eventually, however, towards the end of July, Lord Herries, who had been pleading Mary's case in London, and trying to counter the influence of Murray and his associates, brought news of the result of his labours to Bolton castle in Yorkshire, where the prisoner was now lodged. It was a curious offer, compounded evidently by Elizabeth and Cecil, and designed, so it appeared, in a spirit of compromise; but the prime object was to lure the Scottish queen into submitting her cause to the verdict of a quasi-judicial tribunal. Herries, unfortunately, was a man of dull apprehension, and certainly no match for the clever diplomatists of London, but he vouched for the correctness of his report—he had heard it from the lips of the English queen herself. And this was the tenor of it: if Mary would remit her case to be heard by Elizabeth, but not to make her highness judge over her, but rather as her 'dear cousin and friend' to commit herself to her (Elizabeth's) advice and counsel; and if she would thus do, her highness would surely set her in her seat of regiment and dignity regal in this form and order. Her highness would send for the noblemen of Scotland her adversaries . . . to know their answer why they had deposed their queen; and if they could allege some reason for so doing (which her highness thinks they cannot), then Elizabeth would set Mary in her seat regal, conditional upon her lords and subjects continuing in their honours, states, and dignities; but if they should not be able to allege any reason of their doings, her highness would absolutely set her in her seat regal, and that by hostility if they should resist; upon condition that the queen of Scots should (i) renounce to claim, or have any present title to, the Crown of England, during the life of her highness and issue of her body; and upon condition that the said queen should (2) abandon the league with France, and enter into a league with England; and (3) abandon the Mass in Scotland and receive common prayer after the form of England.

The terms were indeed stiff, but enticing—if the Scottish lords failed to make good their case. So Mary accepted the offer; and Elizabeth, having manœuvred herself into the position of arbiter, which she always coveted, arranged for the 'conference' at York (October 1568).

Although elaborate and careful precautions were taken by Cecil and Murray, acting together, to secure the success of the 'conference', it seemed to go awry almost from the start. Elizabeth became annoyed at its delays, its intrigues, and particularly at the persistent refusal of Murray and his associates to bring forward the 'rigorous accusations' which they had boasted would prove Mary 'privy', or 'consentient', to the murder of her husband. There was, of course, some justification for this reticence: rumours had been spread in Scotland, to the effect that if the queen's accusers soft-pedalled their arguments and abstained from 'touching her honour', she would make with them 'what reasonable end they can devise'. So Murray withheld his trump card—the evidence of the so-called Casket Letters; and he held on to it until he had definite assurance from Elizabeth that, if he played it convincingly, there would be no possibility of a Marian restoration.

Meanwhile the duke of Norfolk, who was the chief member of the English commissioners and chairman of the 'conference', was becoming greatly perplexed by what he called 'this most brykle case'; for, as he said, 'here is nobody of any side, but that for fear or mistrust, makes courtesy to utter plainly their minds in that case, wherein they know not the end'. The situation became more confused and difficult when it transpired that Norfolk himself was beginning to dally with the idea of a marriage alliance with the Scottish queen; and Lethington, Murray's aide-de-camp, became afraid that if an investigation of the Darnley murder took place, his own part in the event might be revealed. As for Murray, his main concern was the maintenance and security of his regency and of the protestant settlement in Scotland. He fell into the category of those 'that seek wholly to serve their own particular turns, the which being done, they care not what becomes neither of Queen nor King'. Thus matters at York reached an *impasse*, and Sir Francis Knollys at

Bolton was inclined to think that the best way out of the tangle would be to marry the queen of Scots to George Carey, son of Lord Hunsdon, and a near relative to Elizabeth.

In the meantime Murray had resolved to break through the murky atmosphere of the 'conference' with a bold and fateful move. On 11 October, in the afternoon, he sent Lethington, James Makgill, George Buchanan, and John Wood (secretary) to submit to the English commissioners copies of the Casket Letters and Documents. Elizabeth was immediately informed by the horrified Norfolk, and excerpts were sent to her. On 16 October she adjourned the 'conference' to Westminster, alleging that the purpose was 'to take away the delay of time, which of force we see likely to ensue, by sending to and fro by way of letters and writing betwixt us and you our commissioners'. Mary was to be encouraged to 'imagine this conference of ours principally to be meant how her restitution may be devised with surety to the prince her son, and the nobility that have adhered to him'. The prisoner of Bolton seems to have accepted the new situation complacently; for on 22 October she wrote to Elizabeth: 'Since you, my good sister, know our cause best, we doubt not to receive presently good end thereof; wherethrough we may be perpetually indebted to you.'

Alas! it is obvious from the records that the principal object of the change in the rendezvous was not—as Elizabeth remarked in a note to her commissioners—'to resolve her of certain difficulties that did arise between both parties at York', but to put Murray and his associates 'on the spot' and to find out the reason why 'they do forbear . . . to charge the queen with guiltiness of the murder'. In other words, the recalcitrant and stubborn Scots were to be coerced, prodded, or cajoled into a full-scale revelation of the 'evidence' they were known to possess concerning their queen's participation in the Kirk-o-Field tragedy; and, to smooth the path for them, a guarantee was given that 'if it may certainly appear to her Majesty and her council, that the said queen was guilty . . . then her Majesty will never restore her to the crown of Scotland, nor permit her to be restored, without such assurance as they [the Scottish lords] shall allow to be good for them'; but 'will make it manifest to the world what she thinketh of the cause'. Cecil was evidently taking no chances of failure. He even took account of the possibility that Mary might escape from Bolton castle, and urged that the preparations for her removal to Tutbury should be hastened!

At the same time the 'adjudicating' body was strengthened at Westminster so as to include not only the commissioners on either side, and the English representatives, but also the following: the lord keeper, Bacon; the earl of Arundel; the earl of Leicester; Lord Clinton; and Sir William Cecil. Mary, of course, knew nothing, or next to nothing, of these manœuvres and preparations: she still believed that Elizabeth's original intention, divulged while the York 'conference' was in session, of striving for an 'appointment' between herself and her subjects, was the guiding principle. At the same time she cannot have been completely blind to what was being brewed for her; for in addition to protesting, through her commissioners, against anything in the nature of a 'judicial trial', since she was a 'free princess', owing her crown to God, she instructed them 'to desire in our name and afore our sister, her nobility, and the ambassadors of strange countries' that she might be licensed to come in person and answer what her rebels had to say against her. And she coupled with this request a threat that if she was not to be admitted to the presence of Elizabeth, as Murray evidently was, and justice required, her commissioners were to 'break the conference, and proceed no further therein'.

Meanwhile, before the Westminster 'conference' commenced its activities, it is advisable to take into account the summing up of the situation at York as seen through the eyes of a cool, unprejudiced, observant Englishman—the earl of Sussex—who represented his government, along with Norfolk and Sadler. After commenting in a letter, dated 22 October, on the inconstancy and subtlety of the Scots 'with whom we deal', he goes on to say that either 'Mary must be found guilty, or the matter must be huddled up "with a show of saving her honour"'. He did not think that the first alternative would be attempted, for two reasons: if the 'adverse party' were to accuse her of the murder by producing her letters (presumably the Casket Letters) 'she will deny them, and accuse the most of them of manifest consent to the murder, hardly to be denied: so as, upon the trial on both sides, her proofs will judicially fall out the best, as is thought'. To Sussex the main object was to retain Mary in England, and at the same time to prevent the Scots from patching up a peace with her. Hence he thought it would be best to let Murray

produce his 'proofs'—of which Sussex had already seen a sample
—and then, if Elizabeth 'by virtue of her superiority over Scotland' would give a verdict against Mary, the whole matter might
be settled. But he was doubtful whether Murray's 'proofs' would
carry any weight, if the Scottish queen denied the letters attributed to her. Therefore, although Sussex does not actually say
so, Mary must not be allowed to appear in court and make her
own defence. And this was the policy followed at Westminster,
and afterwards at Hampton Court.

Proceedings began at Westminster on 25 November, and on
the following day Murray presented his famous 'eik', or
amplification. 'We boldly and constantly affirm', he said, 'that as
James, sometime earl of Bothwell, was the chief executor of the
horrible and unworthy murder, perpetrate in the person of king
Henry of good memory . . . so was *she* of the foreknowledge
counsel, device, persuader, and commander of the said murder
to be done, maintainer and fortifier of the executors thereof, by
impeding and stopping of the inquisition and punishment due
for the same according to the laws of the realm.' Mary's commissioners at once claimed that the queen herself ought to be
present at the conference, to reply to the charge and imputation. On 4 December Elizabeth admitted the reasonableness of
the request, but preferred first to hear how the Scots would verify
their allegation; this being, she said, 'for the better satisfaction
of herself'. After a foolish attempt had been made by the Marian
commissioners—without their mistress's sanction or knowledge
—to stop proceedings from going any farther, by means of a
compromise or 'appointment' between the two parties, Elizabeth rejected the proposal; and her plan of hearing the 'proofs
of the allegations' before allowing the Marian defence to reply
to the 'eik', was permitted to run its course. Accordingly, on
6 December Murray submitted his documentary 'evidence'—
the Casket Letters, the Book of Articles, the Lennox Papers, the
Depositions of witnesses, &c.—until the grand finale on 14 and
15 December, when the calligraphy of the Letters was compared
with that of unquestionable Marian epistles 'of long standing'.
By this time the Scottish commissioners had intimated their
withdrawal from the 'conference', in accordance with instructions
from Mary when she learned that she was not to be allowed to
attend the 'conference' and defend herself in person. Her attitude
was that anything produced by her rebels since 6 December,

when Murray tabled his 'eik', was but 'invented slanders, private writings, which could not prejudice her in any wise'.

This does not mean, however, that no reply was made by the Scottish queen to the charge, or allegation, made by Murray in the 'eik': it only means that since admission to the 'conference' was refused, and consequently no opportunity was given to hear or even read the 'evidence' or 'proofs' advanced by the Scots, Mary could not meet the accusation with anything like a detailed argument. Again and again she appealed for the 'articles, presumptions, and principal writings' submitted by Murray and his associates, or copies of them; and she would 'answer the calumnious accusations of her subjects, and also would accuse them as principal authors, inventors, and executors of that deed'. 'By God's grace', she said, 'we shall make such answers thereto, that our innocence shall be known to our good sister and to all other princes.' But all these appeals were either ignored, side-tracked, or forgotten—all, until the appeal of January 1569, which brought an answer of a sort. Elizabeth, it said, would not refuse the 'doubles' of all that was produced; but she must have 'a special writing sent by the queen of Scots, signed with her own hand, promising that she will answer to the same writings and things laid to her charge without any exception'. Only when she (Elizabeth) received this 'writing of the said tenor' would she send the 'doubles'. It is not surprising that Mary's commissioners regarded this precaution as quite unnecessary; and they repeated their mistress's assertion that 'whatsomever thing was produced by her rebels since the discharging of the conference at Westminster the 6 day of December last past, was but invented slanders, and private writings, which could not prejudice her in any wise'.

It was now apparent that matters had come to an *impasse*; and already Elizabeth had made up her mind to finish off the whole business. On 10 January she had pronounced her verdict. 'Nothing', she declared, 'had been deduced against Murray and his company as yet, that may impair their honour; and on the other part, there had been nothing sufficiently produced by them against the queen their sovereign, whereby the Queen of England should conceive or take any evil opinion of the Queen, her good sister, for any thing yet seen.' In the meantime Elizabeth had been turning over in her mind the possibility of a compromise between Mary and her subjects; and late in December

1568 she had broached a proposal to the Scottish commissioners, viz. that Mary should demit her crown and government to her son, and herself live privately in England: in other words, accept the revolution in Scotland, without prejudice to her own return if the son died before her. Mary, however, would have no such arrangement. 'Je suis résolue', she said, 'et délibérée plustost mourir, que de le faire: et la dernière parole que je feroys en ma vie, sera d'une Royne d'Escosse.'

Some ten days later, after Murray had taken his farewell and set out for Scotland, accompanied by his party, Mary was removed from Bolton to Tutbury in Staffordshire, to begin her long imprisonment in England. The acute Scot, armed with a safe-conduct to see him through the dangerous border country, and with a loan of £5,000 in his pocket, was returning to his native land to complete, if possible, the destruction of the Marian party. In passing through Kingston on 11 January, he wrote a palpably false letter, stating that Elizabeth had promised to maintain 'the king's authority and our regiment'. Actually she had done nothing of the sort, albeit she had made it possible by her actions.

For the moment Elizabeth had seemingly won a victory over her defenceless rival; but she was soon to realize that it was a Pyrrhic victory. By imprisoning Mary in England she all unwittingly lost her own freedom, and for the next nineteen years lived in ceaseless anxiety lest her prisoner might escape. While the two queens lived, there could be no quiet in the realm. Far better would it have been—such is the irony of history—had Elizabeth allowed her defeated and discredited enemy to go whither she pleased. The catholic world, influenced by her recent behaviour, would have treated her with cold contempt: she would have sunk into comparative insignificance, suffered, it may be, complete political eclipse; and her name would have left no mark on history. But the incarceration saved her from this. As the victim of an unjust fate she became invested with a halo of martyrdom, recovered her position in the eyes of her co-religionists, and lived to plague the inventor of her misery. with even greater misery than she herself endured.

IV

YEARS OF CRISIS: 1568–75

Ⲓɴ no department of state action is it more difficult to foresee the future course of events than in that of foreign policy. The enemies of yesterday become the friends of tomorrow, and, vice versa, the friends of yesterday become the enemies of tomorrow, according as interests coincide or clash. The reign began with Spain in a benevolent role and France as the national foe to be combated sword in hand. But before twelve years had elapsed a regrouping became necessary. The conflict with France had given way to a dawning appreciation of the fact that differences were not irremediable, whereas the early protestations of goodwill by Philip II were found to cover a wide range of opposing interests that threatened to become, and did become, insoluble except by the arbitrament of war. These differences were partly political, partly economic; they were in some measure due to the aggressiveness of England; but they were also caused by the refusal of the Spanish king to accept the religious settlement in England as final. Indeed, it would be no exaggeration to say that, in so far as any event in history may be described as inevitable, the great struggle between England and Spain, that convulsed the later years of the century, partook of this nature. Its shadow lay heavy across the path of Anglo-Spanish relations almost from the commencement of Elizabeth's reign.

Let us endeavour to see how the quarrel originated. To begin with, the queen's policy of establishing relations with the elements of disorder in the dominions of the continental monarchies operated no less effectively in the Netherlands than in France. The seventeen provinces which formed this outlying bastion of King Philip's empire had never taken kindly to his rule. On the contrary, their insistence upon old liberties, charters, and immunities, dating back to Burgundian times, ran counter to the royal conception of monarchical authority; while their love of religious liberty, fostered by an intense absorption in material pursuits, collided with the rigid Spanish belief that the catholic religion was indispensable to the maintenance of civil obedience. Grievances multiplied apace when it was seen that the king intended to treat them as possessions, to convert them into a *point d'appui* for the Spanish power in the north of Europe, and to tax them more heavily—because they were wealthier—than any other part of the empire for the furtherance of purely Spanish interests. The fact that Philip was a foreigner, unimaginative, slow of mind, maladroit, and altogether devoid of that higher statesmanship that takes into account the idiosyncrasies of the people committed to its care, probably increased the difficulties in the way of a mutual understanding, and lessened the chances of fruitful co-operation. Nor did it mend matters—rather the reverse—when he abandoned the country for the more congenial soil of Spain, in the summer of 1559, leaving it to be governed by a viceroy and a council of state, whose policy was provocatively Spanish, and whose authority was sustained by an army of 3,000 Spanish veterans. The simmering discontent ripened quickly into defiant outbursts of popular feeling against the cardinal de Granvelle, *le diable rouge*, president of the *consulta*, who, rightly or wrongly, was singled out as the evil genius of the administration.[1] Attacked on the one side by the native nobility, who refused to co-operate so long as they were excluded from the inner counsels of the government, he was exposed, on the other, to the odium of the masses, who regarded him as the instigator of the obnoxious 'placards' against heresy, the activities of the inquisition, and the other repressionist measures undertaken in the interest of public order. The situation, in fact, was precisely the same as that which prevailed in Scotland during the regency of Mary of Lorraine. A nationalist revolt was clearly presaged as soon as the political and religious discontented joined hands.

On this fertile soil fell the seeds of English propaganda. The object aimed at was not to challenge Philip's sovereign rights over the Netherlands, still less to deprive him of his inheritance: it was simply to increase the difficulties of the Spanish authorities in Brussels, to stir up, if possible, a 'Flemish Amboise', and thus prevent the complete absorption of the provinces into the Spanish political system. To this end, therefore, the campaign against Granvelle was fomented by pamphlets written in England and circulated by English agents among the Flemish cities; and at the same time agitators in the pay of England mingled in the Calvinist preachings, with a view to fostering religious

---

[1] De Granvelle was a native of Franche-Comté: 'sa vraie patrie était la Cour et sa fidélité au prince lui tenait lieu de patriotisme.' (Pirenne, *Histoire de la Belgique*, iii. 400.)

discontent. The extent of the propaganda cannot be fully known, because it was carried out with great secrecy and relied for its success upon nameless individuals, often renegade Spaniards as well as Flemings, and high-placed officials in the government, who chafed at the autocratic rule of the cardinal.[1] That the king knew of it is certain from the dispatches of his ambassadors as well as from the correspondence of Granvelle himself. But it was impossible for him to check it, owing to the close commercial intercourse of England and the Low Countries at this time, and the comparative ease with which the disturbed areas could be reached. So serious did the situation become that not only was chaos produced in the administration of the Netherlands itself, but the European policy of Spain was also profoundly affected. The dismissal of Granvelle by the king in 1564 appeased, but did not end, the turmoil; for the nationalist movement was only just beginning to take definite shape, and the protestant agitation stimulated by huguenot immigrants from the south, received a fresh access of strength. A climax came in 1566, when the fanatical populace, fired by the preachers, began a widespread attack on the churches, creating general anarchy. With this direct challenge to social order and the royal power, Elizabeth was careful not to identify herself. Her purpose had been served: she could afford now to condemn the rebels who had hitherto been her tools, and profess to the Spanish ambassador in London that her sympathies were entirely with his master. Meanwhile thousands of fugitive Flemings—there were from eighteen to twenty thousand of them in London and Sandwich in 1563, and thirty thousand in 1566—escaping from the troubled country flocked over to England to be warmly received by the queen, who gave them permission to settle, practise their trades, and worship in their own Calvinist conventicles. Thus England was doubly the gainer by the convulsed state of the Netherlands—Spain was weakened and held in check, and the immigrant foreigners were a valuable asset to the economic and industrial life of the English nation.

But if Elizabeth was treading on dangerous ground with respect to Spain's authority in the Netherlands, Philip was far from passive in his relations with the queen's catholic subjects in England. Although he remained outwardly friendly, and the

---

[1] e.g. Simon Renard, formerly Spanish ambassador in England, and Erasso, secretary to the holy inquisition, both of whom were enemies of Granvelle.

instructions he gave to his ambassadors were uniformly prudent, it soon became common knowledge that the Spanish embassy in London dispensed largesse to needy catholics, opened its doors to all who desired to practise the forbidden ritual of the Mass in secret, and compromised itself with notorious rebels like Shane O'Neill. The consequence was that a careful watch was kept on its activities—so strict, indeed, that de Quadra grumbled of the 'distrust that is publicly shown to all who associate with me'. 'Not a prisoner is arrested for state reasons', he remarked, 'without his being asked whether he had any conversation with me.' But worse was to follow. In the summer of 1562 Cecil bribed the secretary to the embassy, Borghese Venturini, to turn queen's evidence against his master, and de Quadra found it difficult to reply to the formidable *dossier* of unfriendly acts which the council drew up. A few months later (January 1563) he was charged with sheltering a criminal who attempted the life of the vidame de Chartres, an envoy of the huguenots, and deprived of the keys of his house, a government custodian being placed in charge. At the same time de Quadra was solemnly warned that if he overstepped his duties as ambassador he would be tried by the laws of the land, his extra-territorial privileges notwithstanding. In February his privacy was invaded by the marshal of the court with a company of halberdiers in search of certain English catholics, who were said to be at Mass in the embassy chapel; and a number of Flemings, Italians, and Spaniards were carried off to prison in defiance of his remonstrances. Although de Quadra complained bitterly to the king, the only comfort he received was an instruction to bear his trials with fortitude. Matters improved under his successor, de Silva, who was caution personified; but the potential danger from the embassy continued, as may be seen from the fact that, during the year 1565–6, it became the principal channel of communication between Mary Stuart and Spain. All this, however, was merely preliminary to the period of turmoil that set in when de Silva was replaced by Don Guerau de Spes, in 1568. To him we shall return presently.

Political friction was bad enough, but not so dangerous to the maintenance of good relations as the economic rivalry which followed as a necessary consequence upon England's expanding trade. Hitherto, as a result of the opening up of the world in the fifteenth century, the most delectable parts of the earth had fallen to Spain and Portugal. West Africa from Senegal to the Congo, a region of incalculable resources, was in the possession of the Portuguese, who claimed and exercised a prescriptive right to political jurisdiction and an exclusive trade monopoly over the entire area. A still more extensive and equally rigid monopoly was maintained by Spain in Central America, both on the mainland, from the Orinoco to the cape of Florida, and in the islands of the Caribbean sea. Although both monopolies had some legal basis, they cannot be said to have commanded general respect in a world ruled by force and not by right. The Portuguese sphere of influence had been invaded frequently by English traders before Elizabeth's accession, in defiance of protests from Lisbon, and the activities of the Portuguese naval squadron based on El Mina; and it was only a matter of time when the lure of tropical America would entice enterprising traders to the more remote and less familiar Spanish preserves on the other side of the Atlantic.

In 1561 Cecil scandalized de Quadra by remarking that the pope had no right to partition the earth and bestow kingdoms on whom he pleased—a significant indication that England at least did not recognize existing monopolies. A year later the validity of the Spanish monopoly was put to the test by John Hawkins of Plymouth, whose father, William, had trafficked with Guinea, and probably supplied his son with the initial incentive for his enterprise. Hawkins's idea was to effect an entry into the lucrative trade in African negroes which now formed an important constituent element in the internal economy of Spanish America. Relying on the urgent needs of the Spanish planters for slave labour to make good the wastage of the aboriginal population, and on the help of friendly Spaniards in the Canaries, who were prepared to furnish him with pilots for the journey across the Atlantic, he easily procured a cargo of negroes, partly by raiding native villages on the African coast south of Cape Verde and partly by purchase from Portuguese slavers, and set sail for Hispaniola in the autumn of 1562. As Hawkins was in no sense a pirate but a peaceful trader, reasonable in his charges and professing to be a friend of King Philip, the success of the venture surpassed expectations. He returned to Europe with a valuable freight of gold, silver, pearls, hides, and sugar, and with the consciousness that, in the Indies at least, the Spanish monopoly was not seriously regarded.

Moreover, he had taken the precaution of obtaining certificates from the authorities as to his good behaviour and honourable intentions. But his moderation had little weight with the government at Madrid; for when he sent part of his cargo to be sold in Seville, as a further proof that his actions were above board, it was seized and confiscated by the port officials. In spite of this set-back, however, his ardour for the enterprise was in no way damped; and two years later he planned a second expedition on the same lines as the first but more elaborate. On this occasion he had the patronage of the queen, who loaned him one of her own ships, the earls of Leicester and Pembroke, and Cecil—all of whom took shares in the undertaking. Meantime, in view of the attitude of the Spanish government, which had issued strict injunctions to the administration in the Indies not to allow trade with the English, Hawkins had armed his flotilla. Fortunately there was no need as yet to abandon the pretence of peaceful trade; and although the Spaniards were reluctant to do business with him, Hawkins managed by cajolery and threats to dispose of his cargo of negroes at Borburata and Rio de la Hacha. He returned to Europe again with a substantial profit.

Spain was now thoroughly on the alert. Precautions were redoubled both in Europe and in America and at the Canaries, and every move of Hawkins was carefully watched by the Spanish ambassador in England, who reported his doings to Madrid. The consequence was that when he prepared his third expedition the circumstances from the start were far from favourable, and Hawkins must have known that his appearance in America might lead to trouble. The secrecy with which the details of the enterprise were screened from the prying eyes of de Silva seems to be a proof of this. Nevertheless in the autumn of 1567 he set out once more for America, supported on this occasion by no less than seven well-armed ships—the *Jesus, Minion, Judith, William and John, Swallow, Angel, Gratia Dei*—with Francis Drake in command of the *Judith*.

At every stage of the journey difficulties and troubles assailed him. An attempt was made at Plymouth to prevent his departure by the Flemish admiral, de Waachen. On the African coast he had to engage in inter-tribal war in order to obtain his negro cargo. At Teneriffe the Spanish governor tried to lure him under the guns of the fort. And when he arrived at his base of operations in America no one would have anything to do with him. But Hawkins was not to be denied. At Rio de la Hacha he opened fire on the treasurer's house, blockaded the port, and fought a pitched battle with the Spaniards on land; and it was only when he had partially burnt the town and seized its treasure that the inhabitants consented to take part of his wares. Cartagena, his next port of call, proved to be too strong for intimidation; and Hawkins was compelled to put into the harbour of San Juan de Ulloa to refit his ships and refresh his men (20 September 1568). Three days later, and some time before it was expected, the Spanish fleet appeared in the offing, with the viceroy of Mexico, Don Martin Enriquez, on board. Hawkins was now in a position of some danger, for the Spanish ships were in the majority and he could not refuse to admit them to the roadstead. He therefore made terms with them, and the two flotillas anchored side by side. The viceroy, however, was bent on treachery from the first; and on a preconcerted signal, aided by troops secretly brought from Vera Cruz, the Spaniards attacked Hawkins's ships. A battle ensued, in the course of which several English ships were lost, including the *Jesus*, together with part of the treasure it contained. In January and February the remnant of the expedition, consisting of the *William and John*, the *Minion*, and the *Judith* arrived in England, much dilapidated, with over 120 men missing, dead or prisoners of the Spaniards or Indians.

It was impossible any longer to disguise the fact that although England and Spain were nominally at peace in Europe, a state of war prevailed 'beyond the line'. The bad blood engendered by the affray had an incalculable effect in embittering the growing enmity between the two peoples, however much their political leaders might disguise the fact by diplomacy.

Meanwhile another field of economic rivalry was opening up in Europe. The main export trade of England at this time was conducted with the Spanish Netherlands, where the cloth from English looms found a ready vent in the busy market of Antwerp. There was, of course, no monopoly in this traffic; nor was there any necessary opposition from Flemish merchants to the entrance of English goods: on the contrary both countries profited by the economic interchange. But government action introduced an element of unfairness into the traffic, which acted disastrously on the maintenance of good relations. Guided by the prevailing mercantilist ideas of the age, the Elizabethan government endeavoured to establish an advantage in favour of England against the Netherlands by restricting the privileges of Flemish merchants in England. Customs dues and other charges on many articles imported into England from Flanders were raised, and others were prohibited altogether, while the preference in the carrying trade was given to English ships. At the same time the Flemish merchants were placed under the obligation of spending the proceeds of their sales on the purchase of English goods before leaving the country. To this undoubtedly severe attack on the prosperity of the Netherlands the Spanish government at Brussels retorted with corresponding restrictions on English traders in Flanders, and on English goods imported into Flanders by Englishmen. Likewise the shipment of goods from Flemish ports in English ships was interdicted. Thus arose the economic *impasse* of 1563–4, when many English merchants temporarily abandoned Antwerp for the German port of Emden. The aggressive commercial thrust of England was undoubtedly an additional cause of friction.

In the third place there was the question of piracy on the high seas. The main sea-borne traffic of northern Europe passed along the commercial gut of the English Channel, and a large part of it was conducted between Spain and Antwerp, either in Flemish or Spanish ships. For the greater part of its route this traffic was subject to piratical attack, for the Channel swarmed with freebooters. Some were French, others English; but generally their lairs were situated on the English rather than on the French side of the Channel, because of the greater convenience of the numerous bays and creeks of the south and south-east coast of England. English shipping suffered little by the disorder at first, except by reprisals; but it was obviously to the interest of all countries abutting on the Channel to co-operate in its suppression. Spain naturally looked to England to give a lead in the matter, and numerous complaints were addressed to Elizabeth from Madrid as well as Brussels urging drastic action. The difficulty, however, of giving effect to measures against the pirates was great; and restitution was exceedingly hard to obtain. De Silva, writing in August 1564, was inclined to lay the blame not on the lack of energy of the English government, which indeed had behaved well, but on the remissness of admiralty judges, and the fact that the rogues, when captured, were usually unable to pay for their depredations. The desire of the government to combat the evil is apparent from the repeated efforts of the Privy Council in 1564, 1565, and 1566 to devise a satisfactory plan for tracking down the pirates and keeping a careful watch on their accomplices on land and their bases and sources of supply. Yet, in spite of all preventive measures, and the barbaric severities meted out to pirates taken red-handed, the pillage continued. Matters were made even worse when the huguenots and the Dutch *gueux de mer*, or sea beggars,[1] turned piracy into a weapon against the political aims of the French and Spanish monarchies. Although the Elizabethan government cannot be held responsible for the losses incurred by Spanish shipping in the Channel, the fact that the pirates were frequently English undoubtedly raised a presumption in the mind of Philip that Elizabeth was hand in glove with the nefarious traffic; and in this he was encouraged by de Spes, who, unlike his predecessor, refused to credit the queen with a single friendly act towards his master. Piracy, therefore, may be added to the causes producing trouble between England and Spain.

There were, of course, other matters, notably the treatment of English sailors in Spanish ports by officials of the inquisition, the arbitrary action of port authorities in both England and Spain, and the patronage by Spain of the polemical catholic literature introduced into England from the continental presses. But the prime source of antagonism was the clash of economic interests, and the political opposition induced by the religious changes in England.

By 1568 it must have been apparent that Anglo-Spanish relations were fast approaching a crisis. Everywhere the interests of the two countries were colliding. In the Netherlands the duke of Alva, who had taken over control from Margaret of Parma in the previous autumn, was engaged in extinguishing the last embers of the nationalist revolt, preparatory to a thorough-going 'hispanicization' of the provinces. His 'council of blood' with its proscriptions, judicial murders, and confiscations was as efficient an engine of repression as the revolutionary tribunal in Paris during the Terror. The whole country was soon cowed into abject submission, and Alva was now in a position to proceed

---

[1] '*Gueux* signifie autant que *vagabond* ou *ribaud*' (M. Van Vaernewyck, *Troubles religieux en Flandres . . . au XVIe siècle*): in English *gueux de mer* is usually rendered as 'sea beggars'. For the incident out of which the term *gueux*, as applied to the rebels, arose, see Motley, *The Rise of the Dutch Republic*, vol. i, chap. vi.

with the second and more important part of his programme, viz. the conversion of the Netherlands into a *citadelle d'acier*, from which the king of Spain could lay down the law to the rest of Europe.[1] All pretence of constitutional government was abandoned in favour of a purely military dictatorship wielded by the duke and the little group of Spaniards who formed his immediate entourage—Vargas, del Rio, and Albornoz. For England the worst feature of the tyranny was not so much its ruthlessness as its complete disregard of the delicate machinery of industry and commerce, which was brought to a standstill, with disastrous repercussions on England's principal overseas market. Nor was this all. It was hardly possible to mistake the ultimate significance of Alva's measures, for it was observed that while he sedulously crushed the spirit of the Netherlanders, he expressly favoured the bands of English catholics who had taken refuge in the country for conscience' sake, and encouraged them to enlist in his armies. They, for their part, looked to him as the champion of the catholic cause to crown his career by reducing England to the Roman obedience. Thus there was every incentive to Elizabeth to be on her guard against a possible hostile move from the Low Countries, and to take such precautionary steps as would prevent it.

There were two obvious methods of doing this, without, at the same time, throwing down the gage openly to Spain. She might on the one hand permit secret assistance to be sent to the patriot cause in the Netherlands from the Flemish and Dutch communities in England; and, on the other hand, she might recognize the *gueux de mer*, who, acting under commissions from William of Orange, were engaged in harassing Spanish commerce in the Channel. Neither action could be regarded as friendly to Spain, and either might lead to complications; but the risk had to be taken, for the need was urgent. Consequently a good deal of assistance, in the shape of money collected among the refugees in England and volunteers recruited in the same quarters, was dispatched from English ports to the Low Countries; and at the same time pirate commanders like La Marck, who flew the flag of Orange, were permitted to load ordnance and munitions in England. Of a similar nature, only more dangerous in its possible consequences, was the seizure of Spanish treasure in December 1568. It is difficult to believe that this action was not related in some way to the disaster at San Juan earlier in the year,

[1] Pirenne, op. cit. iv. 16.

for news of the Mexican occurrence had reached England by 3 December. In a letter to Cecil, written on this date, William Hawkins urged the secretary to 'advertise the queen's majesty thereof, to the end there might be some stay made of king Philip's treasure here in these parts till there be sufficient recompense made for the great wrong offered, and also other wrongs done long before this'. In any case, when the Spanish bullion ships, carrying the considerable sum of 800,000 ducats, the property of Italian bankers, who had loaned it to the king for the payment of Alva's troops in the Netherlands, put into Plymouth and Southampton to escape the clutches of the Channel pirates, a convenient pretext was easily discovered for detaining it. Obviously the queen could not be expected to have it convoyed to its destination in her own ships, and to let it proceed on its way unconvoyed was tantamount to making a present of it to the enemy lying in wait outside. For a few days she played the honest broker; and then, on learning that the money was not technically the king's, according to the contract, until it was delivered in the Netherlands, she decided to borrow it for her own use. Instantly, and without waiting to learn all the facts of the case, de Spes wrote to Alva urging immediate reprisals, and in the last days of December an embargo was laid on all property belonging to Englishmen in the Low Countries. News of the duke's action reached London on 3 January: on the 7th, orders were issued by the council for corresponding arrests of Spanish property in England; and on the following day de Spes was placed under arrest in his house, for acting without the king's orders to the prejudice of the ancient alliance and commerce of the two kingdoms.

Ostensibly de Spes had been sent to England, in July 1568, as a peace-maker. His instructions were to satisfy the queen about the alleged ill-treatment of her ambassador, Dr. John Man, whom the king had forbidden his presence because he had publicly shown contempt for the catholic religion—a serious offence in Spain—and had uttered opprobrious words about the pope. De Spes seems to have imagined, however, that his mission was in the nature of a crusade. Even before he set foot on English soil his fiery zeal for the catholic faith led him to overstep his instructions. When passing through France he informed Mary Stuart's ambassador, the bishop of Glasgow, that he had orders to do something for the royal captive as soon as he reached his destination. A few weeks later, when he had established contact with Mary's partisans in England, he expressed the opinion that it would not be difficult to release the queen of Scots and 'even raise a revolt against this queen'. On 9 November he thought the propitious hour for action was approaching.

To de Spes the crisis provoked by the seizure of the treasure, the embargoes, and the trade stoppage was nothing less than a heaven-sent opportunity: it would provide him with the necessary lever for overthrowing Elizabeth's government, restoring catholicism, and seating Mary Stuart on the throne. Early in January Mary conveyed to him the message: 'Tell the ambassador that if his master will help me, I shall be queen of England in three months, and Mass shall be said all over the country.'[1] In communicating this news to the king, de Spes stressed the necessity of developing and extending the economic blockade. 'If they cannot work', he wrote, 'or there is any obstacle to the disposal of their goods, they usually take up arms.' Let the king check the vital imports—oil, alum, sugar, spices, and iron from Biscay—as well as the exports, and he would have the fate of the queen in the hollow of his hand. Philip was not impressed by his ambassador's assurance; and, on 18 February, he consulted Alva as to the feasibility of the scheme.

In the meantime the indefatigable de Spes had established connexion with a conspiracy that had been brewing for some time among the older nobility for the displacement of Cecil. The causes of the antagonism were many and varied—discontent with the policy pursued in regard to Mary Stuart and the succession: irritation at the growing estrangement from Spain: personal pique at the power enjoyed by one who did not belong to the ranks of the aristocracy; and, in some cases, a profound antipathy to the ecclesiastical innovations and the severance of the kingdom from Rome. The conspirators thought that if they could unseat Cecil and destroy his influence over the queen it would be possible to settle the succession in favour of Mary, set her free, and restore her to Scotland, with guarantees safeguarding Elizabeth during her lifetime. At the same time Anglo-Spanish relations might be rectified by restoring the treasure; and the peril created by the breach with Rome might be averted by a return to catholicism. In fact what the malcontents aimed at was a complete reversal of national

---

[1] Probably an 'improved version' of what Mary really said. (Pollen.)

policy. The plot arose in the minds of the duke of Norfolk and the earl of Arundel; but it was soon participated in by the northern earls, Northumberland and Westmorland, the earls of Pembroke, Leicester, and Derby, and Lords Montague, Dacre, Morley, and Lumley. On 29 February 1568 de Spes notified the king that he had been approached by a certain Roberto Ridolfi, a Florentine, in the name of Norfolk and Arundel, who had sent him to say that they were in favour of a settlement with Spain, that although they were not yet strong enough to challenge Cecil, they were gathering friends and hoped to turn out the present government, replacing it with a catholic one. They also thought that they could bring the queen to consent thereto. Behind them stood the serried ranks of a phantom catholic host who, de Spes fondly believed, were preparing to move at the command of the duke and his supporters.

Undoubtedly the situation was becoming serious—all the more so since relations with France were far from satisfactory. After several years of uneasy peace, that country had again plunged into the throes of civil war, and public opinion in England expressed itself strongly on the side of the distressed protestants. Although the queen professed her neutrality in the struggle, she did not prohibit her subjects from sending munitions and money to the huguenot stronghold of La Rochelle, and bands of enthusiastic volunteers were flocking to Coligny's help under Sir Henry Champernoun, Walter Raleigh, and other west-country gentlemen. In the Channel, too, English privateers co-operated with the huguenots in the destruction of 'Guisan' commerce. So intolerable did the state of affairs become that on 15 January 1569, at the very moment when the crisis with Spain began, Charles IX ordered the arrest of English goods at Rouen. It was a retaliatory step, he said, undertaken in order to reimburse his merchants for the losses they had sustained by piracy. The tension lasted for some months, and de Spes was in high hopes of bringing France into the plot for Elizabeth's overthrow. Fortunately, however, although the French tried to make some capital out of the queen's embarrassment, they refused to play the Spanish game, being afraid that, owing to the intimate economic ties between England and the Netherlands, Alva and the queen might at any time make up their differences and leave France in the lurch. Nevertheless Anglo-French relations were strained almost to the breaking-point in March, when La Mothe Fénelon, Charles IX's ambassador in London, presented a formidable list of grievances, and required Elizabeth to declare within fifteen days whether it was to be peace or war.[1] If the rupture was avoided, it was only by the exercise of considerable tact on the queen's part.

Meanwhile Alva's statesmanlike mind was assailed by grave doubts about the practicability of de Spes's plan for the reduction of England. On 10 March he wrote to Philip discountenancing war, and pointing out that he lacked both ships and money for the enterprise. The ambassador, however, was not to be thwarted. Norfolk and Arundel, he said, only wanted Spain to stand firm in regard to the trade stoppage, and the people, who were already beginning to move, would rise. It would not be difficult to bring the 'barefaced thieves' to account: he knew that the queen and Cecil were now 'suspicious even of the birds of the air', and that the former was 'abandoned by many and hardly any one really liked her'. If only Alva could seize the English cloth fleet on its way to Hamburg, it would precipitate the revolution. But the duke was not to be stampeded from reality by the heated imaginings of a fanatic. On 4 April he wrote to the king: 'Notwithstanding what Don Guerau writes, I am not yet convinced that they are not deceiving him.' Philip, too, was veering round to the view that it would be better to come to an agreement with Elizabeth, for his own subjects were petitioning him to bring about an early restoration of trade and of their confiscated property. About the middle of May two letters crossed one another on the way to Madrid and Brussels, respectively. The first, from Alva to the king, stated that it was imperative that the restitution of the goods should precede the breach with England; the second, from the king to Alva, explained that the Spanish council of state had decided that war was undesirable, since it would not help the major matter, the recovery of the lost property. In other words, the plot was at an end so far as Spain was concerned, and the 'climb down' had begun.

In England the conspiracy was also at a standstill; for the leaders were afraid to move, and were waiting in vain for a sign from Alva and the expected popular demonstrations against the

---

[1] 'Tout ce royaume est en suspens de la guerre, craignant de l'avoir tout à la fois avec la France et l'Espagne, ou séparément avec l'une ou l'autre.' (La Mothe to Charles IX, 8 March 1569: *Correspondance diplomatique de La Mothe Fénelon*.)

government. Nor was the blockade working according to plan. In spite of the trade stoppage, English goods were being passed into Europe through the friendly ports of La Rochelle and Hamburg, and imports were coming into England in Venetian and Ragusan bottoms. De Spes became more and more frantic in his efforts to stop the leakages. Spain, he said, must enlist the pope's help in arresting English trade with the seigniories of Venice, Genoa, Lucca, and the dukedom of Florence, get the emperor to seize Hamburg and the mouth of the Elbe, and keep the English out of Poland, Muscovy, and the Easterling country. It would be advisable, too, to harass English ships in the Channel and neighbouring waters. In short, he had discovered that before England could be brought to her knees every port in Europe would have to be closed against her and a Spanish naval supremacy established on the high seas!

While de Spes was vapouring about blockades, the Norfolk–Arundel plan for seizing Cecil and overthrowing the government collapsed: partly through its betrayal by Leicester, who had been admitted into the plot in order to strengthen the attack: partly by the astuteness of Cecil, who had got wind of it from Leicester and talked over Norfolk; and partly by a dispute between Norfolk and Dacre over the Dacre inheritance. Alva, too, had been busy separating the property-restitution question from the political revolution which de Spes was trying to promote; and on 12 June he had written to Philip stating that in his opinion war with England, which would assuredly follow any attempt to help Mary Stuart with men, was clearly impossible, and that money and advice was all that could safely be sent. He therefore proposed to sound the English government as to the possibility of a restitution by sending over a trustworthy Genoese merchant, Thomas Fiesco, to broach the matter unofficially.

In view, however, of de Spes's ardent advocacy of intervention by Spain in the internal affairs of England, it was necessary for Alva, if his new plan was to succeed, to stop the activities of the ambassador. On 2 July he wrote ordering him not to entertain any approaches made to him against the queen and her councillors, but to exercise the greatest reticence and neutrality in the internal affairs of the country. On 14 July he again wrote: 'I must again press this upon you and tell you that I am informed from France to-day that the queen of Scotland is being utterly ruined by the plotting of her servants with you, as they never enter your house without being watched. This might cost the queen's life, and I am not sure that yours would be safe.' On 8 August he complained to the king that in spite of all warnings de Spes would not do as he was told. De Spes, in fact, was still in full correspondence with the malcontent group of nobles. They had abandoned their plan of a *coup d'état* against Cecil, but they were still pressing forward their general plan for the declaration of Mary's title to the succession, and her liberation, coupled with a scheme for her marriage to Norfolk. In this they had the support of the whole council including Leicester, but the queen was in the dark and Cecil doubtful. Help from France was also invoked.[1]

The plotters, however, were soon to be disillusioned. About the middle of September Elizabeth got wind of what was on foot, and peremptorily forbade the marriage. Before the end of the month the back of the conspiracy was broken. Norfolk had been severely warned, Leicester had sought and obtained the royal pardon, de Spes was being carefully watched and his dispatches opened. Even La Mothe's correspondence was inspected, showing that the government was leaving nothing to chance. Moreover, throughout the country preparations were made to meet any emergency. Commissions were sent down from London to see to the musters: every family was ordered to possess itself of at least one serviceable weapon and practise its use: the coast defences from Yarmouth to the Lizard were placed in a state of preparedness: the fleet was augmented and provisioned, and lay at the mouth of the Thames: warships convoyed the cloth fleet to and from Hamburg, and the wine fleet to and from La Rochelle. Mary Stuart at Tutbury felt the rigour also, for in September she wrote to La Mothe: 'Si je demeure un temps ici, je ne perdrai seulement mon royaume mais la vie.'

While the tension was still at its height, the Northern Rebellion broke like a thunderclap over the country. In Tudor times the valley of the Trent marked, as it had done for centuries before, the great divide between northern and southern England. Beyond Trent, stretching from the Peakland to the Cheviots, lay a country whose aspect grew more and more forbidding as

---

[1] Early in September Norfolk negotiated with Charles IX for the dispatch of a French force of 5,000 or 6,000 to Dumbarton; and the king agreed (20 Sept.) to give him all the help he could—'de gens et d'argent que Dieu m'a donné'. (*Correspondance diplomatique de La Mothe Fénelon.*)

the great *massif* of the Pennines dominated the landscape and
broke the plains into a tumbled mass of isolated dales and pas-
turelands, rocky uplands, bleak moors, forests, bogs, and wastes.
To the southerner this distant and inaccessible region, with its
sunless and tempestuous winters, its comparative lack of roads
and bridges, its sparse and rude inhabitants, and its general suggestion of niggardliness, must have seemed little better than the
unredeemed wilderness. The agrarian and industrial changes
that had transformed the face of southern England, and were fast
destroying the last vestiges of the old medieval economy, here
found themselves impeded by natural obstacles and by a people
whose spirit was opposed to change and slow to adapt itself to
new conditions. Agriculture was largely confined to the vale of
York and the coastal plains, and the woollen industry had
made only a rudimentary beginning in the West Riding of
Yorkshire, eastern Lancashire, and the palatinate of Durham.
It was inevitable that a region so circumstanced should give rise
to serious administrative problems, for its lack of an ordered life
based upon economic pursuits perpetuated the turbulence of its
inhabitants and made them a drag on the wheels of progress.
For the young there was no choice of a career apart from service
in the households of the nobility and gentry. In fact feudalism
was a necessary element in the northern economy: it provided
both a means of livelihood and a rallying-point for the general
life of the community. But it was a different kind of feudalism
from that which prevailed in the south—less affluent, but deeper
and stronger of root, more intimate, more militant. The great
families of Percy, Neville, and Dacre, whose honours, baronies,
tenements, and dependencies covered the bulk of the land between Yorkshire and the Border, were more like petty sovereigns
than subjects, for the feudal tie was so strong that it was commonly said of the Northumbrians that they 'knew no prince but
a Percy'. Even the authority of the Crown, which made itself
felt only intermittently when subsidies were levied or statutes
proclaimed, or when justice was to be executed, was interpreted
in terms of feudalism, the great magnates being the intermediaries through whom the commands of the queen were transmitted to the people. As lords-lieutenant, justices of the peace,
and dispensers of patronage they were at one and the same
time Crown officials and the natural leaders of society.

But feudalism was not the only bond of union in the north, nor, perhaps, was it the most powerful. Lord and tenant were drawn closer together by a common interest in the defence of the old faith than they were by ties of a material kind; for the religious innovations of the queen and the reconstruction of the church which followed seemed to portend a complete overthrow of the main bulwark of the old order north of Trent. This was a matter on which all classes could combine, for it affected all. Hence as soon as the new Elizabethan bishops essayed to enforce the prayer book and church attendance they found themselves thwarted at every turn by a recalcitrant laity, backed by disloyalty among the Crown officials and stimulated by the obvious shortage of a protestant clergy. Recusancy began almost at once; and if in some parts the people conformed so far as to go to church, the 'lees' of the old faith still lay 'at the bottom of men's hearts' ready to come to the surface if 'the vessel was ever so little stirred'. It was not the policy of the queen, however, to stir the vessel too much during the first ten years of her reign, and the despairing cries of the bishops were not heeded. The council in the north, which had done great service since its re-establishment by Henry VIII in removing many social grievances, was not disposed to interfere in the matter of religion; for its presidents were, with one exception, complacent men, moderate in their opinions, and friendly to catholicism. The consequence was that England beyond Trent remained an overwhelmingly catholic country—so much so that it almost seemed as if the government were content to recognize the territorial principle, *cuius regio eius religio*, as applicable to these parts.

There were dangers, of course, in such a situation; for the cleavage in religion might easily become the basis of a political antagonism, which, in its turn, might lead to another conflagration of the 'inly working north', similar in kind to that which shook the throne of Henry VIII. And if there was plenty of combustible material, there was no lack of flying sparks to set it aflame. Ever since the beginning of the reign Elizabeth had shown a disposition to weaken her over-mighty subjects by transferring important offices from their hands to new men, on whose reliability she could depend. Custodianships of castles, stewardships of royal manors in the north, posts of responsibility like the wardenship of the marches were taken out of their control. Similarly, when the youthful heir to the Dacre inheritance at Naworth died accidentally, in May 1569, the estates were conferred upon the duke of Norfolk, to the exclusion of Leonard, uncle of the deceased, who by ancient usage should have taken both the title and the lands. Moreover, it was part of the royal policy to insist on the northern earls residing at court—no doubt because the queen believed they would behave themselves better under her eye than if they were left to brood in their native fastnesses. Residence at court entailed expense, and expense was a serious consideration to men whose revenues, like the countryside from which they were derived, were smitten by the blight of poverty. Finally to these private rancours were added public grievances—discontent with the queen's stubborn refusal to settle the succession question in favour of Mary Stuart, her peremptory veto of the Norfolk marriage proposal, and her imprisonment of the Scottish queen. Over all flickered the hostility to Cecil and his policy.

Strictly speaking, the rebellion should have begun when Norfolk, disappointed of his purpose, left the court in high dudgeon in September, and betook himself to his country house at Kenninghall. De Spes thought he had gone to raise the standard of revolt, and Mary counselled him to be bold. But the duke was a coward. Fearing the queen's resentment, and believing that his imprisonment was imminent, he craved the royal pardon in a letter of 24 September, and wrote to his fellow conspirators to dissuade them from action. He probably knew that Pembroke and Arundel were already under arrest, and that all who were privy to the plot were being watched. Eventually, trusting to Cecil's assurance that he would be leniently treated if he made his submission, he consented to set out for the court, and was intercepted at Burnham by Sir Francis Knollys and Sir Henry Neville, who conducted him to the Tower. Meanwhile the two northern earls, hearing on 10 October of Norfolk's imprisonment, met the following day in Northumberland's house at Topcliffe in Yorkshire, to decide what course to take. Northumberland, who was loath to take extreme measures because of the danger in which Mary Stuart might be placed, and also because he had no stomach for rebellion, was overborne by the more fiery Westmorland, and by his 'company' who 'threatened him with daggs', saying, 'If ye will not cast yourself away, ye shall not cast us.'

About the same time the earl of Sussex, lord president of the council at York, had received instructions from the queen to warn all justices of the peace in his shire and throughout the north to keep good watch and ward in all boroughs, market towns, and places where people congregated, and to advertise any unlawful action attempted. Sons of northern families at the universities were detained in residence until the situation cleared. The lord president, whose information appears to have been defective, was inclined at first to make light of the rumours of rebellion, but in accordance with orders took preliminary measures for the defence of York, Hull, Pomfret, and Knaresborough, and obtained assurances from Northumberland and Westmorland that the 'bruits' were false. On 13 October he reported all quiet to the queen, and trusted 'the time of the year would cool hot humours'. But Elizabeth was troubled by the messages reaching her from other sources, and instructed Sussex to order the earls to repair to court forthwith (24 October). The lord president did so on 30 October, but still maintained that he had heard of no conventions of multitudes at unlawful times and places. Sir Thomas Gargrave at Pomfret, however, had better information, and on 2 November reported to Cecil the names of the 'great doers in these matters'—Robert Tempest, John Swinburn, Thomas Markinfield, Francis Norton, Thomas Hussey, Christopher Danby, and Highingham of Yorkshire— but was also inclined to think there would be no rebellion. On 4 November Sussex, replying to the earls, who excused themselves from obeying his command, issued a fresh and more peremptory summons ordering them to be at York by the following morning. Before his messenger left Topcliffe on the return journey, he heard the church bells sounding the tocsin for rebellion. But Sussex repeated his attempt to keep the earls to their obedience—to be informed on this occasion, by the countess of Northumberland, that her husband was gone, having received alarming messages from his friends at court. On the 12th it transpired that the earls were at Brancepeth, Westmorland's castle, with their followers in armour. He therefore decided to order a general mobilization of the armed forces of the north in Richmondshire and the bishopric; while at the same time he issued a proclamation denouncing the treason of the earls. Nevertheless, in spite of this, he made a fifth and last attempt to recall the misguided noblemen to their duty: 'If you have slipped', he wrote on 13 November, 'your friends will be suitors for you to the queen, who never shows herself extreme and has always borne you affection.' Two days later news arrived that the rebels had entered Durham, celebrated Mass in the cathedral, and trodden the prayer book under foot. The die was cast. Westmorland, who now took the lead, informed Sussex that he proposed to remain at Brancepeth and fortify himself against his enemies who sought his destruction. No further parley was possible, and Sussex prepared himself for the worst.

Meanwhile the poor response to his call to arms was giving him grave concern: 'Except it be a few protestants and some well affected to me', he wrote, 'every man seeks to bring as small a force as he can of horsemen, and the footmen find fault with the weather and besides speak very broadly.' It was obvious that the north could not provide for its own defence; so Sussex had to be content with the protection of York itself, and dispatched an urgent appeal for help to the government.

The proclamation published by the earls after the occupation of Durham made it appear that their hostility was directed not against the queen, but against 'divers evil disposed persons about the queen', who by their 'crafty dealing have overthrown the catholic religion, abused the queen, dishonoured the realm, and seek the destruction of the nobility'. Force, they said, must be resisted by force. The ancient customs and liberties must be restored 'lest if we do it not ourselves strangers will do it to the great hazard of the estate of our country'.

On 20 November Sussex, having received more ample commission from the queen, proclaimed the earls rebels, offering pardon to all who repaired to their houses before the 22nd. On the same date he explained to Elizabeth that he had only 400 horsemen, ill horsed and badly furnished, and a great number with only bows and arrows: that the rebels had interrupted his mobilization, spoiling the men of their weapons and money: that the justices of the peace and gentlemen were mostly holding aloof; and that the rebels were strong in horse, having the reivers of Tynedale and Redesdale with them. Lord Hunsdon, who had been sent from the court to take command at Berwick, found his progress barred beyond Doncaster, and was compelled to go round by Hull; but he had heard from Lord Darcy's men, who were holding Doncaster for the queen, that the rebels intended to attempt the rescue of Mary Stuart at Tutbury. Sadler, who followed Hunsdon, also went round by Hull in order to reach York. Both men in their reports to the queen dwelt on the seriousness of the position and justified Sussex's inactivity in the face of heavy odds.

The march of the rebel host southwards indicates that the intention of its leaders was, as Hunsdon learned at the bridge of Don, to spring a surprise on Mary Stuart's guardians at Tutbury. Passing York, which would, in any case, have defied a force lacking artillery, they followed the line—Richmond, Ripon, Wetherby, Knaresborough, Tadcaster, Cawood, Selby, arriving at this last and southernmost limit of their march about 24 November. Whether a swift raid was actually made from here on Tutbury—a distance of over 50 miles—by a band of horsemen under Northumberland is uncertain but highly improbable. The fact that Mary was removed to Coventry on the 25th and that the whole expedition was back again in Richmond on the 28th, and at Brancepeth by the 30th—a rapid retreat—suggests, if it does not prove, that the retirement was not due to the failure of the projected *coup* but to other causes. In all probability the earls had heard of the great concentration of royal troops taking place on the south side of Trent, in Lincolnshire, Leicestershire, and Warwickshire, and determined to extricate themselves as speedily as possible from what might easily prove to be a death-trap.

Lord Clinton and the earl of Warwick, who were in charge of this southern army, were now completing the mobilization and were in touch with Sussex, although it was not until 10 December that they were able to begin effective co-operation. Meanwhile the retreating rebels, taking advantage of Sussex's immobility at York, captured Barnard Castle from Sir George Bowes—a useless piece of bravado which delayed them several days and very nearly jeopardized their safety. The royal forces had now begun to move. On 11 December Sussex, reinforced by some of Clinton's men, set out in pursuit of the rebels, leaving the main army to follow him a day's march behind. The fleet was also in occupation of Hartlepool, which the rebels had captured in November, in order to keep a port open for the reception of expected succours from Alva; and far away on the Scottish border Sir Henry Percy with garrison troops from Berwick was on his way southward to Newcastle.

The earls now realized that the game was up. At Durham, which they reached on 15 December, they decided on flight; and disbanding their weary and tattered footmen they themselves, with a handful of horse, made for Hexham and thence across the Pennines to Naworth and the Dacre country. Sir John Forster with the horsemen of the East and Middle Marches now took up the pursuit; but on the night of 20 December, with the help of Edward Dacre, they slipped past Scrope at Carlisle and reached the shelter of Liddesdale. Here they were safe for the moment, for the Scottish border families, the Scotts, Kers, Maxwells, Humes, and Hepburns gave them protection, esteeming it 'a liberty incident to all nations to succour banished men'.

The crisis was now past, but the danger was by no means over; and the queen's order for demobilization, issued on 16 January 1570, was somewhat premature. Elizabeth probably calculated on the kind services of the Scottish regent to secure the surrender of the fugitives; for Murray had been kept informed of their movements by Sussex. This, however, was a task beyond the regent, who, although he captured the earl of Northumberland by the treachery of a Liddesdale reiver, could not deliver him to the English because of the hostile attitude of the Scots. Nor could he do anything to effect the arrest of the others. Northumberland was therefore taken a prisoner to Edinburgh.

In the meantime further troubles were brewing on the frontier. The Scottish borderers who had given hospitality to the fugitives from England, being staunch catholics, now made common cause with their guests; and rumours were rife that Leonard Dacre was in league with them, albeit he had helped Scrope to round up the stragglers of the rebel cavalcade in the West March. Old wrongs were rankling in Dacre's heart, and he probably suspected that the queen would attribute the escape of her rebels to him as well as to his brother. As a matter of fact Elizabeth had already ordered Sussex and Sadler to effect his arrest, early in January, and they were in correspondence with Forster, Hunsdon, and Scrope with a view to an attack on Naworth. But the castle was strongly fortified, and the lack of artillery delayed operations. Eventually, however, the assassination of Murray on 23 January, and the aggressiveness of the Scots, made the immediate arrest of Dacre imperative; and on 8 February a peremptory message from the queen forced Hunsdon and Forster to attempt the task without waiting for siege artillery.

Leaving Berwick with the comparatively slender force of 1,500 men on 15 February, Hunsdon reached Hexham on the 19th, where he was joined by Forster. Then followed a night march to Naworth through the Dacre country, where 'the beacons burned all night and every hill was full of horse and foot crying and shouting as if they had been mad'. A surprise attack was obviously out of the question; and Hunsdon decided to continue his march past Naworth, it being still dark, in the hope of reaching Scrope at Carlisle. The move was undoubtedly wise, as Scrope had news of a considerable army of the Scots hastening to Dacre's assistance. Happily, however, Dacre attempted to hold up Hunsdon's march at the crossing of the Gelt, four miles west of the castle, and a general engagement ensued. After 'the proudest charge upon my shot that ever I saw', the rebel troops broke themselves against Hunsdon's arquebuses, and their leader fled, leaving 300 dead and over 200 prisoners in the hands of his opponents. Hunsdon then moved on to Carlisle, descrying in the distance, as he approached his objective, the Scottish reinforcements on which Dacre had counted. 'If we had tarried until Wednesday', he remarked in a letter to the queen, 'as Dacre thought I should, he had been past dealing with, for he would have had four or five thousand men more out of Scotland, besides increasing his own power'. It was clearly a narrow thing; and Hunsdon confided in Cecil that if he had 'taken the repulse, from Trent hitherward had been in great danger, and Carlisle would have been gone'. On 26 February the queen lavished her praise and thanks on her victorious general: 'I doubt much, my Harry, whether that the victory were given me more joyed me, or that you were by God appointed the instrument of my glory; and I assure you for my country's good, the first might suffice, but for my heart's contentation, the second more pleased me.'

While these decisive events were being transacted on the border, the main 'southern army' under Clinton and Warwick began an irregular spoliation of the north from Doncaster to Newcastle, driving cattle before them, seizing lands, goods, and leases, putting the miserable people to ransom 'as if all be rebels from Doncaster northwards'. Sussex tried to stop the reign of terror by a stern proclamation against the indiscriminate plunder, forbidding under penalty anyone to take or spoil men's goods except the sheriffs or their officers. But Gargrave was afraid that the queen would 'lose most of the forfeitures', and could not 'get knowledge of the twentieth part of the goods bruited to be carried out of the country'. On 18 January he wrote to Cecil: 'I think a difference should be made between a rebellion in the queen's own dominions and a foreign realm.' And Hunsdon, who was likewise irritated by the behaviour of the southerners, commented with pardonable sarcasm: 'If the earl of Sussex had not been where he was, neither York nor Yorkshire had been at her [i.e. the queen's] discretion, and then the lusty southern army would not have returned laden with such spoils, nor put their noses over Doncaster bridge; but others beat the bush and they have had the birds.' The wastage of livestock was appalling. 'Cattle and sheep have come to my hands by seizure', wrote Gargrave, 'and I have no meat for them; if I buy it, they will soon eat up their value. Some have died by driving and lack of meat. The queen orders me to keep the goods without diminishing, but it would be better husbandry to sell some than keep all.' It was a cruel visitation upon an already poverty-stricken land.

By 4 February 500 of the rebels had suffered execution by martial law; they were of the poorer sort, and were put to death to overawe the people. Another 129 were indicted of treason, conspiracy, and rebellion, respectively, at York, Durham, and Carlisle. And in March the queen sent instructions to Sussex and others associated with him to wind up the work by compounding with such offenders as were deemed 'meet for mercy and pardon', subject to their making their submission and taking an oath of obedience to the queen. Thus persons in possession of lands worth £5 annually or under might redeem them by paying a reasonable sum: retainers of rebels might be pardoned if their relatives were wealthy enough to pay their fines for them: those who held office under the Crown were to be discharged from their offices; and all payments were to be in ready money or goods to be sold for the queen's use. The lands of the important rebels, however, were reserved to be attainted and resumed by the Crown, their valuation being entrusted to royal surveyors to be certified to the court of king's bench. By July the fine rolls and the valuation were complete, and Sir Thomas Gargrave placed his accounts with the balance of the money in the hands of Valentine Browne, treasurer of Berwick.

Altogether there suffered for the rebellion some 800 persons; but the chief loss was in goods and property. If the north had been poor, it was now reduced to the verge of starvation. In September 1570 Gargrave wrote to Cecil: 'I have not heard the complaint so general of poverty as it now is. They have been much touched with the late troubles, payments for armour,

assessment for repair of above a dozen bridges overthrown last
winter, payment of fines, enhancement of rents, lack of traffic
with Flanders, commissioners for concealed lands and goods,
and for the sale of wines, outlawries, &c.'

The collapse of the northern rebellion undoubtedly cleared
away Elizabeth's most pressing danger at home; but, inter-
nationally considered, her position was far from reassuring. On
the contrary, the political sky was everywhere clouded, nowhere
more so than in Scotland. Here, the assassination of Murray
had withdrawn the main pillar of English influence north of the
Tweed; and the Marian party, leagued with Elizabeth's rebels,
again raised the standard of the queen of Scots. France, too, was
eager to take advantage of the situation in order to increase
England's predicament. Already, in February, Sir Henry
Norreys found it necessary to warn his government from Paris
of the naval preparations in Brittany for a descent on Dumbarton
in aid of the Marians: 'all men's mouths' being 'full of the
invasion of England'. But Elizabeth was in no mood at first to
pay much attention to these rumours of French aggression. 'It
were a great folly and danger and against common sense', she
said, 'to restore the queen of Scots.' One policy alone seemed
feasible, to lend immediate aid to the party led by Morton and
Mar, on whose shoulders had fallen the mantle of Murray, and
at the same time to secure redress for the unfriendly action of
the borderers during the late rebellion. In pursuance of this
plan, Sussex was authorized to carry out a great punitive raid
into the border country, which he did in April, in conjunction
with Scrope and Forster, burning and destroying the castles of
'all such as helped the queen's rebels' as far as Kelso, Jedburgh,
and Hawick. A few weeks later Sir William Drury was dispatched
from Berwick with an English contingent to strengthen Morton's
hands at Edinburgh; and very soon he was engaged along with
King James's troops in the siege of Dumbarton castle. La Mothe
protested vigorously in the name of France against this violation
of Scottish territory, but was told that it would cease as soon as
the English rebels were expelled from Scotland.

If Cecil and Bacon had had the sole direction of affairs at
this time, the forward policy would have been followed by a
thorough-going subjection of Scotland to England's will, defiance of France, and the utter ruin of Mary Stuart's cause. But

other voices were now whispering caution in Elizabeth's ear; and with that sensitiveness to danger that always characterized her movements, she began to doubt the wisdom of becoming further embroiled in Scottish affairs. The publication of the papal bull in England (May 1570),[1] and the uncertainty of her relations with Spain, coupled with the menacing attitude of France, lent weight to the suggestions of Leicester and Arundel that she ought to pacify both France and Scotland by seeking a diplomatic restoration of Mary Stuart. Towards the end of May, therefore, Elizabeth suddenly reversed her Scottish policy, recalled Drury to Berwick, and sent Randolph to intimate her changed intentions to the king's party at Stirling. It was a sad blow to the hopes of Morton and Mar; but on being assured that ample guarantees would be exacted for their security and that of the prince, they acquiesced in Elizabeth's will, and elected the earl of Lennox, her nominee, as Murray's successor in the regency (July). The next step was to bring about an armistice between the rival parties and begin negotiations for a treaty. Sussex took the matter in hand, and in September announced that a suspension of arms was arranged for six months. The way was now open for a settlement by diplomacy.

While events were moving towards peace in Scotland, great anxiety prevailed in England as to the activities of Alva in the Netherlands, where elaborate preparations were being made during the summer for the reception and escort of Anne of Austria, Philip II's bride elect, on her way to Madrid. The royal flotilla was to be accompanied from Antwerp by the Spanish fleet; but fears were expressed in London that under cover of this apparently legitimate display of Spanish courtesy some blow was intended against England. France was also thought to be in the plot, and it might even be that both powers were preparing to carry out the papal decree. The consequence was that during the month of July England was in the grip of an acute scare. 'They are so alarmed here', wrote Antonio de Guaras, 'that they fear their own shadows.' Throughout the country sheriffs were busy enrolling men for home defence: hackbut practice was instituted on every village green: mobilization of the fleet under Clinton was ordered at Rochester: Lord Charles Howard was sent with ten great ships to guard the narrow seas; and signalling beacons were set up in various parts

[1] See p. 167.

to notify any attempted landing of the Spaniards. Howard was instructed to be punctilious about exacting the salute when the Spanish ships passed through the strait of Dover.[1] In August the whole coast from the Thames to Berwick, from Dover to Cornwall, was guarded as if the enemy were in sight, and scouting pinnaces were patrolling the French side of the Channel, while Hawkins was on the look-out at Plymouth, and watch was kept night and day on the hill near Margate. This state of tension lasted all summer until the Spaniards had completed the double journey. It was the month of October before the government felt justified in ordering a general relaxation of precautions.

Eventually, after the excitement over the movements of the Spanish fleet had subsided, the terms on which Elizabeth was prepared to restore the queen of Scots to her kingdom were communicated to the royal captive at Chatsworth by Cecil and Sir Walter Mildmay. They were necessarily severe—involving, among other things, the surrender of her son as a hostage for his mother's good behaviour, the conclusion of a defensive alliance with England, an undertaking not to contract any marriage without Elizabeth's consent, and the retention by the English of Hume castle until restitution was made for the spoils committed by the borderers in England. Objection was raised by the French ambassador to the surrender of James and the defensive alliance with England; but the real obstacle to a convention arose not from the French, nor from the queen of Scots, who was willing to purchase her liberty at almost any price, and apparently satisfied Cecil as to her substantial acceptance of all the articles, but from the king's party in Scotland, who had become increasingly afraid of their position in the event of Mary's return. After a long delay of more than three months, Morton and his fellow commissioners ventured to explain to Elizabeth, in a personal interview, that they could not enter into any treaty that invalidated the abdication signed by Mary at Loch Leven and legalized by the Scottish estates, or involved any abridgement of the king's sovereignty, or his removal to England. If, therefore, Mary returned to Scotland, it must be as a private person. Elizabeth was visibly annoyed with this recalcitrant reply, and threatened Morton with her hostility if he persisted in his attitude; and La Mothe also exerted pressure on him 'par prières et même par menaces'. But the Scots refused to modify

[1] The strait of Dover was 'her majesty's stream'.

their position, and returned to Edinburgh in March 1571, on the plea that they must consult parliament, but really resolved to fight out their quarrel with the Marians to the bitter end. The restoration of the queen of Scots was now an impossibility, for Elizabeth could not coerce the party on whom alone she must rely for the maintenance of English influence in Scotland. Meanwhile, the armistice having come to an end, the rival parties plunged again into war for the mastery of the kingdom; and with the return of anarchy, all hope of achieving an Anglo-French agreement with regard to Scotland temporarily vanished.

The principal conclusion to be drawn from the failure was that the solution of the Scottish question must wait until more substantial grounds of co-operation with France could be discovered. Nor was it difficult to see that public opinion on the other side of the Channel was also moving towards the same conclusion, albeit from a different point. As early as 1568, the house of Châtillon had mooted the idea of an Anglo-French alliance, based upon the marriage of the duke of Anjou and Queen Elizabeth: hoping thereby to get rid of the fanatical and superstitious heir apparent to the Crown, rescue their country from the recurring chaos of civil war, and restore foreign policy to its traditional anti-Habsburg groove. The idea, though creditable to the prescience of its promoters, was somewhat premature and found less support than it was entitled to, at the time it was first discussed; but two years later, when the pacification of St. Germain freed the hands of Charles IX for a more ambitious role in European affairs, it had much to commend it. Like his father and grandfather before him, Charles aspired to strike a blow at the Habsburgs; and like them, too, he determined to build up a system of alliances between France and the protestants abroad. The first step was the treaty of St. Germain, which established liberty of worship for the huguenots and gave them legal security: the next was the summons of Coligny to the council, a token that co-operation was to be the watchword of the future; and on this solid foundation could be established alliances with the protestants of Germany and the Netherlands. The union of the houses of Bourbon and Valois by the marriage of Henry of Navarre and the king's sister Margaret would complete the protective circle which Charles, magician-wise, hoped to draw round himself; and if he could marry his brother Anjou to the English queen, he might even draw England into his schemes for the dismemberment of the Spanish empire.

The isolation of England, owing to the rupture with Spain and the hostility of the pope, and the troubles in Scotland, had likewise created the need for an ally; and, as we have seen, there was a strong pro-French party in the council, headed by Leicester ('plus français que nul autre de ce royaume'), who were largely responsible for the new Scottish policy announced by the queen in May 1570. Cecil, too, began to turn over in his mind the 'commodities' that might result from a marriage between Elizabeth and Anjou. The consequence was that unofficial feelers were put out during the winter of 1570-1 with a view to discovering whether France was sufficiently interested in the matter for it to be committed to diplomacy. Then, in February 1571, Lord Buckhurst went to Paris, ostensibly to congratulate Charles on his marriage, but really to announce in Elizabeth's name that England was ready to entertain official *pourparlers* on the subject of the Anjou match. Thereafter the negotiations passed into the capable hands of Sir Francis Walsingham, the resident English ambassador in Paris, and became the main substance of Anglo-French diplomatic correspondence until January 1572.

If the failure of her negotiations for the pacification of Scotland drove Elizabeth into seeking a *rapprochement* with France, it found the queen of Scots deeply involved in the dangerous mazes of the Ridolfi conspiracy. This pretentious but thoroughly impracticable plot took shape in England at the very moment when Lord Buckhurst initiated the Anjou conversations in Paris. Its notoriety lies chiefly in the irreparable damage it did to Mary Stuart's cause and its tragic consequences for the duke of Norfolk. Essentially a Hispano-papal plot, it was the work of the cosmopolitan financier Roberto Ridolfi, who had already graduated in conspiracy by taking a hand in the intrigues of 1569. Being an Italian, versed in the swift and sudden revolutions characteristic of his own country, he conceived it possible, by combining the elements of unrest in England with the queen's enemies abroad, to stage a spectacular *coup* against the English state, overthrow Elizabeth, and seat Mary Stuart on the throne of a catholic England. He was nothing if not methodical; and he conducted his conspiracy as he conducted his business transactions, in the best counting-house manner, procuring signatures, letters of recommendation, statistical proofs of his assertions, and carefully noting the obligations of everybody. But he was too masterful, too confident of his own ability, and too much given to make light of difficulties he could not understand and still less foresee. His ideas on international politics were bound by the horizons of an ordinary Italian *cittadino*, in whose eyes the decisive power in European politics lay with the catholic powers under the hegemony of the pope.[1] Of the intricate, involved, and complex relationships of the powers to each other he knew nothing; nor was he really conversant, in spite of his elaborate array of figures, with the feelings and aspirations of the English catholics. His greatest weakness, however, was his gullibility, and his confidence that a conspiracy entailing the co-ordination of centres so far apart as London, Rome, Madrid, and Brussels could be controlled and directed by one man, or could long escape the eyes and ears of the English government and of other governments friendly to Elizabeth. It is difficult to see how the Ridolfi plot could have achieved success even in the most favourable circumstances.

The focus of the conspiracy was of necessity England, where the decisive events would occur. Here, the cause of Mary Stuart would provide the battle-cry: the papal bull, news of which spread through the country during the year 1570, would supply the incentive to action; and the duke of Norfolk with his associates among the nobility, whom Ridolfi numbered at over sixty, would give the plot its natural leaders. Behind the nobility, massed in their tens of thousands, would rally the discontented catholics. Then, on a preconcerted signal to be given by the landing of a Spanish expeditionary force composed of veterans from the Netherlands and Spain, on the coast of Norfolk, the queen would be seized or assassinated, the Tower and the fleet captured, parliament overawed or broken up, and Mary Stuart freed from prison. Such was the substance of this grotesque conspiracy.

The first to be drawn into Ridolfi's net was the queen of Scots, who readily gave her assent to it, with the pope's approval, in February 1571, and furnished the arch-conspirator with letters of credence for Alva, the pope, and the king of Spain. Norfolk was harder to win; for he disliked Ridolfi's 'Italian

[1] J. H. Pollen, *The English Catholics in the Reign of Queen Elizabeth*, p. 132.

devices', doubted the possibility of keeping the matter secret, and insisted upon knowing what help might be expected from Spain. Eventually, however, he allowed himself to be overborne by Ridolfi and the persuasive arguments of the bishop of Ross, his chief coadjutor, who showed him that, as Morton had returned to Scotland, nothing further could be done towards a Marian restoration by negotiation; and about 10 March he gave by word of mouth his assent to do what he could for the queen of Scots and the advancement of the catholic religion. Probably also, though the point is not verifiable, he acknowledged himself a catholic.

Having thus laid the mine to his own satisfaction in England Ridolfi then left for the Continent on 25 March with his copious notes and documents to concert measures with Alva, the pope, and Philip II. He was in Brussels in April; in May he was in Rome; and late in June he reached Madrid. His reception varied in accordance with the political acumen of the men with whom he dealt. Rome welcomed his scheme with open arms: in Madrid it was submitted to a long and careful scrutiny before it was accepted; but Alva was from the first sceptical, critical, irresponsive. The astute governor of the Netherlands, who desired above everything else the recovery of his confiscated treasure and the property lost in England by the embargoes, poured cold water on Ridolfi as he had already done on de Spes in 1569, and let it be known that he thought as little of the ability of the one as he did of the other. He described Ridolfi as a *gran parlaquina*: a great chatterbox. Nor would he abandon his stubborn resistance to the plot unless and until he had proof positive that the English were prepared to carry out the essential part of the business themselves. In several letters to his master he analysed with merciless cogency the dangers and difficulties in the way of success, and the fatal consequences of failure: the disastrous effects a war with England would have on Spanish policy both in northern Europe and in the Mediterranean, and the impossibility of sending an army from the Netherlands at the present juncture of international affairs. At the back of Alva's mind lay the fear that England would seize the occasion to accelerate the alliance with France which was already beginning to loom over the horizon, and the complementary fear of French aggression in the Low Countries, which was also coming daily nearer. So far as England was concerned, failure of the plot would probably mean ruin of the catholic cause and the forfeiture of Mary Stuart's life. In the face of this opposition from Alva, it was impossible for Philip to move, for he had complete trust in the judgement of his lieutenant. Thus by the end of August the bottom had fallen out of Ridolfi's elaborate scheme.

Meanwhile the activities of the plotters were gradually coming within the purview of the English government. The first authentic evidence of Mary's relations with Alva came from Scotland, where it fell into the hands of Regent Lennox after the capture of Dumbarton castle on the night of 2–3 April, and was remitted to Cecil. News of Ridolfi's plans was sent to Elizabeth by the grand duke of Tuscany, with whom he had stayed during his journey from Rome to Madrid. From the queen of Navarre came information extracted from the dispatches of a Spanish courier intercepted in the Pyrenees. In the month of May a certain Charles Bailly was arrested at Dover with a packet of letters and books consigned by Ridolfi to the bishop of Ross, and this led to the discovery of Ross's implication in the conspiracy, and his arrest. 'Trente' and 'Quarante' (Norfolk and Lumley), the addressees of the letters, to whom Ross had distributed them before his arrest, were not yet indentifiable. But shortly afterwards the arrest of Higford, the duke of Norfolk's secretary, and his agents, Barker and Bannister, in connexion with the transmission by Norfolk of a sum of money to Mary Stuart's supporters in Scotland, brought guilt home to the duke, and he was arrested and taken to the Tower on 7 September. Finally, in October, Ross revealed the whole plot, under threat of torture, and placed the government in possession of a damning case against Norfolk. Further revelations led to the implication of Arundel, Southampton, Cobham, and others of Norfolk's associates, and they were likewise arrested. As the ramifications of the conspiracy were discovered, excitement grew. The catholic nobles were carefully watched, the port guards were changed, the watch was reinforced in London and other cities by day and night, and all roads leading to and from the capital were picketed.

In January 1572 a process for treason was begun against Norfolk, and on the 16th, he was sentenced to death by his peers. Six months later, after prolonged hesitation on the part of the queen, he was executed. Thus perished the greatest noble in England—the last aristocratic champion of reaction—a victim to his own inordinate ambition and crooked ways.

While Ridolfi was posting across Europe endeavouring to weave together the various strands of his complicated plot, Walsingham was busy in Paris wrestling with the exasperating problem of the Anjou marriage. From the first his task was practically hopeless; for as soon as the articles were reduced to writing it was seen that no compromise was possible on the question of religion. The French insisted upon freedom of worship for the duke, on the plea that he could not be expected to abandon the faith in which he was nurtured. Elizabeth, for political reasons no less cogent, could not yield on the point that he must conform to the religious observances established by law in England. Nor could the wit of man devise a formula that would meet the objections on either side. Walsingham's efforts to cajole or browbeat the duke into acceptance of Elizabeth's demand were countered at every step by the combined influence of the papal nuncio, the cardinal of Lorraine, and the ambassadors of Spain and Portugal, who played on the fears and ambitions of Anjou with consummate skill. He stoutly refused to do violence to his conscience even with the hope of a kingdom dangled before him. By the month of July something very like an *impasse* had been reached in the negotiations, and the promoters of the match on both sides were reduced to despair. Charles IX, who longed to see his brother safely out of the kingdom, was angered at his intransigence; and the queen mother 'never wept so much since her husband died'. Burghley[1] and Leicester were no less helpless and distraught before the obstinacy of the queen, who flatly refused to sanction the use of the Mass in England 'how secret soever', and seemed wilfully blind to the gravity of the issues involved. 'This amity', lamented Burghley, 'were needful to us; but God hath determined to plague us, the hour is at hand, His will be done with mercy!' 'God protect and defend us,' wrote Leicester; 'thus we are with our neighbours, in all places without friendship!' A last desperate effort was made, in August, by a mission of Paul de Foix and the marshal de Montmorency, to procure some concession from the queen; but it only served to prove the utter impossibility of solving the problem by diplomacy. About a month

---

[1] Cecil was promoted to the peerage in 1571, taking the title of Baron Burghley.

later Leicester, who had means of knowing the queen's mind better perhaps than any one, concluded that there would be no marriage. 'Surely', he remarked in a letter to Walsingham, on 20 September, 'I am persuaded that her Majesty's heart is nothing inclined to marry at all, for the matter was ever brought to as many points as we could devise, and always she was bent to hold with the difficultest.'

This avowal doubtless came as a great relief to Walsingham, for his interest and sympathies were elsewhere than in the interminable marriage negotiations. Deep in the confidence of the huguenot leader Coligny and his brother in arms Lewis of Nassau[1]—kindred spirits with whom he could converse on terms of perfect equality and frankness—he had become convinced, like them, that the need of the hour was a combined onslaught on 'the proud Spaniard'. In August he adumbrated to Burghley a grandiose scheme, emanating from the fertile brain of Lewis of Nassau, whereby the Spaniards could be ejected from the Netherlands, and their inheritance divided between France, England, and Germany. France would take Artois and Flanders: Brabant, Guelderland, and Luxemburg would fall to the Empire; and England would annex Zeeland. It was a brilliant conception, satisfying at one and the same time the crusading impulse in Walsingham, the territorial ambitions of France, and the aspirations of the Flemish and Dutch patriots. Spain would be thoroughly humiliated, and England, at a small cost of financial assistance and the loan of a few ships, would see all her dangers vanish in the smoke of a European conflagration. In urging Burghley to recommend the project to the queen, Walsingham strongly emphasized the latter point: if the scheme prospered, 'the fire that is now kindling may grow to a flame and we take comfort at the heat thereof'. But although Leicester 'never found cause . . . that moveth me more to further it', the cautious Burghley, whose insular mind and self-regarding ideas of foreign policy cut sharp across the imaginative schemes of dreamers and firebrands like Coligny and Nassau, refused to be tempted. 'I fear the offers of so great amity', he wrote, 'will diminish or divert the former intention of the marriage without which the French amity shall serve to small purpose but to make us ministers of their appetites, and those fulfilled, to cast us off.' A French occupation of the Netherlands was in his

[1] Brother of William of Orange.

opinion a contingency more to be feared than all the threats of Spain—a subject on which he would have more to say when the storm broke over the Low Countries early in the following summer. So Walsingham was gently but firmly shepherded back again to the main purpose of his mission. He protested, it is true, but acquiesced, and the 'great enterprise of Flanders' was shelved so far as England was concerned.

Meanwhile the inexorable logic of events was steadily driving home the conviction, both in France and in England, that an immediate settlement, marriage or no marriage, was imperative in the interest of national defence. The continued anarchy in Scotland, leading to the *coup d'état* of the Marians at Stirling (September), in which Lennox was killed, together with the discovery of Spanish machinations in the Ridolfi plot, accelerated the pace on the English side; while the French were likewise stimulated by the victory of the Spaniards over the Turks at the battle of Lepanto (October), and the rumours of a treaty between Alva and the Marian party in Scotland for the invasion of that country and the removal of James to Spain. Accordingly, when Sir Thomas Smith and Sir Henry Killigrew went over to Paris at the end of December, the Anjou match was quietly dropped, and diplomacy addressed itself in earnest to the elaboration of an Anglo-French defensive league based upon the real needs of both countries. Difficulties were encountered, of course, owing to the reluctance of the French to abandon the cause of Mary Stuart, and the insistence by the English on the inclusion of an *etiamsi religionis causâ* clause in the *casus foederis*.[1] Eventually, however, the French agreed to withdraw their opposition in regard to Scotland, and Elizabeth contented herself with a 'letter missive' from Charles IX granting the substance of what she asked, although the matter was omitted from the text of the treaty. On 21 April 1572 the document giving effect to the settlement arrived at was signed at Blois; and the diplomatic revolution, as it has been called, was complete.

In actual fact the Treaty of Blois was more of a diplomatic convenience than a diplomatic revolution. It did not abrogate the Anglo-Burgundian alliance on the one hand, nor did it impose a veto on a reconstruction of a Franco-Scottish on the other. Briefly, it committed England and France to mutual

---

[1] England desired the treaty to be operative even in the event of invasion for religious reasons.

military and naval assistance if attacked by a third power, arranged for the establishment of a 'staple' in France to compensate England for the loss of her Flemish trade, and provided for a joint effort to pacify Scotland. The importance sometimes attached to the treaty is probably excessive. The promised staple in France was never set up, because the settlement between England and Spain in 1573 rendered it unnecessary. Nor were the military and naval clauses ever put into operation. In fact the only substantial result was the triumph of Elizabeth's policy in Scotland, and the abandonment of Mary Stuart by the French. From this standpoint England rather than France was the real gainer by the treaty.

Some three weeks before the Treaty of Blois was concluded, a revolution broke out in the Netherlands, which upset all the calculations of the diplomatists, plunged France into one of the gravest crises in her history, and shook the Anglo-French alliance to its foundations. The immediate cause of this sudden and unexpected sequence of events was the expulsion of the *gueux de mer* from English waters by a decree of Queen Elizabeth on 1 March. The measure was undertaken primarily to protect English commerce, and that of countries friendly to England, against the indiscriminate plunder indulged in by the disorderly crews of La Marck, the accredited admiral of the prince of Orange. Previously the queen had recognized the prince's right to issue naval commissions, and La Marck was granted the freedom of the port of Dover for victualling and munitioning purposes. But the exercise of the privilege led to gross abuses, to the slander and disgrace of the realm, and the time had come to teach the offenders a salutary lesson. Elizabeth, however, was not responsible, either as accomplice or accessory, for the action of the sea rover after his expulsion: that was due solely to the urgent need of a fresh base from which to continue his depredations on Spanish shipping in the Channel.[1] On 1 April La Marck made a surprise descent on the Dutch coast, captured Brill from the Spaniards, and proceeded to fortify it with a view to permanent occupation. It was the first foothold of the patriot cause on the soil of the Netherlands, and was taken as a signal for a widespread revolt against Spanish authority. Within a very

[1] See J. B. Black, 'Queen Elizabeth, the Sea Beggars and the Capture of Brill', in *Eng. Hist. Rev.* (1931).

short time the inhabitants of Flushing, Rotterdam, Schiedam, Gouda, and many other towns followed the lead given by Brill, expelled their garrisons, and placed themselves under the flag of Orange, who was proclaimed stadholder of Holland, Zeeland, Friesland, and Utrecht.

Great was the excitement when news of the rebellion reached London. 'The least thing they shout on 'change and in the street', wrote Guaras, the Spanish *chargé d'affaires*, to Alva, 'is that the states are utterly lost to us and that your Excellency and the Spaniards will have to leave.' The Flemish refugees organized expeditions in support, sending money and munitions, and presently a steady stream of adventurers, English as well as huguenot, began to join the movement. Although the enterprise had been achieved without the knowledge or sanction of Orange and Nassau, they realized quickly that the critical moment was at hand for launching their long-projected offensive in the Netherlands. In May Nassau, accompanied by the huguenot La Noue, led an army of French levies across the frontier. Valenciennes and Mons fell before them, to the cry of 'France et Liberté'; and with Orange on the move from Germany with powerful reinforcements, it must have seemed as if the 'great enterprise' was fairly on the way to success.

Clearly the time was ripe for Elizabeth to make some pronouncement on English policy; for the French were daily strengthening their hold on the country, especially in the island of Walcheren, the key to the entire Netherlands from the seaward side. In June Burghley analysed the situation for the benefit of the council, pointing out that the encroachment of the French in the maritime parts constituted a direct menace to England, to be resisted at all costs, even if it meant giving help to the duke of Alva. Shortly afterwards (11 July) Sir Humphrey Gilbert landed with a strong company of volunteers at Flushing, and was instructed by the queen—in the spirit of Burghley's memorandum—not to embark on any inland adventures, but to prevent the occupation of Flushing by the French. Not a word was said about the defence of Dutch and Flemish liberty: the eyes of the English government were directed exclusively to the danger from France, whose designs on the Low Countries were well known through Walsingham's dispatches of the previous year.

The drama unrolled itself with surprising swiftness, for Alva left no stone unturned in his anxiety to drive the French back again across the frontier. He retook Valenciennes, invested Mons, and cut to pieces a relieving army under the huguenot Genlis, who had been sent by Coligny with Charles IX's approval to assist Nassau. Mons then surrendered by capitulation, and the whole undertaking collapsed in ruin. Orange was compelled to beat a retreat into France with a rapidly dwindling army. Not only so: the capture of Genlis led to the discovery of information showing the French king's complicity in the affair. Charles IX was now confronted with the probability of an imminent war, single-handed, against Spain—a contingency he had made no provision for, and Coligny alone accepted with complacency. The queen mother, backed by the catholics in the council, protested that war could only lead to the triumph of the huguenots and the subjection of the king to their will; and hot words passed between her and the admiral. In order to escape from his dilemma, and at the same time avert a possible catastrophe, Charles decided to denounce the 'enterprise'. It was now Coligny's turn to fall into the pit he had unwittingly dug for his master. Regarded with suspicion by the king as the author of the disaster to Genlis, he found himself exposed to the concentrated animosity of all who resented his power in the state. The chronology of events places it beyond doubt that his removal by assassination was now the uppermost thought in the minds of Catherine de Médicis and the Guise faction.

News of Genlis's overthrow reached Paris when the huguenot leaders from all over France were assembling for the celebration of Navarre's marriage to the king's sister. On 19 August the wedding was solemnized with festivities and revelries; and on the 22nd, before the dispersal began, Coligny was shot at and wounded in the streets of the city. Charles IX, unaware of the part his mother had played in the deed, and thinking it was simply another event in the interminable private feud between the houses of Guise and Châtillon, vowed vengeance on the culprits, and ordered an inquiry. But the suspicions of the huguenots were roused, and accusing fingers were pointed at the queen mother and the duke of Anjou: with the result that Catherine determined to destroy the leading men of the party, including Coligny, before the inevitable revelations came out. She took Tavannes, Nevers, Guise, and others of the admiral's enemies into her confidence, concocted a bogus plot of the huguenots to kill the king and all the members of the royal family, and induced her son to sanction the murder of the ring-leaders. Navarre and Condé, being of the blood royal, were to be spared. Thus on the early morning of 24 August, St. Bartholomew's day, the 'caged birds' were brutally done to death; and the fanatical mob converted an act of private and essentially political vengeance into a signal for a wholesale massacre.[1]

Catholic Europe did not hide its satisfaction at the atrocity. 'Canticles of holy joy' resounded in the churches of France. At Rome, Pope Gregory XIII avowed himself better pleased than with fifty Lepantos. He ordered the *Te Deum* to be sung at St. Peter's and *feux de joie* to be lit at the Castle of St. Angelo, and summoned Vasari from Florence to decorate the hall of kings at the Vatican with paintings of the massacre. Profane minds everywhere gave a cynical approval to the skill with which the trap had been set; and the pious acknowledged the genuine religious spirit of the French court. In Italy the 'stratagem of Charles IX' became a byword. Philip II, relieved of his anxiety about Flanders, mirthfully referred to the 'long dissimulation' of his most christian brother, while Alva dismissed the bogy of the Anglo-French alliance as a thing of the past. The general impression was that France had vindicated her catholicity and thrown in her lot irrevocably with the cause of the counter-reformation. Protestant countries, however, were struck dumb with amazement and horror at the cruelty and barbarity of the deed. So far as England was concerned it came like a bolt out of a rapidly clearing heaven. The summer had begun with rejoicings and festivities over the ratification of the treaty, and Walsingham in Paris had no glimmering of what was brewing round him, the only thing that troubled him being the parlous position of William of Orange, and the seeming indifference of Elizabeth to his fate. The queen was palavering, now hot, now cold, with Catherine de Médicis's new proposal that she should marry her younger son Alençon, if she could not see her way to accommodate Anjou. On 6 June the execution of Norfolk had closed the episode of the Ridolfi plot, and Northumberland, who had been surrendered by the Scots, paid

---

[1] For details of the massacre, its causes and consequences, see Lord Acton, *History of Freedom and Other Essays*. In spite of the vast accumulation of literature on the subject, and the differences of opinion among historians, Acton's essay still commands the highest respect. But it would be advisable for the reader to pay attention to Herbert Butterfield's *Man on his Past*, chap. vi (Cambridge, 1955), where he will find an interesting account of the long controversy.

the same penalty on 22 August for his share in the rising of 1569. Scottish affairs were also proceeding towards a settlement under the joint guidance of England and France. Against this brightening landscape was suddenly projected the grim spectre of a France dyed red in the blood of the huguenots. Crowds of panic-stricken fugitives from Dieppe began to arrive at Rye on 27 August with harrowing details of their sufferings, and the news spread like wildfire through England. 'Il n'est pas à croire', wrote La Mothe, 'combien cette nouvelle émeut grandement tout ce royaume.'

In the absence of authentic tidings—for Walsingham's dispatches were held up, and the French king was slow to send his ambassador the official account of the occurrence—the worst construction was put upon the motives and intentions of the French court. The interview between Catherine de Médicis and Alva at Bayonne (June 1565) was recalled as a proof that the massacre had been planned long before.[1] Nor did the horror and excitement abate when Charles IX first threw the blame on Guise and then retracted this specious excuse in favour of the huguenot murder-plot theory advanced by the queen mother. When Elizabeth heard this revised version of the responsibility for the massacre she commented caustically on the barbarity of the French method of administering justice, and urged an early publication of the details of the alleged conspiracy. The council was more outspoken in its criticism. La Mothe was told that France had been guilty of the most heinous crime since the days of Jesus Christ. The general impression, so far as the ambassador was able to gauge public opinion, was that the word of a Frenchman was no longer to be trusted. 'Leur défiance est si grande', he wrote, 'qu'ils croient que tout que je leur dis de votre part est pour les surprendre et tromper.'

The difficulty of believing the official assurances of the French court that the matter was now finished and done with was greatly increased by the spread of the atrocities to Rouen and

---

[1] The Conference of Bayonne discussed the question of a marriage between Margaret of Valois and Don Carlos, and the enforcement in France of the decrees of the Council of Trent. It is certain that Catherine undertook to have the decrees of the Council examined by a body of prelates and to expel the protestant clergy from France on condition that the marriage took place. There is no record, however, of any talk about a massacre of the huguenot leaders. In any case the conference produced no tangible result. (Lavisse et Rambaud, *Histoire Générale*, v. 132.) For full details see E. Marcks, *Die Zusammenkunft von Bayonne*, esp. pp. 234–8.

other centres of population, and by the pessimistic reports received from Walsingham. It was impossible to disguise the fact that the mortal enemies of the huguenots were now directing the government, and that the edict of pacification had been abandoned. Everything pointed to the enthronement of the principles of the counter-reformation as the presiding genius of French domestic policy. Navarre and Condé, who had escaped death, were offered the alternative of the Mass or the Bastille, and the papal legate, the Cardinal Orsini, was on his way to Paris. To make matters worse, hostility to England was beginning to show itself in suspicious movements of the French fleet under Strozzi and the pillaging of English merchants at Rouen and on the high seas. Not all the eloquence of Cicero or Demosthenes, said La Mothe, could obliterate the bad impression created in England by the notorious evidence of the facts. 'I think it less peril', wrote Walsingham, summing up the situation, 'to live with them as enemies than as friends.'

Elizabeth's attitude during the crisis was a curious blend of dignity, restraint, fear, and dissimulation. She could not penetrate the ultimate designs of the French court, for Walsingham found it increasingly difficult, after the massacre, to learn what went on in the council. On the all-important matter of France's relations with the pope and Spain conjecture alone was possible, and, in the circumstances, the worst was apprehended. On the other hand, the conciliatory tone of the king's communications, and his evident desire to retain the goodwill of England, together with the queen mother's hasty revival of the Alençon marriage proposal, seemed to indicate that Walsingham was probably over-severe in his judgements. All things considered, Elizabeth decided to move cautiously in her dealings with France. Distrust must not be allowed to endanger the continuance of amicable relations, nor must the Treaty of Blois be regarded as a dead letter; but at the same time every necessary precaution must be taken to protect England's interests and to render France incapable of doing any harm. The first object was served by retaining Walsingham at his post in Paris, and by the dispatch of the earl of Worcester, in January, to represent Elizabeth at the christening of Charles IX's infant daughter, to whom she had consented to act as godmother. The renewal of the Alençon negotiations, however, was coldly received, it being pointed out by Burghley to La Mothe that no good could come of discussing the question so long as the French government maintained its unsatisfactory attitude to the huguenots.

From Elizabeth's point of view the dangerous position of the huguenots was the crux of the situation. The shock of the massacre had driven the province of Gascony into armed rebellion, and the terrified sectaries were now concentrated in La Rochelle, with nothing to shelter them from their enemies but the walls of the fortress. If they succumbed, England would be deprived of the one effective means she possessed of influencing French policy. To aid them overtly was, of course, impossible if the Treaty of Blois was to be rigidly observed; but to refuse assistance might be more dangerous to England than a breach of the treaty. It was imperative that the French government should be kept busy within its own borders. Elizabeth therefore compromised. Publicly she proclaimed her neutrality: privately she connived at assistance being sent by her subjects; and when La Mothe protested against the activities of the count de Montgommery, the huguenot agent, on English soil, she disclaimed all responsibility and denied that any ship, man, or gun of hers was engaged in the enterprise.

With regard to Scotland, the only really weak point in her armour, where France, if evilly disposed, could do her serious injury, she proceeded more vigorously to work. Here the crucial matter was the strong position of the Marian party in Edinburgh castle and their confident hope that France would rally to their assistance as soon as the huguenots were disposed of. Edinburgh castle was, in effect, England's La Rochelle. For a brief space (September–October) Elizabeth toyed with the idea of destroying the Marian cause altogether by handing over Mary Stuart to Regent Mar, to be tried by process of justice and executed by the Scots themselves. But Mar died in October, and the plan was dropped. Killigrew, who was entrusted by Elizabeth with the negotiation, now applied himself to the task of procuring a settlement by agreement; and in February 1573 he succeeded in inducing Huntly and the Hamiltons, under guarantee of English protection, to make their peace with the new regent, Morton, at Perth. A similar proposal was made to Grange and Lethington at the castle, but it met with a summary refusal, and Elizabeth was reluctantly compelled to authorize the reduction of the fortress by English artillery. On 17 April Drury once more crossed the border at Berwick, his siege-guns being conveyed by ship to Leith. A month later the bombardment began; and on 28 May, disappointed by the failure of France to lend any help, overcome by the intensive artillery fire, and cut off from their only water-supply, the garrison capitulated. Of the gallant defenders, Lethington only survived the surrender by eleven days, and Grange was put to death some months later by order of the regent; but Elizabeth's recommendation to mercy saved the others from reprisals. Thus ended the contest that had raged in Scotland since 1570; and the 'postern gate' that had worried Walsingham was temporarily closed. It was an unexpected result of the turmoil in France, but a happy one for England.

The triumph of Elizabeth's Scottish policy was followed by the failure of Charles IX to subdue the Rochellois. The great huguenot fortress, defended by a desperate population in receipt of continuous help from England and the Netherlands, defied the concentrated might of catholic France; and in July peace was restored by the grant of freedom of conscience to the protestants, with full liberty of worship in the specified *enclaves* of La Rochelle, Montauban, Nîmes, and Sancerre. Now was the king's opportunity to attempt the restoration of Anglo-French relations to their former cordiality, and with this in view he reopened the question of the Alençon marriage. Elizabeth, who made it clear that the oppression of the huguenots was the only serious obstacle in the way, received his advances favourably; with the result that an arrangement was arrived at, in March 1574, whereby Alençon should cross the Channel secretly and meet the queen near Dover.

But the duke had other schemes on hand which wrecked the project. Desirous of playing the leading role in French politics that his brother Anjou had played before him, he had become associated with Montmorency, Navarre, Condé, and Montgommery in a combined movement of catholics and huguenots to force 'politique' doctrines on the court. As a result he involved himself in conspiracy and rebellion and was thrown into the prison of St. Germain along with Montmorency and Navarre. Shortly afterwards Charles IX died (30 May), and the succession passed to Anjou, the 'tyrant from Poland'.[1] As the new king was well known for his fanatical catholicism and his subservience to the clergy and the Guises, it was confidently

---

[1] Anjou had been elected king of Poland in February 1574: his reign lasted only a few months.

expected that his accession would initiate a fresh outburst of religious strife, the abandonment of the league with England, and the championship by France of the counter-reformation in its most aggressive form. The danger was fully realized in England and Germany, and diplomatic pressure was immediately brought to bear on Henry III by Elizabeth and the protestant princes to avert the threatened catastrophe. For nine months the weak-willed king 'floated between the storm and the rock', tormented by his natural desire to follow the counsel of the Guises and the queen mother, but afraid to take a step that would rally protestant Europe to the support of the huguenots. The situation was so menacing that in February 1575 Elizabeth entered into communication with the count palatine about dispatching assistance to Condé. Eventually, however, Henry III ended the period of tension by sending an envoy to England with the news that he was ready to confirm the Treaty of Blois. On St. George's day he was elected to the Order of the Garter at a chapter held at Greenwich, and within a month the league was formally confirmed by both governments. Elizabeth could now rest assured that she had nothing further to fear from France, for the treaty was a guarantee that the French government would not indulge in excesses against the huguenots, and the strength of the huguenots was a guarantee that the treaty would not be overthrown.

Meanwhile the shock of the reaction against France consequent upon the massacre of St. Bartholomew had generated a strong feeling in England in favour of a settlement with Spain. For three years Alva had struggled in vain, interrupted by the foolish plotting of de Spes and Ridolfi with the English catholics, to end the deadlock created by the seizures of 1568-9; but every ambassador he had sent to England—d'Assonleville, Chapin Vitelli, Fiesco, Sweveghem—had returned with the same tale: Elizabeth refused to negotiate unless Spain would agree to bring all the outstanding questions at issue between the two governments within the scope of the settlement. The first indication that a change was coming was given by Burghley in a conversation with Antonio de Guaras, at the time when the league with France was nearing completion. Burghley, whose interest in the Anglo-French alliance was never very keen, stated that a concord between England and Spain was eminently desirable, and might be brought about on the basis of 'the most just restitution of the confiscated property', the reopening of trade, the mutual banishment of rebels, and the confirmation of all the old treaties. It was not, however, until the catastrophic events of the summer opened every one's eyes to the shifty, incalculable, and untrustworthy tactics of the French court that the question entered the field of practical politics. The ill treatment of English merchants in France during the troubles, the insecurity and inadequacy of Rouen as a market in lieu of Antwerp, and the shrinkage of trade converted many others of the privy council, including Leicester, to Burghley's standpoint; and negotiations were begun through Guaras with Madrid and Brussels.

In April 1573 an agreement was reached between Alva and Elizabeth, in virtue of which traffic was restored for a period of two years in order to allow diplomacy to get to work on the economic and political questions involved in the projected settlement. A year later (July 1574) Bernardino de Mendoza arrived in London as representative of the king of Spain, and was given a cordial reception. On 28 August of the same year there followed the Treaty of Bristol, which wound up the matter of the confiscated property by assessing the losses on both sides and striking the balance. The Spanish claim was placed at the net figure of £89,076 and the English at £68,076; thus leaving Spain England's creditor to the extent of £21,000. In the meantime Requesens, who had succeeded Alva during the previous year as governor of the Netherlands, had busied himself with the problems arising out of the navigation of the Scheldt and the banishment of Elizabeth's rebels from the Spanish dominions. Both questions raised difficulties; for Orange and the Dutch, who were at war with the king of Spain and commanded the mouth of the Scheldt, insisted upon controlling the traffic on the river, and the English catholic refugees were anxious about their future and the pensions they received from Spain.

A satisfactory settlement, however, was reached in March 1575. Requesens agreed to banish all English refugees from the Netherlands and to allow English merchants to trade with Antwerp provided they gave their bond not to have any dealings with the Flushingers. He even granted them freedom to practise their religion so long as they did nothing scandalous or derogatory to the established religion of the country. In return, a month later, Elizabeth forbade the prince of Orange, his aiders and abettors, to frequent English ports or her subjects to give them any succour until they returned to the obedience they owed to their natural sovereign. The good relations now established between England and Spain seemed to presage a happier future. They are reflected in the friendly reception accorded to the Spanish fleet which put into Portsmouth, Dartmouth, and the Isle of Wight in October—a marked contrast to the hostile preparations that were made only a few years before, when a similar armament passed along the Channel on its way to the Netherlands.

V

CATHOLIC AND PURITAN

W E have seen that the bulk of the laity found no great difficulty in transferring its allegiance from the old church to the new. The queen, for her part, had made the establishment as comprehensive as possible, taking her stand on the principle that all members of the state were *ipso facto* members of the state church. Consequently, since the existence of dissent was not admitted, there was no persecution; and the first decade of the reign passed away without any serious challenge to the established order. This does not mean, of course, that acquiescence was complete, or that those who clung to the Mass in defiance of the law escaped hardship. Whenever the political heaven became overclouded, by reason of diplomatic tension with Spain, or uncertainty as to the attitude of Rome, the peace of the London catholics was disturbed by domiciliary visits and the rounding up of those who were suspected of celebrating Mass in secret. But these petty vexations, harassing enough to the sufferers, perhaps, cannot be described as persecution, at all events in the sense in which the word was then understood. It was intermittent, variable, and not due to any fixed or deliberate government policy, but rather the result of fluctuations of the political barometer. After ten years had elapsed, however, a number of new and far-reaching influences began to affect the course of events; and the government, confronted with a possible catholic break away, was compelled to modify greatly its attitude to church attendance and the exercise of the old religion.

In the first place must be reckoned the effect of the papal bull of 1570. Pius V, who succeeded to the tiara in the last days of 1565, is generally regarded by his co-religionists as the greatest pope of the counter-reformation period. Unlike his predecessor, Pius IV, he was not a politician, nor did he set much store by the many secular and worldly factors entering into the organization of religion; but he had the gift of leadership in a marked degree, a remorselessly logical and sanguine temperament, and a very clear conception of his duty as head of the catholic church.[1] Originally a Dominican friar trained in the service of the Inquisition, of which he became in due course the supreme officer, he was essentially a medievalist in his mode of life and thought; and when he was promoted to the Holy See, he resolved to cut the gordian knot of the English question in a manner that would have commended itself to Innocent III. The actual circumstances leading to his fateful pronouncement against the queen are not clear, but there can be no doubt that he was strongly influenced by the optimistic reports reaching him from his agents in England and elsewhere as to the rising temper of the northern catholics in the autumn of 1569. He determined to strike while the iron was hot. Without communicating his plan to any secular prince, he opened a process for heresy against Elizabeth at Rome on 5 February 1570. Eight days later sentence was passed, and on the 25th a bull[2] excommunicating and deposing the queen was published by the papal chancery.

So slowly did news travel in those days that Rome was still without authentic tidings, at the moment the bull was released, of the outbreak of the northern rebellion in England three months before. And what is even more striking, the date of the publication of the bull practically coincided with Hunsdon's dramatic defeat of Dacre's men on the banks of the Gelt— a defeat that completed the subjugation of the north to the queen's government. Thus from the standpoint of mere timeliness the pope's action failed to assist the cause it was intended to promote. Another three months were to elapse before a copy of it was smuggled into England and affixed by one John Felton to the door of the bishop of London's palace in Paul's churchyard; and by this time the terroristic measures employed by the government in the disaffected districts had crushed the spirit of the northern catholics.

Historically, a special interest attaches to Pius V's pronouncement. It was the last effort of the papacy to check the progress of the reformation by medieval methods, and its spectacular character turned it into something of a *cause célèbre*. Writers

---

[1] Ranke describes him thus: 'A strange medley of singleness of purpose, loftiness of soul, personal austerity, and entire devotion to religion with grim bigotry, rancorous hatred, and sanguinary zeal for persecution.' (*History of the Popes*, bk. iii, § 8, pp. 361–83.)

[2] Printed *in extenso* in Camden.

have examined not only the grounds on which the pope acted, but also the form and substance of the bull itself, with a minuteness which is probably excessive and unnecessary. It has been shown, for example, that Elizabeth is styled the 'pretended queen of England' (*pretensa Angliae Regina*), as if her right to the crown had never been acknowledged at Rome: whereas both Paul IV and Pius IV had recognized her as queen without qualification. Again, part of the charge on which she was condemned rested on the assumption that she had claimed the supreme headship of the church—a title which, as we have seen, she definitely declined. Furthermore, one of the iniquities imputed to her was the adoption of Calvinism: although she cordially disliked, and continued to dislike, this form of church government. Finally, attention has been drawn to the fact that she was allowed no time for recantation—the excommunication and the sentence of deposition being simultaneous, which was a departure from canonical procedure in regard to the treatment of heretical princes. These and other criticisms seem to point to a certain confusion at Rome as to the real situation in England, and also to undue haste.[1] But when all is said and done, the errors and defects of the papal enactment are of trifling importance compared with the effect it was intended to produce as a sovereign remedy for the English question, and the consequences it drew in its train.

Briefly stated, the bull was directed to the achievement of a twofold result. In the first place, by declaring the queen excommunicate and deposed, it aimed at destroying the allegiance of her subjects. In the second place, by coupling all who continued to obey her laws and mandates in the same anathema,[2] it not only legalized rebellion but, by implication, positively commanded it. Thus to every one who in his heart respected the authority of the Holy See, the bull must have come as an ultimatum, ordering him to choose between his conscience and his political obligation. The dual obedience and the tacit compromise of conscience, on which the vast majority of catholics in England had hitherto acted, was for ever destroyed, and in its place was restored the duty of unqualified allegiance to the church of Rome. Theoretically, also, the sentence of

---

[1] For a full discussion of the subject see Meyer, *England and the Catholic Church under Queen Elizabeth*, pp. 78–83.

[2] 'Qui secus egerint, eos simili anathematis sententia innodamus.'

excommunication involved the severance of all diplomatic and commercial relations with the doomed country, whose ruin would be completed by the invading army of any catholic power that felt itself strong enough to act as executor of the papal will.

Normally, then, the bull ought to have stricken the queen and her protestant subjects with dismay. And if the world had moved at the bidding of Pius V as it had done at Innocent III's, the result might have been disastrous enough. Caught between the fire of rebellion at home and the advancing tide of invasion from abroad the Elizabethan government would have been in a parlous position. But in reality there was little likelihood of either event taking place. The only disaffected catholics in England had already shot their bolt in the winter of 1569–70, and the rest remained outwardly at least quiescent. On the other hand, the interested catholic powers on the Continent betrayed no inclination to shoulder the unenviable task of making war on England. On the contrary, both the king of Spain and the emperor Maximilian II were astonished and angry at the pope for not consulting them before he proceeded to extreme measures, and they branded his action as a political blunder, protesting to the queen that they had no hand in it. Maximilian, in fact, made an unavailing effort to get the bull rescinded. In England the reception of the news that the queen was excommunicated and deposed varied greatly among the different individuals and classes affected by it. Elizabeth, it was said, displayed her indifference by inditing some Latin verses scoffing at the papal authority, and saying that no ship of Peter would enter her ports. In certain protestant circles, however, the position was regarded as dangerous in the extreme, and the pulpits resounded with appeals to patriotism and adjurations to both catholics and protestants to rally to the queen's support 'lest we all go together and row in the galleys of Spain'. Cecil, according to the Spanish ambassador, began to think of flight! Bishop Jewel, on the other hand, attacked the pope as a foolish Balaam, whose curses could not harm the people of God. 'O vain man!' exclaimed the worthy prelate: 'as if the coasts and ends of the earth were in his hands, or as if no prince in the world might rule without his sufferance.' The coarse jest and the vulgar lampoon supplied an outlet for the pent-up feelings of others; and pamphlets appeared ridiculing the 'bull of Bashan', 'the monster bull that roared at my lord bishop's gate', &c. In short, nothing was too scurrilous to say about the pope's folly.

Nevertheless the government resolved to leave nothing to chance. A vigilant watch was kept on the ports for papal emissaries and the importation of seditious books: the movements of the Spanish fleet were shadowed; and all catholics in England were regarded with suspicion, as people in whom the principles of sedition were, so to speak, in suspension and ready to be deposited whenever a favourable moment arrived. In 1571 a statute was passed (13 Eliz., cap. 1) by which it was declared to be high treason to affirm that Elizabeth was not, or ought not to be, queen: that any other person ought to be queen during her lifetime; or that she was a heretic, schismatic, tyrant, infidel, or usurper of the Crown.[1] Since the main question at issue, from the government's standpoint, was one of jurisdiction rather than of religion—namely, the maintenance of national sovereignty against the 'false, usurped, and alien authority of Rome'—stress was laid on the fact that to reconcile the queen's subjects to Rome was to withdraw them from their natural and due allegiance, to create sedition, and to connive at the overthrow of the state. Hence it was made a treasonable offence to introduce and 'put in ure' papal bulls and instruments of absolution and reconciliation, or to act in accordance with them (13 Eliz., cap. 2). By the same act the importation of *Agnus Dei*'s, crosses, beads, pictures, and other gear from beyond the sea was brought under the pains and penalties of the statute of *Praemunire*. By a further enactment (13 Eliz., cap. 3) confiscation of property was decreed against all who had fled abroad without permission since the beginning of the reign and refused to return within a year.

For the moment, however, the only effect of the bull so far as the catholics in England were concerned was a certain 'frowardness' and 'stubbornness' in the matter of church attendance. Recusancy, or deliberate abstention from the anglican service, made its appearance as a phenomenon to be reckoned with in the national life.

I wis, I wis, [cried Dr. Overton of East Grinstead] there are many cursed calves of Basan abroad, which, since they have sucked

---

[1] Some members of the house of commons were in favour of extending the act by introducing a provision excluding the queen of Scots from the succession; but Elizabeth rejected this severity.

the bull that came from Rome, have given over all obedience and allegiance to God and the queen; for before that time they could be content to come to the church and hear sermons and to receive the sacraments, and to use the common prayer with the rest of the congregation of Christ, and so forth. They were conformable in all respects, and content to do anything that beseemed good christians to do; but since they sucked that mad bull, they are become even as brainsick calves, froward, stubborn, disobedient in word and deed, not to be led nor ordered by any reason.[1]

Something more, however, was needed to awaken the English catholics from their lethargy and to drive them out of the establishment in considerable numbers; and this was supplied by the missionary efforts of priests from the Continent. Shortly before the publication of the bull, an English college was set up at Douai (1568) by William Allen—himself a refugee—to provide a rallying-point for the scattered bands of catholics who had fled from their native land for conscience' sake, together with educational facilities for the young. The success of the scheme and the enthusiasm it evoked led its promoter to the conviction that something might be done by its agency towards the revival of the old faith in England. Thus, from being merely an asylum for refugees, Douai rapidly became the centre of a great missionary effort to wrest England from the grasp of heresy.

Accepting only youths of from fourteen to twenty-five years of age, of respectable family,[2] the college supplied them with an excellent education based on the curriculum of the jesuit schools. The key-note to the system of instruction was given in the vow taken by the novice shortly after entrance: 'I swear to Almighty God that I am ready and shall always be ready to receive holy orders, in His own good time, and I shall return to England for the salvation of souls, whenever it shall seem good to the superior of this college to order me to do so.' With this self-dedicatory motto for their inspiration, the youths who entered the seminary bent their energies to a seven years' study of theology, philosophy, dialectic, and the history of the English church, under the severest bodily and mental discipline then known. But at the same time as they were trained to co-operate in the struggle for dogmatic mastery over protestantism, they were also

[1] J. O. W. Haweis, *Sketches of the Reformation* . . . *taken from the Contemporary Pulpit* (1844), pp. 193–4.
[2] 'Non ex faece hominum . . . sed nobilibus plerumque orti familiis.'

nurtured in the idea that the apotheosis of the religious life was martyrdom, to die, if need be, for England. The walls of their rooms were hung with pictures of torture-chambers and the glory of Christ's sacrifice: prayer, meditation, and seclusion were carefully provided for in the daily routine; and everything was done to concentrate the mind of the neophyte on that 'glorious conquest of human nature' which was deemed necessary for the success of his mission. Self was extinguished by the overpowering belief that God had saved them from the disasters overtaking their country in order to make them instrumental in saving others. Without a doubt no body of missionaries ever set about their task with a deeper conviction of the majesty of the cause for which they contended. So popular did the calling become, in spite of its dangers, or perhaps in virtue of them, that the English government grew alarmed at the numbers fleeing overseas, and instituted heavy penalties to check the stream. But it was in vain: the movement spread from Douai to other centres, like Rome (1579), Valladolid (1589), Seville (1592); and the colleges could hardly cope with the influx of students.

There is no reason to suppose—indeed the evidence is conclusively against such a supposition—that political aims entered into Allen's scheme, or that the priests who enlisted under his banner were other than they professed to be, crusaders for the catholic faith. The *via dolorosa* that led from Douai to Tyburn could not have been trod by men who were not profoundly imbued with the spiritual character of their work. But the fact that the pope and the Spanish king were the chief patrons of the colleges afforded a strong presumption against the alleged innocence of the missionaries. It was difficult to disconnect the seminary movement from the avowed policy of Pius V, or to avoid the conclusion that under the guise of saving souls the priests were really acting as executors of the bull. Moreover, even if the mission was devoted to exclusively religious ends, the law, as we have seen, made it treason to reconcile the queen's subjects to Rome. Consequently, when they began operations in England, in 1574, the unfortunate priests walked straight into the trap which circumstances had prepared for them. The very word 'seminarist' came to mean in common parlance 'conspirator'. Nevertheless their ministrations gave a great impetus to the growth of recusancy. By 1580 there were a hundred seminary priests working in England.

The third influence affecting the attitude of the Romanists came into play after Gregory XIII succeeded Pius V in the chair of St. Peter (1572). The latter part of the period covered by Gregory's pontificate (1579–85) is the most dramatic, if not the most critical, in the conflict between the English government and the forces of the counter-reformation. The new pope was as great a believer in coercive methods as his predecessor. He took his stand unflinchingly on the bull of 1570, professed supreme contempt for policies that truckled to worldly considerations, and gave himself to the advancement of the campaign against the 'Jezebel' of England with all the vigour of his fiery nature. His confidence in the strength of the catholic cause was unbounded. Daily he saw the sword of the counter-reformation driven deeper and deeper into Europe, and it seemed to him that a few more resolute blows shrewdly administered would give him the mastery of England. The destruction of Elizabeth and all her works was the master purpose of his life. The great pope Gregory I had been the instrument of England's conversion from heathenism a thousand years before: the rescue of England from heresy would be the crowning glory of his sixteenth-century namesake.

As a man of action Gregory had many admirable qualities— optimism, initiative, concentration of thought, unquenchable zeal; but he was strangely ignorant of the complexity of international affairs, and hopelessly failed to combine his actions in one coherent plan. His schemes for the overthrow of Elizabeth were confused, impulsive, self-contradictory, and lacking in that steady purpose which is the essence of statesmanship. Every weapon that ingenuity could devise he pressed into his service without scruple, and with an almost criminal disregard of consequences. Nor was he helped but rather hindered by his secretary of state, the cardinal of Como, whose rashness in the field of action was even more pronounced than his master's.[1]

Gregory's main contribution to the solution of the English question was his patronage of the jesuit mission, which materialized at Rome during the winter of 1579–80, and began operations in England the following summer. Substantially there was little difference between this mission and that of the

---

[1] J. H. Pollen (*The English Catholics in the Reign of Elizabeth*) describes him as a shallow, imprudent man, with little of that traditional caution for which papal diplomacy is generally distinguished.

seminarists. The instructions with which the leaders were provided (April 1580) make it clear that the object aimed at was
the 'preservation and augmentation of the faith of the catholics
in England': they were not to have any political contact with
heretics, to speak, or to allow others in their presence to speak,
against the queen, or to correspond with Rome on political
matters. But a certain discretionary power, to be used with the
utmost caution, was granted them in regard to political conversations with 'those whose fidelity has been long and stead-
fast'. It is impossible to say how far, if at all, this permissive
clause in the instructions, which ran counter to the whole tenor
of the mission, was used or abused during the first year of its
existence. But the good faith of Rome need not be questioned;
for the clause was withdrawn in 1581, and the conditional prohibition of politics was made an absolute prohibition. On the
other hand, the fact that the original instructions fell into the
hands of Burghley enabled him to brand the enterprise as a
disingenuous attempt to destroy the queen's government under
the guise of saving souls.

But this was not all. The mission was dogged from the first
moment of its appearance by unfortunate accompaniments. In
his desire to meet the grievances of the English catholics, who
had long been complaining of the intolerable position thrust
upon them by Pius V's action in 1570, Gregory issued an
Explanatio (April 1580), which he entrusted to the jesuits to
publish in England. It was to the effect that, while the policy
of the Holy See remained in principle unchanged, and the bull
must be regarded as still operative against Elizabeth and the
heretics, it did not bind catholics except when public execution
of the said bull should become possible. The pope's intention was
obviously not to establish peace with the English government,
for that could only be done by a complete withdrawal of his
predecessor's enactment—an impossible supposition in any case
—but to proclaim a truce for an indefinite period, thereby
saving the catholics in England from the formal imputation of
treason, unless, of course, an overt act could be proved against
them. But as a matter of fact the *Explanatio* produced quite the
reverse effect. It increased the suspicion with which the jesuits
were regarded by the government, and afforded Burghley
stronger grounds for the accusation he brought against them.

A further blow was struck at the mission by the pope himself on the very eve of its departure from Rome. For many years Gregory had been urging the need for an expedition against England, either in the shape of a direct attack from Spanish Flanders or indirectly through Ireland. His efforts to give this *empresa* (enterprise), as it was called in the papal documents of the time, a concrete embodiment in men, money, and ships were warmly supported by his cardinal secretary, by papal nuncios like Ormanetto in Madrid, by leading English catholic exiles who longed to return to their native country, and by swashbucklers like Thomas Stukeley, who was prepared to sell his sword to any man for any cause.

This remarkable man was a knight of Ilfracombe in north Devon, who had changed sides several times during the Tudor period, and had grown rich on the plunder of churches and monasteries. He was a gambler and a spendthrift by nature, whose word was not to be trusted. But his strange career seems to have run through the whole gamut of almost unbelievable experiences—from soldiering with the armies of England, France, and Spain to fighting with Don John in the naval battle of Lepanto; from piracy to legacy hunting; from floating a company to explore and settle Florida to 'purchasing' the office of marshal of the Irish army from Sir Nicholas Bagenal—without defraying the cost of either; but so plausible was he in his roguery that he turned deception into a fine art. Lord Burghley, Sir Henry Sidney, and King Philip of Spain fell victims to his wiles, and doubtless many others. When England became too hot for him, he set sail for Spain to offer his services as a crusader for catholicism, an embittered enemy of England, which he never wanted to see again. His head swarmed with ideas and plans, mostly fantastic, for the invasion of his native land, the liberation of Mary Stuart, the overthrow of Elizabeth, and the establishment of Don John on the throne. In short, he was the type who could worm his way into even the papal good graces.

But Pope Gregory was at the moment confronted with a veritable tangle of difficulties. He wanted to stop the Turk in the Mediterranean and hold him at bay, by bringing France and Spain together in a holy phalanx of the church. He also wanted to destroy Elizabethan England as the chief enemy to the peace of Europe; and at the same time he was prepared to move heaven and earth to get the duke of Anjou married to a

Spanish princess. But neither France nor Spain was prepared to move by directives from Rome. France had just made the Treaty of Blois with England, and was now swinging into the English orbit of diplomacy; and Spain was troubled with a host of problems stretching from Morocco to the Low Countries, which made her exceedingly anxious not to antagonize Elizabeth. Altogether the pope was in no position to organize an *empresa* against England, lacking the full support of Spain and France.

Cardinal Como, however, refused to be pessimistic. He took Stukeley into his confidence, brought the pope round to his own point of view, and informed the nuncio at Madrid that if the king was not willing to be openly associated with the coming attack on England, the Holy See would take the responsibility at least in the initial stages; but Spain would have to provide the hard cash. Progress was held up by the outbreak of turmoil in the Netherlands, the sacking of Antwerp, the mutiny of the Spanish troops. But in the spring of 1577, Como determined to push on with the Stukeley plan regardless of the difficulties and dangers. On 12 April 1577 he drafted a letter to Don John, outlining his ideas and urging support. The crucial passage runs thus: 'Although your Highness should discover difficulty in the said enterprise, you should see the need for at least thinking of supporting an "Orange" on the flanks of that wicked woman [i.e. Elizabeth], to harass her and wear her out as Orange has worn us out; and such an "Orange" would be Stukeley, who with a few ships and a few troops would be able in this case to do great things.' Pope Gregory, however, had a brighter idea. Perhaps Don John's troops, who would soon be evacuating Flanders in accord with the 'Pacification' agreement of February 1577, might be available for a swift and unexpected descent upon the English coast—provided they were evacuated by sea. In the event, however, thanks to the states-general and the alertness of the English government, the ruse was detected and destroyed: the Spaniards were ordered to leave the country by the land route. Thus Como's scheme stood fast, and preparations were made for the Stukeley naval enterprise.

The outcome was ludicrous in the extreme. The so-called fleet, which sailed from Civita Vecchia in the spring of 1578, consisted of one ship, six hundred 'choice' men, and arms and munitions for another 3,000: these were the paper figures. But actually, no more dilapidated, ill-conceived, and badly fitted ship ever left the coast of Europe than that for the Irish enterprise. It carried four small guns, one of them being a Turkish saker, and another discharging stone missiles; and the victuals put aboard were calculated to last until Marseilles! 'The ship lacks everything', was the comment of the captain; and he was probably right. The crew mutinied before the voyage began. And Stukeley informed Como from Porto Palamos: 'As the ship is very ill-furnished with gear, and the timbers are weak and ill-caulked, I shall be compelled, as soon as I find a safe port, which will perhaps be Lisbon, to land the soldiers and refit the ship with timbers, ropes, and gear and sails, and have her well caulked, as otherwise she runs a risk of going all to pieces in the sea.'

After a 'terrible' voyage, Stukeley managed to reach the port of Lisbon with a ship 'totally unfit' to proceed farther. There the Odyssey came to an end so far as the crew were concerned; but King Sebastian came to the rescue of the now disillusioned Stukeley. He was about to lead an army to Moorish Africa, and it took little persuasion to enlist the Englishman, whose career came to a sanguinary end at Alcazar, where he died at the hands of the Moors.

With the subsequent history of this grotesque and ill-starred expedition—the desertion of Stukeley at Lisbon, the reorganization of the enterprise by the papal nuncio in Spain, the rebel Irishman James Fitzmaurice Fitzgerald, and Dr. Nicholas Sanders, and its final destruction at Smerwick by the English under Lord Grey—we need not at present concern ourselves.[1] The important fact to be grasped is its relation to, and reaction on, the jesuit mission in England. Thanks to Stukeley's bravadoes, which had been circulated in every port of call between Italy and Lisbon, the news that the pope was at war with England percolated to all European countries months before Campion and Persons left Rome on their journey to London. Is it to be wondered at that the two jesuits were much perplexed at the ill-timed action of the pope which exposed not only their own

---

[1] There is no authoritative biography of Stukeley, but reference should be made to the *Dict. of Nat. Biog.*; to Z. N. Brooke's article in *Eng. Hist. Rev.* xxviii. 330–7; and to Pollen's in the *Month*, ci. 69–85; cf. also R. Simpson, *The School of Shakespeare* (1878). See also chapter xii, below.

lives but also the whole future of their mission to imminent and dire peril? 'We plainly foresaw', wrote Persons on 31 May 1580, 'that this would be taken in England as though we had been privy or partakers thereof, as in very truth we were not, nor ever heard or suspected the same until this day.' Thus if the original instructions of 1580 compromised the jesuits deeply in the eyes of the English government, the coincidence of their arrival in London with the *empresa* against Ireland placed them in a still more sinister light, and gave colour to the belief entertained by most protestants that they were the advance guard of the main onslaught on England which, it was believed, the catholic powers might at any moment decide to launch.

Confusion could hardly be worse confounded when, in addition to sanctioning the 'Irish enterprise', the pope grasped at a still more doubtful weapon against Elizabeth, political assassination. The lawfulness of tyrannicide was much discussed at this time in Europe by both catholic and protestant writers; but the only example of its use by a responsible authority was in 1580, when the king of Spain outlawed William of Orange and put a price on his head. Unfortunately there can be no doubt that Gregory XIII was also a disciple of the doctrine, or that he advocated its use against the queen. Two plotters who were racked and executed in England in 1581 and 1584, Anthony Tyrrell and Dr. Parry, confessed that they had undertaken the murder of Elizabeth under promise of a plenary indulgence. But the decisive proof that they did not confess more than the truth is to be found in a letter written (December 1580) by the cardinal secretary, Como, to the papal nuncio, Sega, at Madrid. The letter was in answer to a question addressed by the latter to the pope at the instigation of two English nobles, who, having entered into an agreement to take the queen's life, desired to know if they would thereby incur sin. They wanted to be assured on this point because the deed might cost them their lives. The reply was clear and decisive.

Since that guilty woman of England [writes the papal secretary] rules over two such noble kingdoms of Christendom and is cause of so much injury to the Catholic faith, and loss of so many million souls, there is no doubt that whosoever sends her out of the world with the pious intention of doing God service, not only does not sin but gains merit, especially having regard to the sentence pronounced against her by Pius V of holy memory. And so if these English nobles decide actually to undertake so glorious a work, your lordship can assure them that they do not commit any sin.[1]

Thus, if Pius made assassination lawful by his bull of excommunication, Gregory positively encouraged it. Clearly he was not above his age, but rather deeply immersed in it. In his impetuous desire to make an end of heresy in England, he virtually cast aside the moral weapon—to the best catholics, the only legitimate weapon with which to combat heresy—and dragged the cause of religion in the mire. Fortunately the vast bulk of the catholic priests, engaged in the attempt to recover England for the faith, believed in moral heroism. But the rash action of the head of the church seriously compromised them in their single-minded work.

Under these unhappy auspices the jesuit campaign was begun. The two men selected by the general of the jesuits for command of the expedition, Edmund Campion[2] and Robert Persons,[3] were remarkably diverse in character, temperament, and genius. Englishmen both and Oxford bred, they were at one only in the enthusiasm and loyalty with which they embraced the perils of the journey to England. Campion was the *beau sabreur* of spiritual gladiators—a radiant figure, whose nonchalance in the face of danger won for him an imperishable renown among his followers, and a high place in the gallery of great Elizabethans. His saintliness, transparent sincerity, and glowing rhetoric were infectious, and it was largely through his ministrations that catholicism in England rose to the heights of heroism it reached during the 'eighties. Many a time he owed escape from death to the deep affection in which he was held by the populace; and to the very end he protested the non-political and essentially spiritual nature of his mission. 'We are dead men to the world,' he cried on the scaffold: 'we travelled only for souls; we touched neither state nor policy: we had no such commission.'

Of Persons, his coadjutor and immediate superior in the enterprise, it is impossible to speak with the same assurance and lack of reserve. His was a subtle and complex character.

[1] Meyer, op. cit., p. 271.
[2] For Campion's life see R. Simpson, *Edmund Campion* (Catholic Standard Library).
[3] There is no complete biography of Persons, but the *Dict. of Nat. Biog.* should be consulted, also Persons's 'Memoirs', ed. Pollen (*Cath. Rec. Soc. Misc.* ii), and *Letters and Memorials of Father Robert Persons, S.J.* (Catholic Record Soc., 1942, ed. Leo Hicks, S.J.) especially the admirable Introduction.

Gifted with a trenchant personality, he had all the qualities—resourcefulness, perseverance, foresight—that show the man of action rather than the saint or the pastor. His mind never ran on small things; and it is more than likely that the general of the order marked him down from the very first as too valuable a man to be 'expended' in the narrow field of the English mission. His remarkable talent for organization quickly raised him to the forefront of the counter-reformation. Nevertheless, there is plenty of evidence to show that Persons's sympathy lay with the men who served as the 'shock troops' of the church, in the front line of battle. In a letter to the general on 12 November 1583, he made the following confession: 'A slight feeling of sadness arises at times when I consider how many, indeed nearly all, of my comrades who set out together with me on this work [their number was thirteen] have attained their reward, or are still undergoing their contest, whilst I alone am left out for my sins.'

When he escaped from the clutches of the government pursuivants after Campion's execution, and settled in Rouen, he was careful to point out that it was not fear of martyrdom that drove him abroad, but grim necessity (1) to establish a closer connexion with Allen and the missionaries at Rheims; (2) to set up an overseas printing press, beyond the reach of the English government, for the supply of propaganda—controversial, educational, and devotional; (3) to prepare and organize the 'onslaught' on Scotland, which was now regarded as the only possible gateway to success in England; and (4) to persuade and urge the French king to exercise his influence in favour of the suffering English catholics. Thus did Persons drift towards politics; and although professional diplomatists like Mendoza, the Spanish ambassador in London, gravely doubted his capacity or trustworthiness 'in matters of state', he quickly established himself as a kind of factotum, counsellor, and confidant of all the queen's enemies. Everyone consulted him—the pope, the duke of Guise, Philip II of Spain—as the best informed man on the subject of English affairs. His consuming ambition was to be the instrument *par excellence* for the overthrow of the Elizabethan state; and to this end he spent—and wasted—much of his time in prodding on the slow-moving, procrastinating Spaniard to war with England.

But we must not anticipate events. The mission began its work with the so-called 'Synod of Southwark', where the two jesuits clarified the purpose of their coming before a select group of 'old' priests and laymen, and at the same time settled the vexed question of church attendance by catholics. On the first point they declared that, by their oaths and protestations made before God and their consciences, they came to England 'apostolically'—only to treat of matters of religion, and to attend to the winning of souls, 'without knowledge or intention in the realm of state affairs'; and on the second point, they demolished the widespread belief that catholics might obey the law about attendance at Anglican services, without detriment to their souls and without censure, thereby escaping the fine for non-attendance. It was made perfectly clear by the two jesuits that no papal dispensation was to be expected on so vital a matter. In short, there was to be no more easy 'compromise of conscience': on the contrary, war against the establishment was to be the order of the day. Campion then drew up his manifesto known as the 'Challenge' for the privy council, and Persons wrote a lengthier *Confessio Fidei* for the London magistrates. The documents run on similar lines; but that of Persons is perhaps the more vigorous. 'You are persecuting a corporation', he says, 'that will never die, and sooner will your hearts and hands, sated with blood, fail you, than there will be lacking men eminent for virtue and learning, who will be sent by this Society and allow their blood to be shed by you for this cause.' He goes on to explain that, contrary to what their adversaries say, they were to do nothing more than their comrades were doing in other parts of the world, viz. 'to teach those Christians who will receive us, the rudiments of the catholic faith, and to make their habits conform to the most holy commandments of God'. Both documents challenge the clergy of the Anglican church to a debate on doctrine and taunt them with their confident anticipation of victory.

The two missioners then set out: Persons to make a circuit of the counties of Northampton, Derby, Worcester, and Gloucester, and Campion to tackle Berkshire and Oxford, and later when he became the most sought after man in England, to focus on the north and north-west—Lancashire and Yorkshire. 'We passed', says Persons, 'through most of the shires of England, preaching and administering the sacraments in almost every gentleman and nobleman's house that we passed by, whether he himself were a catholic or no, if he had any catholics in the house.' Mass was celebrated and communion given either in the early morning or at dead of night. Of course the strain was considerable on both the missionaries and those who harboured them. The astonishing thing is that in spite of the government spies, intelligencers, and pursuivants the mission managed to survive so long as it did. Persons gives a lively picture of what happened.

Sometimes [he writes] when we are sitting at table quite cheerfully conversing familiarly about matters of faith or piety . . . if it happens that someone rings at the front door a little insistently, so that it can be put down as an official; immediately like deer that have heard the voice of hunters and prick their ears and become alert, all stand to attention, stop eating and commend themselves to God in the briefest of prayers: no word or sound is heard until the servants report what is the matter; and if it turns out that there is no danger of the scare they have had, they become still more cheerful.

That considerable success was achieved may be gathered from the remarks of a Lancashire J.P., who apparently found himself taxed beyond his power: 'We strive in vain', he says; 'we hoped that these papistical priests [i.e. the priests of the old régime] dying, all papistry should have died and ended with them, but this brood [the seminarists and jesuits] will never be rooted out: it is impossible . . . to extirpate the papistical faith out of the land.' He spoke too pessimistically perhaps; for the net closed round Campion and Persons—to such an extent that Campion was trapped on 17 July 1581, and shortly afterwards Persons fled overseas to Rouen.

Yet the purely personal work of winning souls, confuting errors, reforming sinners, and 'crying alarm spiritual against foul vice and proud ignorance', great as it was, was not sufficient in itself: literature was necessary to help in upbuilding converts and supplying the mental and spiritual needs of those who could not be reached by a personal visit. Hence the idea of a secret printing-press arose and took shape in 1581. It was a matter of extreme difficulty to arrange, because the government was fully alive to the dangers of a catholic press, while the supervision of literature was in the hands of the bishop of London, and the stationers' company controlled the presses. Every week the various printing-houses in the capital were visited: every one was known, and the type it used; and outside London the luxury of a press was limited to Oxford and Cambridge. Yet in spite of the difficulties, the new catholic press was set up—first in 'a suitable house' at Greenstreet some six or seven miles from London, and later, when the government got on its track, in Stonor Park at Henley-on-Thames. Workmen dressed up in gentlemen's attire, with ruffs, cocked hats, and swords supplied the necessary camouflage; but the scheme had a short life if a merry one. While it lasted, books were printed, marked 'Douai' to mislead the government, and carried by night to London, where they were packed in smaller bundles and dispatched to Oxford and Cambridge, or colported even farther afield among the catholic population. In the morning, so to speak, scholars and laymen, town and gown, awoke to find the new propaganda on the breakfast table.

But the experiment lasted only a year. Its migrations would make a subject in itself: here it must suffice to say that the flight of Persons, who had taken a lion's share in the work, and the subsequent dispersal of the company, ended the venture. Nevertheless, in its short life, it had accomplished the task of beginning the counter-offensive and showing the catholic population who avidly drank this 'water of Bethlehem' that all was not lost. Two influential books, or pamphlets, were published— Campion's *Decem Rationes*, and Persons's *Brief Discours contayning certayn Reasons why Catholiques refuse to go to church*—before the end came. Meanwhile the indefatigable jesuit turned to the organization of the *empresa*, and for the next few years became a political agent pure and simple.

'Book-running' from the Continent was easier to organize than printing under the eyes of the queen. And when Persons fled, he devoted much of his time to developing this branch of activity from the safer vantage-ground of Rouen. Thus the infiltration of 'seditious and papistical literature' into England received a new stimulus from the energy of the fugitive jesuit. Boxes of books, printed at the seminaries and continental presses, were brought over under the guise of general cargo, and landed at remote places on the coast. Thence they were taken by an army of receivers and distributed to London and other centres.

One of the most daring of the band of professional 'book-runners' was a certain Ralph Emerson, who came over from France in the company of Father Weston, with a considerable package of books 'and other blest things of importance'. It was his last journey. They landed in 'broad daylight' on the 'open coast' of Norfolk, at a point 'between two ports'. Weston went on to London, leaving the intrepid Ralph to manage the transit of the baggage to the capital. After his departure, Emerson got his books conveyed up the river to Norwich, 'where the carriers take the goods and merchandise to London'. Unfortunately the package was delayed for inspection at an inn; and Ralph, fearing the worst, continued his journey without it. When he arrived at the address in London given him by the priest, without the invaluable gear, a hurried conference was held as to what to do. It was cowardice, they thought, to abandon the books, and yet 'to cling to them and redeem them was full of peril'. The upshot was that Ralph went back, was arrested, brought before a magistrate, and thrown into prison, where he remained for a year or more; and 'no one could tell where he had been taken'.

The career of Emerson is typical of many another, and shows the perils to which the traffic in illicit books was exposed.

Naturally the intensification of the catholic campaign by seminarist and jesuit caused the government the liveliest anxiety; and in order to meet the impending, or probable, dangers the penal laws were greatly amplified and strengthened. Recusancy, which hitherto was punished by a fine of 1s. per Sunday, in accordance with the provision of the Act of Uniformity, was now (23 Eliz., cap. 1) subjected to the relatively enormous fine of £20 per month, and at the same time the offender had to be bound by two securities for his good behaviour with a £200 guarantee. Saying or singing Mass, again, was punishable with a fine of 200 marks[1] and a year's imprisonment, while 'hearing' Mass 'willingly' entailed the forfeiture of 100 marks and the same term of imprisonment. Since the collection of recusancy fines now became a matter of difficulty, the new law had to be reinforced a few years later by a further enactment (28 & 29 Eliz., cap. 6), which provided that if a recusant failed to meet the exactions laid upon him, the Crown might 'seize and enjoy' his goods and chattels, and two-thirds of his lands and tenements, leaving only one-third for the maintenance of the individual, his wife, and family. By another enactment (23 Eliz., cap. 11) the utterance of seditious or slanderous rumours in defamation of the queen was made punishable by the pillory, mutilation (loss of both ears), and

---

[1] The English 'mark' was worth 13s. 4d.

a fine of £200 for the first offence, and a felon's death for the second; while the publishing of a seditious book, or prophesying the queen's death, or forecasting the name of her successor, was also branded as a felonious offence. By the act already alluded to (23 Eliz., cap. 1) all priests who sought to withdraw the queen's subjects from their natural obedience, or to withdraw them 'for that intent' from the religion by law established, were to be adjudged traitors, and their proselytes with them. Thus, to become a catholic was a much more serious offence than to be a catholic; for whereas the latter offence was commutable for a monetary fine, the former could only result in the death of the culprit. The severity of the government towards the priests probably reached its climax in the act (27 Eliz., cap. 11) which ordered all jesuits, seminary priests, and other priests to leave the country within forty days on pain of death for high treason, their aiders and abettors being threatened with a charge of felony. English students residing abroad in the seminaries were ordered by the same act to return, and take the oath of supremacy, under penalty for default of being declared traitors. Then came the last enactment in the Elizabethan penal code against catholics, the statute of 1593. This measure (35 Eliz., cap. 2) struck heavily at popish recusants who 'wander and shift' about the country, and 'seduce and corrupt' the queen's subjects. All such, being above the age of sixteen years, were ordered to repair to their normal place of abode, and not henceforth remove above five miles from it, under pain of forfeiture of goods, chattels, and land: if too poor to have confiscable goods and lands, the only option was to abjure the realm. By the same enactment, suspected jesuit or seminarist priests, who refused to answer when questioned, were to be imprisoned without bail or mainprise until they made true answer.

The application of these laws constitutes the bulk of the 'persecution' attributed to the Elizabethan government, and we must see what it amounted to. First, however, let it be understood that under whatever guise the issue appears, not only the reformation settlement in England but also the safety of the state was at stake. It was a life-and-death struggle, in which both parties—the medieval catholic church and the English government—were endeavouring to crush each other to powder. That being so, it was natural that the apologists for the state should represent the conflict as political. Those who suffered, said Burghley, did so, not because they believed in transubstantiation or upheld the Mass, but because they were traitors and sedition-mongers. But the catholic priests, on whom fell the burden and heat of the day, were just as convinced that they were martyrs for their faith. Therein lies the profound pathos of this terrible time. Up to a point both were right; but when the whole sweep of the controversy is taken into account, it becomes clear that neither was wholly right. So long as loyalty to the state was interpreted in terms of loyalty to the anglican church, and loyalty to the Roman church involved acceptance of the papal bull, there could be no separation between politics and religion. Moreover, the confusion of religion and politics made it impossible for impartial justice to be administered. Juries were biased, judges were convinced that every priest was a traitor, and convictions were often obtained on evidence supplied by men of worthless character—renegades, spies, and informers—who throve on their nefarious trade. In fact, all the conditions incidental to a reign of terror prevailed. The innocent suffered with the guilty. Nor was it always a question of proving an overt act against an accused person: the opinion he held on such matters as the legality of the pope's power to excommunicate and depose the queen, or the validity of the lay supremacy over the church, or what side he would take in the event of an invasion by a catholic power, was regarded as sufficient warranty for his punishment. Doubtless the government had a right to be informed on these points, particularly the last; but in extracting the information, with the help of torture, and with the hideous penalty for treason lurking in the background, it introduced a system of judicial inquiry as bad as that practised by the Spanish Inquisition, which it professed to abhor. Consciences were racked as well as bodies. The majority of priests who suffered death, died not because they were proved guilty of conspiracies—that was the exception rather than the rule—but because they held opinions that were considered dangerous to the existence of the state—opinions, moreover, from which they could not dissociate themselves without ceasing to be catholics. At the same time, we must remember the abnormal conditions prevailing in the political world, when tyrannicide was sanctioned not only by political thinkers but also by the head of the catholic church, when the queen's life was believed to be in danger from fanatics, and when England was in daily fear of a Spanish invasion. The fairest criticism that can be passed is to say that both parties to the conflict were the victims of a tragic dilemma, from which there seems to have been no escape but by the shedding of blood on the one side, and by self-sacrifice on the other.

The heroism of the priests cannot be denied. Strange as it may seem, they were the real gainers by the ordeal through which they passed. The moral stature of men like Campion and Southwell has won them a place among the truly great. On the eve of his execution, the latter wrote to a friend at Rome: 'We have sung the canticles of the Lord in a strange land, and in this desert we have sucked honey from the rocks and oil from the hard stone. . . . It seems to me that I see the beginning of a religious life set on foot in England, of which we now sow the seeds with tears, that others hereafter may with joy carry in the sheaves to the heavenly granaries.' Campion's death produced a whole cycle of poems, some of which rise to the level of literature:

> God knows it is not force nor might,
> Nor war, nor warlike band,
> Nor shield and spear, nor dint of sword,
> That must convert the land:
> It is the blood of martyrs shed,
> It is that noble train,
> That fights with word and not with sword,
> And Christ their capitaine.

A movement that produced poetry, and could reach such heights of moral and spiritual sublimity, was representative of many of the best elements in the nation. On the other hand, those who plied the penal laws did not escape scatheless from the ordeal to which they subjected their victims. From Walsingham to Topcliffe, the rack-master of the Tower, every one engaged in the tracking down and condemnation of the priests suffered a certain moral loss. Nor was this all. In the catholic countries abroad, nothing was too bad to say about the inhumanity of the English government: indeed the whole nation was calumniated as a herd of ravening wolves:

> Et de loups ravissants l'isle en est toute pleine,
> Qui de patte et de dent, et de puante haleine,
> Font mourir à jamais et les corps et les âmes.[1]

[1] G. Ascoli, *La Grande-Bretagne devant l'opinion française depuis la guerre de cent ans à la fin du XVIᵉ siècle* (1927), p. 154.

Books like the *De Persecutione Anglicana*, published in Rome in 1582 and illustrated with gross pictures of arrests, tortures, and executions, created a foul impression of Englishmen that persisted for a century.

Yet the wonder is that so few suffered death under the Elizabethan penal laws. There were no holocausts of victims, such as blotted the contemporary history of catholic countries abroad. Only some 250 perished during twenty years, including those who died in prison—a notable fact, when we consider that in the five years of Mary's reign more than 300 protestants were put to death. The fact is the Elizabethan government preferred to work by fine, imprisonment, and even banishment rather than by putting into force the full rigour of the law; and few went to the scaffold compared with the number imprisoned in the various castles and strongholds throughout the country—Wisbech, Kimbolton, Wigmore, York, Durham, &c. There they lived under various forms of 'vexation', but at least their lives were spared, and their liberty, though restricted, was not greatly interfered with.

At the same time as the catholic revival threatened the Establishment from one side it was exposed on the other to the running fire of the 'precisians' or puritans, who desired to carry on the reformation to its logical conclusion in a church entirely emancipated from the Romanist tradition. It is probable that the queen regarded the puritan attack with even greater irritation than the catholic; for although the vast majority of puritans remained within the church, and professed to aim not at its overthrow but at its transformation, the political doctrines underlying their religious 'platform' were inimical to the whole structure of Tudor government. Had they triumphed, they would have subordinated the state to the will of a Genevan sanhedrim. Thus puritanism was branded equally with catholicism as a potential, if not actual, danger to the peace of the realm, and punished accordingly.

From the standpoint of its completed development, puritanism may be described as a comprehensive protest against the principle, the method, and the result of the settlement of 1559.

As we have seen, the court reformers had proceeded on the assumption that the church of Rome, despite its corruption in certain points of doctrine and discipline, was nevertheless a true church. They had therefore gone back for their inspiration and guidance to the fourth and fifth centuries, when the see of Rome was still without its universal sway, and by lopping off the 'errors' and 'superstitions' of the medieval church had contrived to preserve all that was essential to the maintenance of pure religion. To the puritan, however, this assumption was untenable. He refused to accord the church of Rome the title of a true church: to him it was simply the Antichrist of the Bible, and to have anything in common with it was to be contaminated. In order to recover the truth in matters of church polity it was necessary to go back, not merely to the fourth and fifth centuries, but to the apostolic age and the Scriptures. The will of God and not the works of man was the final court of appeal.

No less vigorous was the opposition of the puritan to the method by which the religious changes had been effected. A lay settlement of religion seemed to him, no less than it did to the catholic, a gross and unjustifiable encroachment by the state on a domain properly belonging to the clergy; or, as it was put in the second *Admonition to Parliament,* 'Church matters ought ordinarily to be handled by church officers.'

Lastly, the legislation of 1559 had resulted in the erection of a church that was an amalgam of protestant doctrine and catholic ceremonial, which was repellent to the conscience of the purist. To him there was no logical stopping-place between Rome and Geneva, no security for the individual who had left the Roman communion until he found a resting-place within the unassailable fortress of Calvinism. To compromise with Rome in any shape or form was to endanger the future of protestantism. Moreover, to some of the more extreme puritans the sweeping of all and sundry into the established church 'at the blast of Queen Elizabeth's trumpet' seemed a crass betrayal of the first principles of a christian fellowship. To the anglican contention that all members of the state were necessarily members of the state church, and that church and state were different aspects of the same body politic, these puritans replied that the church and state were separate and distinct corporations: that the church was a voluntary association of believers whose aims and ideals were entirely spiritual, whose bond was the acceptance of a common creed, and whose only head was Christ.

Puritanism, however, was more than a protest against religious forms that, in the opinion of its votaries, had no basis in the Scriptures. It was also a protest against the spirit of greed and materialism that saturated society and corrupted the church. In spite of Parker's effort, in the Canons of 1571, to check pluralism by making the holding of more than two benefices illegal,[1] many of the leading clerics indulged in the practice to the top of their bent. Bishop Hughes, who was appointed to the see of St. Asaph's in 1573, held *in commendam* an archdeaconry and ten other livings; and added another six later, nine of the total being sinecures. He also sold livings in his gift, and leased episcopal manors for long terms to his wife, children, sisters, and cousins. Sandys of Worcester was a man of similar stamp, who systematically plundered his see. Even the celebrated Bancroft held canonries in St. Patrick's Dublin, Westminster, Canterbury, and St. Paul's, and, in addition, the rectories of Feversham and St. Andrew's Holborn. Of the simoniacal practices of several of the episcopate there is, unfortunately, no doubt whatever. Scory of Hereford took his see on condition of alienating seventeen manors to the queen; and he gave three sinecure prebends in Bromwich collegiate church to his wife, and another in his own cathedral church to his worthless son. Harington says of him that he 'worshipped images (not saints but angels)', i.e. the coin. When Young entered upon his tenure of the see of York he pulled down the hall attached to the cathedral 'for the greediness of the lead that covered it'. It was indeed a common practice for a new bishop to enter an action against his predecessor for the spoliation of the episcopal lands and impoverishment of the revenues of the see. Nor was there any respect shown by the queen and those about her for the sanctity of church property. The see of Oxford was kept vacant for a long time in order that she and her favourites might enjoy its revenues. Fletcher on becoming bishop of Bristol leased his manors to the queen's personal friends at a nominal rent. When he was promoted to London it cost him more than £2,000 in cash to gratify the queen's nominees. In fact, all the principal laymen battened on impropriations. Cecil surrounded his mansion at Burleigh with estates once belonging to the see of Peterborough, and Christopher Hatton compelled

---

[1] 'Non licebit cuiquam, cujuscunque sit gradus, plusquam duo ecclesiastica beneficia obtinere eodem tempore', &c. (Prothero, *Statutes and Documents*, p. 202.)

Cox of Ely to lease him his London house in Holborn for 21 years. When Coldwell was promoted to the see of Salisbury, he was compelled to alienate the manor of Sherborne, one of his best estates, to Sir Walter Raleigh. Wickham was similarly treated on his entry upon the see of Winchester, having to make over extensive leases to Sir Francis Carew. These are only a few instances of the worldliness that characterized the age and ate like a canker into the church. But they are sufficient to show that the puritans had something to grieve about when they contemplated the condition of religion in England.

Naturally the whole sweep of the puritan objection to the Establishment did not manifest itself at once: it was a slow development, stimulated by conflict and nurtured by persecution; but for all practical purposes it was substantially the detailed exposition of the differences just indicated.

The dispute began in 1559 over what appeared to be a relatively insignificant matter, viz. the vestments prescribed for the use of the clergy by the royal Injunctions. Many took offence at this enforcement of the 'livery of Antichrist', and protested that dress, being a 'thing indifferent', should be left to the discretion of the individual. 'Let the clergy be known', said one, 'by their demeanour and conversation and not by their dress.' 'We confess one faith of Jesus Christ,' said another, 'we preach one doctrine, we acknowledge one ruler over all things; shall we be so used for a surplice; shall brethren persecute brethren for a forkèd cap?' To which the anglican replied that if dress was 'indifferent', it might advisedly be left to the decision of the civil magistrate; but for decency's sake one form of dress was essential, and the vestments prescribed were better than any other because of their hallowed associations. Met on this point, the puritan had recourse to the argument of the 'tender conscience'. The vestments in which he was asked to officiate had been consecrated to Antichrist: they were in the same category as meat offered to idols. Weak brothers, seeing a protestant minister clad in the livery of Rome, would confound the two religions and lose their balance.

The question at issue appeared to be trifling, yet neither side could afford to yield—the puritans, because they had grounded their case on conscience: the queen, because she had merely made a legitimate use of her prerogative for the right ordering of the church service. Several continental reformers—Bullinger, Gualter, and Peter Martyr—tried to ease the deadlock by advising a temporary acquiescence, lest in the conflict of protestants the settlement might be jeopardized, preaching be brought to a standstill, and the Romanists again lift their heads. But they failed to moderate the rising temper of the puritans, and the agitation increased rather than diminished. The use of organs in churches, of the ring in the marriage ceremony, and of the sign of the cross in baptism, kneeling at communion, the excessive number of holy-days, and other 'dregs of popery' were added to the list of puritan *gravamina*. In 1563 the agitators petitioned convocation to make a clean sweep of these obnoxious practices, and to limit the use of vestments to the surplice only. So strong was the movement that the petition was rejected by only one vote, and that was a proxy vote.

Meanwhile great disorder prevailed in the church. In some instances the prayer book was rigidly adhered to, in others psalms in metre were added; in some churches the communion table stood in the middle of the chancel, in others 'altarwise a yard distant from the wall'; some ministers officiated at the sacraments in a surplice, others without it; some used a chalice in the communion service, others were content with a common cup; some favoured unleavened bread, others preferred leavened; some baptized in a font, others in a basin; some made the sign of the cross, others dispensed with it; and so forth. On 25 January 1563 the queen becoming alarmed instructed the archbishops of Canterbury and York 'to take effectual measures that an exact order and uniformity be maintained in all external rites and ceremonies . . .' and to see 'that none hereafter be admitted to any ecclesiastical preferment but who is well disposed to common order and shall formally promise to comply with it'. In virtue of this instruction Parker eventually issued his *Book of Advertisements* (1566) laying down fixed rules for the conduct of public service. He was careful to point out in the preface that his regulations were not prescribed 'as equivalent with the Word of God . . . but as temporal orders mere ecclesiastical'; but he soon found that as many as 37 per cent. of the clergy in the diocese of London alone refused to obey, and were ready to leave the church rather than 'make themselves hypocrites for the queen's sake'. Suspension from office was followed by deprivation, and the first serious split in the ranks of the protestants was consummated. Parker's problem, however, was by no means solved. Many puritans, less conscientious than the stalwarts who went into the wilderness, contrived to remain in the church, albeit openly contemptuous of the *Advertisements* and defiant of the bishops' authority. To cope with this nuisance the archbishop was compelled to give the screw another twist by commanding the clergy to obey their superiors as they obeyed the queen or the letters patent of the council. The only result was to stimulate the puritans to a more resolute and more comprehensive attack on the Establishment. Leaving the question of vestments for the moment, they proceeded to challenge the position of the bishops and the whole hierarchical organization of the church. 'Bishops must be unlorded' became the cry. 'All ministers must be equal.'

For this new development the bishops themselves were partly to blame. Many of them, including Jewel, Sandys, Grindal, Horne, Pilkington, and Parkhurst, had openly avowed their dislike of the vestments regulations, and professed sympathy with the puritans. There were many things, they acknowledged, 'barely tolerable' in the existing state of religion, which ought to be removed as soon as opportunity offered. 'I confess', wrote Pilkington of Durham, 'we suffer many things against our hearts; but we cannot take them away, though we were ever so much set upon it. We are under authority; and we can innovate nothing without the queen; nor can we alter the laws; the only thing left to our choice is whether we will bear these things or break the peace of the church.' Such men were clearly more of a hindrance than a help to the archbishop in his attempt to discipline the clergy: to engage in repression, as they were obliged to do if they remained in office, and at the same time sympathize with the party to be repressed, could only end in trouble. The more honourable course would have been to resign and let others wield the lash: weakness was fatal.

But there were other factors at work than episcopal indecision. When Parker issued his *Book of Advertisements* it was noted by the puritans that it lacked the authority of the broad seal, and this gave rise to the conviction that the archbishop had acted illegally, in which case they were not legally bound to obey him. In actual fact the queen was just as desirous as Parker for uniformity in the church, but for political reasons she did not want the uniformity to be enforced by state action; she believed that the old visitatorial powers vested in the archbishop and the bishops from time immemorial, even if they were deprived of the authority they possessed in former times, were fully sufficient for present needs. Indeed her quarrel with Parker and his successor Grindal was that they did not make enough of the system, and she was inclined to lay all the troubles of the church at their door. But it is now clear that diocesan visitation, backed as it was by ecclesiastical commissions appointed by the Crown from time to time as occasion required, was quite inadequate to ensure that constant supervision which the church stood in need of in a period of emergency. Only at a later date, when the floating commissions were replaced by a permanent court of high commission, was the machinery of control and correction brought into correspondence with the actual requirements of the situation; but that was the work of Richard Bancroft after 1587. Lastly, we have to note that the puritans had many friends among the nobility and those who occupied important positions in the government. The influence of these men was often used to restrain or weaken the hands of the archbishop. The privy council itself was divided in its sympathies, and even Cecil was not altogether on Parker's side. In many ways, therefore, the task of keeping the puritans within bounds was beset by great difficulties.

Meanwhile puritanism had found a stalwart leader in Dr. Thomas Cartwright, the most outstanding figure in the early history of the movement, and a man of considerable learning. As a fellow of Trinity College, Cambridge, and Lady Margaret professor of divinity in the university, Cartwright had convinced himself through his studies in the New Testament that the whole fabric of anglican church government, no less than the Roman, was in flagrant contradiction with that of the primitive church. Diocesan episcopacy, he asserted, had no basis in Scripture, and ought to be abolished root and branch. His conception of the church entailed the removal of archbishops and archdeacons: the restoration of bishops and deacons to their proper apostolic functions—the former to preaching and teaching, the latter to the care of the poor: the substitution of presbyteries for episcopal chancellors and archdeacons in the disciplinary system of the church; and the election of ministers in the first instance by congregations. It will be apparent that

Cartwright's views were simply undiluted Calvinism. His originality did not lie in the reforms he advocated, but in the fact that he was the first puritan to take his stand boldly on Scripture as the court of appeal for discipline as well as doctrine, and to apply this principle with logical completeness. In the face of his sweeping affirmations, based on a seemingly unassailable foundation, the controversy about vestments sank into comparative insignificance; and the anglican appeal to history, which had hitherto been the main pillar in the defence of episcopacy, lost half its validity. Historical precedent was now confronted with the divine will revealed in Scripture.

There was no gainsaying the fact that Cartwright was the most dangerous man in the church. In 1570 he was deprived of his professorship: a year later he lost his fellowship at Trinity; and in 1574, in consequence of a summons issued by the ecclesiastical commissioners for his arrest, he was compelled to seek refuge abroad. But by this time he had set puritanism to march in a new direction, and supplied it with a battle-cry, a creed, and a clearly marked objective. In the year of his flight there appeared the *Ecclesiasticae Disciplinae . . . Explicatio*, by Walter Travers, translated by Cartwright, which became the canonical book of presbyterian nonconformity.

The advance made by puritanism under the impetus communicated by Cartwright may be seen in the *Admonition to Parliament* in 1571 and the *Second Admonition*, published in 1572. Both are distinguished from previous puritan documents by the comprehensiveness of the indictment they bring against the Establishment, although they differ greatly in tone and manner. The first was an emotional diatribe, strong in language and essentially destructive in character, addressed to the general body of the laity as well as to parliament: the second was a systematic exposition of the new discipline, less interesting from a literary point of view, but of more practical value because of its careful statement of the puritan position. After the publication of the second *Admonition*, there could be little doubt that presbyterianism had become the creed of the majority of puritans. Its popularity was so considerable that the bishops took alarm. 'The city will never be quiet', wrote Bishop Sandys of London to Burghley, 'till these authors of sedition, who are now esteemed as gods, as Field, Wilcox, Cartwright, and others be removed from the city; the people resort to them as in popery

they were wont to run on pilgrimages.' Scambler of Peterborough was similarly troubled about the state of Northampton
and Rutland.

But the strengthening of intellectual propaganda was only
one aspect of the movement. The *Admonitions to Parliament*
opened up a fresh line of attack; for it was arguable that just
as the settlement of 1559 had been carried out by parliament,
so it might be altered by parliament. Moreover, it was noticeable that the house of commons was becoming more and more
puritanical in its sympathies, and deeply concerned about the
religious state of the country. In 1566, for example, a petition
was drafted drawing the queen's attention to the evils accruing
from the lack of efficient ministers, pluralism and non-residence,
the absence of a 'true discipline', and the insufficiency of preaching and instruction, 'whereby infinite numbers of your majesty's
subjects are like to perish from lack of knowledge'. The parliamentary campaign did not begin in earnest, however, until
1571, when a bill for the reform of the prayer book was introduced into the commons by Walter Strickland; and the immediate result was a constitutional crisis between the Crown and
parliament on the question of rights and privileges. From the
queen's point of view the intervention of parliament in religious
matters was just as intolerable as that convocation should interfere in the secular government of the country. Through parliament she ruled the state: through convocation she ruled the
church; and neither could be allowed to overstep its legitimate
sphere without upsetting the balance of the constitution. In the
same way as she had prevented convocation from taking an
official part in the settlement of 1559, so now she refused to
sanction the attempt of parliament to intrude into a department
reserved for herself and convocation. In consequence of this
attitude, Strickland was summoned before the privy council and
temporarily forbidden the house 'for the exhibiting of a bill into
the house against the prerogative of the queen'. A year later the
queen found it necessary to inform the commons through the
Speaker that 'henceforth no bills concerning religion shall be
preferred or received into this house unless the same should
be first considered and liked by the clergy'; and at the same
time she impounded two bills 'touching rites and ceremonies'.[1]
It was clear that there could be little hope of ecclesiastical

[1] See also p. 222 for the constitutional issue.

reform through parliament; and the puritans turned to a more useful avenue of self-help.

For some little time there had grown up among the clergy in many of the south-eastern dioceses a practice of holding weekly or fortnightly meetings for the study of the Scriptures and the improvement of morals. To these 'prophesyings' or 'exercises', which were generally supported by the bishops as conducive to greater efficiency in the clergy, it was customary to invite the laity; but the conduct of the meetings, the exposition of scriptural texts, and the discussion that followed were understood to be matters for the clergy alone. In some cases, as in Scambler's diocese of Peterborough, a voluntary discipline was set up in conjunction with the 'prophesyings' whereby offenders against morality, both clerical and lay, could be brought to book and compelled by pressure of public opinion to reform their evil lives. In this way an attempt was made to supplement the canons of the church and to deepen and strengthen the religious life of the community in accordance with the puritan ideal.

Of the efficacy of such a movement there could be no doubt; but it had its dangers. Study of the Scriptures might easily lead to open or covert criticism of the existing rites, ceremonies, and government of the church; and the fact that the laity were present, even although they did not intervene in the debates, might cause the spread of discontent, schism, and rebellion among those who were least able to appreciate the significance of what was said. It was to meet these dangers that Archbishop Edmund Grindal[1] issued his regulations in 1576. His attitude to the 'prophesyings' was that of a sympathizer who believed that every effort of the clergy to better themselves should be recognized by their superiors and incorporated, if possible, in the organization of the church: provided always that ample safeguards were available against unconstitutional innovations. On this point, however, he was destined to be rudely disillusioned by the queen, who saw nothing in the 'prophesyings' but a veiled attempt to carry out a further reformation of the church in defiance of the law and the royal prerogative. On the ground that they were causing disorder in the general body of the laity, she peremptorily ordered the archbishop, in 1577, to take steps immediately for their suppression, and to report the

[1] Appointed to Canterbury on Parker's death (1575).

names of those who refused to desist to the privy council for exemplary punishment. When Grindal, with amazing audacity, declined to carry out these instructions, and pointed out that the *hoc volo sic jubeo* of the queen's letter was no better than the 'anti-christian voice of the pope', he was deprived of office and remained suspended from the exercise of his temporal jurisdiction for five years.

The full severity of the repression, however, did not really begin to break over the puritans until the appointment of John Whitgift as archbishop of Canterbury in 1583. The new prelate was a man after the queen's own heart—hard-working, consistent, and a resolute opponent of dissent. Unlike Grindal he had formed his views in conflict with puritanism, when, as master of Trinity College and Regius professor of divinity at Cambridge, he had been the chief defender of the church against the assault of Cartwright; and by the time he was promoted to Canterbury they had grown to be a kind of second nature to him.

The question [he said] is not whether many things maintained in your platform of discipline [i.e. the puritan] were fitly used in the apostles' time or may now be well used in sundry reformed churches; but whether, when there is a settled order in doctrine and discipline established by law, it may stand with godly and christian wisdom to attempt so great an alteration as this platform must needs bring in, with disobedience to the queen and law and injunctions of the church, and offence to many consciences.

As for the puritan demand for equality of ministers, he was prepared to recognize it *quoad ministerium*, but *quoad politiam et ordinem* there must be degrees of superior and inferior. In short the time for argument was past, and the time for drastic action had come.

Whitgift's panacea for the religious troubles of the time was to erect in England a church as absolute and infallible as that of Rome. His policy is contained in the six articles of 1583, by which the clergy were compelled to accept by unqualified subscription the following three points: (1) the ecclesiastical supremacy of the Crown: (2) the book of common prayer and the ordinal, as containing nothing contrary to Scripture; and (3) the whole of the Thirty-nine Articles as agreeable to the word of God. The immediate effect of this enactment was the suspension of over two hundred ministers in Lincoln, Norfolk, Suffolk, Essex, and Kent, and a great outcry against the inhumanity of the archbishop. There is no doubt that Whitgift's methods were those of a grand inquisitor: in tracking down puritan delinquents he followed, as Burghley pointed out to him in 1584,[1] the example of the Romish Inquisition. His chief weapon of repression was the ecclesiastical commission, which, under his presidency, was drawn more and more into the disciplinary system of the church as an adjunct to the ordinary diocesan machinery whose inadequacy Parker and Grindal had already experienced. The advantage of having some such weapon to combat the spread of puritanism was great: it was swift and secret in action, could dispense with formalities of the law, and had behind it the whole coercive power of the state. Suspects and witnesses who were summoned before the commissioners were tendered an oath (the oath *ex officio*, as it was called) which obliged them to answer all interrogatories. If they refused to take it, they were handed over to the court of star chamber to be punished: if they accepted it, and through their subsequent admissions were convicted, they were sentenced to fines or imprisonment at discretion and without right of appeal. Needless to say the victims complained bitterly against the legality of such a régime. 'This corporal oath', said Cartwright, 'is to inquire of our private speeches and conferences with our dearest and nearest friends; yea, of the very secret thoughts and intents of our hearts, that so we may furnish both matter of accusation and evidence of proof against ourselves, which was not used to be done in causes of heresy or high treason.' By substituting inquiry by oath for indictment and trial by jury in open court the queen, it was said, was over-riding the common law, and setting up a system of legal procedure in flat contradiction with a basic principle of English law—*nemo tenetur seipsum accusare*. On the other hand, it is difficult to see how the integrity of the church could have been protected against puritan disruption otherwise than by some sort of inquisitorial process such as the high commission made possible. Statutory enactments for the repression of dissent were practically impossible when parliament itself was so strongly puritanical in its sympathies. Whitgift was fully convinced that he could not proceed effectively with the purification of the church unless the discretionary

[1] Letter printed in Prothero, pp. 213-14.

power of the commissioners was allowed; for in many cases parishioners were so friendly to puritan ministers that they would not 'present' them nor appear as witnesses against them.

As if to emphasize the need for drastic control, there had developed, shortly after Whitgift's appointment, the so-called 'classical' movement within the ranks of the puritans. The basis of the scheme was the introduction of a presbyterian discipline into episcopacy. The 'classis' was simply a secret synod after the Genevan pattern, and was composed of all the clergy in a district who were willing to follow a new Book of Discipline by Travers.[1] The object aimed at was to keep within the letter of the law, but to seek ways and means of adapting the anglican service and polity to the presbyterian. Wherever possible, offending passages in the prayer book were to be omitted: puritan interpretations of the Scriptures were to be freely used in preaching: congregations were to elect their ministers and recommend them through the 'classis' to the bishop for consecration; and the names of elder and deacon were to be substituted for churchwarden and collector for the poor. Clearly such a movement, however law-abiding, was tendentious in the extreme, and might easily culminate in the overthrow of the Establishment if allowed to run its course unchecked. But owing to the secrecy in which it was wrapped it was difficult to obtain evidence that would secure conviction of any overt breach of the law.

The same could not be said of the other menace to the established religion which began to manifest itself about the same time—the separatist movement. Prior to Whitgift's tenure of the archbishopric of Canterbury, the presbyterian idea of reforming the church by constitutional means had maintained substantial unity of aim within the ranks of the puritans. The only serious attempt to break away from the Establishment and found a 'separatist' organization at Plumbers' Hall in 1567 had ended in failure and the imprisonment of the leaders. Thirteen years later, however, the effort to set up an independent church was resumed with increased vigour under more favourable auspices. By this time a group of men, led by Robert Browne and Henry Barrow, who belonged to a younger generation than Cartwright

---

[1] Not to be confused with the *Ecc. Discip. Explicatio* by the same author (p. 195, above).

and cared nothing for the authority of Calvin or the sacro-sanctity of the Genevan system, had begun to preach a conception of the church that differed radically from both the puritan and the anglican. As against the inclusiveness of the latter and the cast-iron rigidity of the former, they held that voluntaryism or congregationalism was the only possible basis of a christian church. The root principle of their teaching was that the close connexion between church and state, symbolized by anglicanism and upheld by the presbyterians, was unscriptural and ought to be abolished. For the rest, they denied that a learned ministry was essential, laid supreme stress on inspiration, and exalted the idea of a non-hierarchic, non-ritualist form of public worship. In spite of inadequate organization, or possibly because of it, their spiritual enthusiasm gave an emotional touch to religion which neither anglicanism nor presbyterianism could supply, while their denunciations of Rome reached the fervour and intensity of the Hebrew prophets. In short the Brownists and Barrowists formed the spearhead of Elizabethan puritanism. Unfortunately their uncompromising opposition to the Establishment and their determination to effect a further reformation of religion 'without tarrying for any' brought them into conflict with the ecclesiastical supremacy of the Crown; and their democratic theory of church government ran counter to the spirit of the age.

Towards the close of the year 1587 yet another phase of puritan activity took shape in the Martin Marprelate attack on the bishops. It began with the issue of an anonymous pamphlet addressed to convocation, and 'compiled for the behoof and overthrow of the unpreaching parsons, fyckers, and curates that have learnt their catechism and are past grace'. Its ribald humour and bold sallies against the bishops, coupled with the anonymity of the author, at once caught the attention of the public; and very soon a second appeared still more outspoken, declaring war on the 'petty antichrists, proud prelates, intolerable withstanders of reformation, enemies of the gospel and covetous wretched priests'. 'Martin', it announced, would not only publish every one of their mistakes, but also put 'a young Martin in every parish . . . every one of them able to mar a prelate'. In all, seven famous tracts were published: 'The Epistle', 'The Epitome', 'Hay any Work for Cooper', 'Minerall and Metaphysical School-points', 'Theses Martinianae', 'The Just

Censure and Reproof', and 'The Protestation'. If the literary form adopted was novel, the attitude of the mysterious 'Martin' was even more novel: he swept away in a tide of unrestrained jocularity all the traditional reverence for the episcopate. For a time the martinists and anti-martinists bespattered each other to the amusement of the London public, while the government and the bishops conducted an unremitting search for the secret martinist press and the author of the tracts. The episode, however, proved to be of short duration; for no secret press could exist for any length of time in the England of Elizabeth, as the jesuit experiment of 1580–1 had already shown. By Christmas 1589 it was over. Of the chief actors—John Penry and Job Throgmorton—the former escaped for a time to Scotland, but subsequently returned to England to be executed: the latter, for some reason which remains a mystery, was allowed to go free. The others who were associated with the movement in a minor capacity suffered fines and imprisonment, but no clear evidence is available even today as to who Martin actually was. Like the author of the letters of Junius his identity remains an unsolved problem of history.

Although the repressionist campaign conducted by Whitgift went far beyond the comparatively mild measures adopted by his predecessors, it was Richard Bancroft's appearance on the high commission in 1587 that ushered in the period of storm and stress. This rising ecclesiastic, who had worked his way up the ladder of preferment by sheer ability, had latterly acquired a unique knowledge of the ramifications of puritan activity, particularly of the 'classis' movement, and in February 1589 he delivered a bitter philippic against presbyterianism at Paul's Cross. The sermon raised a storm of protest from Scotland, where the presbyterian type of church government now reigned supreme, and the Kirk dominated the state; but Bancroft continued his exposure of the political dangers of the movement, unperturbed by the criticism levelled at him by the irate Scottish Calvinists. Not only was the sermon itself published, but two other publications entitled *A Survey of the Holy Discipline* and *Dangerous Positions* followed later, showing that Bancroft could quote chapter and verse for the accusations he made.

Bancroft lashed out bitterly: 'The Apostle Paul did prophesy that there should be many false prophets; and we do see his sayings therein to be fulfilled by the number of such prophets as now remain among us—Arians, Donatists, Papists, Libertines, Anabaptists, the Family of Love, and sundry others.' In this way all nonconformists were linked together with the anabaptists as politically dangerous to the community. Bishop Cooper followed suit in his *Admonition* (1589), and, going even a step farther, accused the whole group of anti-episcopal sects as guilty of being 'levellers'. Recalling the Peasants' Revolt of 1381, he counselled all wise men to watch lest the sparks from a neighbouring house on fire, might set their own ablaze. 'No bishop, no property' seems to have been his text. 'We see therefore', he wrote, 'how Satan under pretences seeketh to thrust the spirit of the anabaptists and the grounds of their learning into this church of England.'

Of course, there was a good deal of hysteria in all this; and it was inevitable that it should provoke anger and recrimination in those who felt themselves maligned. Henry Barrow, for example, addressed a petition to the queen, pointing out reasonably and logically that 'If a man write in humble, loyal, and dutiful manner, having no purpose and intent to work rebellion, though rebellion should thereof ensue, yet could not such a writer, without great injustice, be drawn within this statute. For he cannot be a felon that hath not a felonious intent and purpose.' Logic and pure reason, however, failed to make any advance against the driving force of endowments and livelihood. The fear of anabaptism was paramount in the minds of all who engaged in the controversy on the side of the Establishment. And Nash, the spell-binding pamphleteer of the age, joined in with his whimsical rhyme on the 'death and burial of Martin':

> O vos Martinistae
> Et vos Brounistae
> Et Famililovistae
> Et Anabaptistae
> Et Omnes Sectistae
> Et Machiavelistae
> Et Atheistae
> Quorum dux fuit iste
> Lugete singuli!

Soon after the February diatribe the presbyterian leaders, including Cartwright himself, who had been lured back to

England in the hope of better times, were summoned before the commission, and on their refusal to take the oath were sent to prison. They remained there until 1592, when the star chamber, as a consequence of Attorney-general Sir John Popham's advice, decided to take no further action in the matter, because no overt breach of the law could be proved against them.

Meanwhile the full rigour of the law was being felt by the extremists. John Udall, the martinist (or supposed martinist), was imprisoned under sentence of death in 1590, and died in prison before the sentence could be executed. Three fanatics— Coppinger, Arthington, and Hacket—were accused of plotting to take the queen's life, and Hacket was executed in 1592. In the following year Barrow and Greenwood, the separatists, were put to death for seditious words: John Penry suffered the same penalty for his share in the marprelate movement; and the drastic conventicle act (35 Eliz., cap. 1) was passed punishing, in the last resort with exile or a felon's death, all who obstinately refused to attend the anglican church or attended separate conventicles.

By these means the back of the puritan movement was effectually broken. The queen, in the meantime, kept a rigorous control over any attempt of parliament to come to the rescue of the suppressed party. When Anthony Cope introduced a bill, in 1587, for the repeal of all existing ecclesiastical laws, and the introduction of a new form of common prayer, both the bill and the book were impounded, and Cope was sent to the Tower for disobeying the royal injunction concerning the submission of all such projects to the bishops. A similar sharp punishment was meted out to Attorney Morrice of the court of wards, who took up the cudgels on behalf of the suffering puritans in 1593, and introduced two bills for the abolition of oaths and subscriptions, and against unlawful imprisonments and restraints of liberty. He was deprived of office, suspended from practising as a lawyer, and imprisoned for several years in Tutbury castle.

Note. Elizabethan England was, comparatively speaking, free from the more fanatical protestant sects, whose politico-religious doctrines, subversive of both church and state, had caused widespread disturbances and bloodshed in many parts of Germany, Switzerland, and the Netherlands during Henry VIII's reign. The anabaptists, in particular, were a very small body, mostly Dutch, who had mingled with the stream of refugees fleeing from Spanish tyranny. In all probability they would have lived peaceably in their English settlements; but the queen, like her father, set her face flintlike against their dangerous creed. In 1561, says Camden, a royal proclamation ordered 'anabaptists and such like heretics' who have come to England under colour of avoiding persecution, to leave the realm within twenty days under penalty of imprisonment and confiscation of goods. In 1568, owing to a fresh wave of immigration, Parker was commanded to undertake, through the bishop of London, an inquiry into the character of the immigrants, and to compile a register. In the same year a second proclamation referred to secret conventicles by which many English people have been corrupted, and ordered all who hold anabaptist principles, and refuse to recant, to leave the country within twenty days under penalty of death. But apparently, in spite of all measures and precautions, the danger from anabaptism continued. In 1575, at Easter, a congregation of the much-feared sect was discovered in Aldgate. The culprits, who were Dutch, were tried before the bishop of London at St. Paul's: five recanted their heresies, fifteen were shipped abroad, and five were condemned to death. Eventually only two of the five were burnt at the stake in Smithfield 'in great horror with roaring and crying'. Extermination of the sect, however, was impossible. In 1589 there were said to be several anabaptist conventicles in London and elsewhere; and in 1591 occurred the Hacket affair mentioned in the text. 'Men talk of it,' wrote a contemporary, 'resemble it to the matter of John of Leyden, who took upon himself the kingdom of the anabaptists, and think this fool [i.e. Hacket] plotted some such kingdom as these prophets might have assembled.' Evidently John of Leyden and the Münster atrocities (1534–5) were still a vivid memory even in Elizabethan England.

VI

THE CONSTITUTION

ELIZABETHAN England produced no book on political theory fit to be compared with the writings of Bodin, Hotman, Duplessis-Mornay, or the other great thinkers of contemporary Europe. Presumably Englishmen were, on the whole, too well satisfied with the form of government under which they lived to probe deeply into first principles, or to question the grounds of their political obligation. If they wrote about the state, they did so in a perfunctory manner, explanatory or laudatory rather than critical or controversial.[1] To the political theorist, therefore, the reign is to a large extent devoid of interest. When we turn from theory to practice, however, a somewhat different picture presents itself. We become aware that the apparent complacency is shot through with a good deal of discontent, and that the Tudor ideal of government, now at its zenith, was already entering upon a period of disintegration. True, the question of defining where the sovereign power lay in the constitution had not yet arisen, for the great corporation and body politic of the kingdom, consisting of king and parliament, was still one and undivided. But to the observant eye the germs of the later conflict, that made definition a necessity, were not only latent but active in Elizabeth's reign. For this reason the constitutional historian will find the period a valuable introductory study to the seventeenth-century struggle: it supplies, in fact, an indispensable connecting link between two epochs.

It has been pointed out[2] that if a strong and vigilant executive was justified in the earlier part of the sixteenth century as a preservative of law and order and national security, it was more than ever justified during the latter part, when the renewal of the breach with Rome, the uncertainty of the succession, the Stuart menace, and the constant threat of invasion combined to create a state of emergency without parallel in English history. Every one realized that if the queen were to

---

[1] e.g. Sir Thomas Smith's *De Republica Anglorum*: Hooker's work will be referred to later in another connexion.

[2] Prothero, *Statutes and Documents*, Preface, p. xix.

die before Mary Stuart, the country would be plunged into the vortex of civil war and all the other evils of a disputed succession, coupled, in all probability, with foreign intervention. Consciousness of this fact provided Elizabeth with the lever by which she moved her world, and at the same time it enabled her to maintain in substantial working order the mechanism of government she inherited from her predecessors. On the other hand, when the sense of omnipresent danger grew less or faded from memory, after the execution of the Scottish queen and the defeat of the Spanish armada, it is noticeable that a spirit inimical to the existing system of government spread itself through the community. Criticism of the executive became more and more pronounced in parliament: privy councillors were treated with less respect than formerly: even the popularity of the queen, great as it was, seemed to wane; and a *fin de siècle* feeling, compounded of irritation and lassitude, hovered like a cloud over the political landscape. The glory of the reign was passing away, and a prosaic age, unattended by dangers from without and within, was soon to pick to pieces the governmental machinery that had made that glory possible.

All this is true, but not the whole truth. As we shall see, the effort of parliament to enlarge the scope of its rights and privileges at the expense of the prerogative, to eat its way into the Tudor edifice, and to grope forward to the ideal of popular sovereignty of a much later day began quite early in the reign, and continued unabated for more than thirty years before the queen's death. The transition, therefore, was not sudden, nor was it, strictly speaking, a consequence of the removal of public apprehension: on the contrary, the friction between Crown and parliament was itself generated by the emergency in which the country stood. And this friction acted like a forcing-house for the development of parliamentary technique, as well as of a corporate feeling and continuity of tradition that must have proved useful once the real contest began under the Stuarts.

The central organ of the Elizabethan administration was the privy council, a body consisting of seventeen or twenty carefully chosen, experienced men, mostly the great ministers of state and officials of the royal household, through whose hands passed all the routine business of the state. Unlike the modern cabinet, which is responsible to parliament, the council of the sixteenth century was simply and solely the executive instrument of the sovereign, by whom it was appointed and from whom it derived its authority. It had no permanent abode, but met where the queen happened to be in residence at the moment. Owing to its size it worked by committees, and only occasionally, when matters of exceptional interest or importance were remitted to it by the queen, did it meet as a body. As a rule its meetings, which were held in secret, were attended by eight or ten members, and not infrequently business was transacted by only half that number.[1] The queen herself never attended, being content to let her wishes be known through one or other of those present or through the secretary, who was in constant communication with her. Normally she accepted the council's decisions for better or worse, but she did not regard herself as bound to follow its advice, nor did she scruple, when questions of policy were in debate, to exercise an over-riding authority if she thought her own or the national interests demanded it.

There is no official evidence to show that the resolutions arrived at round the council table were other than unanimous; but from unofficial sources it may be gathered that when great affairs of state were under consideration differences of opinion bred factions,[2] and factions might easily become feuds.[3] Moreover, there was always a latent rivalry among the members for a leading place in the queen's favour. It is noticeable also that councillors were free to communicate individually and privately, as well as publicly, with any one they pleased, for the purpose of acquiring information, providing always they observed their oath of fealty to the Crown. The queen's ambassadors and dignitaries of all sorts consulted them as to the meaning or implication of their instructions, or supplied them with information which they dared not incorporate in their official reports to her and the council as a whole. Knowledge

---

[1] Mendoza reported to Philip II, in 1578, that although there were seventeen counsellors, the bulk of the business was transacted by Leicester, Walsingham, and Burghley; and towards the close of the reign Robert Cecil, Nottingham, and Buckhurst took their places.

[2] e.g. the marked division between Burghley supported by Sussex, Hunsdon, and Lincoln, on the one hand, and Walsingham and Leicester supported by Warwick, Bedford, and Knollys, during the years 1578–85.

[3] e.g. the Essex–Cecil feud in the nineties.

as well as wisdom was a necessary equipment of any one who aimed at taking a leading part in debate; and all the great figures of the Elizabethan council—Burghley, Walsingham, Leicester, Essex, Robert Cecil—spared themselves no effort to acquire, by an elaborate system of espionage, every scrap of information likely to be of use to them in the discharge of their duties.[1] Elizabeth had a curious way of showing her approval or disapproval of those who supported or opposed her own will; but as a rule she appreciated and respected the man whose opinions were based upon a rational analysis of facts, or who could quote chapter and verse for the advice he tendered. The system was perhaps too casual and unscientific. The field of national interests was too vast to be spanned effectively by any one person however gifted; the accumulation of state papers, official and unofficial, was wasteful and often futile; but a more vigilant, hard-working, and loyal body of men than the privy council in Elizabeth's reign it would be hard to find.

The business that devolved upon the council was widely varied, enormous in bulk, and extremely difficult to classify. Besides the highest matters of state, comparatively trivial concerns affecting the private life of individuals were brought under consideration. Decisions about the army and navy, seminary priests and jesuits, recusants, foreign affairs, commerce, industry, and piracy were interspersed with pronouncements on civil suits, family disputes, and petitions for relief from oppressed persons who could not obtain justice in the ordinary law courts. There was, in fact, no limit to the competence of the council: it could handle any question involving the security of the state or the welfare of the subject; and it could issue proclamations with the validity of law. In Hallam's opinion,[2] England was managed 'as if it had been the household and estate of a nobleman under a strict and prying steward'.

As the supreme centre of authority under the Crown, the council stood in the closest relation with the judicial system, the church, and parliament, and exercised a directing, controlling, and supervisory authority over all officials—bishops,

---

[1] Walsingham, for example, received intelligence not only from every quarter of England, but also from thirteen towns in France, seven in the Low Countries, five in Italy, five in Spain, nine in Germany, three in the United Provinces, and three in Turkey. (F. M. G. Evans, *The Principal Secretary of State* (1923), p. 286.)

[2] *The Constitutional History of England from the accession of Henry VII to the death of George II* (1827), i. 265.

judges of assize, lords-lieutenant, sheriffs, justices of the peace. A constant stream of letters, reports, and petitions poured into it from all parts of the country, to be answered by an equally voluminous outgoing stream of writs, instructions, and summonses. To some extent its labours were lightened by the concurrent and subordinate jurisdictions wielded by the council of the north, which was responsible for the administration of the counties lying beyond Trent, and by the similarly constituted council of Wales and the Marches. Purely judicial cases, again, were as a rule relegated to the court of star chamber. Sometimes matters capable of being handled by the ordinary law courts were ordered to be dealt with there; and there was a practice of devolving certain defined pieces of administrative or judicial work on commissioners, not privy councillors, who were specially appointed for the task. But the council itself remained the final court of appeal and the co-ordinating centre of the political universe.[1]

Particularly important, perhaps, were its duties and responsibilities as guardian of the state against all manner of disturbances. In order to strengthen its hands for the investigation and castigation of offences under this head, especially with regard to suspected treason, it possessed the unique privilege of employing torture and forced confessions. In the troubled times of the sixteenth century, it was useful to have some body of men empowered to 'bolt out' the truth from suspects by extraordinary means; and it was right that this power, which might give rise to abuses, should be vested in the highest and most respected court in the land, where it would be used with moderation and discretion. It will be apparent, however, that men entrusted with such far-reaching powers and a jurisdiction extending over all officials, local as well as central, might easily develop a conception of the state very different from that entertained by parliament and the common law courts, and by treating them all as its agents work for the transformation of England into a centralized bureaucratic state. This did not happen, but circumstances were undoubtedly tending in that direction until the end of the Tudor régime.

The judicial annex or extension of the council was the court

---

[1] For instances of its supervision and control of local affairs see Sir W. H. Holdsworth, *History of English Law*, iv. 78–80: of ecclesiastical affairs, ibid. 81, 82; of the judicial system, ibid. 84, 85.

of star chamber. In the reign of Elizabeth this court, albeit it was officially styled 'the lords of the council sitting in the star chamber', had a separate organic existence, kept its own records, and followed its own practices and precedents. All privy councillors attended its meetings, together with some of the judges who were not privy councillors, and such peers and bishops as were summoned by the Crown in the capacity of assessors. In contemporary phrase, the star chamber was 'the curious eye of the state and the king's council prying into the inconveniences and mischiefs which abound in the common-wealth'. As such, the range of its activities was practically unlimited; but for convenience' sake the cases with which it dealt may be regarded as falling into two main categories: first, those which involved a breach of public order, or might be construed as provocative of such a breach; secondly, those which arose out of a direct violation of royal ordinances, pro-clamations, grants, or commands. In the first category might be grouped riots, conspiracies, challenges to duels, forgeries, libels and defamation of character, disturbances arising out of the game laws, hunting, or inclosures, disputes as to the ownership of land, or between lord and tenant, assaults, and disorderly behaviour of all kinds. When justice Shallow saw Falstaff ill-treating his men, killing his deer, and kissing his keeper's daughter, he exclaimed: 'I will make a star chamber matter of it; if he were twenty Sir John Falstaffs he shall not abuse Robert Shallow, Esquire. . . . The council shall hear of it; it is a riot.'[1] It was a 'star chamber matter', also, to write ballads about one's neighbour, to write abusive letters to jus-tices, or to speak scandal of men in high position. It was an outspoken and scurrilous age, when the 'filthy ballad' set to some trite tune became a regular means, even in polite society, of humiliating a rival; and Sir John Harington was in good company when he noted in his diary: 'I will write a damnable story and put it in goodly verse about Lord A.'[2] Next to rioting and forgery, the 'infamous libel' was more often the cause of action by the star chamber than any other offence.

But the peculiarity of the star chamber was not so much the rich variety of cases it dealt with as the informality of its pro-cedure and the swift and summary punishments it inflicted.

[1] Quoted by E. P. Cheyney, *A History of England from the Defeat of the Armada*, &c p. 90.   [2] Ibid., p. 93.

As opposed to the courts of common law, where accused persons were tried by a jury, the star chamber was a court composed entirely of judges, who proceeded on written depositions and predigested evidence—sometimes even on verbal confessions (*ore tenus*)—and only summoned the accused before its bar in the final stage of the trial. The method was similar in many respects to that of a modern court martial. The penalties inflicted were not according to statute, but at the discretion of the court, and adapted to the nature of the offence, being often of an ingenious and bizarre nature. Capital punishment, it is true, was beyond its province; but heavy fines, imprisonments, corporal punishment, whipping, branding, the pillory, cutting of ears, slitting of noses, and other forms of public humiliation were freely used *in terrorem populi*. On the other hand, it is important to note that the proceedings in the court of star chamber were not conducted in secrecy, but in full view of the public, who were admitted freely, and 'flock thither in great abundance when causes of weight are there heard and determined'. Not only so: all classes might apply to it for redress of wrongs, and its diligence in the discharge of business, together with the rigorous justice it dispensed, made it the most popular court in the realm. Lambarde, speaking of it in 1591, alludes to it as 'this most noble and praiseworthy Court, the beams of whose bright justice, equal in beauty with Hesperus and Lucifer, . . . do blaze and spread themselves as far as the realm is long or wide'. Coke was no less complimentary when he wrote of it as 'the most honourable court (our parliament excepted) that is in the christian world'.

Of the local administration only a brief description can be given. Here again, however, the queen made no innovation in the system she inherited from her predecessors, although two of the offices, the justiceship of the peace and the lord lieutenancy of the shire, took on a greater significance owing to the expanding activities of the central government and the political dangers of the time. As a rule all the chief officers of the local administration—justices of the peace, sheriffs, lords lieutenant, vice-admirals, coroners, and high constables—were drawn from the ranks of the rural gentry, who performed the duties assigned to them, not as a professional class trained for the purpose, but as amateurs. To each was entrusted a definite function or series of functions in the preservation of order, the execution of justice, and the military security of the community; but the diffusion of authority and the exact apportionment of responsibility in particular cases is not always easy to determine. Frequently offices seem to overlap or run into one another, and there was a tendency on the part of the central government to modify the system or interfere with its working without paying too much deference to formality. Efficiency rather than formality was the guiding principle.

It must have been difficult, for example, for an Elizabethan justice of the peace to discover just where he stood with regard to his various responsibilities at any particular time: he was the beast of burden on whose broad shoulders the government continually devolved new tasks.[1] Besides the 'commission of the peace', which implied authority to hear and determine all manner of criminal charges, except those which were indictable, that is, subject to trial by jury in the ordinary courts of law, he was the principal officer through whom council ordinances and parliamentary statutes were brought into touch with local life. The quarter sessions, or general assembly of the justices, held in each shire in October, January, spring, and midsummer, display a remarkable variety of business, covering criminal offences such as murder, assault, burglary, vagabondage, witchcraft, breaches of industrial laws and game laws, and recusancy; and the punishments inflicted ranged from fine and imprisonment to flogging, branding, and hanging. But the justices were also responsible for the repair of roads, licensing of taverns, binding of apprentices, relief of the honest poor in times of inordinate distress owing to famine, fire, or pestilence, fixing of the wage level for the district, regulation of the price and the export of grain, and the making of provision for redeeming English sailors from the Barbary pirates. They did not deal with civil litigation, but in certain circumstances they co-operated with the bishops in the suppression of irregularities in the church, and gradually the responsibility for the entire administration of the poor law was deputed to them. In short, there was no more useful officer in the local administration than the justice of the peace. He was its pivotal point and the guarantee of its efficiency, and his integrity was carefully watched by the council.

[1] W. Lambarde in *Eirenarcha* (1581) takes over 600 pages to describe the powers and responsibilities of the J.P.

The office of the sheriff, on the other hand, was becoming more honorific, and was certainly less arduous than the justice-ship. As the immediate representative of the Crown in the shire, the sheriff was charged with the provision of hospitality in the event of a royal visit, or the sojourn of distinguished strangers from abroad, and the periodical visit from the justices of assize. He had also important financial responsibilities in connexion with the collection of debts due to the Crown and of fines imposed by the law-courts, either locally or at West-minster, together with the enforcement of the queen's right to purveyance. He had nothing to do, however, with the collec-tion of taxes levied by the authority of parliament; but in the county court, over which he presided, he supervised what was by far the most important function of this decaying assembly, the election of members of parliament. In the same place he proclaimed the laws, published outlawries, decided civil suits involving less than 40s., and awarded damages for breach of contract and non-payment of wages. After the close of each parliamentary session writs were sent to him authorizing the payment of wages and travelling expenses to members of par-liament, and these were assessed upon the hundreds and town-ships at the next meeting of the county court. The sheriff also attended the quarter sessions of the justices of the peace and the assize courts for the impanelling of juries, and the due pre-sentment of prisoners from jail, whose safe keeping was part of his duty. These courts could not be properly constituted without his presence, nor could the sentences imposed be dis-charged without his co-operation; and all writs and summonses required his sanction. Certain other powers were also exercised by the sheriff, either on his own initiative or in conjunction with other Crown officials. Such were the suppression of riots and unlawful assemblies and the supervision of the county musters, but in these matters his responsibility was over-shadowed by that of the lord lieutenant.

The lord-lieutenant[1] was, like the justice of the peace, a typically Elizabethan functionary. The constant fear of internal rebellion and invasion from abroad combined to elevate the lord lieutenancy to a position of great importance in the local administration. On this office fell the supreme responsibility for

[1] Appointments to this office were temporary until 1585; after that they became permanent.

holding the musters in the shire, selecting officers and men for
the trained bands or local militia of the time, purchasing and
listing armour and munitions of war, keeping up the beacons,
and generally speaking making all local arrangements for the
defence of the country. In case of invasion or rebellion it was
his duty to lead the county levies; and if men were wanted for
foreign service he supplied them, provided for their equipment,
and saw to their transport.

In the maritime counties there was another typical functionary, the vice-admiral, whose jurisdiction covered all matters
arising out of the naval and commercial exigencies of the age.
He saw to the suppression of piracy, the impressment of seamen
for the navy, the enforcement of embargoes, the registration
of captures at sea, and the salvage of wrecks, together with the
settlement of disputes connected with these matters. He was
directly responsible to the lord admiral in London.

When the wide area covered by prerogative government is
considered, it will be apparent that the Elizabethan parliament
enjoyed a very restricted sphere of activity, and a very imperfect
influence over the executive.[1] The queen in council could issue
proclamations modifying the law without its sanction, except
for the infliction of new penalties, and in finance was dependent
upon it only for the 'extraordinary' revenue, the 'ordinary' or
main part of the revenue being entirely at her own disposal and
derived from sources beyond parliamentary control. In spite,
therefore, of the showy title accorded to the national assembly
by Sir Thomas Smith, it remained constitutionally subordinate
to the council, and was frowned upon by the queen if it ventured to assert an independent judgement in regard to policy. It
is a striking testimony to the relatively humble position it occupied that in a reign of forty-four and a half years the total time
spent in parliamentary discussions was only some thirty-five
months. Sessions were short, and the intervals between them
sometimes long and always irregular—circumstances that made
it difficult for parties to develop or for leaders to arise, who
might focus and direct public opinion or become the centre of
opposition to the executive. The only member of parliament
who showed the makings of a great parliament man was Peter

[1] It had not even obtained full control over its own elections, controversies in
regard to which were in many cases dealt with by the council.

Wentworth,[1] a member for the Cornish borough of Tregony; but his courageous independence of mind and fervid political genius were largely wasted on the sixteenth century. The conservative force of tradition, operative even in parliament itself, was too strong for men of his stamp to take command. Moreover, there was always a number of privy councillors with seats in the house who assumed an informal leadership, and by co-ordinating their actions made it certain that any organization of opinion that existed would be in favour of, rather than against, the royal policy. These councillor members were always men of experience, who did excellent work in committees and by acting as a *liaison* between parliament and the executive; but their weight was invariably thrown on the conservative side when disputes arose concerning the rights and privileges of the house.

The same criticism applies, with reservation, to the Speaker. Nominally he was the freely elected spokesman or prolocutor of the commons; but in actual fact his nomination usually came from one or other of the privy councillors present, and it would be no exaggeration to say that he was as much a Crown official as the 'mouthpiece' of the popular assembly. His conflicting duties in this dual capacity sometimes led to trouble; for, as chairman of the house, he had to allow a certain liberty of discussion, while, at the same time, as an official responsible to the Crown he had to exercise care that members did not trespass upon 'points of sovereignty'. True, he received no special instructions from the queen about the discharge of his duties; but in the speech delivered by the lord keeper or the lord chancellor at the opening of parliament, the purposes for which it was summoned were more or less clearly indicated, and it was the Speaker's task to see that these terms of reference were adhered to. If he permitted an undue liberty of criticism, he might be summoned by the queen and brought to book for his laxity; and generally speaking he was subject to direction as to the receiving and reading of bills. 'Messages from Caesar', or, as Peter Wentworth described them in his speech of 1575, 'rumours and messages', were a common occurrence in Elizabethan parliamentary history.

Nor was this all. It may be assumed that although there

---

[1] For Wentworth's parliamentary career see Professor Neale in *Engl. Hist. Rev.* xxxix. 36–54, 175–205.

was no discrimination against private members' bills, the initiation of all the important legislation lay not with parliament but with the council, where it was carefully prepared beforehand, and the councillor members were the men who piloted it through the house. Sometimes, too, bills were brought from the upper house to the commons 'specially recommended from the queen's majesty'; and if bills were introduced which appeared to touch the royal prerogative, there were always members who 'moved that petition be made by this house to her majesty for her licence and privity to proceed'. Finally, it is to be noted that the summoning and dissolution of parliament, and the validity of the measures it passed, were all dependent upon the will of the sovereign alone. 'It is in me and my power', said Elizabeth to the Speaker, in 1593, 'to call parliaments: it is in my power to end and determine the same: it is in my power to assent or dissent to any thing done in parliaments.' That she made full use of this power may be gathered from the fact that she summoned her parliaments only when it suited her convenience, and dismissed or prorogued them when she thought they had sat long enough. Her hatred of long parliaments and lengthy debates was notorious. Again and again the lord keeper was instructed in his speech on the opening day of the session to emphasize the importance of making existing laws more effective rather than of multiplying new laws. To curtail discussion whenever and wherever possible, to expedite the passing of subsidy bills and other necessary measures, and to send the members back to their constituencies with the minimum of delay—this seems to have been Elizabeth's settled policy in the conduct and control of parliament.

The question therefore arises: how much liberty was allowed in the discussion of public affairs?[1] In the first place, we must note that it was customary for the Speaker of the house of commons to petition the Crown at the commencement of the session for recognition of certain privileges: (1) freedom of access for the house to the royal presence in all matters of urgency and importance; (2) favourable construction of the Speaker's words when reporting resolutions of the house; (3) freedom from arrest of members and their servants during the continuance of

---

[1] For this subject see Neale's excellent chapter in *Tudor Studies*, ed. R. W. Seton-Watson (1924), together with other studies by the same author referred to in the Bibliography below.

parliament; and (4) freedom of speech 'in whatsoever was treated, propounded, and debated in the house'. All four liberties were established in principle before Elizabeth's accession, and the queen found no difficulty in giving her assent to them in 1559 'as largely, as amply, and as liberally as ever they were granted by her noble progenitors'. This did not mean, of course, that they were recognized in an absolute sense, or without qualification as to the use that might be made of them: on the contrary, it rested with the Crown to determine their due limits, and to apply restrictions if liberty threatened to degenerate into licence. Thus freedom of speech was granted to the first parliament of the reign with the condition that members were 'neither unmindful nor uncareful of their duties, reverence, and obedience to their sovereign'. But it was found necessary later to define the condition more narrowly and specifically, for what constituted 'duty', 'reverence', and 'obedience' was apt to be very differently interpreted by Crown and parliament. Consequently, in 1593, after thirty-eight years of more or less continuous friction, the lord keeper, in his reply to the Speaker's petition, summed up the attitude of the Crown as follows:

> For even as there can be no good consultation where all freedom of advice is barred, so there will be no good conclusion where every man may speak what he listeth, without fit observation of persons, matter, times, places, and other needful circumstances. . . . For liberty of speech her majesty commandeth me to tell you that to say yea or no to bills, God forbid that any man should be restrained or afraid to answer according to his best liking, with some short declaration of his reason therein, and therein to have a free voice, which is the very true liberty of this house; not as some suppose to speak there of all causes as him listeth and to frame a form of religion or a state of government as to their idle brains shall seem meetest. She saith that no king fit for his state will suffer such absurdities. . . .

From the queen's standpoint the question was not so much one of free speech as of the topics to which this freedom might be applied. Certain matters she regarded as definitely outside the scope of popular debate, and fit to be handled by herself alone, or by herself in conjunction with the council, viz. the succession, religion, foreign policy, and trade. Since parliament was not prepared to accept all of these extensive reservations, which covered every important national interest, a struggle ensued; and it was only by adroit tactics, or by coercive measures, that the queen was able to obtain the ultimate victory.

As we have seen[1] the first clash occurred over the succession, in the autumn of 1566. Already petitions had been addressed to the queen either to marry (1559) or to marry and declare a successor (1562–3); but in each case the supplication was met by an evasive answer or by the non-committal statement that the matter was weighty and required further consideration. As time passed, however, and nothing was done, the anxiety of the commons increased; and in October 1566, when the second parliament met for its second session, Mr. Molineux moved that their former suit to the queen be revived. Sir Ralph Sadler and others of the council who were present tried to 'stay' the house; but it was resolved to go on with the petitition, in conjunction with the lords. Whereupon Cecil and the vice-chamberlain intimated a message from the queen that 'by the words of a prince, she by God's grace would marry, and would have it believed', but that 'touching the limitation of the succession, the perils be so great to her person . . . that the time will not yet suffer to treat of it'. Despite this assurance and warning, the house went on with the matter in hand. The queen then tried to forestall it by summoning a deputation of both lords and commons before her. She would not, she said, be moved by violence to do anything, for it was 'monstrous that the feet should direct the head', but she would limit the succession when she conveniently could without peril. The report of this speech was communicated to the house by Cecil on the following day (6 November); but the ferment continued. On the 8th Mr. Lambert moved that a further attempt be made. Next day the vice-chamberlain, Francis Knollys, 'declared the queen's majesty's express command to the house that they should proceed no further in their suit, but satisfy themselves with her majesty's promise to marry'. In the debate that took place on receipt of this inhibition, Paul Wentworth desired to know whether the action of the Crown was not against the liberties and privileges of the house. Tempers were obviously rising. Two days later the Speaker was summoned to court, and returned with the news 'that he had received a special command from her highness . . . that there should be no further talk of the matter . . . and that if any person thought himself not satisfied

[1] Above, pp. 95–97.

let him come before the privy council and there show them'.
Even this peremptory veto did not stop the discussion; but later
in the month the queen, confronted with the possibility of having to dissolve parliament and lose her supplies, voluntarily
'revoked her two former commandments'—a concession that
was received with great joy by the commons. But when the
jubilant house then tried to turn its 'victory' to account by
incorporating the queen's promise of 5 November in the pre-
amble to the subsidy bill—a significant move—Elizabeth became very angry: 'as if', she scribbled on the draft, 'my private
answers to the realm should serve for a prologue to a subsidies
book'.[1] At the dissolution, on 2 January 1567, the lord keeper
seized the opportunity to rebuke the house through the Speaker
for 'bringing her majesty's prerogative in question'; and the
queen, who was present as usual in her place, delivered them
a short but caustic lecture on the same text.

> I have in this assembly [she said] found so much dissimulation,
> where I always professed plainness, that I marvel thereat, yea two
> faces under one hood, and the body rotten, being covered with two
> vizors, succession and liberty, which they determined must be either
> presently granted, denied or deferred. . . . But do you think that
> either I am unmindful of your surety by succession, wherein is all
> my care, considering I know myself to be mortal? No, I warrant
> you. Or that I went about to break your liberties? No, it was never
> in my meaning, but to stay you before you fell into the ditch. For
> all things have their time . . . yet beware however you prove your
> prince's patience, as you have now done mine.

At the opening of the third parliament in April 1571, when
Christopher Wraye, the Speaker, made his petitions as usual,
the lord keeper reminded him 'that her majesty having experience of late of some disorder and certain offences, which
though they were not punished, yet were they offences still'; and
'that they should do well to meddle with no matters of state but
such as should be propounded unto them, and to occupy themselves in other matters concerning the commonwealth'.

In spite of this warning off 'state affairs', the parliamentary
session had scarcely begun (14 April) when Mr. Strickland,
'a grave and ancient man of great zeal', broached the question
of reforming the prayer book so as to 'have all things brought to
the purity of the primitive church and the institution of Christ'.

---

[1] See Neale in *Eng. Hist. Rev.* xxxvi. 497–520.

A few days later he introduced a bill 'for reformation of the book of common prayer';[1] and the Speaker, having no authority to refuse it, allowed it to be presented and read for the first time. Mr. Treasurer and Mr. Comptroller pleaded that it was a matter for the queen alone as head of the church, and after 'divers long arguments' the house agreed to petition her majesty for licence to proceed.

Strickland's bill, it should be noted, was only one of a series introduced into the commons at this time for the regulation of ecclesiastical affairs, all of which were subsequently 'dashed' by the queen, on the ground that 'she could not suffer these things to be ordered by parliament'. But as the unfortunate Strickland had taken the lead and was evidently the prime mover, Elizabeth determined to make an example of him. During the Easter recess he was summoned before the council, reprimanded, and commanded to refrain in the meantime from attendance at the house. The consequence was that soon after business was resumed a debate ensued as to the legitimacy of his detention. Mr. Carleton represented it as a breach of parliamentary liberty, and urged that the offending member be sent for to the bar of the house, 'there to be heard, and there to answer'. Mr. Treasurer, on the other hand, advised caution and showed that Strickland 'was in no sort stayed for any word or speech by him in that place offered, but for the exhibiting of a bill into the house against the prerogative of the queen; which was not to be tolerated'. Whereupon Mr. Yelverton, taking his cue from the treasurer's remarks, boldly attacked the prerogative. Characterizing Strickland's detention as a 'perilous precedent', he proceeded to vindicate the authority of parliament in these words: 'It was fit', he said, 'for princes to have their prerogatives; but yet the same to be straitened within reasonable limits.' The prince, he showed, could not of herself make laws, neither might she by the same reason break laws.

The councillor members were obviously uneasy at the turn the discussion was taking, and were observed to 'whisper together': so the Speaker, realizing that matters had gone far enough, moved 'that the house should make stay of any further

[1] This was to provide for the abolition of kneeling at the communion, the removal of copes and surplices, confirmation of children, private baptism, and private administration of the Sacraments.

consultation thereupon'. On the next day, to the joy of the commons, Strickland reappeared in his place, and the committee on religious affairs resumed its discussions. For the remainder of the session there was no further trouble; but when parliament was dissolved on 29 May the lord keeper took occasion, in his reply to the Speaker's speech, to animadvert upon the 'audacious, arrogant, and presumptuous folly' of the house 'thus by superfluous speech spending much time in meddling with matters neither pertaining to them nor within the capacity of their understanding'. A year later, during the first session of the fourth parliament, the commons were informed through the Speaker that 'her highness' pleasure is that from henceforth no bills concerning religion shall be preferred or received into this house, unless the same should be first considered and liked of the clergy'. Coupled with this inhibitory message came another commanding the delivery to the queen of two bills concerning rites and ceremonies, which were then pending in parliament. The house had perforce to surrender them, and they were duly impounded.

Although it must now have been evident that the queen was inflexible, and the vast majority of members disinclined to continue the struggle, there was one man, Peter Wentworth, who determined to protest vigorously against the treatment meted out to parliament. Wentworth was one of the younger members, and perhaps on that account less cautious than his fellows; but his sincerity, eloquence, and courage were of a high order, and his grasp of principle still more remarkable. His speech in the house on 8 February 1575 was as much an invective against the subservience of parliament as it was a calculated indictment of the royal policy.

There is nothing so necessary [he said] for the preservation of the prince and state as free speech, and without it is a scorn and mockery to call it a parliament house, for in truth it is none, but a very school of flattery and dissimulation. . . . Amongst other, two things do great hurt in this place, of the which I do mean to speak: the one is a rumour which runneth about the house, and this it is, take heed what you do, the queen's majesty liketh not such a matter, whoever preferreth it, she will be offended with him. . . . The other: sometimes a message is brought into the house either of commanding or inhibiting, very injurious to the freedom of speech and consultation. I would to God, Mr. Speaker, that these two were buried in hell, I mean rumours and messages. . . . So that to avoid everlasting death and condemnation with the high and mighty God, we ought to proceed in every cause according to the matter, and not according to the prince's mind. . . . Free speech and conscience in this place are granted by a special law, as that without the which the prince and state cannot be preserved or maintained. . . . It is a dangerous thing in a prince to oppose or bend herself against her nobility and people. . . . I beseech the same God to endue her majesty with His wisdom, whereby she may discern faithful advice from traitorous sugared speeches, that will may not stand for a reason; and then her majesty will stand when her enemies are fallen, for no estate can stand where the prince will not be governed by advice. . . . For we are incorporated into this place to serve God and all England, and not to be time-servers, as humour-feeders, cancers that would pierce the bone, or as flatterers that would beguile all the world, and so worthy to be condemned both of God and man. . . .[1]

The commons were so surprised at the vehemence of the speech that 'out of a reverent regard of her majesty's honour' they stopped him before he had fully completed his remarks, and presently committed him to the serjeant's ward, to be examined the same afternoon by a committee of the house. The upshot was that Wentworth was sent to the Tower by a resolution of the house of commons itself and remained there a prisoner until 12 March, when he was released by 'special favour' of the queen.

When the fourth parliament met for its third session in January 1580 puritan feeling again ran high in the commons; and on the initiative of Paul Wentworth, brother of the redoubtable Peter, it was resolved to hold a public fast and a daily preaching, so that God 'might the better bless them in all their consultations and actions'. It was agreed that the preachers to

---

[1] It was during this speech that Wentworth recounted his well-known exchanges with Archbishop Parker in 1571 apropos of the bill on the Articles, which the puritanical section of the commons had modified by the excision of certain non-doctrinal clauses. He along with certain others had been sent to find out the archbishop's reaction to the changes, and the interview proceeded thus. The archbishop asked why the Articles concerning the Homilies and the consecration of bishops had been eliminated from the Book of Articles. Wentworth replied: 'Surely, sir, because we were so occupied in other matters that we had no time to examine them, how they agreed with the word of God.' To which Parker retorted: 'What! surely you mistook the matter. You will refer yourselves wholly to us therein.' 'No', said Wentworth, 'by the faith I bear to God, we will pass nothing before we understand what it is, for that were but to make you Popes. Make you Popes who list, for we will make you none.'

conduct the first service should be selected by such of the privy council as were members of the house 'to the intent that they may be discreet persons and keep convenient proportion of time, without intermeddling with matter of innovation or unquietness'. But the queen was annoyed at the innovation being made without her 'privity and pleasure first known', and a message was sent through Mr. Vice-chamberlain to that effect. The reprimand, however, was tempered by the remark that the 'error' was not 'wilful and malicious', but simply 'rash, ill-advised, and inconsiderate'. The house therefore agreed, on the suggestion of the vice-chamberlain, to make 'humble submission unto her majesty, acknowledging the said offence and contempt'. On the following day answer was brought from the queen 'of her most gracious acceptation of the submission', accompanied by the comment that the cause of the royal displeasure was 'not for that they desired fasting and prayer, but for the manner in presuming to indict a public fast without order and without her privity, which was to intrude upon her authority ecclesiastical'.

Meanwhile the yeast of puritanism continued to ferment beneath the surface, and in the succeeding parliament, on 27 February 1587, Anthony Cope introduced into the house a bill petitioning for the repeal of all existing laws touching ecclesiastical government, and for the authorization of a book containing a new form of public prayer and administration of the sacraments. So sweeping a change virtually meant the complete obliteration of the Establishment, including the Acts of Supremacy and Uniformity, and the book of common prayer. The Speaker, mindful of the queen's previous command not to meddle with such matters, asked to be spared the reading of the book; but the house insisted, and but for lack of time the Speaker would have been overborne. It was agreed to begin the first reading on the morrow. When the queen heard of the intention, she sent for the Speaker and ordered him to deliver up the bill and the book. On the following day (1 March) Peter Wentworth presented a number of articles concerning the liberties of the house, which he desired should be read and put to the question by the Speaker. He was asked to wait until the queen had signified her pleasure with regard to Cope's bill and book; but Wentworth refused, and the Speaker retorted that he must first peruse the articles before he took any further step. The articles were as follows: 'Whether this council be not a fit place for any member of the same here assembled freely and without controlment of any person or danger of laws, by bill or speech to utter any of the griefs of this commonwealth whatsoever touching the service of God, the safety of the prince, and this noble realm? Whether that great honour may be done unto God, and benefit and service unto the prince and state without free speech in this council, which may be done with it? Whether there be any council which can make, add to or diminish from the laws of the realm, but only this council of parliament? Whether it be not against the orders of this council to make any secret or matter of weight, which is here in hand, known to the prince or any other, concerning the high service of God, prince, or state, without the consent of the house? Whether the Speaker or any other may interrupt any member of this council in his speech used in this house, tending to any of the aforesaid high services? Whether the Speaker may rise when he will, any matter being propounded, without consent of the house or not? Whether the Speaker may over-rule the house in any matter or cause there in question; or whether he is to be ruled or over-ruled in any matter or not? Whether the prince and state can continue, stand, and be maintained without this council of parliament, not altering the government of the state?' The Speaker 'pocketed up' the questions and showed them to Sir Thomas Heneage, one of the privy council, 'who so handled the matter that Mr. Wentworth went to the Tower, and the question not at all moved'. Cope and others who had supported him were likewise committed to the Tower, by order of the lord chancellor, on the following day. No explanation was officially given for these arrests, nor did the commons take any steps, either by petitioning or otherwise, to secure the liberation of the prisoners. The conjectural statement made by the vice-chamberlain 'that they might perhaps be committed for somewhat that concerned not the business or privilege of the house', which was accepted, seems to indicate that they were punished not for anything they said or did in parliament but for their actions outside. Meanwhile the heavy artillery of the government—Sir Christopher Hatton, Sir Walter Mildmay, and Sir Thomas Egerton—was turned on to pulverize the puritan proposals. But it was the queen herself who quashed both book and bill by a message sent by one of the privy council members.

'Her Majesty', ran the message, 'taketh your petition herein to be against the prerogative of her crown; for by your full consent, it hath been confirmed and enacted . . . that the full power, authority, jurisdiction, and supremacy in church causes . . . should be united and annexed to the Imperial Crown of this Realm.'

But Wentworth was nothing if not pertinacious. For some time he had been brooding over the still unsettled succession question, which most men were now inclined to leave alone, and in August 1591 was again sent to prison for writing a pamphlet entitled *A Pithy Exhortation to Her Majesty for Establishing the Succession*. On being liberated he proceeded to work up a party in support of his plan; and when the eighth parliament of the reign met, in February 1593, he and Sir Henry Bromley presented a petition to the lord keeper, Puckering, in which they urged the lords of the upper house to join with the commons in a supplication to the queen for 'entailing' the succession, 'whereof a bill was ready drawn up by them'. For this offence against the 'former strait commandment' relating to matters of state they were 'presently sent for' by Sir Thomas Heneage, and ordered not to attend parliament or leave their lodgings. But the queen was so offended at their conduct that she gave instructions for their imprisonment, and Wentworth and Bromley along with others consentient to their proposal were severally sent to the Tower and the Fleet Prison. When the question was raised in the commons, and Mr. Wroth moved that a petition be made to her majesty for their release, on the ground that since they were absent from the debates on the subsidy their constituents might complain of the heavy taxation about to be imposed on them, the councillor members in the house replied that 'her majesty had committed them for causes best known to herself, and for us to press her majesty with this suit, we should but hinder them whose good we seek'. It should be remembered that it was at the opening of this 1593 parliament that Sir John Puckering, lord keeper, replying to the Speaker's request for privilege, made the remarkable announcement which we have already mentioned,[1] in which he stated the queen's view of freedom of speech and its limits.

Meanwhile, two days after the imprisonment of Wentworth and Bromley, Mr. Attorney Morrice of the court of wards

[1] p. 218.

raised the question of tyranny in the ecclesiastical courts, pointing out that the 'hard courses' adopted by the bishops, ordinaries, and other ecclesiastical judges towards 'the godly ministers and preachers of this realm' were 'contrary to the honour of God, the regality of her majesty, the laws of the realm, and the liberty of the subject'. He then presented two bills to be read: the first concerning unlawful 'inquisitions, subscriptions, and offering of oaths'; the second concerning the imprisonments inflicted for refusal to take oaths. Various members spoke in favour of the mover; but Sir Robert Cecil reminded the house that the queen had forbidden its interference in such matters, and advised that as the bill 'seemed to contain matters needful', it should first be 'commended to her majesty', with a view to obtaining her approval. This, however, did not meet with any support; but on the Speaker's protest that the bill was weighty and complicated, and that he could not 'open' it as he should until he understood it, it was agreed to let him have it for his private perusal. The same afternoon he was sent for to the court and questioned as to the content of the bill. He returned to the commons with the information that the queen was highly offended that, in spite of her express prohibition, the house had intermeddled with ecclesiastical affairs. 'Her majesty's present charge', he said, 'and express commandment is, that no bill touching the said matters of state or reformation in causes ecclesiastical be exhibited. And upon my allegiance I am commanded, if any such bill be exhibited, not to read it.' Morrice was reprimanded by the privy council, and his bill confiscated: confinement for several weeks followed.

This really terminated the efforts of the house of commons to legislate in religious matters; for although the queen removed her prohibition in 1597, and a bill against pluralities was read twice and 'committed' in 1601, there is no record that it reached the statute-book. As for the succession question, it was discreetly dropped, as being a subject in which the house had no further interest.

So far no reference has been made to the financial aspect of the relations between Crown and parliament, for, strictly speaking, finance did not enter as a factor into the constitutional struggle of the reign. The permanent hereditary revenue was derived from the income from the Crown lands, feudal incidents, the customs, ecclesiastical first-fruits, the proceeds of justice, recusancy fines, and the right to purveyance and preemption. It was sufficiently large to make the queen in ordinary years more or less independent of parliament, and able to 'live of her own'. Indeed the revenue granted by parliament in the shape of subsidies, tenths, and fifteenths was intended to meet only exceptional expenditure.

Until 1589 it was customary for the subsidy bill to consist of one subsidy and two tenths and fifteenths—roughly £140,000; and although the yield of these taxes had fallen greatly since Henry VIII's time, this was ample enough—thanks to the queen's frugality—not only for the needs of the government, but for the remission of the third instalment of the subsidy, in 1566. But a great change came over the situation after 1588, owing to the intensification of the war with Spain, the commitments in France and the Netherlands, and the growing expenditure in Ireland; and for the first time we hear of parliament being summoned primarily for the provision of 'treasure'. In 1589 the committee for the subsidy in the house of commons, stimulated by the arguments of Sir Walter Mildmay, chancellor of the exchequer, recommended two subsidies and four tenths and fifteenths. This was agreed upon by the house, subject to the proviso that the double subsidy would not become 'the occasion of a precedent to posterity'. But when the next parliament met, in 1593, it was confronted with a fresh request for liberality. The foreign peril and the military and naval needs of the country were strongly emphasized by the lord keeper in his opening speech, and by Sir Edward Stafford, Sir John Fortescue, and others in the commons. It was a question, said Fortescue, 'non utrum imperare sed utrum vivere'. In spite, therefore, of its previous decision not to allow a precedent to be established, the house of commons agreed to repeat the double subsidy and four tenths and fifteenths of 1589, and gave instructions for the bill to be drawn up accordingly.

At this point the lords of the upper house requested a conference with the commons about the subsidy, and the lord treasurer pointed out that whereas the last parliamentary grant brought in only £280,000, the queen had spent over £1,000,000 since the grant had been made. He also stated that the lords could not assent to less than three subsidies payable in the next three years. This at once gave rise to a somewhat acrimonious discussion in the commons on the question of privilege, it being asserted that the amount of the subsidy was a matter for the lower house alone to determine. Eventually, however, it was decided to revise the grant in the light of the treasurer's statement, and a lengthy debate ensued as to the capacity of the country to pay a triple subsidy. Sir Francis Bacon avowed himself in favour of three subsidies, but would have them spread over six years, because 'gentlemen must sell their plate, and farmers their brass pots ere this will be paid'. Mr. Heyle, on the other hand, affirmed 'that of his own knowledge from the Mount to London the country was richer many thousand pounds than heretofore'. Sir Walter Raleigh was of the opinion that 'for the difficulty in getting this subsidy, I think it seems more difficult by speaking than it would be in gathering'. 'Let us let the people blood', remarked Mr. George Moore, using a surgical metaphor, 'and so prevent the danger.' Once again the bogy of undesirable precedents came up, to be quashed by Sir Robert Cecil, her majesty's principal secretary, with the remark that 'precedents have never been perpetual, but begun and ended with the causes. . . . We have no reason to give prejudice to the best queen or king that ever came, for fear of a worse king than ever was.' After 'many long and grave speeches' the house agreed to three subsidies and six tenths and fifteenths. The bill passed the house on 22 March 'very difficultly . . . by reason of the greatness thereof', but the Speaker 'did overreach the house in the subtle putting of the question'. From start to finish the discussions had lasted twenty-four days.

Despite the increased revenue the financial situation had in no way improved when, in October 1597, the queen summoned her ninth parliament. The lord keeper laid great stress on the fact that Crown lands had been sold to maintain the necessary forces by sea and land, 'whereby with such small helps as from her subjects have been yielded, she hath defended and kept safe her dominions'.[1] So serious was the position of the country, he said, that 'he that would seek to lay up treasure and enrich himself, should be like to him that would busy himself to

[1] Loans and benevolences were levied on the wealthy by privy seal, and ship money was imposed on even the inland towns, while the customs were augmented; but still there was a deficit. For the ship money levy see *Acts of the Privy Council*, xvi. 304, 353-4.

beautify his house when the city where he dwelleth were on fire
or to deck up his cabin when the ship wherein he saileth were
ready to drown'. Bacon threw his oratorical weight on the
government side, thus redeeming his *faux pas* of 1593. It was
impossible for the commons to do less than repeat the three
subsidies of the previous parliament and they did so apparently
without any serious criticism. But their troubles were not yet
at an end.[1]

The last parliament of the reign, which sat from October to
December 1601, was in many respects the most interesting, as
it was certainly the most turbulent, of all. The purpose for
which it was called was to provide ways and means of financing
the costly war in Ireland; but trouble was in the air almost
from the very start of the session. When the commons, as was
their wont, repaired to the upper house to hear the opening
speech of the lord keeper, they found the door of the chamber
accidentally barred against them; and a day or two later (30
October), when the queen left the parliament house, after the
Speaker's petitions had been granted, there were few who
greeted her with the customary 'God save your majesty'.[2] It
was a bad beginning, but worse followed, as soon as the commons settled down to business. Acrimony, noise, and confusion
characterized the debates. Speakers were 'cried or coughed
down', or otherwise interrupted in their remarks: voting was
interfered with, members being, on one occasion, pulled back
into the house or pulled out into the lobby against their will;
and even the precincts of the house were disturbed by brawling
and disorder. The two principal matters in dispute were the
subsidy bill and monopolies. In regard to the former it was
pointed out by Cecil, who repeated the substance of the lord
keeper's speech in the house of commons on the following day,
that the rebellion in Ireland and the war with Spain had
created a deficit of £140,000; while the government would
require £300,000 for fresh outlay before Easter. In order to

---

[1] Out of this parliament came two great enactments—for relief of the poor, and
the punishment of sturdy beggars: see below, p. 266.

[2] 'And the throng being great, and little room to pass, she moved her hand to
have more room; whereupon one of the gentlemen ushers said openly, "Back
masters, make room." And one answered stoutly behind, "If you will hang us,
we can make no more room": which the queen seemed not to hear, though she
heaved up her head and looked that way towards him that spake.' (H. Townshend,
Historical Collections, pp. 178, 179.)

meet this, it would be necessary for the house to offer no less than four subsidies, or twice the sum granted under protest in 1589. The commons were greatly perturbed, and in the debates that followed many raised their voices on behalf of the poor, who, it was said, were compelled to sell their 'pots and pans' to meet the already heavy taxation; and a desire was expressed that the incidence of the taxes should be made more equitable by higher assessment of the wealthy. Some thought that the 'three pound men' should be spared; others that the 'four pound men' should pay double, with a correspondingly increased charge on the 'rest upwards'. Cecil reminded the house that 'when Hannibal resolved to sack Rome, he dwelt in the cities adjoining, and never feared or doubted of his enterprise, till word was brought him that the maidens, ladies, and women of Rome sold their ear-rings, jewels, and all their necessaries to maintain the war against him'. Serjeant Heyle averred that the queen 'hath as much right to all our lands and goods as to any revenue of her crown'—a remark that caused the house to 'hem, laugh, and talk'. Eventually, however, after a protracted debate, it was agreed to grant the four subsidies and the eight tenths and fifteenths, and a committee was appointed to draw up the necessary bill.

The climax of the session was reached when the question of monopolies was brought before the house by Mr. Lawrence Hide, for this was a subject that touched every one closely, and on which every one believed he could speak with authority. A monopoly, said Mr. Spicer of Warwick, is 'a restraint of any thing public in a city or commonwealth to a private use, and the user called a monopolitan'. The practice of granting monopolies by royal patent for the manufacture, distribution, or sale of certain articles of commerce had grown up since the sixteenth year of the reign, with disastrous effect on the cost of living and the general welfare of the community. 'I cannot utter with my tongue', said Mr. Francis Moore, 'or conceive with my heart the great grievances that the town and country which I serve suffereth by some of these monopolies; it bringeth the general profit into a private hand, and the end of all is beggary and bondage of the subject.' When Sir Robert Wroth read out the list of fresh patents issued since the last parliament —for currants, iron, powder, cards, ox shin-bones, train oil, oil of blubber, transportation of leather, cloth, ashes, aniseeds, vinegar, sea-coals, salt-petre, lead, calamine stones, pilchards, &c., Mr. Hakewell of Lincoln's Inn stood up and asked: 'Is bread not there?' 'Bread?' quoth one. 'Bread?' quoth another. 'This voice seems strange,' quoth a third. 'No,' quoth Mr. Hakewell, 'if order be not taken for these, bread will be there before the next parliament.'

There was no doubt about the evils of the system: they were admitted by every speaker; but the question was how to proceed towards their amendment. As Francis Bacon pointed out, 'the queen, as she is our sovereign, hath both an enlarging and restraining power. For by her prerogative she may first set at liberty things restrained by statute law or otherwise; and secondly, by her prerogative she may restrain things that be at liberty.' 'Wherefore', he concluded, 'I say and I say again, that we ought not to deal, to judge or meddle with her majesty's prerogative.' But the house found it difficult to reach unanimity as to procedure. Some demanded a bill: others insisted that all patents should be brought before the house and cancelled: others, again, were for petitioning the queen. The confusion was so great that Cecil exclaimed: 'This is more fit for a grammar school than a court of parliament. I have been a counsellor of state this twelve years, yet did I never know it subject to construction of levity and disorder.' Outside the house, in the streets, there were ominous mutterings and cries of 'God prosper those that further the overthrow of these monopolies, God send the prerogative touch not our liberty'. 'Let me give you this note,' said Cecil, 'that the time was never more apt to disorder and make ill interpretation of good meaning: I think those persons would be glad that all sovereignty were converted into popularity.'

Fortunately at this juncture the queen, who had been informed of the debate by her council, and had received many petitions 'both going to chapel and also to walk abroad', intervened with a drastic solution of the problem that took the house by storm, and won for her one of the greatest triumphs of her reign. Summoning the Speaker, she informed him that 'she herself would take present order of reformation'; that 'some [of the monopolies] would presently be repealed, some suspended, and none put in execution, but such as should first have a trial according to the law for the good of the people'. When the news was communicated to the commons they agreed to send a deputation, headed by the Speaker, to express their gratitude to her majesty; and on 30 November, in the council chamber at Whitehall, was transacted one of the most memorable and glamorous scenes in Tudor history. After receiving the thanks of the Speaker, which were couched in a language that must have sounded sweet to her ears, the aged queen replied with a speech full of gracious condescension, fervour, and evident sincerity:

Though God hath raised me high [she said] yet this I count the glory of my crown, that I have reigned with your loves. This makes me that I do not so much rejoice that God has made me to be a queen, as to be a queen over so thankful a people. . . . Neither do I desire to live longer days, than that I may see your prosperity, and that is my only desire. . . . Of myself I must say this, I never was any greedy, scraping grasper, nor a strait fast-holding prince, nor yet a waster; my heart was never set on worldly goods, but only for my subjects' good. . . . Yea mine own properties I count yours to be expended for your good.

Hereupon she bade the kneeling commons to stand up, and thanked them for preventing her from falling 'into the lap of an error, only for lack of true information', and for their zeal for the common good.

Since I was queen [she said] yet did I never put my pen to any grant, but that upon pretext and semblance made unto me that it was both good and beneficial to the subjects in general, though a private profit to some of my ancient servants who deserved well.

But if her 'kingly bounty' had been 'abused', and her grants 'turned to the hurt of my people', she hoped that 'God will not lay their culps and offences to my charge'. 'To be a king and wear a crown', she assured them, 'is more glorious to them that see it, than it is a pleasure to them that bear it.' For herself, she continued,

I was never so much enticed with the glorious name of a king, or royal authority of a queen, as delighted that God hath made me His instrument to maintain His truth and glory, and to defend this kingdom from peril, dishonour, tyranny, and oppression. . . . I speak it to give God the praise as a testimony before you, and not to attribute anything to myself; for I, O Lord, what am I, whom practices and perils past should not fear! O what can I do that I should speak for any glory! God forbid.

On this note of humility Elizabeth ended her speech; and having bade them all kiss her hand, she dismissed the deputation. Although this was not actually her last public speech to her subjects, it has rightly been hailed as the most moving, and by far the most impressive and inspiring. The speech that followed on 19 December when parliament was dissolved, seems by comparison formal and prosaic; but it has the same emphasis on divine providence, and on the fact that she is God's instrument 'in delivering the state from danger and herself from dishonour'.

VII

THE EXPANSION OF ENGLAND
AND THE ECONOMIC AND
SOCIAL REVOLUTION

THE Englishman of the Tudor period was not by nature or tradition an explorer or a conquistador. The cult of the map and the flag was unknown to him: he had no desire to search out the distant places of the earth, or to found a new England beyond the seas. After the nine days' wonder of the Cabot voyages had subsided, leaving nothing behind it but the memory of a new fishing-station for cod off the Canadian coast, sixty years elapsed during which England made no contribution whatever to the extension of geographical knowledge, or to the opening up of new sea routes. Neither the fabled wealth of Cathay, nor the epoch-making achievements of the Spaniard in central and south America, nor the study of the new geography, which created a ferment in all European countries, from Cracow to Seville, could tempt the sea-girt Englishman out of his isolation. To all intents and purposes he remained a passive spectator of the world's far-flung maritime activity. Not even a book appeared, with an English superscription, to commemorate the greatness of human endeavour in the most momentous half-century of the world's history.[1] It was only when the magical movement of trade began, after 1550, when the expansion of industry at home made distant markets a necessity, and when, in Elizabeth's reign, spoliation of the Spaniard became a patriotic duty, that Englishmen took the lead in maritime enterprise, and entered the field as competitors for geographical honours. In other words, it was trading and buccaneering, rather than the lure of the unknown, or the thirst for knowledge, or the vision of empire, that gave birth to the greatest period of English exploit on the sea.

In 1558 the population of England and Wales was probably not more than from two and a half to three millions, with an

---

[1] The first original English work on cosmography was W. Cunningham's *Cosmographical Glasse* (1559): 'I am the first', wrote the author, 'that ever in our tongue have written of this argument.'

average density approximating to that of European Russia in the nineteenth century; and the wealth of the richest London merchants was estimated by the Venetian ambassador in 1557, as between fifty and sixty thousand pounds—a figure that compares very unfavourably with the three and a half million ducats of capital (£875,000) possessed by a first-class continental business firm like the Fuggers of Augsburg. England, in fact, was a relatively poor country, and the standard of living was low. In the production as well as in the consumption of wealth, in industrial technique and scientific skill, she was markedly behind her nearest neighbours on the Continent. Her extractive industries, with the exception of lead and tin mining, which were of ancient standing, were so backward that it was necessary to import Germans to run the copper mines at Keswick; and coal was only beginning to come into its own as a fuel, either for the forge or the domestic hearth.[1] Nor was agriculture in a much better state, for only one-quarter of the soil was under grain crops. One economic asset, however, she did possess, and it was

[1] According to a reliable estimate, the total annual production of coal in the British Isles, about the beginning of Elizabeth's reign, was slightly over 200,000 tons, or, if we exclude Scotland and Ireland, 160,000 tons. The chief coalfields were situated in Northumberland and Durham, Cumberland, the Midlands (Yorkshire, Lancashire, Cheshire, Derbyshire, Shropshire, Staffordshire, Nottinghamshire, Warwickshire, Leicestershire, and Worcestershire), South Wales, Kingswood Chase (near Bristol), the Forest of Dean, and Devonshire. Only some 12,000 tons of the whole output were exported, the rest being consumed mainly in the coal-producing districts and in London and the south-east generally. From this it may be concluded that (1) although the coal industry was not a negligible quantity in the national economy, the consumption of mineral fuel per head of the population was probably only about one hundredweight a year; (2) England had not yet begun to use her coal to any appreciable extent as a means of purchasing food and raw materials from other countries. It cannot be too strongly emphasized, therefore, that Elizabethan England was still in the timber age. Every industry of importance, excepting that of the smith and the lime-burner, in which the use of coal was well established, drew on the timber supplies of the country to a degree almost inconceivable today: so much so, indeed, that, as the reign advanced, the conservation of woods and forests became a serious problem for the government, and the cost of firewood almost trebled. It was this timber shortage—one might call it a crisis—that really gave coal its opportunity: this, and the growing demand of an expanding population for manufactured goods of all kinds. The noxious fumes which rendered coal unpopular at first, both for domestic and industrial purposes, gradually assumed less significance as the potentiality of the new fuel was discovered, and a better technique was invented for handling it in furnaces. Finally, it would be no exaggeration to say that the substitution of coal for wood (or wood charcoal) in industry, which began in Elizabeth's reign, made possible its great industrial development; for the rapid diminution of timber supplies and the consequent enhancement of prices for wood fuel might easily have nipped such a movement in the bud.

of priceless value, viz. the cloth and woollen industry. Here, indeed, she enjoyed a pronounced advantage over all rivals, for English sheep and wool were admitted to be the best in the world; and although 42 per cent. of the export trade in woollen products was still in the hands of the foreigner, and the finer branches of the manufacture were practised only in Flanders, the paramount importance of the industry in the national economy is clearly reflected by the customs statistics. During the year 1564-5 the total value of all goods exported from England amounted to the round sum of £1,100,000, of which no less than 81·60 per cent. accrued from cloth and woollens: the remaining 18·40 per cent. being divided between raw wool, woolfells, lead, tin, corn, beer, coal, and fish in that order of value. It is impossible, therefore, to be mistaken as to the basic source of the national wealth. Not only so: the cloth trade was so far ahead of the others, and so powerfully organized under government favour, as to constitute a 'phalanx of irresistible momentum, to which other nations had nothing similar to oppose'.

When Elizabeth's reign began, the export trade in cloth, so far as it was conducted by English merchants, had a very restricted market, being confined chiefly to Antwerp, where the Merchant Adventurers had their 'staple'. The Muscovy Company, founded in 1555, had just begun to explore the possibilities of the Russian market. And there was a group of London and west country merchants who plied a lucrative if somewhat precarious traffic with Barbary and the Guinea coast. But with the exception of Africa England had no markets of value outside Europe. The habitable part of the north American continent from Newfoundland to Florida was unknown to English navigators, and remained so for another generation: central and south America lay within the monopolist area of the Spaniards; and the Near and Far East were preserves of the Venetians and Portuguese respectively. Nevertheless a beginning had been made by the Muscovy Company to penetrate beyond Russia into Asia by sea and by land. In 1556 Stephen Burrough was sent in the *Searchthrift* to force a passage by the North Cape to Cathay, following the line taken by the ill-fated Willoughby and Chancellor expedition three years before. He succeeded in passing the Kanin peninsula and the Island of Kolgiev, and reached the Bay of Petchora, but was eventually compelled to turn back by drift ice, fogs, and contrary winds at the Straits of

Waigatz. In the next year Anthony Jenkinson, another agent of the company, set out on his first journey overland into Asia via the great rivers of Russia, Astrakhan, the Caspian sea, the Transcaspian desert, and the Oxus, reaching Bokhara about Christmas. Meanwhile Richard Eden had published his *Decades of the New World* (1555), the first compendium in English of information concerning the Spanish exploits in America; and a few years later Burrough placed his countrymen in touch with the latest developments in navigation by inducing the Muscovy Company to publish a translation of Martin Cortes 's *Art of Navigation*, a notable product of the Spanish school of seamanship at Seville.

Although it was now clear that Englishmen were acquiring knowledge and experience in exploration, so far no positive gains had resulted from the efforts of the Muscovy Company, beyond the opening up of the Russian market. The barren tundras of Siberia, and the semi-cannibal tribes of Samoyeds who inhabited them, offered little prospect of trade in this direction; and Jenkinson at Bokhara found that the main import and export traffic of Asia was handled by Venetians, who traded with Persia through the Turkish empire, and by Portuguese from their stations at Ormuz and Malacca. The company therefore suspended its interest for the time being in the north-east passage, but decided to make a bid for the Persian trade. In 1561 Jenkinson was dispatched on his second journey, with instructions to negotiate a commercial agreement with the shah. Following the same route as on the previous occasion as far as Astrakhan, he crossed the Caspian in a more southerly direction to Derbend, and entered Old Persia, where he met the shah at Kasbin. In spite of opposition from the Turk, who sponsored the Venetians, and was unwilling that the fertilizing stream of traffic should be diverted from the Turkish empire to the northerly route through Russia to England, an understanding was reached; and during the next twenty years no fewer than six other commercial missions were sent from England to Persia. Thus a considerable quantity of the finer English cloths, dyed with bright colours to suit the oriental taste, found its way to the markets of Tabriz, Shamakha, and Kasbin. This route to Persia via Russia and Astrakhan continued to be frequented until 1581, when it was superseded by the Mediterranean route used by the Levant Company.

In the meantime the Muscovy Company strengthened its position in Russia. Under the protection of the tsar, Ivan the Terrible, exclusive rights were obtained to trade in the northern regions of the empire, and factories were established linking up Rose Island in the White Sea (the company's headquarters) with Cholmogory, Moscow, Jaroslav, Vologda, and even far distant Kazan and Astrakhan. It was the hope of the promoters to acquire a monopoly of Russian exports and imports, thereby enhancing profits; but this was prevented, partly by the presence of numerous English 'interlopers', partly by Russian resentment at the high prices charged by the company, and partly by the competition of the Dutch. The loss of ships and cargoes on the hazardous sea passage, the dangers to which merchants were exposed in a semi-barbarous land, the plunder of caravans either by the wild tribes in Russia itself or on the farther side of the Caspian, and the dishonest practices of the company's own factors also added to the difficulties of the enterprise. Still the profits were satisfactory for a number of years, and the exports from Russia—train oil, tallow, hides, tar, timber for masts, hemp, cordage, and wax—were of the greatest value to England as raw materials and supplies for the navy and ship-building.

One notable advantage the Muscovy Company enjoyed was its comparative immunity from the political disturbances of western Europe, and the evil consequences of Anglo-Spanish rivalry, which played havoc with the Netherlands market, and compelled the Merchant Adventurers to remove their staple from Antwerp to the German cities of Hamburg, Emden, Stade, and latterly to Middleburg in Zeeland. Nor was it troubled by the severe competition of the Hanse merchants, who fought a long and desperate struggle with the Adventurers for the economic mastery of the German market and the maintenance of their privileged position in the English carrying trade—a struggle that ended with the defeat of the Hanse and the evacuation of the Steelyard in London, but told heavily on the finances of the English company.

While the Adventurers were endeavouring to establish themselves on the Rhine and the Elbe, a new company, the Eastland Company, was formed in 1579, for the purpose of still further weakening the Hanse by capturing the trade of Scandinavia, Pomerania, and Poland. Its depot was at Elbing in Poland,

and later at Danzig. Like the Muscovy Company, it dealt in materials for shipping, which were exchanged for English cloth. The lure of Cathay, however, was irresistible. During the seventies a project began to take shape for the opening up of a passage by the north-west instead of the north-east. For some years the fertile and adventurous brain of Humphrey Gilbert had been busy with the technical aspect of the problem, working over geographical treatises, ancient as well as modern, and old chronicles, and collating every scrap of information available on ocean currents and prevailing winds. The outcome was the celebrated *Discourse to Prove a North-west Passage*. The thesis of this remarkable book, 'that there lieth a great sea between it [i.e. America], Cathaia, and Greenland, by the which any man of our country that will give the attempt, may with small danger pass to Cathaia, the Moluccae, India, and all the other places in the east, in much shorter time than the Spaniard or Portugal doth', was doubtless something of an academic *tour de force*; but it was stated with such fervour and plausibility that it became the signal for a fresh onslaught on the Arctic. Other men had also been thinking on similar lines, notably Martin Frobisher and Michael Lock—the former a practised navigator and the latter a London merchant and member of the Muscovy Company who dabbled in the new geography. Sanction was obtained from the queen to make the venture, and the Muscovy Company waived its monopoly of the 'search for new trades to the northward, north-eastward, and north-westward'. Thus, under the patronage of the earl of Warwick, and with the financial backing of the queen, Burghley, Walsingham, Leicester, Sir Thomas Gresham, and others, Frobisher set out on three voyages to the unknown lands north of Labrador (1576–8). By some mischance he missed the entrance to Hudson Strait, which would have taken him a long way on his journey; but he succeeded in destroying the legend of a *mare glaciale* or frozen sea, and planted the flag on the 'Countess of Warwick Island', in the strait that subsequently became known as Frobisher Strait. Unfortunately the report got abroad that some black stones, which one of the crew brought home with him from the first voyage, contained gold: with the result that the geographical interest of the enterprise was quickly subordinated to mining operations on the Canadian coast. In the end the alleged ore turned out, on being assayed, to be worthless, and was thrown out, says Camden, to mend a road at Dartford in Kent. On the other hand, although Frobisher's 'Cathay Company' failed of its object, a milestone had been set up in Arctic exploration, and England's faith in the existence of a north-west passage was not shaken. The anxiety of the government to keep the achievement a secret from the Spaniard shows the importance attached to it.

Two years later the Muscovy Company revived its interest in the north-east passage; and an expedition was organized (1580) for another attempt to break through the Straits of Waigatz. Of all the voyages of the period none was more elaborately prepared or more carefully thought out. The knowledge gained on previous expeditions was utilized, and the leaders, Arthur Pet and Charles Jackman, bore with them a mass of instructions and advice, in which several of the best-known geographers of the time, Mercator, Dr. Dee, Stephen Burrough, and Richard Hakluyt, had a hand. They were to proceed to the Straits of Waigatz, and push on through the Kara Sea to the 'river of Ob' (Obi); thence 'in God's name proceed eastwards with the land on the starboard side until Cathay is reached'. It was believed that if once the northern trend of the Siberian coast could be circumnavigated, the land would fall away rapidly to the southward, and Cathay would soon be in their grasp. But alas for the hopes of the promoters! After a weary battle for two months with the ice, fog, rain, and contrary winds that had barred Burrough's progress in 1556, Pet and Jackman found it impossible to penetrate into the Kara Sea, and gave up the project in despair. It was the last Elizabethan voyage to the north-east. The task of discovering the passage to Cathay by the North Cape had to be left to the better technique and more scientific equipment of a later age.

So far the only contact which England had established with Asiatic markets was the Muscovy Company's trade with Persia. The older Levant trade, which had flourished in the fifteenth century and given England a share in Turkish markets, and the means of access to the spices, drugs, and gems that came from farther east, had practically died out. In 1578, however, two London merchants, Sir Edward Osborne and Richard Staper, 'seriously considering what benefit might grow to the commonwealth by renewing the aforesaid discontinued trade', sent out an envoy, William Harborne, to the court of Murad III; and in June 1580 this able negotiator secured a *firman* from the

Sultan, granting full rights and privileges to English merchants trading in all parts of the Turkish empire. Immediately afterwards the Levant Company was formed and received a charter from the queen, who hoped to turn the commercial connexion with the Porte to political advantage in the struggle with Spain (1581). Depots were founded at Aleppo, Damascus, Tunis, Alexandria, Tripoli, and other Turkish ports, and an ambassador took up residence at Constantinople, at the company's expense. Prosperity came quickly to the Levant merchants, and also to the Venetian Company, which was formed a few years later for trade with Venice and her possessions in the eastern Mediterranean; for the sweet wines of Candia, olive oil, and dried currants were in great demand in England. Furthermore, the friendship of Turkey opened up an entrancing vista of trade with the countries lying beyond, as far as the Persian Gulf and perhaps even India.

Thus, in 1583, the same two merchants who had floated the Levant Company planned the crowning adventure of the reign into the east by land. In that year a small party of Englishmen led by John Newbery and Ralph Fitch made its way to Jaffa by sea, crossed the Lebanon mountains to Aleppo, and joined a caravan for the Euphrates. Sailing down this river to Basra and the Persian Gulf, they took ship to Ormuz; and from Ormuz crossed the Indian Ocean in a Portuguese vessel to Goa, where the authorities threw them into prison as spies. But they escaped through the good services of an English jesuit, Father Stevens, who had settled in Goa in 1579, and picking their way eastward to Golconda, turned north across the great river and mountain system of India, and eventually arrived at Agra, the residence of the moghul, to whom Newbery presented a letter of credence from Queen Elizabeth. Thereafter the little party broke up. Newbery set out on a perilous return journey to Europe through the Punjab, promising to come back with a ship and pick up Fitch in Bengal in two years. Another member of the expedition took service with the moghul. But Fitch, whose appetite for adventure was only whetted, pursued his way down the Jumna and the Ganges to Bengal, from Bengal to Pegu (Burma), and from Pegu to Malacca. Returning to Bengal in time to keep his appointment with Newbery, he found no trace of him—he had perished on the homeward journey: whereupon he took ship for Goa; and at long last, after nine years of wandering in the east, arrived back in England by approximately the route he had used on the outward expedition. From many points of view he had accomplished the most remarkable journey of the period; and, above all, he had opened communications with India, Burma, and the Malay peninsula.

While these events were taking place in India, John Davis was making the last and greatest attempt of the reign to prove the existence of the north-west passage. Supported by Walsingham, Adrian Gilbert,[1] and William Sanderson, a member of the merchant community in London, this prince of Elizabethan navigators made three voyages into the waters between Greenland and the Canadian coast. In 1585 he reached latitude 66° 40', to the north of Frobisher Strait, and discovered Northumberland Inlet, which he took to be the passage he was in search of. Further investigation, on the second voyage, however, revealed the fact that Northumberland Inlet was merely an arm of the sea. On the third voyage (1587) Davis held on to latitude 73° on the Greenland side, the 'farthest north' of the period, which he named 'Sanderson His Hope'. To the north of this point the sea was invitingly open; but when he turned westwards to look for the passage, he ran into pack ice, and was compelled to return southwards by the Canadian coast to Labrador. Curiously enough he too, like Frobisher, passed Hudson Strait without noticing it. But he was greatly impressed by the 'great sea, free, large, very salt, blue, and of unsearchable depth', which lay northwards from Sanderson's Hope. 'I have been in 73°,' he wrote, 'finding the sea all open, and forty leagues between land and land': wherefore, he concluded, 'the passage is most probable, the execution easy'. Subsequent events hardly justified this optimistic forecast; but Davis had rendered a great service to geography. Besides discovering the strait that now bears his name, he had scattered a number of new names over the coasts of Greenland and North America, such as Mount Raleigh, Dier's Cape, Cape Walsingham, Lumley's Inlet, Warwick's Foreland, Cape Childley, and Darcy's Island. Although he remained confident of ultimate success, and would doubtless have pursued it, if chance had offered, the numerous distractions of the later years of the reign, the war with Spain, and the diversion of the nation's energies into other channels made any resumption of the quest for Cathay impossible.

[1] A younger brother of Sir Humphrey.

Although the search for a passage to the Pacific was the lode-star of Elizabethan navigators, it must have been borne in on the mind of the merchant community after 1580, that the exploration of the Siberian, Greenland, and American coasts, and the increase of geographical knowledge resulting therefrom, was but a poor and unproductive outcome of the effort involved. The need for markets beyond the seas, free from interference by the foreigner, was now more urgent than ever; for English trade, though still prosperous in Europe, was being subjected to increasing restrictions, dangers, and interruptions. Baltic shipping was at the mercy of Danish tolls: the Muscovy Company had likewise to pay an annual tribute to Denmark for the right of passage by the North Cape: the Merchant Adventurers and the Eastland Company were fighting the Hanse for the control of markets in Germany, Norway, Sweden, and Poland; and English ships bound for Mediterranean ports had to run the gauntlet of Barbary and Spanish privateers, which haunted the straits of Messina and Gibraltar. Indeed the Mediterranean became so unquiet a region that merchantmen had to go in convoys heavily armed. Moreover, apart from troubles of this nature, England had a surplus population, always increasing, which her industries could not absorb, and a considerable recusant population whose existence taxed her jails and provided the government with a continual source of anxiety. The question therefore arose whether these various problems and difficulties could not be met by 'planting' Englishmen on some suitable part of the American seaboard, where they could develop and exploit the resources of a great continent, beyond the Spanish sphere of influence. Already Gilbert had hinted at some such plan in his pamphlet of 1567; and Richard Hakluyt had suggested to some of Frobisher's men that they should endeavour to find out whether it was possible to set up a 'stapling place' on the other side of the Atlantic—a sort of American Calais—with an English population to maintain it. Gradually the idea was born of transferring the nation's principal economic activities to America, and a rudimentary 'colonial' policy took shape in the minds of Captain Christopher Carlile and Sir George Peckham, and received the able backing of Hakluyt. All three writers set themselves to show that America could supply all the important raw materials which England obtained from European countries, while her vast native population, together with the English to be settled in their midst, would easily absorb all the cloth England could produce. The fact that the passage was quick and easy, and free from molestation by foreign powers, was an additional advantage of the highest importance. Nor was it overlooked that the American aborigines would profit by the introduction of the christian religion and contact with a more advanced civilization. Even the problem of the sea route to Cathay might be solved if England secured a base of operations on the other side of the Atlantic.

In pursuance of this new policy, Gilbert procured his patent from the queen to 'plant' America, in 1578, and five years later organized his expedition to Newfoundland. If he had been successful, Newfoundland would have become the first English colony in the new world; for the patent gave ample rights to its promoter not only to settle a community but also to provide for its government and administration. Fate, however, decreed otherwise. Gilbert's scheme was wrecked by his own impatient, unstable, and perverse nature. After a hurried survey of the mineral and other wealth of the country, a provisional distribution of the lands round St. John's harbour, and the proclamation of English sovereignty over the island, he determined to push on with a grandiose project for carving out similar settlements farther to the south, and plunged into a hazardous voyage along the American coast, which was just as little known to English navigators at this time as the coast of Siberia or of northern Canada. In the shoals off Sablon Island, Cape Breton, he lost his principal ship, the *Delight*, with all his maps and plans and geological specimens, and was compelled to turn homeward with his two remaining ships, the *Squirrel* and the *Golden Hind*. Then his strong sense of duty to his crews, admirable enough in itself but tragic in its consequences, bade him travel in the *Squirrel*—a tiny frigate, heavily gunned and overloaded with deck hamper—in preference to the larger and safer ship, which his pilot advised. North of the Azores the little flotilla was struck by a storm, 'terrible seas breaking short and pyramid wise'; and during the night of 9–10 September the lights of the *Squirrel* disappeared, and all hands were lost, including the 'general'. So ended the first attempt to build up a greater England on American soil.

The death of Gilbert, however, did not affect the continuance of the project of which he was the pioneer: his mantle fell on the shoulders of Walter Raleigh, who sought and received a similar patent from the queen in 1584, and threw himself into a fresh scheme for appropriating and planting the American mainland. A month after the issue of the patent (April 1584) he dispatched Philip Amadas and Arthur Barlow to reconnoitre the coast north of Florida; and when they returned with a glowing report of the natural resources and friendly natives of Roanoke Island in Pamlico Sound, he decided to plant there the new colony of Virginia. In the spring of 1585 a body of settlers set sail under Sir Richard Grenville, over a hundred of whom elected to remain in America with Ralph Lane as their governor. Next year a ship was sent out from England with supplies, and Grenville followed with three other ships. But by this time (June 1586) the entire community, threatened with starvation and at cross purposes with the Indians, had decided to repatriate themselves by the kind services of Drake, who paid the settlement a visit on his way home from his campaign in the West Indies. Nothing daunted by this unexpected set-back, Raleigh launched a second attempt in 1587, when another batch of over a hundred men and women were transported to the same locality by John White, under the title of the 'Governor, Assistants, and Company of the City of Raleigh in Virginia'. But once again disaster dogged the path of the luckless pioneers; and when White, who had gone back to England for supplies, returned to America in 1590 no trace of the settlement could be found, nor could any information be procured of its fate. In all probability it had perished at the hands of the Indians.

Doubtless the failure is to be attributed, primarily, to the incompetence and lack of foresight shown by Raleigh himself. To remove a group of men and women from the political and social surroundings of an old civilization, and plant them down in the wilderness without ample preparations being made to maintain them during the hard struggle against natural difficulties, was to court defeat from the very start. 'Planting of countries', wrote Bacon,[1] 'is like planting of woods; for you must make account to lose almost twenty years' profit, and expect recompence in the end.' But the spirit of the age was against this slow and careful nursing. A race of adventurers like the Elizabethans, who looked upon the world as an oyster to be opened by the sword, could not readily adapt itself to the hard work of pioneering in a virgin country, or realize that the

[1] Essay *Of Plantations.*

development of natural resources is a surer way to wealth than the robbing of treasure-ships and the spoliation of cities. Spanish loot was a sore distraction to would-be empire-builders. Moreover, the prevalent idea of the period that plantations should be used to rid the mother country of its undesirable population may have contributed its share also, as it did in the case of the Irish plantations, in rendering the Elizabethan experiment in America abortive. To quote the wisdom of Bacon again:

> It is a shameful and unblest thing to take the scum of people and wicked condemned men to be the people with whom you plant, and not only so, but it spoileth the plantation; for they will ever live like rogues, and not fall to work, but be lazy, and do mischief, and spend victuals, and be quickly weary, and then certify over to their country to the discredit of the plantation.[1]

It is easy to be wise after the event: a more generous criticism would perhaps regard the collapse of the Elizabethan experiment in colonization as one of the more or less inevitable disasters that accompany the launching of a great idea into the world of practical affairs.

While the merchants, aided by the geographers and explorers, busied themselves with the search for distant markets, and men of vision were dreaming of establishing a new England beyond the Atlantic, there were adventurers of a different sort who held that the surest way to strengthen England was to weaken Spain. The leader of this class was Francis Drake, the stoutest fighter of the war party in England. Drake's feud with the Spaniard dates from the disaster at San Juan de Ulloa in the autumn of 1568; and from that time to his death in 1595 the fixed and unalterable purpose of his existence was the humiliation of his enemy. 'A single purpose animates all his exploits', says the late Sir Walter Raleigh,[2] 'and the chart of his movements is like a cord laced and knotted round the throat of the Spanish monarchy.'

As a seaman Drake had few rivals; but it was in the leadership of men, in the originality of his designs, and in the superb brilliance with which he executed them, that the genius of the man shone at its brightest. In Europe, where England and Spain were nominally at peace, his talents were lost, at least until nearly thirty years of the reign had passed; but beyond the line,

[1] Ibid.   [2] *English Voyages of the Sixteenth Century* (1906), p. 84.

where the feud originally started, and the reign of law was simply the right of the stronger to enforce his will, an ideal theatre presented itself for the display of his singular ability. Doubtless, also, his strategic eye detected in the Isthmus of Panama the weakest point in the Spanish empire; for it was through this narrow neck of land that all the commerce between Spain and her south American colonies of necessity passed. The silver from the mines of Peru was shipped at Lima to Panama, carried on mules across the mountains to Nombre de Dios, and there transferred to galleons which brought it to Europe.

Most of the route was perfectly safe from marauders; for European pirates had not yet broken into the Pacific, and once the treasure was afloat on the Atlantic it ran no risk of molestation until it reached the coast of Spain. Even there the danger was small, there being no instance of an attack on the treasure-ships in European waters before 1580. The only danger zone lay in the land passage across the Panama isthmus. It was here that Drake scored his first piratical success against the Spaniards. In 1572 he descended on Nombre de Dios, and after ransacking the town ambushed the treasure convoy some distance inland, escaping with his booty to the coast before the garrison at Panama had time to act. Complete surprise and the help of the Simaroon Indians, who hated the Spaniards, account for his triumph. A few years later (1575), when John Oxenham tried to repeat the achievement, he found that the convoy was now heavily armed, and that the only way to lay hand on the treasure was to intercept it between Panama and Lima. This he accomplished by building a pinnace on the Pacific coast, to the north of Panama, while he hid his own ship in a creek on the Atlantic side. But the adventure ended disastrously, for Oxenham was trapped with his booty on the way back across the isthmus and hanged as a pirate at Lima. Oxenham's failure, however, did not deter Andrew Barker from carrying out an extended raid along the mainland of Central America from Cartagena to Honduras in 1576; but Barker himself was killed in a skirmish with the Spaniards, and the ship on which his booty was loaded sank on the way home. The next step was boldly to transfer piratical activity on a grand scale to the Pacific, where the element of surprise might still prove effective; and here, again, it was the genius of Drake that gave the lead.

The motive, or motives, underlying the famous voyage of circumnavigation (1577–80) are still something of a mystery; but the theory is now gaining ground that the plunder of Spanish settlements and shipping in the Pacific was not its sole, or even principal, object. The occupation of the Californian coast in the queen's name, under the title of New Albion, together with the suggested plan of a great English settlement in North America, stretching from California to Florida,[1] and the prominence which Drake gave to his search for the western or Pacific end of the north-west passage,[2] would seem to show that part of his intention at least was to set up a base for some colonial and commercial project in the Pacific. The subsequent treaty with the Sultan of Ternate, in the Moluccas, also lends corroboration to this view. Yet, when the results of the expedition are summed up, it becomes difficult to believe that Drake seriously regarded himself as an ambassador of commerce or an empire-builder. His search for the place where the passage to Cathay debouched on the Pacific was perfunctory in the extreme, perhaps disingenuous, since he abandoned the quest at latitude 48° on the ground of excessive cold and contrary winds—a strange description, as one writer remarks, of the climate of Vancouver in the month of June! Nor should too much importance be attached to the treaty with the native ruler of Ternate, albeit it gained subsequent notoriety as the title-deed of the East India Company. The truth is, Drake went forth with the queen's authority to avenge the wrongs done to England by the Spaniard, to strike a resounding blow at catholicism, perchance as a counterblast to the reverses sustained by protestantism in Europe, and lastly, to make good the losses sustained by Hawkins at San Juan a decade before. It would have surprised him had he been designated a pirate, for he had the royal commission to cover his enterprise; but the fact remains that the substantial result of the voyage, apart from the glory it conferred on its commander, was the colossal treasure the hold of the *Golden Hind* disgorged at Plymouth in the last days of September 1580. It was believed at the time that it amounted to a million and a half sterling, or between a quarter

[1] See 'New Light on Drake' (*Hakluyt Society*, ser. ii, vol. xxxiv, introduction, p. lv, and accompanying map).

[2] The north-west passage was believed by some geographers to slant south-west from the Atlantic to the Pacific, debouching on the latter between latitudes 40° and 50° north.

and a half of the whole annual produce of King Philip's American mines.

The principal geographical interest of the voyage lies in the fact that, after passing into the Pacific by the Strait of Magellan, Drake ran into a storm which drove him 'towards the pole antarctic' as far as 57° south, and it was a month before he recovered the mainland of America. Whether he actually discovered Cape Horn is uncertain; but at least he had disposed of the legend that the Strait of Magellan ran between the American continent and a great southern continent stretching unbroken as far as the pole.

Where Drake had sailed others could follow. In 1586–8 Thomas Cavendish carried out a similar voyage of circumnavigation and plunder, arriving back in London in the autumn of the Armada year, his ships gaily bedecked with blue damask sails, and his men each with a chain of gold.

The voyages of Drake and Cavendish may be said to mark the culmination of distant sea-faring in Elizabeth's reign. The men of war had outrun the traders: it remained for the latter to take advantage of the knowledge gained. Raleigh's failure in Virginia had spelt the end of England's interest in America for the time being. It was now apparent that neither Frobisher's Meta Incognita, nor Gilbert's Newfoundland, nor the lands favoured by Raleigh south of the Chesapeake could offer any profitable outlet for trade. There was left India and the Far East, interest in which had been revived by Drake's visit to the Moluccas in 1579, and by the journey of the jesuit father, Thomas Stevens, to Goa in the same year. Accordingly, in 1589, a group of London merchants applied to the privy council for permission to send a trading expedition to the East; and in 1591 James Lancaster took three ships by the Cape route to Sumatra, Malacca, and Ceylon. Although only twenty-five men and officers returned to England in May 1594, the information acquired, coupled with the full report of Dr. Thorne, who resided at Seville, on the advantages of trade with India, led to the projection of a more pretentious expedition, and eventually to the formation of a company to trade with the East Indies. Probably the action of the merchants was accelerated by Ralph Fitch's return after his long sojourn in India, Burma, and Malacca (1594), and the fact that the Dutch were combining to develop an independent Malaysian trade of their own. A sum of

£30,000 was quickly subscribed, augmented later to £72,000; and the queen's approval of the voyage was secured. On 31 December 1599 the charter of incorporation of the East India Company was granted, being a concession for fifteen years to George Clifford, earl of Cumberland, and 215 knights, aldermen, and merchants for the discovery of trade with the East Indies. Lancaster was appointed general of the fleet, with John Davis of Arctic fame as his pilot-major; and in April 1600 five ships— the *Red Dragon*, the *Ascension*, the *Hector*, the *Susan*, and the *Guest*—set sail from Torbay for Acheen (Sumatra) and Bantam (Java), to launch the Company on its amazing career as the pioneer of imperial England in the East.

Economic history cannot as a rule be written in terms of reigns, for its beginnings and endings do not correspond with the normal punctuation of the political calendar. There is some justification, however, for regarding Elizabeth's reign as coincident with an important phase in England's economic development. For one thing, the gradual substitution of free for servile labour, begun two centuries before, had resulted in the destruction of the economic fabric of the medieval manor. The vast bulk of the landholding population were now either freeholders, copyholders, leaseholders, or tenants at will. Villeinage as a tenure was extinct; and although it still survived as a status in something like one per cent. of the population, the progress of manumission would soon account for this last vestige of the old economy. In this respect at least the transition from medieval to modern conditions was virtually complete. On the other hand, the inclosure movement was still running its course. The conversion of arable land into pasture for the production of wool and the economizing of wages, the fencing in of the 'commons' by the gentry, either for grazing purposes or to provide themselves with enlarged parks, warrens, and chases, and the substitution of 'severalty' (inclosed) for 'champaign' (open field) farming, together with all the other phenomena that accompanied and aggravated the change from a feudal economy to an economy based upon individual enterprise—the building up of great estates by the new moneyed interest, rack-renting, eviction, the decay of husbandry, the drift of the rural population to the towns, ruined villages, pauperism, vagabondage—continued to disturb the countryside throughout Elizabeth's reign.

Nevertheless there were indications before the reign terminated that at least the acuteness of the crisis was past. A new race of landlords, more enterprising than their predecessors, were finding it more and more profitable to break up fresh ground for tillage, and farming for gain was supplanting the old subsistence farming of the Middle Ages. So marked was the change that in 1592 Bacon ventured to assert that England was now in a position to feed other nations instead of being fed by them. Even if he interpreted the signs of the times in too favourable a light, as subsequent events showed, his testimony cannot be entirely overlooked. Meanwhile great strides were being made by the application of capital to economic undertakings of all kinds on a scale unprecedented in history. Manufacturers and merchants rivalled graziers in their prosperity. Indeed it would be no exaggeration to say that the grievances of society were now beginning to veer round from the miseries accompanying the dissolution of the old order to the vices incidental to the introduction of the new. In this connexion it is not without significance that the last great parliamentary controversy of the reign was concerned with patents and monopolies. By this time, too, the terrible problem of pauperism, that had perplexed and baffled earlier Tudor statesmen, was solved, or sufficiently solved to warrant the assumption that the worst menace to social order had been successfully disposed of.

We must be careful, however, not to credit the reign of Elizabeth with more than its due. The most striking feature of rural history between 1558 and 1603 was the prevalence of unrest—an unrest provoked, in large measure, by the continued activity of the inclosers for pasture. Complaints on this subject reached the government from many districts, from Lincolnshire, Derbyshire, Norfolk, Hertfordshire, Bedfordshire, Kent, Monmouthshire, Gloucestershire, and Worcestershire. William Harrison, writing about 1577, alludes bitterly to those who 'for the breed and feeding of cattle do not let daily to take in more, not sparing the very commons, whereupon many townships . . . do live', alleging in excuse that 'we have already too great store of people in England'. 'These inclosures', said Philip Stubbs[1] in 1583, 'be the causes why rich men eat up poor men as beasts do eat grass. . . . They take in and inclose commons, moors, heaths, and other common pastures, whereout the poor commonalty

---

[1] *The Anatomie of Abuses*, ed. F. J. Furnivall, pp. 116, 117.

were wont to have all their forage and feeding for their cattle, and (which is more) corn for themselves to live upon.' In 1596, after several bad harvests, there were inclosure riots in various districts. In south Oxfordshire, where a rising of the peasantry was only checked by the timely intervention of the council, there was talk of throwing down the inclosures, killing the gentry, and seizing their corn to alleviate the sufferings of a hunger-striken multitude. Even the north, hitherto exempt from the movement, was beginning to feel its effects. In 1597 the dean of Durham reported that 500 ploughs had decayed in the bishopric within a few years, and of 8,000 acres lately in tillage, not 8 score were now tilled. Needless to say, contemporary literature continued its wail against the iniquities of the incloser: he was a 'cormorant', a 'greedy gull', a 'cruel kestrel':

> Houses by three, and seven, and ten he raseth,
> To make the common glebe his private land:
> Our country cities cruel he defaceth;
> The grass grows green where little Troy did stand.

Writers have pointed out that much of the outcry must be discountenanced as a gross exaggeration, and that although hardship was undoubtedly inflicted on individuals when the commons were taken away, the total acreage involved in the inclosure movement for the parts most affected, the midlands, was only 6·23 per cent. Moreover, it should be borne in mind that inclosure for arable was proceeding side by side with inclosure for pasture. Thomas Tusser and others who studied the problem at first hand are emphatic on the point that this form of inclosure, while it destroyed the old open-field system, greatly increased the productiveness of the soil—a fact which probably counterbalanced any possible shrinkage of the corn supply owing to the action of the graziers. So far as can be ascertained there was no visible diminution of the food supplies of the kingdom as a whole during the period.[1] Nor can it be said that the chief economic problem of the age arose out of scarcity. In spite of recurrent bad harvests, by all accounts England was a land of plenty. 'Thanks be to God,' wrote Bishop Jewel in 1570, 'never was it better in worldly peace, in health of body, and in abundance of victuals.' Nine years later Thomas

---

[1] According to J. U. Nef (*The Rise of the British Coal Industry*, i. 190), it was the supply of timber rather than the supply of grain that suffered through the extension of inclosures.

Churchyard rhapsodized in verse over the 'blessed state of England':

> Here things are cheap and easily had,
> No soil the like can show,
> No state nor kingdom at this day
> Doth in such plenty flow.

What troubled the economists was not a falling off of the food supply, but the existence of a 'dearth' (or dearness) in the midst of apparent plenty. Why did the price of all commodities, food included, continue to rise, as rise it did, even when harvests were satisfactory? 'All this dearth notwithstanding', said John Stow (1575), 'there was no want of anything to him that wanted not money.' The craftsman blamed the husbandman, and the husbandman blamed the merchant and the landlord. The merchant passed on the blame to the foreigner, who charged more for his wares, and the landlord complained that he could not maintain his position in society unless he increased rents and fines, and inclosed more land for grazing. All classes, in fact, were in the grip of an upward movement of prices, for which no one in particular was responsible, and which had for its efficient cause the influx of American silver and the consequent cheapening of the purchasing power of money.

Public opinion, however, laid the onus for the dearth on the individual who added field to field for grazing purposes; and the government, always afraid of a popular rising, took the same line. Thus the history of Elizabeth's reign, so far as inclosures are concerned, is largely a continuation of her predecessors' policy. While no action was taken against the incloser for tillage, who was really an asset to the community, legislative war was proclaimed against the other type, whose activity caused the destruction of buildings, unemployment, and depopulation. In 1563 an act was passed confirming the agrarian legislation of Henry VII and Henry VIII: all land that had been under the plough for the space of four years since 1528 was to remain in tillage for ever, and no land now under the plough must be converted to pasture. Thirty years later (1593) the 'great plenty and cheapness of grain' tempted the government to repeal this statute, which, it would appear, was 'obscure and imperfect'. But in 1598, under pressure of renewed high prices, famine, and popular outcry against inclosures, there was a reversion to the former policy. Two statutes were passed with a view to increasing the area under tillage and arresting the depopulation of the countryside. In the first it was stated that 'of late years more than in times past there have sundry towns, parishes, and houses of husbandry been destroyed and become desolate, by means whereof a great number of poor people are become wanderers, idle and loose'. It was therefore ordered that the destroyed houses should be rebuilt and suitable land assigned to them for cultivation. The second, in which it was pointed out that since the repeal of the 1563 statute 'there have grown many more depopulations, by turning tillage into pasture, than at any time for the like number of years heretofore', it was enacted that all land that had been under the plough for twelve consecutive years and had been converted to pasture since the first year of the reign should be restored to tillage. Clearly, from the government standpoint, the agrarian question was by no means settled. But the next century was not far advanced when all anti-inclosure legislation was definitely abandoned as unnecessary, showing that the Elizabethan government was perhaps unduly nervous as to the dangers of the movement.

Of the sufferings of the poorer classes there can, unfortunately, be no doubt. Those who were torn away from their moorings in the country by the agrarian changes, and sought an entrance into industry, found their way barred by stringent guild restrictions or exorbitant fees; while the town corporations, resenting the influx of casual labour from the outside, which added to their liabilities in respect of poor relief, legislated against the settlement of aliens in their midst. Begging was of little avail, for private charity had grown cold since the dissolution of the monasteries. 'A poor man', says Robert Greene,[1] 'shall as soon break his neck as his fast at a rich man's door.' 'They lie in the streets', writes Stubbs, 'in the dirt as commonly is seen . . . and are permitted to die like dogs or beasts without any mercy or compassion showed them at all.' Verily it must have seemed a heartless world to those whom the relentless pressure of economic fact drove to beggary. Caught in the maelstrom of forces that swept them hither and thither with a violence as blind as it was merciless, they could do nothing to avert their fate.

But if some classes were sinking in the social scale, others were rising. The freeholders, who had broken away from the manor,

[1] Pamphleteer, dramatist, and novelist (1560?–1592).

and, unlike the 'customary' tenants, enjoyed the protection of the law in the payment of fixed rents, benefited by the cheapening price of money and the higher price of victuals. These men were the yeoman class, the backbone of England, of whom Harrison speaks so enthusiastically, 'who come to great wealth insomuch that many of them are able and do buy the lands of unthrifty gentlemen, and often sending their sons to the schools, to the universities, and the inns of court, or otherwise leaving them sufficient lands whereupon they may live without labour, do make them by these means to become gentlemen'. The prosperous yeoman was a typical product of rural society in Elizabeth's day. Often he was more than a wool grower and supplier of markets with butter, cheese, and beef: he dabbled in the new industrial undertakings of the time, sinking coal pits, setting up mills, digging for alum, opening up salt springs, or supplying the leather-goods manufacturers with material from his own tan-yard.

There is a marked difference of opinion among historians today regarding the precise meaning of the so-called 'agrarian crisis' of the sixteenth century. Some hold that the beneficiaries of the 'crisis' were the class lying between the yeomanry and the peerage, viz. the 'gentry'; and the picture they present of the Elizabethan age, or rather of the entire period beginning with Elizabeth and ending with the civil war, is of an age in which the 'gentry', having acquired knowledge, technical skill, business technique, and 'drive', turn land-holding into a profitable investment, at the expense of the aristocracy, peasantry, church, and Crown alike. Meanwhile, the aristocracy, handicapped by inherited incompetence, heavy overhead charges, obsolete methods, steeply rising prices, and diminishing incomes, find themselves confronted with impending bankruptcy and economic ruin. A few succeed in weathering the storm by ruthlessly curtailing expenditure, raising rents 'amid clamour and lamentations from discharged serving-men and rack-rented tenants'. Many, however, have recourse to borrowing and mortgages; and others are too much bound by tradition, too immersed in amusements, too impoverished and easy-going; and as debts pile up and the sale of estates multiplies they find themselves little better than clients of the *nouveaux riches* of the cities, who indulge in money-lending. Thus by stages was the way prepared for the revolution of 1639–40 and the civil war.

Such, roughly, is the theory, developed at considerable length and well documented, that appears to have held the field until quite recently. A full and admirable exposition of it will be found in three important studies by Professor Tawney.[1] It is undoubtedly a fascinating theory, and it has the support of other historians, notably Mr. Lawrence Stone, in his 'Anatomy of the Elizabethan Aristocracy'. A rival interpretation, however, has emerged, fostered and expounded by Professor H. R. Trevor-Roper, which not only challenges but also appears to undermine and virtually overthrow the accepted view.[2] The controversy is by no means easy to follow—partly because of a certain obscurity in the nomenclature, partly because of the intransigence of the rival parties, but mainly because of the lack of a common ground between them. Professor Tawney is 'unconvinced' by Trevor-Roper's arguments 'save on points of detail': Mr. Stone remarks that 'there are some reasons for believing that a large number of Mr. Trevor-Roper's charges of inaccuracy are either false or disputable'; and the latter retorts icily, 'My views are not modified by Mr. Stone's rejoinder . . . in which he anyway seldom quotes me correctly.' Perhaps we might say that the subject still awaits clarification.

The expansion of industry, however, was the dominant feature of the period. New crafts were springing up, often as the result of the incoming refugee protestants from the Netherlands and France, and the older crafts received an impetus from the same source. The felt industry, thread-making, lace manufacture, silk-weaving, engraving, the manufacture of parchment, needles, and glass were introduced. Manchester benefited by the development of 'cottons',[3] Birmingham by the addition of brass to her iron industry; and in both cases much was due to the skill of the foreign workman. Even the staple industry, cloth, profited by the immigration, especially in the finer branches of the craft, i.e. 'bays'. Not less noteworthy than the acclimatization of new industrial pursuits was the extension of industry to parts hitherto

---

[1] Introduction, *Thomas Wilson's Discourse on Usury* (1925); 'The Rise of the Gentry' (*Ec. Hist. Rev.*, 1951); and 'Harrington's Interpretation of his Age' (*Procs. Brit. Acad.*, 1941).

[2] The course of this argument may be followed in the article entitled 'The Elizabethan Aristocracy: An Anatomy anatomized', (*Ec. Hist. Rev.* 1950); and in the fuller 'brochure', under the title of *The Gentry, 1540–1640* (Camb. Univ. Press, 1951).

[3] 'Cottons' were not cottons in the modern sense, merely a species of woollens.

unaffected. Thus the cloth industry, originally centred in the eastern counties, at Norwich, Bury St. Edmunds, the valleys of the Colne and Blackwater in Essex, and the Kentish Weald, had spread to the north and west, to Yorkshire and Lancashire, Wiltshire, Gloucester, Somerset, Devon, the Welsh border districts, and the southern coastal counties from Kent to Plymouth. Nor was cloth-weaving confined to urban centres: it took root in the cottages of rural workers, who procured their supplies of wool from some neighbouring market, and returned later to the same market to sell the woven cloth. This practice was quite common in the west riding of Yorkshire and in Devon, and may have been more prevalent than we suspect. Moreover, although the circumstances of the time favoured the capitalist employer, like John Winchcombe, who paid his workers a mere pittance of fourpence or sixpence a day and amassed a great fortune, they also contributed to the rise of the 'small master', the urban counterpart of the prosperous yeoman in the country, who worked not for wages but for profit, borrowed capital when necessary, and, if successful, established himself as a capitalist on a small scale. He, too, was a typical product of the later sixteenth century, and his existence materially helped to maintain self-respect among the working classes at a time when effective combination against rapacious employers was impossible.

Although the development of the cloth industry and its allied trades was the outstanding feature of the time, there were other directions in which the ebullient energy of the nation found an outlet. The extractive industries were not neglected. Companies were formed on the joint stock principle for the exploitation of natural resources and the manufacture of metals, e.g. the Company of the Mines Royal and the Mineral and Battery Company, both of which were incorporated in 1568. The 'hostmen' of Newcastle developed the coal industry of Durham and Northumberland, and practically controlled the entire traffic in this commodity, although as yet the consumption was small, owing to the continued use of wood in iron-smelting. So considerable was the wastage in timber at the iron-works in Sussex, Nottinghamshire, and in the neighbourhood of Birmingham that it became a matter of grave concern to the state. 'These iron times', sang the poet Drayton, 'breed none that mind posterity.'

It was, in many ways, a chaotic world. Company promoters

and speculators preyed on the credulity of a penny-come-quick public; and patentees and monopolists, many of them courtiers or friends of courtiers, sought and obtained from the queen the exclusive privilege of dealing in certain articles of commerce, or industrial processes, to the detriment of the common weal and their own enrichment. Everywhere private interests predominated over public: everyone 'gaped' for gain. Money was power —it was more than this, it was the national divinity, whose virtues even poets could hymn:

> Money, the minion, the spring of all joy;
> Money, the medicine that heals each annoy;
> Money, the jewel that man keeps in store;
> Money, the idol that women adore!

Nor was the worship of Mammon confined to the laity. Richard Cox, bishop of Ely, a man of scholarly attainments, was also noted for his meanness and avarice. He began his episcopal career with a lawsuit against his popish predecessor, Thomas Thirlby, for alleged conversion of funds belonging to the see to his own private use, and then proceeded to lease the episcopal lands to graziers and sell the timber, in order to enrich himself and his heirs. Edwin Sandys of Worcester and John Scory of Hereford are similar examples of clerical cupidity. On the whole, however, the church was not a highway to wealth: there were too many greedy cormorants among the laity hovering round ecclesiastical endowments to permit of it. On the other hand, there were hundreds of openings for the lay speculator to establish a fortune, provided he was willing to 'chance his arm' in questionable transactions. Contractors for supplies to the army, treasurers, paymasters, and all who handled public funds or their disbursement were favourably circumstanced for giving reign to their cupidity; for public money was regarded as fair game by the embezzler, and embezzlement was one of the curses of the age. Sir George Carey, the bearer of an honourable name, whose loyalty to the state was above suspicion, made a fortune for himself as treasurer of the war in Ireland during the later years of the reign, by passing falsified clothing accounts, by manipulating the exchange, and by purchasing provisions and paying the troops in the base Irish currency, while he himself received sterling from England. Even Sir Thomas Gresham, the oracle of the city, merchant prince and trusted financial agent of the government, whose munificent benefactions were a feature of the time, finished his career, in 1575, with a substantial sum unaccounted for in his transactions on behalf of the Crown. The plain fact is that public morality was low, and the great officials who died poor, like Edward Baeshe, surveyor-general of the navy victualling department, were the exception rather than the rule.

Yet, although the desire for monetary wealth was great, it was not a hoarding age. Men made money in order to enjoy it, and the surest way to enjoy it, and at the same time to gratify one's social ambitions, was to lay it out in land. The successful burgess, lawyer, industrialist, or merchant who had savings to invest, itched for real estate in the hope of founding a county family. Moreover, land could be acquired in various ways: by the purchase of derelict estates, by lending to thriftless landowners on the security of their estates, and selling them up when they failed to redeem their bonds, or by buying reversions and mortgages. All that was needed for this kind of speculation was shrewdness, prudence, and patience—qualities possessed in ample measure by men like Mr. George Stoddart of London, who in a few years transformed himself from a grocer and usurer into a landed proprietor with broad acres.

Another example of how a man of acute intelligence, business capacity, knowledge of finance, and simple acquisitiveness, could build up a fortune and become a landed proprietor, qualifying for entry into the upper ranks of the country gentry, is the fascinating career of Horatio Palavicino, a foreigner of Genoese extraction, who is first heard of in England about 1578. Like Gresham in the earlier part of the reign, only on a more impressive scale, he filled the years 1579–92 with a bewildering variety of activities connected with finance, money-lending, floating of loans, espionage, commercial dealings, &c., becoming the chief consultant of the government in all its continental undertakings and enterprises. Moving about in the *coulisses* of the political world, he became the friend of kings and magnates, was intimately associated with the two Cecils, Walsingham, and members of the English aristocracy; and above all else, he established himself as a friend of the queen, who raised him to the knighthood, and included him among the select few who received a New Year's gift for his services. By 1600, the year of his death, he was reckoned to be one of the richest men in

England, the proud possessor of capital amounting to £100,000, with lands and properties in three counties—Cambridgeshire, Essex, and Norfolk—and a stately manor house at Babraham, dignified with pillared gates surmounted by the armorial eagle of the Palavicino family. At the height of his career he became ambassador extraordinary to the German princes. But all this, and much more, seems to have subserved his social ambition. 'Rumbling up and down the London road in his private coach', says his biographer,[1] 'Horatio must have been a source of wonder and speculation to the Cambridgeshire rustics.' Although he professed to be bored, like many others who moved from business or industry to 'country delights', his 2,300 acres of pasture-land made him a sheep-master, and apparently he took a 'naive pleasure' in signing his letters—'being among my shepherds clipping my sheep'.

Undoubtedly there was a land-hunger in Elizabethan England. Not only were capitalists dabbling in real estate: the law courts were busy from one end of the country to the other with claims arising out of land, or disputed successions to manors. Men flew to the law on the slightest provocation, if they thought they could thereby establish an advantage to themselves at the expense of their neighbours. The succession of a minor to a great estate was sometimes the occasion for a general scramble after plunder by all who deemed they had a claim, bogus or real, to a share in the inheritance; and a sober, industrious land-lord like William Darrell of Littlecote, Wiltshire, might find himself, through the greed or malice of his neighbours, condemned to a whole lifetime of litigation.

England, to be sure, was a quieter place than it had been in the days of Sir John Paston. The statute of retainers had done its work, and the 'overmighty subject' was now a thing of the past. But respect for the law was still only skin deep. Suits could be won by bribing judges, suborning witnesses, or by the help of a powerful patron; and legal decisions were not infrequently followed by reprisals. Thus a defeated claimant to an estate might avenge himself on his successful rival by leading a band of rioters into his grounds, laying waste his fields, plundering his manor house, and, generally speaking, indulging in a miniature private war, although such a procedure inevitably led to a further action for battery and assault or forcible entry. When

[1] Lawrence Stone, *An Elizabethan: Sir Horatio Palavicino*, p. 282.

the mood was on him, a gentleman would divert himself by hunting deer or felling timber on his neighbour's estate, with singular disregard for the rights of private property. In short, behind the imposing façade of the law, society was at war with itself; and the root of this turbulence and factiousness was covetousness.

The main tendencies of the period are easy enough to detect. It is not so easy, however, to determine what part the government played in shaping or controlling the course of events. From one point of view the forces at work appear to have been entirely economic and beyond the scope of government action; but from another the government figures as the *deus ex machina* of the revolution, guiding with its paternal hand the giant impulses at work, so as to minimize their potentiality for evil and maximize their usefulness to society as a whole. It was, we must remember, the beginning of the mercantilist age, when governments were endeavouring to concentrate under their direction all the sources of national power; and England led the way in this new development. Yet it may be doubted whether the state could do more than remove obstacles, encourage enterprise, and seek by remedial measures to keep the swollen stream from overflowing its banks. Within these limits, the Elizabethan government was exceedingly active. By the reform of the coinage (1561) the confidence of the trading community was strengthened. The statute of apprentices (1563) helped to stabilize industry and encourage agriculture, by insisting on long contracts, and by ensuring a plentiful supply of labour in the fields when labour was most needed. It also instituted a system of wage assessment, based upon the conditions obtaining in different parts of the country, so as to 'yield to the hired person, both in time of scarcity and in time of plenty, a convenient proportion of wages'. This elastic principle was an improvement on the older statutes of labourers, which attempted to fix a flat rate for the entire country. Similarly the legalization of interest at a maximum of 10 per cent. (1571) probably gave a stimulus to the employment of capital in increasing amounts. It is noticeable, too, that the privy council kept a wary eye on the food supplies, in order to mitigate the sufferings of the poor in time of dearth. Markets were watched. The export of corn was checked when prices rose higher than 10s. (1563) and 20s. (1593) per quarter, and totally prohibited to any part of the Spanish dominions after the quarrel with Spain developed. Efforts were also made, not so successfully, perhaps, to check engrossing, forestalling, and regrating at the markets, and to check fraud by standardizing weights and measures. In both cases the government acted through the clerks of the markets. Encouragement was given to enterprises that made for national security, such as the working of metals, the production of sulphur, saltpetre, flax, and hemp, and the manufacture of canvas. The same minute attention was paid to the construction or enlargement of ports and harbours, the preservation of timber, and the development of the fisheries by the enforcement of compulsory fish days. The institution of a 'political lent' was definitely intended to strengthen the maritime population and increase the supply of seamen for the navy.

On the other hand nothing was done to improve communications. The roads or common ways of England were allowed to remain, as they had been for centuries, ill conditioned and neglected. Their upkeep fell upon the parishes, who treated their obligation lightly, fulfilled it reluctantly, or totally ignored it when circumstances permitted. Only the great arterial roads connecting London with Dover, Plymouth, Bristol, Chester, and Berwick, which were necessary for government communications, seem to have been suitable for constant traffic, although they, too, had their 'noisome' corners, 'sloughs', and 'holes'. The smaller roads were little better than mere tracks, deeply rutted for most of the year, and practically impassable for foot passengers in winter. All highways were, of course, plentifully provided with commodious and well-equipped inns—the best in the world, said travellers who had sampled those of other countries. But once the traveller left their friendly shelter, he ran the risk not only of the physical hardships of the road but also of falling a victim to the 'close-booted gentlemen' who lay in wait for fat 'booties' by the wayside. Every exposed place had its gang of desperadoes. Gadshill near Rochester, Shooter's hill by Blackheath, Salisbury plain, Newmarket Heath, &c., were notorious haunts of thieves. Frequently, if we may believe Harrison,[1] these land pirates received their information as to travellers' movements and the nature of their business from the ostlers and tapsters of the inns. Falstaff's disgraceful exploit at Gadshill was probably a not uncommon occurrence.

Nevertheless, in spite of the dangers and difficulties, the main roads were serviceable enough for the needs of the time. Rapid

[1] W. Harrison, *Description of England.*

movement was rendered possible by the provision of post-horses at fixed stages, which could be hired at 3*d*. per mile (for private persons) and 2½*d*. (for persons on government business), with 6*d*. for the post-boy, who returned with the 'mount' after completion of the stage. In addition to post-horses there were wheeled vehicles on the roads—carts, coaches, and 'caroches'. But the day of the vehicle was only just beginning: the lack of springs made coaching a sorely trying experience. In London the old-fashioned horse litter was still in vogue for ladies, and some indulged in the newfangled sedan chair, which became popular in the reign of Charles I. In the far north, again, where the roads were few and mountainous, the saddle-horse and the pack-horse remained the sole means of communication and transport.

If the government neglected the roads, the great floating population of vagabonds who used them presented a problem which could not be ignored. Here the need for action on a nation-wide scale was now more than ever apparent, for in spite of all previous attempts to control the plague of beggars their numbers had increased so greatly as to constitute a grave menace to public order. According to Harrison, the vagabonds or 'sturdy beggars' alone numbered 10,000. Harman,[1] the contemporary anatomizer of roguery, asserts that there were no fewer than twenty-three different categories of thieves and swindlers —'rufflers', who pretended they had been at the wars and lived on charity, extorting by violence 'when they may be bold', or by pity when violence would not pay: 'upright men', who were 'of so much authority that, meeting with any of their profession, they may command a share and snap unto themselves': 'hookers', who pilfered linen and clothes from windows with a six-foot pole: 'palliards' or 'clappendogens', who went about in patched clothes, carrying a testimonial, and blistered their limbs with spearwort, ratsbane, or other corrosive: 'priggers of prancers' or horse-thieves: 'Abraham men', who 'feign themselves to have been mad': 'fresh-water mariners' or bogus sailors, 'whose ship was wrecked on Salisbury plain': 'counterfeit cranks', whose specialty was to dissemble the falling sickness by working their mouths into a lather with soap: 'dummerars', who pretended to be dumb by 'holding down their tongues doubled' and 'holding up their hands piteously': 'demanders for glimmer', who said their goods were consumed by fire; and

---

[1] T. Harman, *A Caveat or Warning*.

so on to the 'bawdy baskets', 'morts', 'doxies', 'dells', and common harlots. Such was the composition of this 'merry England' that slept in haylofts, sheepcotes, or on doorsteps, spreading terror in the country and disease in the towns.

The official attitude to the whole fraternity of vagabonds had always been, and still was, one of fear-ridden ferocity: they were the true 'caterpillars of the commonwealth', who 'lick the sweat from the labourers' brows'. But the impotent poor, the poor by casualty, who were poor 'in very deed', were acknowledged to be a charge on public benevolence. The vital question was what form this public maintenance should take. Slowly and painfully the state was being driven by the colossal dimensions of the problem to the conviction that responsibility in the matter could not be left to the conscience of the individual, but must be enforced by law upon every one. Thus while the first pauper enactment of Elizabeth's reign (1563) simply revived the statutes of Henry VIII and Edward VI with regard to the sturdy beggar, it recognized for the first time, in principle at least, the necessity for a compulsory levy for the maintenance of 'impotent, aged, and needy persons'. Men of 'froward and wilful mind', who refused to yield to the gentle suasion of the bishop and contribute their quota to the parish poor fund, were to be handed over to the justices of the peace and coerced into payment. More precise instructions, however, were necessary before the new weapon of compulsion could be used effectively by the local authorities. Consequently in 1572 a further enactment instructed all justices, mayors, sheriffs, bailiffs, &c., to levy a reasonable rate on all inhabitants dwelling within their respective jurisdictions and to settle the impotent in permanent abiding-places. Pauper children were also to be bound out to service. At the same time the treatment of the rogue was made harsher: he was to be whipped and bored through the gristle of the right ear, and if he continued in his roguery he was to suffer, in the last resort, death for felony. The term 'vagabond' was defined so as to include a remarkable variety of flotsam and jetsam: procurators who went about with counterfeit licences, idle persons who indulged in unlawful games, palmists, physiognomists, fencers, bearwards, players of interludes and minstrels 'not belonging to any baron of the realm', jugglers, pedlars, tinkers, petty chapmen, loiterers, scholars of Oxford and Cambridge who begged without the authority of their university, shipmen 'pretending losses by sea', and all who 'being mighty of body' refused to work for wages. In 1576 this statute was amended by another, which compelled every city and town corporate to provide a store of wool, hemp, flax, iron or other stuff, so that the honest poor, if able of body, might be set to work and paid 'according to the desert of the work'. Rogues, on the other hand, were to be sent to 'houses of correction', two of which were to be erected in each county, and there disciplined to labour. Finally came the comprehensive statute of 1598, which corroborated and exploited the same remedies still further. The contribution for poor relief was fixed at a maximum of 2d. per parish. Provision was made for the compulsory apprenticing of pauper children, until they reached the age of twenty-four (for males) and twenty-one (for females). Begging was prohibited. Justices of the peace in each county were to appoint parish 'overseers' of the poor, whose duty it was to raise 'by taxation for every inhabitant' stocks of material for the workhouses, and be responsible for their management. Parents and children of the impotent, who had the necessary wherewithal, were to relieve them 'of their own charges'— a shrewd concession to the principle of self-help. By the same act the statute of 1576 against vagabonds was repealed in favour of more humane methods. Boring of the ear was dropped, but the sturdy beggar, after being whipped 'until his or her body be bloody', was to be sent back to his birth-place, or, if that was unknown, to the place where he last dwelt, and there to be thrown into a house of correction or the common jail until he could be placed in service. If he was not able to work, his destination was an almshouse. Dangerous rogues were to be banished the realm or sent to the galleys, and, if they returned, were to be treated as felons. Private endowment of hospitals, houses of correction, *maisons de Dieu*, or abiding-places for the poor was to be encouraged, provided the endowment amounted to the 'clear yearly value of £10'. This law, which was at first a temporary one, was published with slight alterations in 1601, and became the final expression of Elizabethan statesmanship in the sphere of poor-law administration.

It will be evident that the act completely secularized the whole question of relieving poverty, and at the same time established the principle of corporate responsibility as fully as the time permitted. If it showed no mercy to the 'work-shy', it did everything that was humanly speaking possible for those who were willing to work, and acknowledged a very significant obligation to the children of paupers.

Between the economic and the social condition of a country a close connexion always subsists. Alterations in the distribution of wealth bring new classes to the forefront of society, and they, in turn, create a new social environment. A hundred different ways of spending are discovered and practised, old fashions give place to new, and the whole outlook of society is transformed. Such a change occurred in Elizabeth's reign side by side with the industrial and commercial expansion.

The *foyer* of this social revolution was London, but it spread with the rapidity of an epidemic through the length and breadth of England. Camden noted the phenomenon for the first time in 1574 when, he observes, 'our apish nation' displayed 'a certain deformity and insolency of mind', 'jetted up and down in silks glittering with gold and silver', and began to indulge in a 'riot of banquetting' and 'bravery in building', to the 'great ornament of the kingdom, but to the decay of the glory of hospitality'. Most of the novelties demanded by society for the adornment of the person came from abroad, and the foreign merchant drove a thriving trade. 'One trifling toy not worth the carriage, coming from beyond the sea,' says a writer of the time, 'is more worth with us than a right good jewel easy to be had at home.' In a play entitled *The Three Ladies of London* (1584), one of the characters says: 'Then, signor Mercator, I am forthwith to send ye from hence to search for some new toys in Barbary and in Turkey.' The economist might point out that the purchase of this 'foreign trash' cost England annually £100,000. The puritan satirist might castigate the garish tastes of society with the fury of a Juvenal. Neither could make any impression on the widespread craving for luxury in every shape and form. 'They be desirous of new-fangles,' said Stubbs, 'praising things past, condemning things present, and coveting things to come; ambitious, proud, light-hearted, unstable, ready to be carried away by every blast of wind.' 'Nothing is so constant', wrote Harrison, 'as inconstancy in attire.' Fynes Moryson,[1] who had travelled more widely than most men of his time, thought his countrymen 'more sumptuous than the Persians', because 'they affect all extremes'.

[1] Author of *An Itinerary: containing his ten years' travell*, &c.

It was not only the rich who flaunted their 'silks, velvets, and chains of gold': all who could come by the necessary means—farmers, peasants, artisans—followed in the train of fashion. Many were the gibes levelled by writers of the period at the vanity and presumption of the lower classes. 'Now', says Greene, 'every lout must have his son a court noll, and these dunghill drudges wax so proud that they will presume to wear on their feet what kings have worn on their heads. A clown's son must be clapped in a velvet pantoufle, though the presumptuous ass be drowned in the mercer's book, and make a convey of all his lands to the usurer for commodities.' 'The ploughman', comments Thomas Lodge, 'must nowadays have his doublet of the fashion with wide cuts, his garters of fine silk of Granada, to meet his Sis on Sundays.' To become a fine gentleman, according to Ben Jonson, it was necessary to hie to the city, 'where at your first appearance 'twere good you turned four or five hundred acres of your best land into two or three trunks of apparel'.

Naturally a 'babylonian confusion' of classes ensued, and the social world turned itself topsy-turvy. The 'mingle-mangle' of dress made it impossible to say who was 'noble, worshipful, gentle, or even a yeoman'. 'To such outrage is it grown now-a-days,' writes Stubbs, 'every butcher, shoemaker, tailor, cobbler, husbandman, and other; yea every tinker, pedlar, and swineherd, and every artificer and other *gregarii ordinis*, of the vilest sort of men must be called by the vain name of master at every word.'

The highly artificial composition of men's dress is portrayed humorously in Thomas Dekker's *Seven Deadly Sins of London*.

The Englishman's dress [says the dramatist] is like a traitor's body that hath been hanged, drawn, and quartered, and is set up in various places; his cod-piece is in Denmark, the collar of his doublet and the belly in France; the wing and narrow sleeve in Italy; the short waist hangs over a Dutch butcher's stall in Utrecht; his huge slops speak Spanishly. . . . And thus we that mock every nation for keeping of one fashion, yet steal patches from every one of them to piece out our pride.

So whimsical was the national taste that even the enterprising tailor had to acknowledge himself beaten. Beneath an old wood-cut depicting a naked Englishman carrying a roll of

cloth over his arm and a pair of tailor's shears in his hand, stands
the following doggerel:

> I am an Englishman, and naked I stand here,
> Musing in my mind what raiment I shall wear;
> For now I will wear this and now I will wear that;
> And now I will wear I cannot tell what.

The permanent elements of male costume, on which all the
elaborate changes were rung, were not really complicated. A
doublet tightly fitting the figure, carrying a small puff at the
shoulder, and a high collar at the neck edged with a frill of
lawn, cambric, or holland: a pair of round breeches, generally
showing the knees: long stockings reaching to the thighs: small
pointed shoes or long wide-mouthed boots: a short cloak hanging
loosely from the shoulders: a flat or elongated hat bearing a
band with a feather; and, finally, a rapier and dagger—such
were the essentials. But foreign 'cuts', individual fancies, and
the enterprise of the sartorial artist embellished and enriched
each item almost beyond recognition. Thus the velvet doublet
and breeches were filled out with 'bumbast' of hair or wool
(5 or 6 lb.), 'slashed' with silk or other costly material, embroidered with gold lacing, and fitted with crystal buttons, or
buttons of gold or silver. The cloak, reaching to the girdle,
knee, or even to the heel, was of the most elaborate workman-
ship, and made of the costliest material, within as well as without. As a rule it was of silk, taffeta, and velvet. The stockings
were seldom of cheaper material than silk, and were frequently
'cross-gartered' above and below the knee. Footwear, whether
boot or shoe, was high-heeled, so as to raise the individual
'a finger or two' above the mire of the streets, and like the other
parts of the dress was of silk, velvet, or costly leather work
'slashed' or 'pinked' (perforated), and variegated with embroidery and silver or gilt buckles. Hats, decorated with bands
and feathers, were sometimes drawn out 'like the battlements of
a house' or elongated 'like a spear or shaft of a steeple'. They
were made of silk, taffeta, velvet, wool, sarcenet, or fine hair.
Even the underwear was of the finest cambric, lawn, or holland,
treated with silk needlework, and flounced or frilled at the neck
and hands. Finally the dagger, sword, and rapier bore gilded or
silvered hilts, 'damasked' engraven blades, and were sheathed
in velvet scabbards. All this fantastic dress, it should be noted,

was a glow of colour of the most bizarre description—popinjay blue, pease-porridge tawny, goose-turd green, lusty-gallant, Judas colour, &c. The cost was, of course, heavy. Ornamental breeches ran from £7 to £100, stockings from 15s. upwards, shirts from 10s. to £5, and boots from £4 to £10.

Women's dress was no less revolutionary than that of the men. 'A ship is sooner rigged', said Stubbs, 'than a gentlewoman made ready.' Elizabethan London showed a strange resemblance to renaissance Venice in regard to feminine fashions. In both places it was the custom to expose the breasts freely, to paint the face and dye the hair, 'almost changing the accidents into the substance'. Apparently, too, the stylish women of England followed their Italian sisters in the quest for the blond, and were not above inveigling children with golden locks to part with them for a penny. On the edge of their 'bolstered' hair they hung 'bugles', 'ouches', 'rings', and other ornaments of silver or gold; and across their foreheads were laid, from temple to temple, a gilded or silvered fillet. The inordinate lust for these 'gee-gaws' of the foreign merchant—for they came from abroad—was the cause of many a sly hit in the drama of the time.

All classes and ranks of feminine society affected similar expensive tastes. The merchant's wife and the gentlewoman had their French hoods, artificers' wives had their hats of velvet, while the humble cottager's daughter had her taffeta or woollen headgear, well lined with silk or velvet. Likewise corked shoes, pantoufles, slippers, 'some of black velvet, some of white, some green, and others yellow', embroidered with gold or silver work, were the prerogative of no special class. But the chief fashionable addictions of the period were the ruff and the farthingale. The ruff was a pleated collar, worn round the neck, made of linen, lawn, or cambric, and stiffened with wire ('supportasses') and starch until it stood out from the person by about a foot. The effect, according to one critic, was of John the Baptist's head on a platter. Sometimes several ruffs were placed *gradatim* one on the top of another, and 'all under the master devil ruff'. As a rule feminine taste demanded that the material should be crusted over with gold, silver, or silk lace—'speckled and sparkled here and there with the sun, moon, and stars'. The other special feature of female attire, the farthingale or *verdugado*, was a Spanish invention. Introduced into England about the same time as the ruff, it supplanted the old-fashioned gothic skirt which clung to the figure. Essentially it was a petticoat of canvas, distended with whalebone, cane, or steel hoops, and covered with rich cloth of taffeta, velvet, or silk. The effect was greatly to enlarge the hips; and this was still further accentuated by the habit of squeezing the upper part of the figure into a stiff, pointed doublet—the so-called 'spagnolized' waist. 'A trussed chicken set upon a bell' is how one critic described the general effect.

In so artificial a society the barber drove a thriving trade. His 'cuts', cosmetics, and perfumes were in great demand. Setting aside the old 'Christ's cut' which gave a man's head the appearance of a 'Holland cheese', as if it had been 'cut round by a dish', the tonsorial artist purveyed the latest styles of Italy, France, and Spain. The Italian manner was 'short and round and frounced with curling irons so as to look like a half moon in a mist': the Spanish cut was 'long at the ears and curled'; while the Frenchman affected a love-lock drooping to the shoulders, 'where you may wear your mistress' favour'. The beard was similarly treated. The 'peak' might be 'short and sharp amiable like an inamorato, or broad pendant like a spade, to be terrible like a warrior and a soldado'. But the physiognomy of the client had to be considered. 'And therefore', says Harrison, 'if a man have a lean and straight face, a Marquess Otto's cut will make it broad and large; if it be platter-like, a long slender beard will make it seem the narrower; if he be weasel-beaked, then much hair left on the cheeks will make the owner look big like a bowdled hen, and grim as a goose, if Cornelius of Chelmsford say true.' The moustaches were separately treated, being 'fostered about the ears like the branches of a vine', or cut down to the lip in the Italian manner. Of the unguents and perfumes in common use, perhaps the most popular were civet, musk, oil of tartar, lac virginis, and camphor dissolved in verjuice.

It was not only a richly dressed and highly perfumed, but also a 'militant civility' that paraded the London streets. Everyone went armed from eighteen years of age and upwards, bearing at least a dagger, a broadsword, or a rapier—sometimes both dagger and rapier. Even the labouring man in the country had his weapons, which he laid down in a corner of the field when working. Apprentices had their knives, and women their bodkins. The tendency of the more lethal weapons was to grow longer; and in 1580 the government was compelled to issue a proclamation limiting the length of swords to three feet and daggers to twelve inches, inclusive of the handle. Obviously street fighting was frequent, for the Englishman at this time aped the Italian: he had a 'factious heart, a discoursing head, and a mind to meddle in all men's matters'. Mercutio's taunt to Benvolio shows him in action: 'Thou wilt quarrel with a man for cracking nuts, having no other reason but because thou hast hazel eyes. . . . Thou hast quarrelled with a man for coughing because he hath wakened thy dog that hath been asleep in the sun.'

If the dress was sumptuous, the Elizabethan house and household appurtenances were no less an expression of the general desire for luxury. The old, rude, timber-and-clay dwelling, with its smoky interior, its rush-strewn floor, and its straw pallet, was no fit habitation for 'velvet breeches', however suitable it might have been for 'cloth breeches'. 'Oak, which, in times past', writes Harrison, 'was dedicated wholly to churches, religious houses, noblemen's lodgings, and navigation', now became the rage. Hornbeam, plum-tree, and sallow willow—the old materials of construction—were discarded, and the 'royal wood' appeared in every pretentious dwelling. Timber, clay, and wattles gave place to stone, lath, and plaster: wainscoting appeared on the inner walls and plaster of Paris on the ceilings: the feather bed replaced the straw pallet: carpets took the place of rushes; and stoves and chimneys confined the wandering smoke of the medieval house within manageable limits, while the use of glass dispelled its darkness and draughts. As tapestry and arras work beautified the walls of the rooms, so goblets of silver, glass, or pewter, metal spoons, chairs, and table linen helped to make the act of dining a more elaborate and less gluttonous performance. In noblemen's establishments the value of the plate amounted to £1,000 or even £2,000: in smaller houses, such as the merchant class occupied, to £500; and in artisans' or farmers' cottages it was not altogether unknown. Some idea of the length to which the wealthiest class was prepared to go in the worship of luxury may be gathered from Laneham's flamboyant description of Kenilworth, Leicester's country seat. This stately pile, one of the 'wonder houses' of the time, was 'all of hard stone, every room so spacious, so well lighted, and so high-roofed within: so seemly to sight, so glittering of glass a-nights by continual brightness of candle-fire and torchlight, transparent through the lightsome winds, as if it were the Egyptian Pharos relucent unto all the Alexandrian coast'. When the queen visited it in 1575 she was treated to a banquet that must have been the *chef d'œuvre* of culinary art in the sixteenth century. It was served in a thousand dishes of glass or silver by two hundred gentlemen.

Apparently all classes fed liberally, save the poor, who confined themselves to 'white meats', bread made of rye or barley, when they were obtainable, and a coarser bread of beans, oats, or acorns in time of dearth. Of the fashionable dinner-table Stubbs writes: 'Nowadays, if the table be not covered from the one end to the other as thick as a dish can stand by another, with delicate meats of sundry sorts, one clean different from another, and to every dish a several sauce appropriate to his kind, it is thought unworthy of the name of a dinner.' The nobleman never wanted, in season, his beef, mutton, veal, lamb, kid, pork, coney, capon, red and fallow deer, fish, and wildfowl, together with sundry 'delicates', 'wherein the sweet hand of the seafaring Portugal is not wanting'. The gentlefolk and the merchants used ordinarily four, five, or six dishes, but on special occasions aped the fuller tables of those above them, showing a keen relish for rare and outlandish delicacies. Beef formed the main constituent in the diet of the husbandman and the artificer; but if they happened to 'stumble upon' a haunch of venison and a cup of very strong beer or wine, 'they think their cheer so great and themselves to have fared so well as the lord mayor of London'.

The money expended on spices and condiments was out of all proportion to that expended on food; but there is no reason to suppose that excessive eating was carried on to any marked degree. Excess in drinking, on the other hand, was probably one of the commonest vices of the time. 'Large garaussing', says Moryson, came over with the soldiers and captains returning from the Low Countries, and was evidently due to contact with the Germans. The wealthy 'garaussed' in their fifty-six different kinds of French wine, and their thirty brands of Italian, Grecian, Spanish, and Canary; while the poorer folk frequented the public inn or alehouse, and became 'cup shotten' on common ale. The chief sinners were not the winebibbers, who drank from Murano glass and silver goblets, but the 'vulgar sort' who copied the vices of the swaggering soldier. 'It is incredible , says

Harrison, 'how our malt bugs lug at their liquor even as pigs lie in a row lugging at their dam's teats till they lie still again and be not able to wag.' Drunkenness, however, was regarded by the better classes as a 'clownish' and 'reproachful' vice; and by a very simple device they prevented over-indulgence. The drinks were kept on a sideboard, not on the table, and the guests drank only when necessity urged, thereby avoiding 'the note of great drinking'.

'Tobacco taking' was another luxury of the age. It was probably introduced by Hawkins from America in 1566, in the form of pipe-smoking. Harrison noted its prevalence some eight years later. By 1598 smoking seems to have become general, for Hentzner, who visited England in this year, observed that the English were constantly puffing 'the Nicotian weed' in public places. It was a costly indulgence, for tobacco was retailed at 3s. per ounce; but the practice of providing a common pipe at the inns, taverns, and alehouses placed it within the reach of everybody. By the end of the reign the novelty had become a social necessity, and was practised equally 'in the courts of princes, the chambers of nobles, the bowers of sweet ladies, the cabins of soldiers'.

The social revolution affected also the gardens of the time, which Harrison thought more wonderful than the gardens of the Hesperides, and Fynes Moryson rated above those of any other nation. 'So curious and cunning are our gardeners now in these days', says Harrison, 'that they presume to do in manner what they list with nature.' The old-fashioned garden of 'humble roots' was, by comparison with the new, no better than a 'dunghill'. The artistic sense of the age demanded that the kitchen garden, with its rank odours, 'which are scarce well-pleasing to perfume the lodgings of any house', should be removed to a distant part of the grounds, and that precedence should be given to the vineyard, the orchard, and the flower-bed. Like the Italian, the English gardening expert made the garden the setting for the house. Surrounded with a wall of stone or a thickset hedge of hornbeam or holly, and formed on the pattern of a square, it was laid out with the utmost stiffness and formality, in path and flower-bed, with arbours and vases of lead and stone to diversify the somewhat monotonous repetition. Strange plants, herbs, and fruits adorned it—grapes, plums, apples, pears, walnuts, apricots, almonds, peaches, figs, oranges, lemons, and wild olives. In short, the gardens of Elizabethan England were symbolic of the luxurious and far-flung life of the period.

But of all the sights of the time none could compare with the city of London. The hundred and twenty thousand inhabitants who thronged its congested and plague-infested streets were an epitome of the energy, enterprise, and indomitable spirit of a great people—a people, says Stubbs, 'audacious, bold, puissant, and heroical ... in all humanity inferior to none under the sun'. The Thames, which formed the principal highway between east and west, was the centre of the Londoner's world, and a source of endless surprise to strangers. Its crowded wharves, 'shaded with masts and sails', gave it the appearance, remarks Camden, of a 'wooded grove'. No less wonderful were the palaces and riverside houses, stretching from Temple stairs to King's bridge, each with its garden and water-gate. In the city itself were many attractions to hold the eye of the curious: West Cheap with its far-famed Goldsmith's Row, noted for its glittering tower and fountain that played continuously: Fleet Street with its puppet-shows, where visitors could view a dead Indian for ten doits, and many other marvels: Holborn, the sixteenth-century Kensington, famous for its gardens and the freshness of its air: the Royal Exchange in Cornhill, the haunt of merchants and loungers: the Tower with its armoury and primitive zoological gardens: the monuments at Westminster; and, if a bird's-eye view of the entire panorama were desired, it could be had for a penny by mounting St. Paul's tower.

The principal places of fashionable resort, where all classes sunned themselves, were St. Paul's, the theatre, and the bear garden. Each, in its own way, represents a facet of the variegated life of the period. St. Paul's, intimately associated with all the epoch-making pronouncements of the reformation from the days of the Henrician settlement, had now become one of the hubs of the social universe. In vain the Homilies supplied for the use of the pulpit inveighed against its desecration: the cathedral, in Elizabeth's day, was a 'house of talking, of walking, of brawling, of minstrelsy, of hawks, and of dogs'. The middle aisle of the nave was the scene of a daily pandemonium. Here the gallants and the idle gentlewomen of the capital met to exchange favours. Here, too, came the hawkers and riff-raff of the streets. In one corner were to be found the lawyers and scriveners; in another, shopkeepers exposed their wares for sale, and indulged in their various cries, using the tombs and the font as counters for the payment and receipt of accounts. 'Lordless' men paraded up and down offering their services for hire. And, to increase the din and confusion, horses and mules were led through the cathedral as a short cut, profaning the sacred precincts with the filth and litter of the streets. Outside, in the churchyard, was the book-market of London, where the 'merry books' of Italy were bought and sold; and, in all probability, it was in this very market that Shakespeare purchased the Italian romances on which many of his plays are based.

It was in the theatre, however, that the mundane spirit of the age found its most acute expression. What drew the Elizabethan populace to the playhouse? We are sometimes invited to consider the high poetic value of a Shakespearian drama, and to marvel at the dizzy heights of appreciation required of audiences at the Globe, the Swan, and Blackfriars, when witnessing masterpieces like *Romeo and Juliet*, *Hamlet*, or *A Midsummer-Night's Dream*. We should remember that plays of this nature rose far above the habitual level of contemporary dramatic art. Normally the Elizabethan play staged scenes that would revolt a modern audience—scenes portraying human nature in the raw, that sometimes appear to us to be no fit subject for art at all. Yet this must have been a main source of attraction to the apprentices, mechanics, and artisans who filled the pit. The plain fact is that the popularity of the theatre lay in its direct appeal to the senses. Just as it was the rough and tumble at the bear garden, the 'biting, clawing, roaring, tugging, grasping, tossing, and tumbling' of the bear, and the nimbleness of the dogs, that delighted the spectators, so it was the vehemence of the action, the licence of expression and sentiment, the resounding declamation, the pageantry, and the fine dresses of the actors that charmed the playgoers. To the puritan, the theatre was an eyesore, to the city fathers a plague-spot, but it was, nevertheless, the glory of Elizabethan London, and a microcosm of the age.

It cannot be said that the Elizabethan invented any new form of sport. He indulged in bear- and bull-baiting, cock-fighting, hunting the deer and the hare, falconry, fowling, and angling—all of old standing; but fox-hunting had not yet reached the dignity of a true sport. The 'sweet and comfortable recreation' of baiting the chained bear with mastiffs was the national sport *par excellence*, being patronized by the queen when official entertainments had to be given in honour of distinguished foreigners. But cock-fighting was probably more popular with the masses, since 'cocks of game' were more easily obtained than bears, and there was more excitement in the sport by reason of the betting that accompanied it. Partisans of both sports were to be found, on Sunday afternoons or holidays, at Paris Garden, in Southwark, close by the theatres, or at Lewin Street, Shoe Lane, and St. Giles-in-the-fields, where the most famous cockpits were situated.

In the country the premier sport was the deer hunt. The Elizabethan loved his fat venison, but he was not over-nice as to the manner of killing it. Sometimes the deer were driven into prepared ambushes and shot down with the cross-bow; sometimes they were chased to bay with hounds. 'Under this thick grown brake we'll shroud ourselves,' says the keeper in *Henry VI*, 'for through this laund the deer will come.' Leicester, who was a keen huntsman, preferred the more active pursuit, 'riding about from bush to bush with a cross-bow on his back'. The queen, too, was an ardent follower of the chase, riding so hard on one occasion that she had to keep her bed for several days, and could not interview the French ambassador. But when the Elizabethan sportsman wanted a real thrill, it was the hare he hunted, not the deer. The hare was the 'king of venerie', the 'most marvellous beast there is'. Shakespeare's stanzas on 'poor Wat', the hare, in *Venus and Adonis*, contain, without doubt, the most memorable literary portrait of animal life in the period.

Next to the chase, falconry was probably the most popular pursuit of the country gentry. The very terms of the sport were household words. 'An a man have not skill in the hawking and hunting language', says Master Stephen in *Every Man in his Humour*, 'I'll not give a rush for him.' Training of the hawk was a science in itself. Sometimes he was unhooded and flown off the fist when the quarry rose, sometimes liberated first, to hover over the falconer while the game was flushed. The long-winged species were used for the killing of heron, bittern, wild duck, when long-distance flights were necessary; but goshawks and sparrowhawks, whose range was shorter, sufficed for partridges, pheasants, and woodcock in woodland or inclosed country.

Dogs, of course, were necessary for retrieving the birds or driving them out of cover. Other methods of bird-taking were practised by the fowler, who used the bow and the bird-bolt, springes, gins, bird-lime, and, more rarely, the caliver and shot.

The use of the caliver as a fowling-piece shows that fire-arms were now beginning to invade the realm of sport. They had already established their supremacy in war—a disturbing fact to all who remembered the glory of the long bow, with which so many battles had been won over the French. But so it was. The man trained in the deadlier arquebus was now more prized than the archer, despite Roger Ascham's spirited defence of the bow in *Toxophilus*. Harrison tells us that Frenchmen and German 'rutters', clad in corslets, derided the English archers, crying 'Shoot, English!' Archery, in fact, was fast becoming a pastime practised for skill rather than a serious preparation for war. Similarly the old-fashioned sword and buckler were giving way to the more stylish and deadly rapier. Justice Shallow remembered the time when 'with a long sword I would have made you four fellows skip like rats'; but every gallant now studied to become an expert in the 'immortal passada' of the Italian and Spanish schools of rapier-fencing. Tybalt's style, as described by Mercutio, was probably copied from the Spaniard, who fought on the 'geometric' system: 'He fights as you sing prick-song, keeps time, distance, and proportion; rests me his minim rest, one, two, and the third in your bosom.' It was a ceremonious age, when men stood on points of honour, and duelling was a common occurrence. A quarrel 'by the book', according to Touchstone, consisted of seven stages: first, the 'retort courteous', then the 'quip modest', the 'reply churlish', the 'reproof valiant', the 'countercheck quarrelsome', the 'lie with circumstance', and, finally, the 'lie direct'.

Doubtless the England of Elizabeth had its saints and martyrs; and in the quiet backwaters of the country, far beneath the troubled surface of the age, the main current of religious life ran its course, as it had done for centuries before. Nevertheless it was a time when, as we have seen, the bulk of men paid little more than lip service to the self-denying virtues of the christian religion. As in politics, so also in society, the prevailing tone was markedly secular and worldly. The day of the puritan ascetics had not yet dawned—they were still voices crying in the

wilderness, whose lamentations and denunciations hardly penetrated to the ears of those for whom they were intended. 'They
speak', wrote Thomas Nash, 'as though they had been brought
up all their days on bread and water . . . as though they had
been eunuchs from their cradle or blind from the hour of their
conception.' 'Dost think, because thou art virtuous,' says Toby
Belch to Malvolio, in *Twelfth Night,* 'there shall be no more
cakes and ale? . . . A stoup of wine, Maria!' The confusing doctrinal changes of the previous generation, the extensive spoliation
of the church and the consequent discredit of religion, coupled
with the rising tide of material prosperity and the unscrupulous
pursuit of gain, had contributed not a little to the atmosphere of
egoism, paganism, and epicureanism in which the Elizabethan
lived and moved and had his being. But it was the infiltration of
Italian vices, brought back by those who had made the 'grand
tour' of that over-civilized land, that gave the age its peculiar
flavour of naughtiness. The Englishman italianate, said a contemporary Italian proverb, is a devil incarnate. 'Thou comest
not alone', wrote Greene—himself no paragon of virtue—'but
accompanied with a multitude of abominable vices hanging
on thy bombast, nothing but infectious abuses and vainglory,
self-love, sodomy, and strange poisonings, wherewith thou hast
infected this glorious isle.' Among other things, the *italianato* was
the patron of the 'bawdy books' that streamed from the press in
ever increasing volume, to the alarm and disgust of sober men
like Roger Ascham. 'Ten *Morte Arthures* do not the tenth part so
much harm', complained the schoolmaster, 'as one of these
books, made in Italy and translated in England. They open,
not fond and common ways to vice, but subtle, cunning, new,
and diverse shifts, to carry young wills to vanity, and young
wits to mischief, to teach old bawds new school points.' No
wonder the pulpit spoke of 'godly preaching heard without
remorse', of 'fasting kept without affliction', of 'almsgiving
without compassion', and of 'Lent holden without discipline'.
It was an age that claimed and exercised the right to unlimited
self-expression—'robustious', ostentatious, licentious: when he
that could 'lash out the bloodiest oaths' was accounted the
bravest fellow. 'Canst thunder common oaths like the rattling
of a huge, double, full-charged culverin?' says a character in
Marston's *Scourge of Villainie*: 'Then, Jack, troop among our
gallants, kiss my fist, and call them brothers.'

VIII

LITERATURE, ART, AND THOUGHT

As a race the Elizabethans set a supreme value on the active life. 'We cannot deny', wrote Lawrence Keymis, Raleigh's companion in the ill-fated Guiana expedition, 'that the true commendation of virtue consists in action: we truly say that *otium* is *animae vivae sepultura*.' Nevertheless a description of the age that concerned itself only with the men of action would rob it of half its glory and many of its greatest names. In the realm of literature the England of Elizabeth stands on a pinnacle by itself, and the writers who contributed most to its brilliance were as distinctively national as the anglican church or the poor law. Some connexion doubtless exists between the two aspects of the period, between the heroic deeds of the seamen and soldiers and the wonderful sunburst of poetry, drama, and speculative thought with which the names of Spenser, of Marlowe, of Shakespeare, and of Bacon are associated; for an age rich in exploit is seldom without its poets and dreamers. The out-goings of the spirit are conditioned by its in-takings, and the imaginative reach of the man of letters keeps pace with the widening horizon of his experience. The countless adventures on land and sea that made England respected and feared, and opened up the world to English enterprise, produced an exaltation of soul which the poet and the philosopher by the alchemy of their genius transmuted into the unforgettable beauties and enduring strength of a great literature. Like Drake and Cavendish, Shakespeare and Bacon circumnavigated the earth and grew rich on its spoils.

Let us beware, however, of supposing that the literature of an age is necessarily a mirror of its history. It is infinitely more than this. The literature of the later sixteenth century, as we have seen, has much to say of contemporary life in its social aspect; but the struggle for power in the political arena, the institutions, laws, policy, and administrative machinery that regulated the political life of society, held as little fascination for the writers of the time as for the multitude in the streets. Politics and literature had not yet come together, but ran their courses in entirely different channels. As for the truly great writers, they are less parochial and more universal in their appeal than at any other period. Those who search for 'political allusions' in their works do not find much to reward them for their pains, and the little they do find is of comparatively small value. The only outstanding exception to this general rule is Richard Hooker, whose *Ecclesiastical Polity* ranks with Shakespeare's *Plays*, Bacon's *Essays*, and Hakluyt's *Voyages*, as one of the representative books of the time. But Hooker's work, for all its massive learning and intellectual power, seldom rises to the height of great literature, and only does so when the author abandons the logomachy of the scholastic divine, and launches out into disquisitions on the nature of law, the structure of society, or the duty of man. The main body of his work belongs to the polemical theology of the day.

If the Elizabethans were non-political in their writings, so too they cannot (Spenser alone excepted) be called romantics —if by romance is meant an imaginative longing for a golden age in the past. Ages of romance are essentially decadent ages, when the present loses its flavour and men turn to the past for their inspiration; but the age of Elizabeth was an age of optimism, of experiment, of constructive achievement. The present was too full of interest for men of letters to fall back on the storehouse of memory, or to indulge in vain regrets for a vanished splendour. They looked forward not backward. They blazed fresh trails and opened up new channels of literary expression which subsequent generations turned into broad, beaten highways. Like pioneers, too, they fumbled and blundered; but their irrepressible exuberance and fertility of mind carried them through to amazing success. In the end they created a great literature worthy of a great people.

Finally it may be observed that the term 'Elizabethan' as applied to literature is not coincident in scope with the beginning and ending of Elizabeth's reign. It connotes a period of time stretching from about the end of the second decade of that reign to almost the closing years of her successor's. The first authentic sign that a great movement was under way in the literary world was the publication of Lyly's *Euphues* and Spenser's *Shepheards Calender* in 1579. Twenty years later, when the queen was already passing into the sear and yellow leaf, the giants of literature began to reach their maturity. When she died the greatest of Shakespeare's plays were still unwritten, and the dramatists who stand nearest to him in the quality of their work—Middleton, Webster, Beaumont and Fletcher, Ford, and Rowley—were still in their 'teens. Ben Jonson had some thirty years of life and work before him, and Bacon was only forty-two. Of the better-known writers only five ended their lives within the confines of the reign, viz. Sidney, Marlowe, Spenser, Nash, and Hooker, and two of them died prematurely —Sidney of a wound received on the battle-field of Zutphen, and Marlowe in a tavern brawl. Clearly, then, we must claim a poetic licence when we speak of Elizabethan literature, and pursue our study to its natural conclusion even if it takes us into Jacobean times. To chop and divide a literary movement in accordance with the political calendar would be neither reasonable nor just, nor would it enable us to appreciate the extent of the debt we owe to the Elizabethans.

It is difficult to describe the manifold literary activities of such a prolific period: a mere catalogue of the authors and their works would almost fill the space at our disposal. Let us begin by noting the salient features of the more ephemeral literature. In the first place, there was a colossal amount of printed matter emanating from, or in some way connected with, the prevailing patriotism and national pride. The self-satisfaction of the individual cast a glamour over his whole environment—his family, his ancestors, the soil of his native land, its history and antiquities. It was as if a search-light had suddenly been turned on history and geography. In consequence of this a continual stream of biographical, historical, and geographical works poured from the press. The labours of Leland, Hall, and Fabyan, which had met the needs of the previous generation in regard to such matters, had to be wrought over again on a grander scale; and a new race of antiquaries, topographers, and chroniclers made their appearance. William Camden followed Leland with a description of England, county by county, borough by borough, noting every natural feature and every point of local antiquarian lore. His *Britannia* and *Remains Concerning Britain* are monuments of patient research and physical toil. Similarly William Lambarde, Richard Carew, and George Owen devoted themselves to descriptive surveys of Kent, Cornwall, and Pembroke.[1] Other learned works—Norden's *Speculum Britanniae*, Saxton's

---

[1] For an excellent account of these and other pioneers, see A. L. Rowse, *The England of Elizabeth*, vol. i, chap. 2.

Atlas of England, Nowell's *Maps of the English Counties,* and Speed's *Theatre of the Empire of Great Britain*—show the awakening interest in geography; while Richard Grafton, John Stow, and Raphael Holinshed enriched historical knowledge by their chronicles. The last-mentioned work was prefaced by William Harrison's *Description of Britain,* probably the most interesting contemporary account of Elizabethan England, and certainly the best known. Sir John Fortescue's *De Laudibus Angliae,* a notable book of the late fifteenth century, was reprinted several times in order to satisfy the demand of those who desired to be told why the laws of England 'are plainly proved far to excel as well the civil laws of the Empire, as all other laws of the world'. Interest in recent history was carried to a high pitch by Foxe's *Book of Martyrs,* Camden's *Annales . . . Regnante Elizabetha,* and Hayward's *Annals of the First Four Years of Queen Elizabeth;* while John Speed's *History of Great Britain* and Samuel Daniel's *History of England* attempted historical surveys on a more extended scale. The best of these historians, Camden and Daniel, were eclipsed in fame by Bacon, whose *History of Henry VII* is generally held to be the most literary work of its kind during the period. But Camden, for all his shortcomings in form and finish, still holds the higher place in the affections of those who value historical research, both for his indefatigable efforts to establish the truth, and his industry in collecting material. Lastly we must note the great 'prose epic' of English exploit— Hakluyt's *Principal Navigations, Voyages, Traffics, and Discoveries of the English Nation:* a work which, in sheer massiveness, stands without a rival in our literature.

Both Camden and Hakluyt believed in what critics describe as an *ouvrage de grande haleine.* Both were confronted with a task which only a profound patriotism and self-effacement could carry through, and both were gifted, or cursed, with the same desire for meticulous accuracy, the same scholarly probity of mind, and the same engaging humility.

Camden's genius has a charm that will never fade. In the Preface to the second edition of his greatest work—the *Britannia* —he states his theme with admirable precision: 'to acquaint the world with the ancient state of Britain . . . to restore Britain to Antiquity and Antiquity to Britain . . . and to recover as far as possible, a certainty in our affairs, which either the carelessness of writers, or the credulity of readers, had bereft us of'.

Humble before the immensity of his task, he describes himself as a mere 'smatterer in Antiquities', who has been induced by the natural love of his country, the glory of the British name, and the persuasions of friends to undertake a task he was 'unfit for'. But Time, he thinks, 'the uncorrupt witness', will determine the value of his work, when 'Envy which preys upon the living' shall hold its peace. And so the great achievement was accomplished. With a delicate irony, Camden warns off from reading the book 'all who desire to be strangers in their own country, foreigners in their own cities, and always children in knowledge'; and likewise also 'those who cavil at the roughness of my style'. 'I frankly confess', he writes, 'that neither is every word weighed in Varro's scale; nor did I deign to gratify the reader with a nose-gay of all the flowers that I could meet with in the garden of Eloquence.' On the other hand, however, he does not attempt to conceal, or belittle, the scope of his labours and researches, which were unique in his own day, and have provided a spur to scholars everywhere. 'I have neglected nothing', he asserts, 'that could give considerable light towards the discovery of truth in matters of antiquity. . . . I have travelled almost all over England and have consulted in each county, the persons of best skill and knowledge in these matters. I have diligently perused our own writers, as well as the Greek and Latin. . . . I have examined the public records of the kingdom, ecclesiastical registers and libraries, and the acts and monuments and memorials of churches and cities.' A truly stupendous undertaking!

The story of his struggle, in compiling the *Annales*, with the mass of manuscripts which Lord Burghley placed at his disposal, 'in the rigging and searching whereof I laboured till I sweat, being covered over with dust', is almost an epic in itself. Twice he threw down his pen in dismay at the magnitude of the task before him, and only at the third attempt did he succeed in bringing it to a successful conclusion. It was perhaps natural, after so exhausting travail, that he should dedicate his *Annales* 'to God, my Country, and Posterity, at the Altar of Truth'. Hakluyt, that 'great zealot of the map and the flag', encountered difficulties no less great; but in his case it was the search for documents that wearied him rather than the 'rigging and searching thereof'. 'What restless nights, what painful days, what heat, what cold I have endured; how many long and

chargeful journeys I have travelled; how many famous libraries
I have searched into; what variety of ancient and modern
writers I have pursued . . . albeit thyself canst hardly imagine,
yet I by daily experience do find and feel, and some of my entire
friends can sufficiently testify.' Only his glorious theme and
ardent love of his country sustained him, and 'as it were with
a sharp goad provoked me and thrust me forward into this most
troublesome and painful action'. By redeeming the exploits of
his countrymen from oblivion he wrote all unwittingly a paean
to imperial England, by far the most impressive that has ever
been written.

The writing and study of history was not simply a reflection
of the growing pride, patriotism, and self-glorification of a
young and puissant nation revelling in its strength. It was inspired by the profound conviction that history repeats itself,
and by so doing creates a magnificent repertoire of information
applicable both to the world in which we live and the world of
the future. The key-note to this pragmatic view of the subject
was struck by Lord Berners in his preface to Froissart's *Chronicles*;
but it was echoed, re-echoed, and expanded in Norton's preface to Grafton's *Chronicle*, in Stow's *Chronicles of England*, and,
most brilliantly of all, in Raleigh's preface to his own masterly
History of the World. 'Is it not a right noble thing', remarked
Berners, 'for us, by the faults and errors of others, to amend and
erect our life into better?' By reading history, he continued, 'the
young acquire the wisdom of age, develop the spirit of emula-
tion, and are stimulated to high and great discoveries'. It is
especially important to princes, 'who can find in it many home
truths unobtainable even from their closest friends'. Stow struck
a picturesque and imaginative note when he wrote: 'It is as
hard a matter for the reader of chronicles to pass without
some colours of wisdom, incitements to virtue, and loathing
of naughty facts, as it is for a well-favoured man to walk up
and down in the hot parching sun and not be therewith sun-
burned.' Norton described history as 'a glass wherein each
man may see things past, and thereby judge justly of things
present, and wisely of things to come'. Being a puritan, he
added: 'and finally, all men in seeing the course of God's
doings, may learn to dread his judgments, and love his providence'.

But history was written in verse as well as prose, for the

popularity of verse at this period was greater. The *Mirror for Magistrates*, a composite work by many hands and based upon Lydgate's *Fall of Princes*, became the acknowledged depositary of England's tragic history. Although of very meagre poetic value and crude in compilation, the *Mirror* was enriched by the pen of Sir Thomas Sackville (afterwards Lord Buckhurst), who wrote the Induction, or Prologue, and set the fashion for a new type of plaintive history. Contrasting with this semi-medieval pageantry of lamentation over the downfall of the great, there appeared the heroic poem, which glorified the achievements of the English race in the present as well as the past. 'Heroical works', writes William Webbe, 'are the princely part of poetry.' Sidney was no less enthusiastic: 'There rests', he remarks in his *Defence of Poesy*, 'the heroical, whose name (I think) should daunt all back-biters.' Thus we have Warner's *Albion's England*, Samuel Daniel's *Wars of the Roses*, and Michael Drayton's *Baron's Wars* and *Poly-Olbion*. The chief importance of these works is their contemporary popularity: they reflect the spirit of the age and pander to its desires; but their pompous garrulity had little enduring poetic worth. Because of the inordinate length of their poems the American critic, Lowell, dubbed Daniel and Drayton the *megalosaurus* and the *plesiosaurus* of the Renaissance!

One last point with respect to the function of history in the contemporary political scene, viz. the growth and development of the 'Tudor Myth'. It is well known that the over-riding aim of the earlier Tudor monarchs was to stabilize the dynasty and to prevent the resurgence of civil strife. But it is not generally understood that, in order to accomplish this object, Henry VII and his son fostered the fanciful tale that the Tudor claim to the throne rested not only on Lancastrian descent and Yorkist marriage, but also on the lineal descent of Owen Tudor from Cadwallader, the last of the old British kings; and to this was coupled the equally mythical tale that Arthur would one day return, thereby creating the idea that the first Tudor was Arthur *redivivus*. All his heirs were to share in the dignity. This cult of Arthur seems to run like a refrain through the whole period, reaching its climax and apotheosis in the 'golden age' of Elizabeth. Thus 'Gloriana' became the final incarnation of the legend, and the England she ruled was 'the providential consummation of the vast process that had its beginning in the

remote and fabulous past, when the Trojans landed in Britain'.
The prophecy of Merlin was fulfilled:

> Then shall a Royal Virgin reign, which shall
> Stretch her white rod over the Belgic shore
> And the great Cast(i)le smite so sore withal
> That it shall make him shake and shortly learn to fall.[1]

Side by side with the awakened interest in history went a
movement for the study of the national literature and language.
This, too, is understandable as an off-shoot of the self-compla-
cency and national pride of the age, its love of things English,
and its desire to glorify the past in the light of the present.
Manifestoes, treatises, epistles on orthography and pronuncia-
tion, on the merits of rhyme as against classical metres, on the
need for purity in the use of the native tongue, on the superiority
of English over all other languages, followed one another from
the press, as writer after writer lent the weight of his authority
to the cause. 'I cannot but wonder', wrote Daniel, 'at the strange
presumption of some men that dare so audaciously adventure
to introduce any whatsoever foreign words, be they never so
strange, and of themselves as it were, without a parliament,
without any consent or allowance, establish themselves as free
denizens in our language.' 'The most English words', said
George Gascoign, 'are of one syllable: so that the more mono-
syllables that you use, the truer Englishman you shall seem.'
There was also a widespread desire that the glories of English
literature, up to this time treated with sublime indifference by
continental peoples, should be made patent to the whole world.
'O that Ocean did not bound our style', sang Drayton,

> Within these strict and narrow limits so:
> But that the melody of our sweet isle
> Might now be heard to Tiber, Arne, and Po:
> That they might know how far Thames doth outgo
> The music of declined Italy.

National pride did not, however, turn the eyes of the Elizabethans entirely inward. If they gloried in their own literature
and history, they appropriated to themselves the history and
literature of other peoples, both ancient and modern. Translators looted the classics and presented their compatriots with
Homer, Herodotus, Aesop, Aristotle, Demosthenes, Plutarch,

[1] See E. M. W. Tillyard, *The History Plays of Shakespeare.*

Theocritus, Ovid, Caesar, Cicero, Terence, Seneca, Lucan, Quintus Curtius, Sallust, Pliny, and many others in English dress. Some of the translations came through the medium of French, for instance North's *Plutarch*; but there were many editions of classical writers in the original. Modern French literature was well represented by John Florio's *Montaigne* (usually regarded along with North's *Plutarch*, Chapman's *Homer*, and Sylvester's *Du Bartas* as the most successful of contemporary translations), and English versions of the writings of La Noue, Estienne, La Primaudaye, Commynes; while Ronsard and the poets of the Pléiade were plundered wholesale by the sonneteers. Spanish literature also found its translators, who introduced their country-men to *Lazarillo de Tormes*, Guevara's *Dial of Princes*, the *Diana* of Montemayor, and medieval romances such as *Palmerin* and *Amadis*. But the foreign literature which commanded the greatest popularity in English garb was that of Italy. Boccaccio, Tasso, Ariosto, Castiglione, Machiavelli[1] were translated either wholly or in part, and there was a constant demand for the *novellieri*—Straparola, Cinthio, Bandello—whose tales furnished the drama-tists with matter for their comedies. Altogether the influx of foreign literature and its consumption by the Elizabethans must have been on a truly vast scale, and the ramifications of its influence on the native literature is a chapter which still re-mains to be completed. Thus was the rich soil of England fertilized by a deep layer of translations.

So far we have only touched the fringe of Elizabethan litera-ture. When we enter into the heart of the subject, the luxuriance and variety make the task of selection difficult. The muse of poetry tried her hand with every species of metrical composition except the epic, whose place was no doubt taken by the drama. The lyric, the ode, the madrigal, the ballad, and the sonnet were all brought to a high pitch of perfection which has never been surpassed. Merry England was in fact 'a nest of singing birds'. Erotic verse, of course, predominated, but not to the exclusion of other types; and even within the eroticism of the age it is possible to mark a distinction between the sensuousness and sensuality of poems like Marlowe's *Hero and Leander*, Shake-speare's *Venus and Adonis* and *Rape of Lucrece*, or Marston's *Pyg-malion*, and Spenser's chaste imagery in his *Amoretti* or Sidney's in the sonnet sequence *Astrophel and Stella*. Hymns to heavenly

[1] Only the *Arte della Guerra*.

love and spiritual sonnets were not wanting, but religious poetry in the strict sense of the word was conspicuously absent from the front rank of literature. The only poem that gained subsequent renown in this direction was Robert Southwell's *Burning Babe*, the creation of a martyred jesuit who saw his 'vision splendid' behind the bars of a state prison.

On the whole it is probably true that much of the poetry of the period sprang from the fancy rather than from the depths of the soul's experience. It is certainly true of the sonnet, the vogue of which was second only to that of the drama. Every one who aspired to poetic honours experimented with this easily mastered and more or less stereotyped form of erotic verse. The Dianas, Delias, Phyllises, Corinnas, Auroras, and other goddesses of the sonneteers were more often than not mere figments of the fancy; and the feigned emotion which they gave rise to palls by its monotony and conventionality. Indeed it may be said that only Sidney, Spenser, and Shakespeare embodied a real experience in their sonnets, and in the case of Shakespeare it is still impossible to determine with any degree of certainty the identity of the celebrated 'dark lady' on whom the poet lavishes his affection. Nevertheless, in sonnet literature as in dramatic, Shakespeare undoubtedly stands out as the greatest genius of his time.

It is perhaps permissible to speak with more warmth of the ballad; for the ballad, being less artificial, less ornate, and more popular in its topics and composition, became the vehicle for a simpler and truer emotion that appealed directly to all who could not appreciate the intricacies and subtleties of the sonnet, but loved to hear of the exploits and sufferings of familiar heroes —Robin Hood, Clymme of the Clough, Sir Patrick Spens, Edom o' Gordon, William of Cloudesley, Percy and Douglas, the Earl of Essex, &c.[1] Everything calculated to move the heart of the multitude was grist to the mill of the ballad-writer, and his range of subject was practically infinite. Even men of letters and scholars could avow themselves lovers of this lowly literature. 'I never heard the old song of Percy and Douglas', wrote Sidney in an oft-quoted passage, 'that I found not my heart moved more than with a trumpet; and yet it is sung but by some blind crowder, with no rougher voice than rude style.'

[1] For a full account of the subject, which is voluminous, see Sir Charles Firth's chapter on Ballads and Broadsides in *Shakespeare's England*, vol. ii.

If we think only of pure poetry, and exclude the drama, there is some justification for saying that the 'golden period' in Elizabethan literature began not with the publication of Spenser's *Shepheards Calender*, which is traditionally given the place of honour, but with the appearance of Sir Philip Sidney's *Arcadia* and his sonnet sequence, *Astrophel and Stella*. This, at any rate, is the opinion of Mr. C. S. Lewis. 'Sidney's work', he remarks, 'rises out of the contemporary Drab almost as a rocket rises: Spenser climbed out slowly and painfully like Christian from the slough.' Continuing the metaphor, perhaps we might say that the 'rocket' soared higher than anything produced in England in the field of poetry since Chaucer died. Of course we must remember that, while Sidney finished his brilliant career on the stricken field of Zutphen, before he had achieved more than a tithe of his ambition, and certainly before his genius reached its full effulgence, the somewhat sombre and melancholy Spenser lived to see the completion of his masterpiece, the *Faerie Queene*—'the only poem in the language', according to Spenserians, 'that a lover of poetry can sincerely wish longer'.

Of course it was Spenser who claimed to be the successor to the Chaucerian tradition; and his burial in Westminster Abbey, in close proximity to the great bard of the fourteenth century, seems to indicate that the nation accepted him at his own valuation:

> Here nigh to Chaucer Spenser; to whom
> In genius next he was; as now in tomb.

But he had a narrow escape. In spite of his devotion to Chaucer, he wobbled for a time towards the so-called classical school of poetry, led by his intimate friend, Gabriel Harvey, who was doing his best to lever English poetry into the metrical mould of Greece and Rome. But, as has been said, 'his ear was too fine and sensitive to endure the fearful sounds uttered by the poets of this procrustean creed'; and when he couched his *Faerie Queene* in the traditional melodious verse now familiar, Harvey gave up the effort to proselytize with ill-concealed annoyance. 'If so be', he wrote, 'the Faerie Queene be fairer in your eye than the nine Muses, and Hobgoblin run away with the garland from Apollo . . . there is an end for this once, and fare you well till God or some good Angel put you in a better mood.' Happily Spenser stood firm and refused to be guided by the pedants.

The source of Spenser's poetry may be found in the impact of his idealism on the crude realities of his material environment. He was a disillusioned man, who consistently aimed at political power and just as consistently failed to attain it. All through life he hovered between satire and pessimism, between veiled attacks on the corruptions and backslidings of the age and lamentations on its degeneracy. Probably no great writer ever found himself less in sympathy with the world in which he lived. In spite of the fact that his lot was cast in the most expansive period in English history, Spenser was essentially a *laudator temporis acti*. His philosophy is largely summed up in the derivation he gives of 'world', namely 'warre-old', or that which gets worse as it grows old. Obsessed by the evils, the misery, and the apparent confusion of contemporary society, he seems to have turned his back on its immense potentialities for good, and to have taken refuge more and more in a platonic world of his own creation, where the love of beauty is equivalent with the love of God, where sensuous desire and spiritual aspiration are one, and where men may 'follow their instincts and call their joys by the same name as their duties'.

Spenser's more important works can be grouped as follows: his satires—*The Shepheards Calender, Mother Hubberd's Tale,* the *Complaints,* and *Colin Clout's Come Home Again*: his erotic verse —the *Amoretti,* the *Epithalamion,* and the four platonic *Hymns* to love and beauty: the *Faerie Queene*; and his prose pamphlet entitled *A View of the Present State of Ireland.*

Of all these works, as well as of others which we have not mentioned, the literary critic has much to say, both in regard to the matter and the form. Here, however, we must limit ourselves to a very brief consideration of the *Faerie Queene,* the poem into which Spenser distilled more of his personality, art, and technique than may be found in all his other poems put together. Critics will always be in doubt as to the meaning or purpose of this strangely exotic romance, with its medieval setting, its allegorical figures, and its classical mythology. The author himself was obviously in some difficulty as to how to describe his brain-child: he called it 'a continuous allegory, or dark conceit', designed 'to fashion a gentleman or noble person in virtuous and gentle discipline'. In other words the poem was to be essentially didactic; but in order to render it 'more plausible and pleasing', it was 'coloured by an historical fiction'—the history of King Arthur—in the best tradition of Homer, Virgil, and Tasso; 'by the example of which excellent poets, I labour to portray in Arthur, before he was king, the image of a brave knight, perfected in the twelve private moral virtues, as Aristotle hath devised'. Without doubt a most ambitious programme! But the curious thing is that there is no trace in the poem of the didactic element, nor is the allegory obtrusive enough to spoil the story. What we get, in effect, is a renaissance version of the old Arthurian romance, shot through with veiled allusions to contemporary personalities in the political world, and transacted against the background of an idealized Irish landscape. All these disparate factors are woven together by the magic of the poet's genius into verse of superb beauty which seems to fit the theme like a glove. 'The plan, the story, the invention are triumphant', writes Mr. C. S. Lewis. 'If they have faults, they are such faults as never deterred any reader except those who dislike romance, and would not be allured to read it by any perfections.' 'We hear a slow music', says M. Legouis, 'whose perpetual return rocks the mind and sways it from out the real world into a world of harmony and order, of which it seems to be the natural rhythm.' The Spenserian stanza, in fact, is the 'regulative clock' of fairyland.

It may seem an abrupt transition to pass at one bound from the ethereal heights of Spenser's verse to the sober levels of Elizabethan prose. But the development of prose as an instrument of literary expression must be regarded as one of the minor triumphs of the age, and the writers who took part in it, although they erected no 'star-y-pointing pyramid', and were, for the most part, overshadowed by the genius of those who indulged in the more popular art, are nevertheless worthy to be remembered. Conventionally the study of Elizabethan prose begins with the publication of John Lyly's *Euphues* (1579) and *Euphues His England* (1580). These books, crammed with far-fetched similes derived from medieval bestiaries, herbaries, and lapidaries, with their tricks of alliteration, ornamentation, prolixities, and pedantries, were merely academic exercises in the ornate—notable only for their novelty of form and elegant moral tone. Lyly was a moralist who set himself the task of teaching the young; but the moral of his tale was of less importance than the studied graces of the style he affected. Much the same might be said of Sir Philip Sidney's pastoral story of love and chivalry, the *Arcadia*,[1] which was written about the same time, although there is more spontaneity in his heavily jewelled prose than in the ponderous conceits of *Euphues*. So infectious, however, was euphuism as a cult that it spread like an epidemic, becoming for many years a kind of universal language of the literary world. In this vein Robert Greene wrote his romantic novels *Mamillia*, *Menaphon*, and *Pandosto*, and Thomas Lodge his *Rosalinde*. Both authors interspersed their prose with exquisite lyrics, and Lodge displayed a remarkable talent for witty dialogue; but the main interest attaching to them is that Greene's *Pandosto* supplied Shakespeare with his plot for *A Winter's Tale*, and Lodge gave him both plot and chief character for *As You Like It*. Clearly writers had not yet realized that the function of prose is not to follow in the eccentric footsteps of poetry or to charm the imagination, but to instruct the reason, and to describe real things with precision, simplicity, and restraint. Lodge probably had some distant glimmering of the truth when he tried to lend verisimilitude to his narrative by composing it, not in the study but at sea, 'where every line was wet with a surge, and every humorous passion counter-checked with a storm'. But it was Greene who first broke new ground in the right direction with his coney-catching tracts (1591-2). Here at least was reality of a sort—the reality of London's underworld, with its thieves, swindlers, and loose women—of which our dissolute, tavern-haunting author could speak with all the vigour and authority of an eye-witness. To the same class belong the writings of Thomas Dekker, the author of the *Gul's Hornbook*, the *Seven Deadly Sins of London*, and many other pictures and sketches of London life, both grave and gay, *macabre* and humorous. With Thomas Deloney we enter yet another field of descriptive prose; for Deloney's novels, *Jack of Newbury* and *The Gentle Craft*, take us into the craftsman's world, among the weavers and cordwainers, and give us intimate pictures of industrial life in the capital. Greene, Dekker, and Deloney led English prose along the path that culminated a century later in the writings of Swift, Addison, Steele, and Defoe. Meanwhile Thomas Nash, a disciple of Greene, had turned his mordant wit to effective use in the acrimonious disputes of the period, particularly the Martin Marprelate controversy; and pamphlet after pamphlet flowed

[1] Sidney was the 'Bayard-cum-Petrarch' of the age.

from his sardonic pen with the force and velocity of an avalanche. In spite of his grotesque style and frequent lapses in taste, no one did so much for the development of Elizabethan prose as the 'frantic' Nash. He was more than a controversialist. He castigated the superstitions and absurdities of his generation with the satire of a Juvenal, or mocked at them with the humour of a Rabelais. He scarified the super-pedant of the age, Gabriel Harvey, tilted at Marlowe's 'spacious volubility', wrote a picaresque novel (*The Unfortunate Traveller, or The Life of Jacke Wilton*) to counteract the vogue of euphuism, and produced perhaps the best burlesque of the period—*Lenten Stuff*, in which he glorified the red herring, the source of Yarmouth's wealth.

Although prose found its descriptive powers and potentialities in the hands of realists and satirists, there were writers who applied it with telling effect in other directions. Sidney's *Defence of Poesy*, Daniel's *Defence of Rime*, and the writings of William Webbe are illustrations of its use in literary criticism. Roger Ascham wrote it brilliantly in his *Scholemaster*, Spenser even more brilliantly in his *View of the Present State of Ireland*, the most valuable contemporary analysis of Irish society in the sixteenth century. Sir Thomas Overbury, John Stephens, and John Earle found it the best medium for their 'character' studies. Dramatists adopted it for many of their comic scenes and less exalted personages. Shakespeare wrote it like a master when occasion served, and Ben Jonson employed it entirely in two of his plays. Finally it reached its highest pitch of perfection in Hooker's *Ecclesiastical Polity*, Hakluyt's *Voyages*, the *Essays* of Bacon, and the *Authorized Version* of the Bible. It is a notable fact, however, that when Bacon wrote his great philosophical work, the *Novum Organum*, he reverted to Latin, as being the more suitable medium for the expression of exact ideas. 'These modern languages', he remarked, 'will at one time or other play the bankrupts with books.'

There remains the drama, the crowning achievement of Elizabethan England in the field of literature. More so than any other literary creation the drama gathered up and expressed the emotional and intellectual life of the age in all its length, breadth, height, and depth. The stage play, in fact, became a truly national cult. Its main function was to amuse or instruct the public; but it also served as a kind of safety-valve for the pent-up 'humours' of society, its stresses and strains, its squabbles and irritations. It provided a 'platform' for the 'lay' politician, who had no other means of finding an audience. Disgruntled men of letters, who had somehow fallen short of their ambition, sometimes used it to discharge their shafts of scorn and satire against those who outshone them, or they used it to 'wash their dirty linen in public'. And it became part of the machinery of propaganda, when the government decided to appeal to the *vulgus profanum* in order to popularize a policy.

The uses of the stage play were manifold; but perhaps the most interesting aspect of this lower level of dramatic art was its adoption of the so-called allegory or 'dark conceit', already alluded to in the poetry of Spenser. It was a method of covering or disguising allusions to individuals which, if openly expressed, might expose the writer to punishment for libel or scandal, the pillory, or the loss of an ear. According to Sir John Harington, 'Allegory' was 'as Plutarch defineth it, when one thing is told and another thing is understood'. The passion for it was universal in the days of Shakespeare, Jonson, and Fletcher: it flung itself like a creeper over the entire literary output of the period.

> When Shakespeare, Jonson, Fletcher ruled the stage
> They took so bold a freedom with the age,
> That there was scarce a knave or fool in town
> Of any note, but had his picture shown.

The secret of the game was to plant a dart on the target, and then escape punishment by 'forswearing the application': that is, protesting that the allusion was either misunderstood or misapplied. The perpetrator could also escape by a public avowal before-hand that the political or personal allusion had no bearing on current politics or living persons. Thus Richard Edwardes, the author of *Damon and Pythias* (1566), protected himself by insinuating:

> Wherein, talking of courtly toys, we do protest this flat
> We talk of Dionysius' court, we mean no court but that.

So long as the writer 'sang *placebo* to the Court', he had nothing to fear. Hence Lyly's plays—*Campaspe, Sapho and Phao, Endymion*, and *Midas*—carried the royal 'imprimatur', for they ministered to the gratification of the queen, or—in the case of

Midas (i.e. King Philip II)—finished with an oracular recommendation to the king to ally himself with her. In other words the playwright was clearly backing the Cecilian policy of peace with Spain. On the other hand, the revival of Shakespeare's *Richard II* in 1599–1600 was treated as an act of *lèse majesté* because it seemed to calumniate the queen and support the Essex revolt. Observe the reference to the contemporary grievance of fiscal oppression:

> And daily new exactions are devised
> As blanks, *benevolences*, and I know not what;

The speed with which the movement progressed is one of its minor surprises. At the beginning of Elizabeth's reign the drama was still struggling to free itself from the worn-out morality and miracle plays of the middle ages: there were no public theatres, and actors were treated as vagabonds by the authorities. Until 1580 dramatic literature could be comprised in a single slender volume, and consisted of academic and scholastic productions like Nicholas Udall's *Ralph Roister Doister*, a comedy based on Plautus; Sackville and Norton's *Gorboduc*, a tragedy in the manner of Seneca; episodical plays with classical themes like *Damon and Pythias*, *Appius and Virginia*, and *Cambyses*; and a roaring farce, *Gammer Gurton's Needle*, which resembled in content the interlude of the old miracle play. All these plays—*Gammer Gurton's Needle* alone excepted—were designed for select audiences at school, university, or inns of court. But the foundation of the first actors' company under the patronage of the earl of Leicester, in 1574, and the erection of the first public theatre, in 1576, indicated that a new age was dawning. Then came the court drama of John Lyly (1581–90), followed by George Peele's *Arraignment of Paris* and *David and Bethsabe*. But these writers with their dainty rhymes, conceits, and flatteries of the queen, which formed the substance of their plays, were quickly swept aside by Thomas Kyd, Christopher Marlowe, and the unknown author of *Arden of Feversham*, who made plain for the first time the immense possibilities of the stage play as an instrument of popular amusement, and a sounding-board for the deeper emotions of the period. Kyd's *Spanish Tragedy* (1586) is a drama of the horrific type, a crude study in realism photographed from life, which makes the flesh creep with its passion and barbarity. In *Arden of Feversham* the crime *motif* again dominates the play; but in this case the author is interested in the psychological accompaniments of the crime rather than the crime itself. Prior to the appearance of the Shakespearian plays, *Arden* is the best psychological drama of the period. But it was Marlowe who invented the true medium of the Elizabethan drama. His 'drumming decasyllabon' and 'bragging blank verse', coupled with the spirit of revolt and defiance which animated all his plays, took the public by storm, and created a tradition which his successors, including Shakespeare, adopted and perfected. More than any of his contemporaries Marlowe displays the *terribilità* of the Italian renaissance. There is a massive simplicity and grandeur in the structure of his dramas, a singleness of aim and concentration of purpose that lift them far above the crude realism of Kyd. If at times he blunders into the grotesque in his effort to obtain effect, he more than redeems himself by passages of exquisite beauty and pathos. His heroes and villains are slaves to the 'will to power'—the power of military might, in *Tamburlaine* (1586), the power of knowledge, in *Doctor Faustus* (1588), the power of wealth, in the *Jew of Malta* (1589), and the power of cunning, in Mortimer (*Edward II*, 1592). It is highly probable that when Marlowe died prematurely, in 1592, he had already revealed the full scope of his genius: he certainly could have added nothing to the quality of his work, though he would undoubtedly have increased its quantity. He was a man of intense but limited vision, a fore-runner with a message preceding the true incarnation of dramatic power—Shakespeare.

All the playwrights before Shakespeare were university men, as, indeed, were the poets and other writers of the period. But Shakespeare was a discovery of the despised actor community, whose phenomenal rise to the dignity of authorship caused no small jealousy among the professed masters of the dramatic art. Greene alluded to him as 'an upstart crow beautified with our feathers', who, with his 'tiger's heart wrapped in a player's hide', imagined himself to be 'the only Shake-scene in the country'. At the time Greene penned his indictment the new playwright had nothing to his credit except *Love's Labour's Lost*, the *Comedy of Errors*, the *Two Gentlemen of Verona*, and three parts of *Henry VI*—none of which displayed much genius or originality, and certainly gave little inkling of the robust vitality that was to follow. If Shakespeare had died, like Marlowe, at the age of twenty-nine his fame would have been entirely overshadowed by that of the author of *Tamburlaine*. But by a curious coincidence chance and circumstance combined to eliminate all rivals from his path, when most he needed a free field for the development of his genius. Marlowe and Greene died in 1592, Kyd in 1594; Lodge gave up letters for medicine; Lyly ceased work; and Peele plunged into dissipation. In fact, from 1592 to practically the close of the century Shakespeare had the stage to himself, and established an unassailable reputation as the greatest living playwright. It was during this period that he wrote the bulk of his historical plays, *King John, Richard II, Richard III, Henry IV*, and *Henry V*; the fairy play, *A Midsummer-Night's Dream*; the lyrical tragedy, *Romeo and Juliet*; and all the romantic comedies, the *Merchant of Venice, Much Ado about Nothing, As You Like It, Twelfth Night*, the *Merry Wives of Windsor*, and the *Taming of the Shrew*. Then came the second and greatest phase of his activity (1601–8), when a pessimistic strain mingled in his work, and the note of tragedy prevailed. It was the period of the gloomy comedies, *Measure for Measure, All's Well that Ends Well, Troilus and Cressida*, of the profound tragedies, *Hamlet, Othello, Lear, Macbeth*, and *Timon of Athens*, and of the Roman plays, *Julius Caesar, Antony and Cleopatra*, and *Coriolanus*. The final phase (1608–16) saw the tragic vein soften into the romance of *Pericles, Cymbeline, The Winter's Tale*, and *The Tempest*. Thus Shakespeare may be said to have completed the cycle of human experience, passing from the fanciful plays of his youth to the tragedy of his mature years, and ending on a note of disillusionment, tolerance, and romance. But it will always be a disputable point how far this evolution was conditioned by his environment, and how far it was the natural development of his mind; for the life of Shakespeare apart from his art is wrapped in much mystery, and the attempted reconstructions of the interplay of environment and genius are usually as futile as they are fanciful.

Books on the subject of Shakespeare are now so numerous that writers are inclined to preface a new one with a 'sort of shame-faced apology'; and yet, in spite of the voluminous research, we are not yet possessed of an agreed canon of his work, or an accepted interpretation of many important passages in the tragedies. His character, personality, and the circumstances of his life seem still to lie in a mist of uncertainty, guesswork, and presupposition. Nevertheless, writers wax lyrical in praise of his genius. 'His mind', says one, 'was co-extensive with the human race': 'As a man', says another, 'he was like most of us, just a little higher than Caliban, one of the earthiest of his creations; but as a teacher of mankind, he seems to belong to another planet, born as if by accident into this puny-minded race of ours.' 'For my part', writes a recent American critic, 'I believe we are nearer to the beginning than to the end of our understanding of Shakespeare's genius'; and again, 'Hamlet criticism seems destined to go on being what it has always been, a sustained difference of opinion.' To understand this seemingly strange remark, we have only to read Richard Flatter's *Hamlet's Father*, one of the most recent critiques of the American vintage. Here we find ourselves in the presence of a refreshingly new—almost revolutionary—interpretation of the play, as different from that of the Victorian and Edwardian giants as chalk is different from cheese. According to Flatter, the ghost is not only the father of the chief character, but also the father of the play—the *deus ex machinâ* of the entire action. 'This dead and insubstantial figure, emerging from darkness and resolving into darkness, will be recognised', says the author in his prefatory note to readers, 'as what he truly is: one of Shakespeare's *most human creations*.' And another American scholar, Mr. Goddard, casts an unusually disconcerting light across the troubled waters when he writes, with obvious sincerity and conviction: 'Shakespeare is like life. There are as many ways of taking him as there are ways of living. . . . Never was there a more Protean genius.' All this may be fascinating to the expert critic; but to the ordinary reader who finds in Shakespeare's plays an endless fount of pleasure, philosophy, and illumination, it is both bewildering and somewhat tedious. With a sigh he turns again to Bradley and Brandes.

The greatness of Shakespeare rests essentially upon the extraordinary range of his gifts. His power of characterization, objectivity, inventiveness, and universality of appeal are all unique. Unlike Lyly, Kyd, Marlowe, or even Ben Jonson, he had no mannerisms that could be copied. He wrote lyrical, historical, tragic, comic, romantic, and fairy plays with equal facility and equal distinction; and a reference to the chronology of his works will show that he could turn from one *genre* to another, even within the same period, without any apparent effort. It has been said with truth that there are more immortal characters

in one of his greatest plays than in all the plays of his contemporaries taken together. When he took up the role of
historiographer he not only revived the past, he recreated it;
and the lineaments of the historical personages that throng his
gallery stand out with greater permanence than reality itself.
So strong was the impress of his genius on national history that
palpably false creations like his Richard III persist in defiance
of historical research; and a great critic, Froude, could aver:
'The most perfect English history which exists is to be found, in
my opinion, in the historical plays of Shakespeare.' In addition
to all this the felicity of his diction, imagery, and thought has
made his plays the mightiest store-house of aphorisms in the
English language. In short, we might apply to him the words,
slightly modified, spoken by Enobarbus of Cleopatra: 'Age cannot wither nor custom stale *his* infinite variety.'

Strictly speaking, Ben Jonson belongs to the generation later
than Shakespeare, and ought to be considered in conjunction
with Dekker, Marston, Middleton, Fletcher, Tourneur, Webster, and Heywood. But his marked individuality and versatility bring him into close juxtaposition to Shakespeare, from
whom, however, he differed profoundly in his whole conception and practice of the dramatic art. Without doubt Jonson
was the most learned of the Elizabethan playwrights. His knowledge of the classics was profound, and his reverence for the
dramatic proprieties, as understood by the Greeks, amounted
almost to fanaticism. In the technique of plot-construction as
well as in accuracy of detail he far surpassed Shakespeare,
whose carelessness in such matters is proverbial. This is particularly noticeable in Jonson's Roman plays, *Sejanus* and *Catiline*, where he indulges in a thousand touches, derived from
extensive reading in Latin literature, which Shakespeare could
never aspire to. But in spite of his wider knowledge of literature
and greater facilities, Jonson failed just where Shakespeare
achieved his greatest success, namely in characterization. All
his characters are caricatures rather than living persons. He
was interested in human eccentricities, or, as he would put it,
in men's 'humours'—a feature of his work which is strikingly
displayed in two of his best-known comedies, *Every Man in His
Humour* and *Every Man out of His Humour*. It is but a short step
from exposing men's eccentricities to satirizing their follies;
and Jonson, as his powers matured, rapidly became the greatest

master of satirical comedy in his time. To this category belong *Volpone, or the Fox* (1605), *Epicene, or the Silent Woman* (1609), *The Alchemist* (1610), and *Bartholomew Fair* (1614), all of which, in plot, character, and incident, are entirely creations of the author's own brain, and results of his observation of contemporary society. Never again did he reach the heights attained in these four plays: they stand, says one critic, amongst the most remarkable dramatic works of the English renaissance.

But Jonson was more than a great playwright. Some of the finest lyrics of the period are from his pen; and as a producer of masques he was without a rival. His worst fault was his egotism and aggressive self-assertion, which drew him into controversy with several of his contemporaries, and filled his life with bitterness and contention. This aspect of his character and career is startlingly reflected in his play *The Poetaster*, in which he apotheosizes himself as the Horace of the age.

Of the plays written by other authors during the great period of the Shakespearian drama and subsequently, special mention may be made of the following: George Chapman's *Tragedy of Biron* (1608) and *Bussy d'Ambois* (1607), Thomas Dekker's *Shoemaker's Holiday* (1599), *Old Fortunatus* (1600), and *Honest Whore* (1604), Thomas Heywood's *A Woman Killed with Kindness* (1603), *Eastward Ho!* by Marston, Chapman, and Jonson (1605), Thomas Middleton's *Witch* (1622), Cyril Tourneur's *Revenger's Tragedy* and *Atheist's Tragedy* (1607 and 1611), John Webster's *White Devil* (1611) and *Duchess of Malfi* (1614), Beaumont and Fletcher's *Knight of the Burning Pestle* (1609) and *Maid's Tragedy* (1611). Few of these plays fail to reach a high level of dramatic art, and some are worthy to be compared with Shakespeare's; but none of the authors mentioned was capable of the sustained brilliance and profound thought that characterized the great dramatist at his best. It was as if Shakespeare's genius had been split into fragments and distributed. Dekker could create living characters, Heywood was a master in pathos, Webster was a specialist in the morbid and the *macabre*, and Beaumont and Fletcher were experts in stage-craft and scenic effects. But the combination of qualities that resulted in the production of great literature as well as drama was the prerogative of Shakespeare alone.[1]

[1] 'All who thirst for art or truth', says M. Legouis, 'the comic or the tender, ecstasy or satire, light or shade, can stoop to drink from its waters, and at almost every instant of their changing moods find the one drop to slake their thirst.'

It is not necessary to carry the study of Elizabethan literature farther. The age of great poetry was drawing to its close with the 'metaphysical' verse of John Donne and the Spenserian imitations of George Wither, William Browne, Giles and Phineas Fletcher, and Drummond of Hawthornden. The drama, though still robust, was entering upon its silver age with the plays of Philip Massinger, John Ford, and William Rowley. In every direction save prose, literature was losing touch with the lively, ebullient spirit of Elizabethan England. It was perhaps a sign of the times; for the shadow of puritanism was already cast over the land.

If Elizabethan literature developed a truly national tradition, the same thing cannot be said, except with considerable reservations, of the fine arts. There were plenty of collectors of pictures among the nobility, like the earl of Leicester and Lord Lumley, whose galleries were famous; and Holbein had created a vogue for portraits. It was also the fashion, according to Harrison, for the walls of houses to be hung with tapestry, arras work, and 'painted cloths', 'wherein divers histories, herbs, beasts, knots, and such like are stained'; and there were art shops in Blackfriars, Fleet street, the Strand, and especially Robert Peake's in Holborn, where pictures could be purchased. But the artists of the day were mostly foreigners trained in the great schools of Flanders and Holland, who had migrated to England to escape the severities of Alva's rule. Among these foreign artists three stand out as particularly noteworthy for their excellence in portraiture, viz. Marcus Gheeraerts of Bruges, Paul van Somer of Antwerp, and Daniel Mytens of The Hague. The only English-born painter of note was Cornelius Johnson (or Jansen), and he, too, was of Netherlandish descent, though born in London. Except perhaps in miniature work, with which the names of Nicholas Hilliard and Isaac Oliver are associated, there was no native school of painting. The humble art of copperplate engraving, either for book illustration or map-making, was in a similar position, largely dependent upon the stimulus from abroad; but there were some English engravers, like Augustine Ryther, the map engraver, and William Rogers and Thomas Cockson, portrait engravers, who made a name for themselves. Probably the best known, if not the most famous, of the engravers who 'devilled' for the bookseller were the Droeshout brothers,

Martin and John, members of a refugee family from Brussels, who gained notoriety from the fact that Martin was responsible for the portrait of Shakespeare which adorned the frontispiece of the First Folio.

In regard to sculpture and architecture the same general criticism applies. It is more than doubtful whether England possessed a single creative genius of outstanding merit fit to be compared with the great masters of the Continent. The sculptors and tomb-makers of Southwark were in the main either Flemings or Germans, or of Flemish or German extraction, and the only vast public building erected during the reign, viz. Gresham's Royal Exchange, begun in 1566 and completed in 1570, was the work of a Flemish architect, Henri de Pas (or Paschen), who was responsible for the *Hôtel des Villes Hanséatiques* at Antwerp. The fact that Gresham employed not only a foreign designer but also foreign workmen, and imported the marble for paving the piazza of the Exchange—an action for which he was severely criticized by contemporaries—might seem to suggest that English craftsmen had not yet mastered the higher technique of the renaissance. As a matter of fact it merely shows that the 'classical' or 'italianate' architecture, that was all the rage abroad, was not fully 'received' into England. Gresham's building was intended to be an imitation of the italianate Bourse at Antwerp, and it was natural that he should make use of Flemings in its construction.

When we turn, however, from public buildings to private, and consider the domestic architecture of the period, a different picture presents itself. The glory of Elizabethan England lies depicted for us in the magnificent dwelling-houses, the 'cloud-capp'd towers' and 'gorgeous palaces' of the rich, and the humbler but no less stately manor houses of the gentry, which were now rising in great profusion all over the country. Here something like a blend was effected between classical models and traditional English design, and the architects or 'surveyors', as they styled themselves, were altogether English, albeit we know very little about their careers and individual achievements. Two of the most famous were John Thorpe, who constructed Kirby Hall, Northamptonshire, and Robert Smithson, the designer of Wollaton Hall, near Nottingham. The general trend of their work has been described as 'a gothic framework with a classical overlay'. It may not have been a very happy

combination from a purist point of view. There was a touch of
the exotic, not to say bizarre, in the balustraded and ornamental
parapets, the fantastic gables, the pilastered, columned, and
entablatured fronts, and many other features which the more
pretentious houses affected. Like the dress of the period, architecture of this sort must have struck observers as outlandish.
This, however, was not the opinion of the enthusiastic Harrison,
who writes with obvious pride: 'If ever curious building did
flourish in England, it is in these our days, wherein our workmen excel and are in manner comparable with old Vitruvius,
Leo Baptista, and Serlo.'

It was perhaps natural that an age when men were rapidly
emancipating themselves from medieval habits of living and
had not yet adapted themselves to the new conditions should
indulge in extravagances. The old militarized architecture of
feudal England, when a man's home was his castle, was out
of date in a society whose peace and security were daily becoming more firmly established. The 'halls', 'courts', and 'places'
of Elizabethan England—the very names are significant—had
no use for moats, drawbridges, portcullises, machicolations,
stanchioned windows, and the other relics of a barbarous past,
except for decorative purposes. The cry now was for comfort,
symmetry, and light—especially light. Rooms were multiplied,
galleries introduced for recreational purposes, windows enlarged
into bays and oriels, and piled one on top of another so as
to form glittering façades of glass. So great, indeed, was the
craze for illumination that Bacon remarked: 'You shall sometimes have fair houses so full of glass that one cannot tell where
to be come to be out of the sun or cold.' As an antidote to over-
illumination he advocated the building of 'double houses' (i.e.
rooms back to back), so 'that you may have rooms *from* the sun,
both for forenoon and afternoon'.

In spite, however, of the demand for light, the Elizabethans
do not appear to have favoured a southern exposure, as we
moderns do. On the contrary there is evidence to show that they
preferred to site their houses so as to avoid it. The south wind
was the English mistral of the sixteenth century. 'A south west
blow on ye and blister you all o'er!' was Caliban's curse on
Prospero. Thomas Tusser, the gardening expert, wrote:

> The south as unkind draweth sickness near:
> The north as a friend maketh all again clear.

And the well-known hygienist of the age, Andrew Boorde, in his advice to builders, urged them to 'order and edify' the house so that the main prospect might be east and west, preferably north-east, 'for the south wind doth corrupt and doth make evil vapours'. The east, on the other hand, is 'temperate, fresh, and fragrant', and the north 'purgeth all vapours'. Wherefore, he concluded, it were better that windows should 'open plain north than plain south'.

Opinion seems to be unanimous that the interpenetration of English architecture by foreign influences during Elizabeth's reign did not fundamentally affect its character. The typical dwelling-house of the period was neither Italian, nor French, nor Flemish, nor German: it was distinctively English. We know it by certain well-marked traits—its high-pitched gables, wreathed chimneys, mullioned and transomed windows with leaded lights, heraldic devices over the doorways, oak-panelled rooms, and central hall with open timbered roof. Sometimes it was constructed of stone, sometimes of timber, sometimes of half-timber with brick filling between the wooden uprights. Local materials were necessarily used in construction because of the difficulty of transport. In the Gloucestershire Cotswolds, in the valley of the Nene in Northamptonshire, and in Yorkshire and Derbyshire, where stone was plentiful, this was the material chiefly used; but elsewhere the preference was for the timbered or half-timbered house, with a slight 'overhang', the upper story projecting beyond the lower. Even in stony Derbyshire this type was to be found side by side with the more fashionable stone structure. Finally we may note that the dependence upon materials locally available made possible the perfect harmonizing of the Elizabethan dwelling with the surrounding landscape —one of the first principles of artistic architecture—and at the same time contributed greatly to the maintenance of conservatism and the national tradition in construction.

The position of music was slightly different. Here England could boast a galaxy of talent, indisputably national in character, and of a high order. This is all the more remarkable in that the Elizabethan composers had no longer the elaborate ritual of the Roman church to stimulate them to the noblest flights of musical genius, but were compelled to cultivate their art mainly for secular purposes. Even so, however, there were several, notably William Byrd, Thomas Tallis, Christopher Tye, and Orlando Gibbons, whose work in the field of sacred music compares not unfavourably with that of the more famous masters abroad. The first three were catholics, the last an anglican. Byrd enjoyed, even in his own day, the reputation of being the *homo mirabilis* of the musical world. He towered above his contemporaries, both in the quality and quantity of his compositions, much in the same way as Shakespeare outdistanced all rivals in the realm of letters. Depth of feeling, spontaneity, the perfect blending of musical form with the sense it is intended to convey, constitute the essence of his title to greatness. 'There is', he remarks in the first book of the *Gradualia*, 'a certain hidden power in the thoughts underlying the words themselves, so that as one meditates upon the sacred words and constantly and seriously considers them, the right notes, in some inexplicable fashion, suggest themselves quite spontaneously.' The secret could not be better expressed; but it remained a secret, even from himself. Byrd was a voluminous composer, and all his works have not yet been published; but it is now generally admitted that the *Gradualia*, *Cantiones Sacrae*, and the four *Masses* place him in a category by himself as the equal of Palestrina.

If, however, we would see the true spirit of the time reflected in its music, we must turn from the sacred to the secular, from the composers of solemn organ music to the song-writers; for it is in the lyric, the ballad and the madrigal, that the soul of Elizabeth's England resides. Byrd could write in both styles, but the strongly religious bias of his temperament restricted his success in lighter music. Here the honours lie with Thomas Morley, John Wilbye, Thomas Weelkes, John Dowland, Thomas Campion, and John Danyel. Morley, Wilbye, and Weelkes excelled in the madrigal, a species of composition resembling the modern part-song, generally set for three or more voices, polyphonic in character, and unaccompanied by any instrument. Dowland, Campion, and Danyel, on the other hand, were writers of solo songs to the accompaniment of the lute. Dowland's 'ayres' are said to represent the high-water mark of English songwriting. On the one side they hark back to the days of the troubadour; on the other they forecast the song of today. Nothing more beautiful in the elegiac vein has ever been written than his 'In darkness let me dwell'; and his contemporaries did no more than justice to his genius when they referred to him as one

. . . whose heavenly touch
Upon the lute doth ravish human sense.

In the realm of physical science the age of Elizabeth coincides with the beginnings of a great revolution in human thought, traceable, in the first instance, to the Polish astronomer Copernicus, who introduced the scientific world to a new cosmic system based upon observation, calculation, and deduction. Copernicus was, in fact, the Columbus of the heavens. His investigations into the movements of celestial bodies, which culminated in the publication, in 1543, of his *De Revolutionibus Orbium Celestium*, exercised an influence on astronomical thought comparable to that which the unveiling of the Atlantic and the discovery of America exercised on geography. For over fourteen hundred years the *Almagest* of Ptolemy, with its conception of a geocentric universe, in which the sun, moon, planets, and stars revolved in their separate concentric 'spheres' (or crystalline envelopes) round the earth, had been the canonical book of astronomers. Copernicus replaced this erroneous thesis with a new solar system of astronomy, wherein the planets, including the earth, revolved about the sun; and he coupled with this an equally revolutionary theory of the rotation of the earth on its own axis, and of the planets, like the earth, in their orbits. He regarded his system as merely an hypothesis; and an hypothesis it remained until the appearance of Kepler's epoch-making treatise *De Motibus Stellae Martis* (1609) and Galileo's *Sidereus Nuncius* (1610). But it spread with great rapidity over Europe, and gained a number of supporters in Tudor England. Robert Recorde, the author of *The Castle of Knowledge* (1556), was familiar with it, and another English astronomical scholar, John Field, avowed himself a convinced Copernican in his *Ephemeris anni 1557 currentis juxta Copernici et Reinhaldi Canones*, published in the following year. In Elizabeth's reign the vogue of the new astronomy increased, and a coterie of enthusiastic Copernicans made its appearance in Dr. John Dee, Thomas Digges, William Gilbert, and Thomas Harriot, who not only corresponded with foreign astronomers and sometimes visited them, but contributed not a little by their researches to the advancement of the science. Harriot was the friend and collaborator of the great Kepler himself; Digges was in touch with Tycho Brahe, Kepler's immediate precursor and the learned author of an important work on comets; and Gilbert published a remarkable book 'on the magnet and magnetic bodies and especially the great magnet of the earth, &c'.

(1600),[1] which has been classed as one of the major books on physical science of the century. It would therefore appear that English scientists were fully abreast of the continental development. In one particular direction, indeed, they may have been actually in advance of it; for they possessed an instrument, referred to at the time as 'perspective glasses', which, in principle at least, anticipated the invention of the telescope.

It is important to note, however, that knowledge of the scientific progress of the period was confined to a very small group of enthusiasts. The lay mind was slow to disabuse itself of the Ptolemaic cosmogony, the very nomenclature of which had become embedded in the language of poetry, philosophy, and everyday life. 'Come, Mephistophiles, let us dispute again, and argue of divine Astrology,' says Dr. Faustus in Marlowe's play, and Mephistophiles responds with a disquisition couched in the best Ptolemaic manner. Shakespeare, again, echoes Pythagoras when he speaks of the 'music of the spheres', and pays homage to the old order in the line, 'And certain stars shot madly from their spheres.' Hooker likewise accepts it when he writes: 'If celestial spheres should forget their wonted motions, and by irregular volubility turn themselves any way . . . what would become of man himself, whom all these things do now serve?' In short, the conventional heaven of the layman remained unaffected by science, not only during the reign of Elizabeth but for a long time afterwards. It was not until the 'age of reason' dawned that the Ptolemaic imagery was finally eradicated.

Side by side with this persistent belief in the old cosmic order there existed in Elizabethan England an inveterate conviction—fostered by the pseudo-science of astrology—that the heavenly bodies exercised a profound influence on human affaires. Eclipses were harbingers of disaster: comets were associated with the deaths of illustrious persons. 'When beggars die', says Calpurnia in *Julius Caesar*, 'there are no comets seen: the heavens themselves blaze forth the death of princes.' The twelve 'signs' of the zodiac and the seven planets fixed men's natures and fates, and each part of the human body was regarded as governed by some particular 'sign' or planet. Aries governed the head and face, Taurus the neck and throat, Gemini the shoulders, arms, and hands, Leo the back and

[1] *De Magnete magneticisque corporibus, et de Magno Magnete Tellure, Physiologia nova.*

heart, Cancer the breast, stomach, and lungs, Libra the reins and loins, Sagittarius the thighs, Capricornus the knees, Aquarius the legs, Pisces the feet, &c. The prognostication of events by the movement of heavenly bodies, the decision as to favourable moments for great public functions, and the drawing of individual horoscopes were, of course, the province of the astrologer or astrologaster, who, accordingly, occupied a far more important place in society than the bona fide observer of celestial phenomena. He was the 'applied scientist' of the age, who linked up the occult influences of the heavens with the daily life of humanity.

Kepler regarded the whole subject of astrology with a tolerant contempt as the 'foolish daughter of a wise mother', but admitted the obvious truth that without the help of her foolish daughter the mother could not have lived. On the other hand it is important to realize that although astrology was deeply rooted in the popular mind, the common sense of the age was beginning to revolt against its absurdities. 'It standeth upon nothing else', wrote Philip Stubbs, 'but mere conjectures, supposals, likelihoods, guesses, observations of times and seasons, conjunctions of signs, stars, and planets, with their aspects and occurrents, and the like, and not upon any certain ground, knowledge, or truth, either of God, or of natural reason'; and again: 'It is the malice of the devil, the corruption of our own nature, and the wickedness of our own hearts that draweth us to evil, and so to shameful destinies, and infamous ends, and not the stars or planets.' Cassius made short work of the pseudo-science in his well-known remark to Brutus:

> The fault, dear Brutus, is not in our stars,
> But in ourselves, that we are underlings.

And Edmund, in *King Lear*, reduces it all to absurdity with the statement: 'When we are sick in fortune—often the surfeit of our own behaviour—we make guilty of our disasters the sun, the moon, and the stars; as if we were villains by necessity, fools by heavenly compulsion, knaves, thieves, and treachers by spherical predominance, drunkards, liars, and adulterers by an enforced obedience to planetary influence; and all that we are evil in, by a divine thrusting on.' By the close of the Elizabethan period astrology was clearly doomed, and its practitioners were falling into the category of charlatans, cozeners, and common swindlers, who hung on the skirts of society.

Alchemy, or the *ars chemica* of the middle ages, was also moribund. Unlike modern chemistry, which was still unborn or struggling to be born, and which rests upon the hypothesis of the indestructibility of matter—an hypothesis supported by the evidence of the balance—alchemy was built on a false theory of the unity of matter, which had no basis except in the imagination of the schoolmen. To describe it as a bastard science would, however, be unjust and unhistorical. Actually the alchemist was not attempting anything miraculous: he was merely endeavouring to carry out artificially in his laboratory what he conceived to be the processes of nature. What was wrong was not the method, but the presuppositions on which the method was founded. Since it was assumed that all substances were composed of one primitive matter—the *prima materia*, which is metamorphosed into different forms by the imposition of different qualities upon it, it seemed reasonable to suppose that if by certain chemical processes these qualities could be abstracted, and the primitive matter laid bare, then by further treatment this primitive matter could be transformed into any particular substance required. The transmutation of metals was thus one of the basic assumptions of the alchemical art. But it had another branch, which allied it with medicine. Besides being a search for the philosopher's stone, contact with which could transform the basest metal into gold, it was also a search for the elixir of life or *aurum potabile*, 'the efficacy of which is so certain and so wonderful that by it all infirmities whatsoever are easily curable, human life is prolonged to its natural limit, and man wonderfully preserved in health and manly strength both of body and mind'. It will be clear that the two aspects of alchemy were analogous to each other. Just as the philosophers' stone could banish baseness or imperfection from metals and create the perfect metal, gold, so the elixir of life could eliminate corruption from the body and create perfect health.

Needless to say, it was the multiplying of the precious metals rather than the prolongation of life that provided the driving force in the pursuit of alchemy, and gave it its great popularity. Although forbidden by the law in England, encouragement was given to it by the queen and by many important personages. In 1564 Dr. Dee was appointed the royal adviser in mystic secrets, including alchemy, and a year later Cornelius Alvetanus (or De Lannoy) dedicated a treatise entitled *De Conficiendo*

Divino Elixire sive Lapide Philosophorum to Elizabeth, which secured for him a contract to produce for her 50,000 marks of pure gold each year at a moderate price. He was given quarters in Somerset House and set to work. Evidently, however, his experiments ended in complete failure, for he was committed to the Tower, in 1567, for 'abusing the queen's majesty by promising to make the elixir'. Dee does not appear to have been any more successful in his studies. The fact is, as Reginald Scot[1] pointed out, that the end of the alchemist was generally poverty. 'They have nothing else left them in lieu of lucre', he remarks, 'but only some few burned bricks of a ruinous furnace, a peck or two of ashes, and such light stuff, which they are forced peradventure in fine to sell, when beggary hath arrested and laid his mace on their shoulders.'

Doubtless there were some who practised alchemy with honest intent; but the great majority were sharks who preyed on the credulity and greed of an acquisitive age. Scot describes them as 'rank cozeners and consuming cankers', 'to be rejected and excommunicated from the fellowship of honest men'. Dramatists poked fun at their pseudo-scientific jargon and deceptions. Thomas Nash was of the opinion that alchemy 'hath wrought such a purgation ... of men's purses ... that it hath clean fired them out of all they have'. But the supreme exposure comes from the pen of Ben Jonson in the *Alchemist*, where he depicts the swindling of Sir Epicure Mammon by Subtle and his gang. After spending a considerable part of his fortune in the vain hope of turning Devonshire and Cornwall into 'perfect Indies' and attaining the longevity of the patriarchs, Mammon sees the experiments come to an end with the blowing up of the furnace at the crucial moment, and is advised to go home and repent, while Subtle has made away with his ill-gotten gains.

Another department of scientific inquiry that came under the revolutionizing influence of renaissance thought was medicine. During the generation immediately preceding Elizabeth's accession the most striking feature of the history of European medicine had been the weakening authority of Galen, the second-century Greek physician, whose encyclopaedic writings on every aspect of the healing art had been accepted without

[1] Author of *The Discoverie of Witchcraft* (1584).

question by everyone. Step by step the doctrines of this great master had been challenged, amended, and re-written by investigators who based their work on first-hand observation and experiment. Paracelsus (1493–1541), the Swiss physiologist of Basel, began the revolt by casting the writings of Avicenna, Galen's medieval Arabic interpreter, into the flames; and he followed up this symbolic act by inaugurating a new study of pharmacy allied with chemistry. The next shock to Galenic ideas came from Vesalius (1504–64), the Belgian professor of anatomy at Padua, who began the dissection of human subjects and created a new school of anatomical research. His book entitled *De Humani Corporis Fabrica*, which was published in the same year as Copernicus's revolutionary treatise on the heavenly bodies, created a mighty ferment in Europe no less far-reaching than that caused by the astronomical revelations. Then followed the startling discovery by Servetus, a Spanish physiologist, of the pulmonary circulation of the blood, which he published to the world in his *Restitutio Christianismi* (1553). These epoch-making innovations were only the more important of a series of extensive inroads into Galenism, the cumulative effect of which was like that of a battering-ram of irresistible momentum.

It is to be noted, however, that so far as the movement had gone, England had taken no active part in it. Until the appearance of William Harvey's *De Motu Cordis* (1628), indeed, this country remained largely in the background—willing enough to absorb the new lore, but unable to take an independent share in the higher creative work. It is a significant fact that although Henry VIII had established professorships of medicine at Oxford and Cambridge (1547), together with the College of Physicians (1518) and the Company of Barber-Surgeons (1540), all of which were in full swing in Elizabeth's day, the pick of English youth who desired a sound education in medical science chose to seek it at the universities of Padua, Montpellier, Basel, Heidelberg, or Leyden rather than in their own native land. Padua was especially favoured because it was the headquarters of the Vesalian school of anatomy. Thither went Harvey, in 1598, to study the action of the venous valves, under Fabricius ab Acquapendente, that led directly to his own wonderful discovery in the early seventeenth century. It is perhaps more significant that when Vicary, surgeon to St. Bartholomew's Hospital, wrote his *Treatise of the Anatomy of a Man's Body*

(1577), he made no mention whatever of Vesalius or any other continental scientist of the century, but contented himself with reproducing a fourteenth-century manuscript!

Nevertheless the study of the new anatomy and physiology was not neglected in England. In 1565 the queen granted the College of Physicians the right to carry out human dissections on its premises, and fellows of the college were compelled, under penalty of fine, to take part in public demonstrations of anatomy. There were also similar demonstrations at Barbers' Hall, where an articulated skeleton was kept for instructional purposes, and at Gonville and Caius College, Cambridge, where the Vesalian surgeon Dr. Caius lectured and dissected. The most notable surgeons of the time were John Gale (1507–87), William Clowes (1540–1604), and John Woodall (1569–?), all of whom gained their technical experience in war. Gale served in the English army in Henry VIII's reign, and later in the Spanish army in the reign of Philip II. He wrote a notable book on the treatment of gunshot wounds (1563). Clowes served with Warwick in France during the English occupation of Havre, and later under Leicester in the Netherlands. He, too, was the author of several works on wounds. And Woodall was sent to France with the troops placed at Henry IV's disposal in the last decade of the reign. He became an expert in amputations. There is no doubt that these men were abreast of their time in regard to anatomical science, but their fame was essentially local.

The progress of medicine, as distinct from surgery, was greatly hindered by the Galenic theory of 'humours', which persisted intact until well into the following century. According to this theory four 'humours' or fluids entered into the composition of the body, viz. blood, phlegm, choler (yellow bile), and melancholy (black bile); and the predominance of one or other of them determined the temperament of the individual. Thus we have the sanguine, the phlegmatic, the choleric, and the melancholic temperaments. Excess of any 'humour' constituted a morbid condition, which could only be cured by 'cupping' or 'purging', i.e. by lessening the quantity of blood or by reducing the bile by drugs. Nor was there any English pharmacopoeia in Elizabeth's time, the first being published in 1618; and the sale and purchase of drugs was in the hands of apothecaries, who were still without a charter and under the supervision of the College of Physicians. If Shakespeare is to be trusted, they were a poor and starveling set of men, whose poverty made them susceptible to bribes.

> And in his needy shop a tortoise hung,
> An alligator stuff'd, and other skins
> Of ill-shaped fishes; and about his shelves
> A beggarly account of empty boxes,
> Green earthen pots, bladders, and musty seeds,
> Remnants of packthread, and old cakes of roses,
> Were thinly scatter'd to make up a show.

It was from such a one that Romeo obtained his poison. Moreover, clinical study of disease was only beginning. Dr. Caius was the first to introduce it with his account of the sweating sickness, which he published in his *Liber de Ephemera Britannica* (1555). Clowes followed in his footsteps with observations on the condition of his patients at St. Bartholomew's. But the first to devote himself wholeheartedly to minute study of the subject was Sir Theodore Mayerne, who became physician to James I. We might also note that the first treatise on tropical medicine to be published in England was issued from the press in 1598. It bore the title *The cure of the diseased, in remote regions: preventing mortality, incident in foreign attempts of the English nation.* The author was G. W. (George Whetstone?), who had suffered from yellow fever while a prisoner in Spain, and was anxious to give his countrymen the benefits of his experience.

Philip Stubbs's account of the physicians and surgeons of his day is far from flattering. He describes them as avaricious and frequently unlearned. 'For now-a-days every man, rag and tag, of what sufficiency soever, is suffered to exercise the mystery of physic, and surgery, and to minister both the one, and the other, to the diseased, and infirm persons.' He also accuses some of gross malpractices, of being in league with the apothecaries, who sell 'druggy baggage' to the ignorant, and of deliberately causing the death of their patients. He is especially bitter on the subject of the itinerant quacks 'who run straggling (I will not say rogueing) over the countries, and bear men in hand of their great knowledge', and 'rake in great sums of money, which when they have got, they leave their cures in the dust, I warrant you, and betake them to their heels as to their best refuge'. Whatever truth there may be in this criticism—and it seems to be grossly exaggerated—it is reasonable to suppose that although the granting of licences to practise by the two qualifying bodies of the time, viz. the College of Physicians and the Company of Barber-Surgeons, was strict enough so far as the London area was concerned, there must have been men who practised illicitly in the country and escaped prosecution. But let us remember, on the other hand, the sympathetic and humane picture of the sixteenth-century doctor drawn by Shakespeare in *Macbeth*. After observing Lady Macbeth's symptoms in the famous sleep-walking scene, he remarks:

> This disease is beyond my practice . . .
>
> . . . .
>
> Unnatural deeds
> Do breed unnatural troubles: infected minds
> To their deaf pillows will discharge their secrets:
> More needs she the divine than the physician.
> God, God forgive us all! Look after her;
> Remove from her the means of all annoyance,
> And still keep eyes upon her. So, good night!

Two other branches of knowledge, allied with medicine, were also making progress during the Elizabethan period, viz. zoology and botany. In 1552 Edward Wotton had published his *De Differentiis Animalium*, the first printed book by an Englishman on zoology. It was not an original work, nor was it, strictly speaking, scientific: it was simply a refurbishing of Greek and Latin animal lore, the fruits of a wide and scholarly reading of Aristotle, Pliny, and the great authors of antiquity. A more valuable work was Dr. Caius's treatise on British dogs, which was published in English in 1576, and became the standard book on that subject for the century. Meanwhile John Maplet had issued his comprehensive study of plants, animals, and stones or metals, under the title of *A Green Forest or a Natural History* (1567), which introduced into England for the first time the term 'natural history'. Once again, however, the matter of the book was derivative, being drawn from medieval sources which, in their turn, were largely dependent upon Aristotle and Pliny. Maplet's method of classification was purely alphabetical, not zoological. His description of the cat is typical both of his matter and style. 'The Cat', he says, 'in Latin is called *Catus*, as if you would say *cautus*, wary or wise. In Greek she is named *Galiootes*, with the Germans *Katz*. She is to the mouse a continual enemy:

very like to the lion in tooth and claw; and useth to pastime or play with the Mouse ere she devoureth her. . . .' Mixed up with these attempts to handle the subject in a scholarly way were unedifying repetitions of mythical lore about dragons, griffins, cockatrices, basilisks, phoenixes, pelicans, salamanders, unicorns, and other fabulous beasts, in the manner of the medieval bestiaries. Quite clearly zoology in England was only in its infancy, and hardly on the level to which it was raised by Conrad Gessner, the great German-Swiss naturalist, and other continental scientists of the period. It was passing from the credulous to the collecting stage, from mere repetition of obsolete authorities to attempts at scientific classification; but it had still to move on to the anatomical and microscopic stage before a proper method of classification could be achieved. Towards the close of Elizabeth's reign a beginning was made in this direction by the application of dissection to animal subjects.

Botany was farther advanced. There was a passion for collecting strange plants in England. Burghley was a great collector, and had a garden of medicinal herbs at Holborn. So, too, were Lord Zouche, Lord Hunsdon, and Nicholas Lete, a London merchant. 'It is a world also to see', said Harrison, 'how many strange herbs, plants, and annual fruits are daily brought unto us from the Indies, Americas, Taprobane, Canary Isles, and all parts of the world.' Not only so: there was a real renaissance of botanical studies, due to the labours of William Turner, the 'father' of English botany. Turner had published, in 1548, a treatise entitled *The Names of Herbs*, which, as its title implies, was an attempt—the first attempt—to bring the popular plant vocabulary in England into line with the nomenclature adopted by scientists abroad. He followed this up with another work, *The New Herball* (1568), in which he tried to define and fix the names of familiar and cultivated plants. Turner's work supplied the connecting link between the old and the new botany so far as England was concerned. A number of other books appeared shortly afterwards, notably Matthias Lobel's *Adversaria* (1571), which attempted to classify plants according to their natural affinities. This was perhaps the greatest book on scientific botany that appeared in England during the reign; and it was written by a Dutchman, who, strangely enough, published it in London. Later on, Lobel was to become botanist to James I. Meanwhile Henry Lyte

superseded Turner's herbal by his *Niewe Herball* of 1578, a copy
of a similar Dutch compilation of 1554; and John Frampton,
a merchant of Seville, added to the widening stream of botanical
knowledge with his *Joyful News out of the New World* (1577)—
a translation of Nicholas Monardes's *De las drogas de las Indias*
(1565)—which introduced his countrymen to the vegetable products of America. Finally, John Gerard summed up the progress
of the times in his comprehensive account of the subject entitled
The Herball, or Generall Historie of Plantes (1597). It was not an
original contribution to learning, but a sound journalistic effort,
accompanied by copious illustrations, and it remained for a
long time a standard work. When all is said and done, however,
it must be admitted that botanical studies in England were
behind those of the Continent. The fact that Cesalpino's *De
Plantis* (1583), the most significant investigation into plant
physiology of the age, was not known in this country until the
next century speaks volumes in itself.

It was probably in the pursuit of geographical studies, rather
than in physical science, medicine, or biology, that Elizabethan
England came most closely into touch with European scientific
thought. Until 1550 or thereabout, as we have seen, the country
had lagged behind the rest of the world in maritime activity,
and consequently in the knowledge of geography. But as soon
as the forward movement began under Elizabeth, and the practical problems of navigation called for solution, astronomers,
mathematicians, and men of science became interested in this
new department of inquiry. Side by side with the old-fashioned
'rutters' of the sea, or sailing-charts, there appeared tracts and
treatises on the subject of navigation, almanacs and sea manuals,
discourses on compass variation, on the method of determining
the position of ships at sea, on the use of nautical instruments,
on surveying, &c. At the same time books of travel, voyages, and
discoveries, ancient and modern, some of them translations
from Spanish, French, Italian, and Portuguese works, others
original contributions by Englishmen who had either taken
part themselves in exploration or were in personal touch with
the pioneers, added yearly to the mass of information available
about the maritime achievements of the chief sea-faring nations.
And what appeared in print was probably a mere fraction of
what circulated in manuscript. The consequence was that before

the third decade of the reign drew to a close there was a school of scientists in England whose knowledge of geography and allied subjects was not so very far behind that of the great continental teachers and researchers. True, there were no cosmographers of the calibre of Gerard Mercator of Duisburg, or Abraham Ortelius of Antwerp; but in Dr. Dee, whose astronomical and alchemical studies we have already referred to, England had a scientist and speculator hardly less famous. Up to 1580 Dee was behind all the leading sea enterprises conducted by Englishmen, and corresponded as an equal with his confrères abroad. There were also surveyors and cartographers, like William Bourne, William Borough, and above all Christopher Saxton, who stood in the forefront of their profession. Saxton's great atlas of England and Wales was issued from the press in 1579. Nor must we forget Richard Hakluyt of the Middle Temple, whose knowledge of geography and interest in the expansion of English trade became the inspiration of his namesake and still more famous cousin. Nevertheless English geography was still in a measure derivative: there was no specifically English geographical literature of sufficient weight and importance to evoke the admiration of continental scholars.

Then came with surprising suddenness Camden's *Britannia* (1586) and the younger Hakluyt's *Voyages and Discoveries* (1589). These two works, very dissimilar in character but animated by the same spirit, placed England in the forefront of geographically minded nations. As monuments of industry and learning, and as historical milestones, they have an imperishable interest. The enthusiasm with which they were received is shown by the fact that Camden's work was republished and enlarged four times before the end of the reign, and Hakluyt's, which was originally a single volume, grew by successive additions to the three-volume edition of 1600.

While full credit should be given to these achievements, both from a literary and historical point of view and as contributions to the progress of geographical knowledge, it is necessary also to realize their limitations. Neither Hakluyt nor Camden was, in the strict sense, a scientific geographer, that is, interested primarily in acquiring information about purely geographical phenomena. Hakluyt interlarded his work with a considerable amount of matter—letters of merchants, reports on trade, political correspondence—that belongs rather to state papers or the conduct of business than to a geographical compilation. His interest lay in the extension of markets, in the development of trade, in the utilizing of products of new territories for the benefit of home industries: questions of climate, vegetation, winds and currents, and earth-knowledge generally were secondary. In short, he was utilitarian in his pursuit of geography, not a disinterested inquirer bent on obtaining information for its own sake. Camden, on the other hand, was essentially an antiquarian. His interest in topography was subordinated to an overpowering love of historical lore of all kinds. The contours of the land, the description of scenery or climate, the accurate positioning of roads, and other matters of first-rate geographical importance find a very limited space, if any, in the *Britannia*.

In my description of each country [he says in the Preface] I will show with as much plainness and brevity as I can, who were the ancient inhabitants, what was the reason for the name, what are the bounds of the country, the nature of the soil, the places of greatest antiquity, and of greatest eminence at present, and lastly, who have been dukes or earls of each, since the Norman Conquest.

Quite clearly the word 'chorographical' (or 'regional') bore a very different meaning in the sixteenth century from what it does today. To Camden a 'region' was interesting mainly because of the people who inhabited it, their manners and customs, religion, origin, and history. Much the same criticism applies to other works of a similar character written during this period. Giles Fletcher's *Russe Commonwealth* (1591) devotes only three chapters to purely geographical detail, and all the rest of the book concerns policy, wars, religion, customs, and other 'human' interests. The truth is that geography, for all the advance it was making, was only beginning to realize its real vocation. Like the other branches of inquiry which we have already dealt with, it was in process of transition to the scientific stage proper, but had not yet clearly grasped its objective. Observers were not observing the right things: instruments were inaccurate: technique was undeveloped. Nevertheless, despite its limitations, the spirit of investigation was steadily and surely moving towards that clearer definition on which the science of geography would one day be built.

Lastly, we come to the sphere of education. To begin with,

let us remember that in the earlier years of the reign it had been publicly announced in the commons that England was sadly lacking in schools, that the universities were decayed, and that many great market towns were without either school or preacher. This was at once a challenge and an incentive—not to the state but to private enterprise, for the creative power lay with the individual. Conscious of the fact that education was the 'open sesame' to honour, distinction, and power, and eager to immortalize themselves in stone and lime, in scholarships and bursaries, and in other aids to learning, the rich merchant on whom fortune had smiled, the prosperous industrialist, the well-to-do yeoman, the wealthy brewer and clothier, and—not the least—the high-minded cleric who valued education as a priceless entity in itself—all put their hands in their pockets to make good the losses caused by the upheaval of the Reformation; and soon the builders were busy not only in the south-east but also in the backward north-west and north. No fewer than five new schools, which became famous at a later date, were founded during the reign—Repton (1557), Merchant Taylors' (1561), Rugby (1567), Uppingham (1584), and Harrow (1590); and Harrison was able to say with pride that now, almost every corporate town had at least one grammar school 'with a sufficient living for a master and usher'. The universities were also expanding. At Cambridge Trinity College chapel was rebuilt (1555–64) and the great court completed (1597), and Sir Walter Mildmay founded Emmanuel College (1584). At Oxford Jesus College was founded (1571) and Sir Thomas Bodley built a notable addition to the ancient library (1587–1602) which was henceforth called by his name. Outside the old universities the only other academic erection was that of Gresham College, London (1596), built by the executors of the great financier from a bequest left by him for that purpose. The distinctive feature of this college lay in the fact that it was intended to provide education in the 'seven liberal sciences' in contradistinction to the traditional curriculum at Oxford and Cambridge.

Internally both universities made progress during the reign. Ten years of constitutional unrest at Cambridge came to an end with the appointment of Sir William Cecil to the chancellorship; and in 1570 the university received its new statutes. Leicester, as chancellor of Oxford, was instrumental in securing for it an act of permanent incorporation (1571), which made it unnecessary to seek a fresh charter from each successive ruler. He also provided it with a new printing-press. Great enthusiasm was evoked by the visit of the queen to Cambridge in 1564 and to Oxford in 1566 and 1592. But in spite of the fact that she held out hopes of doing something, like her forebears, for the advancement of learning at both institutions, nothing appears to have eventuated beyond a small contribution to the foundation of Jesus College. So far as the curriculum was concerned, there was no material change introduced at either university. The subjects taught were virtually the same as those prescribed in the time of Edward VI, viz. theology, civil law (expanded to include the ecclesiastical laws of the realm), the philosophy of Aristotle and Plato (with the addition of Pliny), medicine as expounded by Galen or Hippocrates, mathematics (including arithmetic, geometry, astronomy, with the addition of cosmography), dialectic, rhetoric, Greek, and Hebrew. History was not a part of the *studium*, the pursuit of this subject being the work of the Society of Antiquaries, founded by Parker in 1572.

Yet if we are to believe Harrison, neither university was in a very healthy condition. In the election of scholars gross corruption prevailed. It was difficult, he says, owing to the 'bribage' used, for a poor man's son to obtain a scholarship; and the sons of the rich, when they were placed, 'often bring the universities into much slander'. They 'ruffle and roist it out', says Harrison, 'exceeding in apparel and ranting riotous company', and when they were charged with breach of order, 'say they be gentlemen'. Packing was also used in elections to fellowships, with the same discriminating effect against the poor: so that 'not he which best deserveth, but he that hath most friends, though he be the worst scholar, is always surest to speed'. This indictment was probably just, for it is borne out by Sir Humphrey Gilbert, who was in hope of doing something whereby the universities 'shall better suffice to relieve poor scholars, where now the youth of nobility and gentlemen, taking up their scholarships and fellowships do disappoint the poor of their livings and advancements'.

Within the higher educational bracket must also be placed the famous inns of court—the lawyers' University of London— Gray's Inn, Lincoln's Inn, the Inner Temple, and the Middle Temple. Here all the aspirants after knowledge of the common law received an education rivalling that provided by Oxford and Cambridge, where the canon and civil law formed the backbone of culture, and had for a long time opened the way to high office in church and state. By Elizabeth's day, however, it was clear that the canon law was not only sinking into oblivion (thanks to the Reformation) but was also threatening to drag the civil law with it. It was, of course, necessary—as Henry VIII well knew—to have civilian lawyers to handle treaties, to conduct negotiations in commerce, and to deal with international diplomacy; and they were much in demand for the admiralty courts, the courts of star chamber and requests, where procedure lay outwith the rules of the common law.

But the age of Elizabeth was *par excellence* the hey-day of the common law and the golden age to those who practised it. According to Maitland, 'the training given in the theory and practice of the Common Law was by itself sufficient to guarantee it a flourishing existence'. In the inns the collegiate life of Oxford and Cambridge was reproduced, and the teaching was backed by the fertilizing agency of a common life. What the students learned from each other informally was probably more valuable than the discourses of their teachers. The independent self-government of the colleges, coupled with the numerous stimulating activities developed by the students themselves, and the opportunities offered by the close proximity of London and its wonders—all combined to make their mundane existence a useful preparation for their careers in the legal *forum* later on. No other type of university education could be similarly regarded. Manners were undoubtedly rough. 'The members', we are told, 'had to be restrained from dining in their hats, and from scrambling for their food at the dresser in the Hall. Occasionally they came to fisticuffs, and the Hall furniture generally required mending after revels.' But students are always unruly, and the allurements of London might account for their boisterousness; but it is more likely that this was due to the absence of sport from the communal life. Since there was no natural safety-valve, and play-acting—a popular pastime at all times—was hardly comparable to games in the fields, government action became necessary when the students got out of hand. Nevertheless, the success of the Inns and the rapid increase of the common lawyers, induced Thomas Wilson, one of Elizabeth's secretaries, to attribute the following diatribe to a civilian:

'These temporal lawyers do wholly drown our profession, and make us to have less will to study, because our causes are so few that come before us!'

School education was, of course, conditioned by the higher studies at the university. In all schools the subject-matter of instruction and the method of teaching was much the same: they were laid down by the fathers of English renaissance education, Colet and Lily. Latin predominated—was, in fact, the only *pabulum* in the ordinary schools, Greek being taught only at Eton, Harrow, Westminster, Shrewsbury, and a few others. Lily's Latin grammar was the recognized primer, enlarged by successive editions; but there was a wide variety in the prescribed texts. Works by renaissance scholars, such as the *Bucolica* of Baptista Spagnolo, the *Zodiacus Vitae* of Palingenius, Erasmus's *Colloquia*, an old favourite, and Vives's *Linguae Latinae Exercitatio*, were studied side by side with the ancient classical authors. A new note was also struck by the compulsory inclusion in all school curricula of Christopher Ocland's *Anglorum Praelia*, a long rhymed account in hexameters of England's wars from Edward III's reign to the close of Mary's, and the same author's *Elizabetha*, a panegyric of the queen's peaceful rule. Another interesting innovation, if it could have been carried out, was the proposal made by Richard Mulcaster, head of the Merchant Taylors' and St. Paul's schools, that English should be accorded a place in the curriculum. But, speaking generally, the supremacy of classical literature was not seriously challenged. Modern languages played no part in the Elizabethan system of school education; nor did history, although the great Camden was head of Westminster for many years. This exclusive insistence upon the ancient languages did not, however, meet with the entire approval of intelligent critics who, like Humphrey Gilbert, would have liked to see learning brought into closer relation with active life. In or about 1564 Gilbert published a treatise entitled *Queene Elizabeth's Achademy*, in which he outlined a scheme for the training of youth in 'matters of action meet for present practice, both of peace and war'. English was to be studied: there were to be lectures on 'civil policy'; and boys were to be taught shooting, riding, marching, navigation, with the elements of medicine, surgery, and natural science. The academy was to be provided with a library to which 'all printers in England shall be for ever charged to deliver at their own charges one copy, well bound, of every book . . . that they shall print'. The idea was attractive, but like many other reforms mooted during the reign it remained merely a *ballon d'essai*.

More interest attaches to Roger Ascham (1515–68), the greatest educationist of his time and the author of *The Schole-master*, which was published two years after his death. Ascham was no mere pedagogue versed in the traditional school culture of the renaissance: he was a philosopher, moralist, and reformer, whose supreme aim was to see the youth of England 'so grounded in judgement of learning, so founded in love of honesty, as, when they should be called forth to the execution of great affairs, in service of their prince and country, they might be able to use and order all experiences, were they good were they bad, and that according to the square, rule, and line of wisdom, learning, and virtue'. Like Vittorino da Feltre, Vives, and other schoolmasters of the renaissance, he believed that the study of classical literature, organized on rigorous lines, was the only possible basis of a liberal education; but he combined with this insistence on linguistic training the wider ideal set forth by Castiglione, the great Italian master of courtesy, whose *Corte-giano*, 'advisedly read, and diligently followed but one year at home in England, would do a young gentleman more good, I wis, than three years' travel abroad spent in Italy'. Like Casti-glione, he favoured all manner of 'courtly exercises and gentle-manlike pastimes'—riding, vaulting, leaping, running, tilting, shooting at a mark with bow or gun, wrestling, dancing, singing and playing of instruments—provided they 'be joined with labour, used in open place, and in the day light, containing either some fit exercise for war, or pleasant pastime for peace'. 'I was never either Stoic in doctrine or anabaptist in religion,' he says, 'to mislike a merry, pleasant, and playful nature, if no outrage be committed against law, measure, and good order.' Verily the author of *The Scholemaster* and *Toxophilus* was no believer in a fugitive and cloistered virtue.

Three great principles are announced by Ascham in relation to education, namely the necessity of gentleness in instruction, especially at the initial stage: the importance of cultivating the 'hard wits' rather than the 'quick wits'; and the superiority of learning to experience as a sure and safe way to wisdom. In expounding these principles he criticizes, sometimes bitterly, sometimes even savagely, the prevailing practice of his time. The 'butcherly fear of making latins', which characterized grammar-school instruction, the foolish discrimination against the slow-witted child, the brutality of masters, and the habit of sending young men to Italy to acquire experience—all come under his lash.

'I remember', he says, 'when I was young, in the north, they went to the grammar school little children: they came from thence great lubbers: always learning, and little profiting: learning without book everything, understanding within the book little or nothing.' In order to remedy this defect of learning 'without the book', i.e. of studying accidence apart from syntax—which he describes as 'tedious for the master, hard for the scholar, cold and uncomfortable for them both'—Ascham advocates the combination of both accidence and syntax in one organic system. Once the child is familiar with the parts of speech, the joining of substantives with adjectives, of nouns with verbs, of relatives with antecedents, let the master take some simple passage from one of Cicero's epistles, explain the occasion and purpose of it, construe it into English, parse it over perfectly, and when he is sure that the child has understood it all, ask him to construe and parse in the same manner. The next stage is for the child to make a translation of the passage in his exercise-book, unaided; after which, an hour or so having elapsed, he must retranslate his own English version into Latin, without recourse to Cicero. The pupil's effort is now compared with the original, errors are pointed out, reasons given for this or that turn of expression, case, gender, &c., as against that, the grammar book is consulted for the rules, and questions are invited. 'This', says Ascham, 'is a lively and perfect way of teaching of rules.' But the teacher must have patience: he must not chide his pupil for faults, for 'that shall both dull his wit, and discourage his diligence'. Rather let him praise him for what he has done well, for 'there is no such whetstone to sharpen a good wit and encourage a will to learning as is praise'.

In pointing out the need for gentleness on the part of the master Ascham exposes the fallacy of supposing that, by nature, children dislike learning. It is not a question, he says, of the disposition of the child, but of the method employed by the teacher. Beat a child for dancing ill, and cherish him even if he be backward in learning, and he will shun dancing and fly to his books. This was the secret of Lady Jane Grey's love of books: God had blessed her, she said, with a gentle schoolmaster and sharp and severe parents. Moreover the master must study his pupils, not favouring the quick-witted and punishing the slow-witted, but 'discreetly consider the right disposition of both their natures, and not so much weigh what either of them is able to do now, as what either of them is likely to do hereafter'. Quick wits, he says, are like over-sharp tools, whose edges are very soon turned: they are apt to take, unapt to keep, for 'this I know, not only by reading of books in my study, but also by experience of life abroad in the world, that those which be commonly the wisest, the best learned, and best men also, when they be old, were never commonly the quickest of wit when they were young'. 'Hard wits' on the other hand, provided they are not over-dull, heavy, and lumpish, and are not thwarted and wrought 'against the wood' by schoolmasters, are 'both for learning, and whole course of living, always the best', and in the end 'do come to that perfection of learning . . . that quick wits seem in hope, but do not in deed, or else very seldom, ever attain unto'.

Finally in the attainment of wisdom, the be-all and end-all of education, learning is a better preceptor than experience, for learning is the eye of the mind, 'to look wisely before a man, which way to go right and which not'. It is possible to learn more in one year from books than from experience in twenty, and it is safer and infinitely less costly. Experience often makes one more miserable than wise, and he is an unhappy shipmaster who learns his craft by many shipwrecks. 'We know by experience itself', says Ascham, 'that it is a marvellous pain to find out a short way by long wandering.' Hence the folly of those who search for wisdom by travelling in Italy. Italy was the Circe's court of Europe, where vice was cultivated to a fine art, and whence those who succumbed to her charms returned swine and asses, carrying in one body 'the belly of a swine, the head of an ass, and the womb of a wolf'. 'I was once in Italy myself', he continues, 'but I thank God that my abode there was but nine days. And yet I saw in that little time, in one city, more liberty to sin than ever I heard tell of in our noble city of London in nine years.' To scorn both protestant and papist, to ignore the Scripture, to mock the pope, to rail at Luther, to

be atheists in doctrine and epicures in living, to aim at their
own present pleasure and private profit, to expound all the
mysteries of religion with the formula *Credat Judaeus Apella!*[1]
—these, according to Ascham, were the fruits of copying the
Italians. No wonder he did not think Italy a safe place for
wholesome doctrine, or godly manners, or a fit school for the
young gentlemen of England to be brought up in.

The greatness of Ascham as an educationist has never been
questioned. *The Scholemaster* will remain one of the most instruc-
tive books in the English, or, indeed, in any language on the
subject of linguistic training, but it will be remembered even
more for its wisdom than for its technique.

We may conclude this chapter with a glance at some of the
superstitious beliefs and practices of the time, for in spite of its
learning, culture, and realism Elizabethan England was per-
meated with superstition. The supernatural world pressed in
on the natural and became mingled with it to a remarkable
degree. Apart from the occult influences which the stars were
supposed to rain on human life, there was a widespread belief
in elves and fairies, Robin Goodfellows, lubber fiends, fire-
drakes, hobgoblins, incubuses and succubuses, Tom Thumbs,
and many other incarnations of a supramundane sphere, in so
much that on a dark night 'a polled sheep is a perilous beast,
and many times is taken for our father's soul, especially in a
churchyard, where a right hardy man heretofore scant durst
pass by night, but his hairs would stand on end'. If a raven
croaked from a neighbouring roof, a man made his will: if a
sea voyage was intended, he anxiously consulted the almanac
and chose a Sunday or some other lucky day. The efficacy of
charms, spells, incantations, divinations, and amulets was accepted as part and parcel of everyday existence. 'How super-
stitiously we mind our evils,' says Delio in the *Duchess of Malfi*:

> The throwing down of salt, or crossing of a hare,
> Bleeding at the nose, the stumbling of a horse
> Or singing of a cricket, are of power
> To daunt whole man in us.

Dying men were credited with miraculous insight into the
future. 'Methinks', says Shakespeare's John of Gaunt on his

[1] i.e. Let the Jew Apella believe that (if he likes)!

death-bed, 'I am a prophet new inspired, and thus expiring do foretell of him—' (i.e. King Richard II). Ghosts of the dead walked the earth between midnight and cock-crow, and communed with the living, because they had either some secret to impart, or wrong to set right, or reparation to make. 'My father's spirit in arms!' exclaims Hamlet when informed of the apparition on the battlements at Elsinore: 'all is not well: I doubt some foul play.' Subsequently he meets the ghost and hears a tale of incest and fratricide that starts him off on his career as avenger. Similarly Macbeth is haunted, tormented, and mocked by the ghost of 'blood-boltered' Banquo, and Brutus is visited by the spectre of the murdered Caesar in his tent at Sardis—the harbinger of disaster at Philippi. There were charms for every evil and grief. To be cured of the falling sickness it was advisable to 'drink in the night at a spring water out of the skull of one that had been slain', or 'eat a pig killed with a knife that slew a man'. Headaches could be conjured away by tying 'a halter about your head, wherewith one hath been hanged'; a scorpion's bite could be cured by 'saying to an ass secretly, and as it were whispering in his ear—I am bitten with a scorpion'; a woman in travail could be released by throwing over the house 'a stone or any other thing that hath killed three living creatures, viz. a man, a wild boar, and a she bear'; and the prophylactic against the quotidian ague was to 'cut an apple in three pieces, and write upon the one "The Father is uncreated", upon the other, "The Father is incomprehensible", and upon the third, "The Father is eternal" '. Fairies, again, were friends of 'human mortals', rewarders of their minor virtues and punishers of their shortcomings. Like other supernatural beings, they came and went with the hours of darkness. They had great powers, for Puck, 'that merry wanderer of the night', could 'cover the starry welkin with a fog as black as Acheron' and 'overcast the night'. But since they were sympathetic to mortals they did not provoke nature into war against them. It was only when the fairies were unhappy that things went wrong with the world.

> And this same progeny of evil comes
> From our debates, from our dissensions,

says Titania in *A Midsummer-Night's Dream*. Shakespeare, apparently, has two kinds of fairy queen—the Titania of the moonlit

glades and Mab the mischief-maker, who sometimes gallops
her chariot

> over a courtier's nose,
> And then dreams he of smelling out a suit;
> And sometimes comes she with a tithe-pig's tail
> Tickling a parson's nose as a' lies asleep,
> Then dreams he of another benefice;
> Sometimes she driveth o'er a soldier's neck,
> And then dreams he of cutting foreign throats,
> Of breaches, ambuscadoes, Spanish blades.

A very different creature was the witch. If the fairy was
a denizen of the world of folk-lore, the witch was as grim a
reality as nature herself—or so the age believed. Her powers
were malignant and destructive. Popular belief credited her
with being able to raise and suppress lightning, thunder, hail,
rain, winds, tempests, and earthquakes, pull down the moon
and stars, send needles into the livers of her victims, transfer
corn in the blade from one place to another, cause disease or
sterility in man and beast, fly in the air, dance with devils,
transubstantiate herself and others into animals, keep devils
(i.e. familiars) in the shape of toads or cats, dry up springs,
change the course of nature, turn day into night and night into
day, pass through auger-holes, sail in an egg-shell, cockle-shell,
or mussel-shell through or under tempestuous seas, bring souls
out of graves, slay lambs with a look, deprive a cow of its milk,
&c. The essence of the business was a supposed secret compact
with the Devil. 'A witch', said Coke, 'is a person who hath conference with the Devil, to consult with him or to do some act.'
Reginald Scot put it ironically thus: 'In the estimation of the
vulgar people it [i.e. witchcraft] is a supernatural work contrived between a corporal old woman and a spiritual devil. The
manner thereof is so secret, mystical, and strange, that to this
day there hath never been any credible witness thereof.' The
most famous case recorded in British history of the sixteenth
century both of the power and the fate of those who indulged
in the craft is that of the four witches of North Berwick, who
were accused of conspiring to destroy James VI and his queen,
Anne of Denmark, in 1590. According to the evidence submitted
by themselves—under torture—they raised a storm by their incantations and by casting a 'conjured' cat into the sea at Leith,
hoping thereby to wreck the royal ship on its way from Denmark to Scotland. Failing to achieve their end by this means,

they prepared a waxen image, which they melted, in accordance with their cult, saying, 'This is King James the sixth, ordained to be consumed at the instance of a noble man Francis earl of Bothwell'. Sentence of death was pronounced against them by a court of justice, and they were burnt at the stake on Castle hill, Edinburgh, in 1591.

The universality of belief in witchcraft rendered it almost impossible for the person accused of it to escape. Even the enlightened Bishop Jewel could aver, in a sermon delivered before the queen in 1572: 'These eyes have seen most evident and manifest marks of their wickedness. Your Grace's subjects pine away even unto death, their colour fadeth, their flesh rotteth, their speech is benumbed, their senses are bereft. Wherefore your poor subjects' most humble petition unto your Highness, is, that the laws touching such malefactors may be put in due execution.' Proof of witchcraft was comparatively easy. 'She was at my house,' says the plaintiff: 'she would have a pot of milk: she departed in a chafe, because she had it not: she railed, she cursed, she mumbled and whispered, and finally she said she would be even with me; and soon after my child, my cow, my sow, or my pullet died, or was strangely taken.' Little more than this was sufficient, in ordinary circumstances, to decide the fate of the accused. There were some, however, who refused to believe in such trumpery charges, notably Scot, whose sturdy common sense penetrated the absurdity of the witch's supposed powers, and found naturalistic explanations for the evils attributed to them. Butter would not churn, he says, not because the witch has cast her spells over it, but 'if either the maids have eaten up the cream, or the goodwife have sold the butter before in the market'.

My question [he says in his preface[1]] is not whether there be witches or nay; but whether they can do such marvellous works as are imputed to them. Good Master Dean, is it possible for a man to break his fast with you at Rochester, and to dine that day at Durham with Master Doctor Matthew; or can your enemy maim you, when the Ocean sea is betwixt you? May a spiritual body become temporal at his pleasure? Or may a carnal body become invisible? . . . Alas, I am sorry and ashamed to see how many die, that being said to be bewitched, only seek for magical cures, whom wholesome diet and good medicines would have recovered.

[1]   *The Discoverie of Witchcraft.*

But it was a long time before the illuminating ideas of Scot could penetrate into the ignorance even of the educated, or influence practice. He was severely criticized by his contemporaries, and taken to task by one no less than James I.

There remains the 'impious and damnable' magic of the sorcerer, the fruit of an illicit desire for forbidden knowledge—in a word, the so-called 'black art'. It was a superior craft, and might be defined as the attainment of power by intellectual means. As such it appealed to the learned rather than to the ignorant, to men of science like Paracelsus or Dr. Dee rather than to the humble people who practised the mystery of witchcraft. Sorcerers, says Scot, 'pass the degree of witches, and entitle themselves to the name of conjurors'. Unlike the witch, who went to work with toads and cats, the sorcerer could by his adjurations summon devils from hell 'quicker than the pope could release souls from Purgatory'. The seventy and nine principal and princely orders of infernal spirits, with their massed legions of petty devils, were at his disposal. Each had his special qualities and powers. 'Marbas' could reveal all secrets and cure all diseases: 'Furcas' could impart wisdom and cunning in all mechanical arts: 'Beroth' was master of things present, past, and to come: 'Asmodai' could render men invisible and reveal hidden treasure: 'Allocer' could procure the love of any woman: 'Orias' could give dignities and prelacies, and reconcile enemies: 'Vepar' had the secret of killing men by putrefying their wounds: 'Amduscias' could bring it to pass that trumpets and musical instruments might be heard and not seen: 'Buer' and 'Bifrons' had the power to make men live long: 'Caym' could render intelligible the voice of birds and beasts; and so on through the long list. Popular belief had it that in return for the enjoyment of his power over demons the sorcerer yielded to the Devil the reversion of his soul; but there was a different type, who acquired his magic not by devilish compact but by philosophical and cabalistic studies. The contrast is brought out by Marlowe's Faustus, who sold his soul in order to gratify his senses, and Shakespeare's Prospero, whose 'rough magic' depended upon book, wand, and mantle, and was used simply to deliver himself from evil men who had dispossessed him of his dukedom. Faustus's art was diabolic, Prospero's harmless. The former had as his 'familiar' the satanic Mephistophiles: the latter was served by the dainty sprite Ariel. In the end Faustus, his time accomplished, is carried off by demons; while Prospero, having achieved his purpose, breaks his staff, drowns his book 'deeper than did ever plummet sound', and reverts to his former life as the learned prince of Milan.

Notwithstanding the strong hold which sorcery had on the imagination of the Elizabethan age, there were indisputable indications that its foundations were beginning to crumble. The spread of the true scientific spirit, the gradual demolition of the impressive edifice of medieval 'science' by investigation into natural causes, and, lastly, the application of common sense to psychic phenomena—all contributed to its defeat. Scot asserted that he could see no difference between the practices of the sorcerer and the conjurations of the popish exorcist, except that the 'papists do it without shame openly, the other do it in hugger mugger secretly'.

ELIZABETH AND THE NETHERLANDS
1575–86

IN the field of foreign policy Elizabeth was essentially a machiavellian, although there is no reason to suppose that she actually borrowed her maxims of statecraft from *The Prince*.[1] The chief object of her diplomacy, from which she never consciously wavered, was to establish her throne and kingdom in a position of unassailable security and power. To attain this end she was prepared to use every instrument that gave promise of being serviceable, every ally that chance or necessity threw in her way, while at the same time avoiding commitments that might jeopardize her own freedom of action, or lessen the advantage she possessed as the ruler of an insular state. Both a realist and an opportunist, she made 'interest' the determining factor in all her political manœuvres and combinations, and reason of state a sufficient justification for every act. She was loyal to treaties only so long as they served her purpose, and broke them unscrupulously, in spirit if not in the letter, when they threatened to hamper her freedom of movement. A master of prevarication and deceit, when occasion drove her to it, she was an adept at finding subterfuges for actions of doubtful legality, and always had emergency exits at hand when strategic retreats became necessary. Watchfulness and flexibility were the very essence of her system; for each situation, as it arose, had to be examined afresh in the light of England's vital needs and policy modified or redirected accordingly. Thus while the ultimate goal remained as fixed as the stars the lines of approach to it might be as tortuous as the path of a comet. A more self-centred or less doctrinaire statecraft it would be difficult to imagine: it was the very incarnation of *sacro egoismo*.

Continental protestants, oppressed by tyrannical governments or struggling for their lives against the superior might of catholic armies, beckoned her in vain to a crusade on behalf of the reformed faith. The fervent appeals of her own ministers,

---

[1] The influence of Machiavelli on Tudor political thought and policy was practically nil. For a discussion of the subject see M. Praz, 'Machiavelli and the Elizabethans', in *Proc. Brit. Acad.* xiii, 1928; also L. A. Weissenberg, 'Machiavelli and Tudor England', in *Pol. Sci. Quar.* xlii, 1927.

who believed that the protestant cause was also England's cause, struck no responsive chord in her cold and calculating brain. Her one thought was how she could use their respective idealisms for the furtherance of her own secular aims. Experience had taught her—and she was an apt learner—that to confuse state policy with religion, or to put religion first and the state second, could only lead to chaos, bloodshed, and disaster. Her foreign policy, like her home policy, was entirely free from fanaticism. When the German protestants, sunk in their interminable credal dispute concerning the 'ubiquity and omnipresence of the body of Christ', resisted her efforts to make them think as political beings, she made no secret of her contempt for their 'unprofitable dissensions'. But let any one, be he protestant prince or catholic monarch, infringe upon what she deemed to be the permanent interest of her Crown and country, she acted with a swiftness and truculence that disconcerted her friends as well as her foes.

Yet in spite of her fulminations she was no firebrand. Peace with security was her avowed aim.[1] 'Elle est une femme nourrie à la paix et repos,' wrote La Mothe Fénelon, summing up his impressions after seven years' residence at her court: '. . . veut jouir son état tant qu'elle vivra sans guerre ni trouble.' Substantially he was right in his diagnosis. Although Elizabeth had fought two wars against France in the earlier part of her reign, she quickly realized that diplomacy, not war, was her 'long suit'. War, in fact, she abominated: it was the destroyer of peoples, the enemy of that material well-being which she made it the object of her rule to promote. If she could, she would have eliminated bloodshed from international relations, beaten the swords of the nations into ploughshares, abolished confessional strife, and created a world in which all disputes would be settled by the peaceful method of arbitration. For men of blood she had an unconquerable dislike. It is a notable fact that, for the greater part of her reign, her voice was heard amid the din of a Europe given over to violence in every shape and form, counselling moderation and offering her services as a mediator. Possibly she under-estimated the strength of the forces arrayed

---

[1] 'It may be thought simplicity in me that all this time of my reign I have not sought to advance my territories, and enlarge my dominions; for opportunity hath served me to do it. . . . And I must say, my mind was never to invade my neighbours, or to usurp over any; I am contented to reign over mine own, and to rule as a just prince.' (The queen's speech to parliament at its dissolution in 1593: Townshend, p. 48.)

against her—William of Orange and Henry of Navarre were shrewder judges of mankind than she—but she laboured on in the conviction that even fanatics could be persuaded, cajoled, or coerced into a reasonable frame of mind. It is only fair to add, however, that the peace she envisaged was an English peace; that is, a peace designed to safeguard English interests abroad. And in the second place, if she deprecated war, it was not merely because of her humanitarian impulses: she had neither the means nor the inclination to embark upon the costliest of all gambles. Here again her realism probably came into play, for her parsimony kept her solvent at a time when the continental monarchies, with their much greater resources, were either bankrupt or staggering on the verge of bankruptcy.[1] In a world cursed by prodigal expenditure she stood forth a shining example of the power that comes from thrift. English gold, carefully husbanded and carefully doled out, was more potent, in the long run, than all the precious metals of the Indies; and Europe moved more at Elizabeth's bidding than at the impressive military gestures of King Philip.

In 1575 England's position in Europe, though far from secure, was relatively safe. The foreign debt, which had hung like a millstone round her neck since the commencement of the reign, was practically extinguished. Trade was beginning to boom, and for the next eleven years wealth poured into the country. The queen's credit stood high in Europe—much higher than King Philip's, who could not borrow money at less than from 12 to 18 per cent., while Elizabeth could have it at 8 or 9 per cent. The renewal of the Treaty of Blois with Henry III removed any immediate danger from France: the crisis with Spain had been disposed of by the Treaty of Bristol and the reopening of traffic between England and Antwerp; and Scotland was quiescent under the anglophil government of Morton, the king being a minor of nine years. Apart from the unalterable enmity of Rome and of the exiles who flitted about the Continent like uneasy ghosts, living meagrely on Spanish pensions and hoping for the 'enterprise' that would restore them in triumph to their native land, there was little to trouble the

---

[1] Philip II was bankrupt in 1575 and again in 1596: France was in a chronic state of insolvency

queen except the continued turmoil in the Netherlands. If only peace could be re-established there, without involving a complete Spanish victory, she might at last breathe freely.

Such a pacification was not only desirable: it was imperative for a variety of reasons—first, because Antwerp was still the principal market for English cloth on the Continent; secondly, because so long as the struggle continued, the bugbear of a French intervention could not be effectually dispelled; and thirdly, because if the Spaniards mastered the country they might use the 'sea gate' of Flanders as the starting-point for a conquest of England. But how was it to be accomplished? To Elizabeth, with her intensely English outlook, the only feasible solution of the problem was a return to the *status quo* before the outbreak of the troubles: that is, the country must remain under Spanish sovereignty, but its political and civil liberties must be restored. If this could be secured, she was ready to let Spain settle the religious question in her own way, in accordance with the general formula that rulers had the sole right to prescribe the religion of their subjects. Indeed she could hardly do less, since she claimed and exercised the same right with regard to her own dominions.

But there was little likelihood of either William of Orange or King Philip accepting such a solution. Philip was determined to master the rebellion even if it meant making a desert of the country. He would rather lose the provinces altogether than suffer any diminution of his sovereign rights, or infringement of 'our holy catholic religion'. Unconditional submission, he said, must precede any peace negotiations. Orange was no less uncompromising in his attitude. Eight years of struggle had taught him the futility of seeking a compromise with a monarch who was dominated by a fixed idea, who notoriously kept no faith with heretics, and whose hatred of himself was implacable. So distrustful was he of the Spaniard that he likened peace gestures from Madrid to the piping of children in the market place when they try to ensnare little birds. Hitherto he had masked his intentions with the convenient fiction that his quarrel was with the king's ministers, not the king himself; but the mask was wearing thin. Already the doctrines popularized later by Duplessis-Mornay[1] in his *Vindiciae contra Tyrannos* were beginning to circulate among the huguenots in the prince's

---

[1] The enlightened huguenot adviser of Henry of Navarre.

entourage, and many held the view that oppressed peoples had the right to dispose of the sovereign power in their own interest. The strength of the stadholder, now as always, was concentrated in Holland and Zeeland, whose geographical position gave them control of all approaches to the Netherlands by sea, and rendered them practically invulnerable to attack from Spain. He also possessed a formidable navy, increasing in power each year. But two things were necessary for a rapid triumph over his enemy, viz. a close blockade of the river Scheldt, the only waterway that gave access to the heart of the 'Belgian' parts, and a reliable ally to share the burden of the war on land. Orange apparently attached great importance to the blockade, for he is reported to have said that 'if he could but hinder that in a year's space there come no salt into Flanders, he could win such a peace as he wished for'. On this point, however, he encountered the inflexible opposition of Elizabeth, who refused to allow any interference with the free navigation of the Scheldt: the newly revived trade with Antwerp was just as necessary for England's prosperity as the starvation of Antwerp was, in Orange's opinion, necessary for the success of the rebellion. There was considerable bickering over this question. Similarly when the prince, in his quest for help, turned to France, whose age-long enmity to the house of Habsburg seemed to him the one sure fact on which to build amid the shifting sands of European politics, Elizabeth again interposed her veto, giving him to understand—a favourite expression of hers—that if he brought in the French she would immediately 'bend all her forces to the assistance of the king of Spain'. Public opinion in Holland and Zeeland was pardonably annoyed at this callous indifference to their fate, and Englishmen were severely criticized as 'those that do put on religion, piety, and justice for a cloak, to serve humours withal and please the time, while policy only is made both justice, religion, and God'. Even in England there was some honest heart-burning at the treatment meted out to the prince. 'There is no honest man nor of good religion', said Sir Thomas Smith, 'that doth not pity his case and wish it were better.' But Elizabeth held on her course, impervious to the calls of sentiment and religion. She would neither help the Dutch herself nor permit them to help themselves; and if they flouted her efforts to mediate a peace, and by their stubbornness prolonged the war, she would teach them a lesson. Nay, if they maltreated her merchants, she would exterminate them all!

Nor did the Spaniard escape his share of blame for the unquiet state of the Netherlands. Philip was informed that unless he took steps to remedy the grievances of his subjects the French would march in, and Elizabeth would be compelled 'for our own safety to put in execution that remedy for their relief that we would not willingly yield unto otherwise than constrained thereto'. Again and again—'en une infinité de manières et de termes aigres', said Champagny, Requesens's envoy—the queen came back to her fundamental principle that the Spaniards must not 'impatronize' themselves in the Low Countries. They would be bad neighbours, she said, and would try to encircle (cerner) her dominions. From an economic standpoint, too, they were a danger, for, as Burghley remarked to Guaras, 'You people are of such a sort that wherever you set foot no grass grows.' And Elizabeth herself corroborated this with the sage, if somewhat trite, saying that 'where countries be governed and replenished with men of war, the haunt of merchandise will cease'. If the king really desired peace, let him arrange an armistice and let diplomacy get to work. Should his terms be reasonable, and his subjects refuse to accept them, he might rest assured that she would give him her full support in reducing them to obedience.

Meanwhile the struggle in the Netherlands went on. In September 1575 Requesens began his great attack on the islands of Duiveland and Schouwen, and laid siege to Zerickzee, thereby cutting the communications between Holland and Zeeland. By October both islands were in his hands, and an English eyewitness wrote to Burghley that 'all Holland is like to be lost, and not without great danger to the prince his own person'. Captain Edward Chester was of the same opinion. 'Without present relief', he wrote, 'this state will small while stand.' So serious was the situation in December that Orange dispatched a mission, headed by St. Aldegonde and Paul Buys, with the request that Elizabeth should take the two provinces into her protection, lend them a sum of money for military purposes, and accept as security for its repayment the towns of Flushing, Brill, Dordrecht, and Enckhuizen. For a brief space it looked as if the queen's hand would be forced, for the council was strongly in favour of intervention. But the 'business seemed not to ripen'; and in March 1576 Elizabeth reaffirmed her intention to seek a peace by mediation—'an honourable and advantageous settlement' for both parties. Thus the Orange deputation was turned away empty-handed, much to its chagrin.

Worse still: in the same month an incident in the narrow seas nearly provoked war between the two governments. An English ship returning from Antwerp was attacked within a few miles of Dover by cruisers in the service of Zeeland and taken as a prize to Arnemuiden, her crew and passengers being spoiled of their goods. Apart from the gross insult to the flag 'within her Majesty's stream', which was sufficient in itself to warrant sharp reprisals, the treatment of a distinguished foreigner—the bride of the Portuguese ambassador in London—who happened to be travelling in the ship under a safe-conduct from Elizabeth so incensed the queen that she ordered the immediate seizure of Dutch shipping at Falmouth. The admiralty of Zeeland replied with a similar arrest of vessels belonging to the Merchant Adventurers at Flushing. During the heat of the controversy, which lasted all summer, Elizabeth treated Orange to some pretty plain speaking. He was told, in effect, that he was entirely mistaken if he imagined that England's safety depended upon him, and that 'in the judgement of the world, the aptest mean for her Majesty to withstand or prevent the peril that he conceived might grow to her by his overthrow were to join with the king of Spain against him'.

By this time, however, the tension in Holland and Zeeland had relaxed, owing to the death of Requesens (3 March 1576) and the mutiny of the Spanish troops for arrears of pay. Since there was no hope of financial relief from Spain, for Philip had been unable to meet his creditors during the previous year, and had suspended all payments in September 1575, the mutiny rapidly became a reign of terror in the Flemish provinces. Towns and villages were plundered or held to ransom by a licentious soldiery, who treated the civil population with all manner of barbaric cruelty. In self-defence the peasantry and burghers flew to arms, resistance was organized by the provincial estates, and a cry arose for the expulsion of the Spaniards bag and baggage. This was the moment for which Orange had long hoped and prayed, and for which he had worked assiduously since the beginning of the troubles. His dream of a united Netherlands seemed at last on the verge of realization. Accordingly, soon after the 'terror' broke loose, he entered into negotiations with the nobles of Brabant and Flanders for a general agreement. Time was precious, for at any moment the new governor designate, Don John of Austria, might arrive and frustrate the chance of concerted action. But for once fate smiled upon the efforts of the prince. Stimulated by the atrocities of the Spaniards, which culminated in the 'Fury' of Antwerp (September),[1] the states-general concluded the Pacification of Ghent (8 November), and for the first time for nine years the whole seventeen provinces drew together in a common resolve to rid themselves of military rule and to re-establish their political liberties as in the days of Charles V. Although the question of religious toleration was still too dangerous to be handled, and was left in suspense, it was agreed to abolish the placards against heresy, to declare the illegalities of Alva null and void, to confirm Orange in his stadholderate of Holland and Zeeland, and to insist upon the immediate dismissal of all the Spanish garrisons.

Thus when Don John arrived he was confronted, not with a riot to put down and an aggrieved people to be pacified, but with a population in arms and determined not to receive him until he accepted the terms of the 'Pacification' and removed every Spanish *tercio* from the country. It was hardly the sort of reception that the most renowned military commander in christendom expected at the hands of subjects. He had come with a message of peace, entrusted by the king with power to satisfy the provinces on all points compatible with the maintenance of obedience to the Crown and the catholic church. But it was understood[2] that once this was accomplished he would turn his forces against England. This latter project was veiled in the deepest secrecy and was to be executed without warning; but it was nevertheless the *raison d'être* of Don John's mission to the Netherlands.

The new governor, however, soon found himself in a dilemma.

---

[1] For details see Motley, *The Rise of the Dutch Republic*, iii. 43-56.

[2] i.e. by Don John and his secretary Escovedo and also in Rome, where the *empresa* was the dominant theme in diplomatic circles. There is no ground, however, for believing that Philip II was at this time in favour of a blow at England. He was anxious not to compromise the pacification of the Netherlands by associating it with a crusade against Elizabeth (see P. O. de Törne, *Don Juan d'Autriche et les projets de conquête de l'Angleterre*, 1928).

If he agreed to the withdrawal of the Spaniards, how could he obtain the military force necessary for the invasion of England? On the other hand, if he refused to send away the Spaniards, he would not be received as governor, and would have to fight for his position against a united Netherlands. Whichever policy he adopted, his mission was doomed. In the circumstances he tried dissimulation, and offered to evacuate the troops by sea, hoping to divert them, once they were safely embarked, to some convenient port in England. But the ruse was defeated by the states-general, backed by the vigilance of Elizabeth, whose fears were justifiably roused at the prospect of a Spanish force coasting along her shores, when rumours were afoot that some hostile stroke was intended against herself. Consequently, in February 1577, Don John was compelled to come to terms with the states-general at Marche-en-Famine. By this treaty, which was the work of the catholic party in the Low Countries, and was generally known as the 'Paix des Prêtres', or by the inappropriate title of the 'Perpetual Edict', he undertook to observe the Pacification of Ghent, to respect the ancient liberties of the provinces, and to remove the Spanish troops within twenty days by land to Italy. Having now disarmed himself—for the evacuation was carried out to the letter—Don John was received as governor in Brussels, on 1 May, with the cry 'There was a man sent from God whose name was John'! The only one who refused to join in the general rejoicing was Orange, who had taken no part in the peace negotiations, and remained sullen, mistrustful, implacable.

Elizabeth had little cause to be dissatisfied with the settlement. She had laboured all winter to bring it about, urging the states-general 'in God's name not to lose any occasion for obtaining the said peace', and plying Don John with threats that, if he sought to conquer the provinces, she would 'aid them with all the might and power we can'. But Orange was an insurmountable obstacle to the complete pacification on which she had set her heart. Instead of listening to the pleadings of Don John, who 'surpassed Circe' in his efforts to charm, the prince grumbled his suspicions to Elizabeth, renewed his appeals for an alliance, and pointed out that with the havens, ships, and mariners of Holland and Zeeland on her side she could defy her enemies with impunity.

What was the queen to do? She could not coerce Orange, because she might need his help if he were right about the ulterior designs of the Spaniard; she could not abandon him altogether, for that would throw him into the arms of the French; nor, again, could she support him without involving her whole Netherlands policy in ruin. Her dilemma was the more acute because some of her council, notably Leicester, Walsingham, and Wilson—the leaders of the so-called war party—were openly on the side of the prince, and gravely concerned about the position into which England had drifted as a result of the queen's attachment to the cause of peace. Even Burghley was not happy. 'There is no trusting suspected friends at this time,' wrote Wilson, 'but plain dealing with a protestation to make peace will be the best assurance'; and again, 'Better not to deal at all than not to go roundly to work. . . . Valiant working never wanted good fortune.' But the fire-eaters tendered their advice in vain: Elizabeth clung to her policy of mediation, insisting that the Pacification of Ghent was the only sound basis of peace in the Netherlands. If Orange wanted allies, let him form a 'league of association' secretly with the protestant princes of Germany and the protestant cantons of Switzerland, and she would give it her blessing.

Such was the situation in July 1577, when another kaleidoscopic change occurred in the Low Countries, destroying for good the possibility of peace. For five months Don John had chafed at the restrictions imposed upon him by the states-general, and the stubborn recalcitrance of Orange; and at the end of July, on the plea that his life was in danger from plotters —not an improbable story—he seized Namur with a company of Walloons, and swore to avenge his honour by 'bathing in the blood of traitors'. It was the prelude to another attempt to subdue the country by force of arms. Don John had 'reverted to type', as the Dutch stadholder had prophesied.

From blowing cold, Elizabeth now blew hot. Early in August William Davison was sent to the states-general with the urgent message that they should call upon the prince to take command of the situation, coupling with it an offer of armed help from England for the defence of the country. Davison's report, on arrival, was exceedingly pessimistic. 'Both by what I see and find here', he wrote, 'there is no one thing more certainly projected than to shake the state of her Majesty.' To make matters worse, a rumour was afloat that the duke of Guise was marching to Don John's assistance with 7,000 or 8,000 foot and 4,000 horse. After some hesitation, the states-general decided to fall in with the queen's advice. Orange was summoned to Brussels, and the marquis d'Havré was sent to England to raise a loan and procure a contingent of troops under the command of Leicester. On 22 September, 'with such singular demonstrations of joy . . . as if he had been an angel sent down from Heaven', the prince entered the capital. Havré, meanwhile, obtained from the queen the promise of a loan of £100,000, together with the offer of 5,000 foot and 1,000 horse.

At last it seemed as if Elizabeth had determined to join forces with the rebel cause, and Leicester began to turn over in his mind the details of the forthcoming expedition. But the decisive hour had not yet struck. In December the queen decided to make another appeal for peace, and Sir Thomas Wilks was sent to Spain with instructions to urge the recall of Don John, whose conduct had destroyed that 'mutual confidence which is more than necessary in every well-constituted government'. He was to point out to the king that, if aid had been promised in men and money to the states, it was because they might be compelled by Don John's action to seek the help of some other prince or lose their liberties. As for herself, the queen was concerned only to maintain the obedience of the provinces to Spain and the Pacification of Ghent. Wilks's departure for Madrid was followed by the dispatch of Sir Thomas Leighton to the Low Countries with cogent arguments for an armistice, pending the king's decision. 'When account is made of treasure spent, of the spoils of cities, of the intercourse of merchandise broken off', he was to say to the states, 'it will fall out in truth that he that wins loses, and the conqueror has more cause to lament than rejoice.' If the states were agreeable to a cessation of arms, he was to put the case for mildness and conciliation to Don John, and to point out to him that 'to shed blood, if it can be saved, is greatly repugnant to the nature of a prince'.

Meanwhile Elizabeth's reluctance to plunge into the fray in the Netherlands had brought the danger of French intervention nearer. For two years she had successfully staved it off, partly by playing on the need for amity between the two governments, partly by threats that if France intervened England would side with Spain, and partly by interference in the internal affairs of that kingdom contrary to the spirit as well as the letter of the Treaty of Blois. Volunteers and munitions had been passed across to La Rochelle to assist the huguenots, and German armies under John Casimir, son of the Elector Palatine, had been subsidized with English gold to invade France as an ally of Condé and Navarre—in short, the expedients with which Elizabeth had combated the French government in the days before the treaty were revived again, to the anger of the king and queen mother. 'My son', said Catherine de Médicis to Sir Amyas Paulet, Elizabeth's ambassador in Paris, 'may no longer bear this kind of double dealing: he is ready to be a friend, and if not, he is able to be an enemy.' 'All your dealings', wrote Paulet to the queen, 'are registered and laid up against a day, and nothing is forgotten, no not things done before the last treaty.' The real danger, however, was not from the French government but from the factions in France which had mastered the Crown and were trying, in different ways, to force the country into a foreign policy that boded ill for England. The duke of Guise and the catholic extremists—the party of the League—were in favour of supporting the Spaniards in the Netherlands as the best way of securing the supremacy of catholicism in France. The huguenot-politique combination under the leadership of Anjou (Alençon) were for open intervention on the side of Orange—a reversion, it will be noted, to the policy of Coligny in 1571–2. Anjou, in fact, was the Coligny of 1578. His plan was to wrest the Netherlands from Spain, unite them by a marriage alliance with England, and so create a powerful protestant federation, under French protection, to balance the designs of the Spaniard and Guise. The issue at stake was no other than the domination of northern Europe, for Don John and Guise had entered into a compact to establish catholic supremacy in the same three countries. Both schemes were in the highest degree dangerous to England, although at the moment they existed only in the brains of their promoters.

Elizabeth was between the devil and the deep sea. Her appeal to Don John for an armistice met with no success, nor were the states in favour of it; and months must elapse before she had a reply from Spain to the Wilks mission. Meanwhile Don John piled up a great army at Namur, consisting of Germans, Walloons, Burgundians, and Spaniards, and in January 1578, aided by Alexander of Parma from Italy, inflicted a defeat on the states' army at Gembloux. Further Spanish victories followed quickly in the open country, at Louvain, Tirlemont, Aerschot, and elsewhere; and Orange was compelled to use what troops remained to him for purely garrison work. Davison was in despair at the queen's delays. 'Now seeing that her Majesty cannot abandon them without peril to herself and to them', he wrote to Walsingham in March, '. . . it would in my judgement (under correction) be more profitable and honourable for her Majesty the sooner she gives her determination.' Like the other members of the war party in England, Davison believed with all his heart that the only way to keep the Spaniard 'more terrible in opinion than in effect' was to occupy him in the Netherlands. But Elizabeth was not to be moved. The utmost she would do was to subsidize her faithful John Casimir with £20,000 to hire German horse for a demonstration against Don John; but her name was not to be mentioned in the matter, and the subsidy was to be deducted from the £100,000 she had undertaken to advance to the states. 'By your letter', wrote Davison to Leicester, commenting on the transaction, 'I see that our long doubtfulness and irresolution has at length brought forth an unworthy conclusion.' True enough; but the queen had other things to think about: she was expecting Stukeley in Ireland, and Paulet had bad news to communicate about French preparations in Brittany, Bordeaux, and other parts, the object of which was veiled in profound secrecy, but rumour had it that 'something was intended in favour of the queen of Scots'.

The decision to employ John Casimir had scarcely been taken when Bernardino de Mendoza arrived in England with the eagerly awaited communication from Madrid. As the first resident Spanish representative to be sent to Elizabeth's court since the expulsion of de Spes in January 1572 Mendoza was not a happy choice, being essentially a soldier puffed up with Spanish military pride, and contemptuous of the English. He explained that the king's determination to subdue the Netherlands remained unchanged, but that he intended to recall Don John, and would not abrogate but rather extend the ancient privileges of the country. Meanwhile Elizabeth was to understand that no threats of sending assistance to the rebels from England nor any other consideration 'will cause us to relinquish the determination we have adopted to bring our subjects back to obedience, using against them all the force that human or divine right permit us to employ and our royal dignity demands'. As a friendly neighbour, the queen must prohibit, under severe penalties, any help, direct or indirect, being sent to the Netherlands. At first Elizabeth was inclined to accept this statement of the king's intentions as satisfactory; but when the matter was discussed in the council Mendoza became acutely aware that the majority was hostile to Spain. He learnt also that unless there was an immediate suspension of arms it was the intention of the queen to send 'resolute aid' to the rebels. When he attempted, somewhat foolishly, to shake her decision by alluding to the length of his master's arm, he elicited the sharp retort that she would not allow either the French to set foot in the country or the Spaniards to rule it 'while she had a man left in her country'. On his expressing the hope that at least his dispatches would not be tampered with, he was blandly informed that no such assurance could be given, 'as certain people came here with no very good objects in view'; and as for his complaints about succours being sent to the Netherlands, 'there were so many people leaving and arriving in so large an island that she could not prevent them from leaving without permission'. Intimidation was obviously the wrong way to handle Elizabeth.

Matters were now going from bad to worse in the Low Countries. Two of the provinces, Artois and Hainault, were threatening to go over to Anjou, while great cities like Douai, Arras, Lille, Mons, Courtrai, and St. Omer were strongly in favour of making peace with Don John, and it looked as if the agreement of Ghent would be dissolved. The war party in England, fortified by Davison in the Netherlands and Paulet in France, renewed their clamour for open intervention. 'The loss of a day', wrote Paulet, 'is of great moment; the Spaniard knows it, and therefore seeks to gain time by all feasible means; and when his purpose is served, he may turn his flatterings into threatenings, and rip up old matters to ground his new quarrels.' But Elizabeth, despite her bellicose utterances to Mendoza, was not to be stampeded into war. In April she turned again to Don John, refusing to abandon her efforts 'so long as any spark of hope remains'. At the same time she approached Henry III with a proposal for joint mediation. In neither case was there any chance of success. Don John had become so 'insolent' by reason of his victories that 'he makes his account to be master of all these countries within two months'; and Henry III proved so broken a reed that he could only exclaim, 'You see how I am obeyed: I have no means to stay my brother otherwise than by force, which cannot be done without danger of new civil troubles.'

The resources of diplomacy were almost exhausted, but not quite. In a last effort to avert the peril of French intervention, which was now the only hope of the rebels, Elizabeth decided to send a powerful embassy, headed by Walsingham and Lord Cobham, to moderate the demands of both sides. If they failed to achieve this, they were to come to an understanding with Anjou's representatives that his entrance into the Netherlands would not mean their subjugation by France. 'Do your endeavour for a peace', wrote Wilson to Walsingham, as a final injunction, 'and you shall have thanks on your return. If you tell us of the necessity of war, I tell you plainly that we cannot abide to hear of it.' But the embassy which landed at Antwerp on 28 June 1578 soon found the task confronting it impossible of fulfilment. The states, backed by Orange, insisted on the withdrawal of Don John and the Spaniards, together with the acceptance by Spain of the Pacification of Ghent; while Don John refused to consider such terms 'even if he were a prisoner in the Brodhuis of Brussels'. Walsingham's private opinion was that 'it is greatly to be doubted that "Monsieur" will have a further foot in the country than ever the king of Spain will be able to remove, or we to hinder; of which I fear we shall too soon see an experience'. It did not lessen his fear to know that Monsieur had given his assurance that he would do nothing without the consent of the queen. Less than a fortnight later, on 13 August, a treaty was signed between Anjou and the states, giving the duke the title of 'Défenseur de la liberté belgique' and a joint share in the military command.

Elizabeth had undoubtedly contributed to this result by her dilatory policy, by holding back the bonds for the £100,000 she had promised, and by demanding the surrender of Sluys and Flushing as security for the moneys she had already spent in loans. Her apparently irrational conduct evoked from Walsingham the despairing cry, 'The only remedy left to us is prayer.' 'Where the advice of counsellors cannot prevail with a prince of her judgement', he wrote, 'it is a sign that God hath closed up her heart from seeing and executing what may be for her safety.' The position in the Netherlands was one of increasing chaos. No fewer than four armies were encamped on her soil, for, in addition to the principals in the struggle, John Casimir with his horsemen and Anjou with his motley horde of Frenchmen had arrived on the scene. But since Elizabeth had drawn her purse-strings tight, and Spain could not finance Don John, all four armies were reduced to disorder through lack of pay and supplies. Discipline broke down, and bands of famished soldiers devastated the land as if a cloud of locusts had settled on it. Plague, famine, and pestilence completed the ruin. In September Walsingham and Cobham were ordered to return to England, their presence being no longer useful in the stricken country. A fortnight later (1 October) Don John died a victim to the plague, broken in spirit, as well as in health, by the total collapse of his hopes. Finally John Casimir and Anjou, after taking part in a religious struggle between the people of Ghent and the Walloons, departed the country—the former to be honoured at Elizabeth's court with the Order of the Garter and banqueted by the city of London, the latter to return to France.

While Walsingham and Cobham were in the Netherlands, Elizabeth executed one of her swift and unexpected changes of front in foreign policy—she revived the Alençon (Anjou) marriage project. Her object in doing so was to draw off the restless and ambitious duke from his dangerous designs on the Spanish king's inheritance, or, at all events, to make sure that if he persisted in his enterprise he would be amenable to her advice and control. The bait of the most acceptable marriage in Europe might even turn the would-be liberator of the Netherlands into a champion of England's interests. It is impossible to say whether Elizabeth intended to go farther than this when she reopened the question. If the love palaver failed to produce the political results she hoped for, there were plenty of loopholes for escape from undesirable consequences, or diplomacy would provide them. Nevertheless there was a seriousness about this courtship of Anjou in 1578 entirely absent from all previous manœuvres of a similar nature. Apart altogether from the French danger in the Netherlands, a marriage with Anjou seemed to offer a means of egress from many of the fears that haunted the queen's mind, both domestic and foreign. It might, for example, get rid of the otherwise insoluble succession problem by providing an heir to continue the line of Henry VIII —a matter that troubled Elizabeth more acutely as she grew older. It would greatly strengthen the Anglo-French alliance, which was now honeycombed with distrust and sadly in need of repair. It would go far to dispose of the danger from Mary Stuart. It might even compel Philip II to come to terms with his rebels. In fact, when Burghley considered the benefits likely to accrue from it, and set them against the perils that would have to be provided for if the queen did not marry, he was convinced that the advantages were overwhelming. Sussex was also in favour of the marriage. The only obstacles in the way were the queen's age and Anjou's attachment to the catholic religion; but neither was insuperable. If Elizabeth was forty-five—a risky age at which to contemplate matrimony—the risk, after all, was not abnormal; and as for the duke, he was assuredly no zealot, as his championship of the huguenots showed. It remained to be seen, however, how public opinion in England would regard these matters.

The negotiations began in the summer of 1578; and in November Anjou sent over his agent, Jean de Simier, the most accomplished philanderer of the period, to discuss terms and to prepare the way for his master's 'frenzied wooing'. In a remarkably short time Simier won the queen's affections—so much so, indeed, that she added him to the menagerie of her pet 'beasts', nicknaming him her 'monkey' and the duke her 'frog'. The vicarious wooing went on all winter, while Burghley addressed himself to the business side of the transaction. The articles of 1571 were reviewed, and at the end of March 1579 Simier delivered twelve articles in French, three of which were new. So confident was he of success that on 12 April he wrote: 'I have very good hope, but will wait to say more till the curtain is drawn, the candle out, and Monsieur in bed.' Three weeks later, when the French terms came up for discussion in the council, he was somewhat shaken in his optimism, for some members were for rejecting the three new articles outright, and the majority held that, while the second must be disallowed, the first and third could only be dealt with by parliament, and should be kept in suspense until the duke had been inspected by the queen. The substance of the articles in question was as follows: Monsieur was (1) to be crowned king immediately after the marriage, (2) to share jointly with the queen the authority to grant all benefices, offices, and lands, and (3) to have an annual income of £60,000 during marriage, and the minority of any child of the marriage, being heir to the crown. Simier was dissatisfied with the decision of the council; but after consultation with his master intimated that the duke was prepared to leave all to the queen's determination. Thereafter the whole of the articles were gone over, some being accorded and others reserved for 'colloquy'. On 8 July Simier was handed an 'act of council' sanctioning the duke's visit, together with a safe-conduct, and about the middle of August the Frenchman set out on his adventure, travelling incognito to Greenwich. For the next twelve days—17 to 29 August—his courtship was the talk of London. Then he departed, leaving Simier to capitalize the results of his mission and bring the business to a conclusion.

But England was now alarmed. Hardly had Monsieur returned to France when John Stubbs published his *Discovery of a Gaping Gulf Wherein England is like to be Swallowed by Another French Marriage*, an intemperate puritanical pamphlet, grossly libelling the royal family of France, and picturing, in exaggerated language, the disastrous consequences of an alliance with it. Elizabeth was mortally offended at the insult to a neighbouring power whose friendship she desired to cultivate; and the writer, printer, and publisher were arrested, all three being sentenced to have their right hands chopped off and to be imprisoned during the queen's pleasure. Subsequently the printer was pardoned; but when the barbaric punishment was inflicted on the other two it was clear that they had the sympathy of the multitude, for the spectacle was witnessed in dead silence, broken only by the intrepid Stubbs, who, raising his hat with his left hand, cried with a loud voice, 'God save the Queen'.

When the council met to discuss the question, in October, whether the queen should be advised to go forward with the marriage or not, there was a marked difference of opinion. Five voted for it and seven against it. Burghley, who was its main supporter, concluded that unless Elizabeth herself was definitely in its favour he could not advise her to marry the duke. It was agreed, therefore, to ask the queen to 'open her mind' in the matter. When the news of the council's decision was communicated to her (7 October) Elizabeth was greatly distressed: 'not without tears' she complained 'that her councillors should think it doubtful whether there could be any more surety for her and her realm than to have her marry and have a child to inherit and continue the line of Henry VIII'. On the following day the council revised its decision, and offered, after long consultation, to do all it could to further the marriage 'if it so pleased her'. To the surprise of everyone the queen, who had now recovered her equanimity, received the offer coldly, trouncing those who had opposed the marriage, and reiterating that she had expected a unanimous request urging her to marry. As a matter of fact she realized that the game was lost. Nevertheless to save her face she played it out to the bitter end. On 24 November the articles were signed by Simier and the royal commissioners, two months being allowed for Elizabeth to dispose her subjects in favour of the marriage. A vain hope! What the council had refused to recommend of its own free will there was little likelihood of parliament agreeing to. So Simier returned to France at the end of November, to while away the time of waiting by inditing love-epistles to the queen, adorned with pink silk ribbon. 'Be assured on the faith of a monkey', he wrote, 'that your frog lives in hope.'

Meanwhile the situation in the Netherlands grew worse instead of better. Under the governorship of Parma, the ablest and most astute of all Philip's soldier administrators, and a brilliant diplomatist to boot, the catholic Walloon provinces made their peace with Spain (May 1579), leaving the Calvinist north, leagued in the Union of Utrecht, to continue the grim struggle with the Spaniards. The Pacification of Ghent was now a thing of the past: so, too, was the idea of a united Netherlands, to which Orange had dedicated his life; and there was less hope than ever of a peace by compromise, for the star of the Spaniard was in the ascendant. But the resolute will of the Dutch stadholder remained unimpaired. Beset by perils on all sides, and troubled by Elizabeth's insistence upon repayment of the successive borrowings for which she had stood caution, William now decided to reopen negotiations with Anjou and to offer him the sovereignty. No doubt he was influenced in his decision by optimistic reports of the recent marriage discussions in England: the potential husband of the English queen was an asset of unquestionable value. If, as seemed not at all un-likely, the duke succeeded in his suitorship and accepted the sovereignty of the Low Countries, England would probably rally to his support, and the desperate problem of military defence against the Spaniard would be virtually solved. This, however, was not Elizabeth's way of looking at the matter—she was as opposed as ever, in principle, to any radical change in the status of the Netherlands; she could not contemplate marriage with Anjou in the existing state of English public opinion; least of all did she want a war with Spain. On the other hand, she could not afford to see France step into the breach and profit by the duke's crusade in the Netherlands—assuming he accepted the sovereignty. The readiest way out of the difficulty was to keep the hope of marriage dangling before the eyes of Anjou, thereby securing some sort of control over his actions, so that whatever happened the result would not be unduly harmful to England's interests. If the worst came to pass, and he proved to be un-manageable, she might, as a last resort, defy public opinion at home and marry him.

It was, indeed, an anxious moment. The relative security in which England stood in 1575 was rapidly passing away. Pope Gregory XIII had republished his predecessor's bull of excommunication and declared war on the queen in Ireland: the jesuit mission was about to leave Rome—to prepare the way, it was believed, for the *empresa*: Munster was in revolt under Fitzmaurice, subsidized by money and munitions from Spain; and Scotland was beginning to drift from its moorings in the English alliance, after the fall of Morton's regency and the assumption of personal power by King James. If the outlook was gloomy nearer home, it was all the gloomier because of the prevalent unsettlement abroad, consequent upon the emergence of the Portuguese succession question. Since the death of King Sebastian at the battle of Alcazar (August 1578) statesmen in all countries had been perturbed about the future of Portugal, for no less than six candidates were preparing to contest this rich prize as soon as the aged cardinal-king Henry, Sebastian's uncle and successor and the last representative of the dynasty, breathed his last. Of the six claimants—Don Antonio, a bastard nephew of the late king, the dukes of Braganza and Savoy, Alexander of Parma, Catherine de Médicis, and Philip II of Spain—the only one who was likely to succeed was the king of Spain, whose right was as indisputable as his sword was sharp. It required no imagination to foresee an immediate *bouleverse-ment* of the existing balance of power in Europe if Portugal with its dependencies, its navy and material resources, became an appanage of the Spanish crown. The spectre of Spanish aggrandizement was particularly alarming to Elizabeth: the more so, perhaps, because France, the ancient opponent of the house of Habsburg, was not in a position to resume her traditional role. On the contrary, that country was in imminent danger of being submerged beneath a tide of fanatical catholicism, generated by the League and the pro-Spanish Guise faction. Thus when the crisis in Portugal came, with startling suddenness, at the end of January 1580, the Spaniards were ready to overrun the country without fear of serious opposition. By September they had mastered it, and Don Antonio, after a futile struggle, was driven into exile. Only at Terceira, in the Azores, was he acclaimed king of Portugal. Clearly, if Spain was to be checked, France must be pacified forthwith, and the whole force of the kingdom directed to the support of Anjou in his projected enterprise in the Nether-lands, and of Antonio in Portugal. It was a strange reversal of previous English policy, that what the queen had feared most in the past should now be accepted as imperative for her security. In 1571–2 she had frowned on the Coligny–Nassau plan: in 1580–1 she gave its Anjou–Orange counterpart her ardent blessing. Circumstances had altered her attitude. A European war in which France and Spain would figure as principals, with its main theatre in the Low Countries and a subsidiary one at the Azores, was the only way of dealing with the threat to her own dominions; and to the attainment of this object Elizabeth now devoted all her diplomatic skill and in-genuity. When her efforts to mediate a peace in France failed, she revived the moribund marriage negotiations as a lure both to the duke and his brother, the French king. In the end she partially succeeded. Anjou, who made the Treaty of Plessis-les-Tours with the states, accepting the sovereignty (September 1580), set out on his second adventure into the Netherlands in the following year, a willing servant of the queen. A year later (1582) the French government launched a great offensive against the Spaniards at the Azores. In neither case did England take any material share in the enterprise; but she gained the respite necessary for dealing with her more pressing problems at home, with Ireland, Scotland, and the papal emissaries in England.

The key to the complicated diplomatic history of the period is to be found in the marriage negotiations, which assumed an importance out of all proportion to their intrinsic worth. First came an illustrious embassy from France, in April 1581, headed by the prince dauphin, the duc de Montpensier, the count of Soissons, and Pinart, secretary of state, which was received with a round of banquets, bear-baitings, and 'triumphs', but achieved no positive result. It transpired that Elizabeth could not saddle herself with a war on Monsieur's behalf; for war would be the inevitable result of a marriage, Anjou being committed to the support of the Netherlands. War meant 'charges', and England would not 'digest' charges. It would be better to have a league. The embassy had, of course, no authority to conclude a league: so it returned to France in June, having accomplished nothing. Then came Walsingham's great mission to the French court (July–September) to clear up the matter, or, perhaps, to wrap it in deeper obscurity—probably the most exasperating mission ever committed to this sorely tried statesman. His instructions, as he understood them, were to work for an alliance without marriage, but not to break off the hope of marriage altogether. He was given a free hand, subject to compliance with two conditions: that marriage with a 'present war' could not be entertained, and that the duke of Anjou must not abandon his enterprise for the marriage. If the king was adamant that the marriage must precede the league, Walsingham was to say that 'we shall be content to marry . . . so as the French king and his brother will devise how we shall not be brought into a war therewith, although Monsieur shall continue his actions in the Low Countries'. But the French court was not blind to the purport of this complicated and superfine diplomacy. As Anjou remarked to Walsingham, his brother was afraid that if a league were made without the marriage to consolidate it the queen might 'slip the collar' and leave him 'in the briars'. Walsingham, too, was perplexed by the continually changing instructions he received from England. In August he wrote to Burghley:

I would to God her Highness would resolve one way or the other touching the matter of her marriage. . . . When her Majesty is pressed to marry, thus she seemeth to affect a league, and when a league is proposed, then she liketh better of a marriage. And when thereupon she is moved to assent to marriage, then hath she recourse to a league; when the motion for a league or any request is made for money, then her Majesty returneth to marriage.

If Walsingham was mystified by the queen's variability, he had no doubt about the attitude of Henry III and Catherine de Médicis: they insisted on the marriage—no marriage, no league. Anjou, however, was more pliable. About the middle of August, having completed his preparations, he set his army in motion and crossed the frontier. Cambrai fell into his hands almost at once, Parma withdrawing his forces, all 'his swagger gone and vanished into smoke'. But the campaign did not thrive: it stopped from lack of funds, although subsidies of £10,000 and £4,000 were sent to bolster it up from England and France respectively; and, at the end of October, Anjou placed his men in winter quarters at Le Catelet. On 2 November he paid a visit to Elizabeth at Richmond, which turned into a second courtship of three months' duration, more remarkable than the first. 'The queen', wrote Mendoza, 'doth not attend to other matters but only to be together with the duke in the chamber from morning to noon and afterwards till two or three hours after sunset. I cannot tell what a devil they do.' On the 22nd of November Elizabeth staged a superb piece of acting. Exchanging rings with Anjou, she kissed him in the presence of the French ambassador, Leicester, and Walsingham, adding the words (to the Frenchman): 'You may write this to the king, that the duke of Anjou shall be my husband.' The love palaver continuing, the duke forgot all about the Low Countries, and it became difficult to get him out of England; but eventually at the price of a solatium of another £10,000 he was prevailed upon to take his departure. Elizabeth accompanied him to Canterbury, leaving Leicester and a bevy of nobles to see him safely across from Dover to Flushing, where he arrived on 10 February 1582.

At Antwerp he was awaited 'not otherwise than the Hebrews awaited the coming of the Messiah'; but expectations were cruelly disappointed. He found it impossible to collect an army able to cope with Parma, who had captured Tournai in his absence. The states could provide neither men nor equipment nor money, and to make matters worse Elizabeth began to pester them for the repayment of her loans, and the moneys they had borrowed under cover of her credit. Even in France he could not raise recruits, because Henry III would not recognize the enterprise officially. As the year advanced, his position became more and more unbearable. He found that the sovereignty given to him was hedged about with restrictions, that he and his mercenary levies—a motley rabble—were not well liked by the population or by the older huguenots serving with Orange, and that it was difficult even to procure a church for the exercise of his religion. In July Parma captured Oudenarde, and inflicted an overwhelming defeat on the states at Ghent. This was followed by a crop of fresh surrenders to the Spaniard, and a corresponding diminution of Anjou's prestige, who, strange to say, had taken to tennis, riding, running at the ring, and hunting the otter with spaniels, while Parma was capturing cities.

Meanwhile the French government, after prolonged hesitation, had dispatched a naval force under Philip Strozzi to assist the Portuguese pretender, Antonio, at Terceira. It was a foolish expedition, badly organized and practically unsupported by Elizabeth, who, in virtue of Philip's warning (August 1581) that countenance of Antonio would be taken by Spain as a declaration of war, limited her contribution to a few transports. Its destruction by a Spanish fleet under the command of Santa Cruz (July 1582) seemed to vindicate the verdict registered at Lepanto, twelve years before, that Spain was the greatest seapower of the age. Strozzi was killed in the engagement, and the survivors were hanged as pirates at Villafranca: a testimony to the fact that the Spaniard could be as ruthless as Lord Grey at Smerwick.[1] Coming, as it did, about the same time as Parma's triumph at Oudenarde, the victory of Terceira completed the discredit of French arms, and caused no little consternation in the Low Countries.

Elizabeth was annoyed at the miserable position of Anjou and the lack of support given to him by the states. In August she wrote a sharp letter of remonstrance to Orange. 'If they act in this way', she said, 'and behave so to him as to compel him to withdraw once more, in a manner of speaking in his shirt sleeves, to his dishonour . . . they may be assured . . . we shall be the first to advise him flatly to leave the whole thing

[1] See p. 478.

betimes and to take no more account of them than their ingratitude deserves.' Henry III had also his qualms about his brother's discomfiture. In November he allowed the duc de Biron to conduct reinforcements into the Netherlands. But it was impossible to stop Parma's progress. By the end of the year the Spaniards had recovered all Flanders south of the Lys and the Scheldt with the exception of Alost and Dendermonde: only four cites—Bruges, Ghent, Brussels, and Mechlin—now stood between him and his chief objective, Antwerp. Early in January 1583 Anjou had recourse to desperate measures to re-establish his credit. On a preconcerted signal his troops made an attack on several cities, including Antwerp, Bruges, Ostende, Dixmude, Dunkirk, Nieuport, with a view to getting rid of the limitations placed upon him by the states. The main attack at Antwerp was defeated by the burghers, who afterwards alluded to it as the 'French Fury' and made it impossible for a Frenchman to move about the city without the protection of the burgomaster and magistrates. 'Since France was France', commented Roger Williams, in a letter to Walsingham, 'France never received so great a disgrace.' It practically marked the end of the duke's career as 'liberator of the Netherlands'. Shortly after, he left the country for France, all efforts to patch up an agreement by Elizabeth and Orange proving unsuccessful. He died in May of the following year.

All this time Elizabeth had been keeping a careful eye on Scotland, where the ascendancy she had enjoyed for many years under Morton's iron-handed rule had given place to a feeling of insecurity and foreboding. Trouble began in March 1578, when a combination of the regent's enemies, led by the earls of Atholl and Argyll, succeeded in driving him from office and obtaining control of the young king. Immediately the effect of this revolution was felt abroad. In April the duke of Guise and Vargas, the Spanish ambassador in Paris, were in communication with a view to armed intervention on behalf of Mary Stuart, and Archbishop Beaton, the queen of Scots's ambassador in France, plied both with urgent requests for help. Even the hesitant Philip II began to interest himself in the possibility of using Scotland as a means of checking Elizabeth's interference in the Low Countries. The danger, however, passed. In June Morton recovered his position in the council and there was a respite for a few months. Then in the autumn of 1579 a personage arrived in Edinburgh who was destined to excite the liveliest alarm among Elizabeth's advisers, namely Esmé Stuart, seigneur d'Aubigny, nephew of regent Lennox and cousin to the king's father. This new entrant upon the political stage is one of the most romantic and intriguing figures of the time, albeit surprisingly little is known about him. His polished French manners, which screened a subtle if not profound mind, enabled him to glide with remarkable ease through the interstices of Scottish politics, until he became almost a dictator, outrivalling the dour and repellent Morton. The king took to him at once as a convenient refuge from the imperious mentors who surrounded him on every side, and loaded him with honours and offices. He was granted the valuable abbacy of Arbroath, the earldom of Lennox, the governorship of Dumbarton castle, and the high chamberlainship of the kingdom. Very soon it was said that all Scotland was 'running the French course'. Worse still, there were rumours afloat that the new favourite was an emissary of the duke of Guise and the pope. Under his leadership a confederacy was formed for the overthrow of Morton; and in December 1580 the great man was arrested and thrown a prisoner into Dumbarton castle, despite Elizabeth's frantic efforts to save him. Six months later (June 1581) he was condemned to death and executed for complicity in the Darnley murder thirteen years before—again not without vehement protests from the English queen. For a short time, indeed, it almost seemed as if Morton's fate would plunge the two kingdoms into war, for Hunsdon at Berwick had instructions to prepare a punitive expedition against Edinburgh. But once again the tension slackened. There was no party in Scotland in favour of drastic action, and France was on the watch for a breach of treaty obligations. Thus Lennox and his coadjutor, Captain James Stewart, who had been personally responsible for the prosecution of Morton, became virtually masters of the kingdom. Stewart was rewarded with the earldom of Arran.

Elizabeth's position was one of acute anxiety, much worse than it had been at the time of Mary's triumph over the protestant lords in the autumn of 1566, for the forces of the counter-reformation were now gaining ground every day, and fully one-third of the Scottish nobility was catholic. So formidable were the adherents of the old religion in the northern counties of

Caithness, Sutherland, Inverness, Moray, and Aberdeen, and along the border from Nithsdale to Teviotdale, that it would have required only a small expeditionary army, resolutely handled, from France or Spain to turn the scales definitely against the protestants. Hardly less disturbing from Elizabeth's point of view was the doubtful position of the king. James was now in his sixteenth year, still too young to take a firm grasp of policy, and far from mature in mind and character; but he was already beginning to show traits that set shrewd observers thinking.

According to Fontenay, brother to Claude Nau, Mary Stuart's secretary, who studied him closely in the year 1584, James was a *vieux jeune homme*, a curious blend of youthful audacity and the wisdom of eld, learned in languages, science, and affairs of state, of a quick and penetrating intelligence, clever in debate, whether the subject was theology or any other, and gifted with a long and accurate memory. Supremely confident of his own powers, he hated to be surpassed by others and longed to be accounted a brave fellow, but was really a weakling and a coward. His passion for hunting, in the pursuit of which he spent long hours in the saddle, made him neglectful of affairs and overmuch dependent upon favourites; but he excused himself by boasting that he could discharge more business in an hour than others in a whole day, and that nothing of importance could happen in his realm without his knowing about it, because he had spies at his nobles' doors day and night, who reported to him constantly. His worst fault was his vainglory: he was ignorant of his own insignificance, but esteemed himself superior to all other princes. Not a very pleasing description of a young man in his teens, it may be said, but indicative of latent intellectual force with which the experienced Elizabeth would soon have to try conclusions. More than once his swift and disconcerting manœuvres would outwit her eagle eye and test her patience to the uttermost: so that on one occasion she was heard to remark: 'That villain of Scotland! What must I look for from such a double-tongued scoundrel as this?' No doubt she had a strong hold over him in his hopes of the English crown, but she could not trust his good-will; and although he knew full well the necessity of keeping on good terms with her, he was not prepared, any more than his mother before him, to become her 'thrall'. If she would not accommodate him in the matter of the succession, he was only too ready to play upon her fears by fraternizing with her enemies in the best machiavellian manner of the age. Even his protestantism appeared to sit lightly on him; and many believed, or affected to believe, that if he were withdrawn from the influence of Calvinist clerics and tactfully handled by priests, he would willingly proclaim himself a catholic, especially if his conversion materially improved his chances of the English crown.

It is hardly surprising, therefore, that the interest of the whole catholic world turned again to Scotland as the chief hope of better things in Britain. True, England had an unfaltering ally in the Kirk, whose sleepless vigilance and powerful influence in politics were worth a host in themselves. But Elizabeth would have been singularly regardless of her interests had she not striven with every device at her command, short of open war, to combat the machinations of her enemies on Scottish soil, to regain the ascendancy she had lost by Morton's fall, and to retain Scotland, as the phrase then ran, 'at England's devotion'. The record of her intrigues, plots, and counter-plots makes this one of the most baffling periods in the reign.[1]

Meanwhile the establishment of Lennox in the seat of power opened the way for the realization of the scheme with which his name is always associated—the conversion of the king to catholicism, the catholicization of Scotland, and the restoration of Mary to the sovereignty of which she had been deprived in 1567. This was to be merely the first stage in the main enterprise against England, on which the duke of Guise, the queen of Scots, Mendoza, the jesuits, the pope, and the king of Spain had set their hearts. It was the jesuits, however, who took the initiative in laying the foundations for this wider and more pretentious plan: Philip and the pope remained in the background. First of all Fathers Holt, Crichton, and Hay went to Scotland during the year 1581-2 to establish relations with Lennox and the Scottish catholic nobles, Huntly, Caithness, Seton, Eglinton, and Ferniehirst, to whom they communicated exaggerated and glowing reports of the readiness of the Spanish king and the pope to lend assistance. Then, in May 1582, a conference was held in France, under jesuit auspices, to which Mendoza was invited, but for obvious reasons could not go, and which Guise alone of the responsible political leaders attended. Here the details of the invasion plan were fully discussed. Lennox with the support of Spain and the pope, to the extent of eight thousand troops, was to secure the king's conversion and the subjection of the kingdom to the catholic faith. After this was accomplished, the combined Spanish and Scottish force would cross the frontier into England under the command of Lennox or the king: the English catholics, of whom, according to Holt, there were 'incredible numbers' ready to rise as soon as the signal was given, would join hands with it; and the mastery of England as well as Scotland would be assured. Guise gave his approval to the plan, and even offered to create a diversion by landing a contingent of French troops on the Sussex coast. But it will be obvious that a more flimsy, fantastic, or immature plot for the subversion of a well-established kingdom could hardly have been devised by men unfamiliar with the technique of military enterprises. Mendoza and Mary were astounded at the political ineptitude of the jesuits, who seemed to believe that armies could be conjured out of the ground by the mere stamp of a foot. Moreover, Philip had said nothing so far of a Spanish expeditionary force; nor, indeed, could such a force be available until the affairs of the Netherlands were settled. The time had clearly come for Mendoza, who ought to have been the co-ordinating brain of the whole conspiracy, to reassert political control over the schemers and bring them back to realities. But before he could straighten out the tangle he was beaten by English intrigues in Scotland.

In August 1582 the anglophil faction, led by the earls of Angus, Gowrie, and Mar, captured the king by a stratagem while he was hunting near Ruthven castle, Gowrie's Perthshire residence. Then followed the arrest of Arran, the break-up of the Lennox confederacy, and finally the flight of Lennox himself to Dumbarton, whence he made his way, by Elizabeth's permission, through England to France. This unexpected blow completely upset the calculations of the conspirators, who now realized that Scotland was a harder nut to crack than they had imagined. 'It would be better', said Guise, 'to effect the enterprise by way of England'—a sentiment shared by Tassis, the Spanish ambassador in Paris, who wrote: 'It appears to me that the true road to success is by England rather than by

Scotland.' Mendoza also agreed, for, as he said, the English catholics were unlikely to support James unless they were sure of his conversion and subjection to Spain. Further support for the reconstructed scheme was forthcoming from Mary's agents —Charles Paget, Thomas Morgan, and Charles Arundel; and the jesuits were apparently 'so confident . . . that it is impossible for any one hearing them to help being convinced'. Plans were therefore made for the abandonment of Scotland and a direct invasion of England. Spain was to provide an original striking force of 4,000 or 5,000 men from Parma's army in the Netherlands, which would be joined as soon as it landed in England by 20,000 English catholics. Guise was to be commander-in-chief of the expedition, and the landing-place was to be the Pile of Foudrey in Lancashire. The English catholic exiles on the Continent would accompany him; so too would William Allen, head of the seminary at Rheims, to whom was to be given the title of bishop of Durham and the task of publishing a papal bull justifying the enterprise. Charles Paget was to assure his co-religionists in England that the invading army would be withdrawn as soon as its object was achieved, and Mendoza, after remaining at his post to the last possible moment, was to cross to Dunkirk and join Guise. But alas! The king of Spain who was to be the king-pin of the plan withdrew (September 1583).

Meanwhile Elizabeth, ignorant of the danger threatening from abroad, was anxiously watching Scotland, where another revolution had taken place in July 1583, leading to the overthrow of the Ruthven clique and the return of Arran to power. In September, hearing of a renewal of French machinations in the northern kingdom, she sent Walsingham with a splendid embassy to remonstrate with James, and to see what he could do to restore English influence. The veteran diplomatist was no lover of the Scots, whom he regarded as a mercenary nation to be won only by hard cash—a method of persuasion he knew Elizabeth would never sanction. From the first, therefore, he fought a losing battle. He had nothing to offer—no gifts of money, no promises with regard to the succession: the anti-English party were in a strong position; and the king, though friendly, was in no mood to listen to expostulation on his 'crooked ways'. It is hardly surprising that Walsingham's report was a bitter one. He pronounced James 'an ingrate and such a one as if his power may agree to his will, will be found ready to make as unthankful a requital as ever any did that was so greatly beholding unto a prince, as he hath been unto your Majesty'. Nay, he concluded that the only way to deal with him was to have him 'bridled and forced, whether he will or no'. Since Elizabeth was just as averse to the use of force as to bribery, there was clearly nothing to be done but to recall her ambassador, and work for a more favourable turn in Scottish affairs in conjunction with the now exiled Ruthven nobles. Walsingham therefore returned to London in October.

Although the mission to Scotland had been a failure, it was to some extent offset by the immediate discovery of the Hispano-Guise plot. The revelation came as the result of an accident. Hitherto the government had been on the wrong tack, thinking that if trouble came it would come from France through Scotland. But now Walsingham learned from one of his spies in the French embassy of the suspicious movements of a certain Francis Throckmorton,[1] who, in fact, had been drawn into the Guise conspiracy by Morgan, and had become one of the principal intermediaries through whom Morgan communicated with Mary, and Mary with Mendoza. In November Throckmorton was arrested and his papers confiscated. On the rack he confessed everything he knew. So complete was the disclosure that the plot collapsed on the stocks before it was ready to be launched. Throckmorton was executed for treason: others were arrested and imprisoned; and the government decided to take drastic measures against Mendoza. On 9 January 1584 he was summoned before the council and ordered to leave the realm within fifteen days. It was the second time that a Spanish ambassador had been expelled from England for alleged treason. But Mendoza was no craven. 'The insolence of these people', he wrote to Idiaquez, the Spanish secretary of state, 'has brought me to a state in which my only desire to live is for the purpose of avenging myself upon them, and I pray that God may let it be soon and will give me grace to be His instrument of vengeance, even though I have to walk bare-footed to the other side of the world to beg for it.' When he applied for a ship to carry him across the Channel to France it was refused him; the queen, it was explained, reserved such privileges for her friends. His last words were almost a declaration of war. 'Don Bernardino de Mendoza', he remarked to the officer

[1] A nephew of Sir Nicholas, and a catholic.

who brought the message of refusal, 'was born not to disturb countries but to conquer them.' If war did not follow between England and Spain, it drew appreciably nearer.

There was no denying the fact that the peaceful days of Elizabeth's reign were rapidly passing away. During the year following Mendoza's expulsion, Parma continued slowly but surely his triumphant career in the Netherlands, 'invading deeper and deeper into the land', and drawing his toils closer and closer round Antwerp. In April he recovered Ypres, in May Bruges, in August Dendermonde, and in September Ghent. By the early autumn of 1584 all west Flanders except Ostend and Sluys was in his hands, and the Spaniards had begun to penetrate into the land of Waes, thus cutting the communications between Antwerp and the great cities of Brabant and Flanders. Meanwhile, at the end of May, Anjou had died at Château-Thierry, and a month later Orange fell a victim at Delft to the pistol of Balthazar Gerard, a fanatical 'Burgonian', who had wormed his way into the prince's household for the express purpose of murdering him and winning the reward set upon his head by King Philip in September 1580. It thus seemed only a question of time when the United Provinces, bereft of their native leader and the only foreign prince who was committed to their defence, would be reduced to the Spanish obedience. In their despair they turned again to France, offering the sovereignty to Henry III. But France could not and would not take up the burden, either alone or in conjunction with England. Henry of Valois, a wastrel and a pietist, and the last of his line, was spending his time in devising new spiritual ecstasies, and squandering his treasure on unworthy favourites. 'If he had a foolish toy in his head,' wrote Sir Edward Stafford, 'or a monk's weed to make, or an *Ave Maria* to say, he would let his state go to wrack.' What with his new Order of Jeronomists, his pilgrimages, and his 'mignons', the king of France was fast becoming a mere *roi fainéant*, while the duke of Guise and Henry of Navarre contended with each other over the succession—Navarre for his legitimate rights, and Guise in order to prevent the accession of a huguenot to the throne. In vain Elizabeth tried to rally the miserable king to a sense of his duty by pointing out the danger from Spain and the house of Guise. 'Jesus!' she wrote, 'Was there ever a prince so smitten by the snares of traitors without the courage or counsel to reply to it? . . . For the love of God rouse yourself from this too long sleep.' In January 1585 Guise made the secret treaty of Joinville with Philip of Spain, and in March, subsidized by Spain, unfurled the banner of the Holy League, professing as his aim the coercion of the king, the enforcement of the Tridentine decrees, and the exclusion of Navarre from the succession. Truly the Tagus had at last poured into the Seine and the Loire. France was a negligible factor in the affairs of Europe, or of value only as a satellite of the Spanish monarchy.

The time had come for Elizabeth to bestir herself. During the previous autumn Burghley was of the opinion that if France could not be relied upon to send assistance to the Netherlands, England must enter into the war without delay, if only for the purpose of keeping the inevitable conflict with Spain confined to the dominions of her enemy, and retaining the still uncon-quered Holland and Zeeland as her allies. In November 1584 Elizabeth sent over Davison with a tentative offer to the states that if the towns of Flushing, Brill, and Enckhuizen were handed over as 'caution' for the recovery of expenses and a guarantee that no peace would be made with Spain without her approval succour would be given by England. Negotiations, however, moved slowly, partly because of the conflicting reports as to the resisting power of Antwerp, and partly because of the difficulty in reaching a decision as to the nature of the power Elizabeth was to assume in the Netherlands. The states prof-fered the sovereignty: the queen would accept only a protec-torate. It was June 1585 before the commissioners from the Low Countries reached England, and another seven weeks elapsed before a satisfactory agreement was obtained. Even so, when the treaty was eventually signed on 2 August, it was concerned merely with the relief of Antwerp and not the general defence of the provinces. Only after the fall of the great seaport (7 August) did Elizabeth sanction the conclusion of a general treaty (10 August), binding her to provide an army to serve in the Netherlands at her own cost until the end of the war. The states, for their part, undertook to hand over Flushing, Brill, and the fort of Rammekens as 'cautionary towns' to be held by England until the expenses incurred were repaid in London. In September the earl of Leicester received his commission as lieutenant-general, and shortly after the middle of December set sail with a splendid retinue for the Netherlands. His army totalled 6,000 foot and 1,000 horse.

The campaign that followed—if campaign it can be called—began under brilliant auspices. The earl was welcomed with the cry 'God save Queen Elizabeth!' uttered as heartily, he noted, 'as if the queen herself had been in Cheapside'. Bonfires, fireworks, pageants, and banquets awaited him in every town he visited. The triumphal pomp of his reception at The Hague was celebrated in engravings. At Amsterdam he was greeted with a display of aquatic monsters—'whales and others of great hugeness'—who seized his ship and towed it to the shore. 'Never was there a people in such jollity as these be,' was his gratified comment. Alas for his hopes! Leicester was neither a great general nor a wise administrator. Ominously enough, he began by flagrantly disobeying his instructions and the letter and spirit of the queen's express declaration that she had no intention of governing the Netherlands either directly or indirectly. He accepted the title of 'His Excellency the Governor and Captain-general'. Elizabeth was furious at his indiscretion. 'It is sufficient', she remarked, 'to make me infamous to all princes, having protested the contrary in a book which is translated into divers languages.' In her anger she would listen to no expostulations, either by the earl himself or by his friends among her ministers: the obnoxious title must be rescinded at once, or she would withdraw him. Only after Burghley had threatened to resign and the states had made an earnest supplication for the title to be allowed for the time being, did she relent and relax. It was a bad beginning; but worse was to follow when the question of finance arose. Elizabeth had undertaken to maintain her expeditionary force for the duration of the war, at a cost, it is calculated, of £126,000 per annum—a very considerable sum when her other commitments, actual and prospective, are taken into account, and her entire ordinary revenue was not more than £300,000. Stringent economy in expenditure, always a fundamental matter with Elizabeth, was now more imperative than ever.[1] Yet in spite of instructions to

---

[1] The financial dealings of Elizabeth with the Dutch provinces of the Low Countries, after the break-away of the catholic or Walloon provinces of the south (May 1579), make difficult, confused, and sometimes sordid reading—a tale of continuous bickering about the repayment and recovery of debts and loans, out of

handle the disbursement of the queen's treasure with care, and warnings from Walsingham to beware of 'charges', Leicester appears to have used part of the money transmitted to him to alleviate the condition of the English troops in the service of the states, of whom there was a considerable number, and to have taken no steps whatever to check the widespread peculation that went on among the captains, although this, too, was part of his instructions. Nay, he even increased the officers' pay, his own included. Can it be wondered at that Elizabeth soon grew 'weary of the charges of the war'? Her lieutenant-general had become, in effect, a 'conduit along which English treasure passed into the abyss of Dutch bankruptcy'.[1] To crown all, the queen was supremely anxious for peace: she did not accept the view that she was irrevocably at war with Spain. On the contrary, now that she had the 'cautionary towns' in

which neither party emerged with credit to themselves or even self-respect. The alliance between them, designated 'the common cause', was often shaken to its foundations by the bitterness of disputes; and only the dire necessity of each to ward off the threatening dangers from a militant Spain prevented a complete disruption. In her heart of hearts Elizabeth had no love for the Dutch: she detested them as rebels against a divinely appointed sovereign, despised their bourgeois economy, and had nothing but contempt for their virulent, esoteric Calvinism. The moneys she advanced to them, either by way of direct loans, or loans from Italian financiers backed by English credit, were grudgingly given and their repayment carefully provided for; but the crux of the matter was that, as the indebtedness of the Netherlanders increased, both in capital and interest, so too did their unwillingness to pay; and they were in a strong position, for if England allowed them to be defeated all hope of recovering the war loans would vanish completely. Moreover, the Dutch could point out that it would be unjust to expect them to pay the whole debt, when the southern provinces, now reconciled to Spain, were equally responsible for incurring the original indebtedness. Why should they ruin themselves by shouldering the burden of others? It was a desperate tangle of conflicting claims which could only breed endless friction, anger, and strife, destroying anything in the nature of trust or confidence between the allies.

In 1583 matters came to such a point that the queen ordered Sir Richard Bingham to take two ships of the fleet to the Narrow Seas and, under the pretence of hunting down pirates, seize 'any shipping belonging to the states or subjects of the Low Countries, for certain debts due by themselves unto us . . .'. True, this order was not executed; but it shows how tense relations had become; and there were other devices, less creditable, for breaking the *impasse* with the Dutch over repayment, e.g. the levying of taxes on all in-coming and out-going shipping at ports still within the control of the rebels, and the taxing of Dutch refugees and émigrés still resident in England. But it was not until the Anglo-Dutch treaty was signed and sealed in 1598, after the collapse of the 'common cause', that the Dutch acknowledged their mountainous debt of £800,000, albeit they did not include the private debt they had incurred with the Italian financier Palavicino, which had the backing of Elizabeth. (For a good account of the whole question recourse should be had to Mr. Lawrence Stone's *Sir Horatio Palavicino*, especially chap. iii.)

[1] J. E. Neale, *Queen Elizabeth*, p. 289.

her possession, she was hopeful that she might use them to bargain for a general peace, safeguarding the interests both of the Netherlands and of England. It did not trouble her that this might be considered a gross betrayal of the people she had promised to help. 'We are so greedy for a peace', wrote Walsingham to Leicester, 'as in the procuring thereof we neither weigh honour nor safety.' Nor did Leicester improve matters by quarrelling with Sir John Norreys, the best of his subordinates, or by his bickerings with the states over the extent of the power committed to him. The English army rapidly dwindled. 'To say rightly', wrote Sir William Pelham, marshal of the host, 'such are their miseries as I know not how to turn to satisfy them, for some wanting wherewith to feed them, others almost naked, many falling sick daily, and all in general barefoot wanting hose or shoes, do by hundreds flock about me if I stir abroad amongst them, crying for relief of their troubles.'

In brief, the campaign was a miserable failure. Apart from a few brilliant exploits like the capture of Axel, the check to Parma at Zutphen, the taking of Doesburg—all of them due to individual bravery rather than the scientific organization of the generalissimo, the war added nothing to the stability of the states, and brought no glory to the name of Leicester. The true hero of the campaign was Sir Philip Sidney, who died of a gunshot wound received at Zutphen.[1]

If Elizabeth had been reluctant to strike a blow against Spain in the Netherlands, Philip had done his best to incur her hostility on the sea, with dire consequences to himself. On 19 May 1585 an order had been issued to the corregidor of Biscay to seize any shipping lying in Spanish ports belonging to England, Holland, Zeeland, and 'the other states and seigniories that are in rebellion against me'. As there were a considerable number of

---

[1] Leicester returned to England in November 1586. Seven months later he was sent back to the Netherlands, with a fresh army of 5,000 and £30,000 to prepare the way for peace with Spain, and to secure a cessation of arms. But his temperamental unfitness for leadership, combined with the stubborn resistance of the Dutch to a policy of peace, rendered his mission again a failure. Soon after his arrival he fell foul of the states-general, weakened his own forces by cashiering his old enemy, Sir John Norreys, and irritated the Dutch commander, Maurice of Nassau, with whom he attempted to relieve Sluys, then besieged by Parma. The enterprise failed, and Sluys fell into the hands of the Spaniards in August. In November Leicester was recalled to England, and never again set foot in the Netherlands. His repeated failure did not, apparently, weaken his position at court, for in the following year he was appointed commander of the English forces assembled at Tilbury to meet the armada.

English corn-ships at Bilbao and other ports, the seizures that followed resulted in great losses to the merchant community, together with the imprisonment of hundreds of English sailors. Only a few captains succeeded in getting their ships away, among whom was the captain of the *Primrose* of London, who brought the news to England, along with a copy of the writ authorizing the seizures, and the corregidor of Biscay himself, whom he had captured during the scuffle in the port. The outcry against this act on the part of the Spanish king was so general in England, even among the merchants, who had hitherto been afraid of violent measures, that a retaliatory embargo was at once placed on Spanish goods: letters of reprisal were issued to the merchants; and Drake was ordered to proceed with a fleet for the release of the confiscated vessels. On 14 September the great corsair set sail with a composite flotilla consisting of 30 ships, mainly merchantmen from London and the west country, and 2,300 men—ostensibly for northern Spain; but his real objective was the West Indies and the *flota*. At Vigo, his first landfall, he took plunder to the extent of 6,000 ducats. Then, leaving the Spanish coast, he made for the Canaries and Cape Verde Islands, where he burnt Santiago and Porto Praya. Late in November he stood away across the Atlantic, touched at Dominica and St. Christopher, and launched himself with all his force at San Domingo (Hispaniola), the richest and finest city in the Indies, and the 'Queen of Spain's colonial empire'. San Domingo was ransomed for 25,000 ducats, part of it being burnt in order to extort the payment quickly; and on 1 February Cartagena on the mainland was similarly treated, its shipping burnt, and a payment of 110,000 ducats exacted. At the end of March 1586 Drake put to sea again with a fresh cargo of plundered merchandise, guns, and all the church bells and metal he could lay hands on, together with a great quantity of furniture stolen from private houses. Altogether his loot amounted to more than half a million of our money. After hovering about the Yucatan channel and Havana, in the hope of intercepting the *flota*, he bore off to Florida, destroyed Fort St. Augustine, and finally visited Raleigh's colony at Roanoke, where he rescued the disappointed colonists and brought them back to England in the midsummer of 1586.

This remarkable exploit filled Europe with amazement, not so much by the quantity of plunder it produced as by the moral damage it did to Spain. Spanish credit was temporarily shattered, and the sources of King Philip's wealth and power seemed to be absolutely at Elizabeth's mercy. The aggressive power of England, hitherto not fully realized, was seen to be so great that the Antwerp merchants, on whom both Parma and his Master had relied for loans, tightened their pursestrings. If Leicester had failed to prick the bubble of Spanish might, Drake had shown his countrymen how and where to do it.

Meanwhile the situation in Scotland had righted itself in England's favour. After three years and nine months of continuous intrigue and counter-intrigue, and at least two abortive rebellions, the Arran régime had been at last destroyed by the combined efforts of the exiled Ruthven nobles, the Master of Gray, one of the wiliest intriguers of the age and Arran's deadly enemy, and Sir Edward Wotton, the English ambassador in Edinburgh. In July 1586 James was induced to sign the Treaty of Berwick, thereby becoming a pensioner and ally of England. The two monarchs undertook to maintain the religion professed in their respective realms, to assist each other with armed forces in the event of invasion by a third power, and to make no alliances prejudicial to each other with any foreign state. In return for this agreement the king received a pension of £4,000 per annum from the English exchequer; and although no reference was made to the succession, it was understood that the queen would not permit any measure to be brought forward in parliament detrimental to his right. The name of the queen of Scots was not mentioned either in the discussions leading up to the treaty or in the treaty itself, which was simply a mutual insurance arrangement between Elizabeth and James.

Note on Scotland

The account given in this chapter of the issues at stake in Scotland, though very brief, is more or less the accepted version. It should be noted, however, that a good deal of mystery still hangs about Anglo-Scottish relations in the period; and, strange to say, we are still without a thorough-going critical study of James VI, or a biography of Lennox. Of the existing writings on the king, Mr. D. H. Willson's *King James VI and I* is both readable and knowledgeable, but lacks critical insight; and Tytler's *History of Scotland*, though still a standard work and thoroughly reliable, is becoming antiquated.

On the other hand, Conyers Read's passages on Scotland in his *Mr. Secretary Walsingham* are admirable so far as they go, but would carry more weight if we knew more about the actual state of affairs in Scotland. The first requisite is a reasoned inquiry into the attitude of both the king and Lennox to the catholic 'intrigues' of the time; for until this is forthcoming it will be impossible to arrive at any reliable conclusion as to the method and true object of English diplomacy.

THE EXECUTION OF MARY STUART: THE SPANISH ARMADA

WE have now arrived within measurable distance of the supreme crisis in Mary Stuart's fortunes. The chain of events leading to it forms one of the most melancholy dramas in history—a drama, on the one side, of self-centred ambition and self-destructive plotting, and on the other of illogicality, irresolution, and timorous clemency. For many years Elizabeth had shielded the queen of Scots from the wrath of the English protestants, who made no secret of their opinion that so long as the 'monstrous and huge dragon' lived, not only their own queen's life was in danger, but also the security of the state. In 1572 parliament would have attainted her of treason in the highest degree, or, failing that, would have disabled her from the succession for her complicity in the Ridolfi plot; and convocation plied the queen with many 'godly arguments' to set aside her scruples.

In parliament the bishops provided the spearhead of the onslaught: they showed no mercy. Not only did they 'comb the bloody repertoire' of the Old Testament for suitable precedents, they pointed out that if the queen did not punish the Scottish 'Clytemnestra', according to the measure of the offence; she would offend God in her conscience. On the other hand, if she put the culprit to death, she would 'abash and damp the minds of all the enemies of God and friends of Antichrist'. And so the stream of hatred flowed on, and scarcely a voice was heard in parliament on the side of humanity or moderation. What have we to do with the *jus gentium*, said one; have we not a law of our own to provide for this mischief? In vain the Speaker pointed out to the passionate commons, that the queen of Scots was not a subject or feodary of the English Crown. Cut off her head, said the member for New Windsor, and make no more do about her, for she is a common disturber of the peace of this realm. The last bolt was shot, curiously enough, by Peter Wentworth, who, with singular infatuation, dismissed her with the words: 'the most notorious whore in the whole world'!

One wonders if it was not stark fear, rather than reason, that moved the English parliament at this time—fear lest, in the event of Mary's ultimate triumph, the lands, goods, and lives of the prosecutors would be forfeit. But one wonders even more what Elizabeth thought of it all—if indeed she had the commons' speeches reported to her in full—when only a few years before, she dismissed the Scottish lords from the Westminster 'conference' with the staggering remark that 'nothing had been sufficiently produced or shown against the queen of Scots'.

It was only by a supreme exercise of will-power that Elizabeth saved Mary from the scaffold on which Norfolk perished, and vetoed the retaliatory measures against her title to the English crown which both houses had formally approved. There is no doubt that Elizabeth could have put her rival to death with impunity at this time, had she so wished, for even France would have raised no serious protest. 'They will put her to death', exclaimed Charles IX, when informed of the plotting: 'I see it is her own fault and folly.' But it was not to be. For one reason or another, possibly because she was temperamentally averse to shedding a kinswoman's blood, or afraid of the imputation of cruelty, or simply because she thought that Mary alive in an English prison was a better security for the future than Mary dead with a martyr's halo round her head, Elizabeth refused to 'put to death the bird that had flown to her for safety from the hawk'. She may even have hoodwinked herself into the belief that time and diplomacy would solve the problem. There were moments, of course, when she wavered in her attitude. After the massacre of St. Bartholomew, when 'all men cried out' against the Scottish queen and her Guise relations, she would only too willingly have handed her over to Regent Mar to be executed in Edinburgh for her share in the Darnley murder. But the regent stood upon conditions; and rather than be held in any way responsible for the deed, Elizabeth allowed the matter to drop. She reverted to it in 1574, during Morton's regency, but again was unsuccessful; and Mary remained for the next twelve years the great 'untouchable' in English politics—rebellious, defiant, incorrigible in her hope of ultimate victory. The tragedy of her position lay in the fact that, while there was a chance of elevation to power by way of conspiracy, war, and revolution, she would not honestly accept the *pis aller* of a settlement by treaty. The hope of the English succession, always the dominant ambition of her life, was far too precious a thing to be bartered away for personal security or even freedom. With amazing effrontery she said she would not leave her prison save as queen of England.

From 1569 to 1585 the earl of Shrewsbury acted as her jailer; and except for short intervals when her apartments were being cleansed, or when she visited Buxton for health's sake, her abode was Sheffield castle. Life was far from intolerable, although the restrictions were irksome. She dined as a queen, under a cloth of state. Her servitors, of whom there was a considerable number, were chosen by herself, and Shrewsbury was a man of honour, who interpreted his trust in a just and reasonable spirit. He looked after his prisoner so carefully that escape was out of the question 'unless she could transform herself into a flea or a mouse', but he could not exercise an equally close supervision over her communications with the outside world, and was sometimes unfairly charged with laxity. The fact is that although all correspondence was supposed to pass through his hands, there were numerous ways by which cipher messages could be smuggled into and out of the castle, and Mary was able to keep herself fairly well informed of events not only in England but also abroad. Moreover, since the cost of her maintenance was borne principally by the English treasury (£52 per week), she could use the proceeds of her dowry, which yielded annually £12,000, to finance an intelligence service, subsidize her partisans, and, generally speaking, weave plots with Elizabeth's enemies.[1] While she occupied herself with needlework, the results of which she sometimes sent to the English queen as an earnest of her goodwill, or amused herself with pet birds and small dogs, or listened to court scandal purveyed to her by 'Bess of Hardwick', Shrewsbury's terrible spouse, she kept an eye constantly lifting for the propitious moment when, as the cardinal of Lorraine assured her, her 'patient dissimulation' would be rewarded. Her indefatigable ambassadors, the bishop of Ross[2] and the archbishop of Glasgow, advocated her cause in Rome and Paris. She corresponded with the pope, the kings of France and Spain, the emperor, and

---

[1] But the dowry was systematically plundered by Mary's friends and relatives in France; and Elizabeth cut down her allowance to £30 per week (1575).

[2] But see D. McN. Lockie's article on 'The Political Career of the Bishop of Ross' (*Birmingham Univ. Hist. Rev.*, 1954) for a valuable account of Ross's vagaries.

a number of potentates great and small. Indeed her intrigues ramified through the length and breadth of Europe. Always professing the most amicable intentions, she constantly plotted to bring the whole fabric of society in ruin about Elizabeth's ears. When brought to book—for sometimes her correspondence miscarried into Walsingham's hands—she lied volubly but unconvincingly. She was a credulous and impulsive conspirator, full of exaggerated optimism, unburdened by a conscience, but void of a sense of reality, which is the basis of success in plotting as in all other things. It was a wearing and tearing existence. Disappointment rendered her irritable and frantic: she grew prematurely old: her hair whitened; and her health suffered from the prolonged confinement. The surprising thing is not that she failed, but that Elizabeth persisted so long in the attempt to seek a *modus vivendi* with her.

Of the English queen's desire to reach a settlement without bloodshed there is ample evidence. Even during the dangerous plotting which began in 1580 and culminated in the expulsion of Mendoza she made a serious effort at conciliation, on the plea, put forward by Mary herself, that a joint sovereignty comprehending both mother and son could be established in Scotland (April–May–June 1583). The plan was originally intended to get King James's title to the Scottish crown recognized by France and the other continental countries, which had hitherto refused to acknowledge it; and the purpose was to pave the way for rebuilding the old Franco-Scottish alliance as a counterpoise to England's domination north of the Tweed. For this reason France backed the 'association', or 'condominium' as it might be called, whole-heartedly. But Mary had another purpose in mind. In the first place, she intended the establishment of the joint sovereignty to be a stepping-stone to a full restoration of her rule in Scotland: her son was to be king only in name —she was to enjoy the substance of power. In the second place, she was determined to work out a sweeping policy of revenge upon her enemies—a policy that would have meant the complete *bouleversement* of all political, social, and religious life in Scotland, and the installation of civil war and anarchy. It is all described in an extraordinary letter to the archbishop of Glasgow on 28 October 1581. Meanwhile, Elizabeth was inclined to view the original idea with some degree of interest, for it seemed to provide a means to bring both mother and son into England's 'devotion', acquiring control over both, and thereby demolishing the machinations of France. Everything, of course, depended upon the possibility of complete unity and co-operation between James and his mother. This was the crux of the business; and it proved to be insuperable. Nor was Scotland likely to welcome back the exiled queen with any warmth. On the contrary, the Kirk raised the cry of 'papistry' and the return of the 'bloody gully'; and the possibility of any agreement vanished into thin air.

The final blow to the negotiation was struck by Throckmorton's confession on the rack. 'All this shows', said Elizabeth, summing up her impressions in March 1584, 'that her intention was to lull us into security, that we might the less seek to discover practices at home and abroad.' Yet Elizabeth was slow to admit failure in this, as in all her diplomatic ventures. Only after a further effort had been made and her commissioners, Beale and Mildmay, reported that they could not 'by all the cunning that we have, bring her to make any absolute promise' (May 1584), did she give up the struggle. To have proceeded any farther would have been merely fatuous. At the same time as the negotiations were going on, Mary was in active communication with William Allen about her release by force, pointing out how easily a *coup de main* could be effected at Sheffield!

What was to be done with such a woman? Elizabeth was unable to offer any solution of the problem. She had the 'wolf by the ears' with a vengeance! To let go would be fatal: she could only hold on. And doubtless she would have held on indefinitely, for the long duration of the imprisonment created, so to speak, a kind of vested interest in its continuance. Events, however, were at last beginning to move towards a very different conclusion.

The papal sanction of assassination as a lawful weapon against the heretic ruler had already worked havoc with public morality. In 1582 William of Orange had been shot at and severely wounded by a fanatic, only escaping death by a miracle. Soon afterwards the murder campaign was extended to England. In October 1583 a certain John Somerville, a Warwickshire papist, whose head had been turned by the exploit against Orange, swore he would kill Elizabeth with a pistol, 'for she was a serpent and a viper'. Happily this murderous intention was revealed by his own incautious and boastful words, and he was arrested, sent to the Tower, and executed. The loyalty of the nation was roused to a high pitch; and Mauvissière, the French ambassador, noted that when the queen journeyed to Hampton Court in November great throngs of people knelt by the roadside, wishing her a thousand blessings and expressing the hope that evilly disposed persons who meant her harm would be discovered and duly punished. The portent was unmistakable. The time had come to take stern measures to protect the queen. Consequently, less than four months after the second and successful attempt had struck down the Dutch leader (June 1584), the council drew up the so-called Bond of Association, pledging those who signed it—and thousands of signatures were soon forthcoming from many parts of the country—in the event of an attempt on the queen's life, not only to prevent the succession of any person by whom, or in whose interest, the attempt should be made, but also to pursue the said person to the death.[1] No clearer intimation could have been made to Mary that, if the plotting continued, her life would be in danger, if not actually forfeit. There was a considerable conflict of opinion when the question of legalizing this appeal to Texan justice came before parliament, towards the end of November. The commons were unstrung at the prospect of utter chaos likely to supervene if the events envisaged in the Bond took place. The queen, on the other hand, was averse to having any one put to death 'for the fault of another', but would not give parliament the satisfaction it wanted in regard to the succession. Confusion was increased, and excitement grew, when it transpired, in January 1585, that another plot—the Parry plot—was in train for the murder of the queen. Eventually a bill was passed (27 Eliz., cap. i), incorporating the substance of the Bond so far as 'pursuing to the death' was concerned, but making provision for a proper trial and judgement, followed by disablement from the succession, of the person *with whose privity* the attempt was made, prior to the infliction of the death penalty. The Bond of Association was consequently modified in the same way. In February Parry was sent to the scaffold. Immediately afterwards a motion was

[1] James VI was 'touched' by the Bond of Association owing to the inclusion of the words 'or any that may any way claim by or from that individual'. But this was afterwards rectified, thanks to Elizabeth, by the qualification 'assenting and privy', which practically eliminated James from the operation of the Bond or the subsequent act, if he behaved himself.

made in the commons to revive the proceedings against Mary begun in 1572; for Parry's examination elicited the fact that the Scottish queen's agent in Paris, Morgan, had encouraged the plot. At this point, however, Elizabeth interposed her veto: the matter had been carried far enough for the present.

Meanwhile the watch over the captive was intensified. Early in January 1585 she was removed from Sheffield to Tutbury; and shortly afterwards the puritan Amyas Paulet replaced Shrewsbury as her keeper. The new jailer was a man after Walsingham's own heart—formerly captain of Jersey, and later English ambassador at the court of France, he was a puritan of the puritans, single-minded, devoted to duty, and thoroughly loyal. Elizabeth liked and trusted him: as she said, he was 'towards God religious, towards us most faithful, by calling honourable, by birth, in respect of the antiquity of his house, most noble'. He began his custodianship characteristically by instituting a régime of the most stringent surveillance, following his instructions to the letter. The armed guard of the castle was strengthened: no strangers were permitted to enter the precincts under any pretext whatsoever: Mary's retinue were stopped from walking on the walls overlooking the castle gates: Sharp, the queen of Scots's coachman, was ordered not to dine with the keeper's servants; and when Mary went out for exercise, either on horseback or in a coach, she was accompanied by a *posse* of harquebusiers, pistoliers, and horsemen, who were instructed to prevent contact with the common folk. Thus Paulet carried out his policy of beginning 'roundly' with his prisoner: 'a liberty once granted', he said, 'cannot be withdrawn without great exclamation'. But the laundresses baffled and irritated him: being lodged in the neighbouring village, they passed freely in and out of the castle, and short of stripping them 'to their smocks', he had no means of checking what they carried hidden in their dresses. More difficult still, however, was the inspection of all out-going letters from Mary to her correspondents at home and abroad: they were in French, and although Paulet was familiar with the language, he had no end of trouble looking for hidden messages or meanings; and the phraseology often puzzled him. Thus, when Mary wrote a letter of thanks to Chérelles, secretary to Chateauneuf, the French ambassador in London, for a box of sweetmeats received at Christmas, he boggled over the words 'Je vous mercie des confitures seiches.' He had evidently not heard of dried fruit!

Gradually by the systematic elimination of loop-holes and the tightening of the net, Mary was soon cut off from her friends. Even her contact with the French ambassador had to be carried out through official government channels. By January 1586, Paulet was convinced that it would be quite impossible for any of the Scottish queen's retainers 'to convey a piece of paper as big as my finger' out of, or into, the castle. The cordon was complete. But Walsingham was not satisfied. His object was not so much to procure Mary's isolation as to collect information about her intentions that would ensure her trial, condemnation, and death. In order to do this it was first necessary to establish and maintain in Mary the impression that her correspondence was open to inspection, while, at the same time, creating the illusion that a new and secret post had been invented, whereby letters could be carried into and out of her prison without the knowledge of her jailer. To this task he now addressed himself with characteristic ingenuity. It is not necessary to suppose that he invented the plot that lured the queen of Scots to her doom; but the measures he adopted were such as to make it practically certain that, if Mary was bent upon the queen's destruction, she would become hopelessly entangled in a conspiracy against her life, and therefore liable to the penalties laid down in the statute. In this sense he was the *agent provocateur* in the remarkable sequence of events that culminated in the tragedy of Fotheringay.

About the end of December 1585 the Scottish queen was taken from Tutbury to Chartley, a manor belonging to the young earl of Essex, situated some twelve miles from Tutbury, in south Derbyshire. Here, with the help of Paulet, Walsingham constructed his trap for intercepting, or, as we should say, 'listening in' to the secret plans of Mary and her partisans. By means of a brewer of Burton, who supplied the manor with beer, and Gilbert Gifford, a renegade catholic who consented to play the part of 'confidence man' and intermediary, Mary was led to believe that a perfectly safe line of communication had been found connecting Chartley with the outer world. Since Gifford bore credentials from the redoubtable Morgan, she leapt at the opportunity without the slightest hesitation. The mechanism of the trap was simple in the extreme. Letters coming to Mary were wrapped in a waterproof case (*une petite boîte ou sac de cuir*), inserted through the bung into a cask of ale, and carried into Chartley: outgoing letters, enclosed in the same way, were smuggled out in the returned 'empty'. Each packet, before it was placed in the cask for conveyance to Mary, was carefully examined, deciphered, and copied by Thomas Phelippes, Walsingham's secretary; and the same procedure was applied to the outgoing packets before they were passed on to their destination.

Walsingham had not long to wait for results. His first haul was a batch of old letters, hung up at the French embassy since the Throckmorton conspiracy, of value only for the light they shed on Mary's part in the plotting of the previous two years. In May came a letter from Mary to Charles Paget, urging him to hasten on the invasion project, and about the same time a letter from Paget to Mary stating that one, Ballard a priest, had just returned to France with a report that the English catholics were ready to rise as soon as help arrived from abroad. Ballard, it appeared, was sent back to England for more precise information. Then, in June, Walsingham became aware that a new plot was taking shape—the Babington conspiracy, so called from its chief executant agent, Anthony Babington of Dethick, Derbyshire, who had formerly been a page in Mary's household at Sheffield. This ardent, vainglorious, but essentially simple-minded youth of twenty-five had been brought into the deep waters by the persuasive tales of Ballard, and now offered, with five companions, to attempt the murder of the queen and the release of Mary. They were to be supported by an invading army. Meanwhile a broad hint of what was coming was conveyed in a letter from Morgan to Curle, Mary's English secretary. 'There be many means in hand', wrote Morgan, 'to remove the beast that troubles the world.' On 6 July, at the instigation of Gifford and primed by Ballard, Babington divulged the whole plot in a most imprudent letter to Mary, soliciting her approval and advice, and asking for an assurance that the 'six noble gentlemen' who were to undertake the 'tragical execution' would be rewarded—if they escaped with their lives—or their posterity if they failed. He addressed the Scottish queen as 'My dread Sovereign Lady and Queen, unto whom only I owe all fidelity and obedience'; and then set out the details of the intended 'coup'—including the murder of the 'usurper', Mary's liberation, the landing of an invading force from abroad, and the mustering of supporting catholics in the counties. It was a crude effort at conspiracy, lacking any substantial basis in fact, fantastic in its optimism. Nevertheless, this was the 'letter' that opened up the way for the queen of Scots to the scaffold. It was important enough in the eyes of Walsingham for Phelippes to take it down in person to Chartley, to be passed into the castle by the brewer as usual. Everything now depended on Mary's response. Would she 'fall' for the bait? Would she commit herself? The temptation was great: she could hardly resist it. On 14 July Phelippes wrote to Walsingham with ghoulish glee: 'We attend her very heart at the next.'

Meanwhile on 9 July, the very day on which Phelippes arrived at Chartley to deliver the Babington letter via the brewer to Mary, Walsingham wrote a confidential letter to Leicester, who was then in the Netherlands, informing him that a great event was impending—as important as any that ever occurred since Elizabeth's accession. It was so important that information about it could not be communicated to his own servants; but it would be communicated to Leicester by the bearer of the letter *sotto voce*. 'My only fear', says Walsingham, 'is that her Majesty will not use the matter with the secrecy that appertaineth.' Then follows the clue: 'and surely, if the matter be well handled, it will break the neck of all dangerous practices during her Majesty's Reign.' Finally, Walsingham instructs Leicester 'to make this letter a heretic after you have read the same', i.e. to burn it, and confides in him that 'when the matter is grown to a full ripeness', he intends to send some confidential person 'to acquaint him fully with the matter'. The significance of this remarkable letter, which incidentally seems to have eluded the notice of both Pollen and Read, albeit it is well known to Gauthier, Chantelauze, and Hosack, may be summarized thus: (i) the reference is undoubtedly to the Babington Plot; (ii) Walsingham was, as yet, without a scrap of convincing evidence that Mary was involved in a criminal conspiracy against Elizabeth's life; yet he appears to know *in advance* that her answer to Babington's letter will 'break the neck of all conspiracies during the reign of Elizabeth', or, in plain words, send the queen of Scots to her doom; (iii) his only fear is not that Mary will disappoint him, but that Elizabeth will not handle the matter with 'the secrecy that appertaineth'.

But to resume: Walsingham had not long to wait for the deadly epistle he expected. On 17 July came Mary's reply—a long and frank approval of the plot, accompanied by certain recommendations, viz. that her friends should carefully study the numbers to be mustered in the counties and towns; the ports of debarkation for the invading troops from abroad; the strength and resources of the invaders; the place of the general rendezvous; and a query as to how the 'six gentlemen deliberate to proceed'. Finally, and even more important, Mary gives elaborate advice about the method of her own escape, after the 'design' has been accomplished. Before sending on this letter to Walsingham (duly deciphered) Phelippes sketched on it the grim sign of the gallows—a signal that he deemed the end had come. For eleven days the document lay in Walsingham's possession; and then, after the post-script had been forged and added, asking for the names of the 'six associates', it passed into the hands of Babington (29 July).[1]

Walsingham knew two of them already—Babington and Ballard, and he probably suspected who the others were; for all six had been swaggering about London, toasting the success of the enterprise at tavern dinners, and had even committed the incredible folly of having their pictures taken, in a group, with Babington in the centre and subscribed with the motto: 'Hi mihi sunt comites, quos ipsa pericula ducunt.' But like the good sleuth he was, Walsingham wanted to complete his *dossier* of the plot before striking: it was his duty to the queen and the state.

But time pressed: the birds might take fright and fly. So,

---

[1] Mary's *knowledge* of the plot, which earlier catholic apologists denied, on the ground that the vital passages affecting the murder of the queen were probably interpolations by Phelippes (see Chantelauze, *Marie Stuart, son procès et son exécution*, pp. 57–64), is now generally admitted. J. H. Pollen writes: 'I accept the *textus receptus* [i.e. of the letter] throughout, apart from errors of translation. I believe the postscript was the only forgery which Phelippes was allowed' (*Mary Queen of Scots and the Babington Plot*, App. I, p. 32). Pollen also states: 'If the assassination was a crime, Mary was not free from guilt. If it was not a crime, but an inevitable incident in the struggle for liberty, Mary was free from blame' (ibid., Introduction, p. cxliv). Walsingham's biographer sums up the case as follows: 'On these grounds one is justified in concluding that unless further evidence can be produced to the contrary, the official version of Mary's letter to Babington is in all essential respects the correct version, and that Mary stands guilty of being implicated in Babington's conspiracy to murder Queen Elizabeth' (C. Read, *Mr. Secretary Walsingham*, ii. 44). But consult also Alan Gordon Smith, *The Babington Plot*, 1936, for the modern pro-Marian position.

early in August, without waiting for Babington's reply, he struck his blow. Mary's papers, jewellery, and money were seized at Chartley, and her secretaries arrested. Babington and his confederates were rounded up and lodged in the Tower, where they admitted their guilt. On 20 September, amid general rejoicing, the would-be assassins were dragged across London on hurdles to St. Giles's Fields, to be executed with the utmost barbarity which the treason law permitted. Their deaths were the occasion of numerous ballads, showing the widespread interest and emotion the plot had created.

The prisoner at Chartley still remained to be dealt with. It was the old problem back again in an acuter form, and Elizabeth was gravely perplexed. That Mary was guilty of being consentient to a plot against her life she had no doubt: the straight course was to commit her to the tender mercies of the law. The nation demanded it as a measure of self-preservation, and the statute of 1584 would provide sufficient legal cover. Other considerations were really irrelevant. Nevertheless Elizabeth was tormented by scruples. Mary was still a queen regnant in the eyes of the law, and the trial of a prince was without precedent in English history. Moreover, what would France and Scotland say if justice took its course and Mary was condemned? She was a queen dowager of France, and, if for no other reason, France had an interest in keeping her alive as a bar to the pretensions of Philip II. The king of Scotland, too, would certainly raise the point of honour. He could not be expected to consent to his mother's death, however lightly he might view her strait confinement. Altogether Elizabeth would have preferred, now as earlier, to let Mary live.

Meanwhile protestant England became a prey of rumours, circulated, no doubt, by Mary's enemies. It was reported that the queen had been assassinated, that civil war had broken out, that Parma had landed at Newcastle and Guise in Sussex. The musters were called out for the defence of the coast. The fleet was ordered to sea. The hunt for priests increased in vigour. Paulet became nervous and refused to be responsible for his charge if she remained at Chartley. The council was in favour of sending Mary to the Tower. Elizabeth would not hear of the Tower, nor would she hear of any other place, although many were suggested. Finally, however, she decided on Fotheringay, a royal castle in Northamptonshire. Early in

October, after prolonged deliberation, she appointed a commission consisting of thirty-six judges, peers, and privy councillors to meet there for the trial. It assembled on the 11th of the month, with instructions, laid down in accordance with the statute, to try and judge the queen of Scots. Mary, of course, refused to recognize the jurisdiction of this court, making the most of her unique position as a sovereign anointed prince, and descanting at great length on the injustice of her long imprisonment. Her remonstrances, however, had all been discounted, and the trial went forward notwithstanding.

In accordance with invariable practice in treason trials, Mary was denied the help of counsel, but she conducted her own case with superb confidence and not a little ability. She denied all cognizance of the plot, denied the authenticity of her letter to Babington, denied receiving letters from Babington. 'I would never make shipwreck of my soul', she said, 'by compassing the death of my dearest sister.' The only admission she would make was that she had sought help where she hoped to find it. She even rallied the lawyers, these 'sore fellows' who often make a good cause seem a bad one. But it was all in vain. The evidence against her—the confessions of Babington and of her own secretaries, not to mention the fatal letter she wrote to Babington—was overwhelming, irrefutable.

The court was about to proceed to judgement when Elizabeth's scruples again got the better of her: she prorogued it for ten days, summoning its members to London. Here, in the star chamber, the evidence was gone over again, and the commissioners unanimously found Mary guilty, not only as accessory and privy to the plot, but also as an imaginer and compasser of her majesty's destruction. Under the statute she thus became *ipso facto* incapable of succeeding to the crown. The queen and parliament were left to decide what should be done further; but the commissioners took occasion before they dispersed to relieve the anxieties of the king of Scotland by declaring that 'the sentence derogated nothing from him in title or honour'.

The verdict of parliament was a foregone conclusion. It met on 29 October, settled down to business on 5 November, and after several consultations both houses decided, as they did fourteen years before, to make a joint petition to the queen asking that 'a just sentence might be followed by as just an execution'. This was done on 12 November at Richmond.

Elizabeth's reply was that of an embarrassed woman. She did not know what to do, and virtually said so. In her speech, she alluded to the 'bottomless graces and immeasurable benefits' bestowed upon her by Almighty God; to the twenty-eight years of goodwill from her subjects—a wonder in itself; to her freedom from malice towards the queen of Scots, whom she would willingly have pardoned if only she had confessed to her treasons; to her confidence in God who would have given her grace to be prepared, if a 'bloody death' had come her way; to the 'nice' and 'precise' lawyers, who would have her proceed by ordinary law; to the high place occupied by princes, who must be careful that their proceedings are 'just and honourable'; to the peril in which she stood from assassins who, she knew, had taken an oath a short time ago, 'either to kill her or to be hanged themselves'; and, lastly, to the Bond of Association. A curious medley of emotions, hints, suggestions, and a significant appeal at the close! In short, the speech of a painfully distressed woman. Constitutional timidity in the face of an irrevocable act struggled with the desire to perform a plain duty which her people demanded. After three days' consideration, she sent a message asking whether 'some other way' might not be found. The only other way was to settle the crown on James and keep Mary in permanent solitary confinement. Parliament, however, confirmed its verdict, and a deputation returned to Richmond to uphold it with compelling arguments. Still Elizabeth was unconvinced. She delivered another speech, exposing the grounds of her scruples—the fear to spill the blood of a kinswoman—and ended by saying that they must be content with 'an answer answerless'. On 2 December parliament was prorogued to February, on the assumption that in the meantime the queen would publish the sentence against Mary. This she did without delay, to the great joy of London, which was illuminated to mark the occasion.

Mary had been shown the sentence before its publication, and warned that parliament had ratified it. But she showed no alarm at her desperate position. She would confess nothing, she said, because she had nothing to confess. 'Utterly void of all fear of harm', according to Paulet, she defied the government to do its worst. Perhaps she believed that Elizabeth would not dare to execute the sentence, or imagined that her hesitation, which was daily becoming more and more apparent, bespoke a cowardice on which she might safely rely. More probably, if we may judge by her actions and utterances, she had already made up her mind that death was now inevitable; and if die she must, she would do so in the role of a martyr. When Paulet removed her cloth of state, as a sign that she was now dead in the eye of the law, she hung a crucifix in its place. Becoming transfigured in the light of the coming 'martyrdom', she wrote to the pope committing into his hands the spiritual welfare of her son, and to the duke of Guise declaring that she was about to die for 'the maintenance and restoration of the catholic church in this unfortunate island'. The only thing she feared was that fate, or the malice of her enemies, would deprive her of this glorious and spectacular end.

While Mary thus reached her mount of transfiguration, Elizabeth wrestled alone with her unhappy lot, a victim to her own morbid imaginings. Ambassadors from France and Scotland presented themselves at court with vigorous pleas and petitions for clemency, which could not be ignored, however irritating they might be. It was only too apparent that the affairs of Mary Stuart, in this last phase as in all previous phases, were inextricably bound up with the general European situation. To endanger the completed alliance with Scotland or the goodwill of France, at a time when the great duel with Spain was looming over the horizon, was a heavy price to pay for ridding England of the enemy within the gate. To some extent Elizabeth's anxiety, in regard to Scotland, was relieved by the king's obvious and clearly expressed desire to retain her favour in view of his interest in the succession, and the Master of Gray whispered in her ear the significant words: 'Mortui non mordent.' In January 1587 the intercession of France was largely nullified by the discovery (or was it the invention?) of a fresh plot against the queen's life, emanating, it was said, from the French embassy in London. A 'great fear' swept over the country. It was reported that the Spaniards were at Milford, that Mary had escaped, that the northern counties were in revolt, that the capital was on fire. Elizabeth was heard to murmur the words: 'Aut fer, aut feri; ne feriare, feri.'[1] On 1 February she signed the death-warrant.

Even so, she could not bring herself to part with the document. She tried, in a moment of weakness, to get Paulet to play the executioner on his own responsibility, as a signatory

[1] i.e. Suffer or strike; in order not to be struck, strike.

to the Bond of Association; but the 'nice fellow' refused to soil his conscience with murder. At last Burghley took the intolerable situation in hand, and solved Elizabeth's dilemma for her. At a meeting held in his house on 3 February the privy council decided to brave the royal displeasure and to send off the warrant on the next day. Thus, on the night of the 7th, all unknown to the queen, Mary was told to prepare for death at eight o'clock the following morning. She received the news calmly, supped cheerfully, busied herself with correspondence most of the night, giving instructions for the disposal of her personal effects and jewellery. At two in the morning she slept for a little; and then, at the appointed hour, she was summoned to the scaffold in the great hall of the castle. Here she died, in the presence of her ladies-in-waiting, her surgeon, her apothecary, and Andrew Melvil, the master of her household. In London, when the news arrived, on the following afternoon, the church bells were rung, bonfires lit, and people held banquets in the streets. The festivities lasted for more than a week, in token of the great deliverance.

Elizabeth took no part in the rejoicing. She grieved: she wept: she stormed at the ministers who had acted without her authority. Whether her emotions were real or simulated it is impossible to say. The most charitable explanation is that they were partly true and partly fictitious. Certainly the victims of her wrath had no illusions about the vigour with which it was expressed. Hatton, who as chancellor had affixed the great seal to the warrant, was petrified with fright. Burghley was excluded from the royal presence, and sorely troubled. So, too, was Leicester. And Walsingham only escaped the tempest by temporarily taking refuge in his house at Barn Elms, under pretext of sickness. Beale, who had carried the warrant to Fotheringay, was relegated to a subordinate post at York; while Davison, the unfortunate secretary of state, who had allowed it to pass out of his keeping, was heavily fined and committed to the Tower, where he remained for more than a year and a half.[1] These punitive measures were necessary if Elizabeth desired to give substance to the legend that the execution of Mary was a 'deplorable accident', for which she at least was not responsible. It was an unworthy subterfuge, no less specious than Catherine

---

[1] His fine was subsequently remitted and he retained his fees as secretary till his death.

de Médicis's after the massacre of St. Bartholomew. The play-acting was continued almost to the point of absurdity when the distracted queen went into mourning, and authorized a public burial for Mary's body, with royal honours, in Peterborough cathedral.

Europe was not deceived. In Scotland there was a violent explosion of anger against Elizabeth, and a cry arose for re-prisals. Expecting immediate war, the borderers raided northern England, and for a time communications were interrupted between the two countries. Sir Robert Carey, who was dis-patched with an exculpatory letter from Elizabeth, was stopped at the frontier by the king's command, because of the 'fury of the people'. James, however, was astute enough to realize that however much the occasion might demand a display of filial wrath, war with England would only jeopardize his own inter-ests and ambitions. After a brief interval he professed himself satisfied with the official English version of what had happened. He was probably strengthened in his decision to avoid war by a pointed and significant letter from Walsingham to the Scot-tish chancellor, Maitland of Thirlstane, in which the veteran diplomatist showed that neutrality alone would safeguard the Stuart title to the English succession.

The uproar in Scotland was small compared with the whirl-wind of passion that shook France. In Paris the English am-bassadors, Stafford and Waad, were afraid to be seen in the streets, and were denied access to the court. Jacques de Guesle, the *procureur-général du roi*, drew up a juridical indictment of Mary's trial, which was forwarded by Henry III to England. Funeral orations, books, pamphlets, and poems flowed from the press, commemorating the 'martyrdom of the queen of Scotland', and attacking venomously the character and career of the 'Jezebel' who had put her to death—'this singular bastard and shameless harlot'. The chivalrous youth of the nation were urged to avenge the 'outrage':

> Ravagez-moi leur terre et faites abîmer,
> Sous le faix de vos pieds cette île dans la mer.

All this was to be expected from a country dominated by the catholic League and the duke of Guise. But Henry III had no desire, any more than James of Scotland, to be involved in a war with Elizabeth, especially when his own kingdom was torn by internal convulsions, and the Spanish menace, which threatened him even more than it did the English queen, was daily becoming graver. Still the fear of France operated strongly on Elizabeth until after the defeat of the Spanish fleet at Gravelines. The Gordian knot had been cut. The death of Mary Stuart had a simplifying effect on the problems with which England was confronted, for the catholic cause lost most of its driving force. Except for unforeseen circumstances, the succession was now assured to James, and the king of Scotland was certainly not a catholic. Consequently the hopes of the jesuits turned to Philip II and the infanta. This, in turn, had a repercussion on the attitude of the English catholics, who, while they might conceivably have fought for Mary, had no intention of helping to seat a Spaniard on the throne. Their patriotism, which was never really in doubt, received a brilliant vindication a year later, when the supreme question of the hour was the preservation of national independence.

The decision to launch a great armada against England probably took tangible form in the mind of Philip II during the summer of 1585. In June of that year Olivarez, the Spanish ambassador at the court of Pope Sixtus V, offered his master's forces for the enterprise, provided the pontiff was willing to contribute generously to the equipment of the expedition— 'much more than any one has hitherto imagined'. The gist of the Spanish plan was to represent the undertaking as essentially altruistic and unworldly. Much stress was therefore laid on the good of religion, the conversion of England, the avenging of the blood of the martyrs, the restoration of Mary Stuart to her rights, and the other advantages that might be expected to carry weight with the head of the church; and a discreet veil was drawn over the political motives actuating the king. But the pope was difficult to move. He was not only sceptical and distrustful of Spanish promises: he suspected that under the cover of 'serving the Lord' Philip really intended to reap some personal gain for himself, or, worse still, use the threat of invasion in order to extort a favourable peace from the English queen. As a matter of fact, if Sixtus had been able to read the dispatches that passed between Madrid and the Spanish embassy in Rome, he would have discovered that the king's main concern was to secure a controlling hand in the disposal of the

English succession, in the event of Elizabeth's overthrow. For more than a year Olivarez played his game of mystification at Rome, 'weaving his web' and 'placing his snares' about the pontiff, until at length, in December 1586, the contest ended with the conclusion of a contract pledging the Holy See to contribute a million crowns to the Spanish war chest. The cautious pope, however, stipulated that the payment of the money must depend upon results: the first instalment of 500,000 crowns being payable only after the armada landed in England, and the remainder in smaller sums of 100,000 every four months thereafter.

This was hardly what Philip wanted. He would have preferred to have the money in advance, and an absolutely free hand to determine the time of the expedition. But since the pope was inflexible on the point that the invasion must precede payment, he pocketed his disappointment and proceeded with the next stage of his machiavellian plan. In February 1587 Olivarez was instructed to obtain a secret brief declaring that, failing the queen of Scots, the right to the English succession fell to the king of Spain, in virtue of his descent from the house of Lancaster, and of a will[1] which, it was alleged, had been drawn up by Mary in his favour. If the pope showed any scruple in the matter, it was to be pointed out to him that his majesty could not undertake a war with England merely for the purpose of placing 'a young heretic like the king of Scotland' on the throne; but that there was no intention of adding England to the Spanish dominions, since the right was to be exercised not in the interest of the king himself, but in that of his daughter, the infanta Isabella. As for Mary Stuart, who had figured prominently in Philip's previous utterances on England's future, he was cynical enough to suggest that the heretics in England would almost certainly put her to death as soon as the invasion project materialized. Perhaps the wish was father to the thought; for with the mother out of the way the exclusion of the son on account of his heresy became a more practical proposition, and the king could go forward with his design in comparative confidence.

---

[1] In a letter to Mendoza (20 May 1586) Mary stated that she intended to make a will ceding her right to the English succession to King Philip, 'en cas que mon dit fils ne se réduise avant ma mort à la religion catholique'. This will, however, was never made (see *Scot. Hist. Rev.* xi. 338–44).

But the exclusion of the king of Scotland was a question on which there was bound to be a sharp division of opinion in the catholic world. France could not stand by neutral while Spain interfered with the natural order of the English succession to her own advantage. Nor was the duke of Guise, humble suitor to Spain though he was, likely to acquiesce in the deprivation of his Scottish kinsman without at least making a further attempt to secure his conversion. Europe also would be alarmed at the threat of a Spanish domination. Philip therefore addressed himself to meet these contingencies with accustomed subtlety and foresight. At Rome, Olivarez and the pro-Spanish cardinal, Caraffa, plied the pope with arguments to prove that the conversion of James was neither practicable nor wise, and that reliance on France was dangerous because of the understanding between that country and England. William Allen, who was shortly to be raised to the cardinalate at the request of Spain, was also briefed to plead the Spanish case in the name of the English catholics. In Paris, Mendoza spread the view that the exclusion of the Scot was just as important for the catholic cause in Britain as the exclusion of Henry of Navarre was for the triumph of catholicism in France. At the same time he urged Guise, with substantial offers of assistance, to focus his attention on the overthrow of the huguenots. In short, every possible means was used to bend public opinion in those centres where opposition showed itself, or was feared, into acceptance of the Spanish policy. Eventually the superior weight of Spanish diplomacy bore down most of the obstacles; but no decision was arrived at with regard to the English succession, the matter being deferred, at the express wish of the pope, until after the conclusion of the war. It cannot be said, therefore, that the outcome of the negotiations was altogether satisfactory to Spain. If the expedition failed, the burden must fall entirely on the king; and if it succeeded, the fruits of victory would have to be shared with the pope.

While these diplomatic exchanges were going on, Philip was busy with his other preparations relative to the invasion, poring over memoirs on previous invasions and studying charts of the chief ports and landing-places. He was not without expert advice, for the question of how best to set about the enterprise had been settled by Santa Cruz in a detailed memorandum which this famous admiral had drawn up after his victory over

Strozzi at Terceira in 1582. Santa Cruz favoured a combined naval and military attack, delivered directly from Spain.[1] The advantage of such a plan was that it ensured unity of command during the most critical part of the operations, and involved no difficult system of co-ordination between the naval and military factors. Its disadvantage lay in the fact that it was exceedingly costly, and made no use of the splendid army of Parma in the Netherlands. Three and three-quarter million ducats—the sum demanded by Santa Cruz—was more than Philip could afford to spend on the overthrow of England. So this promising scheme was laid aside as impracticable. Even shorter shrift was given to another which emanated from the pen of Mendoza in December 1586. Mendoza was a soldier of great experience in continental wars, but he was little versed in major operations of the kind now contemplated, nor could he draft a scheme with the meticulous minuteness required by the king. Nevertheless the plan he submitted had merits of its own, and was well worth attention because of its salutary comments on the difficulties of sea enterprises. With commendable insight the ambassador pointed out that it was to the enemy's advantage to be attacked by a force 'which needs great sea fleets for its transport and maintenance'; that fleets are more subject to delays and disasters than land armies; and that in the event of a disaster the loss in ships, men, and guns cannot be replaced except with great difficulty. He therefore advised the king that the naval forces of Spain, already too exiguous for the empire's needs, should be kept for defensive purposes alone, and suggested that a comparatively small military force should be sent to assist the Scottish catholics in the catholicization of their country. If this were successful, and if, later, the English catholics rose, further measures might be taken to increase the strength of the Spaniards with a view to subjecting the whole island. 'It will be no small advantage to your Majesty', he commented, 'that the game should be played out on the English table, just as she [i.e. Elizabeth] has tried to make Flanders and France the arena.' But Philip was evidently not impressed with Mendoza's arguments. He had already made up his mind that the blow must be struck in England and not through Scotland, and that Parma's army was to provide the striking force. A military expedition from the Low Countries supported by a powerful

---

[1] 556 ships, carrying 85,000 landing troops, and 200 flat-bottomed boats.

naval armament from Spain—this was the plan which the king especially favoured, and to which he stood committed.

In making his decision to stake everything on a single throw of the dice, Philip relied to some extent on the help he believed he would receive from the catholics in England. His information on this very important point was derived from mentors like William Allen and Robert Persons, who, in the absence of more direct informants, constituted themselves the spokesmen of their fellow religionists within the enemy country. But neither of these men, however much they were cognizant of the opinion prevailing among the exiles on the Continent, really knew the temper and bearing of the catholics at home during the critical years immediately before the invasion. Thus it was the biased views of those whom self-inflicted banishment had soured and embittered that reached the king's ears rather than the authentic voice of the English catholics. Both Allen and Persons held the view that to be a good catholic was synonymous with being pro-Spanish in politics. Of the intense patriotism which now surged through England they knew and cared nothing. Their own love of their native country was eclipsed by a deeper attachment to the cause for which they would willingly have given their lives. As early as 1582 Persons had asserted in all seriousness that 'almost all catholics without a single exception regard the invasion with approval. Nay, they even burn with longing for the undertaking.' Consequently by 1585 it was generally believed among Spanish diplomatists that if an invasion of England took place it would be supported by a general rising within the country; and a year later a list was compiled for the king of Spain stating the numbers likely to take part in it. The 'Catholic army' was placed by the anonymous informer at the remarkable figure of 25,000! The grotesque character of the report is apparent from its confident assertion that 'almost the whole' of Yorkshire was ready to take up arms. If the true opinion of the English catholics is to be sought for anywhere, it is to be found, not in the biased reports of Spanish intelligencers, but in the glowing words of the Campion ballad.[1]

So badly did Allen misinterpret the feelings of his countrymen in England that after his promotion to cardinal rank in August 1587 he composed a manifesto justifying the invasion, and

[1] See p. 187.

addressed an admonition to the nobility and people of England, urging them to assist the invader on peril of their souls. He was repeating, though probably unaware of it, the tactics of the French Leaguers and of Condé and Coligny, when they bartered the integrity of their country for the help of the foreigner. Nevertheless it was on such false hopes that the king of Spain partially depended for the success of his expedition.

The first reports of Spanish preparations reached England in December 1585; but they were so uncertain that the council did not begin to take precautionary measures for another six months. In July 1586 orders were issued for the mustering of foot-bands by the lords-lieutenant of the shires, the training of men in the use of the arquebus, the setting of watches in the towns by night, the preparation of beacons, the rounding up of seminarists and all who spread seditious rumours. In August alarm was created by the report of a French landing in Sussex, and emergency mobilization orders were issued. Another scare followed in September, when rumours were circulated of a Spanish fleet off Conquet in Brittany. But by November the tension had subsided, and England passed into the new year still nominally at peace. In the meantime, however, Philip had sent instructions to the duke of Parma to carry out his preparations on the coast of Flanders, and to be ready by the summer of 1587; and for nearly a year thousands of workmen were employed in deepening and widening the canals between the Scheldt above Antwerp and the towns of Ghent, Bruges, Nieuport, and Dunkirk, improvising dockyards for the construction of flat-bottomed boats, and making the other arrangements for the transport of the expeditionary force to England. At the same time the mobilization of the fleet in Cadiz harbour was proceeding according to plan, and Philip was making frantic efforts to learn from Mendoza the state of the English preparations. This last point was of capital importance, because the assembling ships were absolutely at the mercy of a raid from England. But in spite of all Mendoza's devices he could obtain very little news from the English ports, so great was the secrecy preserved, and so strictly were strangers watched. On the other hand, Walsingham's excellent spy service kept England closely in touch with every stage of the Spanish preparations. The result was that when the concentration at Cadiz was well advanced in the spring of 1587 Drake was released from

Plymouth on 12 April, with a roving commission to 'distress' it in every way possible—to impeach the assembling of the king of Spain's ships, to cut off their supplies of victuals, to follow them up and fall upon them if they had already set sail for England, to intercept galleons from the East and West Indies, and, above all, to do what damage he could 'within the havens themselves'. Mendoza only learnt of the intended raid on the very eve of Drake's departure; and his warning letter was not received by the king until the English had entered Cadiz harbour, or possibly a little later! Thus the execution carried out among the defenceless Spanish ships was considerable. Thousands of tons of shipping and a vast quantity of stores were destroyed: Santa Cruz's own galleon was captured, gutted, and fired; and six vessels laden with provisions were taken as prizes. But the destruction was probably of less importance than the chaos created in the Spanish naval administration, for while Drake was on the coast, from April to June, not a ship could move without danger of capture. From his improvised base at Sagres Bay, the English commander was master of the situation. Finally, after challenging Santa Cruz at Lisbon to come out and fight, which the Spaniard refused to do, Drake stood away for the Azores, and when sixteen days out from Cape St. Vincent captured the Portuguese galleon, the *San Felipe*, worth nearly a million of our money. On 26 June he returned to Plymouth, conscious that if he had not ruined the king of Spain's plans he had at least delayed the sailing of the armada for another year.

As soon as the terror and confusion inspired by the raid was dispelled, work was resumed on the armada, losses were made good, and the concentration continued with accelerated pace. It would appear that the fear of renewed raiding in the spring decided Philip to dispatch the fleet against England in January (1588); but he was dissuaded from this folly by Santa Cruz, who asserted that March was the earliest practicable date. The plan of the campaign was communicated to Parma in September; and so badly was the secret kept that between this date and the end of the year all Europe was talking of the details of the Spanish strategy. 'The affair is so public', wrote Parma late in January, 'that I can assure your Majesty there is not a soldier but has something to say about it, and the details of it.' Less than three months later the despondency of Parma reached a climax. In a letter of 10 March he counselled the king to come to terms with the English, and so 'escape the danger of some disaster, causing you to fail to conquer England, while losing your hold here'. This was due not merely to the fact that the English had been forewarned, but also to the mortality among the troops in the Netherlands, and the shrinkage of their numbers from 30,000 to 17,000. But Philip was not to be turned from his purpose. Nor was he much disconcerted by the death of Santa Cruz, which had taken place early in February, although it was a patent fact that no other commander had the same experience in handling a great fleet in action. A new admiral was found in the duke of Medina Sidonia, a landsman without experience in sea-faring or war. 'I possess neither aptitude, ability, health, nor fortune for the expedition,' was his comment on learning of the king's decision. Nevertheless the luckless duke was ordered to take command at Lisbon on 8 February, and to be ready to start by 19 February. Finally, after much delay, the armada was got ready for sea in May, and put out from the Tagus in the last days of the month, wafted by the prayers and hopes of the whole Spanish nation.

There is little doubt that the king viewed its departure with some anxiety and misgiving. The year 1588 was regarded by Spanish soothsayers as pregnant with misfortune for their country; and the nervousness of the government is reflected in the Easter proclamation that masses should be celebrated throughout the country for the safety of the fleet. The king himself became as ascetic as a monk, spending many hours daily before the blessed sacrament, commending the enterprise to God. Before the stupendous nature of the issue, the religiosity of the Spanish temperament attained an intensity unparalleled since the days of the crusades. The banner borne by the fleet and blessed by the church was inscribed with the legend 'Essurge, Domine, et judica causam tuam!' Very different was the attitude in England, where the appeal to the God of Battles was mingled with a secular optimism based upon the consciousness of superior naval power and skill. Unlike Spain, England pinned her faith to the patriotism of her people. The defence of the gospel against Antichrist, the cry of the puritan section of the community, was certainly not that of the queen or the government. The difference in the mentality of the two peoples, each at the crisis of its fate, is depicted in the very names of their ships. The Spanish fleet was a calendar of saints—the *San Mateo*, *San Cristobal*, &c.: the English fleet boasted the purely secular names of the *Lion*, *Tiger*, *Dreadnought*, *Revenge*, &c. In fact the other-worldly piety of the middle ages was in conflict with a new order of things which shifted the centre of gravity from heaven to earth. When the decisive moment arrived, King Philip entered the sanctuary of his chapel; but Queen Elizabeth rode among her troops at Tilbury.

It is important to bear in mind that Spanish strategy in 1588 arose out of the fact that the king contemplated not a naval but a military conquest of England. The fleet was to be merely the instrument whereby the forces of the duke of Parma could be brought to English soil. This was in keeping with the Spanish king's confidence in his army, and also with his knowledge that England was militarily weak. Consequently the instructions issued to Medina Sidonia were so devised as to render it impossible for him to take the initiative in an independent naval engagement with the English fleet. He was to proceed to the English Channel and 'ascend' it as far as the 'Cape of Margate', where the junction with Parma might most easily be effected. No diversions, feints, or descents on the coast of Portugal, or of Spain, or at the Azores by Drake were to be allowed to deflect him from this prime objective. If, however (and here Philip showed his strategical grasp), the enemy followed, or came within striking distance, he was to be attacked, particularly if the encounter took place at the mouth of the Channel, because this would mean that the English forces were divided and could be separately beaten, or at least prevented from uniting. Finally, if he met with no obstruction until he encountered the united squadrons of Drake and Howard in the narrow seas, he was to give battle, 'trying to gain the weather gage and every other advantage'. The king adds that the enemy will seek to fight at long range, and that the Spanish tactics must consist in drawing him to close quarters. Supplementary instructions authorized Medina Sidonia, in the event of Parma being unable to cross, or of his army being unable to join him, to consider, in communication with Parma, whether the Isle of Wight might be seized and converted into a base for future operations. But on no account was this to be done during the passage up the Channel: it was merely a precautionary measure to be put into operation if the main design failed.

Many grave flaws have been pointed out in these famous instructions, such as the absence of accurate information where the actual junction with Parma was to take place, the belief that a battle could be joined in the Channel whenever the Spaniard desired it, and the lack of a sound system of co-ordinating the movements of the fleet and the army. But as a general strategical scheme it represents the Spanish school of thought to perfection. If the chief consideration in strategy be to overwhelm the enemy at a decisive point by superior numbers, and if the decisive point for the Spaniard was the passage between the Belgian and Kentish coasts, Philip was not far wrong when he insisted upon the attainment of this point as a principal objective. As an essential preliminary to further movements, his secondary schemes of battling in the Channel and of seizing the Isle of Wight were also perfectly feasible in case of failure in the major action. The real weakness of the plan, taken as a whole, was that it left out of account, and did not provide for, the use of a suitable fortified port on the coast of the Netherlands, where the entire expedition could assemble in safety. Possibly the Spanish king forgot that heavy warships could not approach the shallow Flemish ports and so give Parma the protection he needed, or rest at anchor until he was ready to come out. That Philip was informed of this all-important point is clear from a warning he received from Cabrera of Cordova: in whose opinion the junction of the armada and Parma's flotilla could not be achieved unless such a port was available, and if it was not available the enterprise ought to be abandoned. Of course, the only port capable of fulfilling the requirements was Flushing—and Flushing was in the hands of the enemy.

How did England propose to meet the threat of invasion? Charles, Lord Howard of Effingham, was appointed commander-in-chief on 21 December 1587; and in January three separate fleets were placed in commission for the defence of the realm: a grand fleet, under the lord admiral, consisting of sixteen powerful ships, with its base at Queenborough in the Thames, a light squadron under Sir Henry Palmer to patrol the narrow seas, with its headquarters at Dover, and Drake's smaller scouting force at Plymouth to watch the entrance to the Channel from the west. When reports began to filter in from the Spanish coast giving clearer information as to the size and probable date of departure of the armada, Howard moved the grand fleet from Queenborough to the Downs, and finally to Plymouth, where he joined Drake (May 1588). This rearrangement of England's forces held good until the two fleets met in the Channel in July. So far nothing was wrong with the English naval dispositions: Plymouth was the obvious base for a fleet operating against Spain, and Dover the proper place to keep an eye on Parma. But these were only the preliminary moves, on the completion of which the real strategical battle would begin. What use was to be made of the massed squadrons at Plymouth? Or, putting it otherwise, what counter-strategy did the English government adopt to check or defeat the Spanish scheme of attack? Obviously the only effective reply was to deny the Spaniards the advantage of time and place which they sought to secure; that is, to force the conflict at a point as far away from the critical area as possible—in short, in Spanish waters. This was the uniform advice of the naval commanders. In particular it was urgently put forward by Drake in a celebrated letter to the council. Nevertheless, in the face of expert counsel, the government remained wedded to the landsman's fear that if the naval forces of the realm were on the high seas or the Spanish coast England would be exposed to the enemy. The seas were broad, the possibility of accidents was great; and the Spaniards might slip past Howard by sailing northward to latitude 50° and then 'shoot over to this realm'. Consequently the utmost liberty the council would allow Howard was that he might make reconnaissances in force as far as the entrance to the Channel. The system of provisioning the fleet from month to month, against which Howard complained, also helped to reduce his radius of action, and some stress should perhaps be laid on the prevalence of foul weather during the early summer.

The principal reason for the queen's objection to the salutary measures proposed by her sea captains must be regarded as conjectural. It was probably dictated by military as well as political considerations. Elizabeth was firmly convinced that Anglo-Spanish differences could be liquidated without war, and to the very last minute she pinned her faith to the conferences taking place between Parma and her representatives at Brussels. Everyone else dismissed these as merely a Spanish stratagem: better an open trial by battle, they said, than clandestine and uncertain peace palavers. 'Therefore in my mind', wrote Hawkins, 'our profit and best assurance is to seek our peace by a determined and resolute war.' And again: 'In open and lawful wars, God will help us, for we defend the chief cause, our religion, God's own cause.' It was not until 17 June, when the negotiations with Parma broke down irremediably, owing to the publication of Cardinal Allen's manifesto calling upon the catholics in England to co-operate with the invading forces from Spain, that Howard at last received the liberty he had so long sought. On the 22nd he acknowledged the dispatch: on the following day his victuallers arrived at Plymouth; and shortly afterwards he was at sea on a grand reconnaissance with his squadrons strung out between Ushant and Scilly. While in this position, on 5 July, a Rochellese bark brought him news that the Spanish fleet had left the Tagus in May, had been dispersed by a gale, and was now taking refuge for repairs among the harbours of the Biscay coast of Spain. The wind being in the north, Howard at once held a council of war, and at 3 p.m. on 7 July gave orders to proceed to the coast of Spain. If the wind had held for two days and nights, and if his supplies had been sufficient, he would have fallen upon the helpless Spaniards with more disastrous effect than Drake did during the previous year. Unfortunately when he was eighty leagues south-west from Ushant the wind veered to the south, and fearing to be caught with insufficient provisions on the enemy coast, he turned back and made for Plymouth.

But if the wind balked Howard of his prey, it hastened the emergence of the armada from Corunna (12 July)[1] and on the whole favoured it during the remainder of its journey to the English Channel. At 4 p.m. on 19 July[2] Medina Sidonia sighted the Lizard, and at 7 p.m. gave orders to shorten sail three leagues from the shore. At dawn on the following day he had a glimpse of the beacon fires lit by the English; but it was late in the afternoon before he descried Howard's fleet through the mist and rain, slowly warping its way out of Plymouth. Contact was established between the two fleets on the 21st, and from then until 30 July,[3] when the armada escaped in a battered condition into the North Sea, a more or less continuous battle took place. It is not possible here to do more than chronicle

---

[1] 22 July according to the reformed Spanish Calendar (N.S.).
[2] 29 July (N.S.).
[3] 9 August (N.S.).

the outstanding features of that fateful ten days' struggle; nor perhaps is it necessary, for the story has been told fully and impartially by both Spanish and English naval historians.

Owing to the dispersion of the English forces required by the defensive strategy of the council, Howard could not afford at first to provoke a decisive fight with the Spaniards, but was compelled to hang on their heels, 'plucking their feathers', as he expressed it, when occasion offered. The consequence was that the Spanish fleet, keeping a close and compact array, continued its advance up the Channel as far as the roadstead of Calais without incurring serious material loss. Up to this point (27 July)[1] the vitality of the armada was the dominating fact of the situation. 'This is the greatest and strongest combination, to my understanding,' wrote the English admiral, 'that ever was in christendom,' a remark that seems to reveal his chagrin at not being able to break it up sooner than he did. But although Medina Sidonia was now well on the way to his objective, with his fleet practically intact, his difficulties and troubles were only beginning. Already his *morale* had been badly shaken by the elusive tactics of the English, who steadily refused to come to the 'handstroke'. He was worried also by the fear of being caught by foul weather without a safe port to fly to; and he was far from confident about effecting his junction with Parma, on which the success of the expedition depended. From the moment he entered the Channel this matter had caused him no little anxiety; and the nearer he approached the decisive theatre of action the stronger became his conviction that the safety of his ships was of even greater importance than that of Parma's army. On 28 July[2] he wrote to the duke stating that further advance of the fleet was impossible unless he came out to its rescue, 'so that we may go together and take some port where this armada may enter in safety'. Clearly Medina Sidonia was forgetting his instructions; for nothing was more certain than that Parma could not venture into the open with the English and Dutch squadrons blockading his ports, and the mastery of the sea still undecided, or in the hands of the enemy. In fact, the Spanish plan of campaign had come to a complete deadlock: the expeditionary force being bottled up in Flanders, and the necessary naval escort immobilized in the Calais roadstead some hundred miles away.

---

[1] 6 August (N.S.).   [2] 7 August (N.S.).

It was this unfortunate position of the Spaniards that gave Howard the opportunity of taking the initiative and of planning his master-stroke of the fire-ships. On the night of 28 July,[1] after being reinforced by Seymour and Winter, he sent in eight ships blazing with pitch and other combustibles among the anchored Spanish galleons, creating such confusion that a veritable *sauve qui peut* ensued. On the following day a general engagement took place—the decisive battle of Gravelines. The armada streamed off from Calais along the coast in the direction of Dunkirk, with the wind at south-west; and a running 'off-fight' was maintained from daybreak to dusk, of the kind that suited the genius of the English captains. So effective was the English gunfire that every great ship in the armada was 'very much spoiled'; and, to make matters worse, the wind shifted to the west-north-west, threatening to drive the entire fleet on the treacherous Ruytingen shoals. On the 30th[2] Medina Sidonia was informed by his pilots that if the wind held, only the mercy of God could save him from destruction. Five of his principal ships were now out of action, 'all their people being either slain or wounded', and the *San Felipe* and the *San Mateo* were wrecks on the Nieuport and Blankenberghe banks. Fortunately, when things were at their worst, and the sounding-lead of the flagship registered only six fathoms, the wind went back again to the south-west, and the desperate commander managed to pull the remainder of his fleet out of the shallows into the comparative safety of the North Sea. But his plight had now become such that no recovery was possible. Medina Sidonia therefore resigned himself to a northward course, hoping to reach Spain by circumnavigating the British Isles. Howard followed him as far as the Firth of Forth, and then broke off the pursuit.

Such, in brief, is the story of the first great sea-fight in which sailing-ships only were used; and the victory had gone to those who had mastered the science of the new type of fighting. The essential difference between the two fleets did not lie in the tonnage, which was about equal, but in the superior speed and seaworthiness of the English ships, and the heavier ordnance with which they were armed.[3] It must have been a bitter

---

[1] 7 August (N.S.).   [2] 9 August (N.S.).
[3] For a comparison of the two fleets see J. K. Laughton, *The Defeat of the Spanish Armada*, i, Introduction, pp. xxxix–lii; also J. S. Corbett, *Drake and the Tudor Navy*, ii, 179–90. The strength of the Spanish fleet, when it left the Tagus, was 130 ships

thought to the Spanish commander that long before he could lure the elusive enemy within range of his less effective armament the decks of his ships had become a shambles by artillery fire. But the English practice of salvo-firing without any attempt to grapple and board—the *gran furia de artilleria* of the 'off-fight'—was a new thing on the sea, a revolutionary departure from the accepted usage of centuries. The amazement of the Spaniards when they encountered it only serves to show how far behind they were in the technique of naval warfare.

As soon as the Spanish fleet vanished into the mists of the North Sea the wildest speculation prevailed not only as to its whereabouts but also as to what had happened in the fighting between Plymouth and the Belgian coast. The only people who knew the truth, so far as the truth could be known, were the English and the Dutch; but their knowledge was slow to gain credence in catholic countries, where the might of Spain was regarded as precluding any possibility of disaster. At first, rumour had it that a great victory had been won by the Spaniards, and there were rejoicings in Madrid and among the English, Scottish, and Irish catholics at Rome. Mendoza was probably responsible for this lying report, albeit he based his surmises on what purported to be information from authentic sources. Further heartening news to the Spaniards came from Dunkirk on 20 August, to the effect that a battle had taken place between the armada and the English fleet off Newcastle, in which the English lost forty ships and Sir John Hawkins went to the bottom with all his crew. On the following day a message from Calais stated that the armada was 'at a very fertile Norwegian island, where they will find abundance of victuals without resistance'. Still more fantastic was the belief entertained in Prague, on 29 August, that 8,000 Spaniards and 30 guns had been landed at Plymouth. By this time, however, responsible persons in the Spanish and papal diplomatic services had become alarmed at the continued absence of

and 30,000 men, of whom 19,000 were soldiers. It is doubtful, however, whether more than 120 ships entered the Channel, and the number of men probably did not exceed 24,000. The English fleet, reckoning all ships registered as in the queen's service during the season, consisted of 197 ships and 17,000 to 18,000 men, practically all of whom were seamen. Of the 197 English ships by far the greater number neither had, nor were expected to have, any part in the fighting. But the gun power on the English side was overwhelmingly preponderant, not only relatively to the tonnage of the ships, but also absolutely in the actual weight of the projectiles they could throw.

authentic news from Medina Sidonia, and anxiety began to replace the earlier optimism. In Madrid, at the beginning of September, the first disturbing tidings that a disaster had taken place caused the nuncio to write: 'God grant that the evil tidings are false and the good ones true!' But the king maintained a brave countenance, and gave no outward indication of what was passing through his mind. Meanwhile Medina Sidonia was ploughing his way southward along the western seaboard of the British Isles, leaving ship after ship behind him on the rocky Irish coast. It was late in September before he reached Santander with the first battered remnant of his fleet, full of sick and wounded—a vivid and heart-breaking testimony to the toll of the sea and of the English guns. When the king received the report from his grief-stricken commander of the disaster to his ships, he accepted it without rancour, gave orders for the hapless survivors to be properly looked after, and consoled himself with the melancholy reflection that the catastrophe had not been worse than it was.

Greater perhaps than the actual material loss,[1] which, after all, was not irremediable, was the shock to Spanish pride and the general stupefaction at the mysterious ways of Providence. In that superstitious age, when calamities were interpreted as judgements of God, it was difficult to avoid the conclusion that the hand of God seemed to be against Spain. Philip withdrew himself more than ever from the world, and tried to puzzle out the meaning of the calamity that had befallen his kingdom in the seclusion of the confessional. But his father confessor could supply him with no useful answer, nor was any sympathy vouchsafed to him either at Rome or elsewhere. On the contrary, the pope, who had not shown any degree of warmth for the crusade

---

[1] The loss sustained by the Spaniards cannot be accurately stated; but it has been estimated that 63 ships, or approximately half the armada, suffered destruction, as follows:

Abandoned to the enemy	2
Lost in France	3
Lost in Holland	2
Sunk in the battle	2
Wrecked in Scotland and Ireland	19
Fate unknown	35

The English loss in ships was nil. 'They did not, in all their sailing round about England, so much as sink or take one ship, bark, pinnace, or cockboat of ours, or even burn so much as one sheepcote in this land,' says an anonymous but reliable contemporary writer.

against England, expressed his admiration for the courage and bravery of the English queen, who, he said, would be his favourite daughter if only she were a catholic. Mendoza was ridiculed in the streets of Paris by workmen and children, who followed him with cries of 'Victoria, Victoria!' In the anti-Spanish world, again, jubilation at Spain's discomfiture was unrestrained. The Dutch struck a medal to commemorate England's victory, representing the terrestrial globe slipping from the Spanish grasp; and caricatures of the armada were printed with the legend: 'She came, she saw, and fled.'

Note:—The fullest and most vivid record of the armada is to be found in the *Correspondance de Philippe II sur les Affaires des Pays-Bas*: Tome III, 1585–1591, ed. Joseph Lefèvre, 1956.

XI

THE LATER YEARS OF THE REIGN

SELDOM has the strategic situation in a great war been so manifestly favourable to England as on the morrow after the battle of Gravelines. The enemy had struck his blow, and the blow had totally miscarried. The command of the sea rested with the English fleet; and a resolute, well-sustained counter-offensive, followed by occupation of the Azores or some part of the Spanish coast, might have laid King Philip's empire prostrate at Elizabeth's feet. So might a modern critic argue, and, having argued, proceed to judge the Elizabethan government for failing to deliver the *coup de grâce* when every circumstance was in its favour. But it should be remembered that combined military and naval operations, carried out at a distance of a thousand miles from home, were not understood in the sixteenth century, when standing armies were unknown and national resources were very limited. A rising in Portugal would undoubtedly have rendered the problem easier of solution; but in spite of Don Antonio's hopes and assurances in this direction there was little likelihood of such a rising taking place: the yoke of the Spaniard was too firmly planted on the neck of that country. Moreover, it may be doubted whether the queen really desired to fight her adversary to a finish. A war of annihilation, like that which the Venetians waged against the Genoese in the fourteenth century, was alien to the mind of a princess who believed in the virtue of the old maxim—'Sufficient unto the day is the evil thereof'. Never in her career did Elizabeth risk her all on a single throw of the dice. Thus England's war policy continued in the old groove of fighting the Spaniard mainly on land in alliance with the Dutch, and the struggle on the sea went on spasmodically without any approach to finality. The result was that Spain was given time to recover from her humiliation and to become far stronger as a sea power in the later years of the century than at any previous period in her history.

This inconclusive and unsatisfactory state of affairs is reflected in the atmosphere of uncertainty that prevailed in

England during the post-armada period and lasted unabated to the end of the reign. The confidence inspired by the triumph of 1588 was soon qualified by the presentiment that the Spaniard would come again—as come he did. The general uneasiness was probably increased by the continuance of jesuit propaganda and the publication of Persons's tract (1591),[1] comparing England to the barren fig-tree of the gospels, which the husbandman spared for another year to see if it brought forth fruit. Only far-seeing statesmen like Francis Bacon could afford to allude to Spain contemptuously as a 'barren seed plot of soldiers . . . not, in brief, an enemy to be feared by a nation seated, manned, furnished, and policied as is England'. Lesser minds turned to the perusal of military treatises, with a feeling that the land defence of the country required attention, and that the winds and waves might not be so friendly to England in the next encounter. Sir Henry Knyvett's pamphlet on *The Defence of the Realm* (1596), which advocated the compulsory military training of all men aged eighteen to fifty, is indicative of the widespread anxiety regarding the nation's second line of defence. To the same cause may be attributed the prevalence of invasion scares which kept the government continually on the *qui vive* throughout the nineties. In 1597, for example, a situation developed similar in some respects to that which existed two centuries later, when Napoleon's expeditionary force lay encamped at Ambleteuse and Boulogne. The offices of earl marshal and master of the ordnance, temporarily in abeyance, were re-created and invested with a new significance; and a committee of national defence sat in London, under the presidency of the earl of Essex, to co-ordinate and systematize the mobilization of the county levies. Efforts were made to organize the entire country south of the border defences into military districts under superintendents, so that a mobile army could be placed at the government's disposal for immediate service at the point of danger. The Thames defences were likewise overhauled, and a new system of signals prepared, by which the approach of the enemy could be communicated rapidly to Chatham, the strong point and rendezvous of the London area.

In addition, moreover, to the danger of a direct invasion from Spain, there was also the further possibility, after 1590, that the

---

[1] *Elizabethae Angliae Reginae hæresim Calvinianam propugnantis sævissimum in Catholicos sui regni edictum . . .* (the author used the pseudonym Andreas Philopater).

encroachment of the Spaniard on the Breton and Picardy coast might lead to the establishment of a Spanish naval base within easy striking distance of England—a contingency that roused a lively fear in the queen's mind, and led her to embark on military expeditions to France and to advance considerable sums of money to Henry IV. The situation in Ireland also had to be carefully watched for much the same reason; for a widespread rebellion there would provide Philip II with the opportunity he had long sought after, viz. of converting Ireland into a 'catholic Holland' on England's flank. The danger from this source reached a climax when the earl of Tyrone, in 1596, entered into military relations with Spain. Nor was Scotland wholly dependable, despite her king's expressions of goodwill, as the abortive conspiracy of the 'Spanish blanks'[1] clearly demonstrated. Altogether it is difficult to believe that the international problems confronting Elizabeth in the later years of her reign were appreciably less grave than at any previous period.

The government's anxiety also showed itself in other directions less directly connected with the military question. Catholics were watched with a vigilance and suspicion that made their lot more miserable; and the pursuit of priests was intensified. In 1591 a royal proclamation caused the establishment of commissions in every shire, with sub-commissions in the parishes, for the weekly examination of householders in respect of their beliefs and church attendance. Two years later (1593) parliament passed its last and severest statute against those who professed the Roman faith. By this act catholics were placed under a system of restriction not unlike that which a modern state adopts in time of epidemic, being prohibited from approaching within five miles of any corporate town; and catholic parents were in certain cases deprived of the right to educate their children. At the same time precautionary measures were taken to guard the queen from the shadowy figure of the assassin, and it became difficult for petitioners and even ambassadors to gain access to her presence. The execution of Dr. Lopez, the royal physician, for an alleged attempt to murder the queen by poison (1594) shows the strength of the public apprehension on this score, even if the evidence that sent him to the block was not conclusive.

From an economic point of view, too, the period was far

[1] 1592–3; see T. G. Law, *Collected Essays*, pp. 244–76.

from happy. The country seemed to emerge from one crisis only to fall into another. The eleven years of booming trade and general prosperity (1576–87) were followed by a series of lean years, in which industrial and commercial undertakings of all kinds languished, and losses were incurred by companies trafficking with overseas markets. This was partly due to the disturbing effects of the war, partly to the depredations of the Dunkirk pirates, who became more and more active, and partly to the competition of the Dutch as an exporting community. Harvests were frequently bad during the years 1594–8, and again in 1600, causing 'dearths', when the price of corn and provisions rose to unprecedented heights; while recurrent visitations of the plague in 1592, 1602, and 1603 swept off great numbers of the population, producing temporary cessations of trade.

Stow has a melancholy tale to tell of the years 1594–7. Of the former year he writes: 'This year, in the month of May, fell many great showers of rain, but in the months of June and July much more; for it commonly rained every day or night till S. James' Day, and two days after most extremely.' After admitting that the August harvest was 'fair', he continues dolefully: 'But in the month of September, fell great rains which raised high waters, such as stayed the carriages, and bore down bridges at Cambridge, Ware, and elsewhere in many places.' The aftermath was rising prices of corn and rye. But Stow is inclined to put the blame for the dearth as much on the merchants and over-exporting, as on the tempestuous weather. The dearth seems to have prevailed throughout 1595, when Danish rye and wheat had to be imported, and the prentices of London raided the market at Southwark 'taking' butter at 3d. a pound instead of 5d. demanded by the market people.[1] For this 'disorder' they suffered whipping, the pillory, and 'long imprisonment'. Meanwhile, 'all things else, whatsoever was sustenance for men', rose in price. And more trouble from excessive rains continued in 1596. Of 1597 Stow has this to say: 'This summer by reason of much rain, and great floods, corn waxed scant, so

---

[1] A lively discussion of the problem of 'dearth' is to be found in William Stafford's *Examination of Certain Complaints*, &c., for the year 1581 (New Shakespeare Society, 1876). Although Stafford is not an economist in the strict sense, his dialogue between a knight, merchant, doctor, husbandman, and craftsman is a shrewd analysis of the trouble.

as in London wheat was sold for 10 shillings a bushel, rye for 9 shillings, and oat-meal at 8 shillings.'

In the meantime there was distress in the clothing districts of Gloucestershire and Wiltshire; sheep farmers complained that they could not find a market for their wool at 'any reasonable price'; merchants were falling into bankruptcy from 'loss of traffic'; clothiers could not find a 'vent' for their cloth; and there were occasional bread riots. The chaos was increased by the heavy taxation necessitated by the growing war expenditure in the Netherlands, France, and Ireland, which was greater in the last fifteen years of the reign than in the preceding thirty years. The pressure of taxation is shown by the fact that between 1589 and 1603 the annual burden imposed by parliamentary subsidies was treble that of the earlier part of the reign. Parliament was fractious under the government's constant demand for money and more money. Yet, in spite of the greater sums raised by taxation, they only covered half of the war expenditure, and the queen had to sell crown lands in order to keep solvent.

Let us take first of all the naval war. For the reason already stated it was neither given pride of place in the defensive plans of the queen and her councillors, nor was it waged with sustained and concentrated vigour. There was no falling off in valour or seamanship among those who conducted the enterprises—Essex at Cadiz in 1596 and Cumberland at Porto Rico in 1598 worthily maintained the highest traditions of Elizabethan heroism on sea and land. But a certain lack of simplicity, coherence, and co-ordination in the more pretentious undertakings, due to misconceptions and faults in the drawing up of plans, dogged them with failure from the very start. The questions of victualling and military hygiene were little studied and quite unscientifically handled, men and treasure being squandered with a lavish incompetence that almost baffles description. Nor were the troops employed in attacks on the Spanish coast of the right sort or sufficiently well trained and equipped for their task. They were for the most part raw levies, 'pressed' into the service for the occasion, and stiffened with a leavening of veterans from the Low Countries. And in addition to the lack of organization and technique on the English side must be reckoned the fact that the growing efficiency of the Spanish coastal defences in Europe and America made it difficult to repeat the *coups* of pre-armada days, however cleverly planned. In fact the only branch of naval activity that offered much chance of success was the raiding of commerce and the capture of carracks and treasure-ships; although even here the gains were small in proportion to the outlay, owing to the adoption of the convoy system by Spain, and the efficiency of her intelligence service. All things considered, commerce-raiding was singularly unprofitable, only two carracks being captured in ten years, in 1592 and 1602 respectively; while not one treasure-consignment found its way into the hands of the raiders.

In 1589, when circumstances were especially favourable for a swift and decisive blow at the remnant of the armada lying helpless in the northern part of Spain, an expedition was prepared by Drake and Sir John Norreys, consisting of 150 ships and 18,000 men, and set sail for Lisbon in April, with the following elaborate instructions: to distress the ships of the king of Spain in their harbours, to attempt, if they judged the circumstances favourable, the reinstatement of Don Antonio in Portugal, and to seize an island of the Azores and hold it until the end of the war. In point of size it was the most formidable armament that assembled at Plymouth in the reign of Elizabeth; but in actual fact it was a joint-stock piratical enterprise rather than a properly equipped government undertaking. It was financed partly by the queen, partly by London merchants, and partly by the promoters themselves.[1] Only seven ships of the royal navy accompanied it, the rest being merchantmen and transports; and Don Antonio was present in person to give the intended operations against Lisbon a quasi-legitimate appearance and to rally the expected Portuguese malcontents as soon as the army set foot on his native soil. The first objective selected by the leaders was Corunna, which was plundered and burnt; then the troops were landed at Peniche to be conducted overland to the gates of Lisbon by Norreys, while Drake undertook to co-operate with the fleet in the Tagus. But the exhausting march across the burning sands, the outbreak of disease, the terrorized passivity of the Portuguese, and the failure of supplies, together with the lack of siege-artillery and the refusal of Drake

---

[1] The state of the public finances was now well-nigh desperate: money had to be raised from the London companies by letters of privy seal and forced loans: by the sale of Crown lands, parsonages, tithes, &c., in order to raise a sum of £126,305; and there were borrowings from Germany to the extent of £100,000 at 10 per cent.

to risk his ships under the guns of the Lisbon fortifications, prevented the attack on the city from being more than an impressive demonstration. The quixotic valour of the young earl of Essex,[1] who, having stolen away from court, joined the expedition off Corunna and challenged the Spanish commander of the Lisbon garrison to single-handed combat, did nothing to mitigate the bitterness of the retreat. After burning Vigo on the way homeward, the disappointed commanders reached England in the autumn, only to fall victims to the displeasure of the queen.[2]

While Drake and Norreys were on their way home, Frobisher and Cumberland set out from Plymouth with privately organized squadrons for the Spanish coast and the Azores, where they cruised about until the late autumn in search of the West Indian *flota* or other windfalls from the East Indies, Brazil, or the Rio de la Plata. But their main quarry escaped them, and although they made many captures of less value, some of these were lost in the return journey to England. The following summer saw Hawkins and Frobisher with fresh squadrons in Spanish waters; and Philip became so anxious for the safety of that year's *flota* or treasure-fleet that he took the unprecedented step of ordering it to remain in the West Indies until the spring of 1591. In the interval he equipped a powerful fleet under the command of Alonzo de Bazan to act as its convoy through the danger zone. This fleet sailed from Ferrol in August (1591), and making its way to the Azores fell suddenly on Sir Thomas Howard's squadron at Flores, where it was lying in wait for the *flota*. Howard managed to extricate the bulk of his ships without difficulty; but Sir Richard Grenville who commanded the *Revenge*, either because he did not see the signal for retreat in time or simply out of bravado, allowed himself to be trapped, and for fifteen hours fought a single-handed action against the massed galleons of Spain. With forty men killed and almost all the survivors wounded, with six feet of water in the hold and all powder spent, the crew eventually surrendered against Grenville's orders, who wished

---

[1] Essex (b. 1567; d. 1601), son of Walter Devereux, first earl of Essex, and Lettice Knollys, became Leicester's stepson when, in 1578, the latter married the countess of Essex after her first husband's death.

[2] For a full account of the enterprise see R. B. Wernham's 'Queen Elizabeth and the Portugal Expedition of 1589', in *Eng. Hist. Rev.*, 1951, pp. 1–26 and 194–218.

to blow up the ship, but being mortally wounded could not enforce his will. This remarkable display of berserker valour, which cast an immortal glamour about the name of Grenville, has to some extent obscured the real meaning of the episode, which ought to be regarded as the first triumph of Spain's new naval policy. The adoption of the convoy system was the solution of the *flota* problem.

There was little likelihood, however, of the plan being extended to all Spain's commercial routes; and the English continued their hunt for carracks unabated. In August 1592 a squadron captained by Sir John Burrows and financed by the queen, Raleigh, and London merchants intercepted and captured the *Madre de Dios*, a Portuguese galleon from the East Indies of 1,600 tons burden, off the island of Flores. In the indiscriminate plunder that ensued the English crews got out of hand, the ship's bills of lading disappeared, and a considerable part of the rich cargo, whose total value was estimated at £800,000, passed into the possession of ignorant seamen, who sold their takings to land-sharks at ridiculously cheap prices. For days Plymouth was like a Bartholomew Fair, the atmosphere reeking with the perfume of cinnamon, cloves, musk, and other oriental spices—so much so that Sir Robert Cecil, who went down to the west country to look after the queen's interests, wrote to his father that he 'could well smell' the ships before he reached Exeter. 'There never was such spoil,' he commented. In the final distribution of the prize-money Elizabeth netted between £60,000 and £90,000, her original contribution being £3,000.

In the meantime the centre of interest had veered from the high seas to France, where the protestant Navarre, who had succeeded to the throne in July 1589 on the assassination of Henry III, was struggling to assert his rights against the catholic League. So desperate were the prospects of Henry of Bourbon that he could maintain himself in the field only by the friendly assistance of Elizabeth in men, money, and munitions. A loan of £20,000 in September, followed by an expeditionary force of 4,000 men under Lord Willoughby, did something to restore the situation in the king's favour, and prepared the way for his victory over the League at the battle of Ivry (March 1590). But the triumph was short-lived. England's intervention provoked an appeal by the League to Philip II, who now came forward as the protector of the Crown of France (Jan. 1590), and offered his help on condition that certain towns were placed in his hands, and all harbours within the control of the League opened exclusively to Spanish warships. His intention was not merely to manœuvre himself into a commanding position with respect to the disposal of the French crown, but also to secure a suitable base for the invasion of England. After the conclusion of the agreement considerable Spanish forces began to move into France in support of the League. In August Parma swept down on Paris, where Henry IV had concentrated his army after the battle of Ivry, broke up the siege, and revictualled the city. A few months later (October) Don Juan d'Aguila landed with 3,000 Spaniards at Blavet in Upper Brittany, and proceeded in conjunction with the duc de Mercœur, the League commander in the province, to capture the town of Hennebon. These places were some distance to the south of Brest, whose governor, Sourdeac, was a loyal supporter of the king; but they were sufficiently near the channel coast to cause anxiety in England. Consequently, when the Breton estates applied to Elizabeth for help against the Spaniards, she dispatched Sir John Norreys with an army of 3,000 to Paimpol (May 1591) to co-operate with the royalist leader, the prince de Dombes. A detachment of this force, consisting of 600, was sent to Dieppe under Sir Roger Williams to keep open the main port of entry into Normandy for further English succours. Later, in August, the earl of Essex joined Williams with 3,600 well-equipped troops; and the entire body awaited the king's arrival from Noyon, where he had gone to meet his German mercenaries, before proceeding to the siege of Rouen.

Elizabeth was no philanthropist. Every penny she spent on France, either by way of loans to the king or for the equipment of expeditions, was carefully debited to the recipient's account. Her sole interest was to prevent the Spaniard from mastering Brittany, and the League from gaining control over the Norman ports. Norreys's task was to guard the coast from Brest to St. Malo, and Essex was instructed, much against his sense of chivalry, to retain his troops at Dieppe until the king was ready to invest Rouen. The result was that both armies quickly deteriorated—the one through excessive marching and countermarching in 'Base' (or lower) Brittany, the other through prolonged encampment in one place, desertions, and sickness. When at length Henry IV was ready to begin the attack on the city (October 1591) he found it impossible, owing to lack of artillery and man-power, to make any impression on its fortifications; and in January 1592 Essex was recalled to England. Three months later Parma, making another whirlwind raid from the Netherlands, broke up the siege, and strengthened the garrison of Paris with 1,200 Walloons. It was the last exploit of this great soldier, who died shortly after his return to Brussels. Meanwhile the Spaniards in Brittany inflicted a defeat on Norreys at Craon (May 1592).

It was now fairly evident to the French king that the English alliance alone could not save him from disaster; and the persistent demand of Elizabeth for the concession of a seaport in Brittany, which might be fortified and used as a base of operations, or as a place of retirement in case of need, roused his suspicions of her good faith. Neither would he sanction the dismemberment of his country, nor would he hand over an important town to be converted into another Brill or Flushing, even if the refusal involved him in difficulties with his imperious ally. Thus, while he continued to receive succour from England both in Normandy and Brittany during the year 1592–3, he decided that the only sure way to break the power of the League and rid himself of the Spanish menace was to proclaim himself publicly a catholic (July 1593). The political character of the conversion, summed up appropriately in the celebrated phrase 'Paris is worth a mass',[1] was apparent from the first; but it caused great excitement in protestant countries, especially in England, where it was held to presage an early settlement between France and Spain and the downfall of the 'common cause'. Actually it made no immediate change in the prospects of the king, nor did it affect the international relations of France for another four or five years.

The rebirth of patriotism and the expected rally of the catholics to the king's banner proved to be a very slow process; and before the year ended the alliance with England was renewed. It was almost immediately justified by events in Brittany. During the winter and the early spring of 1593–4 Don Juan, the Spanish commander at Blavet, moved some of his troops northwards to Crozon, where they constructed a fort

[1] 'Paris vaut une messe.'

with a view to cutting off Brest from the sea. In May they began to bring up their siege-guns in the direction of the fortress, and Sir John Norreys, writing to the queen, commented as follows: 'I think there never happened a more dangerous enterprise for the state of your majesty's country than this of the Spaniard to possess Brittany, which under humble correction I dare presume to say will prove as prejudicial for England as if they had possessed Ireland.' Needless to say the danger was fully understood by the queen, who was never a sluggard when dangerous enterprises were afoot; and in July preparations were made for the dispatch of a relief expedition under the joint command of Frobisher and Norreys, consisting of 8 warships and 4,000 men. On 10 August the contract was drawn up pledging the French king to bear all expenses of the undertaking: by mid-September the investment of Crozon by land and sea began; and on 7 November, supported by Frobisher's guns, Norreys carried the fort at the second assault. The 350 Spaniards who had defended it for some seven weeks were either put to death by the sword or perished in the sea, and the fort itself was razed to the ground. The death of Frobisher, who was mortally wounded in the attack, was the only serious loss the English force sustained.

Some idea of the strain which these expeditions to France, from the autumn of 1589 to the fall of Crozon, had imposed on England's resources may be gathered from the fact that 20,000 men had been dispatched overseas, and only about half the number returned. The effort is all the more remarkable when we remember that the army in Ireland had also been kept up to strength, and 4,000 troops maintained in the Netherlands, either in the permanent garrisons at Brill and Flushing or in the service of the Dutch. It was fortunate that affairs in the Netherlands were prospering under the leadership of Maurice of Nassau during this period, for again and again the expeditions to France had to be stiffened with contingents of veterans who had learnt their craft in the contest with Parma.

Owing to the queen's preoccupation with the war in France there had been a lull in major operations against Spain since the return of the Portugal expedition in 1589. But the year after the fall of Crozon saw the offensive resumed with the departure of a powerful squadron under the joint command of Drake and Hawkins for the West Indies. This expedition, which sailed in

August 1595 from Plymouth, consisted of 6 royal ships, 11 other ships, and 2,500 men, the latter being under the command of Sir Thomas Baskerville. Experience had shown that if the treasure-fleet of Spain was to be taken it would have to be attacked, not at the Azores or in Spanish waters, where adequate protection was provided, but at its point of departure in the Caribbean sea. Moreover, information had come to hand that the principal galleon of that year's *flota*, said to be worth £600,000, had been compelled to put in to the harbour of San Juan in Porto Rico, owing to injuries at sea. To capture this ship was part of the task allotted to Drake and Hawkins, after which they were to attack Panama and the Spanish settlements in the Pacific. For this latter task the army was provided.

For some reason or another, however, Drake and Hawkins made bad yoke-fellows; and calamity after calamity dogged their footsteps. First of all they attacked Las Palmas in the Canaries, but the attack failed; and when they crossed the Atlantic they found that news of their intentions had been circulated before their arrival among the Spanish settlements. Hawkins sickened and died as the ships reached Porto Rico, and was buried at sea. Drake, who then assumed sole command, completely failed to master the fortifications of San Juan, and made for the mainland, plundering and burning Rio de la Hacha, Santa Marta, and Nombre de Dios, none of which yielded much in the way of spoil. At the last-named place he landed Baskerville and his troops for the march across the isthmus to Panama. But again the English were balked of success; for they found the way blocked by the Spaniards in considerable numbers, and had to retreat to their ships. This final disappointment made a deep impression on Drake, who succumbed soon after to dysentery at the unhealthy island of Escudo and died at Porto Bello. It was a tragic end to the most brilliant career in Elizabethan history, and the tragedy was unrelieved by the consciousness of purpose achieved. Thus the second offensive against the dominions of King Philip proved to be as great a failure as the first; for with the death of the leaders, the enterprise collapsed, and Baskerville brought the ships back to England in the spring of 1596.

While the fate of the expedition was still unknown in England, the earl of Essex, Lord Charles Howard, and Sir Francis Vere, commander of the English army in the Netherlands, were hatching an ambitious plan for the invasion of Spain. In March the first moves were made to collect the necessary ships and to transport a strong force of veterans from the Netherlands; but the actual destination of the expedition was kept a profound secret, it being given out that its purpose was to cover the return of Drake and Hawkins from the West Indies. Suddenly, however, the most alarming news arrived from France, and for a brief space it appeared as if every ship and man would be required for a renewal of the war in that country. On 29 March the cardinal archduke Albert of Austria, Parma's successor in the governorship of the Netherlands, who had captured Doullens and Cambrai from Henry IV in the previous year, took advantage of Vere's withdrawal to make a swift descent on Calais, and seized the Risbank fort dominating the entrance to the harbour from the sea. By 7 April the town was in his hands and the attack on the citadel began. The speed and ease with which the success had been accomplished caused surprise and consternation in London, where the liveliest anxiety was expressed for the safety of the narrow seas and the security of the realm. Essex was immediately ordered to suspend his preparations for the projected expedition to Spain, and to proceed to Dover to take charge of a Calais relief force. Yet although the urgency was great, Elizabeth hesitated to sanction its departure until she was assured by the king that her troops would be received into the garrison of Calais. It was her last effort to recover control over the seaport which her sister had lost, and she fondly believed that in his extremity Henry IV would consent to her desire. Down at Dover Essex was in a fever of impatience to be off. He could hear the Spanish guns 'playing with great fury' on the citadel; but week after week passed in futile palaver and still the relief force remained confined to port. At length on 29 April the garrison capitulated, and the archduke entered into possession of the most coveted fortress on the northern coast of France, within easy striking distance of England.

The most effective reply to this new threat was to release Essex with all speed for his enterprise against Spain. News of Drake's failure at Porto Rico also emphasized the need for an immediate offensive. Consequently on 3 June the best equipped of all the expeditions that left England for Spanish waters in the reign of Elizabeth set sail for Cadiz. It comprised 17 ships of the royal navy, 47 other warships, and a Dutch squadron of 18, together with 6,000 or 8,000 well-trained troops under the command of Sir Francis Vere. Apart from the three leaders, Essex, Howard, and Vere, who formed a remarkable trio of initiative, prudence, and science, the subordinate commanders —Sir Walter Raleigh, Sir Thomas Howard, Baskerville, Amyas Preston, Sir Conyers Clifford, Sir George Carew, Sir John Wingfield, and Sir Charles Blount—were all men of mark in the naval and military world of the time. So well was the secret of the expedition kept that when it reached Cadiz, on 20 June, the Spaniards were completely taken by surprise. Not only was the city captured by assault, but the Spaniards had to burn the *flota*, which was sheltering in the harbour, in order to prevent it from falling into the hands of the English. Twelve million ducats were thus lost to King Philip. Essex originally intended to remain in occupation of Cadiz for an unlimited period, and doubtless would have done so, but his supplies failed him and there was a general desire to return to England on the completion of the operations: consequently he contented himself with the sack of Cadiz, which he left in flames on 5 July. On the homeward journey two other towns, Faro and Loulé, were subjected to the same fate. It was a brilliant display of the might of England on sea and land, a revival of the Drake 'touch' at its best.

Essex was now at the peak of his fame. His climb to greatness had been phenomenal. From the moment he had set foot in the court (1577), under the patronage of his stepfather, Leicester, he caught the eye of the fastidious queen, who 'loved him for his goodly person, his urbanity, and his innate courtesy'. He had walked beside her when she rode in state, holding her bridle rein as Master of the Horse; and he had often passed the evening with her 'playing at cards or other game until the birds sing in the morning'. When life at court palled, as it frequently did, since he had neither aptitude nor liking for the 'Aulical function', he made his escape abroad and sought fame as a soldier, being made a 'knight banneret' for bravery in the campaign that cost the gallant Sidney his life. Later he had served with Henry of Navarre in his struggle for the crown of France, winning the esteem of that incomparable man of war. Honours seemed to come easily and quickly, for he possessed all the qualities that, according to Machiavelli, fit a young man to master Fortune. He was audacious, impetuous, imperious.

After the crowning achievement at Cadiz it must have seemed to him that the world lay at his feet. The masses adored him; or, as a contemporary put it, 'he took a charter of the people's hearts which was never cancelled': the pulpits sounded his praises as a man of valour, justice, and wisdom; and some enthusiasts compared him with great generals of old. Thus at twenty-nine he stood out as the first courtier of the realm, the greatest swordsman of the age, the man on whose shoulders had fallen the mantles of both Leicester and Drake; and in addition, he had become one of the most generous dispensers of patronage in the kingdom.

Tall and handsome, but not the Adonis he is sometimes painted, he had been nurtured on the classics: Cambridge had set her stamp on him; and when Burghley died in 1598, she would make him her chancellor. His virile and versatile pen could create melodious verse, or limpid prose superior in quality to that of most contemporaries. Nothing was too arduous or too risky for his exuberant and untiring energy. His very soul cried out for action, adventure, achievement; and his love of fighting men was probably the deepest and most vivid thing in his nature. 'I do love them', he wrote, 'for they have been my companions both at home and abroad. . . . I find sweetness in their conversation, strong assistance in their employments with me, and happiness in their friendship.' In short, as Camden, who was the fairest of his critics remarked, 'No man was more ambitious of glory by virtue, and no man more careless of all things else.'

Yet this colourful man, looked to by all who coveted honours, social advancement, and glory, had weaknesses that, like a canker-worm at the root of the growing plant, brought him misery and eventual destruction. He was arrogant, vehement, uncontrollable—'soft to take offence, and hard to lay it down'; and quite unable to disguise his feelings or conceal his thoughts. He could fret and fume like a child when thwarted: he could even show contempt for the queen, when she ventured to differ from him—an unpardonable offence, which never ceased to rankle in her mind, and produced bitterness beyond redemption. And like Achilles, he could retire to his tent in a petulant mood and sulk for days or weeks, until either 'healing time' or an indulgent queen recalled him to his senses. In a word, he was the chartered libertine of the day: his ambition was boundless, his egotism superb; he must be *aut Caesar aut nullus*.

For some time the earl had been engaged in laying the foundations of what he called 'domestical greatness', presumably as a preparation for taking over the reins of power when they slipped from the nerveless grasp of the now aged Burghley. Death had already swept from his path all possible competitors among the elder generation of statesmen who had borne the burden and heat of the day; and the new 'jousters' for power in the political field, who were pressing forward into the magic circle, were all young men, in some respects less happily circumstanced than himself. Raleigh and Cobham headed the list—both potentially dangerous, particularly the brilliant but unstable Raleigh,[1] whose rise to fame had been almost as meteoric as Essex's own, and whose versatility was probably greater. But Raleigh never became at any time a popular figure; and his secret marriage to Elizabeth Throckmorton, one of the queen's maids of honour, had ostracized him from the court for five years. The two Bacons, Anthony and Francis, who were intellectually of the first rank, were also political aspirants; but Anthony was a sufferer from gout and other ailments, which rendered him more or less immobile; and both he and his brother were handicapped by the lack of a patron, since their uncle, Burghley, on whom they had to rely for backing, was devoted to the advancement of his own son Robert. In short, Robert Cecil was Essex's only serious rival; and he, too, suffered from a defect that might, in other circumstances, have proved fatal to his chances—he was a hunchback.

Nature had, indeed, played a scurvy trick on Burghley's younger son; but, as sometimes happens, she made amends for this by endowing him with a natural acuteness of mind, quick

---

[1] Raleigh was not a really serious competitor. Born some fifteen years before Essex (*c.* 1552), he had served in the huguenot wars, in the Netherlands, and in Ireland; became a great favourite at court after 1582; and was appointed captain of the guard in 1587. But he never reached the rank of privy councillor, or any place of first command. He was the great 'improviser' of the age—poet, philosopher, historian, soldier, privateersman, shipbuilder, member of parliament, vice-admiral, explorer, colonizer, and empire-builder. Every activity he took up seemed to 'sparkle at his touch' and then, unaccountably, to lose its fire as soon as his hand was withdrawn. It was not until death removed Essex from his path (1601) that Raleigh received his chance, and then it was too late: the glory of the reign had departed, the queen was an old woman, and Robert Cecil was in power.

observation, and an intense power of concentration that almost amounted to genius. In addition, he had the incomparable advantage of being nursed and 'groomed' by a jealous and distinguished parent, from a comparatively early age, for the highest office under the Crown. Thus in spite of his deformity, the young Cecil slipped with comparative ease into familiarity with affairs of state, and learned valuable lessons in diplomacy and statesmanship. No one knew better than he the whole political layout of the time; and he had studied with care the character, temper, and idiosyncrasies of his royal mistress. He could play the courtier to perfection: he never over-stepped his part, nor underestimated the difficulties that confronted him. In fact, without being in any way brilliant, he seemed to be the type of man who, like his father, could be trusted to navigate the ship of state without danger or disaster. His deformity earned for him the sobriquet of *Mons. le Bossu*; and his reputation for cunning stamped him as *Robert le Diable*. This was the man, then, who stood in Essex's path with a challenging mien.

The first significant step taken by the earl in the jostling for position had been to secure the services of Anthony Bacon, who, having just returned from a long sojourn abroad in 1592, was admirably suited to become the organizing genius of a widespread intelligence service, radiating from Gray's Inn and financed by the earl, that would keep his lordship in touch with what was happening in other countries. In this way Essex was able to compete with the Cecilian efficiency in supplying the queen with the latest news from Scotland, France, Spain, and elsewhere. It cost a fabulous and ruinous expenditure of money; but it enabled him to show the queen that he, too, had his finger on the pulse of Europe, and could play the statesman as well as anyone. In 1593 he was elevated to membership of the privy council, and soon after, it was said that 'all matters of intelligence are wholly in his hands, wherein the queen receiveth great liking'. This is perhaps a slight exaggeration; but there is no doubt at all that he was the outstanding authority on Spanish affairs, which the Cecils seem to have neglected.

The struggle began in earnest in 1594 over a question of patronage. In the spring of the year, the office of attorney-general fell vacant by the promotion of Sir Thomas Egerton to the mastership of the rolls. Essex set his heart on getting the vacancy for his protégé, Francis Bacon; but Cecil was in favour

of Edward Coke, who had the advantage of years. The following wordy conflict is said to have taken place between them:
'My Lord', said Cecil, 'the queen hath resolved ere five days
pass, without any further delay, to make an attorney-general.
I pray your lordship to let me know whom you will favour.'
Essex bridled at once. All the world, he said, knew that he
'stood for Francis Bacon': he therefore wondered that Sir Robert
should ask him such a question. 'Good lord', ejaculated Cecil,
'I wonder your lordship should go about to spend your strength
in so unlikely and impossible a manner. Can you name one
precedent for the promotion of so raw a youth to so great a
place?' (Cecil was younger than Bacon by some years.) Essex
retorted, with sarcasm: 'I have', he said, 'made no search for
precedents of young men who have filled the office of attorney-
general; but I could name to you, Sir Robert, a man younger
than Francis, less learned, and equally inexperienced, who
is seeking and striving with all his might, for an office of
far greater weight.' The reference was obvious: no adequate
riposte was possible. But Cecil went on to worsen his position
by suggesting that if Essex was willing, he might have the
solicitor-generalship for Bacon, as this would be more easy of
digestion to the queen. 'Digest me no digestions', exclaimed the
now irate earl; 'the attorneyship for Francis is that I must have;
and in that I will spend all my power, might, authority, and
amity, and with tooth and nail defend and procure the same
for him against whomsoever; and whosoever getteth this office
out of my hands, before he have it, it shall cost him the coming
by.' In the end Coke got the appointment; and, to Essex's
confusion and anger, Bacon not only failed in the matter of the
attorneyship, but also, a year later, was passed over for the
solicitorship, which went to Sergeant Fleming.

As we have seen, 1596 was to Essex an *annus mirabilis*. London
was dazzled by the brilliance of the Cadiz achievement, and
Anthony Bacon wrote jubilantly to a friend in Venice: 'Our
earl, God be thanked! hath with the bright beams of his valour
and virtue scattered the clouds and cleared the mists that
malicious envy had stirred up against his matchless merit;
which hath made the Old Fox[1] to crouch and whine.' But
'brother Francis', observing the effect of the triumph on the

---

[1] Burghley.

queen with a cold and unprejudiced eye, warned his patron
that the very glory of his success might also be the measure of
the danger in which he stood. In a letter full of prescience and
candour, he counselled his lordship to take heed of the advice
he had once given him, viz. that the most important thing—the
beginning of political wisdom—was to 'win the queen' at all
costs.[1] Then he pointed out that he must remove the impression
that his nature was 'opinionative and ungovernable': that since
her majesty 'loveth peace' and 'loveth not charge', a 'popular
reputation of a military dependence' was a 'dangerous image to
any monarch living, much more to a lady of her majesty's
apprehension'. Having thus diagnosed the nature of the danger
towards which Essex was inadvertently drifting, Bacon evolved
from his accumulated worldly wisdom the counter-measures
that might avoid it. Among other things he advised his patron
to avoid seeking the posts of earl marshal and master of the
ordnance 'because of their affinity with a martial greatness'.
Let him rather seek the office of lord privy seal because 'it hath
a kind of superintendance over the secretary'. Similarly he
should pretend to be 'as bookish as ever you were', and at the
same time 'take all occasions to speak against popularity and
popular courses vehemently and to tax it in all others'.

Admirable worldly wisdom! But quite impracticable to a man
of Essex's temperament. However, for a time he tried to follow
it in some of its branches; and then the strain seems to have been
too much, and Edward Reynolds noted that 'his lordship is
wearied, and scorneth the practices and dissembling courses of
this place' and would rather 'be rid of it all'. In short, the earl
could not change his nature. Nor could he school his imperious
mind to the give-and-take of the council table, or share in the
responsibility of formulating policy. The Baconian oracle had
spoken in vain: the effort to establish 'domestical greatness' had
not been a conspicuous success; and in 1597 Essex was back
again on the quest for military renown.

Meanwhile his rivals were collecting more honours and in-

[1] The prescience of Bacon was praiseworthy. He grasped the factor in the situation which Essex seems to have ignored in his furious quest for power, viz. the
queen herself. Elizabeth was undoubtedly ageing; but declining years had not
brought with them, as yet, any decay of her intellectual faculty. She was as little
inclined as ever to succumb to the control of a favourite, or to entrust the destiny
of the state to a man whose genius shone on the field of battle rather than in the
counsels of peace. Caution was what she wanted in her pilot.

fluence. In 1596, while Essex was away fighting on the beaches of Cadiz, Burghley's son quietly stepped into partnership with his father in the secretaryship, becoming in effect, if not in name, first officer of the Crown. About the same time Cobham was promoted warden of the Cinque Ports; and shortly afterwards, Sir Francis Vere, who was no lover of the earl, became governor of Brill—one of the cautionary towns on the coast of the Netherlands. Following hard upon this came Lord Charles Howard's advancement to the earldom of Nottingham—a title that placed him ahead of Essex in the prerogative of honour. What was especially annoying to the proud and touchy earl was the fact that on the charter or letters patent creating the honour were inscribed not only Howard's services in 1588, but also the words: 'and also jointly with our most dear cousin Robert earl of Essex, hath valiantly and honourably taken by open force the isle and city of Cadiz, and destroyed another whole fleet of the king of Spain'.

This was more than Essex could stomach. The wording of the award seemed to him to be a thinly veiled insult, obscuring his own brilliant services in the recent battle; and his passionate temper blinded him to the fact that the right of the Crown to grant promotions is absolute and above question. It was a grave mistake. But worse was to follow, when the queen made an effort to cool his smouldering wrath by appointing him earl marshal! It was obviously a sop—devised probably by Cecil—to pacify a ruffled and disappointed man; and in spite of Bacon's warning, and his own better thoughts, the disgruntled man accepted the appointment: he could hardly do otherwise in the circumstances. Nevertheless, it was an ominous step for anyone to take whose ultimate objective should have been 'domestical greatness'!

By this time the court was irretrievably divided into two warring factions—the Essex, Bacon, Knollys combine on the one hand, and the Cecil, Raleigh, Cobham on the other; and in 1599 tension was reaching the breaking-point. Burghley had vanished from the scene, having died in 1598; and the queen, presiding over the fluctuating struggle for power, place, and influence, was becoming irritable and irascible. In September Roland Whyte summed up the explosive state of affairs in a letter to Sir Robert Sidney, governor of Flushing: 'It is a very dangerous time here', he wrote, 'for the heads of both

factions being here a man cannot tell how to govern himself towards them. For here is such observation and prying into men's
actions that I hold them happy and blessed that live away.' On
the following day, he asked Sidney to burn the letters 'otherwise
he would be afraid to write'. Rumours of violence were also circulating; but who were to be the users of violence, and who the
victims no man could tell. The queen seemed to be losing that
firmness of grasp that had characterized her earlier rule.

Although Spain was now on the verge of a fresh bankruptcy,
the sack of Cadiz spurred on the king to revenge. In the summer
of 1596, after the English left the coast, he began to collect ships
and men for a second armada, and late in October the *adelantado*
(or governor of Castile) set sail from Ferrol with a fleet of over
a hundred ships and some 16,000 men. Rumour had it that part
of the armament was destined for Calais, where the archduke
was preparing to co-operate with it, and part for Ireland to
support the earl of Tyrone. But the winds and waves effectually
destroyed the hopes of the Spaniards. Before the *adelantado*'s
fleet had cleared Cape Finisterre it was dispersed and partially
wrecked by a gale; and the lateness of the season prevented any
possibility of renewing the attempt that year. Meanwhile elaborate preparations had been made in England to cope with the
danger; and by July of the following year (1597), in anticipation of a further effort by the *adelantado*, Essex, Howard, Vere,
and Raleigh were once more on the sea with 98 sail and 5,000
men *en route* for Ferrol. Their instructions were to burn the
armada in its own harbours or meet and destroy it on the high
seas, and thereafter proceed to the Azores and intercept the
flota. Bad weather, however, drove them back to port; and it was
not until 17 August that the expedition really got under way.
By this time news had come to hand that the *adelantado* would
not sail that year, and it was decided to abandon the attack on
Ferrol and make direct for the Azores. September saw the
English squadrons cruising about the islands in search of the
flota; but, as bad luck would have it, the Spanish ships slipped
past them and ran under the guns of Angra, where they were
perfectly safe from attack. Thereupon the English commanders,
considering the season too late for any longer stay at the Azores,
resolved to return.

On the very day on which they sailed, the *adelantado*, contrary to expectation, put out from Ferrol with his reconstituted fleet of 136 ships and troops to the number of 9,000. His intention was to land at Falmouth and establish a Spanish naval base on English soil—a plan very similar in idea to that of Essex in the previous year. The two fleets thus ploughed their way towards the English channel on converging courses but quite oblivious of each other's existence; while a feeling of profound security prevailed in England. Then suddenly, on 23 October, London was thrown into a state of consternation by a report from Sir Ferdinand Gorges at Plymouth that the Spanish fleet was on the high seas. As a matter of fact it had been seen off Blavet on 12 October; but immediately afterwards it ran into a storm, which scattered it and drove the main body in full retreat to Spain. Only a few ships which failed to see the signal to retire reached the English coast, and they made off again when they realized that they were isolated. The safe return of Essex when the panic was at its height helped to restore public confidence; and by the middle of November all anxiety was at an end for the year.

In May of the following year France abandoned the common cause and made peace with Spain at Vervins,[1] leaving England and Holland to continue the struggle alone, or settle their accounts as best they could with Philip. There was great debate in the council as to the future policy of the country. Essex was unhesitating in his advocacy of war: Burghley was for peace. It was the last appearance of the lord treasurer. When argument failed him he drew out a prayer book and pointed to the verse: 'Bloody and deceitful men shall not live out half their days.'[2] But he was unable to carry the council with him, and in August he died without seeing the fulfilment of his hopes. Little more than a month later he was followed to the grave by the king of Spain. It was as if fate had suddenly swept the pieces from the chess-board and reset them for a new

[1] For an account of the circumstances leading to the Treaty of Vervins, England's attitude to the peace negotiations, and the subsequent course of Anglo-French relations see Laffleur de Kermaingant, *Mission de Jean de Thuméry en Angleterre, 1598–1602* (1886); also Cheyney, *A History of England from the Defeat of the Armada to the Death of Elizabeth* (1914), and J. B. Black, *Elizabeth and Henry IV*, (1914). The principal interest of the period following the treaty, when England and the United Provinces were continuing the struggle with Spain, with France a neutral but subject to English and Dutch contraband laws, is the light thrown on the working of international law and the court of admiralty.

[2] Psalm lv, verse 23.

game. But there was to be no new game. The Dutch were adamant in their determination to fight their adversary to a conclusion, and England was too deeply committed to withdraw without loss of honour. So the war went on. There were brilliant successes like the battle of Nieuport (1600) and the defence of Ostend (1601), in which the English played a noble part; but everything else was overshadowed by the Irish question and the last act in the amazing drama of Essex's career.

Ireland was now uppermost in Elizabeth's thoughts,[1] for the disaster to Sir Henry Bagenall's army at the Yellow Ford on the Blackwater, in August 1598, seemed to portend a general uprising under Tyrone, and a sustained effort to drive the English out of Ireland once and for all. The emergency called for the strongest measures; but the problem was to discover a suitable commander-in-chief, since Sir Richard Bingham, the best soldier in the service, had just died in Dublin, and no one had a comparable experience. The queen and the council were favourable to the appointment of Charles Blount, Lord Mountjoy; but Essex demurred on the ground, apparently, that he was a man of little experience in war, of small estate, and 'too much drowned in book-learning'. The man to be sent, said the earl, should be 'some prime man of the nobility, strong in power, honour, and wealth, in favour with military men, who had been before general of an army'. So, said Camden, 'Essex seemed to point the finger to himself.' It is important, however, to observe that there were certain members of the council who 'wished him rather absent than present' and 'pricked him forward . . . setting before him the hope of eternal glory amongst posterity, and love and honour among the multitude'. The plain truth is that Essex allowed himself to be out-manœuvred by his enemies, and was 'jockeyed' into the Irish command.

Observe carefully the sentiments expressed in the following letter, which the earl sent to his friend Southampton on 4 January 1599, immediately after accepting the 'honour';—

Unto Ireland I go. The queen hath irrevocably decreed it; the council do passionately urge it, and I am tied to my reputation to use no tergiversation. And as it were *indecorum* to slip the collar now, so were it *minime tutum*, for Ireland would be lost, and although it perished by destiny, yet should I be accused for it, because I saw the

[1] See chapter xii for a consecutive account of the Irish question.

fire burn, was called to quench it, and yet gave no help. I am not ignorant what are the disadvantages of absence; the opportunities of practising enemies when they are neither encountered nor over-looked: the construction of princes under whom *magna fama* is more dangerous than *mala*, and *successus minus quam nullus*: the difficulties of a war where the rebel that hath been hitherto ever victorious is the least enemy that I shall have against me; for without an enemy, the disease of that country consumes our armies, and if they live, yet famine and nakedness make them lose both heart and strength. And if victuals be sent over, yet there will be no means to carry it. . . . All these things which I am like to see, I do foresee.

In the light of this remarkable letter, which hardly seems to support the view that the earl wanted the Irish command for himself, there can be little doubt that he was well aware of what awaited him, both in Ireland and in England. It was a thank-less task. Criticism would be prolific, malicious, unrelenting: his every act would be scrutinized by his enemies, his mistakes trumpeted abroad and possibly exaggerated: his successes be-littled or ridiculed; and his absence from court would ensure that machinations there would continue unrestricted. No wonder he wrote to the council before he even reached the scene of action: 'I provided for this service a breastplate and not a cuirass: that is, I am armed on the breast but not on the back.' The auguries were undoubtedly bad; and in the circumstances the only possible answer was for the earl to bring back 'rebellion broached on the point of his sword'. He had reached the supreme crisis of his career. If he failed, his military reputation would vanish 'like an unsubstantial pageant faded': nay, if he even partially failed, he would be ruined. Everyone knew that Ire-land would try him to the uttermost, and some hoped it would bring him down in the dust.

On 27 March 1599 he left London for Beaumaris, accom-panied by a brilliant company of officers, and applauded by the populace; and after running through a storm of thunder, hail, and rain—which some superstitious folk interpreted as a bad omen—he reached Helbry at the mouth of the Welsh Dee on 5 April. It took him some more days to batter his way on post-horses across Penman Mawr, in vile weather and through mountainous country, to the port of embarkation. Eventually he arrived in Dublin on 15 April, a much tempest-tossed man. All the way he had grumbled about the 'moist and rotten' country to which he was going, his 'rheumatic body', the state of the army he was to lead—news of which had come to him *en route*. Even more important was the information that reached him from Edward Reynolds, whom he had appointed to be his agent during his absence, and to look after his interests: 'There are', wrote Reynolds, 'but three of the Council whose affections I hold to be settled on you; the most just Lord Keeper, the most reverend Archbishop, and your Lordship's worthy uncle, Mr. Comptroller; the rest are either opposite or neuter.' Reynolds then proceeded to add a touch of realistic gloom, to the effect that, unless his lordship could get a strong party in the council to weaken the power of his opponents with the queen, 'whose ears are too open to suggesting tongues', and to provide him with supplies from time to time, he would find it impossible to go through with the great service he had undertaken. This passage must have struck a chill to the heart of the earl, albeit it was no more than a corroboration of his own forecast; the malign forces were already at work! And if we may argue from what actually happened shortly after the campaign in Ireland began, we might almost conclude that the Cecilian party in the council were none too anxious for the expedition to succeed.

Essex had not been more than a few weeks in Ireland— sufficient time to take a hurried glance over the situation—when the inevitable question of supplies, particularly the supply of horses, for the projected invasion of Ulster, began seriously to worry him. London got to know of it; and early in May we find Sir William Knollys writing a curiously significant letter to Cecil, which cannot be overlooked. 'I am *not* of opinion', said Knollys, 'you have reason to hearken to any new demands, though he [Essex] show a necessary reason touching the carriage horses, which are there [Ireland] not to be had, and without which he will not be able to march. . . .'[1] It certainly looks as if

---

[1] It seems pretty certain that the grave question of the horses was fully understood by the queen and the council in London. On 1 Dec. 1598, more than a year before Essex took up the Irish command, Elizabeth wrote to the lords justices, the lord-lieutenant (Ormonde), and the Irish council stating that she intended to send a powerful force to Ireland, and emphasizing that 'all good means' were to be used for the conservation of victuals and garrons (i.e. pack-horses) for the army when it arrived. Arrangements were to be made for the collecting of 200 carriage horses in England; and another 200 would be raised in Ireland, for which the necessary money would be provided—in all 400 horses. This was the situation when Essex took over the lord-lieutenancy. A fortnight after he arrived in Dublin, on 28 April, we find him writing to the queen and council that 'there are no means to carry

this extraordinary letter were designed to urge the secretary of state *not* to meet the earl's supplication, as one writer suggests;[1] and coming as it did from the earl's uncle, it throws a flood of light on the rapidly crumbling influence of the Devereux section in the council. But whatever we may think of the episode, there can be no doubt about the state of mind of the commander-in-chief on the eve of the most serious campaign in his career. While he was still at Helbry, waiting for transport, he had written bitterly to the council: 'I must save myself by protestation that it is not Tyrone and the Irish rebellion that amazeth me, but to see myself sent on such an errand, at such a time, with so little comfort and ability from the court of England to effect that I go about.'

Once in Dublin, however, Essex became his own dynamic self again. He summoned the Irish council for consultation, and explained his intention to get to grips with the 'capital traitor' Tyrone at the earliest possible moment. But when the military situation was examined—the state of the army, the time of the year, and the probable lack of fodder and grass for the beeves and horses—it was unanimously decided that the attack on Ulster would have to wait until summer was more advanced. With this decision Essex apparently concurred. The result was that early in May he set his army in motion, not northward to Ulster but southward into Leinster, 'the heart of the whole kingdom', and then into Munster. He justified this deviation on the ground that if he first reduced the south and south-west to order, he would then be able 'with more strength and less distraction to follow the main service in the north'. Whether

overland any competent provisions of dry victuals by reason of the country is not able to supply half so many carriage horses as is requisite for the necessary use of the army, though ready money should be paid for them; and touching garrons, which the country is bound by their tenures to answer to the general hosting, it is not possible to raise them before the time of the hosting, and yet then they will hardly be able to supply half their numbers . . . and as for the proportion of carriage horses levied in England, they are not yet here by reason of the contrariety of the wind.' A month later (26 May) the horses from England were still not forthcoming; and Sir George Carey, who had accompanied Essex as the new treasurer, wrote that he was 'persuaded that the want of carriage horses will be a great hindrance thereto [i.e. the campaign against Ulster] for the country being spoiled they will hardly be had'. No notice appears to have been taken of these appeals so long as Essex was in Ireland. And then after the whole sorry business was over, we find Lord Buckhurst ordering a search for the 'missing' horses, 'where they be', to have them accounted for and handed over to Mountjoy! Who, then, was it who sabotaged the campaign?

[1] Leo Hicks, S.J. in *Robert Cecil, Fr. Persons, and the Succession*, pp. 8, 9.

the earl did wisely in this, or not, is hardly a matter for the layman to decide; but when it was reported to the English privy council there was no official opposition or criticism.

It has been customary with historians to condemn Essex for 'wasting his time' fruitlessly in the south. But it should be borne in mind that the decision to move into Leinster was taken on purely military grounds, was unanimous, and represented the considered opinion of men who knew what they were talking about. In the second place, it would seem that before the campaign started, Essex was warned by his intelligence service that Tyrone was preparing for a raid into Munster in conjunction with the White Knight and other rebel chiefs. Thirdly, Mountjoy followed the same tactics a year later without any disapproval from London. In any case, to say that the campaign was 'a triumphal procession through lands already safe', of no significance or value whatever—as the earl's enemies averred at home—was not only foolish but also malicious. In fact, it gave Essex, as it gave Mountjoy later, time and opportunity to practise his raw levies in savage warfare and to give them a taste of manœuvring in bogs and in mountainous country; and this was what they badly needed. Be that as it may, however, the enterprise lasted from May until July, when the army returned to base in Dublin and began preparations for the reckoning with Tyrone. There were casualties to be looked after, depleted ranks to be filled, and stores to be replenished. Meanwhile the earl had turned his observations during the campaign into a summary report on the measures that would have to be taken if the subjugation of the island was to be accomplished rapidly and completely. On 25 June he sent off the document to the queen. It is undeniably a well-informed, clear-sighted and brief analysis of the circumstances confronting English soldiers in Irish warfare, the difficulties encountered, and the physique of the enemy. It might have served as a sort of blueprint for Mountjoy. But it contained two astonishing blunders. In the first place, the earl went out of his way to emphasize the difficulty of subduing the rebels by force, and commented that 'the war of force will be great, *costly*, and *long*'; and in the second place, he glanced back over his shoulders and made an uncomplimentary remark on the queen's favour to Raleigh and Cobham, 'when they wish the ill-success of your majesty's most important action'.

Essex, who had already been pin-pricked by the recall of three of his friends—Sir Christopher Blount, who was to have been promoted marshal of the forces and second in command, the earl of Southampton, and the earl of Rutland—was now to be subjected to a withering blast of the royal wrath, sedulously fanned and fed by his enemies in London, none of whom seems to have had any real experience in Irish campaigning, but who were jointly determined to destroy his reputation and prestige with the queen. Thus Elizabeth was led to believe that the capture of Cahir castle in Leinster was a matter of no account—nothing in fact but the taking of 'a native hold' from 'a rabble of rogues', that could easily have been done by the president of the province 'with a convenient addition to his numbers'. Gradually there had been built up in the royal mind the picture of a man who was consuming treasure, munitions, and lives on a colossal scale to no purpose, and perpetually deferring the essential matter of reducing Tyrone to obedience. Moreover, to make matters worse, it had come to her ears, indeed it was the common talk of certain circles in London, that this same man, who had been cautioned against conferring too many knighthoods for valour, was literally giving them away on a scale unprecedented. 'It is marvelled', said an observer, 'that this humour should so possess him, that not content with his first dozens and scores, he should thus fall to huddle them up by half hundreds and . . . that if he continues this course, he will shortly bring in tag and rag, cut and longtail, and so bring the order into contempt.' No wonder the queen's anger boiled up until it overflowed in scathing letters on 19 and 30 July and 14 September, which cumulatively reduced Essex to a state of dithering confusion and self-pity, so acute that he cried out: 'Since my services past deserve no more than banishment and proscription into the most cursed of all countries, with what expectation or to what end shall I live longer?'

What disturbed the unhappy man most of all was the cancellation of his 'licence' to return to England, which was included in his original orders and subject only to the provision of a substitute to govern in his absence. Now he was peremptorily told (30 July) to 'adventure not to come out of that kingdom by virtue of any former licence whatever', at least not 'until the Northern action be tried'. 'After you shall have certified us', ran the dispatch, 'to what form you have reduced

things in the north, what has been the success, and whom you
and the council could wish to leave with the charge behind—
that being done, you shall with all speed receive our warrant.'
The whole tone of this letter must have sounded to Essex like
a sentence of indefinite incarceration in the 'accursed country':
for the reckoning with Tyrone was still not in sight and the
prospect was bleak. It may have been at this juncture, therefore, that the earl began to entertain the dangerous and treasonable idea of bringing matters to a summary conclusion in
Ulster by negotiating a quick and provisional settlement with
the arch-rebel—in other words, the 'hollow peace' of Bellaclinthe, which played directly into the hands of the astute Irish
leader, and also alas! into the hands of the anti-Essex faction in
England.

Some critics assert that the earl ought now to have hurled all
his available forces against Ulster in a single concentrated blow,
regardless of risk, with a view to capturing the rebel and destroying his hide-out; but this is mere arm-chair tactics, betraying
a complete misunderstanding of the military situation. If Essex
had attempted, in response to the angry promptings and bitter
criticisms of the queen, to launch an all-out offensive against
Tyrone with the troops at his disposal, in the existing state
of their *morale*, he would have courted irretrievable disaster. On
21 August, just after hearing the news of the catastrophe to Sir
Conyers Clifford's force in the Curlews, while that experienced
general was preparing to deliver a flank attack on Ulster, in
support of the main attack by Essex from the Pale, the earl
summoned a council of his principal officers—lords, colonels,
knights—to consider 'her majesty's special commandment to
pull down the pride of the arch-traitor Tyrone, to redeem the
late scorn of the Curlews, and to hold up the reputation of the
army'. All who took part in the discussion—and there were no
silent tongues—were combatant officers in charge of regiments
and companies. A rational and realistic report was therefore the
outcome. Every factor in the situation was given its full weight:
the condition of the troops; the loss of irreplaceable veterans in
Clifford's army; the likelihood that the available force for the
main attack on Ulster—put at 3,500 or 4,000, many of whom
were fresh recruits from England—would be overwhelmed by
the combined forces of the north (Tyrone and O'Donnell); the
impossibility of establishing strongholds at Lough Foyle and

other places in Ulster at present; the impact on the army of the extensive desertions and sickness—real or feigned; and the uselessness of 'horse'—an asset only in 'open' fighting—in the close country of Ulster. For all these, and doubtless other reasons, the council unanimously agreed that the proposed invasion of Ulster was 'a course full of danger and of little or no hope'; and the report concluded with the words: 'We all were of opinion that we could not with duty to her majesty, and safety to this kingdom, advise or assent to the undertaking of any journey far north.' In short, the English army in Ireland was in a more or less demoralized state, and no one knew it so well as the officers. With extraordinary temerity, but with the spectacle of the Wicklow and Curlews' slaughter still fresh in his mind, Essex penned the following words to Elizabeth: 'your army, which never yet abandoned the body of any principal commander being dead, doth now run away from their chief commander being alone and in fight; and . . . your people had rather be hanged for cowardice, than killed or hurt in service.'

But the queen brushed aside this grave report with vituperation and sarcasm. After the lapse of several weeks when, in fact, Essex had at length set his army in motion against Tyrone, she wrote: 'We have seen a writing in manner of a catalogue, full of challenges that are impertinent, and of comparisons that are needless, such as hath not before this time been presented to a state, except it be done with the hope to terrify all men from censuring your proceedings.' All who attended the council, including men of the reputation and calibre of Sir Henry Docwra, Sir Edward Wingfield, Sir Samuel Bagwell, Sir Arthur Champernowne, &c., were lumped together as 'men of slender judgment'!

When Essex moved off north on 2 September his mind seems to have been made up that all he could safely accomplish was to stage a 'demonstration in force' along Ulster's southern boundary. He had no intention of attempting a penetration into the interior of the province: only if Tyrone allowed himself to be lured out into the open country would he engage him in battle. For this reason the English troops were provided with rations for no more than twenty days. Thus the two armies moved on parallel courses from 3 to 5 September—the English in the open, the Irish through the flanking woods and bogs, and nothing happened save an occasional skirmish. And then Tyrone begged for a parley. His first solicitation was rejected; but on 6 September Essex agreed to meet him at the ford of Bellaclinthe on the river Lagan. Here, unfortunately, a capital mistake was made, which was both irretrievable and unpardonable: for half an hour the earl and the Irish leader conversed without witnesses, Essex from the bank and Tyrone from horseback in midstream. No record was kept of the interview. But on the following day a further conference was held, with six staff officers of either side in attendance, and it was agreed that commissioners should draw up the terms of a truce. On 8 September the terms were mutually accepted and the truce was proclaimed. Immediately afterwards Essex dispersed his army and retired to Drogheda for medical treatment, while Tyrone withdrew into the interior of Ulster to consult with his ally O'Donnell.

The plan agreed upon at Bellaclinthe was briefly as follows: There was to be a cessation of arms, to last 'from six weeks to six weeks' until 1 May 1600, but terminable by fourteen days' notice from either side: no new garrisons were to be planted down during the truce: any Irish confederate [e.g. O'Donnell] refusing to be bound by the agreement could be dealt with by the lord-lieutenant; and Tyrone pledged himself to observe the settlement with an oath, while Essex gave his assurance in writing. Such was the *ridiculus mus* that emerged from this hastily conceived, irregular, and totally inadequate attempt to solve the Irish problem. Worse still: owing to the difficulty of communication with England and Essex's carelessness, Elizabeth was left very much in the dark as to what had actually happened. The net result of the truce was that Tyrone, who had given nothing away, gained more time for the expected Spanish assistance to arrive, and, moreover, he could renew the struggle when he was ready on a fortnight's notice. On the English side, the Pale secured a temporary freedom from inroads from Ulster during the coming winter months. But even this small benefit was problematical unless Essex remained personally in Ireland to watch over the situation. The earl decided otherwise. In defiance of the queen's stringent orders, but with a resolute determination to justify his actions by a personal interview, he made hurried arrangements for Ireland's government in his absence, and arrived in London on the morning of 28 September.

Elizabeth, who was at Nonsuch, was taken completely by surprise. She had just risen and was still *en déshabille* when the earl burst in upon her, bespattered with mud and mire after his break-neck gallop across the country; but she received him graciously, talking to him as if she were glad to see his safe return. In the afternoon, however, her attitude underwent a radical change: the council was summoned, and Essex was ordered to 'keep his chamber'; while his adversaries got their heads together behind the scene. Next day he was examined for three hours by the whole council on the following charges: his disobedience of the queen's will and letters by deserting his command; his presumptuous letters from Ireland; his contrary proceedings—contrary, that is, to what had been resolved upon; his rash manner of coming away; his making of so many 'idle' knights; and his overbold going to her majesty's bed-chamber. So reasonable, however, was Essex's defence that many of the council were in favour of leniency and release; but the queen was not appeased, and the earl was committed to the custody of Sir Thomas Egerton, the lord keeper, in York House. It was the beginning of a long term of imprisonment.

Meanwhile, Tyrone had taken to the fields again—the Irish truce was at an end; and Elizabeth's anger boiled up more furiously than ever. Essex must be taught a lesson: 'such contempt', she said, 'ought to be publicly punished'. Months of misery now supervened for the earl: he was not permitted to see his wife: he was suffering from stone in the kidney; and his beseeching letters to the queen were unanswered. 'By God's son', said the queen to Sir John Harington, who had just come over from Ireland, 'I am no queen. That man is above me. Who gave him commandment to come here so soon?' At Michaelmas Essex was deprived of his monopoly of sweet wines, the proceeds of which formed the main part of his income. 'An unruly beast', remarked Elizabeth, 'must be stopped of his provender.'

Of course the entire populace was with Essex: the church preached clemency, and prayers were offered up for the sufferer; while pamphlets and papers were scattered broadcast in the streets praising his virtues and libelling his supposed enemies. There were moments, it is true, when the queen relaxed her severity; but the breaking and crushing process did not cease. In December, Lady Essex who had at length secured admission to the prisoner—albeit by day only—found him so weak that 'there is little hope of his recovery': and about the same time the royal physicians reported gloomily: 'Salus magis optanda quam speranda fuit', showing that Elizabeth was fully aware of the situation at Essex House. But she was determined to exact the last ounce of punishment from the man who had dared to show contempt for her dignity and pride. Verily—

> Heaven has no rage like love to hatred turned,
> Nor Hell a fury like a woman scorned.

Eventually, in June 1600, after eight months confinement, the earl was brought before a court of eighteen commissioners, presided over by the lord keeper, and condemned to be deprived of his various offices as member of the privy council, earl marshal, and master of the ordnance; but he still remained a prisoner 'at the queen's pleasure'. Then, on 26 August, after beseeching letters and expressions of humble acquiescence— *Domina dedit, Domina abstulit, fiat voluntas Dominae*—Essex was at last given his freedom, albeit he was not permitted to approach the court. The queen's disapproval still hung like a cloud over his spirit, forbidding him even the modest satisfaction of 'kissing the fair corrective hand'. Friends urged him to 'yield to the times', and continue to seek the royal favour. He turned a deaf ear to their counsels. 'The queen', he said, 'had thrust him down into a private life; and he could not serve with base obsequiousness.'

It was impossible for such a tense situation to continue. The humiliated earl must either bow or break under the strain; and in November 1600 he broke, or, as Harington put it, 'he shifteth from sorrow and repentance to rage and rebellion' so suddenly that he seemed to be 'devoid of good reason as of a right mind'. He gave vent to disparaging remarks about the queen, scorning her beauty, calling her 'cankered', her mind being 'as crooked as her carcase'. 'The man's soul', thought Harington, 'seemeth tossed to and fro like the waves of a troubled sea.' The moral collapse was now inevitable. There had grown up in his tortured brain, as he brooded over his misfortunes, the conviction that he was the victim of a conspiracy: a sort of persecution mania seized upon him: he must take revenge on the evil men who had ruined him, and were probably bent upon taking his life: they must be removed from the court; and the queen must be brought to see the truth either by persuasion or, if necessary, by force. At the same time, moreover, there germinated in his mind the belief that Cecil and his followers were in favour of the

Spanish infanta—Clara Eugenia—succeeding to the English crown in preference to James VI of Scotland. If this were true, the state would be in danger of falling into the hands of England's inveterate enemy. It would be the end of all things. Thus did the earl turn plotter in order to destroy a plot. Speed was essential. He must warn the Scottish king of his suspicions, and invite him to send ambassadors to London to insist on an immediate declaration of his title and successional rights; and he himself would draw up their instructions. He would try to get his friend Mountjoy, who had taken over the Irish command, to bring an army to Wales. Meanwhile Essex House had been thrown open to sympathizers—puritan preachers, papists, soldiers out of employ, adventurers, a miscellany of discontented men. Soon a group of picked intimates, including the earl of Southampton, Sir Charles Danvers, Sir Ferdinand Gorges, Sir John Davies, and others, was formed to organize a plan of action; and the scene shifted to Drury House, the town residence of Southampton. Here the details of a *coup d'état*—seizing possession of the court and bringing pressure to bear on the queen, were concocted. It was believed that the earl could calculate on a following of 120, composed of two noblemen of equal rank with himself, several barons, and a considerable body of gentlemen.

At this point, however, disaster overtook the plotters. Gorges seems to have lost his nerve and communicated information to Raleigh: the council was quickly alerted; and it had probably come to Elizabeth's ears that Shakespeare's *Richard II* had been staged, with the sanction of the would-be revolutionaries, at the Globe theatre—an ominous event in itself. Essex was therefore 'sent for' by the council: he refused to obey the summons, pleading indisposition: the original plan, which had been prepared with great care, had now to be jettisoned, and an impromptu scheme substituted in a matter of hours. Everything went wrong. Essex was uncertain what to do in the emergency. Flight was considered only to be dropped. There remained the London populace, whose affection for the earl had been greatly stirred by his 'fireworks' at Cadiz, and was presumably still active. Why not tap this great reservoir of support? Besides, rumour had it that the city sheriff, Sir Thomas Smith, would lend a helping hand with a thousand trained men. Accordingly, on Sunday 8 February Essex decided to stake everything on

a swift and mad-cap irruption into the city at the head of 200
men-at-arms, 'a little before the end of the sermon at St. Pauls'.
Cloak and sword only was the order of the day—a signal that
a military *coup* was not intended. But all taking part had been
assured by the earl, in order to stir up their *morale*, that Raleigh
and Cobham were seeking his life. Meanwhile before the cavalcade left Essex House, it had been deemed advisable to lock up
the lord keeper, the earl of Worcester, Sir William Knollys,
and the lord chief justice, Sir John Popham, who had come
upon the scene unexpectedly at the queen's command to find
out the cause of all the hubbub.

Leaving the queen's representatives to cool their heels in
Essex House, the earl then dashed into the city, accompanied
by his men-at-arms, crying as he rode: 'For the Queen! For the
Queen! The crown of England is sold to the Spaniard! A plot
is laid for my life!' But the people were more amazed than
alarmed, and refused to move. Meanwhile the government proclaimed him a traitor, barricades were thrown up across the
principal thoroughfares, and troops under Sir John Leveson
occupied Ludgate. The attempt had failed; and Essex, finding
his way blocked by land, was compelled to return to his house
by water. Here he found his hostages flown: they had been released by Sir Ferdinand Gorges, one of his own supporters, who
went back with them to the palace. There was nothing to be
done but surrender to the queen's troops, who now surrounded
the house, and stand his trial for sedition.

Before a court of peers on 19 February 1601, Essex and his
aide-de-camp Southampton, were arraigned on a charge of
treason. They were accused of plotting to deprive the queen of
her crown and life: they had broken forth into open rebellion
by imprisoning the councillors of the realm, by stirring up the
Londoners with feigned tales, by setting upon the faithful
subjects of the city, and by defending the house (i.e. Essex
House) against the queen's forces. Essex tried hard to parry the
furious and venomous onslaughts of the prosecuting lawyers—
Yelverton, Coke, Bacon, and Popham—but they bore him down
by their oratory. The first compared him to Catiline: the second
hurled an insult at him:—'It were to be wished that this Robert
might be the last of his name, earl of Essex, who affected to be
Robert the first of that name, king of England'; and the third,
the ungrateful Bacon, accused him of 'deep dissimulation', liken-

ing him to the Athenian Pisistratus, who 'gashed his own body, and then showed it to the people as done by his adversaries'. This was the 'unkindest cut of all'. But to all charges, taunts, and accusations the main reply of the earl was that he had no other purpose but to prostrate himself at the queen's feet, to lay before her his just complaints, and to warn her of the dangers that threatened the country. Southampton threw himself on the royal mercy, pleading his love for Essex; but Sir Christopher Blount, a prominent figure in the whole affair, confessed that, although no violence was intended to the queen, he knew not 'whether the matter could have been accomplished without blood drawn from herself'.

In the end, the five ring-leaders—Essex, Blount, Cuff, Merrick, and Danvers—were sentenced to death and beheaded or hanged: Southampton secured a pardon; and the others were either fined or imprisoned. The interesting thing is that Essex, after putting in a kindly word for Southampton, remarked: 'I would not that any man should give the queen to understand that I condemn her mercy, which notwithstanding I believe I shall not fawningly beg.' Then, turning his eyes to the peers, he said: 'Although you have condemned me in a court of judgment, yet in the court of your conscience ye would absolve me, who have intended no harm against the prince.'

Altogether the episode is one of the most pathetic in the reign; and the inevitability of the end in no way detracts from its pathos. If Essex was to a large extent the architect of his own fate, there is, perhaps, some truth in the indulgent words written by his secretary, Sir Henry Wotton, many years after the event: 'He had to wrestle with a queen's declining, or rather with her very setting age, which, besides other respects, is commonly even of itself the more umbratious and apprehensive, as for the most part all horizons are charged with certain vapours towards their evening.' When he died he was only thirty-three and Elizabeth sixty-seven—a contrast in years that suggests, it has been said, the perennial conflict between youth and crabbèd age.

While the seemingly endless conflict with Spain was running its course, and the endemic troubles in Ireland were beginning to draw to a head in the great Tyrone rebellion, the Elizabethan government found itself face to face with a recrudescence of the unsolved—and insoluble—succession question, in a new and more urgent form than before. The queen of Scots was now dead; but her son was very much alive; and he was no longer the callow stripling depicted by Fontenay in 1584—vainglorious, sophisticated, proud of his learning, and preferring hunting to public business: the *vieux jeune homme* of the clear-sighted, critically-minded Frenchman. He was now twenty-five years of age, thinking seriously of marriage, eager to map out his future career with some degree of certainty, and also eager to cut a figure in European politics.

The dominant idea in his mind, however, was to discover ways and means of extracting from Elizabeth a public recognition of his claim to the English succession, which he felt—now that his mother had been removed from the scene—was his by right. In 1586, when Mary's doom was sealed by the Babington Plot, and sentence of death was authorized by both houses of parliament and published to the nation, James had sent Sir Robert Melville and the master of Gray to London, not so much to plead for his mother's life as to suggest that the successional right should now be demitted to him; but they had met with an uncompromising rebuff. 'How is it possible?', said Elizabeth; 'she is declared "inhabil" and can convey nothing.' When Gray tried to pursue the matter farther, he received a volley: 'What! get rid of one and have a worse in her place? Nay, then I put myself in a more miserable case than before. By God's passion, that were to cut my own throat. . . . No, by God, your master shall never be in that place.' And this same inflexibility prevailed as late as May 1601, when the earl of Mar and the abbot of Kinloss renewed the probe. 'Her majesty', wrote Sir Robert Cecil to Nicholson, the English ambassador in Edinburgh, 'gave nothing but negative answers; the matter being of so sour a nature to the queen, who loves neither importunity nor expostulation.' The only consolation vouchsafed to the impatient Scot was virtually the same as that given to his mother more than thirty years before, viz. a promise that no measure would be permitted to be 'brought forward' in the English parliament 'against any title he might pretend to the succession to the English crown'.

But James was nothing if not persistent, and time was fleeting. If he could not get what he wanted by 'expostulation', there were other and more subtle methods he could try. For example, he might play the role of a humble, docile nephew subservient to the whims and caprices of an ill-natured and *difficile* maiden aunt, who refuses to make him a beneficiary under her will, although he is the rightful legatee. He could do this in consideration of a financial *pourboire* in the shape of a pension. On the other hand, he might try to intimidate her into surrender by flirting with her enemies—in this case Spain, the papacy, and the Irish rebels. All of these methods the king experimented with, singly or in conjunction; for the policy of subserviency by itself did not appeal to his sense of self-respect. As we have seen, he secured his *pourboire* in 1586; but it was not enough, since he was chronically hard up, and the wealth of his kingdom—such as it was—was in the hands of the 'rude and ferocious' nobility, whose one aim in life was to keep him in the position of a *roi fainéant*, while they themselves exercised the power and executed justice as they pleased. Flirtation with Elizabeth's enemies was more alluring, more profitable, and it kept everybody guessing —a useful device in diplomacy. Of course the Kirk might prove troublesome if it came to its ears that the king was in communication with the papacy and the 'Most Catholic' ruler of Spain; but he could always fall back on the role of diligent protestant by attending sermons thrice a week. James was in his own estimation an adept at dissimulation and guile. Thus for many years the 'cold war' went on. The Elizabethan government retorted by methods no less guileful. Every English ambassador who went to Edinburgh was expected to play the double role of spy and intelligencer: his job was not only to transmit news but also to foment trouble, to engage in plots, and to do everything possible to maintain the English ascendancy— in other words, to keep Scotland in England's 'devotion'. Sir James Melville was not romancing when he wrote with sarcasm: 'It is the custom of some countries to hold their neighbours in civil discord, and send ambassadors to and fro to kindle fire under colour of concord.' At the same time, as an adjunct to this 'fire-raising' in Scotland, the English government had a useful instrument in James's mortal enemy, Francis Stewart, earl of Bothwell, who was not only subsidized from London, but permitted to organize punitive expeditions and plots from over the border on English soil.

The plain fact is that James was treated with the utmost distrust by both Burghley and his son; and Randolph's aphorism—

'he hath need of a long spoon that sups with the Devil'—was accepted as a working principle of English diplomacy towards Scotland. Thus, during the years 1596–8, when rumours from many sources were coming to Elizabeth's ears that James was in contact with the principal catholic powers abroad, with regard to the advancement of his title; when Poury Ogilvy was haunting the courts of Spain, Venice, and Rome, trying to persuade everyone that his master was ready to receive instruction in the catholic faith, and to send his son abroad for the same purpose; when Balfour of Burley, acting on instructions from the king, was reported to be purchasing arms from the grand duke of Tuscany; and when Spanish gold was believed to be pouring into the pockets of the northern earls—Huntly, Angus, and Errol—and James, after pronouncing a sentence or treason against them, allowed them to evade punishment; and finally, when the jesuit Persons was credited with the saying: 'May Jesus Christ make him [i.e. James] a catholic; for he would be a mirror to all the princes of Christendom'—when all this information, some of it true and some dubious, was circulating, it is not surprising that in London the fear of a re-catholicized Scotland, with all its possible dangers to England, should be taken seriously. Furthermore, it was about this time that a miscreant, Valentine Thomson by name, boasted that he had been employed by the Scottish king to murder Elizabeth. The queen wisely dismissed the tale as the dream of a madman; but there was such a hubbub that she requested Coke and Bacon to investigate the matter. James, however, was so outraged that he demanded a public refutation of the story. There was more excitement shortly afterwards, when it was reported to Cecil from continental sources—probably from Tuscany, where arms were being bought—that the king of Scotland did not intend to await the death of Elizabeth before he asserted his right to the throne.

In this connexion, it is interesting to note that, for some time back, James's interest in the English succession had drawn him into close relations with Essex who, like the Scot, was no lover of Cecil and his followers. The friendship flourished rapidly; and in 1598 it was said that the earl was entrusted by the king with matters he desired to be negotiated in London. Efforts were made by the Cecilian party to poison the king's mind against Essex, whom they represented to be himself bent upon the crown. But Mountjoy, a staunch friend of the earl, demolished the calumny: at the same time he counselled James not to suffer, if he could prevent it, that the government of England should be wholly in the hands of his enemies. Later, when Mountjoy was about to be sent over to Ireland, he urged the king to prepare an army and declare his intent, while he (Mountjoy) would assist him with the army in Ireland, consistently with his allegiance to the queen. James thought well of the matter; but it would be too much to say that these exchanges amounted to a military alliance, especially in view of Mountjoy's disclaimer. Since the latter was soon involved deeply in Irish affairs, and Essex was to lose his head for treason, we need not follow the matter any farther, except to say that Elizabeth was fully aware of the correspondence between them, and James suspected that she knew!

Meanwhile the Scottish king was moving heaven and earth to let his title be known abroad; and jurisconsults, genealogists, heralds, and literary men of adventurous disposition were called in to assist. Jessé, a Frenchman promoted to be the historiographer royal, was instructed to 'blaw abroad', and secretary Elphinstone discoursed learnedly on the merits of the Stuart claim. Walter Quin, an Irish scholar-poet, wrote Latin verses on the same theme, and Damon, another Frenchman, corrected the proofs, while the king himself ordered their publication by his agent Waldegrave—much to the latter's surprise and fear of consequences. At the same time, James seems to have become very touchy and perturbed about the effect of his mother's condemnation and death (for alleged treason) on his own claim transmitted through her. Could an attainted person transmit an untainted title? Hence his irritation at Spenser's *Faerie Queene* with its transparent allusion to Mary as the 'False Duessa'.

Why was James so nervous about his position *vis-à-vis* the crown; and why, in particular, was he so antagonistic to Sir Robert Cecil? These questions can only be answered by taking a leap forward to the time when Essex, on trial for treason (1601), accused Cecil of saying that the title of the Infanta to the English crown was as good as that of any other claimant. The accusation was instantly rebutted by the secretary in person, who begged permission to answer 'so false and foul a report'; and Essex was challenged to give the name of his informant. He named Sir William Knollys. Thereupon it transpired that Cecil had once remarked—referring to 'Dolman's' *Conference about the next Succession*—'Is it not a strange impudence in that "Dolman" to give an equal right to the succession of the crown to the infanta of Spain as to any other?' On this flimsy ground, according to Knollys, 'was based the slanders upon Mr. Secretary, wherof he is as clear as any man present'.

But Cecil's evident perturbation about so apparently trivial a matter has stimulated further inquiry into the circumstances. Fundamentally, of course, both Sir Robert and his father before him were opposed on principle to the Scottish king sitting on the throne of Elizabeth; and likewise both were in favour of peace with Spain, if it could be attained. But to describe the younger Cecil as 'Spanishly affected', in the sense that he would be a party to 'selling the English crown to the Spaniard'—and this was the gist of Essex's statement—was no better than a shot in the dark. Nevertheless, it is a curious fact that in April 1600 the English secretary of state took the trouble to write to the English ambassador in Edinburgh (Nicholson): 'I have thought good to let you know that we have a flying bruit that the king of Scots apprehendeth that those who wish well to the peace would be glad to have the infanta *pro sole oriente*. . . . I pray you learn whether there be any such opinion in the wiser sort. . . .' On 29 May Nicholson replied that the king had a strong feeling about the Spanish peace, and 'complained that more regard was had for a foreign archduke and the infanta than for him'. The ambassador evidently dismissed the matter as of little significance. Still, towards the close of the previous year (1599) it is definitely demonstrable that Sir Robert was interested in the infanta and her husband the Archduke Albert.

In September 1599 we find him communicating secretly with Filippo Corsini in the Netherlands, concerning the procurement of portraits of both these celebrities.[1] 'I have seen your letter', wrote Corsini (3 September), 'and seen your wish to have the picture'; and on 14 November the same correspondent reported that he had 'received from Antwerp the portraits of the infanta and the Archduke Albert. . . . They are a present to me, and I humbly beg that you will accept them. . . . You may be assured that this affair has been carried out in all secrecy.'

[1] See Leo Hicks, S. J., op. cit. p. 20.

Clearly the secretary's thoughts must have been running on the Spanish princess at the moment; and there may be a grain of truth—probably no more than a grain—in Essex's suspicions and fears.

Meanwhile the succession question was creating much interest abroad in high catholic circles, where it was felt that the early death of Elizabeth might well prove to be a turning-point in European history. The 'Dolman' treatise had already played up the claim of the infanta; and the indefatigable Persons, now head of the English college in Rome, was making himself the centre of a plot to prevent the accession of the unconverted king of Scots by bringing forward a trustworthy catholic successor, who would command the support of Spain and the papacy, and at the same time receive substantial backing in England. With this end in view Persons established contact with a certain Englishman (name not divulged) who professed to be in touch with, and the spokesman of, the 'politique' group in the council, viz. Sir Robert Cecil, Admiral Charles Howard, earl of Nottingham, and the treasurer, Lord Buckhurst. The news from England was sent in cipher to Persons, who deciphered it and passed it on with comments to Sessa, the Spanish ambassador in Rome, who in turn transmitted it to Madrid. The word 'politique', it should be noted, signified to Persons 'not ill-affected to the catholic religion'.[1]

The correspondence began about 25 April 1600, when it was reported that the so-called 'politiques' favoured the eldest daughter of the late earl of Derby as the heir to Elizabeth. 'These gentlemen', says the letter, 'think that this queen cannot live much longer and they fear the Scot. Hence they desire to open negotiations in favour of this lady.' An immediate reply is asked for on the point 'whether this would satisfy the king of Spain'. Persons acknowledged the receipt of the letter and counselled continuance of the negotiation, but pointed out the importance of finding out if 'the gentlemen' (i.e. the 'politiques') would agree to the 'lady'—in the event of her marriage—marrying a foreign prince agreeable to the king of Spain, and of course a catholic? 'Up to the present', commented Persons, 'this is the first proposition that has been made to his majesty by those who hold the reins of government and are in power' (in England).

---

[1] See Hicks, op. cit. pp. 20–47 for a fully documented record of the correspondence connected with the matter.

On 3 May, without awaiting replies from the jesuit or from the Spanish government, the correspondent in England wrote again. The gist of the communication was that he had talked with the men mentioned in his previous letter, and they had told him that if the king of Spain would come to a decision he would find many friends in England, heretics as well as catholics: that the catholics in England had no one to lead them in this matter; and that if the king of Scotland were a catholic they would prefer him, but since he is not, 'they say that most heretics and the catholics will support the infanta'. Eventually on 4 October news from England showed that the choice lay between the king of Scotland and the Spanish infanta, Clara Eugenia. This important information Persons passed on to Sessa with the following remark: 'Thus all parties in England are divided in upholding these two; and the counsellors above mentioned, especially the treasurer and secretary Cecil, and their adherents, are in doubt which of the two factions they ought to join, until they know what decision the king (Philip III) has made. They say, moreover, that they cannot postpone much further coming to terms with the king of Scotland if no decision is forthcoming; "because they are afraid of the queen dying and of what thereafter may be the aims of their enemy, the earl of Essex".' At the same time, continues Persons, 'these gentlemen protest explicitly that, so long as the queen lives, they are unwilling that any change should be made'.

Persons's analysis of the situation is interesting and may be summarized as follows. Since the king of Scotland was a heretic, it would be more advantageous for his majesty to support the archduke and the infanta; but 'it would also be no bad policy to keep the king of Scotland in play by fair words, and to feed his hopes to see if he is willing to be converted'. At the same time, he continues, 'in order not to forsake the catholics . . . it seems necessary for his majesty to declare himself forthwith to these English gentlemen, lest they may be lost to the cause, telling them that he intends to support the claim of the lady infanta very effectually with all his forces'.

These views were sent forward, through Sessa, to Madrid on 14 November 1600, together with another plea for urgency, saying that the time had come to communicate the whole plan to the pope, so that His Holiness may lend his aid, whether James of Scotland was converted or not. As a matter of fact,

Sessa had no belief in the possibility of the Scottish king's conversion, for the pope had told him that he had sent a hortatory brief to Edinburgh, and it had had no effect: the king had neither replied to it, nor shown any interest in it.

This was the position when, on 1 February 1601, the Spanish council of state advised the king to take the plunge, and Philip III concurred. '. . . having considered the matter and recommended it earnestly to God, I have decided that the succession to that kingdom [England] should be procured for the said infanta, not only because it seems a suitable choice for the end in view, the establishment, preservation, and increase of the catholic religion, and of the authority of the Holy See in that kingdom, as well as the welfare of its people, but also because of the qualities and virtues of the infanta.' It should be added, however, that part of the bargain was that as soon as the archduke and the infanta settled down in England, they would restore Flanders to Spain.

In the meantime, trouble began to brew in Rome. The pope in the course of a discussion with Persons, disclosed that while he was pleased to be informed of the great project, he foresaw difficulties. He agreed that the archduke and the infanta were the best claimants to oppose the Scottish king, since they were near England, and had Spanish support; but France would resent this apparent aggrandizement of Spain; indeed the union of England with Burgundy and Flanders would be a greater source of possible danger to her than the union of England and Scotland. Therefore, although the Holy See might welcome the formation of a strong catholic combination in the north, consisting of England and the Low Countries, it would be impossible for His Holiness to make a public declaration in favour of it because of the repercussions in France. Briefly, according to Sessa, 'there was no woman more careful not to arouse suspicions in her husband than was the pope as regards the French king'. But the success of Persons's scheme was imperilled from another quarter. A powerful campaign of slander and denigration of the jesuit order and its Spanish policy was in progress in Rome, led by Cardinal Ossat at the instigation of France; and a cry was raised that under the guise of religion they were aiming at nothing less than the subjection of England to the crown of Spain against the will of good English catholics.

Thus the elaborate and fantastic plan to seat the infanta on the English throne, engendered in the fertile brain of Persons, found its way into the limbo of 'pipe dreams'; and it received its final discharge from the minds of all who had become involved in it by a series of unpredictable events in England, namely, the tragedy of Essex—his revolt, imprisonment, trial, and execution. As by a bolt from the blue, Cecil now saw his one and only rival removed from his path; while at the same time, and for the same reason, the way was opened for reconciliation with James of Scotland. Even so, however, the establishment of good relations between them was by no means easily achieved: suspicion and distrust deeply rooted cannot be quickly uprooted. For one thing, James was uncertain to what extent—if any—he was 'touched' by the revelations made at the Essex trial; and above all, he was anxious to learn what Elizabeth knew and thought about his association with the earl. She had at first refused to give audience to his ambassadors, Mar and Kinloss; and when at length they were admitted to the presence, she dealt stiffly and roughly with them, for she knew all and was pained by what she knew. Actually, however, the great trial passed off without any implications, thanks no doubt to instructions from higher authority.

Being now assured by Elizabeth's apparent intention not to pursue the matter, and knowing that Cecil was now virtually 'king' in England, the cautious Scot prepared to carry out his *volte face*; and at the same time Cecil set about clearing himself of the old charge levelled against him that he favoured the Spanish infanta. And this he did, on 23 May 1601, with perfect aplomb in a secret, carefully worded letter to the king: it was his first.

> When I saw [he wrote] that all those whose eyes were blind to all but high imaginations, had left behind them the dregs of foul impressions against some ministers of this estate (especially against myself, as one that was sold over to the Spanish practise and swollen to the chin with other dangerous plots against your person) I did straight consider how necessary it would be for me . . . to pluck up quickly by the roots those gross inventions of conspiracies, because the multiplying still of such shadows upon me (holding the place I do) might prove in time the cause of some effects very prejudicial to both your majesties' fortunes.

Meanwhile James had dispatched a conciliatory epistle within a month of Essex's execution, assuring Cecil of the good report his ambassador had made of him, and commending to him

Lord Henry Howard as 'a sure and secret interpreter' between them in the opening of their minds to one another. The substance of Howard's commission was that the king approved Cecil's mistrust of the aspiring mind of Essex, since he took it for a sign that he would never allow that a subject should climb so high. But as for the earl's behaviour it was not for the king to judge of it, for although he loved him for his virtues, he was no ways obliged to embrace his quarrels, but to accept of every man according to his deserts. Thus the two planners clasped hands over the dead body of the earl.

The death of Essex removed not only the leader of the war party in England and the 'protector' of the puritans, but also one whom even the catholics appear to have trusted because of his generous outlook and professed attachment to toleration. For some time a movement had been afoot in the catholic camp to procure from the state some relaxation of the severe penal laws to which they were exposed, in return for a public avowal of their loyalty and disavowal of Spain as the national enemy. About 1590 a secular priest, Wryght, framed the question thus: 'Is it lawful for catholics in England to take up arms and in other ways defend the queen and the realm against the Spaniards?' It was a courageous thing to formulate such a question, but Wryght did more: he answered it in the affirmative, basing his argument on the demonstrable truth that the king of Spain was no true crusader for the faith but a time-server, who used religion merely as a cloak for political designs. Rome had therefore erred in making him the executor of the bull, and it was not incumbent upon catholics to follow the papal instructions. Rather, said the priest, let them defend their country, yield to the time, and make the best of their lot. In putting forward these views Wryght simply voiced an opinion that had been gradually leavening the whole lump of catholic discontent in England. Experience had shown that Elizabeth's throne was too securely established to be overturned, and the effort to destroy her had only made the situation harder to bear. Why, said the sufferers, in effect, must we be denied the comforts of religion, which we might enjoy in secret, and that freedom in temporal affairs, which would be ours as soon as the plotting ceased—for the sake of some hypothetical catholic England of the future? Could not a catholic church be created in England from the priests and the laity now in the country, with full recognition of papal supremacy in spiritual matters, but pledged to non-political action in the temporal sphere? Between this point of view and that of the jesuits there was a wide gulf fixed; but the opinion of those who stood for present alleviation, albeit they still were in a minority, was at least based upon tangible realities, while that of their opponents, the jesuits, was the outcome of a wild romanticism.

From the government standpoint, this division in the catholic ranks was eminently satisfactory; for a deadlock was reached during the nineties in the handling of the catholic question. Despite the increased severity of the penal laws, the revival of catholicism in England, which began with the foundation of the seminarist and jesuit missions, had continued to make headway,[1] and the flow of priests from the Continent had not been checked. In nearly all parts of the country men were to be found who acknowledged the pope's supremacy and had their spiritual needs attended to by a regularly ordained itinerant catholic clergy. Secret roads connecting the coast with the inland districts, along which priests could travel in comparative safety, and a secret postal service for the dissemination of news and the conveyance of money contributions abroad existed in defiance of all efforts to track them down. In some places justices of the peace and other local officials, themselves secret catholics, winked at breaches of the law, while in the north and west prisoners were rescued from pursuivants in broad daylight, and houses barricaded against the sheriff and his posse. Even in the streets of London, in the spring of 1602, the arrest of a catholic gentleman, Henry Ponod, led to a fracas in which a man was mortally wounded. A point had been reached when the government, with the imperfect machinery at its disposal, could not carry coercion any farther without the risk of provoking rebellion. Yet it had been demonstrated, not once but

---

[1] The number of catholics in England towards the close of the reign cannot be even approximately determined. We know that the recusants in 1603 totalled 8,630 for the whole country; but this figure takes into account only those who were indicted or presented. Secret catholics who evaded the law must have been many times more numerous. R. G. Usher's guess that 'there were very likely between 750,000 and 1,000,000' is probably an exaggeration. A. O. Meyer seems to accept the figure of 120,000 as the nearest approximation. (See Usher's *Reconstruction of the English Church*, i. 157–9; also Meyer's *England and the Catholic Church under Queen Elizabeth*, pp. 62–63.)

many times, that both the catholic laity and the priests whom they supported were overwhelmingly loyal to the queen. Obviously the time had come to consider the question of extending some measure of toleration, with suitable safeguards, to the large body of non-political catholics in England.

Other influences were shaping men's minds towards the same general thesis. After the collapse of the Spanish attack in 1588, the papal interest in the *empresa* faded. Neither Sixtus V nor Clement VIII thought of renewing the extremist policy of Gregory XIII; on the contrary, both put their trust in spiritual weapons, and gave only a perfunctory attention to Spanish designs for the conversion of England by force. Many of the English catholic exiles also found themselves assailed by a longing to return to their native land, and were prepared to gratify it, if only they were given the least assurance that they would be permitted to practise their religion in peace. Even the veteran Cardinal Allen seems to have recovered something of his lost patriotism, for he protected English protestant travellers in Rome from the Inquisition, making himself responsible for their safety provided they gave no outward cause for scandal. The splendid victory which Elizabeth had won over the Spaniard, and the consequently enhanced prestige of her country, may partly account for this remarkable change of attitude; but it was also due to the fact that England was obviously not withering under the papal curse. The government had taken good care that Europe should know the real facts of the situation. Burghley, in his *Execution of Justice* (1583), laid stress on the material well-being of the realm, and Bacon adopted a similar vein in his *Observations on a Libel* (1591). In those days, when every one was scanning heaven and earth for a sign, such an appeal to the evidence of the senses was not without its weight. Elizabeth herself took up the pen of the propagandist. Writing to the duke of Florence, in April 1591, to confute the misrepresentations of the Florentine historian Girolamo Pollini, she pointed out the moral of England's prosperity. 'It is clear as daylight', she said, 'that God's blessing rests upon us, upon our people and realm, with all the plainest signs of prosperity, peace, obedience, riches, power, and increase of our subjects.'

The main interest, however, lies in the quarrel between the seculars and the jesuits, which became more and more pronounced as the last decade of the reign advanced. The field of controversy was wide: it embraced the seminaries, the question of the English succession, and the organization of the catholic priests in England. In each case jesuit internationalism and centralization collided with the nationalist and separatist policy of the seculars. The jesuits wanted to make the seminaries instruments for the mastering of England by Spanish forces, to place the infanta Isabella on the English throne, and to subject the priests working in England to a control in which the chief say would rest with the Society of Jesus. Spiritual pride played a part, too, in the struggle; for the jesuits claimed a superior sanctity, which the seculars would not brook. 'So holy, so godly, so religious would they seem to be', said one, 'as nothing is holy that they have not sanctified.' But the vital issue was the constitution of the catholic community in England.

Trouble began in earnest in 1594, when Persons published his *Conference about the Next Succession*, defending the infanta's claim in preference to that of James VI and Arabella Stuart, Elizabeth's blood relations. The book was hailed in anti-Spanish circles among the English catholics as 'the most pestilential thing ever written', and provoked a fury of excitement in the English seminary at Rome, where anti-jesuit feeling already ran high. It was the third outburst against the jesuits within fourteen years. Simultaneously the so-called 'stirs' began at Wisbech castle, in the diocese of Ely, occasioned by the attempt of Father Weston, a jesuit, to set up a moral censorship over the little community of priests who were imprisoned there. Thirty seculars refused to acknowledge this assertion of jesuit supremacy (February 1595). The point at issue was perhaps trivial enough; but out of it came the archpriest controversy, and, as we shall see, the eventual submission of a number of the seculars to the queen in the spring of 1603.

Meanwhile the death of Cardinal Allen (1594) had raised the question of appointing some one to supervise the catholic community in England. The seculars would have liked a bishop, chosen by themselves and invested with the usual diocesan authority, under whom they might form themselves into a semi-independent national organization. But jesuit influence prevailed at Rome, and Cardinal Caetani, with the pope's sanction, appointed an archpriest, George Blackwell, with far-reaching disciplinary powers and instructions to consult the jesuits in all important matters (1598). Blackwell was not himself a jesuit;

but his arbitrary character and dependent position roused the ire of the seculars who were placed under his authority. Into the merits of the dispute it is unnecessary to enter. The significant fact is that the centralization for which Blackwell stood precluded any hope of the seculars obtaining a reasonable settlement of their position *vis-à-vis* the government. They therefore sent a deputation to Rome, in the autumn of 1598, to plead their case before the pope, coupling with their request for a bishop a plea that jesuit influence might be excluded from the Roman seminary, and a strict control exercised over the publication of defamatory books against the queen and the English government. To bring forward such a scheme during the heat of the counter-reformation was to court disappointment: the appellants were dismissed from Rome without being allowed to interview the pope; and Blackwell was confirmed in office (April 1599). The archpriest then demanded an acknowledgement of schism from the defeated party, and when they received the support of the university of Paris and remained contumacious, threatened them with an interdict. This only added fresh fuel to the fire of anti-jesuit feeling among the seculars, who now resolved to appeal for help to the government.

Here at last was the heaven-sent opportunity for which the government had been patiently waiting—the opportunity, namely, of destroying for good the unity of the catholic party, and of discomfiting the jesuits by drawing the seculars to its side. In March 1601 Bishop Bancroft, with the knowledge of Cecil and the queen, summoned Father Bluet, the secular leader, to a series of conferences at his palace of Fulham; and after some five months' discussion an agreement was reached, which, if it could have been carried out in every particular, would have gone a long way towards solving the catholic problem. A petition was to be drawn up in the name of the catholics promising complete fidelity of both the clergy and laity in all temporal matters, and requesting the queen to grant liberty of conscience and to suppress jesuit books. It was a case for heroic action on the part of the government. But when the petition was presented to Elizabeth she bristled: 'If I grant this liberty to the catholics,' she said, 'by this very fact I lay at their feet my honour, my crown, and my life.' She was too old to adapt her mind to the changing circumstances of the time. Nevertheless at Bancroft's instance she consented that Bluet and a few companions should be permitted to present a second appeal to Rome (November 1602). Meanwhile Bancroft secretly relaxed the censorship so as to allow a number of books written by seculars and printed in London to be circulated, in order to foment the case against Blackwell and the jesuits. It was part of the campaign.

What the government wanted, now that toleration was out of the question, was that the appellant priests should procure a papal bull, or brief, prohibiting or discountenancing catholic plots and insurrections against the state. If they secured this, it was to be understood that certain favours would be extended to them. Bancroft and Cecil, who were behind the movement, were not interested in the religious issue at all: they were anxious to secure the support of the seculars, and through them of the catholic laity, for the succession of James VI, to whom they were already deeply committed. Such support they believed might well prove to be the decisive factor in the crisis following the queen's demise. But the reed broke in their hands. In the autumn of 1602 the pope gave his answer to Bluet's petition. He trounced the archpriest for exceeding his powers, but would not hear of a submission, which he described as dangerous to the catholic cause, and peremptorily forbade all intercourse with heretics to the detriment of catholics. Clearly the petition was a failure from the standpoint of both the government and the seculars. Subsequently, in November 1602, the queen issued a proclamation ordering all jesuits and secular priests to leave the realm, but granting six weeks' grace to the latter to acknowledge their allegiance to the government. This was Elizabeth's last pronouncement on the catholic question, and it shows that nothing was farther from her thoughts than toleration. She would admit the catholics to her grace only on her own terms—absolute submission.

It remained to be seen what the seculars would do. Could they find a formula expressing their attitude to the government that would pass muster, without at the same time sacrificing their catholicity? They were fully prepared to profess their loyalty, to reveal conspiracies, and even to disregard any papal excommunication of the queen, but they could not, and would not, disavow the apostolic authority: they would rather lose their lives, they said, than infringe the lawful authority of Christ's catholic church. Bancroft was not satisfied with this important reservation. But after Chief Justice Popham had interrogated the priests more particularly, and learnt that they would give their written assurance not to obey the pope if he excommunicated Elizabeth, Cecil decided that this was sufficient. Thus on the last day of grace, 31 January 1603, thirteen secular priests signed a conjoint declaration of loyalty, pledging themselves to obey the queen in all things temporal, to defend her and the state against all enemies, irrespective of any papal command to the contrary, but reserving their spiritual obedience to the catholic church. They were only a fraction of the number then working in England, and their submission was of small consequence; but it was at least an indication that a new age was at hand.

For the problem of puritanism,[1] on the other hand, no solution could be found. As a practical movement for reforming the polity of the church, by introducing 'presbytery in episcopacy', it had been tracked down and suppressed by Bancroft and the high commission. The separatists had also been accounted for. But the intellectual basis of presbyterial puritanism still remained unshaken. Neither Whitgift nor Bancroft had found it possible to give an adequate reply to Cartwright's contention that, if the Scriptures were the authentic Word of God, they must necessarily be a better guide to the right ordering of the church, on its disciplinary as well as its doctrinal side, than the opinion of men. Moreover, so long as the *Book of Discipline* was believed to rest upon the impregnable rock of Holy Writ, and the anglican argument rested only on

[1] The number of puritans in England towards the close of the reign is a very disputable point. It cannot be too strongly emphasized that there was no such thing as a puritan party, in the sense of a unified organization of men pledged to the same aims. There were only groups whose sole element in common was opposition to the form of church government established by law. The strength of the most important, and indeed the only significant of these groups, the presbyterians or disciplinarians, perhaps amounted to between 281 and 350 ministers, and from 50,000 to 100,000 laymen. This estimate is highly conjectural, though not unreasonable; but if it be anywhere near the truth it shows conclusively that the puritans as a body did not number more than an infinitesimal fraction of the total population. Furthermore, it has been calculated that of the 281 puritan ministers whose names have been preserved, only 105 had university degrees, and of these 'degree men' only 31 had higher degrees than master of arts. Hence there is some justification for concluding that the 'party' was not in any way outstanding for its learning. Its real leaders were the thirteen divines who drew up the Millenary Petition at the beginning of James I's reign. (For a full discussion of the subject see Usher, op. cit., vol. i, chap. xi.)

expediency, it was futile to expect the puritan to see the error of his ways. It was to remedy this defect that Richard Hooker embarked upon his immortal treatise *Of the Laws of Ecclesiastical Polity*.

As a controversialist he had no equal in his time, and his learning was encyclopaedic. During the period 1584–91, when he occupied the office of master of the Temple, he had exercised his skill in a prolonged gladiatorial contest with Walter Travers. In the latter year he retired to the country parsonage of Boscombe, in Wiltshire, to begin the composition of his treatise. The first four books appeared in 1594, the fifth in 1597; but the remaining three, though completed before his death (1601), did not see the light until well into the next century.

The importance of Hooker's intervention in the politico-ecclesiastical arena lies in the fact that he set the whole controversy, for the first time, in a wide framework, and brought it into vital touch with the learning of the renaissance. 'Let the vulgar sort amongst you know', he wrote, 'that there is not the least branch of the cause wherein they are so resolute, but to the trial of it a good deal more appertaineth than their conceit doth reach unto.' In the preface to his first book he states the purpose of the entire work as follows: 'My whole endeavour is to resolve the conscience, and to show as near as I can what in this controversy the heart is to think, if it will follow the light of sound judgment, without either cloud of prejudice or mist of passionate affection.' He announces that he has set down in the first place 'an introduction . . . declaring what Law is, how different kinds of laws there are, and what force they are of, according unto each kind'. Next he proceeds to 'sift' the 'main pillar' of the puritan platform, viz. that Scripture is, or ought to be, the sole rule of all our actions. Then he challenges Cartwright's contention that in Scripture 'there *must* of necessity be found some particular form of Polity Ecclesiastical, the laws of which admit *not* of any kind of alteration'. Book iv is brought to a close with a rebuttal of the puritan charge that the anglican system had 'corrupted the right form of church polity with manifold popish rites and ceremonies'. The remaining books, from v to viii, are devoted to a descriptive and technical defence of anglicanism, culminating in the royal supremacy in matters spiritual.

Hooker develops his arguments with remarkable clarity and

cogency. The 'kernel' of his position may be found in his exposure of the puritan fallacy, viz. that the only law which God 'appointeth unto man' is the sacred Scriptures. These, he says, are sufficient for the purpose for which they were intended, viz. to reveal the supernatural way of salvation, undiscoverable by the light of reason; but they have a limited sufficiency. They neither abrogate the use of human reason nor discountenance it; on the contrary they presuppose it, being themselves interpretable by reason. Where they are silent, the church which is invested, like any other society, with the power to make laws for its own well-being and government, may establish any form of polity she pleases, provided she does not infringe upon, or contradict, the laws and commands laid down in Holy Writ. Furthermore, Hooker demonstrates fully and conclusively that no one form of church government is prescribed as an immutable pattern by the divine word. Whence it follows that 'in these things whereof the Scriptures appointeth no certainty, the use of the people of God or the ordinances of our fathers must serve for a law'.

The *Ecclesiastical Polity* met with an enthusiastic reception in many quarters, strangely enough in the intellectual circles of papal Rome. The catholic controversialists, Stapleton and Allen, informed Pope Clement VIII that 'a poor obscure English priest had writ four such Books of Laws and Church-Polity, and in a style that expressed such a grave and so humble a majesty, with such clear demonstration of reason, that in all their readings they had not met with any that exceeded him'. The pope, after sampling a part of the 'poor priest's' work, admitted that 'there is in them [i.e. the volumes submitted to him] such seeds of eternity, that if the rest be like unto this, they shall last till the last fire shall consume all learning'.

Hooker, we must remember, did not write merely to confute the puritan platform. 'My meaning', he said, 'is not to provoke any, but to satisfy all tender consciences.' The *Ecclesiastical Polity* was intended to be an *irenicon*, a book of reconciliation, which all would accept as the basis of agreement. As has been finely said, 'he contrived to unite and hold in a real equilibrium a deep sympathy with the three great spiritual currents of his time. He was sincerely and deeply an evangelical, a catholic, and a rationalist.' The peace of the church was the be-all and end-all of his endeavour.

It may well be doubted whether this noble aim could have been achieved in the acidulated atmosphere of the sixteenth century. Bancroft, the practical administrator, who knew human nature and the puritan mind better than the scholarly recluse, avowed himself convinced that the gulf was too wide to be bridged by any philosophic discussion, and that nothing would induce the presbyterians to abandon their belief in the divine sanction behind their Genevan system. Even Hooker himself seems to have realized this before he died. 'All is vain', he wrote, 'which we do to abate the errors of men, except their unruly affections be bridled; self-love, vainglory, impatience, pride, pertinancy, these be the bane of our peace. And these are not to be conquered or cast out but by prayer. . . . There is no way left but this one; pray for the peace of Jerusalem.'

Thus Hooker's treatise passed into the realm of literature, and Bancroft's estimate of the situation, that the puritans were fundamentally irreconcilable and deserved to be driven out of the establishment, became the basis of church policy in the future. For the moment, however, comparative peace descended on the ecclesiastical field. Both parties turned their eyes speculatively towards the king of Scotland, whose sympathies were believed to be with the reformers—the anglicans with some trepidation, the puritans with hope.

XII

THE IRISH PROBLEM

THE pacification of Ireland was the last great achievement of Elizabeth's reign, and the final act in Irish history during the Tudor period. For the greater part of a century English statesmen had wrestled with the problem, only to retire baffled by the difficulties encountered and the inadequacy of the resources at their disposal. Those who crossed St. George's channel as viceroys or lord deputies sometimes cried to be delivered from 'this hell' of a country, that seemed to devour reputations with the rapacity of one of its own bogs, or came home broken in health and spirit by the severities of the service; and few could be prevailed upon to return for a second spell of office. There was no glamour, no uplift, no satisfaction in their work to compensate them for the hardships endured; on the contrary, much of it was sordid and demoralizing. Humane men like Anthony St. Leger or Sir Henry Sidney, men of iron like Lord Leonard Grey, had to admit themselves beaten by this strange island, whose people, while acknowledging England's sovereign rights, refused either to govern themselves or to be governed. In one of the opening passages of his *View of the Present State of Ireland*, Spenser sums up his impression of the matter in the striking words of his spokesman, Irenaeus:

> Marry, so there have been divers good plots devised, and wise counsels cast already about reformation of that realm; but they say, it is the fatal destiny of that land, that no purposes, whatsoever are meant for her good, will prosper or take good effect, which, whether it proceed from the very genius of the soil, or influence of the stars, or that Almighty God hath not yet appointed the time of her reformation, or that he reserveth her in this unquiet state still for some secret scourge, which shall by her come into England, it is hard to be known, but yet much to be feared.

Yet the blame for the confusion cannot be ascribed solely to the Irish. English statesmanship, even when judged by the standards of that age, was short-sighted, shifty, and incoherent. Tudor Ireland was like some bankrupt estate, which successive owners despairingly thrust upon the shoulders of their heirs, content if only they could, by temporary measures, avert the final day of reckoning. Efforts to eradicate the evils that corrupted and disordered the country were neither comprehensive enough nor sufficiently sustained. Plans were made to be abandoned for, or supplemented by, others of a totally different nature. Policy was woven and unwoven in accordance with the needs of the hour, the convenience of statesmen, and, above all, the limited financial resources of the government. Doubtless there were times when gleams of a higher statesmanship penetrated the gloom, as, for example, when Henry VIII, in the later years of his reign, fathered a scheme for the conversion of the Irish land system into English tenures, with the collaboration of the chiefs. But the spirit of co-operation did not survive him. It was followed by the Edwardian reversion to conquest and extermination, which in its turn gave place to a policy of expropriation, under Mary, and the settlement of English military colonies in Leix and Offaly. Meanwhile the introduction of the religious question still further complicated the issue, and led on to that 'Babylonish confusion' which, in the opinion of Fynes Moryson, 'made the Irish like wild colts having unskilful riders to have all their jadish tricks'.

Of Henry VIII's work in Ireland little remained, when Elizabeth took up the sceptre, save the three earldoms he had conferred on MacWilliam Burke (Clanricard), Murrough O'Brien (Thomond), and Con O'Neill (Tyrone), together with the knighthoods distributed among the lesser chiefs. Mary's reign had witnessed the carving out of King's County and Queen's County from the O'Connor and O'More tribal lands in Leix and Offaly. A number of passes had also been cut for military purposes to the west of this area, in the O'Molloy country and near Athlone on the Shannon, giving access to Connaught. But these were relatively small gains, unlikely to breast the vigorous tide of celticism unless they were consolidated by further advances under Elizabeth.

The Ireland she inherited in 1558 was, as it had been since the beginning of the century, a land without political cohesion or racial homogeneity. A great part of it was not yet reduced to shire ground, and two whole provinces, Ulster and Connaught, were more or less formless, their names being simply geographical expressions for the land north of the Pale and west of the Shannon respectively. Twenty counties are mentioned as being in existence, but only half that number were effective units for administrative purposes, viz. the five counties of the Pale (Dublin, Louth, Meath, West Meath, and Kildare); Kilkenny and Carlow in Leinster; Tipperary, Waterford, and Cork in Munster. The Irish revenue, amounting to less than £5,000, was barely sufficient to meet the maintenance costs of the four or five hundred soldiers who formed the garrison at Dublin, let alone the civil administration. Even in time of peace it had to be heavily augmented from England. As for the Irish parliament, it had only begun to take up its permanent abode in Dublin: as late as Mary's reign it had met wherever the lord deputy found it convenient to hold it—at Limerick and Drogheda as well as Dublin. Nominally it represented all the interests in the island, but actually only the great landed proprietors of the Anglo-Irish race, the dignitaries of the church, and the counties, cities, and boroughs that lay within the 'obedient' districts. Of the native chiefs only those who had accepted earldoms attended it, and their attendance was not regular. Broadly speaking, therefore, the Irish parliament was an organ of English rather than of Irish opinion; its sphere of influence was small, and its freedom of action was curtailed by the operation of Poynings's laws and the dominant position of the lord deputy, who took his instructions from the privy council or the queen.

The racial map of Ireland presented a still more remarkable picture of arrested development. The population consisted of three different types or groups, bracketed together not by any community of interest but by the mere fact that they lived in the same island. First came the English of the Pale and the chartered towns of the southern and western seaboard—Waterford, Youghal, Cork, Limerick, and Galway. This group preserved at least a tincture of English usages in regard to speech, dress, and behaviour; but their position was that of an insufficiently reinforced outpost in a savage land, constantly exposed to the insidious pressure of the surrounding barbarism, which threatened to engulf them. Except in the Pale, where order was maintained by the presence of an English garrison, their loyalty was always precarious and suspect, and in moments of crisis they could not be depended upon. Fynes Moryson noted that the citizens of Cork refused to allow their wives to speak English with the English soldiers in the streets, but insisted on their using Erse as a badge of their independence. The English of the chartered towns, in short, were a source of weakness rather than of strength to the ruling authority in Dublin, and every English visitor to Ireland regarded them with dislike and contempt. The second group, the Anglo-Irish, were a hybrid race, who made no pretence of upholding English traditions. Domiciled in the most fertile lands of Leinster and Munster and southern Connaught, they lived 'Irishly', having become so intermixed with the aboriginal Celtic population that they had lost practically every trace of their Norman origin. In the phrase of the time, they were *ipsis hiberniores hibernis*, as 'very patch-cocks as the wild Irish themselves'. To this group belonged the Butlers of Kilkenny, Tipperary, and Wexford, the northern Geraldines of Kildare, and the southern Geraldines of West Munster, who, in the persons of their respective heads, held the great earldoms of Ormonde, Kildare, and Desmond, and exercised a palatine jurisdiction covering the whole southwest of Ireland from the border of the Pale to the extreme limits of Kerry. Southern Connaught was similarly within the jurisdiction of the earldom of Clanricard, more recently created (by Henry VIII) in favour of the Burkes. Altogether the Anglo-Irish were a powerful group, on whose co-operation the Crown perforce depended for the parts beyond the Pale; but their help was fitful, sometimes disingenuous, and seldom hearty. The third element in the population, the pure Irish, were to be found in all parts of the island where the natural features favoured their existence —in the Wicklow highlands, in the boggy lands of the central districts, in Thomond, in northern Connaught, and in the inaccessible wilds of Ulster. Ulster indeed was the stronghold of the clans, where no fewer than a dozen rival groups headed by the O'Neills of Tyrone, the O'Donnells of Tyrconnel, and the Scoto-Irish septs of Antrim parcelled out the territorial lordships between them. It was a land of untempered anarchy, given over to the pursuit of plunder, war, and barbaric glory, and so little accustomed to civilized ways that its rude inhabitants were as surprised to see an English official in their midst as the shades in Virgil were to see Aeneas alive in Hell. Conversely the citizens of London were more than surprised when they saw Shane O'Neill, paramount chief in Ulster, arrive to do homage to Elizabeth in 1562. He was accompanied by a bodyguard of axe-bearing 'galloglasses' wearing long hair curling down over their foreheads, and clothed with saffron coloured long-sleeved

'surplices' topped with hairy mantles. No wonder the populace 'gazed at them with no less "admiration" than they do
to them of China and America'. But there was probably more
amazement when Shane made his speech of submission to the
queen. He spoke in his native tongue; but to the glittering
assembly his linguistic effort sounded like 'howling'. Truly
Spanish America with all its scenic and savage wonders could
not offer a greater contrast to Renaissance England than the
province of Ulster in the sixteenth century. Elizabeth had
a veritable Mexico on her door-step.

If Shane O'Neill could not speak the English tongue, no more
could the other lords of Ulster—all except the remarkable Hugh
O'Neill, second earl of Tyrone, who had spent several years with
the Sidneys in their home at Penshurst learning the language,
and absorbing as much 'civility' as he could. Sir John Harington,
who visited the earl in his Irish home in October 1600, has
left it on record that Tyrone's two sons not only spoke English
with him, but also wore jerkins of velvet comparable with those
worn by noblemen's sons in England. Evidently a certain degree of civilized life was maintained at the Tyrone homestead
in Ulster; but as a rule the family was content to live 'Irishly'—
like 'wolves that fill their bellies sometime and fast as long
after it'.

It should be noted, however, that two chiefs of the Irish race,
Con O'Neill of Tyrone and Murrough O'Brien of Thomond,
promoted by Henry VIII to the rank of earl, held jurisdictional
rights over their respective territories similar to those exercised
by Kildare, Ormonde, Desmond and Clanricard. This extension
of privileges and responsibilities to the heads of native Irish clans
was in the nature of an experiment, the value of which had still
to be proved.

From this brief account of its condition it will be seen that if
the queen had left Ireland to take care of itself, in all probability the celticization of the whole island would have taken
place within a relatively short time, with disastrous results to
the maintenance of English sovereignty. Such a contingency
was sufficient to warrant a more than usually drastic intervention in Irish affairs; for public opinion, already irritated at the
loss of Calais, would not have brooked a further withdrawal
from Dublin. But although the desire to save the Pale from
destruction may be said to have forced the Irish question into

prominence, it did not acquire its subsequent importance in English politics for that reason alone. The moment Elizabeth reformed the church in England, a new complexion came over Anglo-Irish relations. The establishment of a protestant England over against the catholic monarchies of the Continent was in many ways a dangerous and doubtful experiment; but its continuance side by side with a catholic Ireland was virtually inconceivable. Indeed, before anything like assurance could be felt in government circles, the whole of the British Isles must present a solid phalanx of opposition to possible catholic machinations. Fortunately the danger of Scotland's becoming a *point d'appui* of England's enemies was quickly averted, or rendered highly improbable, by the success of the reformation in that country. Ireland, on the other hand, was a positive menace so long as her people remained spiritually dependent upon Rome and loosely attached to the English Crown. In fact, the protestantization of Ireland must have seemed a necessary measure for England's security. It was perhaps more than this. The anglican church inculcated obedience to the powers that be, and reprobated rebellion; and it was at least arguable that if the wild tribes of Ireland could be brought under its influence the civil magistrate would find his arm lengthened and his authority mightily increased. As one of the lord deputies put it, 'Where there is no knowledge of God, there can be no obedience to the magistrate.' Nevertheless the attempt to make Ireland protestant by parliamentary enactment—which was the method adopted—only serves to show how defective were the ideas animating Tudor statesmen in regard to religious policy.

It is impossible to describe with any degree of accuracy the condition of the catholic religion in Ireland at this time, but there is abundant evidence to show that it had reached a very low ebb. The demoralization of the clergy, caused by the confused revolutions of the preceding reigns, had resulted in the cessation of preaching and teaching; and the people, growing up in ignorance of the sacraments and even of the creed itself, abandoned themselves to all manner of gross excesses contrary to the spirit as well as the letter of the christian religion. The ecclesiastical artillery which, in the last resort, might have kept the anarchy in check played harmlessly over the tribal chieftains, who plundered church property with as little compunction as they plundered other property in their rivals' domains. Nor did it matter what dogma was held in England—the chaos continued uninterruptedly, the catholic prelates of Mary's reign being as helpless against it as the protestant bishops of Edwardian times. Ireland was the despair of the saints.[1] So bad was the spiritual condition of the country that almost any change would have been a change for the better. Circumstances were soon to show, however, that if Ireland was to be saved it would not be by the imposition of protestantism.

The first Irish parliament of the reign met at Christ Church, Dublin, on 11 January 1560, and was dissolved on 1 February 'by reason', apparently, 'of its aversion to the protestant religion'. There is no record of what took place; but there is also no doubt that the Acts of Supremacy and Uniformity were subsequently placed upon the statute book. It was a poor augury for the success of the measures. The true state of Irish opinion soon revealed itself, when only five of the reigning catholic bishops, whose sees lay within the Pale or in close proximity to it—Dublin, Ferns, Leighlin—and in Waterford and Cork, consented to accept the settlement. The rest of the episcopate, who were beyond the reach of the government and consequently escaped deprivation, contented themselves with taking the oath of fealty and allegiance to the queen, and continued to celebrate Mass as before. Thus a kind of ecclesiastical dyarchy came into being—a protestant state church functioning in the obedient areas, and a papal church in all the rest of Ireland; but neither exercised much influence over the people. Nor were the prospects of the former sensibly improved by the concession that Latin might be used in the liturgy instead of English, or the subsequent publication of a catechism (1571) and certain articles of religion in Erse (1566). If Ireland set little store by the ancient faith, it had less use for protestantism in any shape or form. So slowly did the reformation progress that

[1] When the holy woman Brigitta 'inquired of her good angel, of what christian land was most souls damned? the angel showed her a land in the west part of the world where there is most continual war, root of hate and envy, and of vices contrary to charity, and without charity the souls cannot be saved. And the angel did show till her the lapse of the souls of christian folk of that land, how they fell down into hell as thick as any hail showers. . . . For there is no land in the world of so continual war within himself, ne of so great shedding of Christian blood, ne of so great robbing, spoiling, preying, and burning, ne of so great wrongful extortion continually, as Ireland.' (Quoted by J. S. Brewer, *Carew Papers, 1575–88*, Introduction, pp. xv–xvi.)

in 1565 Loftus, dean of St. Patrick's, Dublin, confessed that the gentry of the Pale were going to Mass and giving bed and board to 'massing priests' as if they had never heard a word about reform. A year later Sir Henry Sidney, who had just entered upon his first spell of office as lord deputy, stated that only three sees were occupied by zealous protestants, viz. Dublin, Armagh, and Meath; while in the more remote parts 'order cannot yet be taken . . . until the countries be brought into more civil and dutiful obedience'. Ten years later, when Sidney was again in Ireland on his third spell of office, he found to his surprise that the prospect was as gloomy as ever. In his report (1576) he commented that even in Meath, Bishop Brady's diocese and the best ordered in all the country, no fewer than 105 parish churches were without a resident clergyman, and the pluralist curates who served them were in some cases 'Irish rogues having little Latin, less civility[1] and learning'. Wasted patrimonies, ruined churches, and insufficient supply of trained pastors confronted him on all sides. 'Upon the face of the earth', he concluded, 'there is not a church in so miserable a condition.' But if the position in the Pale was bad, it was much worse in the purely Irish districts. 'So profane and heathenish are some parts', remarked the lord deputy, 'that it hath been preached publicly before me that the sacrament of baptism is not used among them.' No doubt the spiritual needs of the native Irish were to some extent provided for by the ministrations of the jesuit David Wolf, who laboured in Ireland as papal commissary from 1561 until his imprisonment in Dublin castle in 1569, and of wandering friars who lurked about the countryside. But the papal bishops who occupied the remoter sees were by all accounts feeble and ineffective in the discharge of their spiritual functions. It was not, in fact, until after 1580, when the seminaries on the Continent began to pour their scholars and missionaries into the island, that there was any serious attempt on the part of the catholic church to meet the needs of the native Irish. By that time, however, the situation had undergone a great change, and the cause of catholicism had become interlocked with a political revolt against English rule. We shall return to this catholic revival after we have considered other aspects of Elizabeth's Irish policy. For the present we may note simply the failure of protestantism

---

[1] i.e. culture, civilization, refinement.

to secure its position even in the parts subject to inspection and control by the Dublin authorities.

Whatever importance the queen may have attached to the introduction of a protestant state church into Ireland, it was not the whole or even the main object of her intervention. The really fundamental question was not how the Irish were to be proselytized, but how they were to be civilized. However much the new bishops might be regarded as the pioneers of political and social progress, they were evidently unsuited for missionary work in a barbarous society that spurned their advances and plundered their sees with impunity. Civilization must precede the church rather than the church civilization. This was the considered opinion of all competent observers who studied the problem at first hand, and it was fully borne out by the disturbed condition of Ulster and Munster.

In 1559, on the death of Con O'Neill, the province of Ulster was plunged into chaos by a contested succession to the earldom of Tyrone. According to the settlement of Henry VIII (1542) the legal heir was Brian, second baron of Dungannon, whose father, Matthew 'Kelly', despite his illegitimacy, had been promoted by the king to the barony and the position of heir designate. But the heir by Celtic law was Shane, the dead earl's eldest legitimate son, who was elected head, on his father's death, of the clan O'Neill. A year before, this able and ambitious chieftain had removed Matthew 'Kelly' from his path by murder; but the support given by the English government to Brian still blocked the way to his ultimate objective, the earldom. After several futile efforts had been made by the lord deputy, the earl of Sussex, to procure Shane's overthrow, both by force and by fraud, the queen decided to compromise, and summoned the rebel chief to London under promise of pardon. In 1562 a settlement was reached by which Shane made his submission, took the oath of allegiance to the Crown, and received in compensation the captaincy of Tyrone. This agreement was precipitated by the news from Ulster that Brian had been murdered during the chief's absence by his *tanist*, Turlogh Luineach; and a clause was introduced into the agreement with Shane expressly reserving the rights of Matthew's only remaining son, Hugh, who was now removed to England for protection and education. In later years he was to become Elizabeth's most resolute opponent in Ireland; but for the time being the substance of power in Tyrone passed into the hands of Shane.

As captain of Tyrone Shane was pledged to keep the peace within the province, to levy no Irish exactions beyond his own territory, to persuade the other chiefs to take the oath of allegiance, and to attend all hostings of the lord deputy. A year later he was permitted to assume the tribal sovereignty as 'The O'Neill'. But his thirst for power being only partially slaked he now began a campaign of terrorism and conquest, forcing all the tribes of Ulster, including the Scots of Antrim, to acknowledge his supremacy. By 1566 he was paramount from Sligo to Carrickfergus, and began to boast that his ancestors were kings and that he himself was superior in blood to any earl. Pope Pius IV addressed him as 'prince of Ulster', commending him for his constancy in the faith. In April 1566 he appealed to Charles IX of France and the cardinal of Lorraine for help to drive the heretical English into the sea. It was now clear that Shane was aiming at something more than the mastery of Ulster; for he carried his depredations into the Pale, raided Meath, made a forcible entry into Newry and Dundrum, and burned the metropolitan church of Armagh. Sidney was so perturbed at the state of affairs that he advised Elizabeth to take drastic action if she did not wish to lose Ireland as her sister had lost Calais; and in September of the same year he conducted a strong punitive expedition into the province for the purpose of reducing the tyrant to obedience. In a triumphal march through Ulster, lasting less than two months, Sidney succeeded in rallying all the tribes to the English side, burned Shane's crannog at Benburb, and left the beaten chieftain to the tender mercies of his enemies, the O'Donnells, who routed him at the battle of Lough Swilly. In desperation Shane fled for assistance to the Scots of Clandeboy, who first welcomed him and then murdered him in a drunken brawl (June 1567).

From start to finish, the troubles in Ulster had cost England no less than £147,000 and 3,500 lives; but the pacification of the province was as far off as ever, for the *tanist* Turlogh Luineach, who now succeeded to the chieftainship of the O'Neills soon proved himself to be as hostile as Shane to English rule.

During the same period conditions were no better in the south of Ireland, where the earl of Desmond ruled west Munster as tyrannically as O'Neill ruled Ulster, plundering and burning villages and carrying on a frontier warfare against his rival Ormonde. Like Shane he had undertaken, in 1562, to be answerable to the laws, to preserve order within his jurisdiction, and not to make war on the queen's subjects. But in spite of reprimands and warnings to observe his obligations he continued his depredations, and was known to be hand in glove with O'Neill for the overthrow of English sovereignty in the island. 'A man both void of judgement to govern and will to be ruled' was Sidney's summing up of his character, when he visited Munster on his tour of inspection as lord deputy in the spring of 1567. Desmond, in fact, was constitutionally incapable of any sustained policy, either pro-Irish or pro-English: he was loyal when it suited him, disloyal whenever the occasion offered. The lands he governed in the queen's name were among the worst governed in Ireland. If Sidney is to be believed, the queen's name and 'letters of commandment' were no more reverenced in the Desmond country 'than they would be in the kingdom of France'. All the lords and gentry of Cork, except Macarthy More of Muskerry and O'Sullivan Beare of Kerry, complained bitterly of his oppression. 'I never was in a more pleasant country,' wrote Sidney, 'but never saw I a more waste or desolate land,' full of ruined churches and burnt-out villages, and the 'bones and skulls of dead subjects, who partly by murder, partly by famine, have died in the fields.' Desmond was not the only offender—the earl of Thomond in Clare and the sons of Clanricard in southern Connaught were also disturbers of the peace—but he was the ringleader, and the lord deputy did not hesitate to imprison him in Dublin castle for his misdeeds (1567). Later he was transferred to London, where he remained a prisoner until 1573.

Sidney's analysis of the situation in Ireland, based upon his experience with O'Neill and Desmond, went straight to the root of the matter. He recommended, among other things, the establishment of English presidencies in Munster and Connaught to supersede the palatine jurisdictions of the Anglo-Irish earldoms; the abolition of coign and livery, on which the chiefs depended for the maintenance of their armed bands; the introduction of land tenure by royal patent, by which the chiefs would hold their lands directly from the Crown; the planting of English colonists at points of vantage in the island; and the control of Ulster by the construction of roads, bridges, and fortified castles. Several of these recommendations were adopted, with or without modification, within the next few years.

As a first step Sir Edward Fitton was appointed president of Connaught in 1569, and Sir John Perrot was similarly established in Munster in 1570. At the same time (1569) the Irish parliament passed an act abolishing coign and livery. This was the prelude to a determined attempt to break the military power of the chiefs. It was supplemented by a renewal of the effort to replace the Celtic land system by English feudal tenures. The method which had already been applied by Henry VIII to certain districts is generally referred to as 'surrender and regrant'. In other words, the chiefs were invited to give up their lands to the Crown and then receive them back and hold them in tail male by royal patent. They would thus be placed in practically the same position as the Anglo-Irish earls of Ormonde, Desmond, Kildare, and Clanricard; and if they committed treason their lands could be legally confiscated. Doubtless this latter consideration weighed heavily with the English government. But there is no reason to suppose that the scheme involved injustice to the Irish, if, as actually happened, a serious effort was made to understand the prevailing land system and deal equitably with the respective rights of all parties, chiefs as well as dependants. The best example of what happened is the so-called 'composition' of Connaught, which Sidney proposed in 1571 and Sir John Perrot carried out in 1585. The object to be attained was set down by Walsingham in the following words: 'To give each chief his due, with a *salvo jure* to all others that have right.' With this end in view, inquisitions were held to determine the area of the lands to be distributed and who were their rightful owners according to Irish law; and indentures were drawn up between the Crown and the owners, giving them a legal title, fixing the tribute to be paid to the queen (10s. per 120 acres) and the amount of compensation to be paid to the chiefs in lieu of 'cuttings', 'spendings', and other Irish exactions. The same method was applied to county Clare and many other Irish districts.

Nor was this all. On the basis of these changes in the land

system was to be built up a thorough-going revolution in the whole internal economy of Ireland, involving the introduction of English dress, the county system, sheriffs, justices of the peace and of assize, juries, and in short everything characteristic of English life in the sixteenth century. It was not a question of whether these innovations were suitable for Ireland in the present stage of her development, nor was any consideration given to the fact that political and social institutions cannot be made to order, but are the result of a long process of historical evolution. Ireland was to be remade in the English mould, either with or against her will, for the matter was urgent and there was no other mould available.

The attitude of the government is seen very clearly in relation to costume. Just as in the eighteenth century stress was laid on the necessity of abolishing the kilt as a barbarizing agency in Scotland, so in Ireland in the sixteenth century the wearing of mantles and long hair (glibbs) was regarded as an obstacle to progress. The mantle, wrote Spenser, 'is a fit house for an outlaw, a meet bed for a rebel, and an apt cloak for a thief'. Much vituperation was also vented on the bard who by his glorification of the past threw up a defence round everything that was barbaric and un-English. Irishmen, we are told, had a greater respect for the opinion of the bard than for the thunders of the civil magistrate. Thus Sir John Perrot issued the following regulations for the province of Munster, over which he presided, in 1571:

The inhabitants of cities and corporate towns shall wear no mantles, shorts, Irish coats, or great shirts, nor suffer their hair to grow long to glibb, but to wear gowns, jerkins, and some civil garments; and no maid or single woman shall put on any great roll or kirchen of linen cloth upon their heads, neither any great smock with great sleeves, but to put on hats, caps, French hoods, tippets or some other civil attire upon their heads: upon pain of £100 to the head officer of the city or corporate town that shall suffer any such Irish garments, and upon forfeiture of the said Irish garments so worn;

and again:

All carroughs, bards, rhymers, and common idle men or women within this province making rhymes . . . to be spoiled of all their goods and chattels and to be put in the next stocks, there to remain till they shall find sufficient surety to leave that wicked 'thrade' of life and fall to other occupation.

The all-important matter, however, was the general alteration of the social environment. Dress, after all, is merely the adjustment of a people to its environment: if the environment be altered, the dress will alter of its own accord. But how was the Elizabethan government, with its limited resources, to bring about so vast a change in the economy of a people? Sir John Davies, writing in the reign of James I, expressed the view that it could only be done by first breaking the tribes in war and then 'planting' the country with English colonists. Spenser, who also had the advantage of seeing the situation in retrospect, was of the same opinion. 'How then, do you think, is the reformation thereof to be begun', asks Eudoxius, 'if not by laws and ordinances?' 'Even by the sword,' replied Irenaeus; 'for all these evils must first be cut away by a strong hand before any good can be planted.' But it was not the queen's policy to launch out into uncertain financial commitments, nor, perhaps, was she convinced that Ireland was worth such a sacrifice of blood and treasure. She was willing, however, to experiment with plantation provided her subjects shouldered the risk in the event of failure. In this light must be viewed the various attempts to establish colonies during the reign: they were not colonies in the strict sense of the word, but simply expedients whereby what threatened to become a lost cause might be retrieved by private enterprise. The age was rich in individual initiative and company-promotion flourished for all manner of undertakings. Why not a company for the exploitation of Ireland? There was a surplus population in England who might be drawn upon for the pioneering work. In fact the plan was feasible enough provided suitable lands for settlement could be obtained in Ireland: otherwise the attempt to 'plant' the country would mean the forcible dispossession of the Irish—a contingency that must involve the planters in interminable disputes with the natives.

The first three efforts, those of Sir Peter Carew and other west-country adventurers in Leinster and Munster (1568–70), of Thomas Smith, son of Elizabeth's principal secretary of state, in the district of Ards (1572–3), and of the earl of Essex[1] in Clandeboy (1573–5), were little better than armed attempts

[1] i.e. the first earl.

to expropriate the native Irish from their ancestral lands, and they ended in bloodshed and disaster. Every tribal chief from Kilkenny to Kerry, Anglo-Irish as well as pure Irish, including the Butlers, the southern Geraldines, and the Burkes, forgetting their own differences, combined in a great confederacy to defend their patrimonies against the English interlopers; and for several years intermittent war raged in Munster and Connaught. The Ulster enterprises of Smith and Essex met with the same resistance from the owners of the soil. Within a year Smith's colony came to an inglorious end with the murder of the promoter; and Essex could do nothing to retrieve the situation, although he added to the tale of English atrocities in Ireland by a massacre of the Scots of Rathlin and the treacherous murder of Brian McPhelim, the lord of south Antrim. Evidently there was no hope of successful colonization by private enterprise until some other method was devised for procuring land than by forcibly dispossessing the native landowners. For the next ten years interest in the project lapsed; and then it was revived under happier auspices by Sir Walter Raleigh, who at this time was dabbling in his Virginian enterprises. When Raleigh took up the matter the Desmond estates in Munster had passed into the hands of the Crown, owing to the treason and death of Desmond (1583), and it was calculated that half a million acres of the best land in Ireland would be available for settlement. Plans were drawn up accordingly for the distribution of the forfeited estates among 4,200 English settlers, both gentry and peasants, chosen from Cheshire, Lancashire, Somerset, and Dorset. In order to encourage the immigrants and to tide them over the early years of pioneer work, they were to hold their lands free for three years, and thereafter pay only half rent till 1593, after which full rent would be charged. Since the purpose was to establish a solid block of uncontaminated English as a basis for the reorganization of Ireland, it was carefully provided that no Irish should be allowed into the settlement, and that no intermarriage should take place.

No sooner was the scheme launched, however, than difficulties were encountered. Complaints by the Irish that far too much land had been pegged off led to judicial inquiries, and three commissions sat between 1586 and 1593 to investigate the extent of territory really forfeited by Desmond. The upshot was that in place of 500,000 acres only 202,000 were declared legitimately confiscable. This shrinkage in the amount of land available caused competition among the planters for the better lands, and many families returned to England. Thereupon the native Irish, despite all regulations to the contrary, swarmed into the settlement, attracted by its peace and order; and in the end half the colony consisted of 'rebellious Irish'. The effect of the infiltration was not immediately felt; but when the period of stress and strain arrived in 1598, and all Ireland broke into rebellion, the colony could not muster more than a quarter of the forces it should have had at its disposal. Unable to breast the tide of fanaticism that swept the country from end to end, the colonists fled for safety to the shelter of the cities, and no attempt was made to reinstate them. The Munster colony had vanished like those of Clandeboy and Antrim.

In this brief analysis of Elizabeth's Irish policy we have endeavoured to lay emphasis on principles rather than events, and, for the sake of clearness, have emptied the narrative of much detail. We have also, it will be noted, considered the problem of Anglo-Irish relations exclusively from the English standpoint. It is now necessary, if the dramatic occurrences of the latter part of the reign are to be understood, to turn back, change our angle of vision, and look at events from the point of view of the Irish themselves.

The great weakness of Ireland in its resistance to England was its disintegration by clan feuds and consequent lack of a common purpose. Although the aims of the English government were subversive of the whole fabric of traditional Irish life, no leader had as yet arisen capable of uniting all his fellow countrymen in the defence of their heritage, nor had the secret of such a union been discovered. In a general and vague way Shane O'Neill appreciated the needs of the situation, but he had neither the brains nor the character to command the respect of all Ireland. It was James Fitzmaurice, the Geraldine leader in the Munster Confederacy of 1569–73, who first rose to the dimensions of a really great figure in Irish history, and provided his race with a policy and rallying-point. In 1569 he had sent Fitz-Gibbon, the papal archbishop of Cashel, to plead the Irish cause at the court of Spain, and to bring the matter to the notice of the catholic world generally. FitzGibbon played his cards well before both King Philip and the pope. He recalled the ancient fidelity of Ireland to the Holy See from the days of St. Patrick and Pope Celestine—1,127 years; and he went on to point out that for the last fifty years they had been labouring under a heretical tyranny. But they prayed God to inspire the minds of His Holiness and the catholic king, so that they should not be contaminated and destroyed by the accursed and contagious heresy that flourishes in England. They had therefore 'resolved with God's help and the favour of the most clement catholic king, to accept the person of any active catholic prince of his catholic majesty's blood, whether of the Spanish or Burgundian branch . . . and to receive him and crown him as their true, legitimate, and natural king, and thus to re-establish in perpetuity the royal throne of that Island'. Simultaneously, in Ireland, Fitzmaurice constituted himself the apostle of an all-catholic island under the joint patronage of Spain and Rome. It was the first step towards the foundation of a new Ireland, in which inter-tribal disputes would melt away in a blaze of religious enthusiasm and hatred for the heretical English. For the next ten years, says a modern catholic writer,[1] 'the fretful form of *Eire* stands on the southern shore peering into the mists and gazing across the waters watching for the foreign galleys to bring "Spanish ale" or "wine from the Royal Pope"'. Meanwhile the catholic chiefs had written to Don John of Austria inviting him to let himself be proclaimed king of Ireland; and at the same time they instructed 'Cashel' to hurry on his mission in Madrid, to discuss with the king the possibility of Don John's undertaking the task, and to point out that the lack of a king was fatal to the Irish cause: 'Because we have not a king and are divided among ourselves the English attack and rob us daily, and we suffer grievously as a result.'

But the time was not yet ripe for foreign intervention. Neither FitzGibbon nor the renegade Sir Thomas Stukeley, who now offered his sword to Spain and became a diligent frequenter of the Spanish court as the *soi-disant* marquess of Leinster, could prevail upon Philip II to take up the Irish cause seriously. Ireland was merely a pawn in the great game of European diplomacy. The eyes of continental catholics were fixed on the main 'enterprise' of England, which was beginning to monopolize the attention of Spain, rather than upon the Irish, whom the count de Feria contemptuously described as 'a sort of beggarly

[1] M. V. Ronan, *The Reformation in Ireland under Elizabeth, 1558–80* (1930).

people, great traitors to one another, and of no force'. At length
Fitzmaurice, tired of the endless delays and disappointments,
left Ireland for France in 1575, and eventually made his way to
Rome, where he gained the ear of Pope Gregory XIII; and early
in 1577 he was rewarded with a brief appointing him leader in
a holy war in Ireland against 'that woman who . . . has been cut
off from the church'. Disappointments, however, dogged Fitzmaurice's footsteps as soon as he tried to furnish out his intended
expedition to Ireland; for, although he was able to charter
a ship from Lisbon and collect a filibustering force of eighty
Spaniards and Portuguese with the money given to him by the
pope, he got no farther than St. Malo. The fault was not his
but the captain's with whom he sailed, who broke his contract. There was now nothing for it but that the pope himself should organize a fresh expedition from Italy; and this
he did in February 1578, placing the egregious Stukeley in
command.

Once more the project collapsed, for Stukeley, as we have
seen,[1] abandoned his crazy ship at Lisbon and joined Sebastian
of Portugal in his African adventure, to die with him at Alcazar.
But Fitzmaurice was not to be daunted. Again he took the
matter in hand, collected a motley band of Italians, Spaniards,
Portuguese, Flemings, French, and Irish, and along with Dr.
Nicholas Sanders and some papal emissaries set sail from Lisbon
in July 1579, to raise a holy war against Elizabeth in Munster.
Viscount Baltinglas of Leinster, recently returned from a visit
to Rome, responded to the appeal; but with the exception of
him and Desmond the Anglo-Irish nobles held aloof from the
crusade. Connaught was kept quiet by Sir Nicholas Maltby,
who thus prevented the spread of the rebellion to Ulster. Consequently, although Baltinglas cut to pieces an English force
at Glenmalure in the Wicklow mountains, and a fresh contingent of Italians and Spaniards arrived at Smerwick in September 1580, the conflagration was soon localized and mastered.
Lord Grey and the earl of Ormonde, supported by the English
fleet under Winter, compelled the fort at Smerwick to surrender
and put the garrison to the sword as pirates (November). Then
followed a systematic devastation of Munster by the English
in an effort to extinguish the last embers of the revolt—
a devastation so ruthless that more than 30,000 native Irish

[1] p. 177.

perished in six months of starvation, pestilence, and sudden death, and 'the wolf and the best rebel lodged in one inn, with one diet and one kind of bedding'. Spenser paints a lurid picture of what he saw with his own eyes: 'Out of every corner of the woods and glens they came creeping forth upon their hands, for their legs could not bear them; they looked like anatomies of death; they spake like ghosts crying out of their graves; they did eat the dead carrions, happy where they could find them; yea, and one another soon after; insomuch as the very carcases they spare not to scrape out of their graves; and if they found a plot of water-cresses or shamrocks then they flocked as to a feast for the time.'[1] The tragic episode was brought to a close with the capture and decapitation of Desmond in the woods of Glanageenty near Tralee (1583), and the forfeiture of his estates to the Crown. Fitzmaurice and Sanders had already died miserably—the former at the hands of the loyal Burkes (1579) and the latter of hunger and dysentery (1581); while Baltinglas fled abroad, leaving his lands like Desmond's to be forfeited for treason.

Although the first attempt to overthrow English rule in Ireland with foreign help thus ended disastrously for the Irish, the fire of religious fanaticism had been kindled in the island, and the counter-reformation, hitherto unable to establish itself in the British isles, at last found a foothold on the tortured soil of the most vulnerable part of Elizabeth's dominions. Increasing numbers of missionary priests poured into Ireland every year, and Irish youths, flocking to the continental seminaries, returned to their native country imbued with a holy zeal for the expulsion of the heretics. It was only a question of time when this widespread propaganda, working on the prevailing discontent, would succeed in fusing all the Irish together, thereby creating the conditions for a general rising, supported by Spain, of which Fitzmaurice had dreamed. For the moment Philip's attitude was not reassuring. He had shown himself sympathetic to the Irish cause to the extent of welcoming refugees and agitators at his court; but his refusal to give official countenance to the Munster rebellion clearly indicated that in his opinion the time was not yet ripe for Spanish intervention. Nor did his attitude

---

[1] This was not the first devastation of Munster. Compare it with the devastation caused by the Butler–Geraldine conflict, reported by Sir Henry Sidney in 1566–7.

of benevolent neutrality undergo any material change until some little time after the disaster to the armada of 1588. The experiences of the luckless Spaniards who fell into the hands of the native Irish, when many of Medina Sidonia's galleons crashed on the Irish rocks, cannot have inspired much confidence in the Spanish government as to the value of Irish friendship. The uncouth, uncivilized nature of their captors, the wildness of the country, and the hardships, plunder, and even in some cases murder, to which they were exposed—if they did not come to a more terrible end at the hands of the English under Sir Richard Bingham and the lord deputy—must have been a rude dis-illusionment to the Spanish commanders. It has been calculated that some 8,000 of the 'invaders' lost their lives between the Giant's Causeway and Blasket Sound, but how they severally met their deaths is one of the secrets of history: all we know is that over 1,000 were put to the sword by Bingham, and about 400 escaped to Scotland. Nevertheless the possibility of Spanish help for Ireland was not destroyed by this untoward event. Spain needed Ireland as a base of operations against England just as much as Ireland needed Spain as an ally. And there were two outstanding Irishmen of the younger generation, Hugh Roe O'Donnell and Hugh O'Neill, earl of Tyrone, who set themselves with resolute will to bring about the desired alliance.

Although the O'Neills and the O'Donnells had been enemies for generations, the common hatred for England acted as a powerful solvent on their inter-tribal feud, and laid the founda-tion of an Ulster confederacy which was soon to shake the whole structure of English rule in the island from base to roof. In 1592, when Pope Clement VIII sent James O'Hely, bishop of Tuam, to Ulster with renewed promises of Spanish assistance, O'Donnell at once took the lead in planning a fresh rising, and secured the co-operation of many other chiefs. Tyrone at first held aloof from the movement, being too prudent to commit himself until he was convinced that the rebellion had a fair chance of success. But O'Donnell was the heart and soul of the conspiracy. In 1593 he authorized the dispatch of a letter by O'Hely to the king of Spain, pleading the cause of the federated chiefs, and offering 7,000 foot and 600 horse for the common enterprise against England. In the margin of the Spanish original of the document Philip scribbled the words: 'If what they say is true, it would be shameful not to help them.' Immediate assistance was, of course, impossible owing to the war in France; but during the year 1594 a Spanish ship reconnoitred the coast from the Shannon to Wexford. More important still: Tyrone now threw off his mask of reserve and entered into direct relations with Spain. On the death of Turlogh Luineach the following year, he publicly assumed the title of 'The O'Neill', and was hailed with almost kingly honours in Ulster.

The new leader was no charlatan. Ever since his return to Ireland in 1576, as baron of Dungannon, he had watched and waited, always preserving a correct attitude to the English, who rewarded him with the earldom of Tyrone in 1585. His ability as a soldier, based upon the training he had received in the English army in Ireland under Essex[1] (1572-4) and as a cavalry commander in the campaign against Desmond, was only matched by his undoubted genius for unscrupulous intrigue and the plausibility of his tongue. An Irishman at heart, despite his English education, he was intellectually much superior to his compeer, O'Donnell, whose glowing passion left little room for obliquity. Tyrone, in fact, was an accomplished disciple of Machiavelli—flexible, suave, incalculable. When circumstances made it necessary he could appear so reasonable as to deceive even the most hardened negotiators whom Elizabeth sent to deal with him, while all the time his purpose remained fixed and unalterable. The attitude he assumed was that of the extirpator of heresy in Ireland, because he knew that under the banner of religion alone could he win the support not only of his fellow countrymen but also of all foreign powers interested in the suppression of protestantism. But the real object of his crusade was political. It was a question of the preservation of Celtic institutions in the island; and to Tyrone there could be no hope for the Irish cause unless Ulster remained sacrosanct to the old order. It is impossible to doubt, however, that his ultimate ambition was to drive the English bag and baggage out of Ireland, to destroy English sovereignty, and to set up a national kingship. He was easily the most dangerous figure who had so far appeared on the stage of Anglo-Irish politics.

Time was no object to Tyrone. He knew that the struggle

[1] Father of Robert Devereux, and first earl of Essex.

would be long and arduous, and he proceeded with the utmost caution, keeping alive as long as he could, by dexterous dissimulation, his openness to conciliation and compromise with England, while at the same time plying Spain with urgent requests for substantial help in men and money. Without Spanish assistance he realized that he was powerless; and without the possibility of a settlement with England hovering in the background he could not exert the necessary pressure on Spain. Thus he manœuvred between pro-Spanish and pro-English expressions of sympathy, coercing the English into concessions by his dealings with Philip II, and goading the Spaniard into active intervention by his professions of weakness.

This policy of delay and prevarication on Tyrone's part was possible only because of the inadequacy of the English forces in Ireland, the reluctance of the queen to increase her expenditure on armaments, and the lack of a methodical plan of conquest. It was the inevitable result of a hand-to-mouth statesmanship. But let us not under-estimate the difficulties of a general subjugation of the Irish. Geographically the country was ill adapted for the invader. There was no natural rampart or mountain barrier behind which the aboriginal inhabitants could be penned up until they either succumbed to military pressure or accepted the terms of the conqueror. The mountains, distributed in some five detached groups round the central plain, presented a problem of strategical control which a military race like the Romans might have solved without difficulty, but to the Elizabethans it must have seemed practically insoluble. Moreover, Ireland was as barbarous physically as it was socially. In most parts it consisted of virgin bush, bog, and lake separating settlement from settlement and town from town, without roads or regular means of communication. Fynes Moryson depicts it as he saw it: an 'uneven, mountainous' country, 'soft, watery, woody, and open to winds and floods of rain, and so fenny as it hath bogs upon the very tops of mountains, not bearing man or beast, but dangerous to pass'; he adds, 'and such bogs are frequent all over Ireland'. It was a country, in fact, whose conquest was bound to exact a heavy toll from civilized troops accustomed to operate within reach of material comforts and properly organized military bases. Consequently the Irish wars were exceedingly unpopular in England. In Lancashire and the other recruiting counties it was commonly said that men would rather go to the gallows than to Ireland. Hard knocks and stale victuals if not actual starvation was all they could look for. No doubt the very severity of the service transformed raw recruits quickly into good soldiers; but it was difficult at first to keep them from deserting and selling their weapons to the native Irish; and many captains preferred to hire mercenary Irish who were less expensive and better adapted by their training to the conditions of savage warfare. Indeed the queen's parsimony compelled them to this course. Yet to attempt a subjugation of the Irish by the Irish—for this is what the system involved—was, to say the least, a hazardous and short-sighted policy; for, at a pinch, the mercenary was unreliable. More than once English generals were reduced to inaction by the fear that their Irish auxiliaries might play them false. To make matters worse, the plan was adopted of making the Irish pay for their own conquest. The wars were run on the Irish revenue supplemented by 'cess', an exaction levied on the people of the Pale, who were obliged to furnish the troops with victuals at the queen's price. In practice the system was iniquitous, for it left the peasantry at the mercy of bullying soldiers, who often robbed their homesteads and indemnified them with worthless notes of hand. In 1586, under the lord-lieutenancy of Sir John Perrot, 'cess' was abolished in favour of a 'composition' fee of £2,100. Even so, however, it was not until the contest with Tyrone began that the organization of the army and of the method of financing it was placed upon a sound basis. The employment of Irish mercenaries was curtailed as far as possible, and the English exchequer took over the entire responsibility. The arch-rebel could not have been beaten in any other way.

The years 1594–6 mark a crucial period in the history of Elizabethan Ireland; for it was at this time that the crafty, treacherous Tyrone began seriously to prepare for his desperate gamble with fate. The way had been smoothed for him by the activities of seminarist and jesuit priests, and by papal emissaries like O'Hely and MacGauran, who held the titular offices of archbishop of Tuam and primate of Ireland respectively. Moreover, there were signs that Philip II was at last becoming deeply interested in the possibility of using the island as a *pied-à-terre* for the final overthrow of England. Spanish ships were seen to be active in Irish waters, taking soundings and mapping the coast-line between the Shannon and Wexford. Open defiance of Elizabeth and the launching of his grandiose project of an all-catholic Ireland, free from English domination, was Tyrone's next and inevitable step. It came quickly.

In 1595, dropping the mask of friendship, he assumed the forbidden title of 'The O'Neill'; and at once set about coaxing the slow-moving Spaniard into action. The jesuit priest Momford, who acted as go-between, was sent to Spain with the message that Spanish support was necessary at once if peace terms with England were to be avoided: moreover, the support must take the form of fighting men, not merely gold and munitions. Philip responded by dispatching Don Alonzo de Cobos in May 1596, with money and munitions sufficient to keep the Irish in the field for eighteen months, but no soldiers. The disappointed Tyrone at once sent back the envoy with heavier demands—6,000 soldiers and munitions for 10,000; and, in addition, a fast ship carrying 1,000 men and their equipment to rouse the spirits of the Irish and strike dismay into the hearts of the English. Finally, the king was invited to send over the archduke Albert of Austria, now Spanish governor of Flanders, to take charge of the whole country. All this was going on while the wily lord of Ulster was engaged at Dundalk in negotiating peace terms with the English, including 'free liberty of conscience for those who were anxious to exchange the sovereignty of Elizabeth for that of Philip II'.

But troubles were on the way for the planners. In July Essex and Howard carried out their brilliant attack on Cadiz, burning or sinking numerous ships intended for the 'Irish enterprise'. True, the Spaniards tried to belittle the disaster; and Cobos returned to Ireland in September to reassure the chieftains, and to make arrangements for the impending arrival of the invading force. He landed at Killibegs and met Tyrone, O'Donnell, and the other leaders at Donegal, where it was decided that the most suitable landing-place was either Carlingford or Galway. Far away in Lisbon the king had succeeded, despite the losses incurred at Cadiz, in assembling a formidable armada consisting of 98 ships and 10,800 men, to be strengthened by a papal squadron and a squadron from Seville. All were under the command of the *adelantado* of Castile. Early in October the preparations were complete, and the great flotilla moved off wafted by the strains of the psalm *Contra Paganos*.

It was not the first time nor was it the last that those who put their trust in Spanish enterprises on the sea were to be sadly disillusioned. The ships had hardly sailed when they were dispersed and partially wrecked by a storm. A second effort a year later (October 1597) proved to be equally abortive; and then Philip II, after concluding the peace of Vervins with Henry IV, died and was succeeded on the throne by his son Philip III. The Hispano-Irish alliance had not yet begun to bear fruit, albeit Spanish diplomacy stood committed to it.

The effect of these disasters to Spain was seriously to endanger Tyrone's position in Ulster; and in December 1597, he decided to submit, temporarily at least, to the lieutenant-general, the earl of Ormonde. Several conferences were held, during the winter and spring, for the purpose of exploring the basis of a settlement; but Ormonde was far from confident in Tyrone's trustworthiness, and the sole result of the discussions was to reveal the alarming extent of the earl's traffic with Spain, and the futility of peace negotiations until his power was effectually broken. So far as the campaign in Ireland had gone, Tyrone had succeeded in maintaining the integrity of his province. The struggle had been waged along the border for the possession of key positions like the fort on the Blackwater, which commanded Ulster's communications with the south. The fort had changed hands several times, and was now occupied by an English detachment. But soon after hostilities were renewed in 1598, Tyrone retook it and cut to pieces an English force which was marching under the command of Sir Henry Bagenal to its relief (August). The news of this brilliant exploit created a sensation in Ireland, and coupled with the defeat of Sir Conyers Clifford by the O'Rourkes of Connaught was instrumental in spreading the rebellion into the other provinces which had hitherto remained quiescent. Everywhere the native Irish rose *en masse*, and terrible atrocities took place. In Munster a new earl of Desmond—the so-called *sugane* (straw rope) earl—was proclaimed, the old customs were revived, and the English planters were driven from their lands. In all parts the chiefs who had conformed to English rule were superseded by irreconcilables. It was virtually a national revolt. In proportion as the confidence of the Irish increased with their successes the English lost heart; and the legend grew that the Irish bore charmed lives. Now was the time for the Spaniard to strike, for the supreme crisis in

Ireland's history had arrived. Accordingly Philip III, who was well informed of the state of affairs, sent a third armada to Tyrone's assistance in the summer of 1599. Had this expedition reached its destination, it is hard to believe that English sovereignty in Ireland would have survived the onslaught. But once more the Spaniard completely failed. Bad weather forced the fleet to take shelter in Brittany and eventually to double back to Spain, and the favourable moment was irretrievably lost. Meanwhile the English grasp on the situation was gradually restored, first by the young Essex and later by Lord Mountjoy, the greatest of Elizabethan soldier administrators.

Although Essex was probably the most colourful and finished exponent of the art of war in England his assumption of the lord deputyship had been a tragic mistake. He was sadly deficient in the patient organizing genius required for the subjugation of a rebel country, where all problems are problems of detail, and prudence more important than heroism. Ireland in fact found out his weaknesses and gave him no scope for the exercise of his undoubted talents. Mountjoy who arrived in Ireland late in February 1600, to take over the lord deputyship, was a man of very different stamp from Robert Devereux. He may have been 'bookish', and he certainly suffered from chronic poor health, causing him to rest every afternoon in his tent, whether in camp or in the field. He was also a heavy smoker and fond of good wine and good food; but the most noteworthy feature of his character was his extraordinary stamina when in action. He is said to have preferred a winter campaign to campaigning in summer; and normally spent five days each week in the saddle. In some ways he resembled Sir John Perrot: he tackled the Irish problem in the spirit of a Roman general. Thorough, scientific, and infinitely patient, he seemed to grasp the essentials of a situation comprehensively and quickly, and having done so, to move to his objective with precision. He may have gleaned something from Essex's report—if indeed he ever saw it, which is doubtful; and he certainly was well aware of the latter's fatal mistake of parleying with the arch-rebel on the banks of the Lagan. He had several advantages over the unfortunate earl. First he does not seem to have been troubled with the constant necessity of 'looking over his shoulder': secondly, he maintained good relations with the English privy council: thirdly, he had at his disposal a better organization of supplies;

and fourthly, he had as his subordinates such excellent soldiers as Sir George Carew and Sir Henry Docwra, both of whom played a big part in the final show-down with Tyrone. Nevertheless, it was the genius and personality of Mountjoy himself that paved the way to certain victory. One might say of him that he was a living embodiment of the famous saying that, in war, 'the moral is to the material as three to one'.

The task confronting the new lord deputy and his lieutenants was such as to excite the most dismal forebodings. No part of the country was sincerely loyal to the Crown, not even the Pale, for the papal emissaries had done their work only too thoroughly. 'It is incredible', wrote Carew to Lord Buckhurst (April 1600), 'to see how our nation and religion are maligned and the awful obedience that all the nation stands in to the romish priests, whose excommunications are of greater terror unto them than any earthly horror whatsoever.' In the cities of Munster culprits could not be punished because the mayors and aldermen were disloyal, and juries made no more scruple to 'pass against' an Englishman and the queen than to 'drink milk unstrained'.

The gloom was deepened by the constant fear of another Spanish invasion; for Tyrone was moving heaven and earth to bring the Spaniards over, and Philip III, despite his failing finances, was making frantic efforts to launch a fresh armada. The question that was agitating the mind of the king, however, was not so much Ireland, as the English succession. As we have seen, in another connexion, Elizabeth was approaching old age, and all Europe was agog with excitement and anticipation. In Spain the question of the hour was how to secure the coveted crown for the infanta Clara Eugenia; and many were convinced that Ireland, the Achilles' heel of England, might be used as a *point d'appui*, whereby pressure might be brought to bear on London. Thus the council of state in Madrid advised the king to give full support to the Irish cause—not so much by sending help as by a full-scale invasion and occupation of the country.

In working out the detail of such a move, however, it was discovered that the exchequer could not provide the initial outlay—150,000 ducats—and that the whole matter had better be postponed until the following year. Philip was angry: it was God's affair, he said, and all difficulties must be laid aside. Tyrone's wailing that his resources were exhausted, that food and pay were lacking, and his men were deserting to the English, must be listened to. The 'Irish enterprise' must proceed before the end of October. At the same time Tyrone petitioned the pope to issue a ban against all who refused to join the rebel cause. But it was all in vain: the money for the enterprise was not forthcoming. Thus the year 1600 passed without any danger from Spain developing; and every month the work of pacification, guided by Mountjoy, advanced a step farther. By the turn of the year, the rebellion was stamped out in Munster; the Pale and the central districts were secure; and Connaught and Clare were quiet under the friendly earls of Clanricard and Thomond. Only the power of Ulster remained unbroken, and its subjugation became the capital problem in Irish politics. For rather more than a year Mountjoy had hammered at its defences, constructing blockhouses and planting garrisons at strategic points, and keeping Tyrone continually on the *qui vive* with extensive raids. But in the summer of 1601 he began preparations for invasion on a grand scale, and the rebel chiefs watched them with growing anxiety. Then suddenly the lord deputy was informed by Carew that the Spaniards were on the high seas (29 August), and he abandoned the Ulster enterprise in order to cope with the new danger.

Meanwhile, early in 1601, Ovieda and Cerda had returned to Ireland to find the Irish leaders reduced to the verge of despair. And in Spain King Philip was deeply involved in a last effort to collect ships and men and money for the decisive onslaught on the English in Ireland, the occupation of the island and the preparation for the enthronement of the infanta. Eventually about midsummer 35 ships had been assembled at Lisbon under the command of Don Diego Brochero, and 4,500 troops were standing by under Don Juan del Aguila. Weapons for the native Irish were put aboard and also some field artillery; and towards the end of August the whole armament set sail for the port of debarkation, Cork harbour. Cerda wrote to the king triumphantly: 'At the moment when your Majesty's troops win a foot-hold in this land, your trade with the West Indies will be assured, and great economies will be possible in Spain.'

Three weeks later, while the Irish council of state sat at Kilkenny to concert measures of defence, 3,000 Spanish troops under Juan landed at Kinsale, and proceeded to construct a fortified camp. It was fortunate that the blow fell in Munster rather than in Ulster, for the distance of the centre of trouble from Tyrone's country made communication between the Spaniards and the northern Irish, their only possible allies, exceedingly difficult, and at the same time simplified the problem of defence. Moreover, Kinsale was a tiny town of some 200 houses, with no store of provisions or natural defences except on the side of the sea; and as soon as the English fleet under Sir Richard Leveson appeared in Irish waters it was practically impossible for Aguila to receive either supplies or reinforcements from Spain. He could not look for assistance to the Munster Irish, who had been thoroughly cowed by Carew. O'Sullivan Beare of Kerry, it is true, offered him 1,000 men if arms and munitions could be provided; but Aguila could not do this, because Pedro de Zubiaur's squadron carrying the extra supply of equipment had been compelled by adverse weather to return to Spain before the main body reached Kinsale. Nor again was it possible for the Spaniards to provision themselves by foraging, for they had no horses and the surrounding country was immediately swept bare by Mountjoy's cavalry. On the other hand, ample reinforcements, guns, and stores of all kinds from England soon began to pour into Waterford in response to the lord deputy's appeal; and by 26 October Mountjoy was in a position to invest Kinsale with an army of between 8,000 and 10,000 men.

For two months the siege was prosecuted with vigour, but the wintry weather and the open entrenchments took a heavy toll of the besiegers. On 1 November the fort of Rincurren commanding the entrance to the harbour was captured, and the Spaniards were completely bottled up, being unable either to retire or advance. On 12 November Leveson began the bombardment of Ny Parke, the only other defensive work protecting the town on the seaward side, and it fell on the 20th. A premature assault delivered on 1 December failed to dislodge the Spaniards, but enabled Mountjoy to draw his lines nearer. On the 6th Leveson destroyed Zubiaur's ships, which had just arrived at Castlehaven. It was now evident that the Spaniards of themselves could do nothing to avert the impending disaster: everything depended on Tyrone and O'Donnell, who were now approaching Mountjoy's lines, after vainly trying to raise the country on their march south from Ulster.

On 21 December the English found themselves enveloped by the northern Irish, who cut off their communications with the interior, and threatened to starve them out just as they had hoped to starve out the Spaniards. But Aguila could not wait, and on 23 December a joint attack on the English entrenchments was arranged, when Mountjoy's forces caught between two fires would be compelled to abandon the siege and withdraw. By sheer good luck news of the attack reached Mountjoy beforehand, owing to the indiscretion of one of Tyrone's officers; and when the action developed it was the Irish and Spaniards who were surprised. At the cost of a single casualty Mountjoy routed the enemy, driving the Spaniards back into the town and inflicting a loss of 2,000 on the Irish. This, in fact, terminated the fighting, for O'Donnell shortly afterwards escaped to Spain with Zubiaur and Tyrone dejectedly moved off to the north. Aguila saw that the time had come to capitulate, and on 2 January he agreed to evacuate Kinsale and Castlehaven, provided the Spaniards were allowed to retain their arms and the English would bear the cost of their repatriation. Mountjoy found no difficulty in accepting these terms, being only too glad to see the Spaniards out of the country. Aguila's verdict on the whole episode is tersely expressed in his own words: 'This land seems destined specially for the princes of Hell.'

After the withdrawal of the Spaniards the pacification of Ireland was rapidly concluded. Carew besieged and captured O'Sullivan Beare's stronghold of Dunboy; Mountjoy and Docwra closed in on Tyrone in Ulster, and harried him into the inaccessible wilds of Glenconkein; while Leveson set sail for the coast of Spain to retaliate on the Spaniard by capturing a carrack in Cezimbra roadstead. At the end of March 1603 Tyrone surrendered unconditionally.

The cost of the conquest in blood and treasure cannot be computed; but it is significant that the last four years and a half of the war drained the English treasury to the extent of one and a quarter millions—an enormous sum in those days. And what were the gains? *Pacata Hibernia!* For the first time in its history Ireland was completely subjugated. The clan system was destroyed, and the power of the Celtic chief as a war lord was broken beyond hope of recovery. The fall of Ulster proclaimed the end of medieval Ireland and of the elder barbarism which had so long stood like a wall between the Irish race and the cultural life of Europe. Moreover, the triumph of the English had brought with it the establishment of a new land system based upon the principles of the Connaught 'composition', and the reduction of the greater part of the country to shire ground. In 1571 Longford was carved out of the O'Farrell lands and added to Leinster. Five years later (1576) Connaught was subdivided into Galway, Roscommon, Sligo, Mayo, and Clare, the last-named county being subsequently incorporated in Munster. Cavan and Wicklow made their appearance in 1579. Leitrim was created in 1583, and Coleraine, Donegal, Tyrone, Armagh, Fermanagh, and Monaghan in 1586. In fact, with the exception of some minor adjustments, Ireland had acquired by the end of the reign her modern administrative units.

It is harder to determine the economic consequences of the long-drawn-out struggle, for the available evidence is inconclusive. In some respects it was a period of economic retrogression for Ireland. The 'cessing' and billeting of troops, the requisitioning of food-supplies and horses, the destruction of crops by rebels and royalists alike, and all the evils incidental to a military régime reduced many parts of the country to a state of bare subsistence; while the devastation of the five counties of Munster by Lord Grey spread death and starvation over the richest and most productive area in all Ireland. The seaports of the south-west, whose trade with Spain in fish, hides, and beeves depended upon the prosperity of their hinterlands, never recovered from that visitation. Waterford and Galway languished as well as Cork and Limerick. To the devastation of war must be added the deleterious effects produced by the systematic debasement of the coinage—a practice followed by all the Tudors for their own private profit. On the other hand, it may be noted that the increasing demands of the English market for Irish wool, flax, hides, and timber to some extent balanced the account. The rise in importance of Dundalk, Drogheda, Carrickfergus, and the seaports of the north-east, which throve on the English trade, took place side by side with the decay of the Munster seaports. It is probable also that a considerable amount of the money spent by the Elizabethan government on Ireland, during the later phases of the war, remained there to stimulate trade; and the military cantonments of Mountjoy and Carew supplied the peasantry with markets for their produce.

Nor was this all. The cultural life of Ireland benefited by the foundation of Trinity College, Dublin, in 1590, and by the establishment of a printing-press capable of handling texts in Erse. Educationally a new era in Irish history was at hand. But in the matter of religion the population remained overwhelmingly catholic. Indeed the outstanding result of the Elizabethan régime, in the religious sphere, was to deepen the attachment of the Irish race as well as the Anglo-Irish to the church of Rome.

XIII

THE DEATH OF THE QUEEN

THE last years of the reign were years of increasing loneliness for the queen. She had outlived her generation. One by one the great men who had served her passed away. Nicholas Bacon, Lord Clinton, the earl of Bedford, and Sir Thomas Gresham were now mere memories. Leicester died in the year of the armada, Walsingham and Warwick in 1590, Hatton and Shrewsbury in 1591, Hunsdon in 1596, and Burghley in 1598. The latter's death moved Elizabeth profoundly: the loss of such a servant, counsellor, and friend was irremediable; but since she was blessed, as Camden tells us, with remarkably good health by reason of her abstinence from wine and a temperate diet, she showed as yet no signs of decrepitude. In the summer she 'progressed', as always had been her habit when business of state permitted; and in the winter months she was to be found at Whitehall. She continued to celebrate each year the anniversary of her accession (17 November) and Twelfth Night: danced *gaillardes gaîment et de belle disposition*, and went a-maying. Indeed it almost seemed as if in this Indian summer of her life she liked to revive something of the feverish activity that had characterized her youth. As a distinguished historian remarks: 'The further Elizabeth descended into the vale of years, the stronger were her efforts to make ostentation of a youthful gaiety of spirits and an unfailing alacrity in the pursuit of pleasure. ... To remark to her the progress of time, was to wound her in the tenderest part; and not even from her ghostly counsellors would she endure a topic so offensive as the mention of her age.' But the struggle could not be long maintained.

Two letters from Sir Robert Sidney to Sir John Harington in the summer of 1600 depict a rapidly ageing woman. 'I do see the queen often,' said Sidney; 'she doth wax weaker since the late troubles, and Burghley's death often draws tears from her goodly cheeks; she walketh out but little, meditates much alone; and sometimes writes in private to her best friends.' And again: 'her Highness hath done honour to my poor house by visiting me. ... At going up-stairs she called for a staff, and was much wearied in walking about the house.' She was a different lady from the irate woman who, when she read Harington's journal of the campaign against Tyrone, cursed them all 'as idle knaves, and the lord deputy worse'; who 'left us no doubtings whose daughter she was', and by her 'choler, which outran all reason', caused Harington himself to run from her presence 'as if all the Irish rebels were at his heels'.

In October Harington found her 'quite disfavoured and un-attired', and apparently 'much wasted' by her troubles.

She disregardeth every costly dish that cometh to the table [he comments] and taketh little but manchet and succory pottage. Every new message from the City doth disturb her, and she frowns on all the ladies. . . . I must not say much even by this trusty and sure messenger; but the many evil plots and designs hath overcome all her Highness' sweet temper. She walks much in her chamber, and stamps with her feet at ill news; and thrusts her rusty sword at time into the arras in great rage. . . . But the dangers are over, and yet she always has a sword by her table. . . . And so disordered is all order that her Highness hath worn but one change of raiment for many days; and swears much at those that cause her griefs in such wise, to the no small discomfiture of all about her, more especially our sweet lady Arundel, that *Venus plus quam venusta*.

In the following summer, she told Count Harlay de Beau-mont, the French ambassador, that 'she was tired of life, for nothing now contented her spirit, or gave her any enjoyment'. She also spoke to him of Essex 'with sighs and almost with tears', saying that she knew his impatient spirit would involve him in misfortune: that she had warned him, but he took pleasure in displeasing her, *et de mépriser sa personne insolemment*.

When Harington paid another visit to the ailing woman about Christmas 1601, he found her in very low spirits, showing unmistakable 'signs of human infirmity'; and when he tried to divert her by reading some of his verses, she contrived to smile once, remarking 'when thou dost feel creeping age at thy gate, these fooleries will please thee less'. Her memory was beginning to fail her. She asked him if he had seen Tyrone; and when he reminded her that he had seen him in Ireland, with the lord deputy (Essex), she looked up 'with grief and choler in her countenance', and said: 'Oh, yes: now it mindeth me that you was one that saw this man elsewhere', and dropping a tear, smote her bosom.

At the end of January 1603, her climacteric year—much feared in the sixteenth century—she removed from Westminster to Richmond, partly to escape the foulness of the weather in the capital and partly to rest her failing body. She was still well enough to receive the Venetian ambassador, Scaramelli; but it was while she was here that she had the ring (symbolizing her marriage to England) filed off from her finger, it being too deeply embedded in the flesh to be detached in any other way. And when the lord admiral, who enjoyed greater liberty of access than almost any other, asked her about her successor, she answered: 'My throne hath been the throne of kings: neither ought any other than my next heir to succeed me.' But she refused to mention any name.

In the meantime it had become known to the queen that many of her nobility were in secret communication with the king of Scots, seeking to win his favour; and, according to Camden, some desired to have the successor sent for whilst her recovery was still uncertain. 'It is incredible', writes the same author, 'with what flying speed Puritans, Papists, and ambitious persons of all sorts, flatterers and others, every of them forward for their own hopes, posted day and night by sea and land into Scotland, to adore the rising sun and gain his favour.' All this must have deepened the queen's melancholy; and it was further deepened by the death of the countess of Nottingham in the last days of February, for she, too, was one of the privileged friends.

Then came the crisis in March, when 'a heavy dullness, with a frowardness familiar to old age' began to lay hold on her. She would sit for long periods in silence, her mind given wholly to meditation, impatient of conversation except with the archbishop of Canterbury. She refused to touch or taste the physic prescribed for her: neither the council, nor the divines, nor the physicians, nor any of her women could persuade her; nor would she be induced to lie down in her bed, 'because she had a persuasion that if she once lay down she would never rise'. While she was in this condition the secretary, the lord keeper, and the lord admiral visited her, and in the name of the whole council desired to know her mind touching the succession. She replied— or so we are told—'I have said that my throne was the throne of kings, and I would not that any base should succeed me.' When Cecil asked what these words meant, the answer is said to have come: 'I will that a king succeed me, and who but my kinsman the king of Scots.'

So died Elizabeth I, on 24 March 1603; and a few hours later, in accordance with arrangements made by the council, James VI of Scotland entered into his heritage. That night bonfires were lit in the streets of London, while Sir Robert Carey rode post haste for Edinburgh with the news.

A new reign and a new age had begun!

BIBLIOGRAPHY

BIBLIOGRAPHY AND WORKS OF REFERENCE

THE standard bibliography for the history of Elizabeth's reign is Conyers Read's *Bibliography of British History: The Tudor Period, 1485–1603* (1933). Without being exhaustive, it is the only systematic survey of the material in print relative to the period. A. W. Pollard and G. R. Redgrave, *A Short Title Catalogue* (Bibliographical Soc., 1926), gives the most complete list of books printed in England, Scotland, and Ireland, as well as of English books printed abroad, before 1640; it includes valuable information as to the libraries and private collections where copies of the books may be found. Reference may also be made to E. Arber, *Transcripts of the Registers of the Stationers' Company* (5 vols., 1875–94), F. Madan, *Early Oxford Press: a Bibliography of Printing and Publishing at Oxford* (1895), and the *British Museum Catalogue of Printed Books*, with its *Supplement* and *Subject Indexes*, which is the best guide to editions, authorship, &c. (new edition in progress, 1931–). Other useful works of general reference are: R. B. McKerrow, *Dictionary of Printers and Booksellers, 1557–1640* (Bibliog. Soc., 1910), the *Catalogue of English Broadsides, 1505–1897* (Bibliotheca Lindesiana, 1898), T. R. Thomson, *Catalogue of British Family Histories* (1928), H. Hall, *List and Index of the Publications of the Royal Historical Society, 1871–1924, and of the Camden Society, 1840–1897* (1925), and *Poole's Index to Periodical Literature*, supplemented by the *Subject Index to Periodicals* (1915–), which is the most important guide to articles in periodicals dealing with English history.

The chief periodicals, journals, and reviews are: *The English Historical Review*, the premier organ of English historical scholarship; *History* (the quarterly journal of the English Historical Association, which also publishes an annual *Bulletin of Historical Literature*); the *Cambridge Historical Journal*; the *Bulletin* of the Institute of Historical Research (useful for corrections of the *Dictionary of National Biography*, summaries of theses, and information regarding the migration of historical documents); the *American Historical Review*; the *Revue Historique*, which occasionally publishes reviews and articles bearing on English history; the *Economic History Review*; the *Mariner's Mirror* (for articles on

naval history); and the *Innes Review* (a catholic publication concerned principally with Scottish history).

To these may be added the *Transactions of the Royal Historical
Society*; C. L. Kingsford, *Chronicles of London* (1905); and the
Bulletins of the *National Register of Archives*, dealing with local
records, which commenced in 1946.

Three handbooks of considerable value to students are: the
Handbook of British Chronology (ed. Powicke, Johnson, and Hart,
1939); the *Handbook of Dates* (ed. C. R. Cheney, 1945); and
Writings on British History, ed. Taylor Milne for the Royal Historical Society.

Rymer's *Foedera* (20 vols., 1704–35) is the standard work of
reference for treaties and other diplomatic instruments; the *Dictionary of National Biography* (22 vols., 1908–9 ed.) is the most
valuable authority for biographical matter, and indeed for all
other aspects of English history; and the *Victoria County History*
(still in progress) is a mine of information on local history.
J. Foster, *Alumni Oxonienses, 1500–1714* (1891–2), and J. A. Venn,
Alumni Cantabrigienses, part i (1922–7), should be used for the
lives of university men.

The most important guide to the various repositories of public
documents is H. Hall, *Repertory of British Archives*, part i, *England*
(1920). For those contained in the Public Record Office consult
M. S. Giuseppi, *Guide to the Manuscripts Preserved in the Public
Record Office* (2 vols., 1923–4), or Sir Hilary Jenkinson's new
substitute. Detailed inventories and descriptive catalogues of
the records are published in the *Reports* of the deputy keeper of
the public records, and in the official *Lists and Indexes* of the
P.R.O. The British Museum and the Bodleian Library have
printed catalogues of their respective manuscript collections,
and there is a subject-index in the manuscript room of the
British Museum. Manuscript collections in private hands are
listed in the *Historical Manuscripts Commission Reports*. The *18th
Report* (1917) gives a list of all collections examined to 1916, with
a list of materials for diplomatic history in these and the British
Museum manuscripts by Frances G. Davenport, and the *19th
Report* (1926) carries the former list forward to 1925. For a
general account of the Commission's work, and a description of
the principal collections, see R. A. Roberts, *The Reports of the Hist.
MSS. Comm.* ('Helps for Students of History', No. 22, 1922). For
the Scottish records consult M. A. Livingstone, *Guide to the*

Public Records of Scotland (1905). Reference should also be made to C. S. Terry, *Index to the Principal Papers relating to Scotland in the H.M.C. Reports* (1908), and C. Matheson's continuation (1928), under the title *Catalogue of the Publications of Scottish Historical Clubs and Societies and of the Volumes relative to Scotland published by the Stationery Office, &c.* Most of the official Irish records preserved in the Public Record Office, Dublin, were destroyed in 1922, and the principal repositories for material on Irish history now available are Trinity College Library and Marsh's Library, Dublin. Useful guidance to source-material on Irish history may be found in Constantia Maxwell, *Irish History from Contemporary Sources, 1509–1610* (1923), and R. H. Murray, *Ireland, 1494–1603* ('Helps for Students of History', No. 33, 1920).

POLITICAL HISTORY

PRINTED SOURCES. The most important collections for the period are the *Calendars of State Papers*, published by the Public Record Office in London, and the Historical Manuscripts Commission publications (separate from the *Reports*). For the former, the current *List of Record Publications* issued by Her Majesty's Stationery Office should be consulted; and for the latter, the *Reports* mentioned above are the best guides. The most valuable of the Commission's publications for the reign are the 15 volumes of the Hatfield (Cecil) Papers, and the *Calendar of State Papers Domestic* which are now complete to 1603. These official publications, however, must be supplemented by such well-known works as J. Strype, *Annals of the Reformation* (4 vols., 1820–40); E. Lodge, *Illustrations of British History* (3 vols., 1838); the *Hardwicke Papers* (ed. Philip Yorke, 2nd earl of Hardwicke, 2 vols., 1778); the *Egerton Papers* (Camd. Soc., xii, 1840); and the *Sidney Papers* (ed. A. Collins, 2 vols., 1746). The more recently published *Sidney Correspondence* (1934–6) covering the period 1557–82 is invaluable for Elizabethan Ireland and the Low Countries. Other collections are the *Harleian Miscellany* (ed. T. Park, 10 vols., 1808–13: Index, 1885); the *Somers Tracts* (ed. Sir Walter Scott, 13 vols., 1809–15); Murdin's (1759) and Haynes's (1740) collections of the Burghley state papers; F. Peck, *Desiderata Curiosa* (ed. T. Evans, 2 vols., 1779); Sir H. Ellis, *Original Letters* (11 vols., 1824, 1827, and 1846); P. Forbes, *Full View of the Public Transactions in the Reign of Elizabeth* (2 vols., 1740–1);

500 BIBLIOGRAPHY

T. Birch, *Memoirs of the Reign of Queen Elizabeth* (2 vols., 1754);
T. Wright, *Queen Elizabeth and her Times* (2 vols., 1838); *Cabala*
(1691); Harington, *Nugae Antiquae* (ed. T. Park, 2 vols., 1769);
Sir R. Naunton, *Fragmenta Regalia* (ed. Arber, 1895); *The
Losely MSS.* (ed. A. J. Kempe, 1825); *The Sadler Papers* (ed. A.
Clifford, 2 vols., 1809); R. Carey's *Memoirs* (ed. Sir W. Scott,
1808); the *Leicester Correspondence, 1585–6* (Camd. Soc., xxvii,
1844); H. Brugmans, *Correspondentie van Robert Dudley, graaf van
Leycester* (3 vols., 1931); John Chamberlain's *Letters* (Camd.
Soc., lxxix, 1861), or, *The Letters of John Chamberlain* (American
Phil. Soc., 2 vols., ed. N. E. McClure, Philadelphia, 1939);
Walsingham's Journal (Camd. Mis., vol. x, 1902); N. H. Nicholas, *Memoirs of the Life and Times of Christopher Hatton* (1847)—or,
better, E. St. John Brookes, *Sir Christopher Hatton, Queen Elizabeth's Favourite* (Jonathan Cape, 1946), 'the only reliable book
on Hatton'. To these may be added J. Nichols, *Progresses and
Public Processions of Queen Elizabeth* (3 vols., 1823); C. Sharpe,
Memorials of the Rebellion of 1569 (1840); Caspari's *Humanism and
the Social Order in Tudor England* (Chicago and Cambridge,
1955); the Manningham and Machyn Diaries (Camd. Soc., xcix,
1868, and xlii, 1848 respectively); the Gawdy *Letters* (ed. I. H.
Jeayes, Roxburghe Club, 1906); the *Letters and Epigrams of Sir
John Harington* (N. E. McClure, 1930); A. F. Pollard, *Tudor
Tracts* (1903); Fulke Greville, *Life of Sidney* (ed. N. Smith, 1907);
and Bacon, *Collected Works* (ed. J. Spedding and others, 1857–
74). For useful notes on many of these works consult Read's
Bibliography.

Of contemporary histories and chronicles, the following are
the most important: W. Camden, *Annales Rerum Anglicarum et
Hibernicarum Regnante Elizabetha*, 1615 (trans. T. Hearne, 3 vols.,
1717) [the 1630 edition translated by Norton is the more attrac-
tive translation]; Raphael Holinshed, *Chronicles*, 1577 (ed. H.
Ellis, 6 vols., 1807–8); and J. Stow, *Chronicles* or *Annals*, and
Survey of London. The 1605 edition of Stow's *Annals* is the best,
and C. L. Kingsford's edition of the *Survey* (2 vols., 1908) is the
standard one. For the Elizabethan taste for history see L. B.
Wright's paper in the *Journal of Modern History*, iii. 175–97
(Chicago, 1931). Also to be considered is E. M. W. Tillyard,
The Elizabethan World Picture, Macmillan, 1944.

MODERN WORKS. Among these pride of place must be given
to J. A. Froude's *History of England from the Fall of Wolsey to the*

Defeat of the Spanish Armada (revised ed. 12 vols., 1862–70), the most brilliantly written and the most complete for the period it covers, viz. to 1588; but it requires to be checked both in fact and inference by more recent research; and it can be supplemented by E. P. Cheyney's *History of England from the Defeat of the Armada to the Death of Elizabeth* (2 vols., 1914–26). Although the latter work has none of the literary distinction of Froude's, it contains some very important chapters on political institutions, piracy, and economic affairs. Nor must we forget Lucy Aikin's *Memoirs of the Court and Times of Queen Elizabeth* (1818) which, in spite of its age, is in some ways a remarkable performance. M. Creighton's *Elizabeth* (1899) has a certain independent value, and is much better than Beesley's *Elizabeth* ('Twelve English Statesmen' series, 1892), which is a mere sketch. A. F. Pollard's *Political History of England, 1547–1603* (1913) is, as its title suggests, a comprehensive study of the political aspect of its period. Of recent works, J. E. Neale's *Queen Elizabeth* (1934) may be commended as a well-written, accurate, and full account of certain aspects of the reign, albeit it does not pretend to be a definitive history. Lastly, there is, standing in a class by itself, A. L. Rowse's *The England of Elizabeth* (3 vols., two of which have been published, and the third is on the way): a very full, highly descriptive, and richly illustrated analysis of the reign—suffering a little from bias, but otherwise a very commendable work.

On the catholic side, John Lingard's *History*, though still useful, is antiquated. The last edition revised by the author was published in 1849 and has been superseded by A. O. Meyer, *England and the Catholic Church under Queen Elizabeth* (trans. from the German by McKee, 1916), which is based on the Vatican archives and carries the *imprimatur* of the Roman church. It is at once scholarly, dispassionate, and reasonable.

Conyers Read's *Mr. Secretary Cecil and Queen Elizabeth* (1956), and his three companion volumes on *Mr. Secretary Walsingham* (1925), are among the most important modern contributions to Elizabethan history: they are both indispensable, but the former is not yet completed. The best account of Essex is W. B. Devereux, *Lives and Letters of the Devereux, Earls of Essex* (2 vols., 1853); to which may be added Lytton Strachey's penetrating study, *Elizabeth and Essex* (1928). The standard life of Sidney is H. R. Fox Bourne, *Sir Philip Sidney* (1891), and of Raleigh, W. Stebbing's *Sir Walter Ralegh* (1899). The best biography of Hawkins is J. A. Williamson's *Hawkins of Plymouth*, 1949. On the controversial topic of Elizabeth's relations with Leicester and the Amy Robsart affair, perhaps the most significant work is by a German historian, viz. Ernst Bekker, *Elisabeth und Leicester* (Giessener Studien, v, 1890).

THE CHURCH SETTLEMENT. For this aspect of the reign, the most important collections of printed sources are the Parker Society's series (54 vols., 1842–55), which contains the works and correspondence of most of the anglican leaders, e.g. Jewel, Pilkington, Grindal, Sandys, Whitgift, &c., and the invaluable *Zurich Letters*. Jewel's *Apology* is important for an understanding of the principles of the Settlement; and it should be studied in conjunction with Hooker's immortal *Ecclesiastical Polity* (ed. Church and Paget, 1888). Paget's *Introduction to the Fifth Book of the Polity* (separately printed) is the best synoptic account of the 'Platform' and philosophy underlying the Settlement. The most useful general history of the church for the period is still W. H. Frere, *The English Church in the reigns of Elizabeth and James* (1904); but the reader should also consult P. Hughes, *The Reformation in England*, vol. 3 (Hollis and Carter, 1950–6). Details of the settlement may be studied in H. Gee, *The Elizabethan Clergy and the Settlement of Religion* (1898). Neale's articles on 'The Elizabethan Acts of Supremacy and Uniformity', *Eng. Hist. Rev.*, vol. lxv, 1950, and 'Parliament and the Articles of Religion', ibid., vol. lxvii, pp. 510–21, are important. H. N. Birt, *The Elizabethan Settlement of Religion* (1907), which gives the catholic standpoint; F. W. Maitland's chapter in the *Cambridge Modern History*, vol. 2—a brilliant study of the subject; C. G. Bayne, *Anglo-Roman Relations, 1558–65* (1913); the relevant chapters in Pastor's monumental *History of the Papacy* (trans. by F. I. Antrobus and R. F. Kerr) are indispensable. Other sources of information are F. W. Maitland's *Elizabethan Gleanings* (1900–3), included in the same author's *Collected Papers* (ed. H. A. L. Fisher, 3 vols., 1911); *Bishops' Letters, 1564* (Camd. Mis., vol. ix); W. H. Frere and W. P. M. Kennedy, *Visitation Articles and Injunctions* (Alcuin Club, 1910); W. P. M. Kennedy, *Elizabethan Episcopal Administration* (Alcuin Club, 1925)—especially valuable for the later history of the church; F. O. White, *Lives of the Elizabethan Bishops* (1898); W. P. M. Kennedy, *Life of Parker* (1908); and Powel Mills Dawley, *John Whitgift and the English Reformation* (Scribner, 1954).

For a detailed study of catholic history recourse should be had to various volumes of the Catholic Record Society publications, esp. Persons's *Storie of Domestical Difficulties*, and *Letters and Memorials of Fr. Robert Persons, S.J.* (ed. Leo Hicks, S.J., 1942). The *Introduction* to the *Memorials* is admirable. Other sources of information are: William Allen's *Letters and Memorials* (ed. T. F. Knox, 1882); *The First and Second Douai Diaries* (ed. Knox, 1878); Cath. Rec. Soc., ii (1905), 12–218, and iv (1907), 1–161; J. H. Pollen, *Unpublished Documents Relating to the English Martyrs*, 1584–1603 (Cath. Rec. Soc., v, xxi); Nicholas Sanders, *De Origine ac Progressu Schismatis Anglicani* (ed. D. Lewis, 1877), and 'Report to Cardinal Morone on the change of Religion in 1558–9' (ed. Pollen, Cath. Rec. Soc. i. 1–46); T. G. Law, *Jesuits and Seculars* (1889); R. Lechat, *Les Réfugiés anglais dans les Pays-Bas espagnols* (1914); R. Simpson, *Edmund Campion* (1896); and J. H. Pollen, *The English Catholics in the Reign of Queen Elizabeth* (1920). On the other (government) side, consult Burghley's *Execution of Justice in England*, and *A Declaration of the Honourable Dealing of her Majesty's Commissioners*, &c. (*Somers Tracts*, i. 189–208 and 209–12).

For the Puritan movement, Daniel Neal, *History of the Puritans* (3 vols., 1793), although out of date, prejudiced, and chaotic, is still useful. The most valuable books on presbyterial puritanism are A. F. Scott Pearson's *Thomas Cartwright and Elizabethan Puritanism* (1925), and the same author's *Church and State: Political Aspects of Sixteenth Century Puritanism* (1928). Other works of importance are: W. H. Frere and C. E. Douglas, *Puritan Manifestos* (Church Hist. Soc., lxxii, 1907); R. G. Usher, *The Presbyterian Movement* (Camd. Soc., 3rd ser., viii, 1905); and Whitgift's *Works* (ed. J. Ayre, 3 vols., Parker Soc., 1851–3). A highly specialized study of the movement from an unusual angle is M. M. Knappen's *Tudor Puritanism* (1939). For the separatists, consult C. Burrage, *Early English Dissenters* (2 vols., 1912), the same author's *True Story of Robert Browne* (1906); F. J. Powicke, *Henry Barrow* (1900); and R. W. and A. W. W. Dale's *History of English Congregationalism* (1907). The Martin Marprelate controversy may be studied in E. Arber's *Introductory Sketch to the Martin Marprelate Controversy* (1895); Albert Peel's *Note-book of John Penry, 1593* (R. Hist. Soc., 1944); W. Pierce, *Historical Introduction to the Marprelate Tracts* (1909), *The Marprelate Tracts* (1909), and *John Penry* (1923). The standard work on the High Commission is R. G. Usher, *The Rise and Fall of the High Commission* (1913). A. J. Klein, *Intolerance in the Reign of Elizabeth*, 1917, should also be mentioned.

FOREIGN AFFAIRS. The *Calendar of State Papers, Foreign*, whose various volumes now cover the period 1558–89, and are still in process of publication, is the chief authority; but it does not include Anglo-Spanish relations, which are separately treated in the *Calendar of State Papers, Spanish* (4 vols., 1558–1603). The *Calendar of State Papers, Venetian*, covering the relations between England and Venice, is complete for the reign of Elizabeth. The important *State Papers, Spanish*, however, have to be supplemented by material from the great *Colección de Documentos inéditos para la Historia de España* (112 vols., 1842–95), especially vols. 87, 89, 90, 91, and 92. There is a catalogue to these *documentos* by J. Paz (1930–1) and a *Nueva Colección* (6 vols., 1892–6). The principal corpus of material for England's relations with the Netherlands is Kervyn de Lettenhove's magnificent *Relations politiques des Pays-Bas et de l'Angleterre, 1555–79* (11 vols., 1882–1900), and although they overlap, in some cases, those printed in the *Foreign Calendar*, the fact that they are printed *in extenso* renders their value unique. For a fuller understanding of the issues at stake in the Low Countries, recourse should be had to L. P. Gachard's *Correspondance de Philippe II* (5 vols., 1848–79); *de Marguerite d'Autriche* (3 vols., 1867–81); *du Duc d'Albe* (1850), *de Guillaume le Taciturne* (6 vols., 1847–57); and *d'Alexandre Farnèse*, part i (1853); and Groen van Prinsterer's *Archives de la Maison d'Orange-Nassau* (1st ser., 10 vols., 1835–47, 2nd ser., 6 vols., 1857–62). Gachard's great work has been supplemented by Lefèvre's continuations, viz., tome i, tome ii, and tome iii of the *Correspondance de Philippe II*, covering the period 1577–1591, and published in Brussels in 1940, 1953, and 1956 respectively. Add also Lefèvre's *Correspondance de Marguerite d'Autriche avec Philippe II*, tome iii, 1566–7, and van der Essen's *Alexandre Farnèse, Duc de Parme* (5 vols., Brussels, 1937)—a masterly production. The following works are also most helpful: R. B. Merriman, *The Rise of the Spanish Empire* (4 vols., 1932); Henri Pirenne, *Histoire de la Belgique* (vols. iii–iv, 1912–19); P. J. Blok, *History of the Netherlands* (8 vols., trans. and abridged by Bierstadt and Putnam, 1898–1912); P. J. Blok, *Correspondance inédite de . . . Leicester, François, et de Jean Hotman* (deals with Leicester and the popular faction); Teulet, *Relations politiques de la France et de l'Espagne avec l'Écosse* (Paris, 1862); P. Geyl, *The Revolt of the Netherlands* (1932); Kervyn de Lettenhove, *Les Huguenots et les Gueux,* (1883–5); and, by far the most literary, J. L. Motley, *The Rise of the Dutch Republic* and *The United Netherlands* (1855, and 1860–7). Motley, like Froude, is a pleasure to read, but his bias against Philip II must be remembered. In this place also might be mentioned P. O. de Törne, *Don Juan d'Autriche et les projets de conquête de l'Angleterre* (1928), and J. Kretzchmar, *Die Invasionsprojekte der katholischen Mächte gegen England zur Zeit Elizabeths* (1892). Both works are invaluable, the latter being based on the Vatican archives.

For Anglo-French relations the most important collections of documents are A. Teulet, *Relations politiques de la France . . . avec l'Écosse* (5 vols., 1862), and *Correspondance diplomatique de B. Salaignac de la Mothe Fénelon* (7 vols., Bannatyne Club, 1840). These should be supplemented by H. Ferrière-Percy, *Lettres de Catherine de Médicis* (10 vols., 1880–1909); *Lettres Missives d'Henri IV* (ed. Xivry & Gaudet, Paris, 1843–76); Le Laboureur, *Mémoires de Michel de Castelnau, seigneur de Mauvissière* (3 vols., 1731); H. Forneron, *Les Ducs de Guise et leur époque* (2 vols., 1877); the duc d'Aumâle's *Histoire des Princes de Condé*; and, exceedingly important for Walsingham's mission to France in 1570–3 and again in 1581, Dudley Digges, *The Compleat Ambassador* (1655). And, for the later history of Anglo-French relations, the relevant sources are:—Laffleur de Kermaingant's *L'Ambassade de France en Angleterre, sous Henry IV, 1598–1605* (4 vols., 1886–95); Henry Unton's *Correspondence, 1591–2* (ed. J. Stevenson, Roxburghe Club, 1847); Ralph Winwood's *Memorials, 1597–1603* (ed. Sawyer, 3 vols., 1725); and the *Edmondes Papers, 1592–9* (ed. G. G. Butler, Roxburghe Club, 1913).

For French public opinion during the reign, in relation to events taking place in England, consult G. Ascoli, *La Grande Bretagne devant l'Opinion française* (1928). A useful analysis of the various embassies sent to France from England is printed in the *Bulletin of the Institute of Historical Research,* 1926, 1927, 1928, and 1929, by F. J. Weaver. Relations of England and Germany, with special reference to Elizabeth's dealings with John Casimir, may be studied in F. von Bezold, *Briefe des Pfalzgrafen Johann Casimir* (2 vols., 1882–4), and V. von Klarwill's *Queen Elizabeth and some Foreigners* (trans. T. N. Nash, 1928) deals with Elizabeth's marriage negotiations with the archduke Charles.

Although the documents quoted in the latter work are from the Vienna archives, the editing is careless. The only papers of value from Italian archives are the Venetian Papers referred to above, and the *Calendar of State Papers, Rome*, 1558–71 and 1572–8.

CONSTITUTIONAL

The most important collections of printed documents are the following: *The Statutes of the Realm* (ed. Luders, Tomlins, and Raithby, 11 vols., 1810–28); J. R. Tanner, *Tudor Constitutional Documents* (1922); G. W. Prothero, *Select Statutes and Documents* (1898); and R. Steele, *Tudor and Stuart Proclamations* (2 vols., 1910). Tanner, Prothero, and Steele have valuable introductions; but there is no adequate history of the constitution for the period. H. Hallam, *The Constitutional History of England from the Accession of Henry VIII to the Death of George II* (1846) is antiquated, and F. W. Maitland, *The Constitutional History of England* (1908) is too brief; but both are helpful. The best account is to be found in Sir W. S. Holdsworth, *A History of English Law*, vol. iv, 1924. Cheyney's *History*, referred to above, ought also to be consulted. The only contemporary survey of the constitution is Thomas Smith, *De Republica Anglorum* (ed. L. Alston, 1906).

For parliament the authorities are Sir Simonds D'Ewes, *Journals of the Parliaments during Elizabeth's Reign* (1693); H. Townshend, *The Last Four Parliaments of Elizabeth* (1680); the *Journals of the House of Lords* (1846); and the *Journals of the House of Commons* (ed. Vardon and May, 1803). In connexion with the last two works, reference should be made to articles by A. F. Pollard on 'The Authenticity of the Lords' Journals in the Sixteenth Century' (*Trans. R.H.S.*, 3rd ser., viii, 1914, 17–40) and by J. E. Neale on 'The Commons' Journal of the Tudor Period' (*Trans. R.H.S.*, 4th ser., iii, 1920, 136–70). Of modern works on parliament, A. F. Pollard, *The Evolution of Parliament* (1926), and C. H. McIlwain, *The High Court of Parliament* (1910), may be singled out as especially worthy of attention; and Neale's articles in the *E.H.R.*, vols. xxxiv (1919) and xxxvi (1921), are valuable elucidations of particular points connected with Elizabeth's parliamentary tactics. The same author's papers on 'The Commons' Privilege of Free Speech' (*Tudor Studies*, ed. R. W. Seton-Watson, 1924), on 'Peter Wentworth' (*E.H.R.* xxxix, 1924), and on 'Three Elizabethan Elections' (*E.H.R.* xlvi, 1931) are important contributions to parliamentary history. C. G. Bayne's article on 'The First House of Commons of Queen Elizabeth' (*E.H.R.* xxiii, 1908) is also valuable. But all books on parliament and the constitution, hitherto accepted as valid, have been superseded by Sir John Neale's trilogy—*The Elizabethan House of Commons*, and *Elizabeth I and her Parliaments* (2 vols.). These volumes are rich in material hitherto unexplored by researchers.

The best guide to the printed and unprinted sources for the history of the council is E. R. Adair, *Sources for the History of the Council in the Sixteenth and Seventeenth Centuries* ('Helps for Students of History', no. 51, 1924). The standard work of reference for the council is the *Acts of the Privy Council of England*, ed. J. R. Dasent (32 vols., 1890–1907), but it has many gaps. On this subject consult Adair's articles in the *E.H.R.*, vols. xxx and xxxviii. The following modern works will be found helpful: A. V. Dicey, *The Privy Council* (1887); Lord Eustace Percy, *The Privy Council under the Tudors* (1907); Dorothy Gladish, *The Tudor Privy Council* (1915); Rachel R. Reid, *The King's Council in the North* (1921)—an exhaustive study; and Caroline A. J. Skeel, *The Council in the Marches of Wales* (1904). Other useful works on the administrative aspect of government are Florence M. G. Evans, *The Principal Secretary of State, &c.* (1923); Gladys Scott Thomson, *Lords Lieutenant in the Sixteenth Century* (1923); and C. H. Beard, *The Office of Justice of the Peace* (1904). But reference should also be made, as in the case of constitutional history generally, to Holdsworth and Cheyney.

For the public finance of the period consult S. Dowell, *A History of Taxation and Taxes in England* (4 vols., 1888)—the only, albeit far from adequate, general account of the system of taxation; H. Hall, *A History of the Customs revenue in England* (2 vols., 1885); F. C. Dietz, *The Exchequer in Elizabeth's Reign* (Smith Coll. Studies in History, iii, 1918, no. 2); and an article by A. P. Newton on 'The Establishment of the Great Farm of the Customs' (*Trans. R.H.S.*, 4th ser., i, 1918).

SCOTLAND AND MARY STUART

The main source for Anglo-Scottish relations is the *Calendar of State Papers relating to Scotland*, 1547–1603 (ed. by J. Bain, W. K. Boyd, and M. S. Giuseppi in succession, and now complete to 1597). Subsidiary collections of documents are: *The Hamilton*

Papers (ed. J. Bain, 1890–2); the *Warrender Papers* (ed. A. I. Cameron, Scottish Hist. Soc., 3rd ser., 1931, 1932); *The Letters of Queen Elizabeth and James VI* (ed. J. Bruce, Camd. Soc., xlvi, 1849); and *The Correspondence of King James VI with Sir Robert Cecil and others*, &c. (ed. J. Bruce, Camd. Soc., lxxviii, 1861). Sir James Melville's *Memoirs, 1549–93* (ed. T. Thomson, Bannatyne Club, No. 18) are of great value, but should be read with caution: they were written in old age. Of contemporary histories, George Buchanan's *Rerum Scoticarum Historia* (trans. Aikman, 1827) is probably the best; but John Knox's *History of the Reformation in Scotland* and his *Correspondence* (vols. i–ii and iii–vi of his collected *Works*, ed. D. Laing, 1846–54) are more lively and give the spirit of the time. Among modern works, P. F. Tytler's *History of Scotland* (4 vols., 1873–7) may be commended for its fulness, but it is almost exclusively political. P. Hume Brown's *History of Scotland* (3 vols., 1908–9) is dispassionate, but rather dull. Both, however, are to be preferred to Andrew Lang's *History of Scotland* (4 vols., 1900–7), which, though brilliant and suggestive, is not impartial. W. L. Mathieson, *Politics and Religion, 1550–1695* (2 vols., 1902), is to be commended; and the *Scottish Historical Review* (1904–28) and (1947–) is a mine of information in matters connected with Scottish history.

The literature dealing with the queen of Scots is much too voluminous to be given in detail here, and a good deal of it is highly controversial; but the most concise bibliography now available is that of S. A. and D. R. Tannenbaum, 2 vols., 1944–5. J. Scott's *Bibliography of Works relating to Mary Queen of Scots* (Edinburgh Bibliographical Society, 1890) stops at 1700. The standard collection of Mary's correspondence is A. Labanoff's *Lettres, Instructions, et Mémoires de Marie Stuart* (7 vols., 1844); but it is incomplete and should be used in conjunction with A. Teulet's *Lettres de Marie Stuart* (1859) and the *Calendar of State Papers, Scotland* (referred to above). Labanoff excludes the so-called Casket Letters as forgeries: Teulet includes them. For Mary's relations with Rome, consult J. H. Pollen's *Papal Negotiations with Mary, Queen of Scots*, &c. (Scot. Hist. Soc., xxxvii, 1901), and for her relations with the Guises, see the same writer's *A Letter from Mary Queen of Scots to the Duke of Guise* (ibid., xliii, 1904).

Of the books friendly to Mary, Jules Gauthier's *Histoire de Marie Stuart* (2 vols., Paris, 1875); Phillipson's *Histoire de la*

Règne de Marie Stuart (1891–2); and J. Hosack's *Mary Queen of Scots and her Accusers* (2 vols., 1870–4), are the best. On the other side stand T. F. Henderson's *Life* of the queen, and Mignet's and Hay Fleming's—all of which are extremely critical. Apart from these scholarly works, Stephan Zweig's *The Queen of Scots* (1935) is a fascinating, interpretative study, psychological as well as historical. Attention should also be paid to W. Goodall's brilliant *Examination of the Letters said to be written by Mary, Queen of Scots, to James, earl of Bothwell* (2 vols., 1754), and to Leslie's *Defence of the Honour of Marie, Queen of Scotland*, albeit the latter is heavily biased. Among recent books two are well worth reading, viz. R. H. Mahon's *Mary Queen of Scots* (1924), and Mons. Roger Chauviré's *Le Secret de Marie Stuart* (Paris, 1937). The most violent anti-Marian propaganda comes, of course, from Buchanan's *Detection of the Doings of Marie, Queen of Scottis* (1572), which presents the case of the Scottish lords against the queen.

The principal material for Mary's imprisonment in England is to be found in the *Bardon Papers* (Camd. Soc., 3rd ser., xvii, 1909); the *Letter Books of Amias Paulet* (J. Morris, 1874); and J. H. Pollen's *Mary Queen of Scots and the Babington Plot* (Scot. Hist. Soc., 3rd ser., 1922). J. D. Leader's *Mary, Queen of Scots in Captivity* (1880) gives a detailed account of her imprisonment, but lacks substance; and S. Cowan's *The Last Days of Mary Stuart* (1907) is mainly useful for its translation of Burgoyne's Journal—originally printed in M. R. Chantelauze's *Marie Stuart, son procès et son exécution* (1876). The Casket Letter controversy can be followed in Goodall's *Examination*; Hosack's *Mary Queen of Scots and her Accusers*; T. F. Henderson's *The Casket Letters*; and A. Lang's *The Mystery of Mary Stuart*.

Other books of value in connexion with the queen of Scots are: A. Chéruel, *Marie Stuart et Catherine de Médicis* (1858); J. E. Neale's *Elizabeth and her Parliaments*, vols. i and ii, *passim*; also *King James's Secret* by R. S. Rait and A. I. Cameron, 1927, which gives an account of the king's attitude to his mother's trial and death, with illustrative matter from the *Warrender Papers*. J. D. Mackie's *Negotiations between James VI and Ferdinand, Grand Duke of Tuscany* (St. Andrews Univ. Pub. no. xxv, 1927) is illuminating on the subject of the king's foreign policy.

IRELAND

The most important collections of documents (printed)

are: The *Calendar of State Papers, Ireland* (ed. Hamilton and Atkinson, 11 vols.), which are complete for the reign; the *Calendar of Carew MSS.* (ed. Brewer and Bullen, 6 vols.); the *Calendar of Fiants* (published by the deputy keeper of public records in Ireland, 6 vols., 1875–90); the *Statutes of Ireland* (8 vols., 1765); the *Acts of the Privy Council in Ireland* (J. T. Gilbert in H.M.C., 15th report, 45, and Appendix iii, 1–296); the *Calendar of Patent and Close Rolls of Chancery in Ireland* (ed. J. Morrin, 3 vols., 1861–3); R. Lascelles, *Liber Munerum Publicorum Hiberniae*—a record of all official appointments (2 vols., 1852) with Index in App. iii, to 9th Report of the deputy keeper of public records, Ireland (1877); J. Lodge, *Desiderata Curiosa Hibernica* (2 vols., 1772); the *Irish Correspondence of James Fitzmaurice of Desmond* (ed. J. O'Donovan, Royal Soc. of Antiquaries of Ireland, 2nd ser., 1859, 354–69); *Letters from Sir Robert Cecil to Sir George Carew* (ed. J. Maclean, Camd. Soc., lxxxvii); the *Social State of the Southern and Eastern Counties of Ireland in the Sixteenth Century* (ed. H. F. Hore and J. Graves, Kilkenny Arch. Soc., 1868–9); T. Stafford, *Pacata Hibernia*—important for the Tyrone rebellion (ed. S. H. O'Grady, 2 vols., 1896); *Ireland under Elizabeth and James I*, described by Spenser, Moryson, and Davies (ed. H. Morley, Carisbrooke Lib. Ser. x, 1890); O'Clery's *Life of Hugh Roe O'Donnell* (ed. D. Murphy, 1893). For the ecclesiastical history of the period recourse should be had to the following: H. Cotton, *Fasti Ecclesiae Hibernicae* (6 vols., 1848–78), which furnishes brief biographies and details of appointments of prelates of the anglican church; W. M. Brady, *The Episcopal Succession in England, Scotland, and Ireland* (3 vols., 1876–7), and P. F. Moran, *The Episcopal Succession in Ireland during the Reign of Elizabeth* (1866), which give similar information for the church of Rome; E. P. Shirley, *Original Letters and Papers* (1851); *Ibernia Ignatiana* (ed. E. Hogan, 1880), which gives letters and papers from jesuit archives dealing with the activities of the Order in Ireland; the *Spicilegium Ossoriense* (ed. P. F. Moran, 3 vols., 1874–84), valuable for letters of Irish catholics to Philip II; and W. M. Brady, *State Papers concerning the Irish Church in the time of Elizabeth* (1868).

The standard modern history of Ireland in the Tudor period is R. Bagwell, *Ireland under the Tudors* (3 vols., 1890), for which at present there is no adequate substitute. M. Bonn, *Die englische Kolonisation in Irland* (2 vols., Stuttgart, 1906), is an analytical work of high quality, on the sociological side, but unfortunately it still lacks a translator. Of the shorter histories, W. O'Connor Morris, *Ireland 1494–1868* (1909), is probably the best. The ablest ecclesiastical histories are J. T. Ball, *The Reformed Church of Ireland, 1537–1886* (1890), on the anglican side, and Bellesheim, *Geschichte der katholischen Kirche in Irland* (3 vols., 1890–1), for the catholic standpoint. Other works on special subjects are: E. W. L. Hamilton, *Elizabethan Ulster* (1919); H. Wood, 'The Court of Castle Chamber, or Star Chamber of Ireland' (*Proc. Royal Irish Academy,* xxxii, sect. c, no. 90); C. I. Falkiner, 'The Parliament of Ireland under the Tudors' (*Proc. R.I.A.* xxv); A. K. Longfield, *Anglo-Irish Trade in the Sixteenth Century* (1930); M. V. Ronan, *The Reformation in Ireland under Elizabeth* (1930)— informative but not well arranged; J. B. Kelso, *Die Spanier in Irland* (Leipzig Diss., 1902); W. F. Butler, *Gleanings from Irish History* (1925), specially important for the English land policy in Ireland; and the same author's *Confiscation in Irish History* (1917). The 'Journal of the Irish House of Lords in Sir John Perrot's Parliament', ed. F. J. Routledge in *E.H.R.* xxix. 104–17, is important for parliamentary history, and J. H. Pollen, 'The Irish Expedition of 1579' (*The Month,* ci, 1903, 69–85), for Thomas Stukely's enterprise.

The Irish chronicles of greatest value are the *Annals of the Four Masters* (ed. J. O'Donovan, 7 vols., 1856) and the *Annals of Loch Cé* (ed. W. Hennessy, Rolls Series, 2 vols., 1871).

LITERATURE, THOUGHT, AND EDUCATION

The general guide to the literature of the period is the *Cambridge History of English Literature* (A. W. Ward and A. R. Waller, 14 vols., 1907–16); the chapters are by specialists, and there are full bibliographies. But C. S. Lewis's 'English Literature in the 16th Century, exclusive of the Drama' (*Oxford History of English Literature,* vol. iii, 1954), is a much more interesting, critical, and inspiring study, within the limits set by the editors. Failing Lewis, there is Legouis and Cazamian's *History of English Literature,* which is admirable (1948). For the more recent additions to the literature dealing with the subject, consult the bibliographies contained in the March issue of the publications of the Modern Language Association each year, and *The Year's Work in English Studies* (published by the Clarendon Press annually for the English Association). Valuable material will be found in the publications of the Shakespeare Society (1841–53) and of the New Shakspere Society (1874–86); also E. Arber's *English Reprints* (7 vols., 1868–70), the Spenser Society (1867–94) publications, the Ballad Society (1868–73), and the Malone Society *Reprints of Elizabethan Plays*. The standard work on the stage of the period is E. K. Chambers, *The Elizabethan Stage* (4 vols., 1923); it contains a copious bibliography. F. E. Schelling, The *Elizabethan Drama* (2 vols., 1908), and W. M. A. Creizenach, *The English Drama in the Age of Shakespeare* (1916), are useful adjuncts; so also is *Henslowe's Diary* (ed. W. W. Greg, 2 vols., 1904–8).

The most important book on Shakespeare is undoubtedly E. K. Chambers's *William Shakespeare* (1930); but the Shakespeare literature is very extensive, and should be approached under the guidance of Chambers's bibliography, attached to the aforesaid volume. Of the modern critics of the plays, the best known are A. C. Bradley and G. Brandes; the former's *Shakespearean Tragedy* and the latter's *William Shakespeare—a Critical Study*, are masterpieces. But a few of the more recent writers may be mentioned as worthy of notice: viz. M. M. Reese, *Shakespeare, his world, and his work* (1954); Lily B. Campbell, *Shakespeare's Histories—Mirrors of Elizabethan Policy* (Huntington Library, 1947); Richard Flatter, *Hamlet's Father*, an unusual and fascinating approach to the subject; and E. M. Tillyard's *Shakespeare's History Plays* (1951).

The literature on Spenser is also considerable, and guidance should be sought in F. I. Carpenter, *A Reference Guide to Edmund Spenser* (1923). For special studies of aspects of Elizabethan literature, the following references may be found useful: J. Erskine, *The Elizabethan Lyric* (1905); Bernard H. Newdigate, *Michael Drayton and his Circle* (Oxford, 1941); J. J. Jusserand, *The English Novel in the Time of Shakespeare* (trans. E. Lee, 1890); P. Sheavyn, *The Literary Profession in the Elizabethan Age* (1909); G. Gregory Smith, *Elizabethan Critical Essays* (2 vols., 1904); A. C. Southern, *Elizabethan Recusant Prose, 1559–1582* (1950); J. T. Murray, *English Dramatic Companies* (2 vols., 1910); J. T. Buxton, *Sir Philip Sidney and the English Renaissance* (1954); and R. B. McKerrow's edition of the *Works of Thomas Nashe* (5 vols., 1904–10), with its valuable introduction on pamphleteering.

The political thought of the period may be studied in Lord Acton's *History of Freedom and other Essays* (ed. J. N. Figgis, 1909);

in J. N. Figgis, *The Theory of the Divine Right of Kings* (1896), and *From Gerson to Grotius* (1907); in H. O. Taylor, *Thought and Expression in the Sixteenth Century* (2 vols., 1920); in L. Einstein, *The Italian Renaissance in England* (1902) and *Tudor Ideals* (1921); in J. W. Allen, *History of Political Thought in the Sixteenth Century* (1928); and Christopher Morris, *Political Thought in England—Tyndale to Hooker* (Home University Library, 1954). For Machiavelli's influence (or lack of influence) on England, consult M. Praz, 'Machiavelli and the Elizabethans' (*Proc. Brit. Acad.*, xiii, 1928), and L. A. Weissberger, 'Machiavelli and Tudor England' (*Pol. Sci. Quar.* xlii, 1927); but see also *Machiavelli's Prince—An Elizabethan Translation* (H. Craig, N. Carolina Univ. Press, 1945).

For Elizabethan education the best guides are: J. B. Mullinger, *The University of Cambridge* (2 vols., 1873–84), and C. E. Mallet, *A History of the University of Oxford* (3 vols., 1924–7); Anthony à Wood, *Athenae Oxonienses* (2 vols., 1692, ed. Philip Bliss, 6 vols., 1813–20); A. R. M. Stowe, *English Grammar Schools in the Reign of Queen Elizabeth* (1908), and Foster Watson, *The English Grammar Schools to 1660, their Curriculum and Practice* (1908); Joan Simons, 'A. F. Leach and the Reformation' (*Brit. Journal of Educ. Studies*, 1955); Roger Ascham, *English Works* (ed. W. A. Wright, 1904), with special reference to *The Scholemaster*; Richard Mulcaster, *Positions* (abridged ed. by J. Oliphant, 1903); and Foster Watson's translation of Vives's *Linguae Latinae Exercitio* (in *Tudor School Boy Life*, 1908). For a general discussion of Renaissance education consult W. H. Woodward, *Studies in Education during the Age of the Renaissance* (1906).

MUSIC, ART, AND SCIENCE

The most satisfactory history of Elizabethan music is perhaps E. Walker, *A History of Music in England*, chaps. iii and iv (1907). Ecclesiastical music is very fully dealt with in P. C. Buck's *Tudor Church Music* (10 vols., 1923–30). E. H. Fellowes, *The English Madrigal Composers* (1921), is valuable for this aspect of the subject, and F. W. Galpin, *Old English Instruments of Music* (1911), is necessary for an understanding of the various instruments and their uses. G. Grove's *Dictionary of Music and Musicians* (ed. H. Colles, 1927–8) is very useful for biographical detail. The standard work on William Byrd, is E. H. Fellowes's *William Byrd*, Oxford, 1937; and an account of

Musicians in English Society from Elizabeth to Charles I by Walter L. Woodfil (Princeton Studies, vol. ix, 1953), has a special interest.

The authorities on architecture for the period are R. Blomfield, *History of Renaissance Architecture in England* (2 vols., 1897); T. Garner and A. Stratton, *The Domestic Architecture of England during the Tudor Period* (2 vols., 1911, 1929); H. M. Colvin, *Biographical Dictionary of English Architects* (1954)—indispensable. For painting and engraving consult C. H. C. Baker and W. G. Constable, *English Painting of the Sixteenth and Seventeenth Centuries* (1930), and A. M. Hind, *Engraving in the Sixteenth and Seventeenth Centuries* (1952).

The best account of gardening is R. Blomfield, *The Formal Garden in England* (8 vols., 1901). F. W. Fairholt's *Costume in England* (4th ed. by H. A. Dillon, 1896) is the standard book of reference for the dress of the period; and manners and customs may be studied in G. Harris's 'Domestic Everyday Life' (*Trans. R.H.S.* ix, 1881) and F. J. Furnival's *Manners and Meals in Olden Time* (Early Eng. Text Soc., xxxii, 1868). For sport and pastimes consult Mr. Justice Madden, *The Diary of Master William Silence* (1907); Roger Ascham's *Toxophilus*; Egerton Castle's *Schools and Masters of Fence* (1893); J. Strutt's *Sports and Pastimes of the People of England* (1801)—for bull- and bear-baiting; and R. Laneham's *Description of the Entertainment at Kenilworth* (ed. Furnival, New Shakespeare Society, 1890).

P. Smith's *History of Modern Culture*, vol. i (1930), is probably the best guide to the intellectual progress of the age; and the following books should be used for special subjects: Wallace Notestein's *History of Witchcraft in England, from 1558 to 1718* (1911), is useful as a background; but special attention should be given to: Halliwell-Phillips's *Collection of Letters illustrative of the progress of Science in England from Elizabeth to Charles II* (1841); C. F. Smith, *John Dee 1527–1608* (1909); W. W. Bryant, *A History of Astronomy* (1907); J. N. Stillman, *The Story of Early Chemistry* (1924); W. W. R. Ball, *A Short Account of the History of Mathematics* (1915); and above all, William Gilbert, *De Magnete*, &c. (trans. Gilbert Club, London, 1900), the most important contribution of the age to natural science. For medicine and surgery, consult W. Osler, *The Evolution of Modern Medicine* (1921), and J. F. South's *Memorials of the Craft of Surgery in England* (1886). Information about social health and disease may be found in

C. Creighton's *A History of Epidemics in Britain* (1891), and
F. P. Wilson, *The Plague in Shakespeare's London* (1927).

MILITARY

M. J. W. Cockle, *A Bibliography of English Military Books to
1642* (1900), is the best guide to literature on the art of war; but
there is no comprehensive bibliography dealing with campaigns.
Information on this subject must be sought for in Froude,
Cheyney, Motley, Bagwell, and other historians of the period.
But the following books are worthy of consideration: E. van
Meteren, *A True Discourse Historical* (trans. T. Churchyard and
R. Robinson, 1602), which gives an account of Norreys's campaigns, 1577–89, and afterwards in Portugal and elsewhere;
and C. R. Markham, *The Fighting Veres* (1888), which is impor-
tant for the military history of the last ten years of the reign.
C. Falls, *Elizabeth's Irish Wars* (1950) and *Lord Mountjoy* (1956),
are very knowledgeable accounts of the Irish campaigns, and
throw light on the native Irish armies and their Scottish allies.
C. G. Cruickshank's *Elizabeth's Army* (1946) helps to complete
the picture. For the armour of the period, consult C. J. Ffoulkes,
Armour and Weapons (1909) and *The Armourer and his Craft* (1912).
Contemporary books on war that may appeal to the specialist
are: Whithorne's translation of Machiavelli's *Arte della Guerra*
(1588); Barnaby Rich's *Pathway to Military Practice* (1587); Sir
John Smith's *Discourses* (1590); Roger Williams's *A Brief Discourse of War* (1590); and Sir H. Knyvett's *Defence of the Realm*
(1596). The standard account of the British army is, of course,
J. H. Fortescue's monumental *History of the British Army* (13
vols., 1899–1930): vol. i, bk. ii, chaps. 2–5, deal with our period.

NAVAL

Naval bibliographies are best represented by W. G. Perrin,
Admiralty Library, a subject-catalogue of printed books in the
Admiralty Library (1912), part i; G. E. Mainwaring, *A Bibliography of British Naval History* (1930); and the bibliographies
appended to J. S. Corbett's standard volumes on *Drake and the
Tudor Navy* (2 vols., 1898–9) and *The Successors of Drake* (1900),
which are both indispensable. For the administration of the
admiralty consult M. Oppenheim, *History of the Administration of
the Royal Navy* (1896), and R. G. Marsden, *Select Cases from the
Admiralty Courts* (Selden Soc., vol. ii, 1897). The Navy Record

Society publications contain much material of first-rate importance, notably vols. i and ii (*State Papers relating to the Defeat of the Armada*, by J. A. K. Laughton), vol. xi (*Papers relating to the Spanish War, 1585–7*, by J. S. Corbett), vols. xxii, xxiii, xlvi, and xlvii (W. Monson's *Naval Tracts*, ed. M. Oppenheim, with a valuable introduction), and vol. xi, app. A (*Guns and Gunnery in the Tudor Navy*, by J. S. Corbett). The story of the armada from the Spanish angle is given in Fernandez Duro, *La Armada Invincible* (2 vols., 1884–5), and in J. A. Froude, *The Spanish Story of the Armada* (1882), which is also based on the Spanish authorities.

ECONOMIC AND SOCIAL

There is no general or complete bibliography at present available, but many of the works referred to below contain useful bibliographies on aspects of the subject. R. H. Tawney and Eileen Power, *Tudor Economic Documents* (3 vols., 1924), is the best selection of material. E. Lipson, *The Economic History of England* (3 vols., 1915–31), is the most systematic account of the whole subject; but W. Cunningham, *Growth of English Industry and Commerce* (2 vols., 1903–5), which is arranged on an entirely different plan, is also to be commended. For the agrarian revolution the best book is R. H. Tawney, *The Agrarian Problem in the Sixteenth Century* (1912), but the following should also be consulted: R. W. Prothero (Lord Ernle), *English Farming Past and Present* (1919); A. H. Johnson, *The Disappearance of the Small Landowner* (1909); E. C. K. Gonner, *Common Land and Enclosure* (1912); Thomas Tusser, *A Hundred Good Points of Husbandrie* (1557, 1573); F. G. Davenport, *The Economic Development of a Norfolk Manor* (1906); H. L. Gray, *English Field Systems* (Harvard Studies, xxii, 1915); E. F. Gay, 'Inclosures in England in the Sixteenth Century' (*Quar. Jour. Econ.* xvii. 576–97); A. Savine, 'Bondmen under the Tudors' (*Trans. R.H.S.*, 2nd ser., xvii. 235–89) and 'English Customary Tenure in the Tudor Period' (*Quar. Jour. Econ.* xix. 33–80). Lipson uses most of the conclusions arrived at by Gay, Savine, and Johnson in his *History*. Relevant contemporary material will be found in *A Discourse of the Common Weal of this Realm of England* (ed. Elizabeth Lamond, 1929); P. Stubbes's *Anatomy of Abuses* (ed. Furnivall, New Shakspere Society, 1877–9); and W. Harrison's *Description of England* (ed. Furnivall, ibid., 1908). The following modern or more recent writings should be noted: R. H. Tawney, 'The Rise of the Gentry, 1558–1640' (*Econ. Hist. Rev.*, 1941); Mildred Campbell, *The English Yeoman under Elizabeth and the Early Stuarts* (Humphrey Milford, London, 1942); Lawrence Stone, 'The Anatomy of the Elizabethan Aristocracy' (*Ec. Hist. Rev.*, 1948); H. R. Trevor-Roper, 'The Elizabethan Aristocracy: An Anatomy Anatomized' (*Ec. Hist. Rev.* 1950), and, on a fuller scale, *The Gentry, 1540–1640* (Camb. Univ. Press, 1951); W. G. Hoskins, *The Leicestershire Farmer in the Sixteenth Century* (1942); E. E. Rich, 'Elizabethan Population' (*Ec. Hist. Rev.*, ser. 2, vol. 2, pp. 247–65).

For industry and commerce the most important works are: G. Unwin, *Industrial Organization in the Sixteenth and Seventeenth Centuries* (1904), and his collected papers (*Studies in Economic History*, ed. R. H. Tawney, 1927). The history of the joint stock companies should be studied in W. R. Scott, *English, Scottish, and Irish Joint Stock Companies* (3 vols., 1911–12). R. H. Tawney, *Religion and the Rise of Capitalism* (1926), is as important as his *Agrarian Problem* for a proper understanding of the economic tendencies of the age. G. Unwin, *The Guilds and Companies of London* (1908), should also be consulted. For monetary theory and practice consult Thomas Wilson, *A Discourse upon Usury* (ed. R. H. Tawney, 1925): it contains a valuable introduction.

It is impossible to give a list of the books dealing with the different industries, but the following represent a choice of the most significant: J. U. Nef, *The Rise of the British Coal Industry* (2 vols., 1932); H. Heaton, *The Yorkshire Woollen and Worsted Industries* (1920), and *The Wiltshire Woollen Industry in the 16th and 17th Centuries* (1943); E. Lipson, *British Woollen and Worsted Industries* (1921); G. R. Lewis, *The Stannaries* (Harv. Econ. Ser. iii, 1908); H. Hamilton, *The English Brass and Copper Industries to 1800* (1926); M. B. Donald, *Elizabeth and Copper: The History of the Company of Mines Royal, 1568–1605* (London, 1955); Allegra Woodworth, *Purveyance for the Royal Household in the Reign of Elizabeth* (Trans. Amer. Phil. Soc., new ser., vol. xxxv, pt. i); J. T. Jenkins, *The Herring and Herring Fisheries* (1927).

For prices consult J. E. T. Rogers, *A History of Agriculture and Prices in England* (7 vols., 1866–1900), supplemented by N. S. B. Gras, *The Evolution of the English Corn-market from the Twelfth to the Eighteenth Century* (Harv. Econ. Stud. xiii), and A. P. Usher, 'Prices of Wheat and Commodity Price Indexes for England,

1259–1930' (*Harv. Rev. of Econ. Statistics*, xiii. 103–13). The history of poor relief is dealt with by E. M. Leonard, *The Early History of English Poor Relief* (1900), and S. and B. Webb, *English Local Government: English Poor Law History*, part i, *The Old Poor Law* (1927); and there is a good account of monopolies in W. H. Price, *English Patents of Monopoly* (Harv. Econ. Stud. i, 1906).

For England's foreign trade, reference should be made to C. Read's article in *E.H.R.* xxix. 515–24; R. Ehrenberg, *Hamburg und England im Zeitalter der Königin Elisabeth* (1896)—the main authority for the struggle between the Merchant Adventurers and the Hanse; N. R. Deardorff, *English Trade in the Baltic during the Reign of Elizabeth* (1912); T. S. Willan, *The Muscovy Merchants of 1555* (Manc. Univ. Press, 1953); also, by the same author, 'Trade between England and Russia in the Second Half of the Sixteenth Century' (*E.H.R.*, 1948, pp. 307–21); and again by the same author, *The Early History of the Russia Company, 1553–1603* (Manc. Univ. Press, 1950); M. Wretts-Smith, 'The English in Russia during the Second Half of the Sixteenth Century' (*Trans. R.H.S.*, 4th ser., iii, 1920, 72–102); H. Stevens, *The Dawn of British Trade to the East Indies, 1599–1603* (1886); A. C. Wood, *The History of the Levant Company* (1935); and H. G. Rawlinson, 'Embassy of William Harborne to Constantinople, 1583–8' (*Trans. R.H.S.*, 4th ser., v, 1922, 1–27). J. W. Burgon, *The Life and Times of Sir Thomas Gresham* (2 vols., 1839), is valuable for England's borrowings abroad; and R. Ehrenberg, *Das Zeitalter der Fugger* (2 vols., 1896), is the last general account of the sixteenth-century money market. The latter work has been translated and abridged by H. M. Lucas under the title *Capital and Finance in the Age of the Renaissance* (1928).

For voyages, discoveries, and navigation the important repository of material is Richard Hakluyt's *Principal Navigations* &c. (ed. W. Raleigh, 12 vols., 1903–5), and *Hakluytus Posthumus or Purchas his Pilgrims* (ed. W. Raleigh, 20 vols., 1905–7), together with the various publications of the Hakluyt Society. The following books will also be found valuable: Elizabeth G. R. Taylor, *Tudor Geography* (1930) and *Late Tudor and Early Stuart Geography* (1934); E. Arber, *The First Three English Books on America* (1895); G. B. Parks, *Richard Hakluyt and the English Voyagers* (Amer. Geog. Soc. Pub., 1928); J. A. Williamson, *Sir John Hawkins* (1927); J. S. Corbett, *Drake and the Tudor Navy* (2 vols., 1899)—the standard life; H. R. Wagner, *Sir Francis*

Drake's Voyage Around the World (1925); J. A. Williamson's article on 'Books on Drake' (in *History*, xii. 310–21); W. Stebbing, *Sir Walter Raleigh* (1899); or E. Thompson, *Sir Walter Raleigh* (1935); C. R. Markham, *A Life of Sir John Davis*; F. Jones, *The Life of Sir Martin Frobisher* (1878); W. G. Gosling, *The Life of Sir Humphrey Gilbert* (1911); and F. E. Dyer, 'The Elizabethan Sailorman' (*Mariner's Mirror*, x. 133–46). The following recent Hakluyt Society publications should be noted: D. B. Quinn, *The Voyages and Colonizing Enterprises of Sir Humphrey Gilbert* (2 vols., 1940), and *The Voyages of Sir James Lancaster to Brazil and the East Indies, 1591–1603* (1940).

LISTS OF THE HOLDERS OF CERTAIN OFFICES

Archbishops of Canterbury

1559   Matthew Parker.
1575   Edmund Grindal (suspended in 1577; performed only spiritual functions till his death in 1583).
1583   John Whitgift.

Lord Chancellors and Keepers of the Great Seal

1558   Sir Nicholas Bacon, Lord Keeper.
1579   Sir Thomas Bromley, Lord Chancellor.
1587   Sir Christopher Hatton, Lord Chancellor.
1591   Sir John Puckering, Lord Keeper.
1596   Sir Thomas Egerton, Lord Keeper.

Lord Treasurers

1558   William Paulet, marquess of Winchester.
1572   William Cecil, Lord Burghley.
1599   Thomas Sackville, Lord Buckhurst.

Secretaries of State

1558   Sir William Cecil.
1572   Sir Thomas Smith.
1573   Sir Francis Walsingham.   1577
1577   Thomas Wilson (till 1581).
1586   William Davison (till 1587).   1590
1590–6   No principal secretary.
1596   Robert Cecil.
1600   John Herbert (till 1619).
               1612

Lord Chief Justices of the King's Bench

1558   Sir Robert Catlin.
1574   Sir Christopher Wray.

Lord Chief Justices of the Common Pleas

1558   Anthony Brown.
1559   Sir James Dyer.
1582   Edmund Anderson.
1592   Sir John Popham.

Lord High Admirals

1558   Edward, Lord Clinton, afterwards earl of Lincoln.

1585   Charles, Lord Howard of Effingham, afterwards earl of Nottingham.

Chief Governors of Ireland

1560   Thomas Radcliffe, earl of Sussex (Lord-Lieutenant).

1565–7
1568–71 } Sir Henry Sidney (Lord Deputy).
1575–8

1580   Arthur, Lord Grey de Wilton (Lord Deputy).

1584–8   Sir John Perrot (Lord Deputy).

1588–94 Sir William Fitzwilliam (Lord Deputy).

1594–7   Sir William Russell (Lord Deputy).

1597   Thomas, Lord Burgh (Lord Deputy).

1599   Robert Devereux, earl of Essex (Lord-Lieutenant).

1600   Charles Blount, Lord Mountjoy (Lord Deputy).

N.B. Lord-Lieutenant was a title of higher distinction than Lord Deputy, but both offices carried the same, or much the same, powers.

Speakers of the House of Commons

1558   Sir Thomas Gargrave.

1562–3   Thomas Williams.

1566   Richard Onslow.

1571   Christopher Wray.

1572   Robert Bell.

1575   Robert Bell.

1580   John Popham.

1584–5   John Puckering.

1586   John Puckering.

1588–9   Thomas Snagg.

1592–3   Edward Coke.

1597   Christopher Yelverton.

1601   John Crooke.

INDEX

Perrot, Sir John, 472, 473, 474.
Persecution of catholics, 185–8.
Persons, Robert, jesuit, 179–80, 181, 182, 183, 393, 407, 447, 448, 449, 454.
Perth, 40, 161.
Pet, Arthur, 241.
Petchora, bay of, 237.
Phelippes, Thomas, 380, 381, 382.
Philip II, 6, 26–27, 28, 36, 37, 39, 46, 52, 58, 59, 74, 88, 89, 96, 119–20, 121, 127, 128, 130, 132, 133, 145, 150, 158, 169, 172, 175, 336, 365, 368–9, 370, 389–90, 391–2, 393, 394, 395, 396, 397, 398, 404, 407, 414, 419, 426, 427 (death), 483, 484.
Philip III, king of Spain (1597), favours the Hispano-Irish alliance, 486, 487, 488, 489, 490.
Physicians, 314; college of, 315.
Pilkington, James, bishop of Durham, 22, 193.
Piracy, 126, 127.
Pius IV, pope, 27, 28.
Pius V, pope, 88–89, 106, 166, 167, 168, 169.
Plantation of Ireland, see Ireland.
Plate, silver, 272.
Plessis-les-Tours, Treaty of, 353.
Plumbers' Hall, 200
Pluralities, 190; bill against, 227.
Plymouth, 124, 129, 146, 398, 399, 400, 403, 411, 412, 413.
Poetaster, 301.
Pole, Reginald, the 'accursed cardinal', 12.
Pollini, Girolamo, 453.
Poly-Olbion, 286.
Ponod, Henry, 452.
Poor, sufferings of, 255.
Poor Law, 265, 266, 267.
Popham, Sir John, 204, 436, 440, 457.
Population of England and Wales, 235–6.
Porto Bello, 417.
Porto Praya, 369.
Porto Rico, 417.
Portugal, conquest of, 352, 353.
Portuguese monopoly in Africa, 123; in the East, 238.
Portuguese succession question, 352, 353.
Post-horses, 263–4.
Poynings, Sir Adrian, 60.
Poynings' Law, 463.
Prayer book, the, 14, 16.
Preston, Captain Amyas, 419.
Prestonpans, 46.
Primrose, of London, 369.
Principal Navigations (Hakluyt), 281, 283, 318.

Printing press, catholic, 182–3; puritan, 201–2.
Privy council, the, 207–10.
Proclamation re catholics (1591), 408.
'Prophesyings', 197–8.
Prose, Elizabethan, 292–4.
Ptolemy, Ptolemaic system, 307–8.
Puckering, Sir William, Lord Keeper, 226–7.
Puritanism, meaning of, 188; opposition to anglican system, 189; hostility to greed, materialism, and corruption, 190; vestiarian controversy, 191–2; produces disorder in the church, 192; attack on bishops, 193; Parker's difficulties with, 192–3; influence of Thomas Cartwright on, 194–5; effect on parliament, 195–6; 'prophesyings', 197–8; Whitgift's treatment of, 198–9; the 'classical' movement (presbytery in episcopacy), 200; the separatist movement, 200–1; Martin Marprelate conflict, 201–2: Bancroft's attack on presbyterianism, 202–3, 204; severity of the law to extremists, 204 and n., on anabaptists, 204–5.
Puritans, number of, 457 and n.
Pygmalion, 288.

Quadra, Alvarez de, bishop of Aquila, 27, 50, 52, 53, 122, 123, 124.
Queenborough, 44, 398.
Queen's County, 462.
Queensferry, 44.

Rabelais, 64.
Raleigh, Sir Walter, 131, 191, 229, 245, 246, 413, 419, 421 and n., 426, 439, 440, 475.
Ralph Roister Doister, 296.
Rammekens, 365.
Randolph, Thomas, 67, 75, 76, 77, 78, 79, 81, 82, 84–85, 87, 92, 94, 145.
Rapiers, 278.
Rathlin, massacre of, 475.
Recorde, Robert, 307.
Recusancy, 136, 185.
Redesdale, 139.
Remains concerning Britain, 282.
Requesens, Don Luis, 164, 338, 339.
Restitutio Christianismi, 312.
Revenger's Tragedy, 301.
Rheims, seminary of, 23.
Rhinegrave, the, 57.
Richmond, 355; Treaty of, 57–58.
Richmondshire, 138.
Ridley, Nicholas, bishop, 29.
Ridolfi, Roberto, 148, 149, 150, 151, 158, 163.
Rincurren, fort of, 489.

Each dot represents enclosing activities over an area up to 500 acres

THE 'INCLOSURES', 1485–1607

Adapted from E. F. Gay's map in *Quarterly Journal of Economics*,
vol. xvii (1903), p. 576

ENGLAND AND SCOTLAND

To illustrate Anglo-Scottish relations and the rebellion of the earls

NORDEN'S MAP OF LONDON, 1593

THE UNITED PROVINCES

The United Provinces

FRIESLAND
GRONINGEN
Enckhuizen
OVÉRYSSEL
Amsterdam
UTRECHT
Zutphen
ZUTPHEN
Doesburg
Rotterdam Gouda
Schiedam
Brill
Schouwen
Duiveland
Walcheren
ZEELAND
Flushing Middleburg
Ostende Sluys Axel
Nieuport Bruges
Dunkirk Dixmude
FLANDERS Ghent ANTWERP
Ypres Oudenarde Dendermonde MALINES
Alost Aerschot
St.Omer Courtrai Brussels Louvain
Lille Tirlemont
ARTOIS Tournai Gembloux
Douai Mons Namur
HAINAULT
Arras Valenciennes
Cateau-Cambrésis
Le Catelet Marche
LUXEMBURG
LIMBURG
R. Rhine
R. Maas

THE NETHERLANDS

The Azores inset:
- FLORES
- TERCEIRA
- Angra
- S. MICHAEL
- Villafranca
- Miles (approx) 0 50 100
- THE AZORES

Map labels:
- K. OF SCOTLAND
- Firth of Forth
- IRELAND
- KINGDOM OF ENGLAND
- R. Thames
- LONDON
- Queenborough
- Margate
- Chatham
- Dover
- Strait of Dover
- Portsmouth
- Plymouth
- Falmouth
- Scilly Is.
- The Lizard
- Isle of Wight
- ENGLISH CHANNEL
- Blankenberg
- Nieuport
- Dunkirk
- Gravelines
- ANTWERP
- NETHERLANDS
- Doullens
- Dieppe
- Le Havre
- Amiens
- Cambrai
- Ushant
- Brest
- LOWER BRITTANY
- Paimpol
- Rouen
- Noyon
- Vervins
- Crozon
- St. Malo
- NORMANDY
- Ivry
- Dreux
- Château-Thierry
- Hennebon
- Blavet
- Craon
- PARIS
- Vassy
- Orleans
- Troyes
- R. Loire
- Amboise
- Sancerre
- KINGDOM OF FRANCE
- La Rochelle
- C. Finisterre
- Ferrol
- Corunna
- Vigo
- Bilbao
- Bayonne
- Montauban
- Nimes
- PYRENEES
- KINGDOM OF SPAIN
- Peniche
- K. OF PORTUGAL TO SPAIN 1580–1640
- LISBON
- R. Tagus
- MADRID
- Cezimbra
- Loule
- C. St. Vincent
- Faro
- Seville
- Cadiz

→ Course of the Spanish Armada
0 50 100 150 200 250 miles

EVENTS IN FRANCE AND THE WAR WITH SPAIN

IRELAND

VOYAGES AND TRAVELS
(see over)

Kholmogory
Vologda
Moscow
Kolomna
Nijni Novgorod
Kazan
Astrakhan
Derbent
Shemakha
Aleppo
Birejik
Baghdad
Basra
Tripoli
Khiva
Bokhara
Kazvin
Ormuz
Agra
Hyderabad
Chaul
Goa
Bijapur
Cochin
Galle
Achin
C. Comorin
Allahabad
Benares
Patna
Hooghly
Cooch-Behar
Chittagong
Kaspin
Pegu
Zimme
Rangoon
Martaban
Tenasserim
Penang
Malacca
Bantam
JAVA
JAPAN
Ladrone Is.
Mindanao
Moluccas
Zanzibar
Cormoro Is.
S. Mary
C. of Good Hope
Mozamb.

WILLOUGHBY & CHANCELLOR 1553
BURROUGH 1556 PET & JACKMAN 1580
JENKINSON 1557-61
HAWKINS 1562 1565 1568
DRAKE 1568 1572 1577-80
FROBISHER 1576-78
FITCH 1583
GILBERT 1583
DAVIS 1585-87
CAVENDISH 1587-88
LANCASTER 1591 1601 1603
RALEIGH 1595

TRAVELS